A CUP OF TEY

A Mystery Guild
Lost Classics Omnibus

A CUP OF TEY

MISS PYM DISPOSES

BRAT FARRAR

THE DAUGHTER OF TIME

by

Josephine Tey

Mystery Guild
Garden City, New York

Introduction

By Robert Barnard

*M*ystery readers who have never encountered Josephine Tey are in for a delicious treat. Tey belonged to the Golden Age of British crime writing (roughly speaking, 1920–1950), and her place in the pantheon of mystery writers is unassailable.

Josephine Tey (1896 or '97–1952) is a writer who lives by her works alone. Nobody seems to know anything much about her life, in spite of her successful career in the theater, and nobody seems to care. The steady and sustained sale of her novels in the forty-odd years since her death is due to the books themselves, which have proved to have an enduring appeal. And I would hazard the guess that her readers' attitude toward her is different from their attitude toward other classic crime writers: they regard her with love. They give to their favorite Tey novel what they once gave to their favorite books of childhood, to *The Wind in the Willows*, *Little Women*, or whatever: unconditional enthusiasm.

This strong bond between novelist and reader is based on trust—trust in someone who is not only a first-rate storyteller but one who is not content with a formula. Tey, in her best books, seeks to tell different sorts of story, in different ways. This marks her off from the usual purveyors of puzzle-plots, brilliant though they often are. Indeed, in her more straight-forward detective stories Josephine Tey often reveals a sort of impatience with the rules and conventions of the whodunit. In *A Shilling for Candles*, for example, two of the three plot strands are unraveled with information that is either not given readers at the time the detective gets it or only revealed just before the unmasking of the criminal. She was, in other words, not interested enough in that kind of game, and preferred to play other, more varied sports.

Three of her novels occupy that hinterland—often uneasy, but not in her hands—between the crime novel and the "novel proper." They all have crime at their hearts, but they are as far as possible from the "body in the library" formula. Impersonation has been at the heart of many detective stories, but it has seldom carried the emotional charge of *Brat Farrar*, and our sympathies are never in a mere puzzle so skillfully and so surprisingly manipulated. *The Daughter of Time* is an almost unrepeatable success (a historical mystery reanimated and investigated by present-day inquirers), and it has aroused a whole new interest in what previously seemed a dusty and rather sordid period of English history—the reign of King Richard III and the murder of the Princes in the Tower. *The Franchise Affair* also has a basis in fact (an eighteenth-century case in which a maid charged her employers with abduction and mistreatment), but in her hands it becomes a sort of parable of the middle class at bay.

Coming at the tail end of the Golden Age of crime fiction, Tey does not escape some of the less attractive attitudes of her contemporaries: anti-Semitism, contempt for the working class, a deep uneasiness about any enthusiasm (for example, Scottish nationalism) that, to her, smacks of crankiness. If Agatha Christie's "Anthony Astor" in *Three Act Tragedy* is indeed a hit at Tey, then Christie targets Tey's weaknesses squarely when she talks about "her spiritual home—a boardinghouse in Bournemouth," with the implication of dreary respectability and conventionality.

But that is to seize on the inessentials and to ignore the essence: Josephine Tey's brilliant storytelling; her varied, loving characterization; above all, her control of reader sympathies. These are evident in all her novels, whether whodunits or more unconventional structures. If Ngaio Marsh or Christie had died as young as Tey, we would have a good idea of what they could have gone on writing. We can guess that Tey would have written several more whodunits, but *what* she would have written is beyond our guesswork. That in itself is her best tribute.

ROBERT BARNARD is the author of more than thirty crime novels, including, most recently, *Bad Samaritan*, and a collection of short stories, *The Habit of Widowhood*. A seven-time Edgar nominee, and winner of the Anthony, Agatha, Mcavity, and Nero Wolfe awards, he lives in Leeds, England.

CONTENTS

MISS PYM
DISPOSES

Chapter 1

*A*bell clanged. Brazen, insistent, maddening.

Through the quiet corridors came the din of it, making hideous the peace of the morning. From each of the yawning windows of the little quadrangle the noise poured out on to the still, sunlit garden where the grass was grey yet with dew.

Little Miss Pym stirred, opened one doubtful grey eye, and reached blindly for her watch. There was no watch. She opened the other eye. There seemed to be no bedside table either. No, of course not; now she remembered. There *was* no bedside table; as she had found last night. Her watch had had of necessity to be put under her pillow. She fumbled for it. Good heavens, what a row that bell was making! Obscene. There seemed to be no watch under the pillow. But it must be there! She lifted the pillow bodily, revealing only one small sheer-linen handkerchief in a saucy pattern of blue-and-white. She dropped the pillow and peered down between the bed and the wall. Yes, there was something that looked like a watch. By lying flat on her front and inserting an arm she could just reach it. Carefully she brought it up, lightly caught between the tips of first and second fingers. If she dropped it now she would have to get out of bed and crawl under for it. She turned on her back with a sigh of relief, holding the watch triumphantly above her.

Half-past five, said the watch.

Half-past five!

Miss Pym stopped breathing and stared in unbelieving fascination. No, really, did any college, however physical and hearty, begin the day at *half-past five!* Anything was possible, of course, in a community which had use for neither bedside tables nor bedside lamps, but—half-past five! She put the watch to her small pink ear. It ticked faithfully. She squinted round her pillow at the garden which was visible from the window behind her bed. Yes, it certainly was early; the world had that unmoving just-an-apparition look of early morning. Well, well!

Henrietta had said last night, standing large and majestical in the doorway: "Sleep well. The students enjoyed your lecture, my dear. I shall see you in the morning"; but had not seen fit to mention half-past-five bells.

Oh, well. It wasn't her funeral, thank goodness. Once upon a time she too had lived a life regulated by bells, but that was long ago. Nearly twenty years ago. When a bell rang in Miss Pym's life now it was because she had put a delicately varnished fingertip on the bell-push. As the clamour died into a complaining whimper and then into silence, she turned over to face the wall, burrowing happily into her pillow. Not her funeral. Dew on the grass, and all that, was for youth: shining resplendent youth; and they could have it. She was having another two hours' sleep.

Very childlike she looked with her round pink face, her neat little button of a nose, and her brown hair rolled in flat invisible-pinned curls all over her head. They had cost her a spiritual struggle last night, those curls. She had been very tired after the train journey, and meeting Henrietta again, and the lecture; and her weaker self had pointed out that she would in all probability be leaving after lunch on the morrow, that her permanent wave was only two months old, and that her hair might very well be left unpinned for one night. But, partly to spite her weaker self with whom she waged a constant and bitter war, partly so that she might do Henrietta justice, she had seen to it that fourteen pins were pressed to their nightly duty. She was remembering her strong-mindedness now (it helped to cancel out any twinge of conscience about her self-indulgence this morning) and marvelling at the survival of that desire to live up to Henrietta. At school, she, the little fourth-form rabbit, had admired the sixth-form Henrietta extravagantly. Henrietta was the born Head Girl. Her talent lay exclusively in seeing that other people employed theirs. That was why, although she had left school to train in secretarial work, she was now Principal of a college of physical culture; a subject of which she knew nothing at all. She had forgotten all about Lucy Pym, just as Lucy had forgotten about her, until Miss Pym had written The Book.

That is how Lucy herself thought of it. The Book.

She was still a little surprised about The Book herself. Her mission in life had been to teach schoolgirls to speak French. But after four years of that her remaining parent had died, leaving her two hundred and fifty pounds a year, and Lucy had dried her eyes with one hand and given in her resignation with the other. The Headmistress had pointed out with envy and all uncharitableness that investments were variable things, and that two hundred and fifty didn't leave much margin for a civilised and cultured existence such as people in Lucy's position were expected to live. But Lucy had resigned all the same, and had taken a very civilised and cultured flat far enough from Camden Town to be nearly Regents Park. She provided the necessary margin by giving French lessons now and then when gas bills were imminent, and spent all her spare time reading books on psychology.

She read her first book on psychology out of curiosity, because it seemed to her an interesting sort of thing; and she read all the rest to see if they were just as silly. By the time she had read thirty-seven books on the subject, she had evolved ideas of her own on psychology; at variance, of course, with all thirty-seven volumes read to date. In fact, the thirty-seven volumes seemed to her so idiotic and made her so angry that she sat down there and then and wrote reams of refutal. Since one cannot talk about psychology in anything but jargon, there being no English for most of it, the reams of refutal read very learnedly indeed. Not that that would have impressed anyone if Miss Pym had not used the back of a discarded sheet (her typing was not very professional) on which to write:

Dear Mr Stallard,
   I should be so grateful if you would not use your wireless after eleven at night. I find it *so* distracting.
                                                    Yours sincerely,
                                                    Lucy Pym.

Mr Stallard, whom she did not know (his name was on the card outside his door on the floor below), arrived in person that evening. He was holding her letter open in his hand, which seemed to Lucy very grim indeed, and she swallowed several times before she could make any coherent sound at all. But Mr Stallard wasn't angry about the wireless. He was a publisher's reader, it seemed, and was interested in what she had unconsciously sent him on the back of the paper.

Now in normal times a publisher would have rung for brandy at the mere suggestion of publishing a book on psychology. But the previous year the British public had shaken the publishing world by tiring suddenly of fiction, and developing an interest in abstruse subjects, such as the distance of Sirius from the earth, and the inward meaning of primitive dances in Bechuanaland. Publishers were falling over themselves, therefore, in their effort to supply this strange new thirst for knowledge, and Miss Pym found herself welcomed with open arms. That is to say, she was taken to lunch by the senior partner, and given an agreement to sign. This alone was a piece of luck, but Providence so ordained it that not only had the British public tired of fiction, but the intellectuals had tired of Freud and Company. They were longing for Some New Thing. And Lucy proved to be it. So Lucy woke one morning to find herself not only famous, but a best-seller. She was so shocked that she went out and had three cups of black coffee and sat in the Park looking straight in front of her for the rest of the morning.

She had been a best-seller for several months, and had become quite used to lecturing on "her subject" to learned societies, when Henrietta's letter had come; reminding her of their schooldays together and asking her to come and stay for a while and address the students. Lucy was a little wearied of addressing people, and the image of Henrietta had grown dim with the years. She was about to write a polite refusal, when she remembered the day on which the fourth form had discovered her christened name to be Laetitia; a shame that Lucy had spent her life concealing, the fourth form had excelled themselves, and Lucy had been wondering whether her mother would mind very much about her suicide, and deciding that anyhow she had brought it on herself by giving her daughter such a high-falutin name. And then Henrietta had waded into the humourists, literally and metaphorically. Her blistering comment had withered humour at the root, so that the word Laetitia had never been heard again, and Lucy had gone home and enjoyed jam roly-poly instead of throwing herself in the river. Lucy sat in her civilised and cultured living-room, and felt the old passionate gratitude to Henrietta run over her in waves. She wrote and said that she would be delighted to stay a night with Henrietta (her native caution was not entirely obliterated by her gratitude) and would with pleasure talk on psychology to her students.

The pleasure had been considerable, she thought, pushing up a hump of sheet to shut out the full brilliance of the daylight. Quite the nicest audience she had ever had. Rows of shining heads, making the bare lecture-room look like a garden. And good hearty applause. After weeks of the polite pattering of learned societies it was pleasant to hear the percussion of hollowed palm on hollowed palm. And their questions had been quite intelligent. Somehow, although psychology was a subject on their time-table, as shown in the common-room, she had not expected intellectual appreciation from young women who presumably spent their days doing things with their muscles. Only a few, of course, had asked questions; so there was still a chance that the rest were morons.

Oh well, tonight she would sleep in her own charming bed, and all this would seem like a dream. Henrietta had pressed her to stay for some days, and for a little she had toyed with the idea. But supper had shaken her. Beans and milk pudding seemed an uninspired sort of meal for a summer evening. Very sustaining and nourishing and all that, she didn't doubt. But not a meal one wanted to repeat. The Staff table, Henrietta had said, always had the same food that the students had; and Lucy had hoped that that remark didn't mean that she had looked doubtfully upon the beans; but perhaps it hadn't been a success.

"Tommy, Tom-*mee!* Oh, Tommy, darling, waken up. I'm *desperate!*"

Miss Pym shot into wakefulness. The despairing cries seemed to be in her room. Then she realised that the second window of her room gave on to the courtyard; that the courtyard was small, and conversation from room to room through the gaping windows a natural method of communication. She lay trying to quiet her thumping heart, peering down over the folds of sheet to where, beyond the hump of her toes, the foreshortened oblong of the window framed a small piece of distant wall. But her bed lay in the angle of the room, one window to her right in the wall behind her, and the courtyard window to her left beyond the foot of her bed, and all that was visible from her pillow through the tall thin strip of brightness was half of an open window far down the courtyard.

"Tom-*mee! Tom-mee!*"

A dark head appeared in the window Miss Pym could see.

"For God's sake, someone," said the head, "throw something at Thomas and stop Dakers' row."

"Oh, Greengage, darling, you are an unsympathetic beast. I've bust my garter, and don't know *what* to do. And Tommy took my *only* safety-pin yesterday to pick the winkles with at Tuppence-Ha'penny's party. She simply *must* let me have it back before—*Tommy!* Oh, *Tommy!*"

"Hey, shut up, will you," said a new voice, in a lowered tone, and there was a pause. A pause, Lucy felt, full of sign language.

"And what does all that semaphoring mean?" asked the dark head.

"Shut up, I tell you. *She's* there!" This in desperate *sotto voce*.

"Who is?"

"The Pym woman."

"What *rubbish*, darling,"—it was the Dakers voice again, high and unsubdued; the happy voice of a world's darling—"she's sleeping in the front of the house with the rest of the mighty. *Do* you think *she* would have a spare safety-pin if I was to ask her?"

"She looks zip-fastener to me," a new voice said.

"Oh, will you be quiet! I tell you she's in Bentley's room!"

There was a real silence this time. Lucy saw the dark head turn sharply towards her window.

"How do you know?" someone asked.

"Jolly told me last night when she was giving me late supper." Miss Joliffe was the housekeeper, Lucy remembered, and appreciated the nickname for so grim a piece of humanity.

"Gawd's truth!" said the "zip-fastener" voice, with feeling.

Into the silence came a bell. The same urgent clamour that had wakened them. The dark head disappeared at the first sound of it, and Dakers' voice above the row could be heard wailing her desperation like a lost thing. Social gaffes were relegated to their proper unimportance, as the business of the day overwhelmed them. A great wave of sound rose up to meet the sound of the bell. Doors were banged, feet drummed in the corridor, voices called, someone remembered that Thomas was still asleep, and a tattoo was beaten on her locked door when objects flung at her from surrounding windows had failed to waken her, and then there was the sound of running feet on the gravel path that crossed the courtyard grass. And gradually there were more feet on the gravel and fewer on the stairs, and the babble of voices swelled to a climax and faded. When the noises had grown faint with distance or died into lecture-room silence, a single pair of feet pattered in flight across the gravel, a voice saying: "Damn, damn, damn, damn, damn—" at each footfall. The Thomas who slept, apparently.

Miss Pym felt sympathetic to the unknown Thomas. Bed was a charming place at any time, but if one was so sleepy that neither riotous bell-ringing nor the wails of a colleague made any impression, then getting up must be torture. Welsh, too, probably. All

Thomases were Welsh. Celts hated getting up. Poor Thomas. Poor, poor Thomas. She would like to find poor Thomas a job where she would never have to get up before afternoon.

Sleep ran over her in waves, drawing her deeper and deeper under. She wondered if "looking zip-fastener" was a compliment. Being a safety-pin person couldn't be thought exactly admirable, so perhaps—

She fell asleep.

Chapter 2

*S*he was being beaten with knouts by two six-foot cossacks because she persisted in using the old-fashioned safety-pin when progress decreed a zip-fastener, and the blood had begun to trickle down her back when she woke to the fact that the only thing that was being assaulted was her hearing. The bell was ringing again. She said something that was neither civilised nor cultured, and sat up. No, definitely, not a minute after lunch would she stay. There was a 2.41 from Larborough, and on that 2.41 she would be; her goodbyes said, her duty of friendship done, and her soul filled with the beatitude of escape. She would treat herself to a half-pound box of chocolates on the station platform as a sort of outward congratulation. It would show on the bathroom scales at the end of the week, but who cared?

The thought of the scales reminded her of the civilised and cultured necessity of having a bath. Henrietta had been sorry about its being so far to the Staff bathrooms; she had been sorry altogether to put a guest into the student block, but Fröken Gustavsen's mother from Sweden was occupying the only Staff guestroom, and was going to stay for some weeks until she had seen and criticized the result of her daughter's work when the annual Demonstration would take place at the beginning of the month. Lucy doubted very much whether her bump of locality—a hollow according to her friends—was good enough to take her back to that bathroom. It would be awful to go prowling along those bright empty corridors, arriving perhaps at lecture-rooms unawares. And still more awful to ask in a crowded corridor of up-since-dawners where one could perform one's belated ablutions.

Lucy's mind always worked like that. It wasn't sufficient for it to visualise one horror; it must visualise the opposite one too. She sat so long considering the rival horrors, and enjoying the sensation of doing nothing, that still another bell rang and still another wave of drumming feet and calling voices rose up and swamped the quiet of the morning. Lucy looked at her watch. It was half-past seven.

She had just decided to be uncivilised and uncultured and "go in her mock," as her daily woman called it—after all, what was this immersion in water but a modern fad, and if Charles the Second could afford to smell a little high, who was she, a mere commoner, to grin at missing a bath?—when there was a knock on her door. Rescue was at hand. Oh, joy, oh, glory, her marooned condition was at an end.

"Come in," she called in the glad tones of a Crusoe welcoming a landing party. Of course Henrietta would come to say good-morning. How silly of her not to have thought of that. She was still at heart the little rabbit who didn't expect Henrietta to bother about her. Really, she must cultivate a habit of mind more suitable to a Celebrity. Perhaps if she were to do her hair differently, or say over something twenty times a day after the manner of Coué—"Come in!"

But it was not Henrietta. It was a goddess.

A goddess with golden hair, a bright blue linen tunic, sea-blue eyes, and the most enviable pair of legs. Lucy always noticed other women's legs, her own being a sad disappointment to her.

"Oh, I'm sorry," said the goddess. "I forgot that you might not be up. In college we keep such odd hours."

Lucy thought that it was nice of this heavenly being to take the blame for her sloth.

"I do apologise for interrupting your dressing." The blue eye came to rest on a mule which was lying in the middle of the floor, and stayed there as if fascinated. It was a pale blue satin mule; very feminine, very thriftless, very feathery. A most undeniable piece of nonsense.

"I'm afraid it is rather silly," Lucy said.

"If you only knew, Miss Pym, what it is to see an object that is not strictly utilitarian!" And then, as if recalled to her business by the very temptation of straying from it: "My name is Nash. I'm the Head Senior. And I came to say that the Senior students would be very honoured if you would come to tea with them tomorrow. On Sundays we take our tea out into the garden. It is a Senior privilege. And it really is very pleasant out there on a summer afternoon, and we really are looking forward to having you." She smiled with eager benevolence on Miss Pym.

Lucy explained that she would not be there tomorrow; that she was departing this afternoon.

"Oh, no!" protested the Nash girl; and the genuine feeling in her tone caused Lucy a rush of warmth to the heart. "No, Miss Pym, you mustn't! You really mustn't. You have no idea what a god-send you are to us. It's seldom that anyone—anyone interesting comes to stay. This place is rather like a convent. We are all so hard-worked that we have no time to think of an outside world; and this is the last term for us Seniors, and everything is very grim and claustrophobic—Final Exams, and the Demonstration, and being found posts, and what not—and we are all feeling like death, and our last scrap of sense of proportion is gone. And then *you* come, a piece of the outside, a civilised being—" She paused; half laughing, half serious. "You *can't* desert us."

"But you have an outside lecturer *every* Friday," Lucy pointed out. It was the first time in her life she had been a god-send to anyone, and she was determined to take the assertion with a grain of salt. She didn't at all like the gratified feeling that was sniffing round the edge of her emotions.

Miss Nash explained with clarity, point, and no small bitterness that the last three lecturers had been: an octogenarian on Assyrian inscriptions, a Czech on Central Europe, and a bonesetter on scoliosis.

"What is scoliosis?" asked Lucy.

"Curvature of the spine. And if you think that any of them brought sweetness and light into the College atmosphere, you are wrong. These lectures are supposed to keep us in touch with the world, but if I must be both frank and indiscreet"—she was obviously enjoying being both—"the frock you wore last night did us more good than all the lectures we have ever heard."

Lucy had spent a really shocking sum on that garment when first her book became a best-seller, and it still remained her favourite; she had worn it to impress Henrietta. The gratified feeling came a little nearer.

But not near enough to destroy her common sense. She could still remember the beans. And the lack of bedside lamps. And the lack of any bells to summon service. And the everlasting bells that rang to summon others. No, on the 2.41 from Larborough she would be, though every student of the Leys Physical Training College lay down in her path and wept aloud. She murmured something about engagements—leaving it to be inferred that her diary bulged with pressing and desirable appointments—and suggested that Miss Nash might, meanwhile, direct her to the Staff bathrooms. "I didn't want to go prowling through the corridors, and I couldn't find a bell to ring."

Miss Nash, having sympathised with her about the lack of service—"Eliza really should have remembered that there are no bells in the rooms here and come to call you; she's the Staff housemaid"—suggested that, if Miss Pym didn't mind using the students' baths, they were much nearer. "They are cubicles, of course; I mean, they have walls only part of the way; and the floor is a sort of greenish concrete where the Staff have turquoise mosaic with a tasteful design in dolphins, but the water is the same."

Miss Pym was delighted to use the students' bathroom, and as she gathered her bathing things together the unoccupied hall of her mind was busy with Miss Nash's lack of any studentlike reverence for the Staff. It reminded her of something. And presently she remembered what it reminded her of. Mary Barharrow. The rest of Mary Barharrow's form had been meek and admiring young labourers in the field of irregular French verbs, but Mary Barharrow, though diligent and amiable, had treated her French mistress as an equal; and that was because Mary Barharrow's father was "nearly a millionaire." Miss Pym concluded that in the "outside"— strange how one already used Klondyke terms about College— Miss Nash, who had so markedly Mary Barharrow's charming air of social ease and equality, had also a father very like Mary Barharrow's. She was to learn later that it was the first thing that anyone remarked on when Nash's name was mentioned. "Pamela Nash's people are very rich, you know. They have a butler." They never failed to mention the butler. To the daughters of struggling doctors, lawyers, dentists, business men and farmers, he was as exotic as a negro slave.

"Shouldn't you be at some class or other?" asked Miss Pym, as the quietness of the sunlit corridors proclaimed an absorption elsewhere. "I take it that if you are wakened at half-past five you work before breakfast."

"Oh, yes. In the summer we have two periods before breakfast, one active and one passive. Tennis practice and Kinesiology, or something like that."

"What is kin—whatever-it-is?"

"Kinesiology?" Miss Nash considered for a moment the best way of imparting knowledge to the ignorant, and then spoke in imaginary quotation. "I take down a jug with a handle from a high shelf; describe the muscle-work involved." And as Miss Pym's nod showed that she had understood: "But in winter we get up like anyone else at half-past seven. As for this particular period, it is normally used for taking outside certificates—Public Health, and Red Cross, and what not. But since we have finished with these we are allowed to use it as a prep. hour for our Final Exams, which begin next week. We have very little prep. time, so we are glad of it."

"Aren't you free after tea, or thereabouts?"

Miss Nash looked amused. "Oh, no. There is afternoon clinic from four o'clock till six; outside patients, you know. Everything from flat feet to broken thighs. And from half-past six to eight there is dancing. Ballet, not folk. We have folk in the morning; it ranks as exercise, not art. And supper doesn't finish much before half-past eight, so we are very sleepy before we begin our prep and it is usually a fight between our sleepiness and our ignorance."

As they turned into the long corridor leading to the stairs, they overtook a small scuttling figure clutching under one arm the head and thorax of a skeleton and the pelvis and legs under the other arm.

"What are you doing with George, Morris?" asked Miss Nash as they drew level.

"Oh, *please* don't stop me, Beau," panted the startled Junior, hitching her grotesque burden more firmly on to her right hip and continuing to scuttle in front of them, "and *please* forget that you saw me. I mean that you saw George. I meant to waken early and put him back in the lecture-room before the half-past-five bell went, but I just slept."

"Have you been up all night with George?"

"No, only till about two. I—"

"And how did you manage about lights?"

"I pinned my travelling rug over the window, of course," said the Junior, in the testy tones of one explaining the obvious.

"A nice atmosphere on a June evening!"

"It was hellish," said Miss Morris, simply. "But it really *is* the only way I can swot up my insertions, so *please*, Beau, just forget that you saw me. I'll get him back before the Staff come down to breakfast."

"You'll never do it, you know. You're bound to meet someone or other."

"Oh, please don't discourage me. I'm terrified enough now. And

I really don't know if I can remember how to hook up his middle."
She preceded them down the stairs, and disappeared into the front
of the house.

"Positively Through-the-Looking-Glass," commented Miss
Pym, watching her go. "I always thought insertion was something
to do with needlework."

"Insertions? They're the exact place on a bone where a muscle is
attached to it. It's much easier to do it with the skeleton in front of
you than with just a book. That is why Morris abducted George."
She expelled a breath of indulgent laughter. "Very enterprising of
her. I stole odd bones from the drawers in the lecture-room when I
was a Junior, but I never thought of taking George. It's the dreadful cloud that hangs over a Junior's life, you know. Final Anatomy.
It really *is* a Final. You're supposed to know all about the body before you begin practising on it, so Final Anatomy is a Junior exam,
not a Senior one like the other Finals. The bathrooms are along
here. When I was a Junior the long grass at the edge of the cricket
field was simply stiff on Sundays with hidden Juniors hugging their
Gray. It is strictly forbidden to take books out of College, and on
Sundays we are supposed to go all social and go out to tea, or to
church, or to the country. But no Junior in the summer term ever
did anything on a Sunday except find a quiet spot for herself and
Gray. It was quite a business getting Gray out of College. Do you
know Gray? About the size of those old family Bibles that rested
on the parlour table. There was actually a rumour once that half the
girls at Leys were pregnant, but it turned out that it was only the
odd silhouette that everyone made with Gray stuffed up the front
of their Sunday bests."

Miss Nash stooped to the taps and sent a roar of water rushing
into the bath. "When everyone in College bathes three or four
times a day, in the matter of minutes, you have to have a Niagara of
a tap," she explained above the row. "I'm afraid you are going to be
very late for breakfast." And as Miss Pym looked dismayed and
oddly small-girlish at the prospect: "Let me bring something for
you on a tray. No, it won't be any trouble, I'd love to do it. There
isn't any need for a guest to appear at eight o'clock breakfast, anyhow. You'd much better have it in peace in your room." She paused
with her hand on the door. "And do change your mind about staying. It really would give us pleasure. More pleasure than you can
imagine."

She smiled and was gone.

Lucy lay in the warm soft water and thought happily of her breakfast. How pleasant not to have to make conversation among all those chattering voices. How imaginative and kind of that charming girl to carry a tray to her. Perhaps after all it would be nice to spend a day or two among these young—

She nearly leaped from her bath as a bell began its maniacal yelling not a dozen yards from where she lay. That settled it. She sat up and soaped herself. Not a minute later than 2.41 from Larborough, not one minute later.

As the bell—presumably a five-minute warning before the gong at eight o'clock—died into silence, there was a wild rush in the corridor, the two doors to her left were flung open, and as the water cascaded into the baths, a high familiar voice was heard shrieking: "Oh, darling, I'm going to be so late for breakfast, but I'm in a *muck* sweat, my dear. I know I should have sat down quietly and done the composition of plasma, of which I know *ab*solutely *noth*-ing, my dear, and Final Phys. is on Tuesday. But it is such a lovely morning—Now what *have* I done with my *soap?*"

Lucy's jaw slowly dropped as it was borne in upon her that in a community which began the day at half-past five and ended it at eight in the evening, there were still individuals who had the vitality to work themselves into a muck sweat when they need not.

"Oh, Donnie, *darling*, I've left my soap behind. Do throw me over yours!"

"You'll have to wait till I've soaped myself," said a placid voice that was in marked contrast to Dakers' high emphasis.

"Well, my angel, *do* be *quick*. I've been late twice this week, and Miss Hodge looked dis*tinctly odd* the last time. I say, Donnie, you *couldn't* by any chance take my 'adipose' patient at twelve o'clock clinic, could you?"

"No, I couldn't."

"She really isn't so heavy as she looks, you know. You have only to—"

"I have a patient of my own."

"Yes, but only the little boy with the ankle. Lucas could take him along with her 'tortis colli' girl—"

"No."

"No, I was afraid you wouldn't. Oh, dear, I don't know *when* I'm going to do that plasma. As for the coats of the stomach, they simply *baffle* me, my dear. I don't really believe there are four, anyhow.

It's just a conspiracy. Miss Lux says look at tripe, but I don't see that tripe proves anything."

"Soap coming up."

"Oh, *thank* you, darling. You've saved my life. What a *nice smell*, my dear. *Very* expensive." In the momentary silence of soaping she became aware that the bath on her right was occupied. "Who is next door, Donnie?"

"Don't know. Gage, probably."

"Is that you, Greengage?"

"No," said Lucy, startled, "it's Miss Pym." And hoped it wasn't as prim as it sounded.

"No, but really, who is it?"

"Miss Pym."

"It's a very good imitation, whoever you are."

"It's Littlejohn," suggested the placid voice. "She does imitations."

Miss Pym fell back on a defeated silence.

There was the hurr-oosh of a body lifted suddenly from the water, the spat of a wet foot placed firmly on the edge of the bath, tight wet finger-tips appeared on the edge of the partition, and a face peered over it. It was a long pale face, like an amiable pony's with the straight fair hair above it screwed up into a knob with a hasty hairpin. An oddly endearing face. Even in that crowded moment, Lucy understood suddenly how Dakers had managed to reach her final term at Leys without being knocked on the head by exasperated colleagues.

First horror, then a wild flush together with a dawning amusement, invaded the face above the partition. It disappeared abruptly. A despairing wail rose from beyond.

"Oh, Miss *Pym!* Oh, *dear* Miss Pym! I *do* apologise. I *abase* myself. It didn't occur to me even to *think* it might be you—"

Lucy could not help feeling that she was enjoying her own enormity.

"I *hope* you're not offended. Not *terribly*, I mean. We are so used to people's skins that—that—"

Lucy understood that she was trying to say that the gaffe was less important in these surroundings than it would have been elsewhere, and since she herself had been decently soaping a big toe at the operative moment, she had no feelings on the subject. She said kindly that it was entirely her own fault for occupying a students' bathroom, and that Miss Dakers was not to worry about it for a moment.

"You know my *name?*"

"Yes. You woke me in the dawn this morning yelling for a safety-pin."

"Oh, *catastrophe!* Now I shall *never* be able to look you in the face!"

"I expect Miss Pym is taking the first train back to London," said the voice in the further bath, in a now-look-what-you've-done tone.

"That is O'Donnell next door," said Dakers. "She's from Ireland."

"Ulster," said O'Donnell, without heat.

"How d'you do, Miss O'Donnell."

"You must think this is a mad-house, Miss Pym. But don't judge us by Dakers, please. Some of us are quite grown up. And some of us are even civilised. When you come to tea tomorrow you will see."

Before Miss Pym could say that she was not coming to tea, a low murmur began to invade the cubicles, rising rapidly into the deep roar of a gong. Into the tumult Dakers' banshee wail rose like the voice of a sea-gull in a storm. She was going to be *so* late. And she was *so* grateful for the soap, which had saved her life. And *where* was the girdle of her tunic? And if dear Miss Pym would promise to overlook her failings up to date, she would yet show her that she was a sensible female and a civilised adult. And they were *all* looking forward so much to that tea tomorrow.

With a rush and a bang the students fled, leaving Miss Pym alone with the dying pulse of the gong and the throaty protest of bath water running away.

Chapter 3

*A*t 2.41, when the afternoon fast train to London was pulling out of Larborough prompt to the minute, Miss Pym sat under the cedar on the lawn wondering whether she was a fool, and not much caring anyhow. It was very pleasant there in the sunlit garden. It was also very quiet, since Saturday afternoon was, it appeared, match afternoon, and College *en masse* was down at the cricket field playing Coombe, a rival establishment from the other side of the County. If they had nothing else, these young creatures, they had versatility. It was a far cry from the lining of the stomach to the placing of a cricket field, but they seemingly took it in their stride. Henrietta, coming into her bedroom after breakfast, had said that if she stayed over the weekend she would at least find it a new experience. "They are a very varied and lively crowd, and the work is very interesting." And Henrietta had certainly been right. There was no moment when some new facet of this odd existence was not being presented to her. She had sat through luncheon at the Staff table, eating unidentifiable dishes that were "balanced" to a dietetic marvel, and making the closer acquaintance of the Staff. Henrietta sat in lonely state at the top of the table and gobbled her food in an abstracted silence. But Miss Lux was talkative. Miss Lux—angular, plain, and clever—was Mistress of Theory, and as befitted a lecturer on theory had not only ideas but opinions. Miss Wragg, on the other hand, the Junior Gymnast—big, bouncing, young, and pink—had apparently no ideas at all and her only opinions were reflections of Madame Lefevre's. Madame Lefevre, the ballet mistress, spoke seldom, but when she did it was a voice like dark brown velvet and no one interrupted her. At the bottom of the table, with her mother by her side, sat Fröken Gustavsen, the Senior Gymnast, who talked not at all.

It was to Fröken Gustavsen that Lucy found her eyes going during that lunch. There was a sly amusement in the handsome

Swede's clear pale eyes that Lucy found irresistible. The heavy Miss Hodge, the clever Miss Lux, the dumb Miss Wragg, the elegant Madame Lefevre—what did they all look like through the eyes of a tall pale enigma from Sweden?

Now, having spent lunch wondering about a Swede, she was waiting the advent of a South American. "Desterro doesn't play games," Henrietta had said, "so I'll send her to keep you company this afternoon." Lucy had not wanted anyone to keep her company—she was used to her own company and liked it—but the thought of a South American at an English college of physical training teased her. And when Nash, running into her after lunch, had said, "I'm afraid you're going to be deserted this afternoon, if you don't care for cricket," another Senior passing in the crush had said, "It's all right, Beau, The Nut Tart is going to look after her." "Oh, good," Beau had said, apparently so accustomed to the nickname that it had ceased to have either meaning or oddity for her.

But Lucy looked forward to meeting a Nut Tart, and sitting in the sunlit garden digesting the dietetic marvels she pondered the name. "Nut" was Brazil, perhaps. It was also the modern slang for "dippy" or "daft," she believed. But "tart"? Surely not!

A Junior, running past her on the way to the bicycle shed, flashed her a smile, and she remembered that they had met in the corridor that morning. "Did you get George back safely?" she called after her.

"Yes, thank you," beamed little Miss Morris, pausing to dance on one toe, "but I think I'm in a different sort of trouble now. You see, I had my arm round George's waist, sort of steadying him after hanging him up, when Miss Lux came in. I'll never be able to explain away that, I'm afraid."

"Life is difficult," agreed Lucy.

"However, I think I really do know my insertions now," called little Miss Morris, speeding away over the grass.

Nice children, thought Miss Pym. Nice, clean, healthy children. It was really very pleasant here. That smudge on the horizon was the smoke of Larborough. There would be another smudge like that over London. It was much better to sit here where the air was bright with sun and heavy with roses, and be given friendly smiles by friendly young creatures. She pushed her plump little feet a little further away from her, approved the Georgian bulk of the "old house" that glowed in the sunlight across the lawn, regretted the modern brick wings that made a "Mary Ann" back to it, but supposed that as modern blocks go the Leys ensemble was pleasant enough. Charmingly proportioned lecture-rooms in the "old house," and neat modern little bedrooms in the wings. An ideal arrangement. And the ugly bulk of the gymnasium decently hidden behind all. Before she went away on Monday she must see the Seniors go through their gym. There would be a double pleasure in that for her. The pleasure of watching experts trained to the last fine hair of perfection, and the ineffable pleasure of knowing that never, never as long as she lived, would she herself have to climb a ribstall again.

Round the corner of the house, as she gazed, came a figure in a flowered silk dress and a plain, wide-brimmed shady hat. It was a slim, graceful figure; and watching it come Lucy realised that she had unconsciously pictured the South American plump and over-ripe. She also realised where the "tart" came from, and smiled. The outdoor frocks of the austere young students of Leys would not be flowered; neither would they be cut so revealingly; and never, oh never, would their hats be broad-brimmed and shady.

"Good afternoon, Miss Pym. I am Teresa Desterro. I am so sorry that I missed your lecture last night. I had a class in Larborough." Desterro took off her hat with a leisurely and studied grace, and dropped to the grass by Lucy's side in one continuous smooth movement. Everything about her was smooth and fluid: her voice, her drawling speech, her body, her movements, her dark hair, her honey-brown eyes.

"A class?"

"A dancing class; for shop girls. So earnest; so precise; so very bad. They will give me a box of chocolates next week because it is the last class of the season, and because they like me, and because it is after all the custom; and I shall feel like a crook. It is false pretences. No one could teach them to dance."

"I expect they enjoy themselves. Is it usual? I mean, for students to take outside classes?"

"But we all do, of course. That is how we get practice. At schools, and convents, and clubs, and that sort of thing. You do not care for cricket?"

Lucy, rousing herself to this swift change of subject, explained that cricket was only possible to her in the company of a bag of cherries. "How is it that you don't play?"

"I don't play *any* games. To run about after a little ball is supremely ridiculous. I came here for the dancing. It is a very good dancing college."

But surely, Lucy said, there were ballet schools in London of an infinitely higher standard than anything obtainable at a college of physical training.

"Oh, for that one has to begin young, and to have a métier. Me, I have no métier, only a liking."

"And will you teach, then, when you go back to—Brazil, is it?"

"Oh, no; I shall get married," said Miss Desterro simply. "I came to England because I had an unhappy love affair. He was r-r-ravishing, but quite unsuitable. So I came to England to get over it."

"Is your mother English, perhaps?"

"No, my mother is French. My grandmother is English. I adore the English. Up to here"—she lifted a graceful hand, wrist properly leading, and laid it edge-wise across her neck—"they are full of romance, and from there up, plain horse sense. I went to my grandmother, and I cried all over her best silk chairs, and I said: 'What shall I do? What shall I do?' About my lover, you understand. And she said: 'You can blow your nose and get out of the country.' So I said I would go to Paris and live in a garret and paint pictures of an eye and a seashell sitting on a plate. But she said: 'You will not. You will go to England and sweat a bit.' So, as I always listen to my grandmother, and since I like dancing and am very good at it, I came here. To Leys. They looked a little sideways on me at first when I said I wanted just to dance—"

This is what Lucy had been wondering. How did this charming "nut" find a welcome in this earnest English college, this starting-place of careers?

"—but one of the students had broken down in the middle of her training—they often do, and do you wonder?—and that left a vacant place in the scheme, which was not so nice, so they said: 'Oh, well, let this crazy woman from Brazil have Kenyon's room and allow her to come to the classes. It will not do any harm and it will keep the books straight.' "

"So you began as a Senior?"

"For dancing, yes. I was already a dancer, you understand. But I took Anatomy with the Juniors. I find bones interesting. And to other lectures I went as I pleased. I have listened to all subjects. All but plumbing. I find plumbing indecent."

Miss Pym took "plumbing" to be Hygiene. "And have you enjoyed it all?"

"It has been a liberal education. They are very naive, the English girls. They are like little boys of nine." Noticing the unbelieving smile on Miss Pym's face: there was nothing naive about Beau Nash. "Or little girls of eleven. They have 'raves.' You know what a 'rave' is?" Miss Pym nodded. "They swoon if Madame Lefevre says a kind word to them. I swoon, too, but it is from surprise. They save up their money to buy flowers for Fröken, who thinks of nothing but a Naval Officer in Sweden."

"How do you know that?" asked Lucy, surprised.

"He is on her table. In her room. His photograph, I mean. And she is Continental. She does not have 'raves.' "

"The Germans do," Lucy pointed out. "They are famous for it."

"An ill-balanced people," said Desterro, dismissing the Teutonic race. "The Swedes are not like that."

"All the same, I expect she likes the little offerings of flowers."

"She does not, of course, throw them out of the window. But I notice she likes better the ones who do not bring her offerings."

"Oh? There *are* some who do not have 'raves,' then?"

"Oh, yes. A few. The Scots, for instance. We have two." She might have been talking of rabbits. "They are too busy quarrelling to have any spare emotions."

"Quarrelling? But I thought the Scots stuck together the world over."

"Not if they belong to different winds."

"*Winds?*"

"It is a matter of climate. We see it very much in Brazil. A wind that goes 'a-a-a-ah' "—she opened her red mouth and expelled a soft insinuating breath—"makes one kind of person. But a wind that goes 's-s-s-s-ss' "—she shot the breath viciously out through her teeth—"makes another person altogether. In Brazil it is altitude, in Scotland it is West Coast and East Coast. I observed it in the Easter holidays, and so understood about the Scots. Campbell has a wind that goes 'a-a-a-ah,' and so she is lazy, and tells lies, and has much charm that is all of it quite synthetic. Stewart has a wind that goes 's-s-s-s-ss,' so she is honest, and hardworking, and has a formidable conscience."

Miss Pym laughed. "According to you, the East Coast of Scotland must be populated entirely by saints."

"There is also some personal reason for the quarrel, I understand. Something about abused hospitality."

"You mean that one went home with the other for holidays and—misbehaved?" Visions of vamped lovers, stolen spoons, and cigarette burns on the furniture ran through Lucy's too vivid imagination.

"Oh, no. It happened more than two hundred years ago. In the deep snow, and there was a massacre." Desterro did full justice to the word "massacre."

At this Lucy really laughed. To think that the Campbells were still engaged in living down Glencoe! A narrow-minded race, the Celts.

She sat so long considering the Celts that The Nut Tart turned to look up at her. "Have you come to use us as specimens, Miss Pym?"

Lucy explained that she and Miss Hodge were old friends and that her visit was a holiday one. "In any case," she said, kindly, "I doubt whether as a specimen a Physical Training Student is likely to be psychologically interesting."

"No? Why?"

"Oh, too normal and too nice. Too much of a type."

A faint amusement crossed Desterro's face; the first expression it had shown so far. Unexpectedly, this stung Lucy; as if she too had been found guilty of being naive.

"You don't agree?"

"I am trying to think of someone—some Senior—who is normal. It is not easy."

"Oh, come!"

"You know how they live here. How they work. It would be difficult to go through their years of training here and be quite normal in their last term."

"Do you suggest that Miss Nash is not normal?"

"Oh, Beau. She is a strong-minded creature, and so has suffered less, perhaps. But would you call her friendship for Innes quite normal? *Nice*, of course," Desterro added hastily, "quite irreproachable. But normal, no. That David and Jonathan relationship. It is a very happy one, no doubt, but it"—Desterro waved her arm to summon an appropriate word—"it *excludes* so much. The Disciples are the same, only there are four of them."

"The Disciples?"

"Mathews, Waymark, Lucas, and Littlejohn. They have come up

the College together because of their names. And now, believe me, my dear Miss Pym, they *think* together. They have the four rooms in the roof"—she tilted her head to the four dormer windows in the roof of the wing—"and if you ask any one of them to lend you a pin she says: 'We have not got one.'"

"Well, there is Miss Dakers. What would you say was wrong with Miss Dakers?"

"Arrested development," said Miss Desterro dryly.

"Nonsense!" said Lucy, determined to assert herself. "A happy, simple, uncomplicated human being, enjoying herself and the world. *Quite* normal."

The Nut Tart smiled suddenly, and her smile was frank and unstudied. "Very well, Miss Pym, I give you Dakers. But I remind you that it is their last term, this. And so everything is e-norrrmously exaggerated. Everyone is just the least little bit insane. No, it is true, I promise you. If a student is frightened by nature, then she is a thousand times more frightened this term. If she is ambitious, then her ambition becomes a passion. *And* so on." She sat up to deliver herself of her summing-up. "It is not a normal life they lead. You cannot expect them to be normal."

Chapter 4

You cannot expect them to be normal," repeated Miss Pym to herself, sitting in the same place on Sunday afternoon and looking at the crowd of happy and excessively normal young faces clustered below her on the grass. Her eye ran over them with pleasure. If none of them was distinguished, at least none of them was mean. Nor was there any trace of morbidity, nor even of exhaustion, in their sunburnt alertness. These were the survivors of a gruelling course—that was admitted even by Henrietta—and it seemed to Miss Pym that the rigours might perhaps have been justified if the residue were of such excellence.

She was amused to note that the Disciples, by much living together, had begun to look vaguely alike—as husband and wife often do, however different their features. They all seemed to have the same round face with the same expression of pleased expectancy; it was only later that one noticed differences of build and colouring.

She was also amused to observe that the Thomas who slept was most undeniably Welsh; a small, dark aborigine. And that O'Donnell, who had now materialised from a voice in the bath, was equally unmistakably an Irishwoman; the long lashes, the fine skin, the wide grey eyes. The two Scots—separated by the furthest possible distance that still allowed them to be part of the group—were less obvious. Stewart was the red-haired girl cutting up cake from one of the plates that lay about on the grass. ("It's from Crowford's," she was saying, in a pleasant Edinburgh voice, "so you poor creatures who know nothing but Buzzards will have a treat for a change!") Campbell, propped against the bole of the cedar, and consuming bread-and-butter with slow absorption, had pink cheeks and brown hair and a vague prettiness.

Apart from Hasselt, who was the girl with the flat, calm, early-Primitive face and who was South African, the rest of the Seniors were, as Queen Elizabeth said, "mere English."

The only face that approached distinction, as opposed to good looks, was that of Mary Innes, Beau Nash's Jonathan. This pleased Miss Pym in an odd fashion. It was fitting, she felt, that Beau should have chosen for friend someone who had quality as well as looks. Nor that Innes was particularly good-looking. Her eyebrows, low over her eyes, gave her face an intensity, a brooding expression, that robbed her fine bones of the beauty they might have had. Unlike Beau, who was animated and smiled easily, she was quiet and so far Miss Pym had not seen her smile, although they had had what amounted in the milieu to a lengthy conversation. That was last night, when Miss Pym was undressing after having spent the evening in the company of the Staff. There had come a knock on her door, and Beau had said: "I just came to see if you had everything you want. And to introduce you to your next-door neighbour, Mary Innes. Any time you want to be rescued, Innes will see to it." And Beau had said goodnight and gone away, leaving Innes to finish the interview. Lucy had found her attractive and very intelligent, but just a shade disconcerting. She did not bother to smile if she was not amused, and though friendly and at her ease made no effort to be entertaining. In the academic and literary circles that Lucy had recently frequented this would not have been remarkable, but in the gay over-accented College world it had the effect almost of a rebuff. Almost. There was certainly nothing of rebuff in Innes's interest in her book—The Book—and in herself.

Looking at her now, sitting in the cedar shade, Lucy wondered if it were just that Mary Innes did not find life very amusing. Lucy had long prided herself on her analysis of facial characteristics, and was beginning nowadays to bet rather heavily on them. She had never, for instance, come across eyebrows beginning low over the nose and ending high up at the outer end without finding that their owner had a scheming, conniving mind. And someone—Jan Gordon, was it?—had observed that of the crowd round a park orator it was the long-nosed people who stayed to listen and the short-nosed people who walked away. So now, looking at Mary Innes's level eyebrows and firm mouth, she wondered whether the concentration of purpose they showed had forbidden any compensating laughter. It was in some way not a contemporary face at all. It was—was what?

An illustration from a history book? A portrait in a gallery? Not, anyhow, the face of a games mistress at a girls' school. Definitely not. It was round faces like Mary Innes's that history was built.

Of all the faces turning to her so constantly and turning away with chatter and badinage, only two were not immediately likeable. One was Campbell's: too pliant, too soft-mouthed, too ready to be all things to all men. The other belonged to a girl called Rouse; and was freckled, and tight-lipped, and watchful.

Rouse had come late to the tea-party, and her advent had caused an odd momentary silence. Lucy was reminded of the sudden stillness that falls on chattering birds when a hawk hovers. But there was nothing deliberate about the silence; no malice. It was as if they had paused in their talk to note her arrival, but none of them cared sufficiently to welcome her into their own particular group. "I'm afraid I'm late," she had said. And in the momentary quiet Lucy had caught the monosyllabic comment, "Swot!" and had concluded that Miss Rouse had not been able to drag herself away from her textbooks. Nash had introduced her, and she had dropped to the grass with the rest, and the interrupted conversations flowed on. Lucy, always sympathetic to the odd-man-out, had caught herself being sorry for the latecomer; but a further inspection of Miss Rouse's North Country features had convinced her that she was wasting good emotion. If Campbell, pink and pretty, was too pliant to be likeable, then Rouse was her complement. Nothing but a bulldozer, Lucy felt, would make an impression on Miss Rouse.

"Miss Pym, you haven't had any of *my* cake," said Dakers, who, quite unabashed, had appropriated Lucy as an old acquaintance, and was now sitting propped against her chair, her legs straight out in front of her like a doll's.

"Which is yours?" asked Lucy, eyeing the various tuckbox products, which stood out from the college bread-and-butter and "Sunday" buns like Creed suits at a country fair.

Dakers' contribution, it seemed, was the chocolate sandwich with the butter icing. Lucy decided that for friendship's sake (and a little for greed) she would forget her weight this once.

"Do you always bring your own cakes to Sunday tea?"

"Oh, no, this is in *your* honour."

Nash, sitting on her other side, laughed. "What you see before you, Miss Pym, is a collection of skeletons out of cupboards. There is no physical training student who is not a Secret Eater."

"There has been *no* moment in my *whole* college career, my dears, when I wasn't *sick* with hunger. Only *shame* makes me stop eating at breakfast, and half an hour afterwards I'm hungry enough to eat the horse in the gym."

"That is why our only crime is—" Rouse was beginning, when Stewart kicked her so hard in the back that she almost fell forward.

"We have spread our dreams under your feet," mocked Nash, covering Rouse's broken sentence. "And a fine rich carpet of carbohydrate they are, to be sure."

"We also had a *solemn* conclave as to whether we ought to *dress* for you," said Dakers, cutting up chocolate sandwich for the others and unaware that there had been any gaffe in the offing. "But we decided that you didn't look very particular." As this raised a laugh, she added hastily, "In the very *nicest* sense, I mean. We thought you would like us as we are."

They were wearing all sorts of garments; as the taste of the wearer or the need of the moment dictated. Some were in shorts, some in blue linen games tunics, some in washing-silk dresses of suitably pastel shades. There were no flowered silks; Desterro was taking tea with the nuns of a convent in Larborough.

"Besides," said Gage, who looked like a Dutch doll and who was the dark head that appeared at a courtyard window at five-thirty yesterday morning and prayed someone to throw something at Thomas and so put a period to the wails of Dakers, "besides, much as we would like to do you honour, Miss Pym, every moment counts with our Finals so oppressively near. Even a quick-change artist like a P.T. Senior needs five full minutes to achieve Sunday-bests, and by accepting us in our rags you have contributed"—she paused to count the gathering and do some mental arithmetic—"you have contributed one hour and twenty minutes to the sum of human knowledge."

"You can subtract *my* five minutes from that, my dear," said Dakers, licking a protuberant piece of butter-icing into safety with an expert tongue. "I've spent the *whole* afternoon doing the cortex of the brain, and the only result is a firm conviction that I personally haven't *got* a cortex."

"You must have a cortex," said Campbell, the literal-minded Scot, in a Glasgow drawl like syrup sliding from a spoon. But no one took any notice of this contribution to the obvious.

"Personally," said O'Donnell, "I think the vilest part of physiology are the villi. Imagine drawing cross-sections of something that has seven different parts and is less than a twentieth of an inch high!"

"But do you have to know the human structure in such detail?" asked Lucy.

"On Tuesday morning we do," said the Thomas who slept. "After that we can forget it for the rest of our lives."

Lucy, remembering the Monday morning visit to the gymnasium which she had promised herself, wondered if physical work ceased during Final Examinations Week. Oh, no, they assured her. Not with the Dem. only a fortnight ahead. The Demonstration, she was given to understand, ranked only a short head behind Final Examinations as a hazard.

"All our parents come," said one of the Disciples, "and—"

"The parents of all of us, she means," put in a fellow Disciple.

"—and people from rival colleges, and all the—"

"And the civic swells of Larborough," put in a third. It seemed that when one Disciple burst into speech the others followed automatically.

"And all the County big-wigs," finished a fourth.

"It's murder," said the first, summing it up for them.

"I *like* the Dem.," said Rouse. And again that odd silence fell.

Not inimical. Merely detached. Their eyes went to her, and came away again, expressionlessly. No one commented on what she had said. Their indifference left her marooned in the moment.

"I think it's fun to show people what we can do," she added, a hint of defence in her tone.

They let that pass too. Never before had Lucy met that negative English silence in its full perfection; in its full cruelty. Her own edges began to curl up in sympathy.

But Rouse was less easily shrivelled. She was eyeing the plates before her, and putting out her hand for something to eat. "Is there any tea left in the pot?" she asked.

Nash bent forward to the big brown pot, and Stewart took up the talk from where the Disciples had left it.

"What really *is* murder is waiting to see what you pull out of the Post lottery."

"Post?" said Lucy. "You mean jobs? But why a lottery? You know what you apply for, surely?"

"Very few of us need to apply," Nash explained, pouring very black tea. "There are usually enough applications from schools to go round. Places that have had Leys gymnasts before just write to Miss Hodge when they have a vacancy and ask her to recommend someone. If it happens to be a very senior or responsible post, she may offer it to some Old Student who wants a change. But normally the vacancies are filled from Leaving Students."

"And a very fine bargain they get," said a Disciple.

"No one works so hard as a First Poster does," said a second.

"For less money," supplemented a third.

"Or with a better grace," said a fourth.

"So you see," Stewart said, "the most agonising moment of the whole term is when you are summoned to Miss Hodge's room and told what your fate is going to be."

"Or when your train is pulling out of Larborough and you haven't been summoned at all!" suggested Thomas, who evidently had had visions of being engulfed, jobless, by her native mountains again.

Nash sat back on her heels and smiled at Lucy. "It is not nearly as grim as it sounds. Quite a few of us are provided for already and so are not in the competition at all. Hasselt, for instance, is going back to South Africa to work there. And the Disciples *en masse* have chosen medical work."

"We are going to start a clinic in Manchester," explained one.

"A very rheumaticky place."

"Full of deformities."

"And brass"—supplemented the other three automatically.

Nash smiled benevolently on them. "And I am going back to my old school as Games Coach. And The Nut—and Desterro, of course, doesn't want a post. So there aren't so many of us to find places for."

"I won't even be qualified if I don't go back to the liver pretty soon," Thomas said, her beady brown eyes blinking in the sun. "What a way to spend a summer evening."

They shifted their positions lazily, as if in protest, and fell to chatter again. But the reminder pricked them, and one by one they began to gather up their belongings and depart, trailing slowly across the sunlit grass like disconsolate children. Until presently Lucy found herself alone with the smell of the roses, and the murmur of insects, and the hot shimmer of the sunlit garden.

For half an hour she sat, in great beatitude, watching the slow shadow of the tree creep out from her feet. Then Desterro came back from Larborough; strolling slowly by the drive with a Rue de la Paix elegance that was odd after Lucy's hour of tumbled youth at tea. She saw Miss Pym, and changed her direction.

"Well," she said, "did you have a profitable afternoon?"

"I wasn't looking for profit," said Lucy, faintly tart. "It was one of the happiest afternoons I have ever spent."

The Nut Tart stood contemplating her.

"I think you are a *very* nice person," she said irrelevantly, and moved away, leisurely, to the house.

And Lucy suddenly felt very young, and didn't like the feeling at all. How dare a chit in a flowered frock make her feel inexperienced and foolish!

She rose abruptly and went to find Henrietta and be reminded that she was Lucy Pym, who had written The Book, and lectured to learned societies, and had her name in *Who's Who*, and was a recognised authority on the working of the Human Mind.

Chapter 5

*W*hat is the College crime?" she asked Henrietta, as they went upstairs after supper. They had paused by the big fan-lighted window on the landing to look down on the little quadrangle, letting the others precede them up to the drawing-room.

"Using the gymnasium as a short cut to the field-path," Henrietta said promptly.

"No, I mean real crime."

Henrietta turned to look at her sharply. After a moment she said: "My dear Lucy, when a human being works as hard as these girls do, it has neither the spare interest to devise a crime nor the energy to undertake it. What made you think of that subject?"

"Something someone said at tea this afternoon. About their 'only crime.' It was something to do with being perpetually hungry."

"Oh, that!" Henrietta's brow cleared. "Food pilfering. Yes, we do now and then have that. In any community of this size there is always someone whose power of resisting temptation is small."

"Food from the kitchen, you mean?"

"No, food from the students' own rooms. It is a Junior crime, and usually disappears spontaneously. It is not a sign of vice, you know. Merely of a weak will. A student who would not dream of taking money or a trinket can't resist a piece of cake. Especially if it is sweet cake. They use up so much energy that their bodies are crying out for sugar; and though there is no limit to what they may eat at table they are forever hungry."

"Yes, they do work very hard. What proportion of any one set finishes the course, would you say?"

"Of this lot"—Henrietta nodded down to where a group of Seniors were strolling out across the courtyard to the lawn—"eighty per cent are finishing. That is about average. Those who fall by the wayside do it in their first term, or perhaps their second."

"But not all, surely. There must be accidents in a life like this."

"Oh, yes, there are accidents." Henrietta turned and began to climb the further flight.

"That girl whose place Teresa Desterro took, was it an accident that overtook her?"

"No," said Henrietta shortly, "she had a breakdown."

Lucy, climbing the shallow steps in the wake of her friend's broad beam, recognised the tone. It was the tone in which Henrietta, the Head Girl, used to say: "And see that no galoshes are left lying about the cloakroom floor." It did not permit of further discussion.

Henrietta, it was to be understood, did not like to think of her beloved College as a Moloch. College was a bright gateway to the future for deserving youth; and if one or two found the gateway a hazard rather than an opening, then it was unfortunate but no reflection on the builders of the gateway.

"Like a convent," Nash had said yesterday morning. "No time to think of an outside world." That was true. She had watched a day's routine go by. She had also seen the students' two daily papers lying unopened in the common-room last night as they went in to supper. But a nunnery, if it was a narrow world, was also a placid one. Uncompetitive. Assured. There was nothing of the nunnery about this over-anxious, wildly strenuous life. Only the self-absorption was the same; the narrowness.

And yet *was* it so narrow, she wondered, considering the gathering in the drawing-room? If this were any other kind of college that gathering would have been homogeneous. If it were a college of science the gathering would consist of scientists; if it were a college of divinity, of theologians. But in this long charming room, with its good "pieces" and its chintzes, with its tall windows pushed up so that the warm evening flowed in through them full of grass and roses, in this one room many worlds met. Madame Lefevre, reclining in thin elegance on a hard Empire sofa and smoking a yellow cigarette in a green holder, represented a world theatrical; a world of grease-paint, art, and artifice. Miss Lux, sitting upright in a hard chair, represented the academical world; the world of universities, textbooks, and discussion. Young Miss Wragg, busy pouring out coffee, was the world of sport; a physical, competitive, unthinking world. And the evening's guest, Dr Enid Knight, one of the "visiting" Staff, stood for the medical world. The foreign world was not present: Sigrid Gustavsen had retired with her mother, who spoke no English, to her own room where they could chatter together in Swedish.

All these worlds had gone to make the finished article that was a Leaving Student; it was at least not the training that was narrow.

"And what do you think of our students, Miss Pym, now that you have had a whole afternoon with them?" Madame Lefevre asked, turning the battery of her enormous dark eyes on Lucy.

A damn-silly question, thought Lucy; and wondered how a good respectable middle-class English couple had produced anything so like the original serpent as Madame Lefevre. "I think," she said, glad to be able to be honest, "that there is not one of them who is not an advertisement for Leys." And she saw Henrietta's heavy face light up. College was Henrietta's world. She lived and moved and had her being in the affairs of Leys; it was her father, mother, lover, and child.

"They *are* a nice lot," agreed Doreen Wragg happily, not yet far removed from her own student days and regarding her pupils with camaraderie.

"They are as the beasts that perish," said Miss Lux incisively. "They think that Botticelli is a variety of spaghetti." She inspected with deep gloom the coffee that Miss Wragg handed to her. "If it comes to that, they don't know what spaghetti is. It's not long since Dakers stood up in the middle of a Dietetic lecture and accused me of destroying her illusions."

"It surprises me to know that anything about Miss Dakers is destructible," observed Madame Lefevre, in her brown velvet drawl.

"What illusion had you destroyed?" the young doctor asked from the window-seat.

"I had just informed them that spaghetti and its relations were made from a paste of flour. That shattered forever, apparently, Dakers' picture of Italy."

"How had she pictured it?"

"Fields of waving macaroni, so she said."

Henrietta turned from putting two lumps of sugar in a very small cup of coffee (*How* nice, thought Lucy wistfully, to have a figure like a sack of flour and not to mind!) and said: "At least they are free from crime."

"Crime?" they said, puzzled.

"Miss Pym has just been enquiring about the incidence of crime at Leys. That is what it is to be a psychologist."

Before Lucy could protest against this version of her simple search for knowledge, Madame Lefevre said: "Well, let us oblige her. Let us turn out the rag-bag of our shameful past. What crime have we had?"

"Farthing was had up last Christmas term for riding her bike without lights," volunteered Miss Wragg.

"Crime," said Madame Lefevre. "Crime. Not petty misdemeanours."

"If you mean a plain wrong-un, there was that dreadful creature who was man-crazy and used to spend Saturday evenings hanging round the barrack gate in Larborough."

"Yes," said Miss Lux, remembering. "What became of *her* when we tossed her out, does anyone know?"

"She is doing the catering at a Seamen Refuge in Plymouth," Henrietta said, and opened her eyes when they laughed. "I don't know what is funny about that. The only real crime we have had in ten years, as you very well know, was the watches affair. And even that," she added, jealous for her beloved institution, "was a fixation, of course."

"By precedent, I suppose she is now with the Goldsmiths and Silversmiths," said Madame Lefevre.

"I don't know," said Henrietta, seriously. "I think her people kept her at home. They were quite well-to-do."

"Well, Miss Pym, the incidence appears to be point-something per cent." Madame Lefevre waved a thin brown hand. "We are an unsensational crowd."

"Too normal by half," Miss Wragg volunteered. "A little spot of scandal would be nice now and again. A nice change from hand-stands and upward-circlings."

"I should like to see some hand-stands and upward-circlings," Lucy said. "Would it be all right if I came and watched the Seniors tomorrow morning?"

But of course she must see the Seniors, Henrietta said. They were busy with their Demonstration programme, so it would be a private Demonstration all for herself. "They are one of the best sets we ever had," she said.

"Can I have first go of the gym. when the Seniors are doing their Final Phys. on Tuesday?" Miss Wragg asked; and they began to discuss time-tables.

Miss Pym moved over to the window-seat and joined Dr Knight.

"Are you responsible for the cross-section of something called the villi?" she asked.

"Oh, no; physiology is an ordinary college subject: Catherine Lux takes that."

"Then what do you lecture on?"

"Oh, different things at different stages. Public Health. The so-called 'social' diseases. The even more so-called Facts of Life. Your subject."

"Psychology?"

"Yes. Public Health is my job, but psychology is my specialty. I liked your book so much. So commonsensical. I admired that. It is so easy to be high-falutin about an abstract subject."

Lucy flushed a little. There is no praise so gratifying as that of a colleague.

"And of course I am the College medical advisor," Dr Knight went on, looking amused. "A sinecure if ever there was one. They are a disgustingly healthy crowd."

"But—" Lucy began. It is the outsider, Desterro (she was thinking), who insists on their abnormality. If it is true, then surely this trained observer, also from the outside, must be aware of it.

"They have accidents, of course," the doctor said, misunderstanding Lucy's "but." "Their life is a long series of minor accidents—bruises, and sprains, and dislocated fingers, and what not—but it is very rarely that anything serious happens. Bentley has been the only instance in my time—the girl whose room you have. She broke a leg, and won't be back till next term."

"But—it is a strenuous training, a gruelling life; do they never break down under it?"

"Yes. That's not unknown. The last term is particularly trying. A concentration of horrors from the student's point of view. Crit. classes, and—"

"Crit. classes?"

"Yes. They each have to take a gym. and a dancing class in the presence of the united Staff and their own set, and are judged according to the show they make. Nerve-shattering. These are all over, the crit. classes; but there are still the Finals, and the Demonstration, and being given jobs, and the actual parting from student life, and what not. Yes, it is a strain for them, poor dears. But they are amazingly resilient. No one who wasn't would have survived so long. Let me get you some more coffee. I'm going to have some."

She took Lucy's cup and went away to the table; and Lucy leaned back in the folds of the curtain and looked at the garden. The sun had set, and the outlines were growing blurred; there was the first hint of dew in the soft air that blew up against her face. Somewhere on the other side of the house (in the students' common-room?) a piano was being played and a girl was singing. It was a charming voice: effortless and pure, without professional tricks and without fashionable dealing in quarter-tones. The song, moreover, was a ballad; old-fashioned and sentimental, but devoid of self-pity and posing. A frank young voice and a frank old song. It shocked Lucy to realise how long it was since she had heard any voice raised in song that was not a product of valves and batteries. In London at this moment the exhausted air was loud with radios; but here, in this cool, scented garden, a girl was singing for the love of it.

I have been too long in London, she thought; I must have a change. Find a hotel on the South Coast, perhaps. Or go abroad. One forgets that the world is young.

"Who is singing?" she asked, as her cup was handed to her again.

"Stewart, I think," Dr Knight said, not interested. "Miss Pym, you can save my life if you like to."

Lucy said that to save a doctor's life would give her immense satisfaction.

"I want to go to a medical conference in London," Dr Knight said in a conspiratorial undertone. "It is on Thursday, but that is the day of my psychology lecture. Miss Hodge thinks I am forever going to conferences, so I can't possibly beg off again. But if you were to take that lecture for me, everything would be grand."

"But I am going back to London myself tomorrow after lunch."

"No!" said Dr Knight, much dashed. "Do you have to?"

"Oddly enough, I was just thinking how much I should hate going back."

"Then don't go. Stay on for a day or two, and save my life. Do, Miss Pym."

"And what would Henrietta think of the substitution?"

"That, of course, is sheer affectation, and you ought to be ashamed of yourself. *I'm* not a best-seller, *I'm* not a celebrity, *I'm* not the author of the latest textbook on the subject—"

Lucy made a small gesture acknowledging her fault, but her eyes were on the garden. Why *should* she go back to London yet? What was there to take her back? Nothing and nobody. For the first time that fine, independent, cushioned, celebrated life of hers looked just a little bleak. A little narrow and inhuman. Could it be? Was there, perhaps, a lack of warmth in that existence she had been so content with? Not a lack of human contact, certainly. She had her fill of human contact. But it was a very all-of-a-piece contact, now that she thought of it. Except for Mrs Montmorency from one of the suburbs of Manchester, who was her daily help, and her Aunt Celia down in Walberswick, who sometimes had her for weekends, and the tradespeople, she never talked to anyone who wasn't somehow connected with the publishing or the academic worlds. And though all the ladies and gentlemen belonging to these two worlds were, of course, both intelligent and amusing, there was no denying that their interests were limited. You couldn't, for instance, talk to one and the same person about Social Security, hill-billy songs, and what won the 3.30. They each had their "subject." And their subject, she found to her cost, was only too likely to be royalties. Lucy herself had only the vaguest idea about royalties; especially her own, and could never keep her end up in this sort of conversation.

Besides, none of them was *young*.

At least, not young as these children here were young. Young in years a few of her acquaintances might be, but they were already bowed down with the weight of the world's wrongs and their own importance. It was nice to meet a morning-of-the-world youngness for a change. Yesterday morning. It was nice to be liked.

There was no good in trying to diddle herself about why she wanted to stay a little longer; why she was seriously prepared to forgo the delights of civilisation that had seemed so desirable—so imperatively desirable—only yesterday morning. It *was nice* to be liked.

In the last few years she had been ignored, envied, admired, kow-towed to, and cultivated; but warm, personal liking was something she had not had since the Lower Fourth said goodbye to her, with a home-made pen-wiper and a speech by Gladys Someone-or-other, shortly after her legacy. To stay in this atmosphere of youth, of liking, of warmth, she was willing to overlook for a space the bells, the beans, and the bathrooms.

"Knight," said young Miss Wragg, raising her voice from the conversation behind them, "did the Disciples ask you about giving them an introduction to some doctor or other in Manchester?"

"Oh, yes, they asked me. In concert. I said yes, of course. As a matter of fact, I was glad to; I think they will be a great success."

"Individually, the Disciples are null and void," Miss Lux said. "But collectively they have a quadruple ruthlessness that will be very useful in Lancashire. It is the only occasion I have ever come across when nothing multiplied by four became something like six-

and-a-half. If nobody wants the *Sunday Times* I shall take it to bed with me."

No one apparently wanted it. It had been lying unopened in the drawing-room after lunch when Lucy had been the first to look at it, and as far as she had noticed no one except Miss Lux had picked it up since.

"This set of Seniors are planting themselves out very nicely. Almost without our help," Madame Lefevre said. "There will be less heart-burning than usual." She did not sound very sorry about the heart-burning; just sardonic.

"It continually surprises me," said Miss Hodge, not at all sardonic, "how each year the students slip into their appropriate places in the world's work. The openings come up as the students are ready to fill them. Almost like—like two pieces of the same machine. So surprising and so satisfactory. I don't think we have had a misfit in all my years at Leys. I had a letter from the Cordwainers School, by the way; in Edinburgh, you know. Mulcaster is getting married and they want someone in her place. You will remember Mulcaster, Marie?" She turned to Madame Lefevre, who, except for Henrietta, was the Oldest Inhabitant—and who, incidentally, had been christened plain Mary.

"Of course I remember her. A lump without leaven," said Madame, who judged everyone by their capacity to execute *rondes de jambes*.

"A nice girl," Henrietta said placidly. "I think Cordwainers will be a very good place for Sheena Stewart."

"Have you told her about it?" Miss Wragg asked.

"No, oh, no; I always like to sleep on things."

"Hatch them out, you mean," Madame said. "You must have heard about Cordwainers before lunch-time yesterday because that was the last post, and it is only now we hear about it."

"It was not very important," Henrietta said defensively; and then added with what was nearly a simper: "But I *have* heard rumours of a 'plum,' a really wonderful chance for someone."

"Tell us," they said.

But Henrietta said no; that no official notice had come, that no official notice or application might come at all, and until it did it was better not to talk about it. But she still looked pleased and mysterious.

"Well, I'm going to bed," Miss Lux said, picking up the *Times* and turning her back on Henrietta's elephantine coyness. "You are not going before lunch tomorrow, are you, Miss Pym?"

"Well," said Lucy, pitchforked of a sudden into decision, "I wondered if I might stay on for a day or two? You did ask me to, you know," she reminded Henrietta. "It has been so nice—So interesting to watch a world so different—And it is so lovely here, so—" Oh, dear, why must she sound so idiotic? Would she never learn to behave like Lucy Pym the Celebrity?

But her stammerings were swamped in the loud wave of their approval. Lucy was touched to note a gleam of pleasure even on the face of Miss Lux.

"Stay on till Thursday and take my Senior Psychology lecture, and let me go to a conference in London," Dr Knight suggested, as if it had just occurred to her.

"Oh, I don't know whether—" began Lucy, all artistic doubt, and looked at Henrietta.

"Dr Knight is always running away to conferences," Miss Hodge said, disapproving but without heat. "But of course we would be delighted and honoured, Lucy, if you agreed to give the students a second lecture."

"I should like to. It would be nice to feel myself a temporary member of the Staff, instead of a mere guest. I should like to very much." She turned in rising to wink at Dr Knight, who was squeezing her arm in a rapture of gratitude. "And now I think I must get back to the student wing."

She said goodnight and went out with Miss Lux.

Lux eyed her sideways as they moved together to the back of the house, but Lucy, catching the glance, thought that there was a friendly gleam in that ice-grey eye.

"Do you really like this menagerie?" Lux asked. "Or are you just looking for things to stick on cardboard with pins?"

That was what The Nut Tart had asked yesterday afternoon. Have you come looking for specimens? Well, she would make the same answer and see what Lux's reaction would be.

"Oh, I'm staying because I like it. A college of Physical Training wouldn't be a very good place to look for the abnormal, anyhow, would it." She made it a statement, not a question; and waited.

"Why not?" asked Miss Lux. "Sweating oneself into a coma may stultify the reason but it doesn't destroy the emotions."

"Doesn't it?" Lucy said, surprised. "If I were dog-tired I'm certain I wouldn't have any feelings about anything but going to sleep quickly."

"Going to sleep dead tired is all right; normal, and pleasant, and safe. It is when one wakens up dead tired that the trouble begins."

"What trouble?"

"The hypothetical trouble of this discussion," Lux said, smoothly.

"And is wakening up dead tired a common thing, would you say?"

"Well, I'm not their medical advisor, so I can't run round with a stethoscope and fond inquiries, but I should say that five Seniors out of six in their last term are so tired that each morning is a mild nightmare. It is when one is as tired as that that one's emotional state ceases to be normal. A tiny obstacle becomes an Everest in the path; a careless comment becomes a grievance to be nursed; a small disappointment is all of a sudden a suicidal affair."

There swam up in Lucy's mind a vision of that circle of faces at tea-time. Brown, laughing, happy faces; careless and for the most part notably confident. Where in that relaxed and healthy crowd had there been the least hint of strain, of bad temper? Nowhere. They had moaned over their hard lot certainly, but it was a humourous and detached complaint.

Tired they might be; in fact tired they certainly were—it would be a miracle if they were not; but tired to the point of abnormality, no. Lucy could not believe it.

"This is my room," Lux said, and paused. "Have you something to read? I don't suppose you brought anything if you meant to go back yesterday. Can I lend you something?"

She opened the door, exhibiting a neat bed-sitting-room of which the sole decorations were one engraving, one photograph, and an entire wainscotting of books. From next-door came the babble of Swedish chat.

"Poor Fröken," Lux said unexpectedly, as Lucy cocked an ear. "She has been so homesick. It must be wonderful to be able to talk family gossip in one's own tongue again." And then, seeing Lucy's eyes on the photograph: "My young sister."

"She is very lovely," Lucy said; and hoped instantly that there had been no hint of surprise in her tone.

"Yes." Lux was drawing the curtains. "I hate moths. Do you? She was born when I was in my teens, and I have practically brought her up. She is in her third year at Medical school." She came and stood for a moment looking at the photograph with Lucy. "Well, what can I give you to read? Anything from Runyon to Proust."

Lucy took *The Young Visiters*. It was a long time since she had read it last, but she found that she was smiling at the very sight of it. A sort of reflex action; quite involuntary. And when she looked up she found that Lux was smiling too.

"Well, that is one thing I shall never do," Lucy said regretfully.

"What?"

"Write a book that makes all the world smile."

"Not all the world," Lux said, her smile broadening. "I had a cousin who stopped halfway through. When I asked her why, she said: 'So *unlikely*.'"

So Lucy went smiling away towards bed, glad that she was not going to catch that train tomorrow, and thinking about the plain Miss Lux who loved a beautiful sister and liked absurdity. As she turned into the long corridor of the E-wing she saw Beau Nash standing at the angle of the stairs at the far end, in the act of lifting a hand-bell to shoulder height, and in another second the wild yelling of it filled the wing. She stood where she was, her hands over her ears, while Beau laughed at her and swung the evil thing with a will. Lovely, she was, standing there with that instrument of torture in her hands.

"Is ringing the 'bedroom' bell the Head Girl's duty?" Lucy asked, as Beau at last ceased to swing.

"No, the Seniors take week-about; it just happens to be my week. Being well down the list alphabetically I don't have more than one week each term." She looked at Miss Pym and lowered her voice in mock-confidence. "I pretend to be glad about that—everyone thinks it a frightful bore to have to watch the clock—but I *love* making a row."

Yes, thought Lucy; no nerves and a body brimming with health; of course she would love the row. And then, almost automatically, wondered if it was not the row that she liked but the feeling of power in her hands. But no, she dismissed that thought; Nash was the one that life had been easy for; the one who had, all her life, only to ask, or take, in order to have. She had no need of vicarious satisfactions; her life was one long satisfaction. She liked the wild clamour of the bell; that was all.

"Anyhow," Nash said, falling into step with her, "it isn't the 'bedroom bell.' It's 'Lights Out.'"

"I had no idea it was so late. Does that apply to me?"

"Of course not. Olympus does as it likes."

"Even a boarded-out Olympus?"

"Here is your hovel," Nash said, switching on the light and standing aside to let Lucy enter the bright little cell, so gay and antiseptic in the unshaded brilliance. After the subtleties of the summer evening and the grace of the Georgian drawing-room, it was like an illustration from one of the glossier American magazines. "I am glad I happened to see you because I have a confession to make. I won't be bringing your breakfast tomorrow."

"Oh, that is all right," Lucy was beginning, "I ought to get up in any case—"

"No, I don't mean that. Of *course* not. It is just that young Morris asked if she might do it—she is one of the Juniors—and—"

"The abductor of George?"

"Oh, yes, I forgot you were there. Yes, that one. And she seemed to think that her life would not be complete unless she had brought up your breakfast on your last morning, so I said that as long as she didn't ask for your autograph or otherwise make a nuisance of herself, she could. I hope you don't mind. She is a nice child, and it would really give her pleasure."

Lucy, who didn't mind if her breakfast was brought by a wall-eyed and homicidal negro so long as she could eat the leathery toast in peace and quiet, said she was grateful to young Morris, and anyhow it wasn't going to be her last morning. She was going to stay on and take a lecture on Thursday.

"You *are!* Oh, that's wonderful. I'm so glad. Everyone will be glad. You are so *good* for us."

"A medicine?" Lucy wrinkled her nose in protest.

"No, a tonic."

"Somebody's Syrup," Lucy said; but she was pleased.

So pleased that even pushing little hairpins into their appointed places did not bore her with the customary frenzy of boredom. She creamed her face and considered it, unadorned and greasy in the bright hard light, with unaccustomed tolerance. There was no doubt that being a little on the plump side kept the lines away; if you had to have a face like a scone it was at least comforting that it was a smooth scone. And, now she came to think of it, one was given the looks that were appropriate; if she had Garbo's nose she would have to dress up to it, and if she had Miss Lux's cheek-bones she would have to live up to them. Lucy had never been able to live up to anything. Not even The Book.

Remembering in time that there was no bedside light—students were discouraged from working in bed—she switched the light off and crossed to pull aside the curtains of the window looking out on the courtyard. She stood there by the wide-open window, smelling the cool scented night. A great stillness had settled on Leys. The chatter, the bells, the laughter, the wild protests, the drumming of feet, the rush of bath water, the coming and going, had crystallised into this great silent bulk, a deeper darkness in the quiet dark.

"Miss Pym."

The whisper came from one of the windows opposite.

Could they see her, then? No, of course not. Someone had heard the small noise of her curtains being drawn back.

"Miss Pym, we are so glad you are staying."

So much for the college grape-vine! Not fifteen minutes since Nash said goodnight, but already the news was in the opposite wing.

Before she could answer, a chorus of whispers came from the unseen windows round the little quadrangle. Yes, Miss Pym. We are glad. Glad, Miss Pym. Yes. Yes. Glad, Miss Pym.

"Goodnight, everyone," Lucy said.

Goodnight, they said. Goodnight. So glad. Goodnight.

She wound her watch and pulled up a chair to put it on—*the* chair, rather: there was only one—so that there should be no burrowing under pillows for it in the morning; and thought how odd it was that only yesterday morning she could not wait to get out of this place.

And perhaps it was because no self-respecting psychologist would have anything to do with a thing so outmoded as Premonition that no small helpful imp from the Unexplainable was there to whisper in her drowsy ear, "Go away from here. Go away while the going is good. Go away. Away from here."

Chapter 6

*T*he chairs scraped on the parquet floor as the students rose from their kneeling position and turned to wait while the Staff filed out of morning prayers. Lucy, having become "temporary Staff," had made the gesture of attending this 8.45 ceremony as an off-set to the un-Staff-like indulgence of breakfast in bed; and she had spent the last few minutes considering the collective legs of College as spread before her in kneeling rows and marvelling at their individuality. Dress was uniform at this hour of the morning, and heads were bowed in dutiful hands, but a pair of legs were as easy to identify as a face, she found. There they were: stubborn legs, frivolous legs, neat legs, dull legs, doubtful legs—already she needed only a turn of calf and piece of ankle to say: Dakers, or Innes, or Rouse, or Beau, as the case might be. Those elegant ones at the end of the first row were The Nut Tart. Did the nuns not mind that their protégée should listen to Anglican prayers, then? And those rather stick-like ones were Campbell, and those—

"Amen," said Henrietta, with unction.

"Amen," murmured the students of Leys, and rose to their feet with the scraping of chairs. And Lucy filed out with the Staff.

"Come in and wait while I arrange this morning's post," Henrietta said, "and then I'll go over to the gymnasium with you," and she led the way into her own sitting-room, where a meek little part-time secretary was waiting for instructions. Lucy sat down on the window-seat with the *Telegraph*, and listened with only half an ear to the professional conversation that followed. Mrs So-and-so had written to ask the date of the Demonstration, Mrs Someone-else wanted to know whether there was a hotel near-by where she and her husband could stay when they came to see their daughter perform, the receipt for the butcher must be looked at and presented to his disbelieving eyes, the special lecturer for the last Friday of term had cried off, three Prospective Parents wanted prospectuses.

"All quite straightforward, I think," Henrietta said.

"Yes," agreed the meek little secretary. "I'll get on with them at once. There was a letter from Arlinghurst. It doesn't seem to be here."

"No," Henrietta said. "That can be answered later in the week."

Arlinghurst, Lucy's mind said. Arlinghurst. The school for girls, of course. A sort of female Eton. "I was at Arlinghurst," they said, and that settled it. She took her attention from the *Telegraph* leader for a moment and thought that if the "plum" that Henrietta had been waiting for was Arlinghurst then indeed it was going to create more than the usual stir among the interested Seniors. She was on the point of asking whether Arlinghurst was in fact that "plum," but was stopped partly by the presence of the meek little secretary but more immediately by the expression on Henrietta's face. Henrietta there was no denying it—Henrietta had a wary, a sort of guilty, look. The look of a person who is Up To Something.

Oh, well, thought Lucy, if she is merely hugging her lovely secret to herself, let her. I shan't spoil it for her. She followed her friend down the long corridor that ran the length of the wing, and out to the covered way that continued the corridor to the gymnasium. The gymnasium lay parallel to the house and to the right-angled wing, so that from the air the buildings made a complete letter E; the three horizontal strokes being "old house," the right-angled wing, and the gymnasium; the vertical stroke being the connecting wing and the covered way.

The door to which the covered way led was open, and from inside the gymnasium came the sounds of uncoordinated activity; voices, laughter, thudding feet. Henrietta paused by the open door and pointed through to the door on the other side, now closed. "*That* is the College crime," she said. "Crossing the gymnasium to the field-path instead of using the appointed covered way round the building. That is why we have had to lock it up. One wouldn't think that a few extra steps would mean much to students who took so many in the day, but there was no argument or threat which would stop them using the short cut through. So we removed the temptation altogether."

She turned from the open door and led the way to the other end of the building, where a small porch held the stairway to the gallery. As they climbed the stairs Henrietta paused to point to a piece of mechanism on a low trolley, which filled the well of the staircase. "That," she said, "is the most famous College character of all. That is our vacuum-cleaner; known from here to New Zealand as The Abhorrence."

"Why abhorrence?" Lucy asked.

"It used to be Nature's Abhorrence, but it became shortened to The Abhorrence. You remember the tag one is taught at school: Nature abhors a vacuum." She looked a moment longer at the monstrous object, caressing it with her eyes. "It cost us a deplorable sum, The Abhorrence, but it was money well spent. However well the gymnasium was cleaned in the old days, there was always a residue of dust, which was beaten into the air by the students' feet and sucked up, of course, by the students' respiratory passages; and the result was catarrh. Not universal, of course, but there never was a time, summer or winter, when some student or other was not having a bout of catarrh. It was Dr Knight's predecessor who suggested that it might be invisible dust that was responsible, and she was right. Since we squandered that immense sum on The Abhorrence there has been no more catarrh. And of course," she added happily, "it was a saving in the end since it is Giddy the gardener's job to vacuum the gymnasium now, and we don't have to pay cleaners."

Lucy stopped as they reached the top of the stairs, and looked over the railings into the well again. "I don't think I like it. It is very well named, it seems to me. There is something obscene about it."

"It is unbelievably powerful. And very easy to work. It takes Giddy only about twenty minutes every morning, and when he has finished there is, as he says himself, 'nothing left but the fixtures.' He is very proud of The Abhorrence. He grooms it as if it were an animal." Henrietta opened the door at the top of the stairs and they entered the gallery.

A gymnasium as a building does not permit of architecture. It is purely functional. It is an oblong box, lit by windows which are either in the roof or high up the walls. The gymnasium at Leys had windows where the walls met the roof, which is not a beautiful arrangement; but through their far-away panes at no hour of any day could direct sunlight blind a student's eyes, and so cause an accident. The great oblong box of a building was filled with the reflected radiance of a summer morning; golden and soft. Across the floor were scattered the Senior students, limbering up, practising, criticising, and in a few happy instances playing the fool.

"Do they mind an audience?" Lucy asked as they sat down.

"They are very used to one. Hardly a day goes by without a visitor of some kind."

"What is under the gallery? What is it they watch all the time?" "Themselves," said Henrietta succinctly. "The whole wall below the gallery is one long mirror."

Lucy admired the impersonal interest on the faces of the students as they watched their reflected performances. To be able to view one's physical entity with such critical detachment was surely no bad thing.

"It is one of the griefs of my life," the Dutch-doll Gage was saying, looking at her up-stretched arms, "that my arms have that kink at the elbow."

"If you listened to that Friday-friend and used your willpower, you'd have them straight by now," Stewart observed, not pausing in her own contortions.

"Probably bent back the other way," Beau Nash mocked, from a double-up position at the ribstalls.

Lucy deduced that a Friday-friend was the "interest" lecturer who appeared on Friday evenings; and wondered idly whether that particular one had called his subject "faith" or "mind-over-matter"; was it Lourdes or was it Coué?

Hasselt, the South African with the flat Primitive face, was clutching Innes's ankles in the air while Innes stood on her hands. "*Reeeee*-ly on thee *arrrrms*, Mees Innes," Hasselt was saying, in a would-be Swedish accent that was evidently a quotation from Fröken; and Innes laughed and collapsed. Looking at them, flushed and smiling (this, she thought, is the first time I have seen Mary Innes smile), Lucy felt again how out-of-place these two faces were. Hasselt's belonged above a Madonna-blue robe, with a tiny landscape of hills and castles and roads somewhere at her left ear. And Innes's to a portrait on some ancestral staircase—seventeenth century, perhaps? No, too gay, too adaptable, too arched-of-eyebrow. Sixteenth century, rather. Withdrawn, uncompromising, unforgiving; the-stake-or-nothing.

Away by herself in a far corner was Rouse, painstakingly stretching her ham-strings by walking her palms up to her feet. She couldn't really *need* to stretch her ham-strings, not after years of continued stretching, so presumably this was merely a North Country example of "makking siccar." There was no fooling about for Miss Rouse; life was real, life was earnest; life was long ham-strings and a good post in the offing. Lucy wished she liked Miss Rouse better, and looked round for Dakers as a sort of antidote. But there was no tow-head and cheerful pony-face among the collection. And then, suddenly, the desultory noise and the chatter faded. No one had come in by the open door at the far end, but there was beyond doubt a Presence in the place. Lucy could feel it coming up through the gallery floor at her feet. She remembered that there was a door at the foot of the stairway; where The Abhorrence stood. Someone had come in down there.

There was no audible word of command, but the students, who a moment before had been scattered over the floor like beads from a broken string, were now, as if by magic, standing in a still, waiting line.

Fröken Gustavsen walked out from under the gallery, and surveyed them.

"Unt wvere ess Mees Dakers?" she asked in a cool small voice. But even as she said it a flustered Dakers ran in through the open door, and stopped short as she saw the picture that waited her.

"Oh, *catastrophe!*" she wailed, and darted to the gap that someone had accommodatingly left for her. "Oh, I *am* sorry, Fröken. *Abyssmally* sorry. It was just that—"

"Ees eet proposed to be laate at the Demonstraation?" asked Fröken, with almost scientific interest.

"Oh, *no*, of *course* not, Fröken. It was just that—"

"We know. We know. Something was lost, or broke. Eef eet wass possible to come to thees plaace naakid, Mees Dakers would still find something to lose or break. Attention!"

They came to attention, and were motionless except for their quick breathing.

"Eef Mees Thomas were to pull een her stow-mach the line would be improved, I theenk."

Thomas obliged instantly.

"Unt Mees Appleyard shows too much cheen."

The plump little girl with the red cheeks pulled her chin further into her neck. "So!"

They right-turned into file, covered, and marched in single file down the gymnasium; their feet falling so lightly on the hard wood floor that they were almost inaudible.

"Quieter, quieter. Lightly, lightly!"

Was it possible?

But it was possible, apparently. Still more quietly fell those long-trained feet, until it was unbelievable that a collection of solid young females weighing individually anything up to ten stones were marching, marching, round the hall.

Lucy slid an eye round to Henrietta; and almost instantly switched it away again. The fond pride on Henrietta's large pale countenance was startling, almost painful, to see; and for a little Lucy forgot the students below and thought about Henrietta. Henrietta of the sack-line figure and the conscientious soul. Henrietta, who had had elderly parents, no sisters, and the instincts of a mother hen. No one had ever lain awake at night over Henrietta; or walked back and fore in the darkness outside her house; or even, perhaps, sent her flowers. (Which reminded her to wonder where Alan was nowadays; there had been several weeks, one spring, when she had thought quite seriously of accepting Alan, in spite of his Adam's apple. It would be nice, she had thought, to be cherished for a change. What had stopped her was the realisation that the cherishing would have to be mutual. That she would inevitably have to mend socks, for instance. She didn't like feet. Even Alan's.) Henrietta had been apparently doomed to a dull if worthy life. But it had not turned out like that. If the expression on her unguarded face had been any criterion, Henrietta had built for herself a life that was full, rich, and satisfying. She had said, in her first re-union gossip with Lucy, that when she took over Leys a decade ago it had been a small and not very popular college, and that she and Leys had flourished together; that she was, in fact, a partner now as well as Principal, and partner in a flourishing concern. But until she had surprised that look on Henrietta's face, Lucy had not realised how much her old friend identified herself with her work. That College was her world, she knew; Henrietta talked of little else. But absorption in a business was one thing, and the emotion on Henrietta's face was quite another.

She was roused from her speculations by the sound of apparatus being dragged out. The students had stopped arching themselves into bows at the ribstalls, puffed out like figureheads on a ship, and were now bringing out the booms. Lucy's shins ached with remembered pain; how often had she barked her bones against that unyielding piece of wood; certainly one of the compensations of middle-age was not having to do uncomfortable things.

The wooden upright was now standing in the middle of the floor, and the two booms were fitted into its grooved sides and hoisted as high as hands could reach. The iron pins with wooden handles shot home through their appointed holes in the upright to hold the booms up, and there was the instrument of torture ready. Not that it was shin-barking time yet; that would come later. Just now it was only "travelling." Two by two, one at each end, the students proceeded along the boom, hanging by their hands, monkey-wise. First sideways, then backwards, and lastly with a rotary movement, like a travelling top. All this was done with monotonous perfection until it was Rouse's turn to rotate. Rouse had bent her knees for the spring to the boom, and then dropped her hands and looked at her instructor with a kind of panic on her tight, freckled face.

"Oh, Fröken," she said, "I'm not going to be able to do it."

"*Nonsense*, Mees Rouse," Fröken said, encouraging but not surprised (this was apparently a repetition of some previous scene), "you have done eet perfectly since you were a Junior. You do it now of course."

In a strained silence Rouse sprang to the boom and began her progress along it. For half its length she performed with professional expertness, and then for no apparent reason her hand missed the boom as she turned, and her body swung away, suspended by her other hand. She made an effort to recover herself, pulling up with her sustaining hand, but the rhythm had broken and she dropped to her feet.

"I knew it," she said. "I'm going to be like Kenyon, Fröken. Just like Kenyon."

"*Mees* Rouse; you are not going to be like *anyone*. It is knack, that. And for a moment you haf lost the knack, that is all. You will try again."

Rouse sprang once more to the boom above her head.

"*No!*" said the Swede with emphasis; and Rouse came back to the ground looking inquiring.

"*Not* saying: Oh dear, I cannot do eet. But saying: This I do often, with ease, and now al*so*. So!"

Twice more Rouse tried, and failed.

"Ve-ry well, Mees Rouse. That will do. One half of the boom will be put up last thing at night, as it is now, and you will come een the morning early and practise, until the knack has come back."

"Poor Rouse," Lucy said, as the booms were being reversed for balance exercises, flat side up instead of rounded.

"Yes, such a pity," Henrietta said. "One of our most brilliant students."

"Brilliant?" said Lucy, surprised. It was not an adjective she would have applied to Rouse.

"In physical work, anyhow. Most brilliant. She finds written work a difficulty, but makes up for it by hard work. A model student, and a great credit to Leys. Such a pity about this little nervous development. Overanxiety, of course. It happens sometimes. Usually over something quite simple, strangely enough."

"What did she mean by 'being like Kenyon'? That is the girl whose place Teresa Desterro took, isn't it?"

"Yes. How clever of you to remember. That was a case in point. Kenyon suddenly decided that she could not balance. She had always had abnormally good balance, and there was no reason why she should lose it. But she began by being wobbly, took to jumping off in the middle of an exercise, and ended by being unable to get up from sitting position on the boom. She sat there and clung to the boom like a frightened child. Sat there and cried."

"Some inner insufficiency."

"Of course. It was not the balance that she was frightened of. But we had to send her home. We are hoping that she will come back to finish her training when she has had a long rest. She was very happy here."

Was she? thought Lucy. So happy that she broke down. What had reduced the girl who was good at balance to a crying, shivering piece of misery, clutching at the boom?

She watched with a new interest the progress of the balancing that had been poor Kenyon's Waterloo. Two by two the students somersaulted upwards on to the high boom, turned to a sitting position sideways, and then slowly stood up on the narrow ledge. Slowly one leg lifted, the muscles rippling in the light, the arms performed their appointed evolution. The faces were calm, intent. The bodies obedient, sure, and accustomed. When the exercise was finished they sank until they were sitting on their heels, upright and easy, put forward blind hands to seize the boom, descended to sideways sitting once more, and from there to a forward somersault and to the ground again.

No one fluffed or failed. The perfection was unblemished. Even Fröken found no word to say. Lucy found that she had been holding her breath. She sat back and relaxed and breathed deeply.

"That was lovely. At school the balance was much lower, wasn't it, and so it was not exciting."

Henrietta looked pleased. "Sometimes I come in just to see the balance and nothing else. So many people like the more spectacular items. The vaulting and so on. But I find the quiet control of the balance very satisfying."

The vaulting, when it came, was spectacular enough. The obstacles were, to Lucy's eyes, horrific; and she looked with uncomprehending wonder at the delighted faces of the students. They *liked* this. They liked launching themselves into nothingness, flying through the air to problematical landings, twisting and somersaulting. The restraint that had characterised their attitude up to now had vanished; there was verve in their every movement, a sort of laughter; living was good and this was a physical expression of their joy in living. Amazed, she watched the Rouse who had stumbled and failed over the simple boom exercise, performing hair-raising feats of perfection that must require the maximum of courage, control, and "knack." (Henrietta had been right, her physical performance was brilliant. She was also, no doubt, a brilliant games player; her timing was excellent. But still that "brilliant" stuck in Lucy's throat. "Brilliant" meant someone like Beau; an all-round fineness; body, mind, and spirit.)

"*Mees* Dakers! Take the left hand off at *wons*. Is eet *mountaineering* you are?"

"I didn't mean to leave it so long, Fröken. Really I didn't."

"That is understood. It is the not meaning to that ees rrreprehensible. Come again, after Mees Mathews."

Dakers came again, and this time managed to make her rebellious hand release its grip at the appropriate moment.

"Ha!" she said, delighted with her own success.

"Ha indeed," agreed Fröken, a smile breaking. "Co-ordination. All is co-ordination."

"They like Fröken, don't they," Lucy said to Henrietta, as the students tidied away the implements of their trade.

"They like all the Staff," Henrietta said, with a faint return of her Head Girl tone. "It is not advisable to keep a mistress who is unpopular, however good she may be. On the other hand it is desirable that they should be just a little in awe of their preceptors." She smiled in her senior-clergy-making-a-joke manner; Henrietta did not make jokes easily. "In their different ways, Fröken, Miss Lux, and Madame Lefevre all inspire a healthy awe."

"Madame Lefevre? If I were a student, I don't think it would be awe that would knock my knees together, but sheer terror."

"Oh, Marie is quite human when you know her. She likes being one of the College legends."

Marie and The Abhorrence, thought Lucy; two College legends. Each with identical qualities; terrible and fascinating.

The students were standing in file, breathing deeply as they raised their arms and lowered them. Their fifty minutes of concentrated activity had come to an end, and there they were: flushed, triumphant, fulfilled.

Henrietta rose to go, and as she turned to follow Lucy found that Fröken's mother had been sitting behind them in the gallery. She was a plump little woman with her hair in a bun at the back, and reminded Lucy of Mrs Noah, as portrayed by the makers of toy Arks. Lucy bowed and smiled that extra-wide-for-foreigners smile that one uses to bridge the gap of silence, and then, remembering that although this little woman spoke no English she might speak German, she tried a phrase, and the little woman's face lit up.

"To speak with you, Fräulein, is such pleasure that I will even speak German to do it," she said. "My daughter tells me that you are very distinguished."

Lucy said that she had had a success, which was not the same thing as being distinguished unfortunately; and expressed her admiration for the work she had just witnessed. Henrietta, who had taken Classics instead of Modern Languages at school, washed her hands of this exchange of civilities, and preceded them down the stairs. As Lucy and Fru Gustavsen came out into the sunlight the students were emerging from the door at the other end, running or dawdling across the covered way to the house. Last of the group came Rouse, and Lucy could not help suspecting that her emergence was timed to coincide with the passing of Henrietta. There was no need for her to linger a yard or two behind the others like that; she must see out of the tail of her eye that Henrietta was bearing down on her. In similar circumstances Lucy would have bolted, but Rouse was lingering. She liked Miss Rouse even less than usual.

Henrietta overtook the girl and paused to speak to her; and as Lucy and her companion passed them Lucy saw the expression on the tight freckled face turned up to receive the Principal's words of wisdom, and remembered what they had called that at school. "Being smarmy." And laying it on with a trowel, too, she thought with vulgar satisfaction.

"And I've always liked freckles, too," she said regretfully.

"*Bitte?*"

But this was not a subject that could be done justice to in German. The Significance of Freckles. She could see it: a thick tome full of portmanteau words and portentousness. No, it would need French to do it justice. Some distilled essence of amiable cynicism. Some pretty little blasting phrase.

"Is this your first visit to England?" she asked; and instead of entering the house with the others they strolled together through the garden toward the front of the house.

Yes, this was Fru Gustavsen's first visit to England, and it amazed her that a people who created gardens like this should also create the buildings in them. "Not this, of course," she said, "this old house is very pleasant. It is of a period that was good, yes? But what one sees from train and taxi; after Sweden it is horrible. Please do not think that I am Russian about things. It is—"

"Russian?"

"Yes. Naive, and ignorant, and sure that no one can do anything as well as my own country can do it. It is just that I am used to modern houses that are good to look at."

Lucy said that she might as well get over the subject of our cooking while she was at it.

"Ach, no," said the little woman surprisingly, "it is not so, that. My daughter has told me. Here in College it is according to regime"—Lucy thought that "according to regime" was tact of the most delicate—"and so is not typical. Nor in the hotels is it typical, my daughter says. But she has stayed in private houses in holiday time, and the dishes of the country, she says, are delicious. Not everything she liked. Not everyone likes our raw herring, after all. But the joint roasted in the oven, and the apple tart with cream, and the cold ham very pink and tender, all that is most admirable. Most admirable."

So, walking through the summer garden Lucy found herself expatiating on herrings fried in oatmeal, and parkins, and Devonshire splits, and hot-pot, and collops, and other regional delicacies. She concealed the existence of the pork pie, which she privately considered a barbarism.

As they turned the corner of the house towards the front door, they passed the windows of a lecture-room where the Seniors were already engaged in listening to Miss Lux. The windows were pushed up from the bottom as far as they would go, so that the room was visible in all its details, and Lucy cast an idle glance at the assembled profiles presented to her.

She had looked away before she realised that these were not the faces she had seen only ten minutes ago. She looked back again, startled. Gone was the excitement, the flush of exercise, the satisfaction of achievement. Gone for the moment was even the youth. The faces were tired and spiritless.

Not all of them, of course. Hasselt still had her air of calm well-being. And Beau Nash's face had still its bright indestructible good looks. But the majority looked sunken; indescribably weary. Mary Innes, seated nearest the window, had a marked line from nostrils to chin; a line that had no business there for thirty years yet.

A little saddened and uncomfortable, as one is at the unexpected discovery of an unhappiness in the middle of delight, Lucy turned her head away, and her last glimpse as she walked past was the face of Miss Rouse. And the expression on the face of Miss Rouse surprised her. It reminded her of Walberswick.

Now why Walberswick?

The wary freckled countenance of Miss Rouse had nothing in common with that formidable grande dame who was Lucy's aunt.

Certainly not.

Then why—but stop! It wasn't her aunt; it was her aunt's cat. The expression on that North Country face in the lecture-room was the expression on the face of Philadelphia when she had had cream instead of milk in her saucer. And there was only one word for that expression. The word smug.

Lucy felt, not unreasonably, that someone who had just failed to perform a routine exercise had no right to be looking smug. And the last faint lingering inclination to be sorry for Miss Rouse died in her.

Chapter 7

*M*iss Pym," said The Nut Tart, materialising at Lucy's elbow, "let us run away together."

It was Wednesday morning, and College was sunk in the thick
silence of Final Examinations. Lucy was leaning over a five-barred
gate behind the gymnasium, staring at a field of buttercups. It was
here at the end of the Leys garden that the country began; the real
country, free of the last tentacles of Larborough, unraped and un-
littered. The field sloped to a stream, beyond which was the cricket
field; and beyond that into the far distance stretched the unbroken
pattern of hedge and tree and pasture; yellow, and white, and green;
asleep in the morning sunshine.

Lucy took her eyes with difficulty from the shimmering yellow
of the buttercups that had been mesmerising her, and wondered
how many flowered silk frocks the Brazilian possessed. Here was
yet another one, shaming the English subtleties with its brilliance.

"Where do you propose that we run to?" she asked.

"Let's go to the village."

"Is there a village?"

"There is always a village in England; it is that kind of country.
But more especially there is Bidlington. You can see the weather
thing of the church steeple just over those trees there."

"It looks a long way," said Lucy, who was no great walker and
was greatly content where she was; it was a long time since she had
had a field of buttercups to look at and all time to do it in. "Is it
much of a place?"

"Oh yes. It is a two-pub village," Desterro said, as one quoting a
calibre. "Besides, it has everything a village in England should have.
Queen Elizabeth slept there, and Charles the Second hid there; and
Crusaders are buried in the church—there is one just like the manager of our ranch in Brazil—and all the cottages are obtainable on
postcards at the shop; and it appears in books, the village does—"

"Guide books, you mean?"

"No, no. It has an author who specialised in it, you understand. I read one of his books when I came first to Leys. *Rain Over the Sky* it was called. All breasts and incest. And it has the Bidlington Martyrs—that is six men who threw stones at the police station last century some time and got put in jail. Imagine a country that remembers a thing like that! In my country they use knives—when they can't afford revolvers—and we smother the corpses with flowers, and cry a lot, and forget all about it next week."

"Well—"

"We can have some coffee at The Teapot."

"A little Hibernian, surely?"

But that was too much for even an intelligent stranger to these shores. "It is *real* coffee, I may tell you. It both smells and tastes. Oh, come on, Miss Pym. It is a small fifteen minutes away, and it is not yet ten o'clock. And there is nothing to do in this place until we are summoned to eat beans at one o'clock."

"Are you not taking any of the examinations?" Lucy asked, passing meekly through the gate that was held open for her.

"Anatomy I shall take, I think. Just, as you say, for the hell of it. I have taken all the lectures, so it will be fun to find out how much I know. It is worth knowing anatomy. It is a great labour, of course; it is a subject in which imagination is not appreciated, but it is worth learning."

"I suppose so. One wouldn't feel a fool in an emergency."

"Emergency?" said Desterro, whose mind had apparently not been running along these lines. "Oh, yes, I see. But what I meant is that it is a subject that does not get out of date. Now *your* subject, if you will forgive me, Miss Pym, is continually getting out of date, no? To listen to it is charming, but to work at it would be very foolish. An idea today may be nonsense tomorrow, but a clavicle is a clavicle for all time. You see?"

Lucy saw, and envied such economy of effort.

"So tomorrow, when the Juniors take their Final Anatomy, I take it too. It is a respect-worthy thing; my grandmother would approve of it. But today they are busy about conundrums, and so me, I walk to Bidlington with the charming Miss Pym and we have coffee."

"Conundrums?"

The Nut Tart fished a folded paper from the minute pocket of her frock and read from it: "If the ball is over the touch line but has not reached the ground and a player standing inside hits or catches the ball and brings it into the court again, what decision would you give?"

In a silence more eloquent than speech she folded up the cyclostyled sheet and put it away again.

"How did you get a copy of their paper if they are still busy on the subject of games?"

"Miss Wragg gave me one. She said it might amuse me. It does."

Down between the yellow field and the may-white hedge the path led them to the stream. They paused by the small bridge to stare at the shadowed water under the willows.

"Over there," Desterro said, pointing at the level ground across the stream, "is the games field. In winter it is deep in mud, and they have bars across their shoes to keep them from slipping in it." Lucy thought that if she were saying, "They wear rings through their noses to add to their attraction," the tone would be identical. "Now we walk down-stream to the next little bridge and get on to the road there. It is not a road; just a lane." She moved in silence down the shaded path, a bright dragon-fly of a creature, graceful and alien; and Lucy was surprised to find that she was capable of so unbroken a quiet.

As they came up on to the road at last she said: "Have you any money, Miss Pym?"

"No," said Lucy, stopping in dismay.

"Neither have I. But it is all right. Miss Nevill will finance us."

"Who is Miss Nevill?"

"The lady who runs the tea-house."

"That is rather unusual, isn't it?"

"Not with me. I am always forgetting my money. But Miss Nevill is charming. Do not feel bad about it, dear Miss Pym, I am in good standing in the village, you will see."

The village was all that Desterro had claimed for it; and so was Miss Nevill. So, indeed, was The Teapot. It was one of those teashops so much despised by the bread-and-cheese-and-beer school, and so gladly welcomed by a generation of tea-drinkers who remember the fly-blown rooms behind village bakers' shops, the primitive buns with currants like dead insects, the cracked and ill-washed cups, and the black evil tea.

It had all the properties stigmatised by the literary frequenters of village inns: the Indian-tree-pattern china, the dark oak tables, the linen curtains in a Jacobean design, the herbaceous bouquets in unglazed brown jugs; yes, even the arts and crafts in the window.

But to Lucy, who in the Alan period had had her share of undusted "snugs," it was quite frankly charming. There was a rich scent of spiced cakes straight from the oven; there was, as well as the long window on the street, a further window that gave on a garden bright with colour; there was peace, and coolness, and welcome.

Miss Nevill, a large lady in a chintz apron, received Desterro as an old and valued acquaintance, and asked if she were "playing hookey, as you say on your side of the Atlantic." The Nut Tart ignored this identification with the back streets of Brooklyn. "This is Miss Pym, who writes books about psychology and is our guest at Leys," she said, politely introducing Lucy. "I have told her that here one can drink real coffee, and be in general civilised. We have no money at all, either of us, but we will have a great deal to eat and pay you back later."

This appeared to Miss Nevill to be quite a normal proposition, and she went away to the kitchen to get the coffee with neither surprise nor demur. The place was empty at this hour of the morning, and Lucy wandered round inspecting the old prints and the new crafts—she was pleased to observe that Miss Nevill drew the line at Brummagem brass door-knockers even if there were raffia mats—and then sat down with Desterro at the table looking on to the village street. Before their coffee arrived, they were joined by a middle-aged couple, husband and wife, who drove up in a car as if they were searching for the place. The car was the kind that a provincial doctor might use; low in petrol consumption and in its third or fourth year of wear. But the woman who came round from the further seat with a laughing remark to her husband was not a typical doctor's wife. She was grey, and slim, with long legs and narrow feet in good shoes. Lucy watched her with pleasure. It was not often nowadays that one saw good bones; smartness had taken the place of breeding.

"In *my* country," said Desterro, looking with a considering eye at the woman and with a contemptuous eye on the car, "that woman would have a chauffeur *and a footman.*"

It was not often, moreover, that one saw a middle-aged husband and wife so pleased with each other, Lucy thought, as she watched them come in. They had a holiday air. They came in and looked about them expectantly, questioningly.

"Yes, this is it," the woman said. "That is the window on the garden that she talks about, and there is the print of Old London Bridge."

They moved about looking at things, quietly, unself-consciously, and then took the table at the other window. Lucy was relieved to see that the man was the mate she would have chosen for such a woman; a little saturnine, perhaps, more self-absorbed than the woman; but quite admirable. He reminded her of someone, but she could not think of whom; someone whom she admired. The eyebrows, it was. Dark level brush-marks low over the eyes. His suit was very old, she noticed; well-pressed and kept, but with that much-cleaned air that overtakes a garment in its old age. The woman's suit, a tweed, was frankly shabby, and her stockings were darned—very neatly darned—at the heels. Her hands, too, looked as if they were accustomed to household tasks, and her fine grey hair was washed at home and unwaved. What had she got to look so happy about, this woman who struggled with straitened means? Was it just being on holiday with a husband she loved? Was it that that gave her grey luminous eyes their almost childlike happiness?

Miss Nevill came in with the coffee and a large plate of spiced cakes shining with newness and crisp at the edges. Lucy decided to forget her weight just this once and enjoy herself. This was a decision she made with deplorable frequency.

As she poured the coffee she heard the man say: "Good morning. We have come all the way from the West Country to taste your griddle cakes. Do you think you could make us some, or are you too busy at this hour of the morning?"

"If you are too busy it doesn't matter," said the woman with the hard-worked hands. "We shall have some of the cakes that smell so good."

But Miss Nevill would not be a minute in preparing the griddle cakes. She had no batter standing, she said, so the griddle cakes would not be as wonderful as when the batter was allowed to stand; but she was not often asked for them in summer time.

"No, I expect not. But our daughter at Leys has talked so often of them, and this may be our only chance of tasting them." The woman smiled, half it seemed at the thought of her daughter, half at their own childish desire.

So they were College parents.

Whose? Lucy wondered, watching them over the rim of her coffee cup.

Beau's, perhaps. Oh, no; Beau was rich, of course. Then whose?

She wouldn't mind giving them to Dakers, but there were objections. That tow-head could not be sired by that dark grave man; nor could that adult and intelligent woman have given birth to the through-other piece of nonsense that was Dakers.

And then, quite suddenly, she knew whose eyebrows those were. Mary Innes's.

They were Mary Innes's parents. And in some odd way they explained Mary Innes. Her gravity; her air of belonging to a century other than this one; her not finding life very amusing. To have standards to live up to, but to have little money to live up to them with, was not a happy combination for a girl burdened with the need to make a success of her training.

Into the silence that had succeeded Miss Nevill's departure, Lucy heard her own voice saying, "Forgive me, but is your name Innes?"

They turned to her, puzzled for a moment; then the woman smiled. "Yes," she said. "Have we met somewhere?"

"No," said poor Lucy, growing a little pink as she always did when her impulsiveness had led her into an unexpected situation. "But I recognised your husband's eyebrows."

"My *eyebrows*," said Mr Innes.

But his wife, quicker-witted, laughed. "Of course," she said. "Mary! Are you from Leys, then? Do you know Mary?" Her face lit and her voice sang as she said it. Do you know Mary? Was it because she was going to see her daughter that she was happy today?

Lucy explained who she was, and introduced Desterro, who was pleased to find that this charming couple knew all about her. "There is very little we don't know about Leys," Mrs Innes said, "even if we have never seen the place."

"Not seen it? Won't you come over and have your coffee with us, by the way?"

"It was too far for us to inspect it before Mary went there. So we decided that we would wait until her training was finished and then come to the Demonstration." Lucy deduced that if fares had not been a problem, Mary Innes's mother would not have had to wait these years before seeing Leys; she would have come if only so that she could picture her daughter in her setting.

"But you are going there now, surely?"

"No. Oddly enough, we are not. We are on our way to Larborough, where my husband—he's a doctor—has to attend a meeting. We *could* go to Leys, of course, but it is the week of the Final Examinations, and it would only distract Mary to have her parents descending suddenly on her for no reason. It is a little difficult to pass by when we are so near, but we have waited so long that we can wait another ten days or so. What we couldn't resist was turning off the main West road as far as Bidlington. We didn't expect to run into any College people at this hour of the morning, especially in Examination Week, and we did want to see the place that Mary had talked so much about."

"We knew that we shouldn't have time on Demonstration Day," Dr Innes said. "There will be so much to see then. A surprisingly varied training, isn't it?"

Lucy agreed, and described her first impression of the staffroom with its varying worlds.

"Yes. We were a little puzzled when Mary chose that for her career—she had never shown any great interest in games, and I had thoughts that she might take a medical training—but she said she wanted a career with a great many facets; and she seems to have found it!"

Lucy remembered the concentration of purpose in those level brows; she had been right in her face-reading; if Mary Innes had an ambition it would not lightly be given up. Really, eyebrows were the most *helpful* things. If psychology ever went out of fashion she would write a book about face-reading. Under another name, of course. Face-reading was not well seen among the intelligentsia.

"She is very beautiful, your daughter," said Desterro unexpectedly. She polished off a large mouthful of spice cake, and then, feeling the surprise in their silence, looked up at them. "Is it not a proper thing in England to compliment parents on their daughter's looks?"

"Oh, yes," Mrs Innes said hastily, "it is not that, it is just that we had not thought of Mary as beautiful. She is nice to look at, of course; at least we think so, but then parents are apt to be fatuous about an only daughter. She—"

"When I came first to this place," Desterro said, reaching out for another cake from the plate (how *did* she keep that figure!), "it was raining, and all the dirty leaves were hanging down from the trees like dead bats and dripping on everyone, and everyone was rushing round College and saying: 'Oh *darling*, how *are* you? Did you have nice hols? Darling, you won't believe it but I left my new hockey stick on *Crewe platform!*' And then I saw a girl who was *not* running about and *not* talking, and who looked a little like my great-grandmother's grandmother who is in the dining-room at the house of my grandmother's great-nephew, so I said: 'It is not after all a barbarism. If it were as it seems to be that girl would not be here. I shall stay.' Is there more coffee, Miss Pym, please? She is not only beautiful, your daughter, she is the only beautiful person at Leys."

"What about Beau Nash?" asked Lucy loyally.

"In England at Christmas time—*very* little milk, Miss Pym, please—the magazines go all gay and give away bright pretty pictures that one can frame and hang above the kitchen mantelpiece to make glad the hearts of the cook and her friends. Very shiny, they are, with—"

"Now that," said Mrs Innes, "is sheer libel! Beau is lovely, quite lovely, and you know it. I forgot that you would know Beau, too," she turned to Lucy, "that you would know them all, in fact. Beau is the only one we know because she came to us for the holidays once; at Easter time when the West is kinder than the rest of England; and Mary went to them once for some weeks in the summer. We admired Beau so much." She looked to her husband for confirmation; he had been too withdrawn.

Dr Innes roused himself—he had the wrung-out look of the overworked G.P. when he sank into repose—and the saturnine face took on a boyish and faintly malicious, if tender, amusement. "It was very odd to see our competent and self-reliant Mary being looked after," he said.

Mrs Innes evidently felt that this was not the contribution she had been looking for, but decided to make the best of it. "Perhaps," she said, as if thinking of it for the first time, "we have always taken Mary's self-reliance so much for granted that she finds it pleasant to be looked after." And to Miss Pym: "It is because they are complementary, I think, that they are such great friends. I am glad about it because we like Beau so much, and because Mary has never made intimate friends easily."

"It is a very strenuous training, isn't it?" Dr Innes said. "I sometimes look at my daughter's notebooks and wonder why they bother with stuff that even a doctor forgets as soon as he leaves medical school."

"The cross-section of the villi," remembered Lucy.

"Yes; that sort of thing. You seem to have picked up a remarkable amount of physical lore in four days."

The crumpets came, and even without the ritual standing of the batter they were worth coming even from the West Country for, supposing that had been true. It was a happy party. Indeed, Lucy felt that the whole room was soaked in happiness; that happiness bathed it like a reflexion from the sunlight outside. Even the doctor's tired face looked content and relaxed. As for Mrs Innes, Lucy had rarely seen such happiness on the face of a woman; merely being in this room that her daughter had used so often was, it seemed, a sort of communion with her, and in a few days' time she would see her in the flesh and share her achievement.

If I had gone back to London, Lucy thought, I would have had no share in this. What would I be doing? Eleven o'clock. Going for a walk in the Park, and deciding how to get out of being guest of honour at some literary dinner. Instead I have this. And all because Dr Knight wanted to go to a medical conference tomorrow. No, because once long ago Henrietta stood up for me at school. It was odd to think that this sun-lit moment in an English June began to take shape thirty years ago in a dark crowded school cloakroom filled with little girls putting on their goloshes. What were first causes, anyhow?

"This has been *very* pleasant," said Mrs Innes, as they stood once more in the village street. "And it is nice to think that we shall meet again so soon. You will still be at Leys when the Demonstration comes off, won't you?"

"I hope so," Lucy said, and wondered if she could cadge a bed from Henrietta for so long.

"And you have both promised, solemnly and on your word of honour, not to tell anyone that you saw us today," Dr Innes said.

"We have," they said, waiting to see their new friends get into their car.

"Do you think I can turn the car in one swoop without hitting the Post Office?" Dr Innes said, consideringly.

"I should hate to make any more Bidlington martyrs," his wife said. "A tiresome breed. On the other hand, what is this life without some risk?"

So Dr Innes encouraged his engine and swung into this risky evolution. The hub of his off front wheel left a faint smudge on the Post Office's virgin white-wash.

"Gervase Innes, his mark," said Mrs Innes, and waved her hand to them. "Till Demonstration Day, and pray for fine weather for it! Au revoir!"

They watched the car grow small up the village street, and turned towards the field-path and Leys.

"*Nice* people," Desterro said.

"Charming. Odd to think that we should never have met them if you had not had a craving for good coffee this morning."

"That is the kind of English, let me tell you in confidence, Miss Pym, that make every other nation on earth sick with envy. So quiet, so well-bred, so good to look at. They are poor, too, did you notice? Her blouse is quite washed-out. It used to be blue, the blouse; you could see when she leaned forward and her collar lifted a little. It is wrong that they should be so poor, people like that."

"It must have cost her a lot not to see her daughter when she was so near," Lucy said reflectively.

"Ah, but she has character, that woman. She was right not to come. None of the Seniors has one little particle of interest to spare this week. Take away even one little particle, and *woops!* the whole thing comes crashing down." She plucked an ox-eyed daisy from the bank by the bridge and gave the first giggle Lucy had ever heard from her. "I wonder how my colleagues are getting on with their one-leg-over-the-line puzzles."

Lucy was wondering how she herself would appear in Mary Innes's Sunday letter home. "It will be amusing," Mrs Innes had said, "to get back home and read all about you in Mary's Sunday letter. Something to do with relativity. Like coming back the previous night."

"It was strange that Mary Innes should have reminded you of someone in a portrait," she said to Desterro. "That is how she seemed to me, too."

"Ah yes, my great-grandmother's grandmother." Desterro dropped the daisy on to the surface of the water and watched the stream bear it down under the bridge and away out of sight. "I did not say it to the nice Inneses, but my great-grandmother's grandmother was a little unpopular with her generation."

"Oh? Shy, perhaps. What we call nowadays an inferiority complex."

"I would not know about that. Her husband died too conveniently. It is always sad for a woman when her husband dies too conveniently."

"You mean that she murdered him!" Lucy said, standing stock-still in the summer landscape, appalled.

"Oh, no. There was no *scandal*." Desterro sounded reproving. "It was just that her husband died too conveniently. He drank too much, and was a great gambler, and *not* very attractive. And there was a loose tread at the top of the stairs. A long flight of stairs. And he stepped on it one day when he was drunk. That was all."

"And did she marry again?" Lucy asked, having absorbed this information.

"Oh, no. She was not in love with anyone else. She had her son to bring up, and the estates were safe for him now that there was no one to gamble them away. She was a very good estate manager. That is where my grandmother got her talent from. When my grandmother came out from England to marry my grandfather she had never been further from her own county than Charles Street, West One; and in six months she was running the estate." Desterro sighed with admiration. "They are wonderful the English."

Chapter 8

*M*iss Pym was invigilating at the Senior Pathology Final, so as to give Miss Lux more time for the correction and marking of previous papers, when Henrietta's meek little secretary tiptoed in and laid the day's letters reverently on the desk in front of her. Miss Pym had been frowning over a copy of the examination paper, and thinking how badly words like *arthritis gonorrhoica* and *suppurative tenosynovitis* went with the clean air of a summer morning after breakfast. *Emphysema* was not so bad; it might be the gardener's name for a flower. A sort of columbine. And *kyphosis* she could picture as something in the dahlia line. *Myelitis* would be a small creeping plant, very blue, with a tendency to turn pink if not watched. And *tabes dorsalis* was obviously an exotic affair of the tiger lily persuasion, expensive and very faintly obscene.

Chorea. Sclerosis. Pes Varus.

Dear goodness. Did those young things know all that? Differentiate the treatment of something-or-other according to whether it is (a) congenital (b) traumatic (c) hysterical. Well, well. How had she ever erred so far as to feel patronizing about these young creatures?

She looked down from her dais with affection on them; all writing away for dear life. The faces were sober but not on the whole anxious. Only Rouse looked worried, and Lucy decided that her face looked better worried than smug, and withheld her sympathy. Dakers was ploughing steadily over the paper with her tongue protruding and an automatic sigh as she came to the end of each line and began a new one. Beau was confident and detached as if she were writing invitations; doubt was something that had never entered her life; neither her present standing nor her future life was in jeopardy. Stewart's face under the bright red hair was pale, but a faint smile played around her mouth; Stewart's future, too, was as-

sured; she was going to the Cordwainers School, going home to
Scotland bringing her sheaves with her, and Lucy was going to the
party she was giving in her room on Saturday night to celebrate.
("We don't ask Staff to individual parties, but since you are not
quite Staff you could rank as just a friend.") The Four Disciples,
spread across the front row, cast each other communal and encouraging glances now and then; this was their own particular subject
and obviously what they did not know about it was not worth mentioning; Manchester was going to get its money's worth. Innes, by
the window, lifted her head every now and then to look out at the
garden, as if seeking refreshment; that it was not inspiration she
sought was apparent from her unhurried progress through the
questions; she turned to the garden for some spiritual comfort; it
was as if she said: "Ah yes, you are still there, Beauty; there is a
world outside this lecture-room." Innes was beginning to look as if
College might be too much with her. That tired line from nostril to
mouth was still there.

Lucy picked up the paper-knife from Miss Lux's neat desk,
and considered her post. Three bills, which she need not disturb
the holy hush by opening. A receipt. An Annual Report. A large,
square, deep-blue, and very stiff and expensive envelope with
MILLICENT CRAYE embossed in scarlet across the flap (really there
was no end to the self-advertising instinct in actresses) which
would be five lines of thanks with a broad nib and outsize capitals
for her contribution to the Benevolent Fund. That left only
Mrs Montmorency. So into Mrs Montmorency she inserted the
paper-knife.

Maddam (wrote Mrs Montmorency),
    I as done as you sed an sent the urgent by passel post. Reg-
istered. Fred put it into Wigmore Street on is way to work re-
ceit enclosed I as packed the blue and the blouses also under-
close as per instruxions your pink nitie not having come back
from the laundry I as put in the hedge instead hopping this
will be all rite.
    Maddam, please dont think that I presoom but this is a
good thing. It is no life for a woman writin books and not
havin no young company please dont think I presoom but I as
your welfare at heart you ben one of the nicest ladies I ever
worked for Fred says the same. A nice lady like that he says

when look at the things thats around not write it isnt please
dont think I presoom

yrs respectfully
Mrs Montmorency.

P.S. Wire brush in toe of swede shoe

Lucy spent the next fifteen minutes being touched by Mrs
Montmorency's concern for her, being furious with the laundry,
and wondering why she paid education rates. It wasn't public
schools for everyone that was needed but a great many elementary
school classes of not more than a dozen, where the future Mrs
Montmorencys could be adequately taken care of in the matter of
the Three Rs. Old McLean, their jobbing gardener at home, had
left school when he was twelve, but he could write as good a letter
as any University acquaintance of hers; and why? Because he came
from a small village school with small classes and a good school-
master.

And of course because he lived in an age when the Three Rs
were more important than Free Milk. They made him literate and
left the rest to him. He lived on white-flour scones and stewed tea
and died hale and hearty at the age of ninety-two.

She was roused from her musings by Miss Rouse. There was a
new expression on Miss Rouse's face, and Lucy didn't like the new
expression at all. She had seen Miss Rouse look despairing,
smarmy, smug, and worried, but till now she had never seen her
look furtive.

Why should she be looking furtive?

She watched her for a moment or two, curiously.

Rouse looked up and caught her gaze and looked quickly away
again. Her furtive expression had gone; what had taken its place
was one labelled Consciously Carefree. Lucy knew all about that
expression. She had not been Form Mistress of the Lower Fourth
for nothing. Every eater of illicit sweets wore that expression. So
did those who were doing their arithmetic in French lesson.

So did those who were cheating at an examination.

What was it Henrietta had said? "She finds written work difficult."

So.

Emphysema and all those flowery sounding things were too
much for Miss Rouse, and so she had provided some aids to memory. The question was what kind of aids and where were they? Not

on her knee. The desks were open in front, so that a lap was no safe billet for a crib. And one could hardly write enough pathology on one's fingernails to be of much help; fingernails were useful only for formula. The obvious solution would be the notes up the sleeve, with or without an arrangement of elastic, but these girls had no sleeves below the elbow. Then, what? Where? Or was it that she was just having glimpses of O'Donnell's paper in front of her? Or Thomas's to her right?

Lucy went back to her letters for a moment or two, and waited. All schoolmistresses know this gambit. She looked up casually at the Seniors in general and again went back to her letters. When next she looked up it was straight at Rouse. Rouse's head was low over her paper and in her left hand she held a handkerchief. Now even on a handkerchief it is not possible to write anything that is helpful on so large a subject as pathology, nor is it an easy affair to manipulate; on the other hand, handkerchiefs were not common objects at Leys, and certainly no one else was clutching one and dabbing a nose occasionally with it. Lucy decided that whatever sources of information Rouse had lay in her left hand. Her desk was at the back on the window side, so that the wall was to her left; whatever she did with her left hand was not overlooked by anyone.

Well, thought Lucy, what does A do?

Walk down the room and demand the handkerchief and find that it is a square piece of white linen, nine inches by nine inches, with the owner's initials properly marked in one corner, and as candid as a good laundry can make it?

Demand the handkerchief and unearth a scandal that will blast the Senior set like a hurricane at their least stable moment?

See that Rouse gets no chance to use her source of information, and say nothing?

The last was certainly the most sensible. She couldn't have obtained very much aid from anything so far; it would be doing no injustice to anyone to make her a present of that small amount.

Lucy left the desk and strolled down the room to the back, where she stood leaning against the wall, Thomas to her right and Rouse to her left. Thomas stopped writing for a moment and looked up at her with a quick smile. But Rouse did not look up. And Lucy watched the hot blood dye her sandy neck a dull red. And presently she put away the handkerchief—and whatever else that hand contained—in her tunic pocket.

Well, she had foiled the machinations of the evil-intended, but she could feel no satisfaction about it. For the first time it occurred to her that what was very naughty and deplorable in the fourth form was quite sickening in a Senior Final. She was glad that it was Rouse and not anyone else. Presently she strolled back to her desk on the dais, and as far as she could see Rouse made no further effort to obtain help with her paper. On the contrary, she was very obviously in deep waters. And Lucy was infuriated to find herself feeling sorry for her. Yes, *sorry*. Sorry for *Rouse*. After all, the girl had worked. Worked like a madman, if all reports were true. It was not as if she had been taking an easy way out to save herself effort. It was just that she found acquiring theoretical knowledge difficult almost to the point of impossibility, and had succumbed to temptation in her desperation.

This point of view made Lucy feel much better about it, and she spent the rest of her invigilating time speculating quite undistressedly about the nature of the crib. She would look again at the examination paper, and consider the enormous range of material it covered, and wonder how Rouse had devised anything at once helpful and invisible. She longed to ask her.

The most likely explanation was that there were two or three particular subjects that Rouse was afraid of, and that help with them was scribbled on a piece of paper.

Innes was the first to shuffle the written sheets together and slip the waiting clip over the upper edge. She read through the pages, making a correction now and then, laid the sheaf down on her desk, sat for a few relaxed moments taking in the beauty of the garden, and then rose quietly and came forward to leave her work on the desk in front of Miss Pym.

"Oh, *catastrophe!*" wailed Dakers; "is somebody *finished?* And I have a whole question and a half to do yet!"

"Hush, Miss Dakers," said Lucy, as in duty bound.

Dakers favoured her with a radiant smile, and went back to her steady plodding.

Stewart and Beau Nash followed Innes very shortly; and presently the pile of papers in front of Miss Pym began to grow. With five minutes of the allotted time still to go there were only three students left in the examination room: the little dark Welsh Thomas, who presumably slept too much to be a good "study"; the imperturbable Dakers still plodding steadily; and a flushed and unhappy Rouse, who was plainly making heavy weather of it. With two minutes still to go there was only Rouse; she was looking confused and desperate; making hasty little excursions back and fore through her papers, deleting, amending, and adding.

The distant yelling of the bell put an end to her indecisions and to her chances; whatever she had done must now abide. She shoved her papers hastily together, aware that the bell meant an instant appearance in the gymnasium and that Fröken would not consider the ordeal of an examination paper any excuse for being late, and brought them up to Lucy at the double. Lucy had expected her to avoid her eye, or otherwise to display symptoms of awkwardness or self-consciousness. But Rouse surprised her by a frank smile and a still franker remark.

"Whoo!" said Rouse, blowing her breath out expressively, "that was a horror." And she ran out to join the rest of her set.

Lucy opened the much-scored offering and looked at it with compunction. She had been imagining things. Rouse had not been cheating after all. Or at least not systematically. That furtive look might have been the guilt of inadequacy, now she came to think of it; or perhaps, at the worst, a hope of hints from her neighbour's paper. And that flush that had dyed her neck was due to her awareness of being suspected; Lucy could remember very well even yet times at school when the very knowledge that her innocent act was capable of sinister interpretation was enough to make her face burn with false guilt. Really, she owed Rouse an apology. She would find some way of making it up to her.

She stacked the papers neatly together, put them in alphabetical order from sheer force of habit, checked their number, and carried them upstairs to Miss Lux's room, glad that it would not be her chore to correct them. There was no one in the room, so she left them on the desk and stood for a moment wondering what to do with the hour before lunch. She toyed with the thought of watching the gymnastics, but decided that she must not allow the performance to become familiar, and consequently devoid of wonder, before Demonstration Day. Having induced Henrietta to keep her until then—Henrietta had not required much inducement, it is true—she was not going to mar her own pleasure in the day by too many tastings beforehand. She went downstairs, lingering by the tall window on the landing—how well eighteenth-century architects had understood how to build houses; nowadays landings were not things to linger on, but breakneck little corners lit, if at all, by a small circular light like a ship's port-hole—and from there, beyond the courtyard and the opposite wing she could see the elms of

the field that led to the stream. She would go and look at the buttercups for a little. There was no better way of wasting a summer
hour than staring at a field of buttercups. So down she went, and
along the wing, and so out to the covered path to the gymnasium,
for beyond the gymnasium were the buttercups.

As she went down the covered way her eye caught a spot of
colour in the grass that bordered the path. At first she took it for a
flower petal and was going to ignore it, when she noticed that it was
square, and certainly not a petal. She turned back and picked it up.
It was a tiny address-book in faded red leather. It looked as if it had
formed part of the fittings of a handbag; an old-fashioned handbag
probably since one did not see leather nor workmanship like that
nowadays. Idly, with her thoughts on the femininity of that vanished bag with its miniature fittings—there would of course have
been a little tube of scent, and a gold pencil, and one of those ivory
tablets to scribble engagements on—she opened it, and read, on a
page crowded with writing in a tiny script: "Path. anat. changes as
in traumatic. Fibrin in synov. memb. Tissues contr. by fibr. and fold
of caps. joined to bone. Anchylosis. Fever."

It meant nothing to Lucy as information but its meaning was
obvious. She turned the pages, finding nearly all of them crowded
with the same succinct information. Even the X page—devoted by
the keepers of address-books to measurements for new curtains or
that good story that would do for the W.R.I. speech next Tuesday—even the X page had cryptic remarks about rays. What
bowled Lucy over was the comprehensiveness of it; the premeditation. This was no product of a last-minute panic; it was a coldblooded insurance against failure. By the neatness and method
shown in the compiling, it looked as though the entries had been
made as each subject was studied. Had the notebook been of a normal size, in fact, it would have been nothing more than a legitimate
précis of a subject. But no one making a précis would have chosen
a book not much larger than a good-sized postage stamp when an
equally portable but normal-sized notebook could be had for a few
pence. The use of a book so tiny that a mapping pen had been necessary in order to make the entries legible could have only one explanation.

Lucy knew very well what had happened. Rouse had pulled out
her handkerchief as she ran. She had never before carried the little
book in a pocket, and her mind was divided urgently between the
bad paper she had done and the fear of being late for gymnastics,

so there was no care in the pulling out of the handkerchief. And so the little book dropped on to the grass at the edge of the path.

She walked on beyond the gymnasium and through the five-barred gate into the field, but she had no eye for the buttercups. She walked on slowly down the field to the coolness under the willows and the quiet green water. She hung over the rail of the bridge watching the weeds trail and the occasional fish dart, and thought about Rouse. There was no name on the flyleaf, nor as far as she could see any means of identification in the book itself. Most schools taught script as well as current form in writing nowadays; and script was much less easily recognisable than current writing. A handwriting expert would no doubt be easily able to trace the author, but to what end? There was no evidence that the book had been used for any illegitimate purpose; no evidence even that it had been compiled with any sinister intent—although the presumption was strong. If she handed it over to Henrietta as lost property what would happen? No one would claim it, and Henrietta would be faced with the fact that one of her Seniors had prepared a précis that could be conveniently palmed at an examination.

If nothing was ever said about the book, then Rouse's punishment would be a perpetual and lifelong doubt as to what had become of it. Lucy felt that such a punishment fitted the crime admirably. She thumbed the tiny India-paper pages once more, wondered again what Edwardian elegancy had given it birth, and leaning over, dropped it into the water.

As she walked back to the house she wondered how Rouse had managed the other Final Examinations Pathology could be no less easy to memorise than Kinesiology or any of the other obscurities studied by the budding P.T.I. How had Rouse, the difficult "study," managed with these? Was the little red leather book only one of five or six? Did one invest in a mapping pen for one subject only? One *could*, she supposed, buy very tiny address-books if one searched long enough; though not perhaps so fine or so tiny as the little red one. It may have been the possession of the little red one which first put the thought of insurance against failure into Rouse's mind.

She remembered that the result of the previous examinations would be exhibited on the letter-board by the students' entrance, so instead of walking round to the front of the house as she had meant to she turned in at the quadrangle door. There were several Junior lists pinned to the green baize, and three Senior lists. Lucy read them with interest.

FINAL PHYSIOLOGY

Honours
Mary Innes	93

First Class
Wilhelmina Hasselt	87
Pamela Nash	86
Sheena Stewart	82
Pauline Lucas	79
Janet Gage	79
Barbara Rouse	77

Second Class
Dorothy Littlejohn	74
Beatrice Appleyard	71
Joan Dakers	69
Eileen O'Donnell	68
Margaret Campbell	67
Ruth Waymark	66
Lilian Mathews	65

and the rest, below that mark, mere Passes.

Well, Rouse had scraped into a First by two marks, it seemed. Lucy turned to the next list.

FINAL MEDICALS

First Class
Pauline Lucas	89
Pamela Nash	89
Mary Innes	89
Dorothy Littlejohn	87
Ruth Waymark	85
Wilhelmina Hasselt	82
Sheena Stewart	80
Lilian Mathews	79
Barbara Rouse	79

Second Class
Jenny Burton	73
Janet Gage	72
Eileen O'Donnell	71
Joan Dakers	69

and the rest mere Passes.
And again Rouse managed to scrape a First.

FINAL KINESIOLOGY

Honours
Mary Innes	96

First Class
Pauline Lucas	89
Pamela Nash	88
Sheena Stewart	87
Wilhelmina Hasselt	85
Ruth Waymark	80
Janet Gage	79
Joan Dakers	78
Barbara Rouse	78

Another First! Three Firsts out of three tries. The girl who found written work so difficult? There was surely a strong case for the existence of more little notebooks?

Oh, well; this being Friday, tomorrow would see the end of examinations and it was not likely that Rouse would, after this morning's experience, bring any extraneous help to the test tomorrow morning. The little book prepared for tomorrow, if it existed, would be still-born.

While she mused over the lists (it was nice to see that Dakers had managed at least one First) Miss Lux arrived with the results of yesterday's Final.

"Thank you for bringing up the Path. papers," she said. "And thank you for invigilating. It helped me to get these done."

She thumbed the drawing-pin into the board and stood back to look at the list.

FINAL HYGIENE

Honours
Mary Innes	91

First Class
Pamela Nash	88
Wilhelmina Hasselt	87
Sheena Stewart	86

Pauline Lucas   81
Barbara Rouse   81

"Barbara Rouse, eighty-one," Lucy said, before she thought.
"Yes, surprising, isn't it?" Miss Lux said placidly. "But she works
like a black. She is so brilliant in her physical work that I think it
maddens her to be far down any list."
"Innes seems to make a habit of heading the lists."
"Oh, Innes is wasted here."
"Why? The more intelligence one brings to a profession the better surely?"
"Yes, but with an intelligence like Innes's one could head much
more thrilling lists than these. It's a waste."
"I somehow don't think that Rouse will get eighty-one in today's
paper," Lucy said, as they moved away from the board.
"Why? Was she in difficulties?"
"Bogged down," said Lucy; and hoped that she did not sound
too pleased. "*What* a life it is," she added, as the five-minute bell
rang, and the dripping Seniors came running in from the gymnasium, ripping off their tunics as they tore into the bathrooms for a
shower before the gong went. "When you think of the leisurely way
we acquired knowledge. At university, I mean. If we sat a Final Examination, the rest of the day would almost certainly be our own to
recover in. But these young creatures do it as part of their time-
table."
From the bathrooms came cursing and chaos. "Oh, Donnie, you
swine, that was *my* shower!" "Mark, you brute, get off my foot!"
"Oh, no, you don't, my girl; these are *my* tights!" "God, look at my
blisters!" "Kick over my shoe, Greengage, the floor's sopping."
"*Must* you shoot the cold water round like that, you chump!"
"They like it, you know," Lux said. "In their heart they like the
rush and the overwork. It makes them feel important. Very few of
them will ever have any legitimate reason for feeling important, and
so it is comforting for them to have the image of it at least."
"Cynic," said Lucy.
"No, psychologist." She inclined her head towards the row as
they moved away. "It sounds like a free fight, doesn't it? Everyone
sounds desperate and furious. But it is all play-acting. In five minutes they will be sitting like good children in the dining-room with
not a hair out of place."
And so they were. When the Staff filed in to the top table five

minutes later, there were the scramblers of the bathroom, standing dutifully behind their chairs, calm, and combed, and neat, their interest already absorbed by the thought of food. Truly, they *were* children. Whatever heartbreaks they suffered would be forgotten in tomorrow's toy. It was absurd to think of them as harassed adults, trembling on the precipice edge of breakdown. They were volatile children; their griefs were loud, and vocal, and transient. For five days now, ever since The Nut Tart had been so knowing under the cedar tree last Saturday afternoon, she had looked for some hint of abnormality, of aberration, of lack of control, and what had she found? One very normal and highly controlled piece of dishonesty; unremarkable except for its neatness.

"Isn't it nice," Henrietta said, helping out something that looked like cheese-and-vegetable pie, "I've got a post in Wales for little Miss Thomas. Near Aberystwyth. I am so delighted."

"A very soporific atmosphere, Wales," Madame Lefevre said, consideringly; blasting Henrietta's whole conception with five gentle words.

"Yes," said Miss Lux, "who is going to keep her awake?"

"It's not who is going to *keep* her awake, it's who is going to wake her in the first place," Wragg said, with a greedy eye on the pie. Wragg was still near enough her College days to be possessed of a large hunger and no gastronomic judgment.

"Wales is her native atmosphere," Henrietta said, repressive, "and I have no doubt she will know how to deal with it. In any case she is not likely to have any great success *outside* Wales; the Welsh are extraordinarily provincial, using the word in its literal sense. I have noticed before how they gravitated back to their own province. It is as well for them to go there in the first place if the chance offers. And luckily, in this case, it has offered very conveniently. The junior gymnast of three. That will suit Miss Thomas very nicely. She has no great initiative, I'm afraid."

"Is Thomas's the only new post?" Wragg asked, falling on the pie.

"No, there was one that I wanted to discuss with you."

Aha, thought Lucy, here comes Arlinghurst at last.

"Ling Abbey wants someone to be wholly responsible for the younger children, and to take dancing as well all through the school. That is to say, the dancing would have to be of a high standard. I wanted to give the post to Miss Dakers—she is very good with small children—but I wanted to know what you thought of her dancing, Marie."

"She is a cow," said Madame.

"She *is* very good with little ones, though," Wragg said.

"A *heavy* cow," said Madame.

"It isn't her personal performance that is important," Henrietta said. "It is her power to inspire performance in others. Does she understand the subject sufficiently, that is the point?"

"Oh, she knows the difference between three-four time and four-four, certainly."

"I saw Dakers teaching the babies at West Larborough their dances for their do last Christmas," Wragg said, "and she was wonderful. I was there to crit. her, and I was so fascinated I forgot to make any notes at all. I think she would be just right for that post."

"Well, Marie."

"I can't imagine why anyone bothers," Madame said. "The dancing at Ling Abbey is quite frightful anyhow."

This Pilatian washing of hands, in spite of its negative quality, seemed positive enough to all concerned. It was apparent that Dakers was going to Ling Abbey. And since Ling Abbey was a good place to be going to—if one had to be going to a school—Lucy was glad for her. She glanced down the room to where, even above this babel, Dakers' high voice could be heard italicising her opinion of the Pathology paper. "I said that a joint went *gummy*, my dear, and I'm certain that's not the *technical* word."

"Shall I warn them both, Miss Hodge?" Wragg asked, later. (Warn?)

"No, just Miss Thomas today, I think. I shall tell Miss Dakers tomorrow. It is better to spread the excitement out."

As the Staff rose from their table and filed out, Wragg turned to the politely standing and temporarily silent students and said: "Miss Hodge will see Miss Thomas in her office when luncheon is over."

This was apparently a ritual pronouncement, for the buzz broke out almost before the Staff had reached the door. "A post, Tommy!" "Congrats., Tommy." "Hoorah, old Thomas." "Up the Welsh!" "Hope it's a thousand a year, Tom." "Iss nott thatt the lucky thing, now!" "Cheers, Tommy!"

And still no one had mentioned Arlinghurst.

Chapter 9

*W*hen Lucy first heard Arlinghurst mentioned it was not by any of the Staff but by the students themselves. She had spent Saturday afternoon with Fröken and her mother, helping to finish the Swedish folk costumes which the Juniors would wear for some of the country dances at the Demonstration. It was a lovely day and they had taken the piles of bright primitive colour to the furthest corner of the garden, where they could sit and look over the English countryside. Both cricket and tennis matches were "away" this week, so the garden was deserted, and no toiling figures marred the virgin green of the field beyond the stream. They had sewed in great beatitude, and Fru Gustavsen seemed to have reported well of Lucy to her daughter, for Fröken's reticence had largely vanished, and Lucy was delighted to find that a young woman who had always reminded her of sunlight on snow was the possessor of a rich warm chuckle and a sense of humour to match. (It is true that Lucy's sewing considerably shook Fru Gustavsen's faith in her, but much must be forgiven the English.) Fru Gustavsen had gone back to the subject of food, and held forth at great length on the virtues of something called "frikadellar"; which, it appeared, was a kind of mince. Lucy (whose cooking consisted of chopping up a few tomatoes in a pan at the last moment, adding whatever was to be cooked, and pouring some cream over the lot) thought it a very lengthy and complicated affair, and decided to have nothing to do with it.

"Are you doing anything tonight?" Fröken had asked. "My mother and I are going into Larborough to the theatre. She has not yet seen an English company. We would be delighted if you would care to come with us."

Lucy explained that tonight she was going to a party in Stewart's room to celebrate her post. "I understand that Staff don't usually go, but I am not real Staff."

Fröken slid an eye round at her and said: "You ought to be. You are very good for them."

That medicinal phrase again. As if she were a prescription.

"How?"

"Oh, in ways too subtle for my English—and *much* too subtle for the German language. It is, a little, that you wear heels; a little, that you have written a book; a little, that they don't have to be just a tiny bit afraid of you; a little, that—oh, a thousand littles. You have come at a good time for them; a time when they need a distraction that is not—distracting. Oh, dear, I wish my English was better."

"You mean, I am a dose of alkali on an acid stomach."

Fröken gave her unexpected chuckle. "Yes, just that. I am sorry you will not be coming to the theatre, but it is a great mark of favour to be invited to a students' party, and you will enjoy it, I think. Everyone will be happy tonight, now that the examinations are over. Once they come back from the match they are free for the week-end. So they will be gay this Saturday. Off the chain," she added, in English.

And off the chain they certainly were. As Lucy came in by the quadrangle door, leaving Fröken and her mother to go round to the front of the house where they lived, a blast of sound rose up round her. The rush of bath water on two floors, the calling of innumerable voices, the drum-fire of feet on bare oak stairs, singing, whistling, crooning. Both teams had apparently come back—victorious to judge by the atmosphere—and the place was alive. The place was also excited, and one word was woven like a leit-motif through the babble. Arlinghurst. Arlinghurst. As she walked past the ground-floor bathrooms on her way to the stairs, she heard the first of it. "*Have you heard*, my dear! *Arlinghurst!*"

"What?"

"*Arling-hurst!*"

A tap was turned off.

"I can't hear with the blasted water. Where, did you say?"

"Arlinghurst!"

"I don't believe it."

"But yes," said another voice, "it's true."

"It can't be; they don't send First Posters to Arlinghurst."

"No, really it's true. Miss Hodge's sec. told Jolly in confidence and Jolly told her sister in the village and *she* told Miss Nevill at The Teapot, and Miss Nevill talked about it to The Nut Tart when she was there to tea this afternoon with that cousin of hers."

"Is that gigolo here again?"

"I say, *Arlinghurst!* Who would believe it! Whom do you think they'll give it to?"

"Oh, that's easy."

"Yes, Innes of course."

"Lucky Innes."

"Oh, well, she deserves it."

"Just imagine. *Arlinghurst!*"

And on the first floor it was the same; the rushing of bath water, the splashing, the babble, and Arlinghurst.

"But who told you?"

"The Nut Tart."

"Oh, my dear, she's dippy, everyone knows."

"Well, it's a cert for Innes, anyhow, so it's nothing to do with me. I'll probably wind up in the L.C.C."

"She may be dippy, but she's not M.D., and she'd got it pat. She didn't even know what Arlinghurst *was*, so she wasn't making it up. She said: 'Is it a school?' "

"*Is it a school!* My hat!"

"I say, won't The Hodge be just dizzy with pride, my dears!"

"D'you suppose she'll be dizzy enough to give us tart for supper instead of that milk pudding?"

"I expect Jolly made the puddings yesterday and they're all standing waiting in rows on the hatch."

"Oh, well, they can wait as far as I'm concerned. I'm for Larborough."

"Me, too. I say, is Innes there?"

"No, she's finished. She's dressing."

"I say, let's throw Innes a party, all of us, instead of letting her give a little private one. After all, it's—"

"Yes. Let's do that, shall we? After all, it isn't every day that someone gets a post like that, and Innes deserves it, and everyone will be glad about it, and—"

"Yes, let's have a do in the common-room."

"After all, it's a sort of communal honour. A decoration for Leys."

"Arlinghurst! Who'd have believed it?"

"Arlinghurst!"

Lucy wondered if the meek little secretary's indiscretion had been prompted by the knowledge that the news was about to be made public. Even the cautious and secretive Henrietta could not sit on such a piece of information much longer; if for no other reason than that Arlinghurst would be expecting an answer. Lucy supposed that Henrietta had been waiting until the "bad" week was over before providing her sensation; she could not help feeling that it was a very neat piece of timing.

As she walked along the corridor to her cell at the end, she met Innes, buttoning herself into a fresh cotton frock.

"Well," said Lucy, "it seems to have been a successful afternoon."

"The row, you mean?" Innes said. "Yes, we won. But the row is not a war chant. It's a paean of praise that they will never have to live this week again."

Lucy noticed how unconsciously she had used the word "they." She wondered for a moment at the girl's calm. Had she, possibly, not yet heard about the Arlinghurst vacancy? And then, as Innes moved from the dimness of the corridor into the light from Dakers' wide-open door, Lucy saw the radiance on her face. And her own heart turned over in sympathy. *That* was how it felt, was it? Like seeing Heaven opened.

"*You* look happy, anyhow," she said, falling back on bald platitude since there were no words to describe what was shining in Innes's eyes.

"To use a phrase of O'Donnell's, I wouldn't call the king my cousin," Innes said, as they moved apart. "You are coming to Stewart's party, aren't you? That's good. We'll meet again there."

Lucy powdered her nose, and decided to go over to the "old house" and see how the Staff were reacting to the news of Arlinghurst. Perhaps there would still be some tea; she had forgotten all about tea and so apparently had the Gustavsens. She re-arranged the bottle of champagne which was waiting for Stewart's party in the ice she had begged from Miss Joliffe, regretted yet once more that the Larborough wine merchant had not been able to supply a better year, but trusted (rightly) that Rheims and all its products were simply "champagne" to a student.

To go over to the "old house" one had to pass both the Seniors' bedrooms and the first-floor bathrooms again, and it seemed to Lucy that the orchestration of sound had reached a new pitch of intensity, as more and more students heard the news and passed it on and commented on it above the roar of water, and banging of doors, and the thudding of feet. It was strange to come from that blare of sound and excitement into the quiet, the cream paint and mahogany, the tall windows and space, the waiting peace of the "house." She crossed the wide landing and opened the door of the drawing-room. Here too there was quiet, and she had shut the door behind her and come forward into the room before becoming aware of the exact quality of that quiet. Before realising, in fact, that the quiet was electric, and that she had walked into the middle of a Staff row. A row, moreover, if one was to judge from the faces, of most unholy proportions. Henrietta was standing, flushed and defensive and stubborn, with her back to the fireplace, and the others were staring at her, accusing and angry.

Lucy would have beaten a retreat, but someone had automatically poured out a cup of tea and thrust it at her, and she could hardly put it down again and walk out. Though she would have liked to for more reasons than one. The tea was almost black and quite cold.

No one took any notice of Lucy. Either they accepted her as one of themselves, or they were too absorbed in their quarrel to realise her fully. Their eyes had acknowledged her presence with the same absent acquiescence that greets a ticket collector in a railway carriage; a legitimate intruder but not a partaker in discussion.

"It's monstrous," Madame was saying. "Monstrous!" For the first time within Lucy's experience she had discarded her Récamier pose and was sitting with both slender feet planted firmly on the floor.

Miss Lux was standing behind her, her bleak face even bleaker than usual, and two very unusual spots of bright red high on her cheek-bones. Fröken was sitting back in one of the chintz-covered chairs looking contemptuous and sullen. And Wragg, hovering by the window, looked as much confused and embarrassed as angry; as if, having so lately come up from the mortal world, she found this battling of Olympians disconcerting.

"I fail to see anything monstrous about it," Henrietta said with an attempt at her Head Girl manner; but even to Lucy's ears it had a synthetic quality. Henrietta was obviously in a spot.

"It is more than monstrous," Madame said, "it is very nearly criminal."

"Marie, don't be absurd."

"Criminal from more than one point of view. You propose to palm off an inferior product on someone who expects the best; and you propose at the same time to lower the credit of Leys so that it will take twenty years to recover it, if it ever recovers. And for what, I ask you? For what? Just to satisfy some whim of your own!"

"I fail to see where the whim comes in," Henrietta snapped,

dropping some of her Great Dane dignity at this thrust. "No one here can deny that she is a brilliant student, that she has worked hard and deserved her reward. Even her theoretical work has been consistently good this term."

"Not consistently," said Miss Lux in a voice like water dropping on to a metal pan. "According to the paper I corrected last night, she could not even get a Second in Pathology."

It was here that Lucy stopped wondering what to do with her tea, and pricked up her ears.

"Oh, dear, that is a pity," Henrietta said, genuinely distracted from the main point by this news. "She was doing so well. So much better than I had dared to hope."

"The girl is a moron, and you know it," Madame said.

"But that is nonsense. She is one of the most brilliant students Leys has ever—"

"For God's sake, Henrietta, stop saying that. You know as well as any of us what they mean by brilliant." She flourished a sheet of blue note-paper in her thin brown hand, and holding it at arm's length (she was "getting on" was Madame, and she hated to wear glasses), read aloud. "'We wondered if, among your Leaving Students, you had one brilliant enough to fill this place. Someone who would be "Arlinghurst" from the beginning, and so more part of the school and its traditions than a migrant can ever be, and at the same time continue the Leys connection that has been so fortunate for us.' The Leys connection that has been so fortunate! And you propose to end it by sending them Rouse!"

"I don't know why you are all so stubbornly against her. It can be nothing but prejudice. She has been a model student, and no one has ever said a word against her until now. Until I am prepared to give her the rewards of her work. And then you are all suddenly furious. I am entirely at a loss. Fröken! Surely you will bear me out. You can never have had a better pupil than Miss Rouse."

"Mees Rouse is a very good gymnast. She is also, I understand from Mees Wragg, a very fine games player. But when she goes out from thees plaace it will not matter any longer that she can do a handstand better than anyone else and that she ees a good half-back. What will matter then is character. And what Mees Rouse has of character is neither very much nor very admirable."

"Fröken!" Henrietta sounded shocked. "I thought you liked her."

"Did you?" The two cold, disinterested little words said: I am expected to like all my students; if you had known whom I liked or disliked I should be unworthy.

"Well, you *asked* Sigrid, and you've certainly been told," Madame said, delighted. "I could not have put it better myself."

"Perhaps—" began Miss Wragg. "I mean, it *is* for gymnastics they want her. They are separate departments at Arlinghurst: the gym., and the games, and the dancing; one person for each. So perhaps Rouse wouldn't be too bad."

Lucy wondered whether this tentative offering was inspired by Rouse's performance for Miss Wragg's department at half-back, or by a desire to smooth things over and draw the two edges of the yawning gap even a little nearer.

"Doreen, my pet," said Madame, in the tolerant tones that one uses to a half-wit, "what they are looking for is not someone who 'wouldn't be too bad'; what they are looking for is someone so outstanding that she can step straight from College to be one of the gymnasts at the best girls' school in England. Does that sound to you like Miss Rouse, do you think?"

"No. No, I suppose not. It does sound like Innes, I must admit."

"Quite so. It does sound like Innes. And it is beyond the wit of man why it doesn't sound like Innes to Miss Hodge." She fixed Henrietta with her enormous black eyes, and Henrietta winced.

"I've told you! There is a vacancy at the Wycherley Orthopaedic Hospital that would be ideal for Miss Innes. She is excellent at medical work."

"God give me patience! The Wycherley Orthopaedic Hospital!"

"Doesn't the unity of the opposition persuade you that you are wrong, Miss Hodge?" It was Miss Lux, incisive even in her anger. "Being a minority of one is not a very strong position."

But that was the wrong thing to say. If Henrietta had ever been open to persuasion, she was by now far past that stage. She reacted to Miss Lux's logic with a spurt of fury.

"My position as a minority may not be very strong, Miss Lux, but my position as Principal of this college is unquestioned, and what you think or do not think of my decisions is immaterial. I took you into my confidence, as I always have, about the disposal of this vacancy. That you do not agree with me is, of course, regrettable, but of no consequence. It is for me to make decisions here, and in this case I have made it. You are free to disapprove, of course; but not to interfere, I am glad to say."

She picked up her cup with a hand that shook, and put it away on the tea-tray, as was her habit; and then made for the door. Lumbering and hurt, like a wounded elephant, thought Lucy.

"Just a minute, Henrietta!" Madame said, her eyes having lighted on Lucy and a spark of amused malice appearing therein. "Let us ask the outsider and the trained psychologist."

"But I am *not* a trained psychologist," said poor Lucy.

"Just let us hear what Miss Pym thinks."

"I don't know what Miss Pym has to do with the vacancies—"

"No, not about the appointment. Just what she thinks of these two students. Come along, Miss Pym. Give us your frank opinion. After a mere week among us you cannot be accused of bias."

"You mean Rouse and Innes?" asked Lucy, playing for time. Henrietta had paused with her hand on the door. "I don't know them of course; but it certainly surprises me that Miss Hodge should think of giving that appointment to Rouse. I don't think she is at all—in fact I think she would be *quite* the wrong person."

Henrietta, to whom this was apparently the last straw, cast her an *et tu Brute* look and blundered out of the room, with a muttered remark about it being "surprising what a pretty face can do to influence people." Which Lucy took to refer to Innes, not to herself.

In the drawing-room was a very crowded silence.

"I thought I knew all about Henrietta," Madame said at last, reflective and puzzled.

"I thought one could trust her to do justice," Miss Lux said, bitter.

Fröken got to her feet without a word, and still looking contemptuous and sullen, walked out of the room. They watched her go with gloomy approbation; her silence was comment enough.

"It is a pity that this should have happened, when everything was going so well," Wragg said, producing another of her unhelpful offerings. She was like someone running round with black-currant lozenges to the victims of an earthquake. "Everyone has been so pleased with their posts, and—"

"Do you think she will come to her senses when she has had time to think it over?" Lux asked Madame.

"She has been thinking it over for nearly a week. Or rather she has had it settled in her mind for nearly a week; so that by now it has become established fact and she will not be able to see it any other way."

"And yet she couldn't have been sure about—I mean, sure of our reaction—or she would not have kept it to herself until now. Perhaps when she thinks it over—"

"When she thinks it over she will remember that Catherine Lux questioned the Royal Prerogative—"

"But there is a Board in the background. There is no question of Divine Right. There must be someone who can be appealed to against her decision. An injustice like this can't be allowed to happen just because—"

"Of course there is a Board. You met them when you got the job here. You see one of them when she comes to supper on the Friday nights when the lecture happens to be on Yoga, or Theosophy, or Voodoo, or what not. A greedy slug in amber beads and black satin, with the brains of a louse. She thinks Henrietta is wonderful. So do the rest of the Board. And so, let me say it here and now, do I. That is what makes it all so shocking. That Henrietta, the shrewd Henrietta who built this place up from something not much better than a dame's school, should be so blind, so suddenly devoid of the most elementary judgment—it's fantastic. Fantastic!"

"But there must be *something* we can do—"

"My good if tactless Catherine," Madame said, rising gracefully to her feet, "all we can do is go to our rooms and pray." She reached for the scarf that even in the hottest weather draped her thin body as she moved from one room to another. "There are also the lesser resorts of aspirin and a hot bath. They may not move the Almighty but they are beneficial to the blood pressure." She floated out of the room; as nearly without substance as a human being can be.

"If Madame can't do anything to influence Miss Hodge, I don't see that anyone else can," Wragg said.

"I certainly can't," Lux said. "I just rub her the wrong way. Even if I didn't, even if I had the charm of Cleopatra and she hung on my every word, how can one reduce a mental astigmatism like that? She is quite honest about it, you see. She is one of the most honest persons I have ever met. She really *sees* the thing like that; she really sees Rouse as everything that is admirable and deserving, and thinks we are prejudiced and oppositional. How can one alter a thing like that?" She stared a moment, blankly, at the bright window, and then picked up her book. "I must go and change, if I can find a free bathroom."

Her going left Lucy alone with Miss Wragg, who obviously wanted to go too but did not know how to make her departure sufficiently graceful.

"It is a mess, isn't it?" she proffered.

"Yes, it seems a pity," Lucy said, thinking how inadequately it summed up the situation; she was still stunned by the new aspect presented to her. She became aware that Wragg was still in her outdoor clothes. "When did you hear about it?"

"I heard the students talking about it downstairs—when we came in from the match, I mean—and I bolted up here to see if it was true, and I walked straight into it. Into the row, I mean. It *is* a pity; everything was going so well."

"You know that the students take it for granted that Innes will get the post," Lucy said.

"Yes." Wragg sounded sober. "I heard them in the bathrooms. It was a natural thing to think. All of us would take it for granted that Innes would be the one. She is not very good for me—in games, I mean—but she is a good coach. She understands what she is doing. And of course in other things she is brilliant. She really should have been a doctor or something brainy like that. Oh, well, I suppose I must go and get out of these things." She hesitated a moment. "Don't think we do this often, will you, Miss Pym? This is the first time I have seen the Staff het up about anything. We are all such good friends as a rule. That's what makes this such a pity. I wish someone could change Miss Hodge's point of view. But if I know her no one can do that."

Chapter 10

No one can do that, they said; but it was just possible that she, Lucy, might. When the door closed behind Wragg she found herself faced with her own dilemma. She had reason to know that Miss Lux's first view of Henrietta's reaction was much truer than her second. That mental astigmatism that Lux talked about was not great enough to exclude a doubt of her own judgment; Lucy had not forgotten the odd guilty look on Henrietta's face last Monday morning when her secretary had tried to bring up the subject of the Arlinghurst letter. It had been an up-to-something look. Not a Father Christmas up-to-something, either. Quite definitely it was something she was a little ashamed of. Astigmatic enough she might be to find Rouse worthy, but not cock-eyed enough to be unaware that Innes had a prior claim.

And that being so, then it was Lucy's duty to put certain facts before her. It was a great pity about the little red book now dissolving into pulp among the weeds—she had been altogether too impulsive about its disposal—but book or no book, she must brave Henrietta and produce some cogent reasons for her belief that Rouse was not a suitable person to be appointed to Arlinghurst.

It surprised her a little to find that an interview with Henrietta on this footing brought back a school-girl qualm that had no place in the bosom of any adult; least of all one who was a Celebrity. But she was greatly fortified by that remark of Henrietta's about "pretty faces." That was a remark that Henrietta really should not have made.

She got up and put the cup of black, cold tea on the tray; noticing regretfully that they had had almond-fingers for tea; she would have very much liked an almond-finger ten minutes ago, but now she could not have eaten even an éclair. It would not be true to say that she had discovered feet of clay in Henrietta, since she had never made any sort of image in Henrietta's likeness. But she *had* looked up to Henrietta as a person of superior worth to her own, and the habit of mind acquired at school had stayed with her. She was therefore shocked to find her capable of what was at worst cheating, and at the very least a *bêtise*. She wondered what there had been in Rouse to unseat so solid a judgment as Henrietta's. That remark about "pretty faces." That unconsidered, blurted remark. Was there something in that plain, North Country face that had touched a woman so used to good looks in her students? Was there something in the plain, unloved, hardworking, ambitious Rouse that Henrietta identified with herself? Was it like seeing some old struggle of her own? So that she adopted, and championed, and watched over her unconsciously. Her disappointment over Rouse's comparative failure in Pathology had been so keen that it had distracted her even from the urgent quarrel with her Staff.

Or was it just that Rouse had made good use of those admiring—not to say adoring—looks that she had sampled on the covered way the other morning?

No, not that. Henrietta had her faults but silliness was not one of them. She had, moreover, like everyone else in the scholastic world, served a long apprenticeship to adoration, both real and synthetic. Her interest in Rouse might be heightened by Rouse's obvious discipleship, but the origin of that interest was elsewhere. It was most likely that the Henrietta who had been plain, and unloved, and ambitious, had viewed the plain, and unloved, and ambitious young Rouse with a kindliness that was half recognition.

Lucy wondered whether to go to Henrietta at once, or to wait until she simmered down. The snag was that as Henrietta simmered down, so would her own determination to beard Henrietta on the subject. All things considered, and with the memory of previous fiascos, she thought that she had better go now while her feet would still carry her in the proper direction.

There was no immediate answer to her tap at the office door, and for a moment she hoped that Henrietta had retired to her own room upstairs and so reprieved her from her plain duty for a few hours longer. But no; there was her voice bidding her come in, and in went Lucy, feeling horribly like a culprit and furious with herself for being such a rabbit. Henrietta was still flushed and wounded-looking, and if she had not been Henrietta, Lucy would have said that there were tears in her eyes; but that was manifestly impossible. She was very busy about some papers on her desk, but Lucy felt that until she had knocked Henrietta's only activity had been mental.

"Henrietta," she began, "I'm afraid you thought it presumptuous of me to express an opinion about Miss Rouse." (Oh dear, that sounded very pompous!)

"A little uncalled-for," Henrietta said coldly.

Of all the Henrietta phrases! "Uncalled-for!" "But it *was* called for," she pointed out. "That is just what it was. I should never have dreamed of offering my opinion unasked. The point is, that opinion—"

"I don't think we need discuss it, Lucy. It is a small matter, anyhow, and not one to—"

"But it *isn't* a small matter. That is why I've come to see you."

"We pride ourselves in this country, don't we, that everyone has a right to his opinion, and a right to express it. Well, you expressed it—"

"When I was asked to."

"When you were asked to. And all I say is that it was a little tactless of you to take sides in a matter of which you can know very little, if anything at all."

"But that is just it. I *do* know something about it. You think I am just prejudiced against Miss Rouse because she is not very attractive—"

"Not very attractive to *you*, perhaps," amended Henrietta quickly.

"Shall we say not very obviously attractive," Lucy said, annoyed and beginning to feel better. "You think I have judged her merely on her social graces, but that is not so."

"On what else could you judge her? You know nothing of her work."

"I invigilated at one of her examinations."

Lucy observed with satisfaction that this brought Henrietta up short.

There was silence while one could count five.

"And what quality of a student could you possibly test by invigilating at an examination?"

"Her honesty."

"Lucy!" But the tone was not shocked. It was a warning. It meant, if it meant anything: Do-you-know-what-the-punishment-for-slander-is?

"Yes, I said her honesty."

"Are you trying to tell me that you found Miss Rouse—obtaining help during an examination?"

"She did her best. I haven't spent the best years of my life in fourth-form circles without knowing the routine. It was at the beginning that I noticed what she was about, and since I didn't want to make a scandal of it I thought the best way was to prevent her from using it."

"Using it? Using what?"

"The little book."

"You mean that you saw a student using a small book at an examination, and *said nothing about it?*"

"No, of course not. It was only afterwards that I knew about the book. All that I knew at the time was that there was something she was trying to refer to. She had a handkerchief in her left hand—although she hadn't a cold, and seemed to have no legitimate use for the thing—and she had that bag-of-sweets-under-the-desk look that you know as well as I do. There wasn't anything under her desk, so I deduced that whatever she had was in her hand with the handkerchief. As I had no proof—"

"Ah! You had no proof."

"No. I had no proof, and I didn't want to upset the whole room by demanding any, so I invigilated from the back of the room, where I was directly behind her, and could see to it that she got no help from anything or anybody."

"But if you did not ask her about the affair, how did you know about a book?"

"I found the book lying by the path to the gymnasium. It was—"

"You mean the book was not in her desk? Not *in the room at all?*"

"No. If it had been in her desk you would have known about it five minutes later. And if I had found such a book in the examination room I would have brought it to you at once."

"Such a book? What kind of book?"

"A tiny address-book filled with Pathology notes."

"An address-book?"

"Yes. A, arthritis—and so on."

"You mean that the book was merely a book of reference compiled by a student in the course of her study?"

"Not 'merely.' "

"And *why* not 'merely.'?"

"Because the whole thing was not much bigger than an outsize postage stamp."

Lucy waited for this to sink in.

"And what connection is there between this book you found and Miss Rouse?"

"Only that no one else in the room had a bag-of-sweets-under-the-desk expression; in fact, no one else seemed to be particularly worried about the paper. And that Rouse was the last to leave the room."

"What has that to do with it?"

"If the book had been dropped before Rouse came out of the examination room it would almost certainly have been picked up by one of the other students. It was a sort of dahlia red, and was lying very obviously on the grass at the edge of the path."

"Not *on the path?*"

"No," said Lucy, reluctantly. "About half an inch off it."

"So that it could have been passed many times by a crowd of chattering students excited over an examination, and anxious not to be late for their next class?"

"Yes, I suppose it could."

"And was there a name on the book?"

"No."

"No name? No means of identification?"

"Nothing except the script. It was in script, not current form."

"I see." One could see Henrietta bracing herself. "Then you had better bring me the book and we will take the proper steps to have the owner identified."

"I haven't got it," said poor Lucy. "I drowned it."

"You what?"

"I mean, I dropped it into the stream by the games field."

"That was surely a very extraordinary thing to do!" *Was* there a spark of relief in Henrietta's eye?

"Not really. I suppose it was impetuous. But what was I to do with it? It was a précis of Pathology, and the Pathology Final was over and the book had not been used. Whatever had been planned had not been carried out. Why, then, worry you by bringing the book to you? It seemed to me that the best punishment for who-ever had compiled the thing was never to know what had become of it. To live the rest of her days with a question at the back of her mind."

" 'Whoever had compiled it.' That describes the situation, doesn't it? There is not one iota of evidence to connect the book with Miss Rouse."

"If there had been evidence, as I said before, I would have brought it to you. There is only presumption. But the presumption is very strong. A great many people are ruled out altogether."

"Why?"

"Those who don't consider themselves likely to be at a loss don't waste time insuring against it. That is to say, those who are good on the theoretical side are innocent. But you yourself told me that Rouse finds written work extraordinarily difficult."

"So do a great many others."

"Yes. But there is another factor. A great many no doubt find difficulty with theory but don't particularly care as long as they struggle through. But Rouse is brilliant at practical work, and it galls her to be also-ran in examinations. She is ambitious, and a hard worker. She wants the fruits of her labours, and she is very doubtful of getting them. Hence the little book."

"That, my dear Lucy, is psychological theorising."

"Maybe. But psychological theorising is what Madame asked me to do, in the drawing-room. You thought I had based my opinion on a mere prejudice. I thought you ought to know that I had some better foundation for my theorising." She watched Henrietta's flushed face, and wondered if she might venture into the minefield again, now that she had proved that she was not merely wantonly trespassing. "As one friend to another, Henrietta, I don't understand why you even consider sending Rouse to Arlinghurst when you have someone as suitable as Innes." And she waited for the explosion.

But there was no explosion. Henrietta sat in heavy silence, making a dotted pattern with her pen on the fine clean blotting-paper; a measure of her troubled state, since neither doodling nor wasting paper was a habit of Henrietta's.

"I don't think you know much about Innes," she said at length, in a reasonably friendly tone. "Because she has a brilliant mind and good looks you credit her with all the other virtues. Virtues that she quite definitely does not possess. She has no sense of humour, and she does not make friends easily—two serious disabilities in anyone who plans to live the communal life of a residential school. Her very brilliance is a drawback in that it makes it difficult for her to suffer fools gladly. She has a tendency—quite unconscious, I am sure—to look down her nose at the rest of the world." (Lucy remembered suddenly how, this very afternoon, Innes had automatically used the word "they" in referring to the students. Old Henrietta was shrewd enough.) "In fact, ever since she came here she has left me with the impression that she despises Leys, and is using it only as a means to an end."

"Oh, surely not," Lucy protested mechanically, while her inner self was wondering whether that were indeed so, and whether that accounted for a great deal that had puzzled her about Mary Innes. If being at Leys had indeed been a secret purgatory, a trial endured as a means to an end, that might explain that too-adult reticence, that air of concentration in a person who had no natural need of concentration, that inability to smile.

She remembered, irrelevantly, Desterro's lighthearted account of how she changed her mind and decided to stay at Leys when she saw Innes. It was because Innes was not "of" Leys that Desterro had noticed her on that dreary autumn afternoon, picking her out from the milling crowd as someone from an alien, more adult world.

"But she is very popular with her colleagues," Lucy said aloud.

"Yes, her own set like her well enough. They find her aloofness—intriguing I think. She is not so popular with children, unfortunately; they find her intimidating. If you look at her crit. book—the book that the Staff use for reports when they go to outside classes with students—you would find that the word 'antagonistic' appears again and again in describing her attitude."

"Perhaps it is just those eyebrows," Lucy said. She saw that Henrietta, uncomprehending, thought this a mere frivolousness, and added: "Or perhaps like so many people she has an inner doubt about herself, in spite of all appearances to the contrary. That is the usual explanation of antagonism as an attitude."

"I find psychologists' explanations a little too glib," Henrietta said. "If one has not the natural graces to attract friendship, one can at least make an *effort* to be friendly. Miss Rouse does."

(I bet! thought Lucy.)

"It is a great tragedy to lack the natural graces; one is not only denied the ready friendship of one's colleagues but one has to overcome the unreasoning prejudice of those in office. Miss Rouse has fought hard to overcome her natural disabilities: her slowness of mind and her lack of good looks; she goes more than halfway to meet people and puts herself to great pains to be adaptable and pleasant and—and—and acceptable to people. And with her pupils she succeeds. They like her and look forward to seeing her; her reports from her classes are excellent. But with the Staff in their private capacity she has failed. They see only her personal—unattrac- tiveness, and her efforts to be friendly and adaptable have merely annoyed them." She looked up from her pen-patterns and caught Lucy's expression. "Oh, yes, you thought my preference for Rouse as a candidate was the result of blind prejudice, didn't you? Believe me, I have not brought up Leys to its present position without un- derstanding something of how the human mind works. Rouse has worked hard during her years here and has made a success of them; she is popular with her pupils and sufficiently adaptable to make herself acceptable to her colleagues; she has the friendliness and the adaptability that Innes so conspicuously lacks; and there is no rea- son why she should not go to Arlinghurst with my warm recom- mendation."

"Except that she is dishonest."

Henrietta flung the pen down on its tray with a clatter.

"That is a sample of what the unattractive girl has to struggle against," she said, all righteousness and wrath. "You think that one out of a score of girls has tried to cheat at an examination, and you pick on Rouse. Why? Because you don't like her face—or her ex- pression, if one must be accurate."

So it had been no use. Lucy drew her feet under and prepared to go.

"There is nothing at all to connect the little book you found with any particular student. You just remembered that you hadn't liked the looks of Miss Rouse; and so she was the culprit. The culprit— if there is one; I should be sorry to think that any Senior student of mine would stoop to such a subterfuge—the culprit is probably the prettiest and most innocent member of the set. You should know enough of human nature, as distinct from psychology, to know that."

Lucy was not sure whether it was this last thrust or the accusa- tion of fastening crime on to plain faces, but she was very angry by the time she reached the door.

"There is just one point, Henrietta," she said, pausing with the door-knob in her hand.

"Yes?"

"Rouse managed to get a First in all her Finals so far."

"Yes."

"That is odd, isn't it?"

"Not at all odd. She had worked very hard."

"It's odd, all the same; because on the occasion when someone was prevented from using the little red book she could not even get a Second."

And she closed the door quietly behind her.

"Let her stew over that," she thought.

As she made her way over the wing her anger gave way to depression. Henrietta was, as Lux said, honest, and that honesty made arguing with her hopeless. Up to a point she was shrewd and clear-minded, and beyond that she suffered from Miss Lux's "astigmatism"; and for mental astigmatism nothing could be done. Henrietta was not consciously cheating, and therefore could not be reasoned, frightened, nor cajoled into a different course. Lucy thought with something like dismay of the party she was to attend presently. How was she going to face a gathering of Seniors, all speculating about Arlinghurst and rejoicing openly over Innes's luck?

How was she going to face Innes herself, with the radiance in her eyes? The Innes who "wouldn't call the king her cousin."

Chapter 11

*S*upper at Leys was the formal meal of the day, with the Seniors in their dancing silks and the rest in supper frocks, but on Saturdays when so many had "Larborough leave" it was a much more casual affair. Students sat where they pleased, and, within the bounds of convention, wore what they pleased. Tonight the atmosphere was even more informal than usual since so many had departed to celebrate the end of Examination Week elsewhere, and still more were planning celebration on the spot after supper. Henrietta did not appear—it was understood that she was having a tray in her room—and Madame Lefevre was absent on concerns of her own. Fröken and her mother were at the theatre in Larborough, so Lucy shared the top table with Miss Lux and Miss Wragg, and found it very pleasant. By tacit consent the burning question of Arlinghurst was not referred to.

"One would think," said Miss Lux, turning over with a fastidious fork the vegetable mysteries on her plate, "that on a night of celebration Miss Joliffe would have provided something more alluring than a scranbag."

"It's *because* it's a celebration night that she doesn't bother," said Wragg, eating heartily. "She knows quite well that there is enough good food waiting upstairs to sink a battleship."

"Not for us, unfortunately. Miss Pym must put something in her pocket for us when she is coming away."

"I bought some cream puffs in Larborough on the way home from the match," Wragg confessed. "We can have our coffee in my room and have a gorge."

Miss Lux looked as if she would have preferred cheese straws, but in spite of her chill incisiveness she was a kind person, so she said: "I take that very kindly of you, so I do."

"I thought you would be going to the theatre, or I would have suggested it before."

"An out-moded convention," said Miss Lux.

"Don't you like the theatre?" asked the surprised Lucy, to whom the theatre was still a part of childhood's magic.

Miss Lux stopped looking with a questioning revulsion at a piece of carrot, and said: "Have you ever considered what you would think of the theatre if you were taken to it for the first time, now, without the referred affection of childhood pantomimes and what not? Would you really find a few dressed-up figures posturing in a lighted box *entertaining?* And the absurd convention of intervals— once devoted to the promenade of toilettes and now perpetuated for the benefit of the bar. What other entertainment would permit such arbitrary interruption? Does one stop in the middle of a symphony to go and have a drink?"

"But a play is made that way," Lucy protested.

"Yes. As I said; an out-moded convention."

This dashed Lucy a little, not because of her lingering affection for the theatre, but because she had been so wrong about Miss Lux. She would have said that Miss Lux would be a passionate attender of try-out performances in the drearier suburbs of plays devoted to a Cause and Effects.

"Well, I nearly went tonight myself," Wragg said, "just to see Edward Adrian again. I had a terrific rave on him when I was a student. I expect he's a bit passé now. Have you ever seen him?"

"Not on the stage. He used to spend his holidays with us when he was a boy." Miss Lux ran her fork once more through the heap on her plate and decided that there was nothing further worth her attention.

"*Used to spend the holidays!* At your *house?*"

"Yes, he went to school with my brother."

"Good heavens! How absolutely incredible!"

"What is incredible about it?"

"I mean, one just doesn't think of Edward Adrian as being an ordinary person that people *know*. Just a schoolboy like anyone else."

"A very horrid little boy."

"Oh, *no!*"

"A quite revolting little boy. Always watching himself in mirrors. And possessed of a remarkable talent for getting the best of everything that was going." She sounded calm, and clinical, and detached.

"Oh, Catherine, you shatter me."

"No one I have ever met had the same genius for leaving someone holding the baby as Teddy Adrian."

"He has other kinds of genius though, surely," Lucy ventured.

"He has talent, yes."

"Do you still see him?" asked Wragg, still a little dazzled to be
getting first-hand news of Olympus.

"Only by accident. When my brother died we gave up the house
that our parents had had, and there were no more family gatherings."

"And you've never seen him on the stage?"

"Never."

"And you didn't even go to a sixpenny bus-ride into Larborough
to see him play tonight."

"I did not. I told you, the theatre bores me inexpressibly."

"But it's Shakespeare."

"Very well, it's Shakespeare. I would rather sit at home and read
him in the company of Doreen Wragg and her cream puffs. You
won't forget to put something in your pocket for us when you leave
your feast, will you, Miss Pym? Anything gratefully received by the
starving proletariat. Macaroons, Mars bars, blood oranges, left-over
sandwiches, squashed sausage rolls—"

"I'll put a hat round," promised Lucy. "I'll pass the hat and qua-
ver: 'Don't forget the Staff.' "

But as she lifted the champagne bottle out of its melting ice in
her wash-bowl she did not feel so gay about it. This party was going to be an ordeal, there was no denying it. She tied a big bow of
ribbon to the neck of the bottle, to make it look festive and to take
away any suggestion of "bringing her own liquor"; the result was
rather like a duchess in a paper cap, but she didn't think that the
simile would occur to the students. She had hesitated over her own
toilette, being divided between a rough-and-tumble outfit suitable
to a cushions-on-the-floor gathering, and the desire to do her hosts
honour. She had paid them the compliment of putting on her "lecture" frock, and doing an extra-careful make-up. If Henrietta had
taken away from this party by her vagaries, she, Lucy, would bring
all she could to it.

Judging by the noise in other rooms, and the running back and
fore with kettles, Stewart's was not the only party in Leys that
evening. The corridors smelt strongly of coffee, and waves of laughter and talk rose and died away as doors were opened and shut.
Even the Juniors seemed to be entertaining; if they had no posts to

celebrate they had the glory of having their first Final behind them. Lucy remembered that she had not found out from The Nut Tart how she had fared in that Anatomy Final. ("Today's idea may be nonsense tomorrow, but a clavicle is a clavicle for all time.") When she passed the students' notice-board again she must look for Desterro's name.

She had to knock twice at the door of Number Ten before the sound penetrated, but when a flushed Stewart opened the door and drew her in a sudden shyness fell on the group, so that they got to their feet in polite silence like well-brought-up children.

"We are so glad to have you," Stewart was beginning, when Dakers sighted the bottle and all formality was at an end.

"*Drink!*" she shrieked. "As I live and breathe, *drink!* Oh, Miss Pym, you are a *poppet!*"

"I hope that I am not breaking any rules," Lucy said, remembering that there had been an expression in Miss Joliffe's eye that she had still not accounted for, "but it seemed to me an occasion for champagne."

"It's a triple occasion," Stewart said. "Dakers and Thomas are celebrating too. It couldn't be *more* of an occasion. It was lovely of you to think of the champagne."

"It will be sacrilege to drink it out of tooth-glasses," Hasselt said.

"Well, anyhow, we drink it now, as aperitif. A course by itself. Pass up your glasses everyone. Miss Pym, the chair is for you."

A basket-chair had been imported and lined with a motley collection of cushions; except for the hard chair at the desk it was the only legitimate seat in the room, the rest of the party having brought their cushions with them and being now disposed about the floor or piled in relaxed heaps like kittens on the bed. Someone had tied a yellow silk handkerchief over the light so that a golden benevolence took the place of the usual hard brightness. The twilight beyond the wide-open window made a pale blue back-cloth that would soon be a dark one. It was like any student party of her own college days, but as a picture it had more brilliance than her own parties had had. Was it just that the colours of the cushions were gayer? That the guests were better physical types, without lank hair, spectacles, and studious pallor?

No, of course it wasn't that. She knew what it was. There was no cigarette smoke.

"O'Donnell isn't here yet," Thomas said, collecting tooth-glasses from the guests and laying them on the cloth that covered the desk.

"I expect she's helping Rouse to put up the boom," a Disciple said.

"She can't be," a second Disciple said, "it's Saturday."

"Even a P.T.I. stops work on a Sunday," said a third.

"Even Rouse," commented a fourth.

"Is Miss Rouse still practising rotatory travelling?" Lucy asked.

"Oh, yes," they said. "She will be, up to the day of the Dem."

"And when does she find time?"

"She goes when she is dressed in the morning. Before first class."

"Six o'clock," said Lucy. "Horrible."

"It's no worse than any other time," they said. "At least one is fresh, and there is no hurry, and you can have the gym to yourself. Besides, it's the only possible time. The boom has to be put away before first class."

"She doesn't have to go," Stewart said, "the knack has come back. But she is terrified she will lose it again before the Dem."

"I can understand that, my dear," Dakers said. "Think what an *immortal* fool one would feel hanging like a sick monkey from the boom, with all the élite looking on, and Fröken simply *stabbing* one with that eye of hers. My dear, *death* would be a happy release. If Donnie isn't doing her usual chore for Rouse, *where* is she? She's the only one not here."

"Poor Don," Thomas said, "she hasn't got a post yet." Thomas with her junior-of-three in Wales was feeling like a millionaire.

"Don't worry over Don," Hasselt said, "the Irish always fall on their feet."

But Miss Pym was looking round for Innes, and not finding her. Nor was Beau there.

Stewart, seeing her wandering eye, interpreted the question in it and said: "Beau and Innes wanted me to tell you how sorry they were to miss the party, and to hope that you would be their guest at another one before the end of term."

"Beau will be giving one for Innes," Hasselt said. "To celebrate Arlinghurst."

"As a matter of fact, we're *all* giving a party for Innes," a Disciple said.

"A sort of general jamboree," said a second Disciple.

"It's an honour for College, after all," said a third.

"You'll come to that, won't you, Miss Pym," said a fourth, making it a statement rather than a question.

"Nothing would please me more," Lucy said. And then, glad to skate away from such thin ice: "What has happened to Beau and Innes?"

"Beau's people turned up unexpectedly and took them off to the theatre in Larborough," Stewart said.

"That's what it is to own a Rolls," Thomas said, quite without envy. "You just dash around England as the fit takes you. When *my* people want to move they have to yoke up the old grey mare—a brown cob, actually—and trot twenty miles before they reach any place at all."

"Farmers?" Lucy asked, seeing the lonely narrow Welsh road winding through desolation.

"No, my father is a clergyman. But we have to keep a horse to work the place, and we can't have a horse and a car too."

"Oh, well," said a Disciple arranging herself more comfortably on the bed, "who wants to go to the theatre anyhow?"

"Of all the boring ways of spending an evening," said a second.

"Sitting with one's knees in someone's back," said a third.

"With one's eyes to opera glasses," said a fourth.

"Why opera glasses?" asked Lucy, surprised to find Miss Lux's attitude repeated in a gathering where sophistication had not yet destroyed a juvenile thirst for entertainment.

"What would you see without them?"

"Little dolls walking about in a box."

"Like something on Brighton pier."

"Except that on Brighton pier you can see the expression on the faces."

They were rather like something from Brighton pier themselves, Lucy thought. A turn. A sort of extended Tweedledum and Tweedledee. They were apparently not moved to speech unless one of their number made a remark; when the others felt called upon to produce corroborative evidence.

"Me, I'm only too glad to put my feet up and do nothing for a change," Hasselt said. "I'm breaking in a new pair of ballet shoes for the Dem. and my blisters are spectacular."

"Miss Hasselt," said Stewart, obviously quoting, "it is a student's business to preserve her body in a state of fitness at all times."

"That may be," said Hasselt, "but I'm not standing in a bus for five miles on a Saturday night to go anywhere, least of all to a theatre."

"Anyhow, it's only Shakespeare, my dears," Dakers said. " 'It is the cause, my soul!' " she burlesqued, clutching at her breast.

"Edward Adrian, though," volunteered Lucy, feeling that her beloved theatre must have one champion.

"Who is Edward Adrian?" Dakers asked, in genuine inquiry.

"He's that weary-looking creature who looks like a moulting eagle," Stewart said, too busy about her hostess's duties to be aware of the reaction on Lucy: that was a horribly vivid summing-up of Edward Adrian, as seen by the unsentimental eyes of modern youth. "We used to be taken to see him when I was at school in Edinburgh."

"And didn't you enjoy it?" Lucy asked, remembering that Stewart's name headed the lists on the notice-board along with Innes's and Beau's, and that mental activity would not be for her the chore that it probably was for some of the others.

"Oh, it was better than sitting in a class-room," Stewart allowed. "But it was all terribly—old-fashioned. Nice to look at, but a bit dreary. I'm a tooth-glass short."

"Mine, I suppose," O'Donnell said, coming in on the words and handing over her glass. "I'm afraid I'm late. I was looking for some shoes that my feet would go into. Forgive these, won't you, Miss Pym." She indicated the bedroom slippers she was wearing. "My feet have died on me."

"Do *you* know who Edward Adrian is?" Lucy asked her.

"Certainly I do," O'Donnell said. "I've had a rave on him ever since I went to see him at the age of twelve in Belfast."

"You seem to be the only person in this room either to know or to admire him."

"Ah, the heathen," said O'Donnell, casting a scornful eye on the gathering—and it seemed to Lucy that O'Donnell was suspiciously bright about the eyes, as if she had been crying. "It's in Larborough I would be this minute, sitting at his feet, if it wasn't practically the end of term and I lacked the price of a seat."

And if, thought Lucy pitying, you hadn't felt that backing out of this party would be put down to your being the only one present not yet to have a post. She liked the girl who had dried her eyes and thought of the bedroom slipper excuse and come gaily to the party that was none of hers.

"Well," said Stewart, busy with the wire of the cork, "now that O'Donnell is here we can open the bottle."

"Good heavens, champagne!" O'Donnell said.

The wine came foaming into the thick blunt tooth-glasses, and they turned to Lucy expectantly.

"To Stewart in Scotland, to Thomas in Wales, to Dakers at Ling Abbey," she said.

They drank that.

"And to all our friends between Capetown and Manchester," Stewart said.

And they drank that too.

"Now, Miss Pym, what will you eat?"

And Lucy settled down happily to enjoy herself. Rouse was not going to be a guest; and she was by some special intervention of Providence in the shape of rich parents in a Rolls-Royce going to be spared the ordeal of sitting opposite an Innes bursting with happiness that had no vestige of foundation.

Chapter 12

But by noon on Sunday she was much less happy, and was wishing that she had had the foresight to invent a luncheon engagement in Larborough and so removed herself out of the area of the explosion that was coming. She had always hated explosions, literal and metaphorical; people who blew into paper bags and then burst them had always been regarded by Lucy with a mixture of abhorrence and awe. And the paper bag that was going to be burst after lunch was a particularly nasty affair; an explosion whose reverberations would be endless and unpredictable. At the back of her mind was the faint hope that Henrietta might have changed her mind; that the silent witness of those tell-tale lists on the noticeboard might have proved more eloquent than her own poor words. But no amount of encouragement could make this hope anything but embryonic. She remembered only too clearly that a shaking of Henrietta's faith in Rouse would not mean a corresponding access of belief in Innes as a candidate. The best that could be hoped for was that she might write to the Head at Arlinghurst and say that there was no Leaving Student good enough for so exalted a post; and that would do nothing to save Innes from the grief that was coming to her. No, she really should have got herself out of Leys for Sunday lunch and come back when it was all over. Even in Larborough, it was to be supposed, there were people that one might conceivably be going to see. Beyond those over-rich villas of the outskirts with their smooth sanded avenues and their pseudo everything, somewhere between them and the soot of the city there must be a belt of people like herself. Doctors, there must be, for instance. She could have invented a doctor friend—except that doctors were listed in registers. If she had thought in time she could have invited herself to lunch with Dr Knight; after all, Knight owed her something. Or she could have taken sandwiches and just walked out into the landscape and not come home till bed-time.

Now she sat in the window-seat in the drawing-room, waiting for the Staff to assemble there before going down to the dining-room; watching the students come back from church and wondering if she had sufficient courage and resolution to seek out Miss Joliffe even yet and ask for sandwiches; or even just walk out of College with no word said—after all, one didn't starve in the English country even on a Sunday. As Desterro said, there were always villages.

Desterro was the first to come back from church; leisured and fashionable as always. Lucy leant out and said: "Congratulations on your knowledge of the clavicle." For she had looked at the board on the way to bed last night.

"Yes, I surprised myself," said The Nut Tart. "My grandmother will be so pleased. A 'First' sounds so well, don't you think? I boasted about it to my cousin, but he said that was most unseemly. In England one waits to be asked about one's successes."

"Yes," agreed Lucy, sadly, "and the worst of it is so few people ask. The number of lights under bushels in Great Britain is tragic."

"Not Great Britain," amended Desterro. "He says—my cousin—that it is all right north of the river Tweed. That is the river between England and Scotland, you know. You can boast in Dunbar but not in Berwick, Rick says."

"I should like to meet Rick," Lucy said.

"He thinks you are quite adorable, by the way."

"*Me?*"

"I have been telling him about you. We spent all the intervals talking about you."

"Oh you went to the theatre, did you?"

"He went. I was taken."

"Did you not enjoy it, then?" asked Lucy, mentally applauding the young man who made The Nut Tart do anything at all that she did not want to do.

"Oh, it was as they say, 'not too bad.' A little of the grand manner is nice for a change. Ballet would have been better. He is a dancer manqué, that one."

"Edward Adrian?"

"Yes." Her mind seemed to have strayed away. "The English wear all one kind of hat," she said reflectively. "Up at the back and down in front."

With which irrelevance she trailed away round the house, leaving Lucy wondering whether the remark was occasioned by last night's audience or Dakers' advent up the avenue. Dakers' Sunday hat was certainly a mere superior copy of the hat she had worn at school, and under its short brim her pleasant, waggish, pony's face looked more youthful than ever. She took off the hat with a gesture when she saw Miss Pym, and loudly expressed her delight in finding Lucy alive and well after the rigours of the night before. This was the first morning in *all* her college career, it seemed, when she had positively *failed* to eat a fifth slice of bread and marmalade.

"Gluttony is one of the seven deadly sins," she observed, "so I had need of shriving this morning. I went to the Baptist place because it is nearest."

"And do you feel shriven?"

"I *don't* know that I *do*, now you come to mention it. It was all very *conversational*."

Lucy took it that a shamed soul demanded ritual.

"Very friendly, though, I understand."

"Oh, *frightfully*. The clergyman began his sermon by leaning on one elbow and remarking: 'Well, my friends, it's a very fine day.' And everyone shook hands with everyone coming out. And they had some fine warlike hymns," she added, having thought over the Baptist good points. She looked thoughtful for a moment longer and then said: "There are some Portsmouth Brothers on the Larborough road—"

"Plymouth."

"Plymouth what?"

"Plymouth Brethren, I suppose you mean."

"Oh, yes; I know it had something to do with the Navy. And I'm Pompey by inclination. Well, I think I shall sample *them* next Sunday. You don't suppose they're *private* or anything like that?"

Miss Pym thought not, and Dakers swung her hat in a wide gesture of burlesque farewell and went on round the house.

By ones and twos, and in little groups, the students returned from their compulsory hour out of College. Waving or calling a greeting or merely smiling, as their temperaments were. Even Rouse called a happy "Good morning, Miss Pym!" as she passed. Almost last came Beau and Innes; walking slowly, serene and relaxed. They came to rest beneath the window looking up at her.

"Heathen!" said Beau, smiling at her.

They were sorry they missed the party, they said, but there would be others.

"I shall be giving one myself when the Dem. is over," Beau said. "You'll come to that, won't you?"

"I shall be delighted. How was the theatre?"

"It might have been worse. We sat behind Colin Barry."

"Who is he?"

"The All-England hockey 'half.' "

"And I suppose that helped *Othello* a lot."

"It helped the intervals, I assure you."

"Didn't you want to see *Othello?*"

"Not us! We were dying to go to Irma Ireland's new film—*Flaming Barriers*. It sounds very sultry but actually, I believe, it's just a good clean forest fire. But my parents' idea of a night out is the theatre and a box of chocolates for the intervals. We couldn't disappoint the old dears."

"Did *they* like it?"

"Oh, they *loved* it. They spent the whole of supper talking about it."

"You're a fine pair to call anyone 'heathen,' " Lucy observed.

"Come to tea with the Seniors this afternoon," Beau said.

Lucy said hastily that she was going out to tea.

Beau eyed her guilty face with something like amusement, but Innes said soberly: "We should have asked you before. You are not going away before the Dem., are you?"

"Not if I can help it."

"Then will you come to tea with the Seniors next Sunday?"

"Thank you. If I am here I should be delighted."

"My lesson in manners," said Beau.

They stood there on the gravel looking up at her, smiling. That was how she always remembered them afterwards. Standing there in the sunlight, easy and graceful; secure in their belief in the world's rightness and in their trust in each other. Untouched by doubt or blemish. Taking it for granted that the warm gravel under their feet was lasting earth, and not the precipice edge of disaster.

It was the five-minute bell that roused them. As they moved away, Miss Lux came into the room behind, looking grimmer than Lucy had ever seen her.

"I can't imagine why I'm here," she said. "If I had thought in time I wouldn't be taking part in this Godforsaken farce at all."

Lucy said that that was exactly what she herself had been thinking.

"I suppose there has been no word of Miss Hodge having a change of heart?"

"Not as far as I know. I'm afraid it isn't likely."

"What a pity we didn't *all* go out for lunch. If Miss Hodge had to call Rouse's name from a completely deserted table, College would at least be aware that we had no part in this travesty."

"If you didn't have to mark yourself 'out' on the slate before eleven, I would go now, but I haven't the nerve."

"Oh well, perhaps we can do something with our expressions to convey that we consider the whole thing just a bad smell."

It's the being there to countenance it she minds, thought Lucy; while I just want to run away from unpleasantness like a child. Not for the first time, she wished she was a more admirable character.

Madame Lefevre came floating in wearing a cocoa-brown silk affair that was shot with a metallic blue in the high-lights; which made her look more than ever like some exotic kind of dragon-fly. It was partly those enormous headlamps of eyes, of course; like some close-up of an insect in half-remembered Nature "shorts"; the eyes and the thin brown body, so angular yet so graceful. Madame, having got over her immediate rage, had, it seemed, recovered her detached contempt for the human species, and was regarding the situation with malicious if slightly enjoyable distaste.

"Never having attended a wake," she said, "I look forward with interest to the performance today."

"You are a ghoul," Lux said; but without feeling, as if she were too depressed to care greatly. "Haven't you done anything to alter her mind?"

"Oh, yes, I have wrestled with the Powers of Darkness. Wrestled very mightily. Also very cogently, may I say. With example and precept. Who was it who was condemned to push an enormous stone up a hill for ever? Extraordinary how appropriate these mythological fancies still are. I wonder if a ballet of Punishment would be any good? Sweeping out stables, and so forth. To Bach, perhaps. Though Bach is not very inspirational, choreographically speaking. And a great many people rise up and call one damned, of course, if one uses him."

"Oh, stop it," Lux said. "We are going to connive at an abomination and you speculate about choreography!"

"My good, if too earnest, Catherine, you must learn to take life as it comes, and to withdraw yourself from what you cannot alter.

As the Chinese so rightly advise: When rape is inevitable, relax and enjoy it. We connive at an abomination, as you so exquisitely put it. True. But as intelligent human beings we concern ourselves with the by-products of the action. It will be interesting to see how, for instance, the little Innes reacts to the stimulus. Will the shock be a mortal one, will it galvanise her into action, or will it send her into crazy throes of galvanic activity that has no meaning?"

"Damn your metaphors. You are talking nonsense and you know it. It is someone else's rape we are invited to countenance; and as far as I know there is nothing in the history of philosophy, Chinese or otherwise, to recommend that."

"Rape?" said Fröken, coming in followed by her mother. "Who is going to be raped?"

"Innes," Lux said dryly.

"Oh." The twinkle died out of Fröken's eye, leaving it cold and pale. "Yes," she said, reflectively. "Yes."

Fru Gustavsen's round "Mrs Noah" face looked troubled. She looked from one to another, as if hoping for some gleam of assurance, some suggestion that the problem was capable of being resolved. She came over to Lucy in the window-seat, ducked her head in a sharp Good-morning, and said in German:

"You know about this thing the Principal does? My daughter is very angry. Very angry my daughter is. Not since she was a little girl have I seen her so angry. It is very bad what they do? You think so too?"

"Yes, I'm afraid I do."

"Miss Hodge is a very good woman. I admire her very much. But when a good woman makes a mistake it is apt to be much worse than a bad woman's mistake. More colossal. It is a pity."

It was a great pity, Lucy agreed.

The door opened and Henrietta came in, with a nervous Wragg in tow. Henrietta appeared serene, if a little more stately than usual (or than circumstances demanded), but Wragg cast a placatory smile round the gathering as if pleading with them to be all girls together and look on the bright side. Their close-hedged antagonism dismayed her, and she sent an appealing glance at Madame, whose dogs-body she normally was. But Madame's wide sardonic gaze was fixed on Henrietta.

Henrietta wished them all good-morning (she had breakfasted in her own room) and she had timed her entrance very neatly, for before her greeting was finished, the murmur of the distant gong made the moment one for action, not conversation.

"It is time for us to go down, I think," Henrietta said, and led the way out.

Madame rolled her eye at Lux in admiration of this piece of generalship, and fell in behind.

"A wake indeed!" Lux said to Lucy as they went downstairs. "It feels more like Fotheringay."

The demure silence waiting them in the dining-room seemed to Lucy's heightened imagination to be charged with expectation, and certainly during the meal College seemed to be more excited than she had ever seen it. The babble of conversation deepened to a roar, so that Henrietta, coming-to between her busy gobbling of the meat course and her expectation of the pudding, sent a message by Wragg to Beau, asking that College should contain themselves.

For a little they were circumspect, but soon they forgot and the talk and laughter rose again.

"They are excited to have Examinations Week over," Henrietta said indulgently, and let them be.

This was her only contribution to conversation—she never did converse while eating—but Wragg served up brave little platitudes at regular intervals, looking from one to the other of the shut faces round the table hopefully, like a terrier which has brought a bone to lay at one's feet. One could almost see her tail wag. Wragg was to be the innocent means of execution, the passive knife in the guillotine, and she felt her position and was tacitly apologising for it. Oh, for Pete's sake, she seemed to be saying, I'm only the Junior Gymnast in this set-up, it's not my fault that I have to tag along in her rear; what do you expect me to do?—tell her to announce the damned thing herself?

Lucy was sorry for her, even while her pious pieces of the obvious made her want to scream. Be quiet, she wanted to say, do be quiet, there is nothing for a situation like this but silence.

At last Henrietta folded up her napkin, looked round the table to make sure that all her Staff had finished eating, and rose. As the Staff rose with her, College came to its feet with an alacrity and a unanimity that was rare. It was apparent that they had been waiting for this moment. Against her will, Lucy turned to look at them; at the rows of bright expectant faces, half-smiling in their eagerness; it did nothing to comfort her that they looked as if at the slightest provocation they would break into a cheer.

As Henrietta turned to the door and the Staff filed after her, Wragg faced the delighted throng and said the words that had been given her to say.

"Miss Hodge will see Miss Rouse in her office when luncheon is over."

Chapter 13

*L*ucy could no longer see the faces, but she felt the silence go suddenly blank. Become void and dead. It was the difference between a summer silence full of bird-notes and leaves and wind in the grasses, and the frozen stillness of some Arctic waste. And then, into the dead void just as they reached the door, came the first faint sibilant whisper as they repeated the name.

"Rouse!" they were saying. "Rouse!"

And Lucy, stepping over the warm sunlight, shivered. The sound reminded her of frozen particles being swept over a snow surface by a bitter wind. She even remembered where she had seen and heard those particles: that Easter she had spent on Speyside when they had missed the Grantown bus and they were a long way from home and they had to walk it every foot of the way, under a leaden sky into a bitter wind over a frozen world. She felt a long way from home now, crossing the sunny courtyard to the quadrangle door, and the sky seemed to her as leaden as any Highland one in a March storm. She wished for a moment that she were at home, in her own quiet little sitting-room, settling down for a Sunday afternoon of unbroken peace, untouched by human problems and unhurt by human griefs. She toyed with the idea of inventing an excuse to go when tomorrow morning's post would give her a chance; but she had looked forward like a child to the Demonstration on Friday, and she had now a quite personal interest in what had promised to be for her merely something new in spectacles. She knew all the Seniors personally and a great many of the Juniors; she had talked "Dem." with them, shared their half-fearful anticipation of it, even helped to make their costumes. It was the summit, the triumphant flower, the resounding full-stop of their College careers, and she could not bear to go without seeing it; without being part of it.

She had dropped the rest of the Staff, who were bound for the front of the house, but Wragg, coming behind her to pin a notice on the students' board, mopped her forehead in frank relief and said: "Thank heaven that is over. I think it was the worst thing I have ever had to do. I couldn't eat my lunch with thinking of it." And Lucy remembered that there had indeed been the phenomenon of a large piece of tart unfinished on Miss Wragg's plate.

That was life, that was. Innes had Heaven's door shut in her face, and Wragg couldn't finish her pudding!

No one had yet come out of the dining-room—College appetites being so much larger than Staff ones, their meals lasted at least ten or fifteen minutes longer—so the corridors were still deserted as Lucy went up to her room. She resolved to get away from Leys before the crowd of students overran the countryside. She would go away deep into the green and white and yellow countryside, and smell the may and lie in the grass and feel the world turning on its axis, and remember that it was a very large world, and that College griefs were wild and bitter but soon over and that in the Scale of Things they were undeniably Very Small Beer.

She changed her shoes to something more appropriate to field-paths, crossed to the "old house" and ran down the front stairs and out by the front door so as to avoid the students who would now be percolating out of the dining-room. The "old house" was very silent and she deduced that there had been no lingering in the drawing-room after lunch today. She skirted the house and made for the field behind the gymnasium, with vague thoughts of Bidlington and The Teapot stirring in her mind. The hedge of may was a creamy foam on her right and on her left the buttercups were a golden sea. The elms, half-floating in the warm light, were anchored each to its purple shadow, and daisies patterned the short grass under her feet. It was a lovely world, a fine round gracious world, and no day for—Oh, poor Innes! *Poor* Innes!—no day for the world to turn over and crush one.

It was when she was debating with herself whether to cross the little bridge, to turn down-stream to Bidlington, or up-stream to the unknown, that she saw Beau. Beau was standing in the middle of the bridge watching the water, but with her green linen dress and bright hair she was so much a part of the sunlight-and-shadow under the willows that Lucy had been unaware that anyone was there. As she came into the shade herself and could see more clearly, Lucy saw that Beau was watching her come, but she gave her no greeting. This was so unlike Beau that Lucy was daunted.

"Hullo," she said, and leaned beside her on the wooden rail. "Isn't it beautiful this afternoon?" *Must* you sound so idiotic? she asked herself.

There was no answer to this, but presently Beau said: "Did you know about this appointment?"

"Yes," said Lucy. "I—I heard the Staff talking about it."

"When?"

"Yesterday."

"Then you knew this morning when you were talking to us."

"Yes. Why?"

"It would have been kind if someone had warned her."

"Warned whom?"

"Innes. It isn't very nice to have your teeth kicked in in public."

She realised that Beau was sick with rage. Never before had she seen her even out of temper, and now she was so angry that she could hardly talk.

"But how could I have done that?" she asked reasonably, dismayed to be taken personally to task for something that she considered none of her business. "It would have been disloyal to mention it before Miss Hodge had announced her decision. For all I knew she might have altered that decision; when I left her it was still possible that she might see things from—" She stopped, realising where she was headed. But Beau too had realised. She turned her head sharply to look at Miss Pym.

"Oh. You argued with her about it. You didn't approve of her choice, then?"

"Of course not." She looked at the angry young face so near her own and decided to be frank. "You might as well know, Beau, that no one approves. The Staff feel about it very much as you do. Miss Hodge is an old friend of mine, and I owe her a great deal, and admire her, but where this appointment is concerned she is 'on her own.' I have been desolated ever since I first heard of it, I would do anything to reverse it, to waken up tomorrow and find that it is just a bad dream; but as to warning anyone—" She lifted her hand in a gesture of helplessness.

Beau had gone back to glaring at the water. "A clever woman like you could have thought of something," she muttered.

The "clever woman" somehow made Beau of a sudden very young and appealing; it was not like the confident and sophisticated Beau to look for help or to think of her very ordinary Pym self as clever. She was after all a child; a child raging and hurt at the wrong that had been done her friend. Lucy had never liked her so well.

"Even a hint," Beau went on, muttering at the water. "Even a suggestion that there might be someone else in the running. *Anything* to warn her. To make the shock less shattering. To put her on her guard, so that she wasn't wide open. It had to be punishment, but it needn't have been a massacre. You could have sacrificed a little scruple in so good a cause, couldn't you?"

Lucy felt, belatedly, that perhaps she might have.

"Where is she?" she asked. "Where is Innes?"

"I don't know. She ran straight out of College before I could catch her up. I know she came this way, but I don't know where she went from here."

"She will take it very badly?"

"Did you expect her to be brave and noble about the hideous mess?" Beau said savagely, and then, instantly: "Oh, I'm sorry. I do beg your pardon. I know you're sorry about it too. I'm just not fit to be spoken to just now."

"Yes, I am sorry," Lucy said. "I admired Innes the first time I saw her, and I think she would have been an enormous success at Arlinghurst."

"Would have been," muttered Beau.

"How did Miss Rouse take the news? Was she surprised, do you think?"

"I didn't wait to see," Beau said shortly. And presently: "I think I shall go up-stream. There is a little thorn wood up there that she is very fond of, she may be there."

"Are you worried about her?" Lucy asked; feeling that if it were merely comforting that Beau planned, Innes would surely prefer solitude at the moment.

"I don't think she is busy committing suicide, if that is what you mean. But of course I am worried about her. A shock like that would be bad for anyone—especially coming now, at the end of term when one is tired. But Innes—Innes has always cared too much about things." She paused to look at the water again. "When we were Juniors and Madame used to blister us with her sarcasm—Madame can be simply unspeakable, you know—the rest of us just came up in weals but Innes was actually flayed; just raw flesh. She never cried, as some of the others did when they'd had too much for one go. She just—just burned up inside. It's bad for you to burn up inside. And once when—" She stopped, and seemed to decide that she had said enough. Either she had been on the verge of an indiscretion or she came to the conclusion that discussing her friend with a comparative stranger, however sympathetic, was not after all the thing to do. "She has no oil on her feathers, Innes," she finished.

She stepped off the bridge and began to walk away up the path by the willows. "If I was rude," she said, pausing just before she disappeared, "do forgive me. I didn't mean to be."

Lucy went on looking at the smooth silent water, wishing passionately that she could recover the little red book which she had consigned so smugly to the brook two days ago, and thinking of the girl who had no "duck's back"—no protective mechanism against the world's weather. The girl who could neither whimper nor laugh; who "burned up inside" instead. She rather hoped that Beau would not find her until the worst was over; she had not run to Beau for sympathy, she had run as far and as fast from human company as she could, and it seemed only fair to let her have the solitude she sought.

It would do Beau no harm at any rate, Lucy thought, to find that the world had its snags and its disappointments; life had been much too easy for Beau. It was a pity that she had to learn at Innes's expense.

She crossed the bridge into the games field, turned her face to open country and took the hedge gaps as they came; hoping that she might not overtake Innes, and determined to turn a blind eye in her direction if she did. But there was no Innes. No one at all moved in the Sunday landscape. Everyone was still digesting roast beef. She was alone with the hedges of may, the pasture, and the blue sky. Presently she came to the edge of a slope, from which she could look across a shallow valley to successive distances, and there she sat with her back against an oak, while the insects hummed in the grass, and the fat white clouds sailed up and passed, and the slow shadow of the tree circled round her feet. Lucy's capacity for doing nothing was almost endless, and had been the despair of both her preceptors and friends.

It was not until the sun was at hedge level that she roused herself to further decision. The result of her self-communing was a realisation that she could *not* face College supper tonight; she would walk until she found an inn, and in the half-dark she would come back to a College already hushed by the "bedroom" bell. She made a wide circle round, and in half an hour saw in the distance a steeple she recognised, whereupon she jettisoned her thoughts of an inn and wondered if The Teapot was open on Sundays. Even if it wasn't perhaps she could persuade Miss Nevill to stay her pangs with something out of a can. It was after seven before she reached the outskirts of Bidlington, and she looked at the Martyr's Memorial— the only ugly erection in the place—with something of a fellow interest, but the open door of The Teapot restored her. *Dear* Miss Nevill. Dear large clever business-like accommodating Miss Nevill.

She walked into the pleasant room, already shadowed by the opposite cottages, and found it almost empty. A family party occupied the front window, and in the far corner were a young couple who presumably owned the expensive coupé which was backed in at the end of the garden. She thought it clever of Miss Nevill to manage that the room should still look spotless and smell of flowers after the deluge of a Sunday's traffic in June.

She was looking round for a table when a voice said: "Miss Pym!"

Lucy's first instinct was to bolt: she was in no mood for student chat at the moment; and then she noticed that it was The Nut Tart. The Nut Tart was the female half of the couple in the corner. The male half was undoubtedly "my cousin"; the Rick who thought her adorable and who was referred to in College parlance as "that gigolo."

Desterro rose and came over to meet her—she had charming manners on formal occasions—and drew her over to their table. "But this is lovely!" she said. "We were talking of you, and Rick was saying how much he would like to meet you, and here you are. It is magic. This is my cousin, Richard Gillespie. He was christened Riccardo, but he thinks it sounds too like a cinema star."

"Or a band leader," Gillespie said, shaking hands with her and putting her into a chair. His unaccented manner was very English, and did something to counteract his undoubted resemblance to the more Latin types of screen hero. Lucy saw where the "gigolo" came from; the black smooth hair that grew so thick, the eyelashes, the flare of the nostrils, the thin line of dark moustache were all according to the recipe; but nothing else was, it seemed to Lucy. Looks were what he had inherited from some Latin ancestor; but manner, breeding, and character seemed to be ordinary public school. He was considerably older than Desterro—nearly thirty, Lucy reckoned—and looked a pleasant and responsible person.

They had just ordered, it seemed, and Richard went away to the back premises to command another portion of Bidlington rarebit.

"It is a cheese affair," Desterro said. "But not those Welsh things you get in London teashops. It is a very rich cheese sauce on very soft buttery toast, and it is flavoured with odd things like nutmeg— I think it is nutmeg—and things like that, and it tastes divine."

Lucy, who was in no state to care what food tasted like, said that it sounded delicious. "Your cousin is English, then?"

"Oh, yes. We are not what you call first cousins," she explained as Richard came back. "The sister of my father's father married his mother's father."

"In simpler words," Richard said, "our grandparents were brother and sister."

"It may be simpler, but it is not explicit," Desterro said, with all the scorn of a Latin for the Saxon indifference to relationships.

"Do you live in Larborough?" Lucy asked Richard.

"No, I work in London, at our head office. But just now I am doing liaison work in Larborough."

In spite of herself Lucy's eye swivelled round to Desterro, busy with a copy of the menu.

"One of our associated firms is here, and I am working with them for a week or two," Rick said smoothly; and laughed at her with his eyes. And then, to put her mind completely at rest: "I came with a chit to Miss Hodge, vouching for my relationship, my respectability, my solvency, my presentability, my orthodoxy—"

"Oh, be quiet, Rick," Desterro said, "it is not my fault that my father is Brazilian and my mother French. What is saffron dough-cake?"

"Teresa is the loveliest person to take out to a meal," Rick said. "She eats like a starved lion. My other women friends spend the whole evening reckoning the calories and imagining what is happening to their waists."

"Your other women friends," his cousin pointed out a trifle astringently, "have not spent twelve months at Leys Physical Training College, being sweated down to vanishing point and fed on vegetable macédoine."

Lucy, remembering the piles of bread wolfed by the students at every meal, thought this an overstatement.

"When I go back to Brazil I shall live like a lady and eat like a civilised person, and it will be time then to consider my calories."

Lucy asked when she was going back.

"I am sailing on the last day of August. That will give me a little of the English summer to enjoy between the last day of College and my going away. I like the English summer. So green, and gentle, and kind. I like everything about the English except their clothes, their winter, and their teeth. Where is Arlinghurst?"

Lucy, who had forgotten Desterro's abrupt hopping from one subject to another, was too surprised by the name to answer immediately and Rick answered for her. "It's the best girls' school in England," he finished, having described the place. "Why?"

"It is the College excitement at the moment. One of our students is going there straight from Leys. One would think she had at least been made a Dame, to listen to them."

"A legitimate reason for excitement, it seems to me," Rick observed. "Not many people get professional plums straight out of college."

"Yes? It really is an honour, then, you think?"

"A very great one, I imagine. Isn't it, Miss Pym?"

"Very."

"Oh, well. I am glad of it. It is sad to think of her wasting the years in a girls' school, but if it is an honour for her, then I am glad."

"For whom?" Lucy asked.

"For Innes, of course."

"Were you not at lunch today?" asked Lucy, puzzled.

"No. Rick came with the car and we went over to the Saracen's Head at Beauminster. Why? What has that to do with this school affair?"

"It isn't Innes who is going to Arlinghurst."

"Not Innes! But they all said she was. Everyone said so."

"Yes, that is what everyone expected, but it didn't turn out like that."

"No? Who is going, then?"

"Rouse."

Desterro stared.

"Oh, no. No, that I refuse to believe. It is quite simply not possible."

"It is true, I am afraid."

"You mean that—that someone—that they have preferred that *canaille*, that *espèce d'une—!*"

"Teresa!" warned Rick, amused to see her moved for once.

Desterro sat silent for a space, communing with herself.

"If I were not a lady," she said at length in clear tones, "I would *spit!*"

The family party looked over, surprised and faintly alarmed.

They decided that it was time they were going, and began to collect their things and reckon up what they had had.

"Now look what you have done," Rick said. "Alarmed the lieges."

At this moment the rarebits arrived from the kitchen, with Miss Nevill's large chintz presence behind them; but The Nut Tart, far from being distracted by the savoury food, remembered that it was from Miss Nevill that she had first had news of the Arlinghurst vacancy, and the subject took a fresh lease of life. It was Rick who rescued Lucy from the loathed subject by pointing out that the rarebit was rapidly cooling; Lucy had a strong feeling that he himself cared nothing for the rarebit, but that he had somehow become aware of her tiredness and her distaste for the affair; and she felt warm and grateful to him and on the point of tears.

"After all," pointed out Rick as The Nut Tart at last turned her attention to her food, "I don't know Miss Innes, but if she is as wonderful as you say she is bound to get a very good post, even if it isn't exactly Arlinghurst."

This was the argument with which Lucy had sought to comfort herself all the long afternoon. It was reasonable, logical, and balanced; and as a sort of moral belladonna-plaster it was so much red flannel. Lucy understood why The Nut Tart rejected it with scorn.

"How would *you* like to have *that* preferred to you?" she demanded through a large mouthful of rarebit. "That" was Rouse. "How would you like to believe that they were going to pay you honour, a fine public honour, and then have them slap your face in front of everyone?"

"Having your teeth kicked in," Beau had called it. Their reactions were remarkably similar. The only difference was that Desterro saw the insult, and Beau the injury.

"And we had such a lovely happy morning in this very room the other day with Innes's father and mother," Desterro went on, her fine eyes wandering to the table where they had sat. This, too, Lucy had been remembering. "Such nice people, Rick; I wish you could see them. We were all nice people together: me, and Miss Pym, and the Inneses *père et mère*, and we had an interval of civilisation and some good coffee. It was charming. And now—"

Between them, Lucy and Rick steered her away from the subject; and it was not until they were getting into the car to go back to Leys that she remembered and began to mourn again. But the distance between Bidlington and Leys as covered by Rick's car was so short that she had no time to work herself up before they were at the door. Lucy said goodnight and was going to withdraw tactfully, but The Nut Tart came with her. "Goodnight, Rick," she said, casually. "You are coming on Friday, aren't you?"

"Nothing will stop me," Rick assured her. "Three o'clock, is it?"

"No, half-past two. It is written on your invitation card. The invitation I sent you. For a business person you are not very accurate."

"Oh, well, my business things I naturally keep in files."

"And where do you keep my invitation?"

"On a gold chain between my vest and my heart," Rick said, and went the winner out of that exchange.

"Your cousin is charming," Lucy said, as they went up the steps together.

"You think so? I am very glad. I think so too. He has all the English virtues, and a little spice of something that is not English virtue at all. I am glad he is coming to see me dance on Friday. What makes you smile?"

Lucy, who had been smiling at this typically Desterro view of her cousin's presence on Friday, hastened to change the subject.

"Shouldn't you be going in by the other door?"

"Oh, yes, but I don't suppose anyone will mind. In a fortnight I shall be free to come up these steps if I like—I shall not like, incidentally—so I might as well use them now. I do not take well to tradesmen's entrances."

Lucy had meant to pay her respects to the Staff before going to her room in the wing, but the hall was so quiet, the air of the house so withdrawn, that she was discouraged and took the line of least resistance. She would see them all in the morning.

The Nut Tart paid at least a token obedience to College rules, and it was apparent from the hush in the wing corridor that the "bedroom" bell must have gone some minutes ago; so they said goodnight at the top of the stairs, and Lucy went away to her room at the far end. As she undressed she found that her ear was waiting for a sound from next door. But there was no sound at all; nor was there any visible light from the window, as she noticed when she drew her own curtains. Had Innes not come back?

She sat for a while wondering whether she should do something about it. If Innes had not come back, Beau would be in need of comfort. And if Innes had come back and was silent, was there perhaps some impersonal piece of kindness, some small service, that she could do to express her sympathy without intrusion?

She switched off her light and drew back the curtains, and sat by the open window looking at the brightly lit squares all round the little quadrangle—it was considered an eccentricity to draw a curtain in this community—watching the separate activities of the now silent and individual students. One was brushing her hair, one sewing something, one putting a bandage on her foot (a Foolish Virgin, that one; she was hopping about looking for a pair of scissors instead of having begun with the implement already laid out, like a good masseuse), one wriggling into a pyjama jacket, one swatting a moth.

Two lights went out as she watched. Tomorrow the waking bell would go at half-past five again, and now that examinations were over they need no longer stay awake till the last moment over their notebooks.

She heard footsteps come along her own corridor, and got up, thinking they were coming at her. Innes's door opened quietly and shut. No light was switched on, but she heard the soft movements of someone getting ready for bed. Then bedroom slippers in the corridor, and a knock. No answer.

"It's me: Beau," a voice said; and the door was opened. The murmur of voices as the door closed. The smell of coffee and the faint chink of china.

It was sensible of Beau to meet the situation with food. Whatever demons Innes had wrestled with during the long hours between one o'clock and ten she must now be empty of emotion and ready to eat what was put in front of her. The murmur of voices went on until the "lights out" bell sounded; then the door opened and closed again, and the silence next-door merged into the greater silence that enveloped Leys.

Lucy decided to stay awake a little and think of some way in which she could express to poor Innes how great was her own sympathy and how deep her own indignation; and fell instantly asleep.

Chapter 14

*M*onday was an anti-climax. Lucy came back into a community that had talked itself out on the subject of Arlinghurst. Both Staff and students had had a whole day's leisure in which to spread themselves over the sensation, and by night-time there was nothing more to be said; indeed every possible view had already been repeated *ad nauseam*; so that with the resumption of routine on Monday the affair had already slipped into the background. Since she still had her breakfast brought to her by the devoted Miss Morris, she was not there to see Innes's first public appearance; and by the time she came face to face with the students as a body, at lunch, habit had smoothed over the rough places and College looked much as usual.

Innes's face was composed, but Lucy thought that its normal withdrawn expression had become a shut-down look; whatever emotions she still wrestled with, they were under hatches and battened down. Rouse looked more than ever like Aunt Celia's cat, Philadelphia, and Lucy longed to shut her out-of-doors and let her mew. The only curiosity she had had about the affair was to know how Rouse took that unexpected announcement; she had even gone the length of asking Miss Lux on the way down to lunch.

"What did Rouse look like when she heard the news?"

"Ectoplasm," said Miss Lux.

"Why ectoplasm?" Lucy had asked, puzzled.

"It is the most revolting thing I can think of."

So her curiosity remained unsatisfied. Madame twitted her about her desertion of them yesterday, but no one wanted to harp on the probable reason for it. Already the shadow of the Demonstration, only four days away, loomed large over them all; Arlinghurst was yesterday's sensation and already a little stale. College was once more into its stride.

Indeed only two small incidents livened the monotony of routine between Monday and Friday.

The first was Miss Hodge's offer to Innes of the post at the Wycherley Orthopaedic Hospital, and Innes's refusal of it. The post was then offered to and gratefully accepted by a much-relieved O'Donnell. (*"Darling,* how *nice!"* Dakers had said. "Now I can sell you my clinic overalls which I shall *never* use again, my dear." And sell them she did; and was so delighted to have good hard cash in her purse so near the end of term that she instantly began to hawk the rest of her belongings round the wing, and was only dissuaded when Stewart asked caustically if the safety-pins were standard equipment.)

The second incident was the arrival of Edward Adrian, thespian.

This unlooked-for occurrence took place on Wednesday. Wednesday was swimmming afternoon, and all the Juniors and such Seniors as had no afternoon patients were down at the pool. Lucy, who by prayer, counting, and determination, could just get across the bath, took no part in this exercise in spite of warm invitations to come in and be cool. She spent half an hour watching the gambols, and then walked back to the house for tea. She was crossing the hall to the stairs when one of the Disciples—she thought it was Luke, but she was still not quite certain about them—dashed out of the clinic door and said:

"Oh, Miss Pym, would you be an angel and sit on Albert's feet for a moment?"

"Sit on Albert's feet?" repeated Lucy, not quite sure that she had heard aright.

"Yes, or hold them. But it's easier to sit on them. The hole in the strap has given way, and there isn't another that isn't in use." She ushered the dazed Lucy into the quiet of the clinic, where students swathed in unfamiliar white linen superintended their patients' contortions, and indicated a plinth where a boy of eleven or so was lying face down. "You see," she said, holding up a leather strap, "the thing has torn away from the hole, and the hole in front is too tight and the one behind too loose. If you would just hang on to his feet for a moment; if you wouldn't rather sit on them."

Lucy said hastily that she would prefer to hang on.

"All right. This is Miss Pym, Albert. She is going to be the strap for the nonce."

"Hullo, Miss Pym," said Albert, rolling an eye round at her.

Luke—if it was she—seized the boy under the shoulders and

yanked him forward till only his legs remained on the plinth. "Now clamp a hand over each ankle and hang on, Miss Pym," she commanded, and Lucy obeyed, thinking how well this breezy bluntness was going to suit Manchester and how extremely heavy a small boy of eleven was when you were trying to keep his ankles down. Her eyes strayed from what Luke was doing to the others, so strange and remote in this new guise. Was there no end to the facets of this odd life? Even the ones she knew well, like Stewart, were different, seen like this. Their movements were slower, and there was a special bright artificially-interested voice that they used to patients. There were no smiles and no chatter; just a bright hospital quiet. "Just a *little* further. *That's* right." "That is looking much better today, isn't it!" "Now, we'll try that once more and then that will be all for today."

Through a gap in Hasselt's overall as she moved, Lucy caught a glimpse of silk, and realised that she was already changed for dancing, there being no interval between finishing her patient and appearing in the gym. Either she had already had tea, or would snatch a cup en route.

While she was thinking of the oddity of this life of dancing silks under hospital clothes, a car passed the window and stopped at the front door. A very fashionable and expensive car of inordinate length and great glossiness, chauffeur-driven. It was so seldom nowadays that one saw anyone but an invalid driven by a chauffeur that she watched with interest to see who might emerge from it.

Beau's mother, perhaps? That was the kind of car that went with a butler, undoubtedly.

But what came out of the car was a youngish man—she could see only his back—in the kind of suit one sees anywhere between St. James's Street and the Duke of York's Steps any time between October and the end of June. What with the chauffeur and the suit Lucy ran through in her mind the available Royalties, but could not find an appropriate one; Royalty drove itself nowadays, anyhow.

"Thank you very much, Miss Pym. You've been an enormous help. Say thank you, Albert."

"Thank you, Miss Pym," Albert said dutifully; and then, catching her eye, winked at her. Lucy winked back, gravely.

At this moment O'Donnell erupted into the room clutching the large sifter of talcum powder that she had been having refilled by Fröken in the further room, and hissed in an excited whisper: "What do you think! *Edward Adrian!* In the car. *Edward Adrian!*"

"Who cares?" Stewart said, relieving her of the sifter. "You were a damned long time getting the talc."

Lucy closed the clinic door behind her and emerged into the hall. O'Donnell had spoken truth. It was Edward Adrian who was standing in the hall. And Miss Lux had also spoken truth. For Edward Adrian was examining himself in the mirror.

As Lucy climbed the stairs she met Miss Lux coming down, and as she turned to the second flight could see their meeting.

"Hullo, Teddy," Miss Lux said, without enthusiasm.

"Catherine!" Adrian said, with the most delighted enthusiasm, going forward to meet her as if about to embrace her. But her cool solitary hand, outstretched in conventional greeting, stopped him.

"What are you doing here? Don't tell me you have developed a 'niece' at Leys."

"Don't be a beast, Cath. I came to see you, of course. Why didn't you tell me you were here? Why didn't you come to see me, so that we could have had a meal together, and a talk about old—"

"Miss Pym," Miss Lux's clear accents came floating up the staircase, "don't run away. I want you to meet a friend of mine."

"But Catherine—" she heard him say in quick low protest.

"It's the *famous* Miss Pym," Miss Lux said, in a you'll-like-that-you silly creature tone, "and a great admirer of yours," she added as a final snare.

Does he realise how cruel she is being? she wondered as she waited for them to come up to her, or is his self-satisfaction too great to be pierced by her rating of him?

As they went together into the deserted drawing-room, she remembered suddenly Stewart's description of him as a "weary-looking creature who looked like a moulting eagle" and thought how apt it was. He had good looks of a sort, but although he could not be much older than forty—forty-three or -four, perhaps—they already had a preserved air. Without his paints and his pencils and his toupees, he looked tired and worn, and his dark hair was receding. Lucy felt suddenly sorry for him. With the youth and strength and beauty of Desterro's Rick fresh in her mind, she found the spoiled and famous actor somehow pitiful.

He was being charming to her—he knew all about her book; he read all the best-sellers—but with one eye on Miss Lux while she examined what was left of tea, inspected the contents of the tea-pot, and apparently deciding that a little more hot water would meet the case, lit the burner under the tea-kettle again. There was something in that consciousness of Catherine Lux's presence that puzzled Lucy. It wasn't in the part, as she had imagined the part for him. The successful star calling on the humble lecturer at a girls' college should surely show more detachment; more willingness to peacock in front of the stranger, after the matter of actors. He was "doing his act" for her, of course; all his charm was turned full on, and it was a very considerable charm; but it was mere reflex action. All his interest was centered round the cool scraggy woman who rated him at some washy tea. It couldn't be very often, Lucy thought with amusement, that Edward Adrian arrived on any doorstep without trumpets; for nearly twenty years—ever since that first heart-breaking Romeo had brought tears to the eyes of critics sick of the very name of Montague—his comings and goings had been matters of moment, he had moved in a constant small eddy of importance; people ran to do his bidding and waited for his plea- sure; they gave him things and asked nothing in return; they gave up things for him and expected no thanks. He was Edward Adrian, household word, two feet high on the bills, national possession.

But he had come out this afternoon to Leys to see Catherine Lux, and his eyes followed her round like an eager dog's. The Catherine whose estimate of him was a little hot water added to the tea-pot. It was all very strange.

"I hope you are doing well in Larborough, Teddy?" Lux asked, with more politeness than interest.

"Oh, yes; fair. Too many schools, but one must put up with that when one plays Shakespeare."

"Don't you like playing to young people?" Lucy asked, remem- bering that the young people she had met lately had not greatly liked having to listen to him.

"Well—they don't make the best audience in the world, you know. One would prefer adults. And they get cut rates, of course; which doesn't help the takings. But we look on it as an investment," he added with generous tolerance. "They are the future theatre- goers, and must be trained up in the way they should go."

Lucy thought that the training, if judged by results, had been singularly unsuccessful. The way the young went was in a bee-line to something called *Flaming Barriers*. It wasn't even true to say that they "didn't go" to the theatre; it was much more positive than that: they fled from it.

However, this was a polite tea-party and no time for home truth. Lucy asked if he was coming to the Demonstration—at which

Miss Lux looked annoyed. He had never heard of a Demonstration and was all eagerness. It was years since he had seen anyone do any more P.T. than putting their toes under the wardrobe and waving their torso about. Dancing? Goodness, was there dancing? But of course he would come. And what was more, they should come back with him to the theatre and have supper with him afterwards.

"I know Catherine hates the theatre, but you could stand it for once, couldn't you, Catherine? It's *Richard III* on Friday night, so you wouldn't have to put up with me in a romantic effort. It isn't a good play, but the production is wonderful, even if it is I who say it that shouldn't."

"A criminal libel on a fine man, a blatant piece of political propaganda, and an extremely silly play," Lux opined.

Adrian smiled broadly, like a schoolboy. "All right, but sit through it and you shall see how good a supper the Midland at Larborough can provide when egged on by a miserable actor. They even have a Johannisberger."

A faint colour showed in Lux's cheek at that.

"You see I remember what you like. Johannisberger, as you once remarked, tastes of flowers, and will take the stink of the theatre out of your nostrils."

"I never said it stank. It creaks."

"Of course it does. It has been on its last legs for quite two hundred years."

"Do you know what it reminds me of? The Coronation Coach. A lumbering anachronism; an absurd convention that we go on making use of because of inherited affection. A gilded relic—"

The kettle boiled, and Miss Lux poured the hot water into the pot.

"Give Miss Pym something to eat, Teddy."

An almost nursery tone, Lucy thought, taking one of the curled-up sandwiches from the plate he offered her. Was that what attracted him? Was it a sort of nostalgia for a world where he was taken for granted? He would not like such a world for long, that was certain, but it was quite possible that he wearied sometimes of the goldfish life he led, and would find a refreshment in the company of someone to whom he was just Teddy Adrian who used to come in the holidays.

She turned to say something to him, and surprised the look in his eyes as he watched Catherine spurning the various eatables. The amusement, the affection, that lit them might be a brother's, but there was something else. A—hopelessness, was it? Something like that. Something, anyhow, that had nothing to do with brotherliness; and that was very odd in a Great Star looking at the plain and ironic Mistress of Theory at Leys.

She looked across at the unconscious Catherine, and for the first time saw her as Edward Adrian saw her. As a woman with the makings of a *belle laide*. In this scholastic world one accepted her "good" clothes, her simple hairdressing, her lack of make-up, as the right and appropriate thing, and took her fine bones and lithe carriage for granted. She was just the plain and clever Miss Lux. But in the theatre world how different she would be! That wide supple mouth, those high cheek-bones with the hollow under them, the short straight nose, the good line of the lean jaw—they cried aloud for make-up. From the conventional point of view Lux had the kind of face that, as errand boys say, would "stop a clock"; but from any other view-point it was a face that would stop them eating at the Iris if she walked in at lunch-time properly dressed and made-up.

A combination of *belle laide* and someone who knew him "when" was no inconsiderable attraction. For the rest of tea-time Lucy's mind was busy with revision.

As soon as she decently could she retired, leaving them to the tête-à-tête that he had so obviously sought; the tête-à-tête that Miss Lux had done her best to deny him. He pleaded once more for a theatre party on Friday night—his car would be there and the Dem. would be over by six o'clock and College supper would be nothing but an anti-climax, and *Richard III* might be a lot of nonsense but it *was* lovely to look at, he promised them, and the food at the Midland was really wonderful since they had lured the chef away from Bono in Dover Street, and it was a very long time since he had seen Catherine and he had not talked half enough to the clever Miss Pym who had written that wonderful book, and he was dead sick anyhow of the company of actors who talked nothing but theatre and golf, and just to please him they might come—and although what with his practised actor's charm and his genuine desire that they should say yes, it was agreed that on Friday night they should go back to Larborough with him, witness his production of *Richard III*, and be rewarded with a good supper and a lift home.

As she crossed to the wing, however, Lucy found herself a little depressed. Yet once more she had been wrong about Miss Lux. Miss Lux was not an unwanted plain woman who found compensation in life by devoting herself to a beautiful younger sister. She was a potentially attractive creature who so little needed compensation that she couldn't be bothered with one of the most successful and handsome men in the world today.

She had been all wrong about Miss Lux. As a psychologist she began to suspect she was a very good teacher of French.

Chapter 15

*T*he only person who was moved by Edward Adrian's incursion into the College world was Madame Lefevre. Madame, as the representative of the theatre world in College, evidently felt that her own share in this visit should have been a larger one. She also gave Miss Lux to understand that she had, in the first place, no right to know Edward Adrian, but that, in the second place, having known him she had no right to keep him to herself. She was comforted by the knowledge that on Friday she would see him in person, and be able to talk to him in his own language, so to speak. He must have felt greatly at sea, she gave them to understand, among the aborigines of Leys Physical Training College.

Lucy, listening to her barbed silkinesses at lunch on Thursday, hoped that she would not ingratiate herself sufficiently with Adrian to be included in the supper party; she was looking forward to Friday night, and she most certainly would not look forward any more if Madame was going to be watching her all evening with those eyes of hers. Perhaps Miss Lux would put a spoke in her wheel in time. It was not Miss Lux's habit to put up with something that was not to her mind.

Still thinking of Madame and Miss Lux and tomorrow night, she turned her eyes absently on the students, and saw Innes's face. And her heart stopped.

It was three days, she supposed, since she had seen Innes for more than a moment in passing; but could three days have done this to a young girl's face? She stared, trying to decide where the change actually lay. Innes was thinner and very pale, certainly, but it was not that. It was not even the shadows under her eyes and the small hollow at the temple. Not even the expression; she was eating her lunch with her eyes on the plate in apparent calm. And yet the face shocked Lucy. She wondered if the others saw; she wondered that no one had mentioned it. The thing was as subtle and as obvious as the expression on the face of the Mona Lisa; as indefinable and as impossible to ignore.

So that is what it is to "burn up inside," she thought. "It is bad to burn up inside," Beau had said. Verily it must be bad if it ravaged a face like that. How could a face be at the same time calm and— and look like that? How, if it came to that, could one have birds tearing at one's vitals and still keep that calm face?

Her glance went to Beau, at the head of the nearer table, and she caught Beau's anxious look at Innes.

"I hope you gave Mr Adrian an invitation card?" Miss Hodge said to Lux.

"No," said Lux, bored with the subject of Adrian.

"And I hope you have told Miss Joliffe that there will be one more for tea."

"He doesn't eat at tea-time, so I didn't bother."

Oh, stop talking little sillinesses, Lucy wanted to say, and look at Innes. What is happening to her? Look at the girl who was so radiant only last Saturday afternoon. *Look* at her. What does she remind you of? Sitting there so calm and beautiful and all wrong inside. What does she remind you of? One of those brilliant things that grow in the woods, isn't it? One of those apparently perfect things that collapse into dust at a touch because they are hollow inside.

"Innes is not looking well," she said in careful understatement to Lux as they went upstairs.

"She is looking very ill," Lux said bluntly. "And would you wonder?"

"Isn't there something one can do about it?" Lucy asked.

"One could find her the kind of post she deserves," Lux said dryly. "As there is no post available at all, that doesn't seem likely to materialise."

"You mean that she will just have to begin to answer advertisements?"

"Yes. It is only a fortnight to the end of term, and there are not likely to be any more posts in Miss Hodge's gift now. Most places for September are filled by this time. The final irony, isn't it? That the most brilliant student we have had for years is reduced to application-in-own-handwriting-with-five-copies-of-testimonials-not-returnable."

It was damnable, Lucy thought; quite damnable.

"She *was* offered a post, so that lets Miss Hodge out."

"But it was a medical one, and she doesn't want that," Lucy said.

"Oh, yes, yes! You don't have to convert me; I'm enlisted already."

Lucy thought of tomorrow, when the parents would come and radiant daughters would show them round, full of the years they had spent here and the new achievement that was theirs. How Innes must have looked forward to that; looked forward to seeing the two people who loved her so well and who had by care and deprivation managed to give her the training she wanted; looked forward to putting Arlinghurst in their laps.

It was bad enough to be a Leaving Student without a post, but that was a matter susceptible to remedy. What could never be remedied was the injustice of it. It was Lucy's private opinion that injustice was harder to bear than almost any other inflicted ill. She could remember yet the surprised hurt, the helpless rage, the despair that used to consume her when she was young and the victim of an injustice. It was the helpless rage that was worst; it consumed one like a slow fire. There was no outlet, because there was nothing one could do about it. A very destructive emotion indeed. Lucy supposed that she had been like Innes, and lacked a sense of humour. But did the young ever have the detachment necessary for a proper focusing of their own griefs? Of course not. It was not people of forty who went upstairs and hanged themselves because someone had said a wrong word to them at the wrong moment, it was adolescents of fourteen.

Lucy thought she knew the passion of rage and disappointment and hate that was eating Innes up. It was enormously to her credit that she had taken the shock with outward dignity. A different type would have babbled to all and sundry, and collected sympathy like a street singer catching coins in a hat. But not Innes. A sense of humour she might lack—oil on her feathers, as Beau said—but the suffering that lack entailed was her affair; not to be exhibited to anyone—least of all to people she unconsciously referred to as "them."

Lucy had failed to think of a nice non-committal way of expressing her sympathy; flowers and sweets and all the conventional marks of active friendship were not to be considered, and she had found no substitute; and she was disgusted with herself now to realise that Innes's trouble, even though it was next-door to her all night, had begun to fade into the background for her. She had remembered it each night as Innes came to her room after the "bedroom" bell, and while the small noises next-door reminded her of the girl's existence. She had wondered and fretted about her for a little before falling to sleep. But during the crowded many-faceted days she had come near forgetting her.

Rouse had made no move to give a post party on Saturday night; but whether this was due to tact, an awareness of College feeling on the subject, or the natural thrift with which, it seemed, she was credited, no one knew. The universal party that had been so triumphantly planned for Innes was no more heard of; a universal party for Rouse was something that was apparently not contemplated.

Although, even allowing for the fact that Lucy had not been present at the height of the excitement when presumably tongues would have wagged with greater freedom, College had been strangely reticent about the Arlinghurst appointment. Even little Miss Morris, who chattered with a fine lack of inhibition every morning as she planked the tray down, made no reference to it. In this affair Lucy was for College purposes "Staff"; an outsider; perhaps a sharer in blame. She did not like the idea at all.

But what she liked least of all, and now could not get out of her mind, was Innes's barren tomorrow. The tomorrow that was to have been such a triumph. Lucy longed to provide her with a post at once, instantly, here and now; so that when tomorrow that tired happy woman with the luminous eyes came at last to see her daughter she would not find her empty-handed.

But of course one could not hawk a P.T.I. from door to door like a writing-pad; nor offer her to one's friends like a misfit frock. Goodwill was not enough. And goodwill was practically all she had.

Well, she would use the goodwill and see where it got her. She followed Miss Hodge into her office as the others went upstairs, and said: "Henrietta, can't we *invent* a post for Miss Innes? It seems all wrong that she should be jobless."

"Miss Innes will not be long jobless. And I can't imagine what consolation an imaginary post would be to her meanwhile."

"I didn't say imagine, I said invent; manufacture. There must be dozens of places all up and down the country that are still vacant. Couldn't we bring the job and Innes together somehow without her going through the slow suspense of applying? That waiting, Henrietta. Do you remember what it used to be like? The beautifully written applications and the testimonials that never came back."

"I have already offered Miss Innes a post and she has refused it. I don't know what more I can do. I have no more vacancies to offer."

"No, but you could get in touch with some of those advertised vacancies on her behalf, couldn't you?"

"I? But that would be most irregular. And quite unnecessary. She naturally gives my name as a reference when she applies; and if she were not commendable—"

"But you could—oh, you could ask for particulars of the post since you have a particularly brilliant student—"

"You are being absurd, Lucy."

"I know, but I want Innes to be very much sought-after by five o'clock this afternoon."

Miss Hodge, who did not read Kipling—or indeed, acknowledge his existence—stared.

"For a woman who has written such a noteworthy book—Professor Beatock praised it yesterday at the University College tea—you have an extraordinarily impulsive and frivolous mind."

This defeated Lucy, who was well aware of her mental limitations. Punctured, she stood looking at Henrietta's broad back in the window.

"I am greatly afraid," Henrietta said, "that the weather is going to break. The forecast this morning was anything but reassuring, and after so long a spell of perfect summer we are due for a change. It would be a tragedy if it decided to change tomorrow of all days."

A tragedy, would it! My God, you big lumbering silly woman, it is you who have the frivolous mind. I may have a C3 intelligence and childish impulses but I know tragedy when I see it and it has nothing to do with a lot of people running to save their party frocks or the cucumber sandwiches getting wet. No, by God, it hasn't.

"Yes, it would be a pity, Henrietta," she said meekly, and went away upstairs.

She stood for a little at the landing window watching the thick black clouds massing on the horizon, and hoping evilly that tomorrow they would swamp Leys in one grand Niagara so that the whole place steamed with damp people drying like a laundry. But she noticed almost immediately the heinousness of this, and hastily revised her wish. Tomorrow was their great day, bless them; the day they had sweated for, borne bruises and sarcasm for, been pummelled, broken, and straightened for, hoped, wept, and lived for. It was plain justice that the sun should shine on them.

Besides, it was pretty certain that Mrs Innes had only one pair of "best" shoes.

Chapter 16

*E*ach successive day of her stay at Leys saw Lucy a little more wide awake in the mornings. When the monstrous clamour of the 5.30 bell had first hurled her into wakefulness, she had turned on her other side as soon as the noise stopped and had fallen asleep again. But habit was beginning to have its way. Not only did she not fall asleep again after the early waking, but for the last day or two she had been sufficiently conscious to know in some drowsy depths of her that the waking bell was about to ring. On Demonstration morning she made history by wakening before the reveille.

What woke her was a faint fluttering under the point of her sternum: a feeling that she had not had since she was a child. It was associated with prize giving days at school. Lucy had always had a prize of sorts. Never anything spectacular, alas—2nd French, 3rd Drawing, 3rd Singing—but she was definitely in the money. Occasionally, too, there was a "piece" to be played—the Rachmaninoff Prelude, for one; not the DA, DA, DA one but the Da-de-de-de; with terrific concentration on the de-de-de—and consequently a new frock. Hence the tremor under the breastbone. And today, all those years afterwards, she had recaptured the sensation. For years any flutterings in that region had been mere indigestion—if indigestion can ever be mere. Now, because she was part of all the young emotion round her, she shared the thrill and the anticipation.

She sat up and looked at the weather. It was blank and grey, with a cool mist that might later lift on a blazing day. She got up and went to the window. The silence was absolute. Nothing stirred in the still greyness but the College cat, picking its way in an annoyed fashion over the dew-wet stones, and shaking each foot in turn as protest against the discomfort. The grass was heavy with dew, and Lucy, who had always had a perverted affection for wet grass, regarded it with satisfaction.

The silence was ripped in two by the bell. The cat, as if suddenly reminded of urgent business, sprang into wild flight. Giddy crunched past on his way to the gymnasium; and presently the faint whine of his vacuum-cleaner could be heard, like some far-distant siren. Groans and yawns and inquiries as to the weather came from the little rooms all round the courtyard, but no one came to a window to look; getting up was an agony to be postponed to the last moment.

Lucy decided to dress and go out into the dew-grey morning, so cool and damp and beneficent. She would go and see how the buttercups looked without the sun on them. Wet gamboge, probably. She washed sketchily, dressed in the warmest things she had with her, and slinging a coat over her shoulders went out into the silent corridor and down the deserted stairs. She paused by the quadrangle door to read the notices on the students' board; cryptic, esoteric, and plain. "Students are reminded that parents and visitors may be shown over the bedroom wings and the clinic, but not the front of the house." "Juniors are reminded that it is their duty to wait on the guests at tea and so help the domestic staff." And, by itself, in capitals, the simple statement:

DIPLOMAS WILL BE PRESENTED
ON TUESDAY MORNING AT 9 O'CLOCK

As she moved on towards the covered way, Lucy visualised the diploma as an imposing roll of parchment tied up with ribbon, and then remembered that even in the matter of diplomas this place was a law unto itself. Their diploma was a badge to stick in their coat; a little enamel-and-silver affair that, pinned to the left breast of their working garment, would tell all and sundry where they had spent their student years and to what end.

Lucy came out into the covered way and dawdled along it to the gymnasium. Giddy had long since finished his cleaning operations—she had seen him from her window before she left her room contemplating his roses at the far side of the lawn—and it was apparent that Rouse had already performed her morning routine—the faint damp marks of her gym. shoes were visible on the concrete path—so the gymnasium was deserted. Lucy paused as she was about to turn along the path by its side wall, and stepped in at the wide-open door. Just as a race-course is more dramatic before the crowds blur it or an arena before its traffic writes scribbles over it, so the great waiting hall had a fascination for her. The emptiness, the quiet, the green subaqueous light, gave it a dignity and a mysteriousness that did not belong to its daytime personality. The single boom that Rouse used swam in the shadows, and the liquid light of the mirrors under the gallery wavered at the far end in vague repetition.

Lucy longed to shout a command so as to hear her voice in this empty space; or to climb a ribstall and see if she could do it without having heart-failure; but she contented herself with gazing. At her age gazing was enough; and it was a thing that she was good at.

Something winked on the floor halfway between her and the boom; something tiny and bright. A nailhead or something, she thought; and then remembered that there were no nailheads in a gymnasium floor. She moved forward, idly curious, and picked the thing up. It was a small filigree rosette, flat, and made of silvery metal; and as she put it absently into her jersey pocket and turned away to continue her walk, she smiled. If the quiver under her sternum this morning had reminded her of school days, that small metal circle brought back even more clearly the parties of her childhood. Almost before her conscious mind had recognised it for what it was she was back in the atmosphere of crackers-and-jellies and white silk frocks, and was wearing on her feet a pair of bronze leather pumps with elastic that criss-crossed over the ankle and a tiny silver filigree rosette on each toe. Going down the path to the field gate, she took it out again and smiled over it, remembering. She had quite forgotten those bronze pumps; there were black ones too, but all the best people wore bronze ones. She wondered who in College possessed a pair. College wore ballet shoes for dancing, with or without blocked toes; and their gymnasium shoes were welted leather with an elastic instep. She had never seen anyone wear those pumps with the little ornament at the toe.

Perhaps Rouse used them for running down to the gymnasium in the mornings. It was certainly this morning the ornament had been dropped, since The Abhorrence under Giddy's direction was guaranteed to abstract from the gymnasium everything that was not nailed down.

She hung over the gate for a little but it was chilly there and disappointing; the trees were invisible in the mist, the buttercups a mere rust on the grey meadow, and the may hedges looked like dirty snow. She did not want to go back to the house before breakfast, so she walked along to the tennis courts where the Juniors were mending nets—this was odd-job day for everyone, they said, this being the one day in the year when they conserved their energies against a greater demand to come—and with them she stayed, talking and lending a hand, until they went up to College for breakfast. When they marvelled at her early rising little Miss Morris had suggested that she was tired of cold toast in her room, but when she said frankly that she could not sleep for excitement they were gratified by so proper an emotion in an alien breast, and promised that the reality would beggar expectation. She had not seen anything yet, it seemed.

She changed her wet shoes, suffered the friendly gibes of the assembled Staff at her access of energy, and went down with them to breakfast.

It was when she turned to see how Innes was looking this morning that she became aware of a gap in the pattern of bright heads. She did not know the pattern well enough to know who was missing, but there was certainly an empty place at one of the tables. She wondered if Henrietta knew. Henrietta had cast the usual critical eye over the assembly as she sat down, but as the assembly was also at that moment in the act of sitting down the pattern was blurred and any gap not immediately visible.

Hastily, in case Henrietta did not in fact know about the gap, she withdrew her gaze without further investigation. It was none of her wish to call down retribution on the head of any student, however delinquent. Perhaps, of course, someone had just "gone sick"; which would account for the lack of remark where their absence was concerned.

Miss Hodge, having wolfed her fish-cake, laid down her fork and swept the students with her small elephant eye. "Miss Wragg," she said, "ask Miss Nash to speak to me."

Nash got up from her place at the head of the nearest table and presented herself.

"Is it Miss Rouse who is missing from Miss Stewart's table?"

"Yes, Miss Hodge."

A stolid amiable Junior called Tuttle, who was always having to take the can back, was sent on the mission, and came back to say that Rouse was not in her room; which report Beau bore to the head table.

"Where was Miss Rouse when you saw her last?"

"I can't remember actually seeing her at all, Miss Hodge. We were all over the place this morning doing different things. It wasn't like sitting in class or being in the gym."

"Does anyone," said Henrietta addressing the students as a whole, "know where Miss Rouse is?"

But no one did, apparently.

"Has anyone seen her this morning?"

But no one, now they came to think of it, had seen her.

Henrietta, who had put away two slices of toast while Tuttle was upstairs, said, "Very well, Miss Nash," and Beau went back to her breakfast. Henrietta rolled up her napkin and caught Fröken's eye, but Fröken was already rising from table, her face anxious.

"You and I will go to the gymnasium, Fröken," Henrietta said, and they went out together, the rest of the Staff trailing after them but not following them out to the gymnasium. It was only on the way upstairs to make her bed that it occurred to Lucy to think: "I could have told them that she wasn't in the gymnasium. How silly of me not to think of it." She tidied her room—a task that the students were expected to perform for themselves and which she thought it only fair that she likewise should do for herself—wondering all the time where Rouse could have disappeared to. And why. Could she suddenly have failed again this morning to do that simple boom exercise and been overtaken by a *crise des nerfs?* That was the only explanation that would fit the odd fact of any College student missing a meal; especially breakfast.

She crossed into the "old house" and went down the front stairs and out into the garden. From the office came Henrietta's voice talking rapidly to someone on the telephone, so she did not interrupt her. There was still more than half an hour before Prayers; she would spend it reading her mail in the garden, where the mist was rapidly lifting and a shimmer had come into the atmosphere that had been so dead a grey. She went to her favourite seat at the far edge of the garden overlooking the countryside, and it was not until nine o'clock that she came back. There was no doubt about the weather now: it was going to be a lovely day; Henrietta's "tragedy" was not going to happen.

As she came round the corner of the house an ambulance drove away from the front door down the avenue. She looked at it, puzzled; but decided that in a place like this an ambulance was not the thing of dread that it was to the ordinary civilian. Something to do with the clinic, probably.

In the drawing-room, instead of the full Staff muster demanded by two minutes of nine o'clock, there was only Miss Lux.

"Has Rouse turned up?" Lucy asked.

"Yes."

"Where was she?"

"In the gymnasiuim, with a fractured skull."

Even in that moment of shock Lucy thought how typical of Lux that succinct sentence was. "But *how?* What happened?"

"The pin that holds up the boom wasn't properly in. When she jumped up to it it came down on her head."

"Good heavens!" Lucy could feel that inert log crash down on her own skull; she had always hated the boom.

"Fröken has just gone away with her in the ambulance to West Larborough."

"That was smart work."

"Yes. West Larborough is not far, and luckily at this hour of the morning the ambulance hadn't gone out and once it was on the way there was no traffic to hold it up."

"What dreadful luck for everyone. On Demonstration Day."

"Yes. We tried to keep it from the students but that was hopeless, of course. So all we can do is to minimise it."

"How bad is it, do you think?"

"No one knows. Miss Hodge has wired to her people."

"Weren't they coming to the Dem.?"

"Apparently not. She has no parents; just an aunt and uncle who brought her up. Come to think of it," she added after a moment's silence, "that is what she looked like: a stray." She did not seem to notice that she had used the past tense.

"I suppose it was Rouse's own fault?" Lucy asked.

"Or the student who helped her put up the thing last night."

"Who was that?"

"O'Donnell, it seems. Miss Hodge has sent for her to ask her about it."

At that moment Henrietta herself came in, and all the vague resentments that Lucy had been nursing against her friend in the last few days melted at sight of Henrietta's face. She looked ten years older, and in some odd fashion at least a stone less heavy.

"They have a telephone, it seems," she said, continuing the subject that was the only one in her mind, "so I shall be able to talk to them perhaps before the telegram reaches them. They are getting the trunk call for me now. They should be here before night. I want to be available for the telephone call, so will you take Prayers, Miss Lux. Fröken will not be back in time." Fröken was, as Senior Gymnast, second in rank to Miss Hodge. "Miss Wragg may not be at Prayers; she is getting the gymnasium put to rights. But Madame will be there, and Lucy will back you up."

"But of course," said Lucy. "I wish there was something more that I could do."

There was a tap at the door, and O'Donnell appeared.

"Miss Hodge? You wanted to see me?"

"Oh, in my office, Miss O'Donnell."

"You weren't there, so I—"

"Not that it matters, now that you are here. Tell me: when you put up the boom with Miss Rouse last night—It *was* you who helped her?"

"Yes, Miss Hodge."

"When you put up the boom with her, which end did you take?"

There was a tense moment of silence. It was obvious that O'Donnell did not know which end of the boom had given way and that what she said in the next few seconds would either damn her or save her. But when she spoke it was with a sort of despairing resolution that stamped what she said with truth.

"The wall end, Miss Hodge."

"You put the pin into the upright that is fixed to the wall?"

"Yes."

"And Miss Rouse took care of the upright in the middle of the floor."

"Yes, Miss Hodge."

"You have no doubt as to which end you attended to?"

"No, none at all."

"Why are you so certain?"

"Because I always did do the end by the wall."

"Why was that?"

"Rouse is taller than I am and could shove the boom higher than I could. So I always took the end by the wall so that I could put a foot in the ribstalls when I was putting the pin in."

"I see. Very well. Thank you, Miss O'Donnell, for being so frank."

O'Donnell turned to go, and then turned back.

"Which end came down, Miss Hodge?"

"The middle end," Miss Hodge said, looking with something

like affection on the girl though she had been on the point of letting her go without putting her out of suspense.

A great wave of colour rushed into O'Donnell's normally pale face. "Oh, thank you!" she said, in a whisper, and almost ran out of the room.

"Poor wretch," said Lux. "That was a horrible moment for her."

"It is most unlike Miss Rouse to be careless about apparatus," Henrietta said thoughtfully.

"You are not suggesting that O'Donnell is not telling the truth?"

"No, no. What she said was obviously true. It was the natural thing for her to take the wall end where she would have the help of the ribstalls. But I still cannot see how it happened. Apart from Miss Rouse's natural carefulness, a pin would have to be very badly put in indeed for it to be so far *not* in that it let the boom come down. And the hoisting rope so slack that it let the boom fall nearly three feet!"

"I suppose Giddy couldn't have done something to it accidentally!"

"I don't know what he could have done to it. You can't alter a pin put in at that height without stretching up deliberately to it. It is not as if it were something he might possibly touch with his apparatus. And much as he prides himself on the strength of The Abhorrence there is no suction that will pull a pin out from under a boom."

"No." Lux thought a little. "Vibration is the only kind of force that would alter a pin's position. Some kind of tremor. And there was nothing like that."

"Not inside the gymnasium, certainly. Miss Rouse locked it as usual last night and gave the key to Giddy, and he unlocked it just after first bell this morning."

"Then there is no alternative to the theory that for once Rouse was too casual. She was the last to leave the place and the first to come back to it—you wouldn't get anyone there at that hour of the morning who wasn't under the direct compulsion—so the blame is Rouse's. And let us be thankful for it. It is bad enough as it is, but it would be far worse if someone else had been careless and had to bear the knowledge that she was responsible for—"

The bell rang for Prayers, and downstairs the telephone shrilled in its own hysterical manner.

"Have you marked the place in the Prayer book?" Lux asked.

"Where the blue ribbon is," Miss Hodge said, and hurried out to the telephone.

"Has Fröken not come back?" asked Madame, appearing in the doorway. "Ah, well, let us proceed. Life must go on, if I may coin a phrase. And let us hope that this morning's ration of uplift is not too apposite. Holy Writ has a horrible habit of being apposite."

Not for the first time, Lucy wished Madame Lefevre on a lonely island off Australia.

It was a silent and subdued gathering that awaited them, and Prayers proceeded in an atmosphere of despondency that was foreign and unprecedented. But with the hymn they recovered a little. It was Blake's and had a fine martial swing, and they sang it with a will. So did Lucy.

"Nor shall the sword sleep in my hand," she sang, making the most of it. And stopped suddenly, hit in the wind.

Hit in the wind by a jolt that left her speechless.

She had just remembered something. She had just remembered why she had been so sure that Rouse would not be found in the gymnasium. Rouse's damp footprints had been visible on the concrete path, and so she had taken it for granted that Rouse had already been and gone. But Rouse had not been. Rouse had come later, and had sprung to the insecure boom and had lain there until after breakfast when she was searched for.

Then—whose footprints were they?

Chapter 17

"Students," said Miss Hodge, rising in her place after lunch and motioning the rest of the Staff to remain seated, "you are all aware of the unfortunate accident which occurred this morning—entirely through the carelessness of the student concerned. The first thing a gymnast learns is to examine apparatus before she uses it. That a student as responsible and altogether admirable as Miss Rouse should have failed in so simple and fundamental a duty is a warning to you all. That is one point. This is the other. This afternoon we are entertaining guests. There is no secret about what happened this morning—we could not keep it secret even if we wanted to—but I do ask you not to make it a subject of conversation. Our guests are coming here to enjoy themselves; and to know that this morning an accident took place sufficiently serious to send one of our students to hospital would undoubtedly take the edge off their pleasure; if indeed it did not fill them with a quite unnecessary apprehension when watching gymnastics. So if any of you have a desire to dramatise today's happenings, please curb it. It is your business to see that your guests go away happy, without reservations or regrets. I leave the matter to your own good sense."

It had been a morning of adjustment; physical, mental, and spiritual. Fröken had come back from the West Larborough hospital to put a worried lot of Seniors through a routine that would allow for the fact that they were one short. Under her robust calm they took the alterations, and necessity for them, with a fair degree of equanimity; although she reported that at least a third of them shied like nervous colts each time they handled the right-hand front boom, or passed the place where it had fallen. It was going to be a miracle, Fröken said with resignation, if they got through this afternoon's performance without someone or other making a fool of themselves. As soon as Fröken had released them Madame Lefevre took them over for a much lengthier session. Thanks to her physi-

cal prowess, Rouse had been part of almost every item on the ballet programme; which meant that almost every item had to undergo
either patching or reconstruction. This thankless and wearisome
business had lasted until nearly lunchtime, and the echoes of it were
still audible. Most of the lunch-table conversation appeared to consist of remarks like "Is it you I give my right hand to when Stewart
passes in front of me?" and Dakers lightened the universal anxiety
by being overtaken by one of those sudden silences common to all
gatherings, which left her announcing loudly that my *dears*, the last
hour had *proved* that one could be in two places at the same time.

The most fundamental adjustment, however, occurred when
both Fröken and Madame had finished their respective revisions. It
was then that Miss Hodge had sent for Innes and offered her
Rouse's place at Arlinghurst. Hospital had confirmed Fröken's diagnosis of a fracture, and there was no chance that Rouse would be
able for work until many months had passed. How Innes had taken
this no one knew; all that anyone knew was that she had accepted.
The appointment, having all the qualities of anti-climax and being
overshadowed by an authentic sensation, was taken as a matter of
course; and as far as Lucy could see neither Staff nor students gave
it a thought. Madame's sardonic "The Deity disposes" was the solitary comment.

But Lucy was less happy about it. A vague uneasy stirring
plagued her like some mental indigestion. The patness of the thing
worried her. The accident had happened not only opportunely but
at the last available moment. Tomorrow there would have been no
need for Rouse to go to the gymnasium and practise; there would
have been no boom set up and no pin to be insecurely placed. And
there were those damp footmarks in the early morning. If they were
not Rouse's own, whose were they? As Lux had very truly observed,
no one could be dragged anywhere near the gymnasium at that
hour by anything less compelling than wild horses.

It was possible that they were Rouse's prints and that she had
done something else before going into the gymnasium for her few
minutes on the boom. Lucy could not swear that footprints actually
went into the building; she could remember no actual print on either of the two steps. She had merely seen the damp marks on the
covered way and concluded, without thinking about it at all, that
Rouse was ahead of her. The prints may have continued round the
building, for all she knew. They may have had nothing to do with
the gymnasium at all. Nothing to do with the students, even. It was

possible that those heelless impressions, so vague and blurred, were made by a maid-servant's early-morning shoes.

All that was possible. But allied to the steps that were not likely to be Rouse's was the oddity of a small metal ornament lying on a floor that had been swept twenty minutes before by a powerful vacuum-cleaner. An ornament lying directly between the door and the waiting boom. And whatever was conjecture, one thing was certain: the ornament was not lost by Rouse. Not only had she almost certainly not been in the gymnasium this morning before Lucy entered it, but she did not possess a pair of pumps. Lucy knew, because one of her helpful chores today had been to pack poor Rouse's things. Miss Joliffe, whose task it would nominally have been, was overwhelmed by preparations for the afternoon's entertainment, and had passed the duty on to Wragg. Wragg had no student to enlist as substitute, since they were all busy with Madame, and it was not a duty that could be entrusted to a Junior. So Lucy had willingly taken over the job, glad to find a way to be of use. And her first action in Number Fourteen had been to take Rouse's shoes out of the cupboard and look at them.

The only pair that were not there were her gymnastic shoes, which presumably had been what she wore this morning. But to be sure she summoned O'Donnell when she heard the Seniors come back from the gymnasium and said: "You know Miss Rouse very well, don't you? Would you cast your eye over these shoes and tell me whether they are all she had, before I begin packing them?"

O'Donnell considered, and said yes, these were all. "Except her gym. shoes," she added. "She was wearing those."

That seemed to settle it.

"Nothing away being cleaned?"

"No, we clean our own—except for our hockey boots in winter."

Well, that seemed to be that. What Rouse had worn this morning were regulation College gym. shoes. It was not off any shoes of Rouse's that the little filigree rosette had come.

Then from where? Lucy had asked herself as she packed Rouse's belongings with a care she never accorded her own. From where?

She was still asking herself that as she changed her dress for the party. She put the rosette into one of the small drawers of the dress-table-desk affair, and dully looked over her scanty collection of clothes for something that would be suitable to a garden-party afternoon. From her second window, the one looking out on the garden, she could see the Juniors busy with small tables and basket-

chairs and tea-umbrellas. Their ant-like running about was producing a gay border of colour round three sides of the lawn. The sun
streamed down on them, and the picture in its definition and variety of detail was like a Brueghel gone suddenly gay.

But Lucy, looking down at the picture and remembering how
she had looked forward to this occasion, felt sick at heart; and could
not bring herself yet to acknowledge why she should be heartsick.
Only one thing was clear to her. Tonight she must go to Henrietta
with the little rosette. When all the excitement was over and Henrietta had time to be quiet and consider, then the problem—if there
was a problem—must be handed over to her. She, Lucy, had been
wrong last time when she had tried to save Henrietta suffering by
dropping the little red book into the water; this time she must do
her duty. The rosette was no concern of hers.

No. It was no concern of hers. Certainly not.

She decided that the blue linen with the narrow red belt was sufficiently Hanover Square to satisfy the most critical of parents from
the provinces, brushed the suede shoes with the brush so dutifully
included by Mrs Montmorency, and went down to help wherever
she could be useful.

By two o'clock the first guests were arriving; going into the office to pay their respects to Miss Hodge, and then being claimed by
excited offspring. Fathers prodded doubtfully at odd gadgets in the
clinic, mothers prodded the beds in the wing, and horticultural un-
cles prodded Giddy's roses in the garden. She tried to find distraction in "pairing" the parents she met with the appropriate student.
She noticed that she was searching unconsciously for Mr and Mrs
Innes and anticipating their meeting with something that was half
dread. Why dread? she asked herself. There was nothing in the
world to dread, was there? Certainly not. Everything was lovely.
Innes had after all got Arlinghurst; the day was after all a triumph
for her.

She came upon them unexpectedly, round the corner of the
sweet-pea hedge; Innes walking between them with her arms
through theirs and a light on her face. It was not the radiance that
had shone in her eyes a week ago, but it was a good enough substitute. She looked worn but at peace; as if some inner battle was over,
the issue settled for good or bad.

"You knew them," she said to Miss Pym, indicating her parents,
"and you never told me."

It was like meeting old friends, Lucy thought. It was unbelievable that her only traffic with these people had been across a coffee table for an hour on a summer morning. She seemed to have known them all her life. And she felt that they in their turn felt like that about her. They really were glad to see her again. They remembered things and asked about them, referred to things she had said, and generally behaved as if she not only was of importance in their scheme of things, but was actually part of that scheme. And Lucy, used to the gushing indifference of literary parties, felt her heart warm afresh to them.

Innes left them together and went away to get ready for the gymnastic display that would open the afternoon's programme, and Lucy walked over to the gymnasium with them.

"Mary is looking very ill," her mother said. "Is there anything wrong?"

Lucy hesitated, wondering how much Innes had told them.

"She has told us about the accident, and about falling heir to Arlinghurst. I don't suppose she is very happy at profiting by another student's bad luck, but it can't be just that."

Lucy thought that the more they understood about the affair the better it would be if—well, the better it would be anyhow.

"Everyone took it for granted that she would get the appointment in the first place. I think it was a shock to her when she didn't."

"I see. Yes," said Mrs Innes, slowly; and Lucy felt that more explanation was not necessary; the whole tale of Innes's suffering and fortitude was clear to her mother in that moment.

"I think she might not approve of my having told you that, so—"

"No, we will not mention it," said Innes's mother. "How lovely the garden is looking. Gervase and I struggle along with our patch but only his bits look like the illustration; mine always turn out to be something else. Just look at those little yellow roses."

And so they came to the gymnasium door, and Lucy showed them up the stairs and introduced them to The Abhorrence—with pricking thought of a little metal rosette—and they found their seats in the gallery, and the afternoon had begun.

Lucy had a seat at the end of the front row. From there she looked down with affection on the grave young faces waiting, with such tense resolution, Fröken's word of command. "Don't worry," she had heard a Senior say, "Fröken will see us through," and one could see the faith in their eyes. This was their ordeal, and they came to it shaken, but Fröken would see them through.

She understood now the love that had filled Henrietta's eyes when she had watched with her on that other occasion. Less than a fortnight ago, that was, and already she had a proprietorial interest and pride in them. When the autumn came the very map of England would look different to her because of these two weeks at Leys. Manchester would be the place where the Disciples were, Aberystwyth the place where Thomas was trying to stay awake, Ling the place where Dakers was being good with the babies, and so on. If she felt like that about them after a matter of days, it was not much wonder that Henrietta, who had seen them come untried into their new life, had watched them grow and improve, struggle, fail, and succeed, not much wonder that she looked on them as daughters. Successful daughters.

They had got through their preliminaries, and a little of the strain had gone from their faces; they were beginning to settle down. The applause that marked the end of their free-standing work broke the silence and warmed them and made the affair more human.

"What a charming collection," said a dowager with lorgnettes who was sitting next to her (now who owned that? she couldn't be a parent) and turning to her confidentially asked: "Tell me, are they hand-picked?"

"I don't understand," murmured Lucy.

"I mean, are these all the Seniors there are?"

"You mean, are these just the best? Oh, no; that is the whole set."

"Really? Quite wonderful. So attractive, too. Quite amazingly attractive."

Did she think we had given the spotty ones half a crown to take themselves off for the afternoon? wondered Lucy.

But of course the dowager was right. Except for a string of two-year-olds in training, Lucy could think of nothing more attractive to mind and eye than that set of burnished and controlled young creatures busy dragging out the booms below her. The ropes rushed down from their looped position near the roof, the window-ladder came to vertical, and over all three pieces of apparatus the Seniors swarmed in easy mastery. The applause as they put ropes and ladder away and turned the booms for balance was real and loud; the spectacular had its appeal.

Very different the place looked from that mysterious vault of greenish shadows that she had visited this morning. It was golden, and matter-of-fact, and alive; the reflected light from the sunlit roof showering down on the pale wood and making it glow. Seeing once more in her mind's eye that dim empty space with the single waiting boom, she turned to see whose lot it might be to perform her balance on the spot where Rouse had been found. Who had the inner end of the right-hand front boom?

It was Innes.

"Go!" said Fröken; and eight young bodies somersaulted up to the high booms. They sat there for a moment, and then rose in unison to a standing position, one foot in front of the other, facing each other in pairs at opposite ends of each boom.

Lucy hoped frantically that Innes was not going to faint. She was not merely pale; she was green. Her opposite number, Stewart, made a tentative beginning, but, seeing that Innes was not ready, waited for her. But Innes stood motionless, apparently unable to move a muscle. Stewart cast her a glance of wild appeal. Innes remained paralysed. Some wordless message passed between them, and Stewart went on with her exercise; achieving a perfection very commendable in the circumstances. All Innes's faculties were concentrated on keeping her standing position on the boom long enough to be able to return to the floor with the rest, and not to ruin the whole exercise by collapsing, or by jumping off. The dead silence and the concentration of interest made her failure painfully obvious; and puzzled sympathy settled on her as she stood there. Poor dear, they thought, she was feeling ill. Excitement, no doubt. Positively green, she was. Poor dear, poor dear.

Stewart had finished, and now waited, looking at Innes. Slowly they sank together to the boom, and sat down on it; turned together to lean face-forward on it; and somersaulted forward on to the ground.

And a great burst of applause greeted them. As always, the English were moved by a gallant failure where an easy success left them merely polite. They were expressing at once their sympathy and their admiration. They had understood the strength of purpose that had kept her on the boom, paralysed as she was.

But the sympathy had not touched Innes. Lucy doubted if she actually heard the applause. She was living in some tortured world of her own, far beyond the reach of human consolation. Lucy could hardly bear to look at her.

The bustle of the following items covered up her failure and put an end to drama. Innes took her place with the others and performed with mechanical perfection. When the final vaulting came, indeed, her performance was so remarkable that Lucy wondered if she were trying to break her neck publicly. The same idea, to judge by her expression, had crossed Fröken's mind; but as long as what Innes did was controlled and perfect there was nothing she could do. And everything that Innes did, however breath-taking, was perfect and controlled. Because she seemed not to care, the wildest flights were possible to her. And when the students had finished their final go-as-you-please and stood breathless and beaming, a single file on an empty floor as they had begun, their guests stood up as one man and cheered.

Lucy, being at the end of the row and next to the door, was first to leave the hall, and so was in time to see Innes's apology to Fröken.

Fröken paused, and then moved on as if not interested, or not willing to listen.

But as she went she lifted a casual arm and gave Innes a light friendly pat on the shoulder.

Chapter 18

*A*s the guests moved out to the garden and the basket-chairs round the lawn, Lucy went with them, and while she was waiting to see if sufficient chairs had been provided before taking one for herself, she was seized upon by Beau, who said: "Miss Pym! There you are! I've been hunting for you. I want you to meet my people."

She turned to a couple who were just sitting down and said: "Look, I've found Miss Pym at last."

Beau's mother was a very lovely woman; as lovely as the best beauty parlours and the most expensive hairdressers could make her—and they had good foundation to work on since when Mrs Nash was twenty she must have looked very like Beau. Even now, in the bright sunlight, she looked no older than thirty-five. She had a good dressmaker too, and bore herself with the easy friendly confidence of a woman who has been a beauty all her life; so used to the effect she had on people that she did not have to consider it at all and so her mind was free to devote itself to the person she happened to be meeting.

Mr Nash was obviously what is called an executive. A fine clear skin, a good tailor, a well-soaped look, and a general aura of mahogany tables with rows of clean blotters round them.

"I should be changing. I must fly," said Beau, and disappeared.

As they sat down together Mrs Nash looked quizzically at Lucy and said: "Well, now that you are here in the flesh, Miss Pym, we can ask you something we are dying to know. We want to know *how you do it?*"

"Do what?"

"Impress Pamela."

"Yes," said Mr Nash, "that is just what we should like to know. All our lives we have been trying to make some impression on Pamela, but we remain just a couple of dear people who happen to be responsible for her existence and have to be humoured now and then."

"Now *you*, it seems, are quite literally something to write home about," Mrs Nash said, and raised an eyebrow and laughed.

"If it is any consolation to you," Lucy offered, "I am greatly impressed by your daughter."

"Pam *is* nice," her mother said. "We love her very much; but I wish we impressed her more. Until you turned up no one has made any impression on Pamela since a Nanny she had at the age of four."

"And that impression was a physical one," Mr Nash volunteered.

"Yes. The only time in her life that she was spanked."

"What happened?" Lucy asked.

"We had to get rid of the Nanny!"

"Didn't you approve of spanking?"

"Oh yes, but Pamela didn't."

"Pam engineered the first sit-down strike in history," Mr Nash said.

"She kept it up for seven days," Mrs Nash said. "Short of going on dressing and forcibly feeding her for the rest of her life, there was nothing to do but get rid of Nanny. A first-rate woman she was, too. We were devastated to lose her."

The music began, and in front of the high screen of the rhododendron thicket appeared the bright colours of the Juniors' Swedish folk dresses. Folk-dancing had begun. Lucy sat back and thought, not of Beau's childish aberrations, but of Innes, and the way a black cloud of doubt and foreboding was making a mockery of the bright sunlight.

It was because her mind was so full of Innes that she was startled when she heard Mrs Nash say, "Mary, darling. There you are. How nice to see you again," and turned to see Innes behind them. She was wearing boys' things; the doublet and hose of the fifteenth century; and the hood that hid all her hair and fitted close round her face accentuated the bony structure that was so individual. Now that the eyes were shadowed and sunk a little in their always-deep sockets, the face had something it had not had before: a forbidding look. It was—what was the word?—a "fatal" face. Lucy remembered her very first impression that it was round faces like that that history was built.

"You have been overworking, Mary," Mr Nash said, eyeing her.

"They all have," Lucy said, to take their attention from her.

"Not Pamela," her mother said. "Pam has never worked hard in her life."

No. Everything had been served to Beau on a plate. It was miraculous that she had turned out so charming.

"Did you see me make a fool of myself on the boom?" Innes asked, in a pleasant conversational tone. This surprised Lucy, somehow; she had expected Innes to avoid the subject.

"My dear, we sweated for you," Mrs Nash said. "What happened? Did you turn dizzy?"

"No," said Beau, coming up behind them and slipping an arm into Innes's, "that is just Innes's way of stealing publicity. It is not inferior physical powers, but superior brains the girl has. None of us has the wit to think up a stunt like that."

Beau gave the arm she was holding a small reassuring squeeze. She too was in boys' clothes, and looked radiant; even the quenching of her bright hair had not diminished the glow and vivacity of her beauty.

"That is the last of the Juniors' efforts—don't they look gay against that green background?—and now Innes and I and the rest of our put-upon set will entertain you with some English antics, and then you shall have tea to sustain you against the real dancing to come."

And they went away together.

"Ah, well," said Mrs Nash, watching her daughter go, "I suppose it is better than being seized with a desire to reform natives in Darkest Africa or something. But I wish she would have just stayed at home and been one's daughter."

Lucy thought that it was to Mrs Nash's credit that, looking as young as she did, she wanted a daughter at home.

"Pam was always mad on gym. and games," Mr Nash said. "There was no holding her. There never was any holding her, come to that."

"Miss Pym," said The Nut Tart, appearing at Lucy's elbow, "do you mind if Rick sits with you while I go through this rigmarole with the Seniors?" She indicated Gillespie, who was standing behind her clutching a chair, and wearing his habitual expression of grave amusement. The wide flat hat planked slightly to the back of her head on top of her wimple—Wife of Bath fashion—gave her an air of innocent astonishment that was delightful. Lucy and Rick exchanged a glance of mutual appreciation, and he smiled at her as he sat down on her other side.

"Isn't she lovely in that get-up," he said, watching Desterro disappear behind the rhododendrons.

"I take it that a rigmarole doesn't count as dancing."

"Is she good?"

"I don't know. I have never seen her, but I understand she is."

"I've never even danced ballroom stuff with her. Odd, isn't it. I didn't even know she existed until last Easter. It maddens me to think she has been a whole year in England and I didn't know about it. Three months of odd moments isn't very long to make any effect on a person like Teresa."

"Do you want to make an effect?"

"Yes." The monosyllable was sufficient.

The Seniors, in the guise of the English Middle Ages, ran out on to the lawn, and conversation lapsed. Lucy tried to find distraction in identifying legs and in marvelling over the energy with which those legs ran about after an hour of strenuous exercise. She said to herself: "Look, you have to go to Henrietta with the little rosette tonight. All right. That is settled. There is nothing you can do, either about the going or the result of the going. So put it out of your mind. This is the afternoon you have been looking forward to. It is a lovely sunny day, and everyone is pleased to see you, and you should be having a grand time. So relax. Even if—if anything awful happens about the rosette, it has nothing to do with you. A fortnight ago you didn't know any of these people, and after you go away you will never see any of them again. It can't matter to you what happens or does not happen to them."

All of which excellent advice left her just where she was before. When she saw Miss Joliffe and the maids busy about the tea-table in the rear she was glad to get up and find some use for her hands and some occupation for her mind.

Rick, unexpectedly, came with her. "I'm a push-over for passing plates. It must be the gigolo in me."

Lucy said that he ought to be watching his lady-love's rigmaroles.

"It is the last dance. And if I know anything of my Teresa her appetite will take more appeasing than her vanity, considerable as it is."

He seemed to know his Teresa very well, Lucy thought.

"Are you worried about something, Miss Pym?"

The question took her by surprise.

"Why should you think that?"

"I don't know. I just got the impression. Is there anything I can do?"

Lucy remembered how on Sunday evening when she had nearly cried into the Bidlington rarebit he had known about her tiredness and tacitly helped her. She wished that she had met someone as understanding and as young and as beautiful as The Nut Tart's follower when she was twenty, instead of Alan and his Adam's apple and his holey socks.

"I have to do something that is right," she said slowly, "and I'm afraid of the consequences."

"Consequences to you?"

"No. To other people."

"Never mind; do it."

Miss Pym put plates of cakes on a tray. "You see, the proper thing is not necessarily the right thing. Or do I mean the opposite?"

"I'm not sure that I know what you mean at all."

"Well—there are those awful dilemmas about whom would you save. You know. If you knew that by saving a person from the top of a snow slide you would start an avalanche that would destroy a village, would you do it? That sort of thing."

"Of course I would do it."

"You would?"

"The avalanche might bury a village without killing a cat—shall I put some sandwiches on that tray?—so you would be one life to the good."

"You would always do the right thing, and let the consequences take care of themselves?"

"That's about it."

"It is certainly the simplest. In fact I think it's too simple."

"Unless you plan to play God, one has to take the simple way."

"Play God? You've got two lots of tongue sandwiches there, do you know?"

"Unless you are clever enough to 'see before and after' like the Deity it's best to stick to rules. Wow! The music has stopped and here comes my young woman like a hunting leopard." He watched Desterro come with a smile in his eyes. "Isn't that hat a knockout!" He looked down at Lucy for a moment. "Do the obvious right thing, Miss Pym, and let God dispose."

"Weren't you watching, Rick?" she heard Desterro ask, and then she and Rick and The Nut Tart were overwhelmed by a wave of Juniors come to do their duty and serve tea. Lucy extricated herself from the crush of white caps and Swedish embroidery, and found herself face to face with Edward Adrian, alone and looking forlorn.

"Miss Pym! You are just the person I wanted to see. Have you heard that—"

A Junior thrust a cup of tea into his hand, and he gave her one of his best smiles, which she did not wait to see. At the same moment little Miss Morris, faithful even in the throes of a Dem., came up with tea and a tray of cakes for Lucy.

"Let us sit down, shall we?" Lucy said.

"Have you heard of the frightful thing that has happened?"

"Yes. It isn't very often, I understand, that a serious accident happens. It is just bad luck that it should be Demonstration Day."

"Oh, the accident, yes. But do you know that Catherine says she can't come to Larborough tonight? This has upset things, she says. She must stay here. But that is absurd. Did you ever hear anything more absurd? If there has been some kind of upset that is all the more reason why she should be taken out of herself for a little. I have arranged everything. I even got special flowers for our table tonight. *And* a birthday cake. It's her birthday next Wednesday."

Lucy wondered if any other person within the bounds of Leys knew when Catherine Lux's birthday was.

Lucy did her best to sympathise, but said gently that she saw Miss Lux's point of view. After all, the girl was seriously injured, and it was all very worrying, and it would no doubt seem to her a little callous to go merrymaking in Larborough.

"But it isn't merrymaking! It is just a quiet supper with an old friend. I really can't see why because some student has had an accident she should desert an old friend. You talk to her, Miss Pym. You make her see reason."

Lucy said she would do her best but could offer no hope of success since she rather shared Miss Lux's ideas on the subject.

"You, too! Oh, my God!"

"I know it isn't reasonable. It's even absurd. But neither of us would be happy and the evening would be a disappointment and you don't want that to happen? Couldn't you have us tomorrow night instead?"

"No, I'm catching a train directly after the evening performance is over. And of course, it being Saturday, I have a matinée. And anyhow, I'm playing Romeo at night and that wouldn't please Cath at all. It takes her all her time to stand me in *Richard III.* Oh dear, the whole thing is absurd."

"Cheer up," Lucy said. "It stops short of tragedy. You will be coming to Larborough again, and you can meet as often as you like now that you know she is here."

"I shall never get Catherine in that pliant mood again. Never. It was partly your doing, you know. She didn't want to appear too much of a Gorgon in front of you. She was even going to come to see me act. Something she has never done before. I'll never get her back to that point if she doesn't come tonight. Do persuade her, Miss Pym."

Lucy promised to try. "How are you enjoying your afternoon, apart from broken appointments?"

Mr Adrian was enjoying himself vastly, it appeared. He was not sure which to admire most: the students' good looks or their efficiency.

"They have charming manners, too. I have not been asked for an autograph once, all the afternoon."

Lucy looked to see if he was being ironic. But no; the remark was "straight." He really could not conceive any reason for the lack of autograph hunters other than that of good manners. Poor silly baby, she thought, walking all his life through a world he knew nothing about. She wondered if all actors were like that. Perambulating spheres of atmosphere with a little actor safely cocooned at the heart of each. How nice it must be, so cushioned and safe from harsh reality. They weren't really born at all; they were still floating in some pre-natal fluid.

"Who is the girl who fluffed at the balance exercise?"

Was she not going to get away from Innes for two minutes together?

"Her name is Mary Innes. Why?"

"What a wonderful face. Pure Borgia."

"Oh, no!" Lucy said, sharply.

"I've been wondering all the afternoon what she reminded me of. I think it is a portrait of a young man by Giorgione, but which of his young men I wouldn't know. I should have to see them again. Anyhow, it's a wonderful face, so delicate and so strong, so good and so bad. Quite fantastically beautiful. I can't imagine what anything so dramatic is doing at a girls' Physical Training College in the twentieth century."

Well, at least she had the consolation of knowing that someone else saw Innes as she did; exceptional, oddly fine, out of her century, and potentially tragic. She remembered that to Henrietta she was merely a tiresome girl who looked down her nose at people less well endowed with brains.

Lucy wondered what to offer Edward Adrian by way of distraction. She saw coming down the path a floppy satin bow-tie against a dazzling collar and recognized Mr Robb, the elocution master; the only member of the visiting Staff, apart from Dr Knight, that she knew. Mr Robb had been a dashing young actor forty years ago—the most brilliant Lancelot Gobbo of his generation, one understood—and she felt that to hoist Mr Adrian with his own petard would be rather pleasant. But being Lucy her heart softened at the thought of the wasted preparations he had made—the flowers, the cake, the plans for showing off—and she decided to be merciful. She saw O'Donnell, gazing from a discreet distance at her one-time hero, and she beckoned to her. Edward Adrian should have a real, authentic, dyed in the wool fan to cheer him; and he need never know that she was the only one in College.

"Mr Adrian," she said, "this is Eileen O'Donnell, one of your most devoted admirers."

"Oh, Mr Adrian—" she heard O'Donnell begin.

And she left them to it.

Chapter 19

When tea was over (and Lucy had been introduced to at least twenty different sets of parents) the drift back from the garden began, and Lucy overtook Miss Lux on the way to the house.

"I'm afraid that I am going to cry off tonight," she said. "I feel a migraine coming."

"That is a pity," Lux said without emotion. "I have cried off too."

"Oh, why?"

"I'm very tired, and upset about Rouse, and I don't feel like going junketing in town."

"You surprise me."

"I surprise you? In what way?"

"I never thought I should live to see Catherine Lux being dishonest with herself."

"Oh. And what am I fooling myself about?"

"If you have a look at your mind you'll find that that's not why you're staying at home."

"No? Why, then?"

"Because you get such pleasure out of telling Edward Adrian where he gets off."

"A deplorable expression."

"Descriptive, though. You simply jumped at the chance of being high and mighty with him, didn't you?"

"I own that breaking the engagement was no effort."

"And a little unkind?"

"A deplorable piece of self-indulgence by a shrew. That's what you're trying to say, isn't it?"

"He is looking forward so much to having you. I can't think why."

"Thanks. I can tell you why. So that he can cry all over me and tell me how he hates acting—which is the breath of life to him."

"Even if he bores you—"

"If! My God!"

"—you can surely put up with him for an hour or so, and not use Rouse's accident as a sort of ace from your sleeve."

"Are you trying to make an honest woman of me, Lucy Pym?"

"That is the general idea. I feel so sorry for him, being left—"

"My—good—woman," Lux said, stabbing a forefinger at Lucy with each word, "*never* be sorry for Edward Adrian. Women spend the best years of their lives being sorry for him, and end by being sorry for it. Of all the self-indulgent, self-deceiving—"

"But he *has* got a Johannisberger."

Lux stopped, and smiled at her.

"I could do with a drink, at that," she said reflectively.

She walked on a little.

"Are you really leaving Teddy high and dry?" she asked.

"Yes."

"All right. You win. I was just being a beast. I'll go. And every time he trots out that line about 'Oh, Catherine, how weary I am of this artificial life' I shall think with malice: That Pym woman got me into this."

"I can bear it," Lucy said. "Has anyone heard how Rouse is?"

"Miss Hodge has just been on the telephone. She is still unconscious."

Lucy, seeing Henrietta's head through the window of her office—it was known as the office but was in reality the little sitting-room to the left of the front door—went in to compliment her on the success of the afternoon and so take her mind for at least a moment or two off the thing that oppressed it, and Miss Lux walked on. Henrietta seemed glad to see her, and even glad to have repeated to her the platitudes she had been listening to all the afternoon, and Lucy stayed talking to her for some time; so that the gallery was almost filled again when she took her seat to watch the dancing.

Seeing Edward Adrian in one of the gangway seats she paused and said:

"Catherine is coming."

"And you?" he said, looking up.

"No, alas; I am having a migraine at six-thirty sharp."

Whereupon he said, "Miss Pym, I adore you," and kissed her hand.

His next-door neighbour looked startled, and someone behind

tittered, but Lucy liked having her hand kissed. What was the good of putting rose-water and glycerine on every night if you didn't have a little return now and then?

She went back to her seat at the end of the front row, and found that the dowager with the lorgnettes had not waited for the dancing; the seat was empty. But just before the lights went down—the hall was curtained and artificially lit—Rick appeared from behind and said: "If you are not keeping that seat for anyone, may I sit there?"

And as he sat down the first dancers appeared.

After the fourth or fifth item Lucy was conscious of a slow disappointment. Used to the technical standards of international ballet, she had not allowed in her mind for the inevitable amateurism of dancing in this milieu. In everything she had seen the students do so far they had been the best of their line in the business; professionals. But it was obviously not possible to give to other subjects the time and energy that they did and still reach a high standard as dancers. Dancing was a whole-time job.

What they did was good, but it was uninspired. On the best amateur level, or a little above. So far the programme had consisted of the national and period dances beloved of all dancing mistresses, and they had been performed with a conscientious accuracy that was admirable but not diverting. Perhaps the need for keeping their minds on the altered track took some of the spontaneity from their work. But on the whole Lucy thought that it was that neither training nor temperament was sufficient. Their audience too lacked spontaneity; the eagerness with which they had watched the gymnastics was lacking. Perhaps they had too much tea; or perhaps it was the cinema had brought to their remotest doors a standard of achievement that made them critical. Anyhow their applause was polite rather than enthusiastic.

A piece of Russian bravura roused them for a moment, and they waited hopefully for what might come next. The curtains parted to reveal Desterro, alone. Her arms raised above her head and one slim hip turned to the audience. She was wearing some sort of native dress from her own hemisphere, and the "spot" made the bright colours and the barbaric jewels glitter so that she looked like one of the brilliant birds from her Brazilian forests. Her little feet in their high-heeled shoes tapped impatiently under the full skirt. She began to dance; slowly, almost absent-mindedly, as if she were putting in time. Then it became evident that she was waiting for her lover and that he was late. What his lateness meant to her also became rapidly apparent. By this time the audience were sitting up. From some empty space she conjured a lover. One could almost see the hang-dog look on his swarthy face. She dealt with him: faithfully. By this time the audience were sitting on the edge of their seats. Then, having dealt with him, she began to show off to him; but did he not realise his luck in having a girl like her, a girl who had a waist, an eye, a hip, a mouth, an ankle, a total grace like hers? Was he a boor that he could not see? She therefore showed him; with a wit in every movement that brought smiles to every face in the audience. Lucy turned to look at them; in another minute they would be cooing. It was magic. By the time she began to relent and let her lover have a word in, they were her slaves. And when she walked away with that still invisible but undoubtedly subdued young man, they cheered like children at a Wild West matinée.

Watching her as she took her bow, Lucy remembered how The Nut Tart had chosen Leys because for the proper dancing schools "one must have a métier."

"She was modest about her dancing after all," she said aloud. "She could have been a professional."

"I am glad she didn't," Rick said. "Coming here she has learned to love the English countryside. If she had trained in town she would have met only the international riff-raff that hang around ballet."

And Lucy thought that he was probably right.

There was a distinct drop in temperature when the conscientious students reappeared to continue their numbers. Stewart had a Celtic verve that was refreshing, and Innes had grace and moments of fire, but the moment Desterro came among them even Lucy forgot Innes and all the others. Desterro was enchanting.

At the end she had an ovation all to herself.

And Miss Pym, catching the look on Rick's face, felt a small pang.

It was not enough to have one's hand kissed.

"Nobody told me that Desterro could dance like that," she said to Miss Wragg as they went over to supper together when the guests had at last taken their departure with much starting up of engines and shouted goodbyes.

"Oh, she is Madame's little pet," Wragg said in the unenthusiastic voice of Madame's follower speaking of a creature so far gone in sin that she did not play games. "I think she is stagey, myself. Out of place here, somehow. I honestly think that first dance wasn't quite nice. Did you think that?"

"I thought it delightful."

"Oh, well," Wragg said, resignedly; and added: "She must be good, or Madame wouldn't be so keen on her."

Supper was a quiet meal. Exhaustion, anti-climax, and the recollection (now that they were idle) of this morning's accident all served to damp the students' spirits and clog their tongues. The Staff, too, were tired after their shocks, exertions, social efforts, and anxieties. Lucy felt that the occasion called for a glass of good wine, and thought with a passing regret of the Johannisberger that Lux was drinking at that moment. Her heart had begun to thud in a horrid way when she thought that in a few moments she must take that little rosette into the office, and tell Henrietta where she found it.

She had still not taken it out of the drawer where she had left it, and after supper she was on the way up to fetch it when she was overtaken by Beau, who slid an arm into hers and said:

"Miss Pym, we are brewing cocoa in the common-room, the whole shoot of us. Do come and cheer us up. You don't want to go and sit in that morgue upstairs"—the morgue was presumably the drawing-room—"do you? Come and cheer us up."

"I don't feel particularly cheerful myself," Lucy said, thinking with loathing of the cocoa, "but if you put up with my gloom I shall put up with yours."

As they turned towards the common-room a great wind out of nowhere swept down the corridor through all the wide-open windows, dashing the green branches of the trees outside against one another and tearing the leaves upward so that their backs showed. "The end of the good weather," Lucy said, pausing to listen. She had always hated that restless destroying wind that put paid to the golden times.

"Yes, it's cold too," Beau said. "We've lit a wood fire."

The common-room was part of the "old house" and had an old brick fireplace; and it certainly looked cheerful with the flame and crackle of a freshly lit fire, the rattle of crockery, the bright dresses of the students lying about in exhausted heaps, and their still brighter bedroom slippers. It was not only O'Donnell who had had recourse to odd footwear tonight; practically everyone was wearing undress shoes of some sort or another. In fact Dakers was lying on a settee with her bare bandaged toes higher than her head. She waved a cheerful hand at Miss Pym, and indicated her feet.

"Haemostosis!" she said. "I bled into my *best* ballet shoes. I suppose no one would like to *buy* a pair of ballet shoes, slightly soiled? No, I was afraid not."

"There's a chair over by the fire, Miss Pym," Beau said, and went to pour out the cocoa. Innes, who was sitting curled up on the hearth superintending a Junior's efforts with a bellows, patted the chair and made her welcome in her usual unsmiling fashion.

"I've cadged the rest of the tea stuff from Miss Joliffe," Hasselt said, coming in with a large plate of mixed left-overs.

"How did you do that?" they asked. "Miss Joliffe never gives away even a smell."

"I promised to send her some peach jam when I got back to South Africa. There isn't really very much though it looks a plateful. The maids had most of it after tea. Hullo, Miss Pym. What did you think of us?"

"I thought you were all wonderful," Lucy said.

"Just like London policemen," Beau said. "Well, you bought that, Hasselt."

Lucy apologised for the cliché, and sought by going into further detail to convince them of her enthusiasm.

"Desterro ran away with the evening, didn't she, though?" they said; and glanced with friendly envy at the composed figure in the bright wrap sitting upright in the ingle-nook.

"Me, I do only one thing. It is easy to do just one thing well."

And Lucy, like the rest of them, could not decide if the cool little remark was meant to be humble or reproving. On the whole she thought humble.

"That's enough, March, it's going beautifully," Innes said to the Junior, and moved to take the bellows from her. As she moved, her feet came out from under her and Lucy saw that she was wearing black pumps.

And the little metal ornament that should have been on the left one was not there.

Oh, *no*, said Lucy's mind. No. No. No.

"That is your cup, Miss Pym, and here is yours, Innes. Have a rather tired macaroon, Miss Pym."

"No, I have some chocolate biscuits for Miss Pym."

"No, she is going to have some Ayrshire shortbread, out of a tin, and *fresh*. None of your pawed-over victuals."

The babble went on round her. She took something off a plate. She answered what was said to her. She even took a sip of the stuff in the cup.

Oh, no. No.

Now that the thing was here—the thing she had been afraid of, so afraid that she would not even formulate it in her mind—now that it was here, made concrete and manifest, she was appalled. It had all suddenly become a nightmare: the bright noisy room with the blackening sky outside where the storm was rushing up, and the missing object. One of those nightmares where something small and irrelevant has a terrifying importance. Where something immediate and urgent must be done about it but one can't think what or why.

Presently she must get up and make polite leave-taking and go to Henrietta with her story and end by saying: "And I know whose shoe it came from. Mary Innes's."

Innes was sitting at her feet, not eating but drinking cocoa thirstily. She had curled her feet under her again, but Lucy had no need for further inspection. Even her faint hope that someone else might be wearing pumps had gone overboard. There was a fine colourful variety of footgear present but not a second pair of pumps.

In any case, no one else had a motive for being in the gymnasium at six o'clock this morning.

"Have some more cocoa," Innes said presently, turning to look at her. But Miss Pym had hardly touched hers.

"Then I must have some more," Innes said, and began to get up.

A very tall thin Junior called Farthing, but known even to the Staff as Tuppence-Ha'penny, came in.

"You're late, Tuppence," someone said. "Come and have a bun." But Farthing stood there, uncertainly.

"What is the matter, Tuppence?" they asked, puzzled by her shocked expression.

"I went to put the flowers in Fröken's room," she said slowly.

"Don't tell us there were some there already?" someone said; and there was a general laugh.

"I heard the Staff talking about Rouse."

"Well, what about her? Is she better?"

"She's dead."

The cup Innes was holding crashed on the hearth. Beau crossed over to her to pick up the pieces.

"Oh, nonsense," they said. "You heard wrong, young Tuppence."

"No, I didn't. They were talking on the landing. She died half an hour ago."

This was succeeded by a dismayed silence.

"I *did* put up the wall end," O'Donnell said loudly, into the silence.

"Of course you did, Don," Stewart said, going to her. "We all know that."

Lucy put down her cup and thought that she had better go upstairs. They let her go with murmured regrets, their happy party in pieces round them.

Upstairs, Lucy found that Miss Hodge had gone to the hospital to receive Rouse's people when they arrived, and that it was she who had telephoned the news. Rouse's people had come, and had taken the blow unemotionally, it seemed.

"I never liked her, God forgive me," said Madame, stretched at full length on the hard sofa; her plea to the Deity for forgiveness had a genuine sound.

"Oh, she was all right," Wragg said, "quite nice when you knew her. And the most marvellous centre-half. This is frightful, isn't it. Now it will be a matter of inquiry, and we'll have police, an inquest, and appalling publicity, and everything."

Yes, police and everything.

She should not do anything about the little rosette tonight. And anyhow she wanted to think about it.

She wanted to get away by herself and think about it.

Chapter 20

*B*ong! Bong! The clock in that far-away steeple struck again.
Two o'clock.

She lay staring into the dark, while the cold rain beat on the
ground outside and wild gusts rose every now and then and rioted
in anarchy, flinging her curtains out into the room so that they
flapped like sails and everything was uncertainty and turmoil.

The rain wept with steady persistence, and her heart wept with
it. And in her mind was a turmoil greater than the wind's.

"Do the obvious right thing, and let God dispose," Rick had
said. And it had seemed a sensible ruling.

But that was when it had been a hypothetical affair of "causing
grievous bodily harm" (that was the phrase, wasn't it?) and now it
had ceased to be hypothesis and it wasn't any longer mere bodily
harm. It was—was *this*.

It wouldn't be God who would dispose this, in spite of all the
comforting tags. It would be the Law. Something written with
ink in a statute book. And once that was invoked God Himself
could not save a score of innocent persons being crushed under the
juggernaut wheels of its progress.

An eye for an eye and a tooth for a tooth, said the old Mosaic
law. And it sounded simple. It sounded just. One saw it against a
desert background, as if it involved two people only. It was quite
different when one put it in modern words and called it "being
hanged by the neck until you are dead."

If she went to Henrietta in the—

If?

Oh, all right, of course she was going.

When she went to Henrietta in the morning, she would be putting in motion a power over which neither she nor anyone else had
control; a power that once released would catch up this, that, and

the next one from the innocent security of their peaceful lives and fling them into chaos.

She thought of Mrs Innes, happily asleep somewhere in Larborough; bound home tomorrow to wait for the return of the daughter in whom she had her life. But her daughter would not come home—ever.

Neither will Rouse, a voice pointed out.

No, of course not, and Innes must somehow pay for that. She must not be allowed to profit by her crime. But surely, surely there was some way in which payment could be made without making the innocent pay even more bitterly.

What was justice?

To break a woman's heart; to bring ruin and shame on Henrietta and the destruction of all she had built up; to rub out for ever the radiance of Beau, the Beau who was unconditioned to grief. Was that a life for a life? That was three—no, four lives for one.

And one not worth—

Oh, no. That she could not judge. For that one had to "see before and after," as Rick said. A curiously sober mind, Rick had, for a person with a play-boy's face and a Latin lover's charm.

There was Innes moving about again next-door. As far as Lucy knew she had not slept yet either. She was very quiet, but every now and then one heard a movement or the tap in her room ran. Lucy wondered whether the water was to satisfy a thirst or to cool temples that must be throbbing. If she, Lucy, was lying awake with her thoughts running round and round inside her skull like trapped mice, what must Innes be going through? Humourless she might be, unenamoured of the human species she probably was, but insensitive she most certainly was not. Whether it was thwarted ambition, or sheer anger and hate, that had driven her down to the gymnasium through the misty morning, she was not the sort to be able to do what she had done with impunity. It might well be indeed, that given her temperament it was herself she had destroyed when she tampered with that boom. In the case-histories of crime there were instances of women so callous that they had come to a fresh blooming once the obstacle to their desires was out of the way. But they were not built like Mary Innes. Innes belonged to that other, and rarer, class who found too late that they could not live with themselves any more. The price they had paid was too high.

Perhaps Innes would provide her own punishment.

That, now she came to think of it, was how she had first thought of Innes, on that Sunday afternoon under the cedar. The stake or nothing. A self-destroyer.

That she had destroyed a life that stood in her way was almost incidental.

It had not, in any case, been intended as destruction; Lucy was quite sure of that. That is what made this business of starting the machine so repellent, so unthinkable. All that the insecure pin was meant to achieve was a temporary incapacity. An assurance that Rouse would not go to Arlinghurst in September—and that she would.

Had she had that in mind, Lucy wondered, when she refused the appointment at the Wycherley Orthopaedic Hospital? No, surely not. She was not a planner in cold blood. The thing had been done at the very last moment, in desperation.

At least, it had been *achieved* at the very last moment.

It was possible that its lateness was due to lack of previous opportunity. The way to the gymnasium might never have been clear before; or Rouse may have got there first.

"A Borgia face," Edward Adrian had said, delightedly.

And Teresa's great-grandmother's grandmother, whom she resembled, *she* had planned. And had lived a long, secure, and successful life as a widow, administering rich estates and bringing up a son, without apparently any signs of spiritual suicide.

The wind flung itself into the room, and Innes's window began to rattle. She heard Innes cross the room to it, and presently it stopped.

She wished she could go next-door, now, at this minute, and put her hand down. Show Innes the ace she held and didn't want to play. Together they could work something out.

Together? With the girl who loosened that pin under the boom?

No. With the girl she had talked to in the corridor last Saturday afternoon, so radiant, so full of dignity and wisdom. With the girl who could not sleep tonight. With her mother's daughter.

Whatever she had done, even if she had planned it, the result had been something she had neither planned nor foreseen. The result was catastrophe for her.

And who in the first place had brought that catastrophe?

Henrietta. Henrietta with her mule-like preference for her inferior favourite.

She wondered if Henrietta was sharing Innes's vigil. Henrietta who had come back from West Larborough so strangely thin and old-looking. As if the frame she was strung on had collapsed and the stuffing had shifted. Like a badly stuffed toy after a month in the nursery. That is what Henrietta had looked like.

She had been truly sorry for her friend, bereft of someone she had—loved? Yes, loved, she supposed. Only love could have blinded her to Rouse's defects. Bereft; and afraid for her beloved Leys. She had been truly moved by her suffering. But she could not help the thought that but for Henrietta's own action none of this would have happened.

The operative cause was Innes's vulnerability. But the button that had set the whole tragedy in motion was pressed by Henrietta.

And now she, Lucy, was waiting to press another button which would set in motion machinery even more monstrous. Machinery that would catch up in its gears and meshes, and maim and destroy, the innocent with the guilty. Henrietta perhaps had bought her punishment, but what had the Inneses done to have this horror unloaded on them? This unnameable horror.

Or *had* they contributed? How much had Innes's upbringing been responsible for her lack of resilience? Given that she had been born without "oil on her feathers," had they tried to condition her to the lack? Who could ever say where first causes lay?

Perhaps after all, even through the Law, it was the Deity who disposed. If you were a Christian you took that for granted, of course. You took for granted that nothing ever happened that there was no cause for. That everyone who would be tortured incidentally by Innes's trial for murder had in some way "bought" their punishment. It was a fine comfortable theory, and Lucy wished that she could subscribe to it. But she found it difficult to believe that any deficiency on the part of parents as responsible and as devoted as the Inneses could warrant the bringing down on their heads of a tragedy so unspeakable.

Or perhaps—

She sat up, to consider this new thought.

If God did dispose—as undoubtedly He did in the latter end—then perhaps the disposing was already at work. Had begun to work when it was she and not someone else who found the little rosette. It had not been found by a strong-minded person who would go straight to Henrietta with it as soon as she smelt a rat, and so set the machinery of man-made Law in motion. No. It had been found by a feeble waverer like herself, who could never see less than three sides to any question. Perhaps that made sense.

But she wished very heartily that the Deity had found another instrument. She had always hated responsibility; and a responsibility of this magnitude was something that she could not deal with at all. She wished that she could throw away the little rosette—toss it out of the window now and pretend that she had never seen it. But of course she could not do that. However rabbity and inadequate she was by nature, there was always her other half—the Laetitia half—which stood watching her with critical eyes. She could never get away from that other half of herself. It had sent her into fights with her knees knocking, it had made her speak when she wanted to hold her tongue, it had kept her from lying down when she was too tired to stand up. It would keep her from washing her hands now.

She got up and leaned out into the wet, lashing, noisy night. There was a puddle of rain water on the wood floor inside the window. The cold shock of it on her bare feet was somehow grateful; a physical and understandable discomfort. At least she did not have to mop it up, or wonder about a carpet. All the elements came into this place at their will and everyone took it for granted. One of Innes's few volunteered remarks had been how lovely it had been one morning to waken and find her pillow crusted with snow. That had happened only once, she said, but you could always tell the season by what you found on your pillow in the morning: spiders in the autumn and sycamore seeds in June.

She stayed so long cooling her burning head that her feet grew cold, and she had to wrap them in a jersey to warm them when she got back into bed. That completes it, she thought: cold feet mentally and physically. You're a poor thing, Lucy Pym.

About three o'clock when she was growing sleepy at last, she was shot wide awake by the realisation of what she was proposing to do. She was seriously considering keeping back evidence in a capital charge. Becoming an accessory after the fact. A criminal.

She, respectable, law-abiding Lucy Pym.

How had she got to that point? What could she have been thinking of?

Of course she had no choice in the matter at all. Who disposed or did not dispose was no concern of hers. This was a matter of public inquiry, and she had a duty to do. A duty to civilisation, to the State, to herself. Her private emotions had nothing to do with it. Her views on justice had nothing to do with it. However unequal and wrong-headed the Law might be, she could not suppress evidence.

How in the name of all that was crazy had she ever thought that she could?

Rick was right: she would do the obvious right thing, and let God dispose.

About half-past four she really did fall asleep.

Chapter 21

The morning was bleary and sodden, and Lucy regarded it with distaste. The waking-bell had sounded as usual at five-thirty, although on the morning after the Demonstration there were no classes before breakfast. College might make concessions but it did not discard its habits. She tried to fall asleep again, but reality had come with the daylight, and what had been feverish theory in the dark hours was now chill fact. In an hour or two she would have pressed that button, and altered beyond computing lives of whose existence she was not even aware. Her heart began to thud again.

Oh, dear, why had she ever come to this place!

It was when she had finished dressing and was sticking a few invisible hairpins into appropriate places that she realised that she could not go to Henrietta about the rosette without first going to Innes. She was not sure whether this was a remnant of some childish conception of "playing fair" or whether she was just trying to find a way of breaking the matter that would make her own personal responsibility less absolute.

She went to Innes's door, quickly before the impulse to action should evaporate, and knocked. She had heard Innes come back from her bath and reckoned that by now she must be dressed.

The Innes who opened the door looked tired and heavy-eyed but composed. Now that she was face to face with her Lucy found it difficult to identify her with the Innes of her disturbed thoughts last night.

"Do you mind coming into my room for a moment?" she asked.

Innes hesitated, looked uncertain for a second, and then recovered herself. "Yes, of course," she said; and followed Lucy.

"What a night of rain it was," she said brightly.

It was unlike Innes to bother with remarks about the weather. And it was exceedingly unlike Innes to be bright.

Lucy took the little silver rosette out of her drawer and held it out on her palm for Innes to see.

"Do you know what that is?" she asked.

In a second the brightness had disappeared and Innes's face was hard and wary.

"Where did you get that?" she snapped.

It was only then that Lucy realised how, deep down, she had counted on Innes's reaction being different. How, unconsciously, she had expected Innes to say: "It looks like something off a dancing pump; lots of us have them." Her heart stopped thudding and sank into her stomach.

"I found it on the gymnasium floor very early yesterday morning," she said.

The hard wariness melted into a slow despair.

"And why do you show it to me?" Innes said dully.

"Because I understand that there is only one pair of those old-fashioned pumps in College."

There was silence. Lucy laid the little object down on the table and waited.

"Am I wrong?" she asked at last.

"No."

There was another silence.

"You don't understand, Miss Pym," she said in a burst, "it wasn't meant to be— I know you'll think I'm just trying to white-wash it, but it was never meant to be—to be the way it turned out. It was because I was so sick about missing Arlinghurst—I practically lost my reason over that for a time—I behaved like an idiot. It got so that I couldn't think of anything in the world but Arlinghurst. And this was just to be a way of—of letting me have a second chance at it. It was never meant to be more than that. You must believe that. You must—"

"But of course I believe it. If I didn't I don't suppose I should be sharing the knowledge of this with you." She indicated the rosette.

After a moment Innes said: "What are you going to do?"

"Oh, dear God, I don't know," said poor Lucy, helpless now that she was face to face with reality. All the crimes she had met with were in slick detective stories where the heroine, however questionable, was invariably innocent, or in case-histories where the crime was safely over with and put away and a matter only for the scalpel. All those subjects of case-history record had had friends and relations whose stunned disbelief must have been very like her own, but the knowledge was neither comfort nor guide to her. This was the kind of thing that happened to other people—happened daily if one could believe the Press—but could not possibly happen to oneself.

How *could* one believe that someone one had laughed and talked with, liked and admired, shared a communal life with, could be responsible for another's death?

She found herself beginning to tell Innes of her sleepless night, of her theories about "disposing," of her reluctance to destroy half a dozen lives because of one person's crime. She was too absorbed in her own problem to notice the dawning hope in Innes's eyes. It was only when she heard herself saying, "Of course you cannot possibly be allowed to profit by Rouse's death," that she realised how far she had already come along the road that she had had no intention of travelling.

But Innes pounced on this. "Oh, but I won't, Miss Pym. And it has nothing to do with your finding the little ornament. I knew last night when I heard that she was dead that I couldn't go to Arlinghurst. I was going to tell Miss Hodge this morning. I was awake too last night. Facing a lot of things. Not only my responsibility for Rouse's death—my inability to take defeat and like it. But—oh, well, a lot of things that wouldn't interest you." She paused a moment, considering Lucy. "Look, Miss Pym, if I were to spend the rest of my life atoning for yesterday morning will you—would you—" She could not put so brazen a suggestion into words, even after Lucy's dissertation on justice.

"Become an accessory after the fact?"

The cold legality of the phrase discouraged Innes.

"No, I suppose it is too much to expect anyone to do. But I *would* atone, you know. It wouldn't be any halfhearted affair. It would be my life for—hers. I would do it gladly."

"I believe you, of course. But how do you plan to atone?"

"I thought of that last night. I began with leper colonies and things like that, but they were rather unreal and didn't make much sense in connection with a Leys training. I have a better idea. I decided that I would work alongside my father. I hadn't planned to do medical work, but I am good at it and there is no orthopaedic clinic in our home town."

"It sounds admirable," Lucy said, "but where is the penance?"

"My one ambition since I was a little girl has been to get away

from living in a little market town; coming to Leys was my passport to freedom."

"I see."

"Believe me, Miss Pym, it would be penance. But it wouldn't be
a barren one. It wouldn't be just personal flagellation. I would be
doing something useful with my life, something that would—
would make it good value for exchange."

"Yes, I see."

There was another long silence.

The five-minute bell rang, but for the first time since she came
to Leys Lucy was unconscious of a bell.

"Of course you have nothing but my word for it—"

"I would accept your word."

"Thank you."

It seemed too easy a way out, she was thinking. If Innes was to
be punished, the living of a dull and useful life hardly seemed a sufficient exaction. She had forfeited Arlinghurst of course; that would
cost her something. But would it pay for a death?

What, in any case, would pay for a death? Except a death.

And Innes was offering what she obviously considered a living
death. Perhaps after all it was not so poor an exchange.

What she, Lucy, was faced with was the fact that her delibera-
tions, her self-communing and comparing of arguments, fused at
this moment into one single and simple issue. Was she going to
condemn to death the girl who was standing in front of her?

It was, after all, as simple as that. If she took that little rosette to
Henrietta this morning, Innes would die before the first students
came back to Leys in the autumn. If she did not die she would
spend her twenties in a living death that would indeed be "barren."

Let her spend her years in the prison of her choice, where she
could be useful to her fellows.

Certainly she, Lucy Pym, was quite unequal to the task of con-
demning her.

And that was that.

"I am entirely in your hands," she said slowly to Innes, "because
I am quite incapable of sending anyone to the gallows. I know what
my plain duty is and I can't do it." Odd, she thought, that I should
be in her reverence rather than she in mine.

Innes stared at her, doubtfully.

"You mean—" Her tongue came out and ran along her dry lips.
"You mean that you won't tell about the rosette?"

"No. I shall never tell anyone."

Innes went suddenly white.

So white that Lucy realised that this was a phenomenon that she had read about but never seen. "White as a sheet," they said. Well, it was perhaps an unbleached sheet but it certainly was "going white."

Innes put her hand out to the chair by the dressing-table and sat down abruptly. Seeing Lucy's anxious expression she said: "It's all right, I'm not going to faint. I've never fainted in my life. I'll be all right in a minute."

Lucy, who had been antagonised by her self-possession, her ready bargaining—Innes had been far too lucid on the subject, she felt—was seized with something like compunction. Innes had not after all been self-possessed. It had been the old story of emotion clamped down and taking a mean revenge when it found escape.

"Would you like a drink of water?" Lucy said, moving to the wash-basin.

"No, thank you, I'm all right. It's just that for the last twenty-four hours I've been so afraid, and seeing that silver thing on your hand was the last straw, and then suddenly it is all over, you've let me buy a reprieve, and—and—"

Sobs came up in her throat and choked the words. Great rending sobs without a single tear. She put her hands over her mouth to stop them, but they burst through and she covered her face and struggled for composure. It was no use. She put both arms on the desk with her head between them and sobbed her heart out.

And Lucy, looking at her, thought: Another girl would have begun with this. Would have used it as a weapon, a bid for my sympathy. But not Innes. Innes comes self-contained and aloof, offering hostages. Without the breakdown no one would have guessed that she was suffering. Her present abandonment was the measure of her previous torture.

The first low murmur of the gong began in a slow crescendo.

Innes heard it and struggled to her feet. "If you'll forgive me," she said, "I'll go and dash some cold water on myself. That will stop it."

Lucy thought it remarkable that a girl so racked with sobs that she could hardly speak should prescribe for herself with such detachment; as if she were another person from this hysterical individual who had taken possession of her and was making such an exhibition of herself.

"Yes, do," Lucy said.

Innes paused with her hand on the door-knob.

"Some day I'll be able to thank you properly," she said, and disappeared.

Lucy dropped the little silver rosette into her pocket and went down to breakfast.

Chapter 22

*I*t was a horrible week-end.

The rain poured down. Henrietta went about looking as though she had had a major operation that had not proved a success. Madame was at her worst and not at all helpful, either actually or verbally. Fröken was furious that such a thing should have happened in "her" gymnasium. Wragg was an ever-present Cassandra scattering depressing truisms. Lux was quiet and tired.

Lux had come back from Larborough bearing a small pink candle wrapped in pale green tissue paper. "Teddy said I was to give you this," she said. "I can't think why."

"Oh? From a cake?"

"Yes. It's my birthday about now."

"How nice of him to remember."

"Oh, he keeps a birthday diary. It's part of his publicity. It is his secretary's duty to send telegrams to all the appropriate people on the appropriate days."

"Don't you ever give him credit for anything?" Lucy asked.

"Teddy? Not for a real emotion, I don't. I've known him since he was ten, don't forget. He can't fool me for more than five seconds together."

"My hairdresser," Lucy said, "who lectures to me while he is doing my hair, says that one should allow everyone three faults. If one makes that allowance, one finds that the rest is surprisingly nice, he says."

"When you allow for Teddy's three faults there is nothing left, unfortunately."

"Why?"

"Because his three faults are vanity, selfishness, and self-pity. And any one of the three is totally destructive."

"Whew!" said Lucy. "I give up."

But she stuck the silly little candle on her dressing-table, and thought kindly of Edward Adrian.

She wished she could think as kindly of her beloved Beau, who was making things as difficult as possible by being furious with Innes for giving up Arlinghurst. In fact Lucy understood that things had come as near a quarrel between them as was possible between two people so mutually devoted.

"Says she wouldn't be happy in dead men's shoes," said Beau, positively giving off sparks with wrath. "Can you imagine anything more ridiculous? Turning down Arlinghurst as if it were a cup of tea. After nearly dying of chagrin because she didn't get it in the first place. For God's sake, Miss Pym, you talk to her and make her see sense before it is too late. It isn't just Arlinghurst, it's her whole future. Beginning at Arlinghurst means beginning at the top. You talk to her, will you? Talk her out of this absurd notion!"

It seemed to Lucy that she was always being implored to "talk to" people. When she wasn't being a dose of soothing syrup she was being a shot of adrenaline, and when she wasn't being that she was being just a spoonful of alkaline powder for general consumption.

When she wasn't being a *deus ex machina;* a perverter of justice. But she tried not to think of that.

There was nothing she could say to Innes, of course, but other people had said it. Miss Hodge had wrought with her long and faithfully; dismayed by the defection of the girl she had not wanted to appoint in the first place. Now she had no one to send to Arlinghurst; she must write and tell them so and see the appointment go elsewhere. Perhaps when the news of the fatal accident leaked round the academic world Arlinghurst would decide to look elsewhere next time they wanted a gymnast. Accidents shouldn't happen in well-conducted gymnasiums; not fatal accidents, anyhow.

That, too, was the police point of view. They had been very nice, the police, very considerate. Very willing to consider the harm that undesirable publicity would do the establishment. But there had to be an inquest, of course. And inquests were painfully public and open to misconstruction. Henrietta's lawyer had seen the local Press and they had promised to play down the affair, but who knew when a clipping might catch the eye of a sub-editor at a temporary loss for a sensation? And then what?

Lucy had wanted to go away before the inquest, to get away from the perpetual reminders of her guilt in the eyes of the Law, but Henrietta had begged her to stay. She had never been able to say no to Henrietta, and this pathetic aged Henrietta was someone whom she could not refuse. So Lucy stayed; doing odd jobs for Henrietta and generally leaving her free to deal with the crowd of extraneous duties that the accident had saddled her with.

But to the inquest she would not go.

She could not sit there with all her load of knowledge and not at some point be tempted to stand up and tell the truth and have the responsibility off her soul.

Who knew what rat the police might smell out? They had come and viewed the gymnasium, and measured things, and reckoned the weight of the boom, and interviewed all and sundry, and consulted the various experts on the subject, and listened and said nothing. They had taken away the pin that had been so fatally insecure; and that may have been mere routine, but who could tell? Who could tell what suspicions they might be entertaining in their large calm breasts and behind their polite expressionless faces?

But as it turned out, a quite unexpected saviour appeared at the inquest. A saviour in the person of Arthur Middleham, tea importer, of 59 West Larborough Road; that is to say, a resident in one of the villas which lined the highroad between West Larborough and the gates of Leys. Mr Middleham knew nothing about College except that it was there, and that the scantily attired young women who flew about the district on bicycles belonged to it. But he had heard about the accident. And it had struck him as odd that a pin in the gymnasium at Leys had moved out of place on the same morning, and presumably about the same time, as a pane of glass had been shaken out of his drawing-room window by a passing convoy of tanks from the works at South Larborough. His theory was, in fact, the same as Miss Lux's: vibration. Only Miss Lux's had been a hit in the dark and of no value. Mr Middleham's was reasonable and backed by three-dimensional evidence: a pane of broken glass.

And as always when someone has given a lead, there were gratuitous followers. (If someone invented a story and wrote to the Press that they had seen a green lion in the sky at 5.30 the previous evening, at least six people would have seen it retrospectively.) An excited woman, hearing Mr Middleham's evidence, got up from the body of the hall and said that her ginger jar that she had had for years had dropped off the little table in her window of its own accord at the same time.

"Where do you live, madam?" the coroner asked, when he had winkled her out of the crowd and installed her as evidence.

She lived in the cottages between Leys and Bidlington, she said. On the highroad? Oh, yes, much too much on the highroad; in the summer the dust was a fair sickener, and when the traffic was them there tanks— No, she had no cat. No, there had been no one in the room. She had just come in after breakfast and found it on the floor. It had never happened before.

Poor O'Donnell, very nervous but clear and decided, gave evidence that she had put up the end by the wall and that Rouse had attended to the middle end. "Puting it up" meant hoisting the boom by the pulley rope and pushing the pin under it to keep it up. It was also kept up, to a certain extent, by the rope, the hanging end of which was given a turn round a cleat on the upright. No, they had not tested the apparatus before going.

Fröken, asked about the rope which had not proved a substitute for the pin, said that it had not been wound tightly enough to prevent sagging when the pin was removed. The twisting of the rope round the cleat was an automatic gesture, and no student thought of it as a precautionary measure. It was that, in fact, of course. The metal of the pin might break through some fault, and the rope in that case took the strain. Yes, it was possible that a rope, unaccustomed to a greater strain than the weight of a boom, stretched under the sudden addition of a ten-stone burden, but she thought not. Gymnasium ropes were highly tested and guaranteed. It was much more likely that the twist Miss Rouse gave it had been inadequate.

And that seemed to be all. It was an unfortunate accident. The pin the police had abstracted had been used by all and sundry during the Demonstration, and was no evidence of anything.

It was obviously Death by Misadventure.

Well, that was the end of it, Lucy thought, when she heard the news. She had waited in the drawing-room, looking out at the rainy garden, not able to believe that something would not go wrong. No crime was ever committed without a slip-up somewhere; she had read enough case-histories to know that.

There had been one slip-up already, when that little ornament came loose from a shoe. Who knew what else the police might have unearthed? And now it was over, and Innes was safe. And she knew now that it was for Innes that she had put herself in the Law's reverence. She had thought it was for Innes's mother, for Henrietta, for absolute justice. But in the latter end it was because whatever

Innes had done she had not deserved what the Law would do to her. She had been highly tried, and her breaking-point was lower than normal. She lacked some alloy, some good coarse reinforcing stuff, that would have helped her to stand tension without giving way. But she was too fine to throw away.

Lucy noticed with interest the quality of the cheer that greeted her as she went up to receive her diploma on Wednesday morning. The cheers for the various Seniors varied not only in intensity but in quality. There was laughter, for instance, and affection in the reception they gave Dakers. And Beau got a Head Senior's tribute; the congratulations of her inferiors to a highly popular Senior. But there was something in the cheer that they gave Innes that was remarkable; a warmth of admiration, a sympathy, and a well-wishing, that was accorded to no one else. Lucy wondered if it was merely that her inability to take the Arlinghurst appointment had moved them. Henrietta had said, during that conversation about Rouse and her examination tactics, that Innes was not popular. But there was something more in that cheer than mere popularity. They admired her. It was their tribute to quality.

The giving of diplomas, postponed from Tuesday to Wednesday because of the inquest, was the last event of Lucy's stay at Leys. She had arranged to catch the twelve o'clock train to London. She had been touched during the last few days to receive an endless string of small presents, which were left in her room with written messages attached. She hardly ever returned to her room without finding a new one there. Very few people had given Lucy presents since she grew up, and she still had a child's pleasure in being given something, however small. And these gifts had a spontaneity that was heart-warming; it was no concerted effort, no affair of putting the hat round; they had each given her something as it occurred to them. The Disciples' offering was a large white card which said:

THIS WILL ADMIT
MISS LUCY PYM
TO THE FOUR DISCIPLES CLINIC
AT MANCHESTER
AND WILL PROVIDE
A COURSE OF TREATMENTS
OF ANY KIND WHATEVER
AT ANY TIME WHATEVER.

Dakers had contributed a small untidy parcel, labelled "To remind you every morning of our first meeting!" which on being opened proved to be one of those flat loofahs for back-scrubbing. It was surely in some other life that she had been peered at over the bathroom partition by that waggish pony's-face. It was certainly not this Lucy Pym who had sat in the bath.

The devoted Miss Morris had made her a little felt purse—Heaven alone knew when the child had found time to fabricate it—and at the other end of the scale of worldly magnificence was Beau's pigskin case, which bore the message "You will have so many parting gifts that you will need something to put them in," and was stamped with her initials. Even Giddy, with whom she had spent odd half hours talking about rheumatism and rats, had sent up a plant in a pot. She had no idea what it was—it looked fleshy and faintly obscene—but was relieved that it was small. Travelling with a pot plant was not her idea of what was fitting.

Beau had come in between breakfast and Diploma-giving to help her pack, but all the serious packing was done. Whether anything would close once everything was in was another matter.

"I'll come back and sit on them for you before morning clinic," Beau said. "We are free until then. Except for clinic there is nothing much to do until we go home on Friday."

"You'll be sorry to finish at Leys?"

"Dreadfully. I've had a wonderful time. However, summer holidays are a great consolation."

"Innes told me some time ago that you were going to Norway together."

"Yes, we were," Beau said, "but we're not any more."

"Oh."

"Innes has other plans."

It was evident that this relationship was not what it had been.

"Well, I'd better go and see that the Juniors haven't hogged all the best seats at the Diploma Do," she said, and went.

But there was one relationship that showed satisfactory progress.

The Nut Tart knocked at her door and said that she had come to give dear Miss Pym a luck-piece. She came in, looked at the piled cases, and said with her customary frankness: "You are not a very good packer, are you? Neither am I. It is a pedestrian talent."

Lucy, whose luck-pieces in the last few days had ranged from a Woolworth monkey-on-a-stick to a South African halfpenny, waited with some curiosity to see what The Nut Tart's idea of the thing might be.

It was a blue bead.

"It was dug up in Central America a hundred years ago and it is almost as old as the world. It is very lucky."

"But I can't take that from you," Lucy protested.

"Oh, I have a little bracelet of them. It was the bracelet that was dug up. But I have taken out one of the beads for you. There are five left and that is plenty. And I have a piece of news for you. I am not going back to Brazil."

"No?"

"I am going to stay in England and marry Rick."

Lucy said that she was delighted to hear it.

"We shall be married in London in October, and you will be there and you will come to the wedding, no?"

Yes, Lucy would come to the wedding with pleasure.

"I am so glad about it," she said. She needed some contact with happiness after the last few days.

"Yes, it is all very satisfactory. We are cousins but not too near, and it is sensible to keep it in the family. I always thought I should like to marry an Englishman; and of course Rick is a parti. He is senior partner although he is so young. My parents are very pleased. And my grandmother, of course."

"And I take it that you yourself are pleased?" Lucy said, a shade dashed by this matter-of-fact catalogue.

"Oh yes. Rick is the only person in the world except my grandmother who can make me do things I don't want to do. That will be very good for me."

She looked at Lucy's doubtful face, and her great eyes sparkled.

"And of course I like him very much," she said.

When the diplomas had been presented, Lucy had mid-morning coffee with the Staff and said goodbye to them. Since she was leaving in the middle of the morning no one was free to come to the station with her. Henrietta thanked her, with undoubted tears in her eyes this time, for the help she had been. (But not in her wildest imaginings would Henrietta guess how much the help amounted to.) Lucy was to consider Leys as her home any time she wanted to come and stay, or if she ever wanted a lecturer's job, or if—or if—

And Lucy had to hide the fact that Leys, where she had been so happy, was the one place in the world that she would never come back to. A place that she was going, if her conscience and the shade of Rouse would let her, to blot out of her mind.

The Staff went to their various duties and Lucy went back to her room to finish packing. She had not spoken to Innes since that so-incredible conversation on Saturday morning; had hardly seen her, indeed, except for the moment when she had taken her diploma from Miss Hodge's hands.

Was Innes going to let her go without a word?

But when she came back to her room she found that word on her table. A written word. She opened the envelope and read:

Dear Miss Pym,

Here it is in writing. For the rest of my life I shall atone for the thing I can't undo. I pay forfeit gladly. My life for hers.

I am sorry that this has spoiled Leys for you. And I hope that you will not be unhappy about what you have done for me. I promise to make it worth while.

Perhaps, ten years from today, you will come to the West Country and see what I have done with my life. That would give me a date to look forward to. A landmark in a world without them.

Meanwhile, and always, my gratitude—my unspeakable gratitude.

Mary Innes.

"What time did you order the taxi for?" Beau asked, coming in on top of her knock.

"Half-past eleven."

"It's practically that now. Have you everything in that is going in? Hot water bottle? You hadn't one. Umbrella downstairs? You don't possess one. What do you do? Wait in doorways till it's over, or steal the nearest one? I had an aunt who always bought the cheapest she could find and discarded it in the nearest waste-paper-bin when the rain stopped. More money than sense, as my Nanny used to say. Well, now. Is that all? Consider well, because once we get those cases shut we'll never get them open again. Nothing left in the drawers? People always leave things stuck at the back of drawers." She opened the small drawers of the table and ran her hands into the back of them. "Half the divorces in the Western Hemisphere start through the subsequent revelations."

She withdrew her right hand, and Lucy saw that she was hold-

ing the little silver rosette; left lying at the back of the drawer because Lucy had not been able to make up her mind what to do with
it.

Beau turned it over in her fingers.

"That looks like the little button thing off my shoe," she said.

"*Your* shoe?"

"Yes. Those black pump things that one wore at dancing class. I
hung on to them because they are so lovely when one's feet are
tired. Like gloves. I can still wear the shoes I wore when I was fourteen. I always had enormous feet for my age, and believe me it was
no consolation to be told that you were going to be tall." Her attention went back to the thing she was holding. "So *this* is where I lost
it," she said. "You know, I wondered quite a lot about that." She
dropped it into her pocket. "You'll have to sit on the case, I'm
afraid. You sit on it and I'll wrestle with the locks."

Automatically Lucy sat on it.

She wondered why she had never noticed before how cold those
blue eyes were. Brilliant and cold and shallow.

The bright hair fell over her lap as Beau wrestled with the locks.
The locks would do what she wanted, of course. Everything and
everyone, always, since the day she was born, had done what she
wanted. If they hadn't, she took steps to see that they did. At the
age of four, Lucy remembered, she had defeated a whole adult
world because her will to have things her way was greater than all
the wills combined against her. She had never known frustration.

She could not visualise the possibility of frustration.

If *her* friend had the obvious right to Arlinghurst, then to Arlinghurst she should go.

"There! That's done it. Stand by to sit on the other if I can't
manage it. I see Giddy's given you one of his loathsome little
plants. What a bore for you. Perhaps you can exchange it for a bowl
at the back door one day."

How soon, Lucy wondered, had Innes begun to suspect? Almost
at once? Certainly before the afternoon, when she had turned green
on the spot where it had happened.

But she had not been sure until she saw the silver rosette on
Lucy's palm, and learned where it had been found.

Poor Innes. Poor Innes, who was paying forfeit.

"*Tax-i!*" yelled a voice along the corridor.

"There's your cab. I'll take your things. No, they're quite light;

you forget the training I've had. I wish you weren't going, Miss Pym. We shall miss you so much."

Lucy heard herself saying the obvious things. She even heard herself promising Beau that she might come to them for Christmas, when Beau would be home for her first "working" holidays.

Beau put her into the cab, took a tender farewell of her, and said, "The station" to the driver, and the taxi slid into motion and Beau's face smiled a moment beyond the window, and was gone.

The driver pushed back the glass panel and asked: "London train, lady?" Yes, Lucy said, to London.

And in London she would stay. In London was her own, safe, nice, calm, collected existence, and in future she would be content with it. She would even give up lecturing on psychology.

What did she know about psychology anyhow?

As a psychologist she was a first-rate teacher of French.

She could write a book about character as betrayed by facial characteristics. As least she had been right about that. Mostly.

Eyebrows that sent people to the stake.

Yes, she would write a book about face-reading.

Under another name, of course. Face-reading was not well seen among the intelligentsia.

BRAT
FARRAR

Chapter 1

"*A*unt Bee," said Jane, breathing heavily into her soup, "was Noah a cleverer back-room boy than Ulysses, or was Ulysses a cleverer back-room boy than Noah?"

"Don't eat out of the point of your spoon, Jane."

"I can't mobilise the strings out of the side."

"Ruth does."

Jane looked across at the twin, negotiating the vermicelli with smug neatness.

"She has a stronger suck than I have."

"Aunt Bee has a face like a very expensive cat," Ruth said, eyeing her aunt sideways.

Bee privately thought that this was a very good description, but wished that Ruth would not be quaint.

"No, but which was the cleverest?" said Jane, who never departed from a path once her feet were on it.

"Clever-*er*," said Ruth.

"Was it Noah or Ulysses? Simon, which was it, do you think?"

"Ulysses," said her brother, not looking up from his paper.

It was so like Simon, Bee thought, to be reading the list of runners at Newmarket, peppering his soup, and listening to the conversation at one and the same time.

"Why, Simon? Why Ulysses?"

"He hadn't Noah's good Met. service. Whereabouts was Firelight in the Free Handicap, do you remember?"

"Oh, away down," Bee said.

"A coming-of-age is a little like a wedding, isn't it, Simon?" This was Ruth.

"Better on the whole."

"Is it?"

"You can stay and dance at your own coming-of-age. Which you can't at your wedding."

"I shall stay and dance at *my* wedding."

"I wouldn't put it past you."

Oh, dear, thought Bee, I suppose there are families that have *conversation* at meals, but I don't know how they manage it. Perhaps I haven't been strict enough.

She looked down the table at the three bent heads, and Eleanor's still vacant place, and wondered if she had done right by them. Would Bill and Nora be pleased with what she had made of their children? If by some miracle they could walk in now, young and fine-looking and gay as they had gone to their deaths, would they say: "Ah, yes, that is just how we pictured them; even to Jane's ragamuffin look."

Bee's eyes smiled as they rested on Jane.

The twins were nine-going-on-ten and identical. Identical, that is to say, in the technical sense. In spite of their physical resemblance there was never any doubt as to which was Jane and which was Ruth. They had the same straight flaxen hair, the same small-boned face and pale skin, the same direct gaze with a challenge in it; but there the identity stopped. Jane was wearing rather grubby jodhpurs and a shapeless jersey festooned with pulled ends of wool. Her hair was pushed back without aid of mirror and held in the uncompromising clasp of a kirby-grip so old that it had reverted to its original steel colour, as old hairpins do. She was slightly astigmatic and, when in the presence of Authority, was in the habit of wearing horn-rimmed spectacles. Normally they lived in the hip pocket of her breeches, and they had been lain-upon, leant-upon, and sat-upon so often that she lived in a permanent state of bankruptcy: breakages over the yearly allowance having to be paid for out of her money-box. She rode to and fro to lessons at the Rectory on Fourposter, the old white pony; her short legs sticking out on either side of him like straws. Fourposter had long ago become a conveyance rather than a ride, so it did not matter that his great barrel was as manageable as a feather-bed and almost as wide.

Ruth, on the other hand, wore a pink cotton frock, as fresh as when she had set off on her bicycle that morning for the Rectory. Her hands were clean and the nails unbroken, and somewhere she had found a pink ribbon and had tied the two side-pieces of her hair in a bow on the top of her head.

Eight years, Bee was thinking. Eight years of contriving, conserving, and planning. And in six weeks' time her stewardship would come to an end. In little more than a month Simon would be twenty-one, and would inherit his mother's fortune and the lean years would be over. The Ashbys had never been rich but while her brother lived there was ample to keep Latchetts—the house and the three farms on the estate—as it should be kept. Only his sudden death had accounted for the near-poverty of those eight years. And only Bee's own resolution accounted for the fact that her sister-in-law's money would, next month, come to her son intact. There had been no borrowing on the strength of that future inheritance. Not even when Mr. Sandal, of Cosset, Thring and Noble, had been prepared to countenance it. Latchetts must pay its way, Bee had said. And Latchetts, after eight years, was still self-supporting and solvent.

Beyond her nephew's fair head she could see, through the window, the white rails of the south paddock, and the flick of old Regina's tail in the sunlight. It was the horses that had saved them. The horses that had been her brother's hobby had proved the salvation of his house. Year after year, in spite of all the ills, accidents, and sheer cussedness that afflict horseflesh, the horses had shown a profit. The swings had always paid a little more than the round-abouts. When the original small stud that had been her brother's delight seemed likely to be a doubtful prop, Bee had added the small hardy children's ponies to occupy the colder pastures half-way up the down. Eleanor had schooled doubtful hacks into "safe rides for a lady," and had sold them at a profit. And now that the manor was a boarding-school she was teaching others to ride, at a very respectable price per hour.

"Eleanor is very late, isn't she?"

"Is she out with La Parslow?" Simon asked.

"The Parslow girl, yes."

"The unhappy horse has probably dropped dead."

Simon got up to take away the soup plates, and to help out the meat course from the sideboard, and Bee watched him with critical approval. At least she had managed not to spoil Simon; and that, given Simon's selfish charm, was no small achievement. Simon had an air of appealing dependence that was quite fallacious, but it had fooled all and sundry since he was in the nursery. Bee had watched the fooling process with amusement and something that was like a reluctant admiration; if she herself had been gifted with Simon's particular brand of charm, she felt, she would in all likelihood have made it work for her as Simon did. But she had seen to it that it did not work with her.

"It would be nice if a coming-of-age had something like brides-maids," Ruth observed, turning over her helping with a fastidious fork.

This fell on stony ground.

"The Rector says that Ulysses was probably a frightful nuisance round the house," said the undeviating Jane.

"Oh!" said Bee, interested in this sidelight on the classics. "Why?"

"He said he was 'without doubt a—a gadget-contriver,' and that Penelope was probably very glad to be rid of him for a bit. I wish liver wasn't so *smooth.*"

Eleanor came in and helped herself from the sideboard in her usual silent fashion.

"Pah!" said Ruth. "What a smell of stables."

"You're late, Nell," Bee said, inquiring.

"She'll never ride," Eleanor said. "She can't even bump the sad-dle yet."

"Perhaps loony people can't ride," Ruth suggested.

"Ruth," Bee said, with vigour. "The pupils at the Manor are not lunatic. They are not even mentally deficient. They are just 'diffi-cult.' "

"Ill-adjusted is the technical description," Simon said.

"Well, they *behave* like lunatics. If you behave like a lunatic how is anyone to tell that you're not one?"

Since no one had an answer to this, silence fell over the Ashby luncheon table. Eleanor ate with the swift purposefulness of a hun-gry schoolboy, not lifting her eyes from her plate. Simon took out a pencil and reckoned odds on the margin of his paper. Ruth, who had stolen three biscuits from the jar on the Rectory sideboard and eaten them in the lavatory, made a castle of her food with a moat of gravy round it. Jane consumed hers with industrious pleasure. And Bee sat with her eyes on the view beyond the window.

Over that far ridge the land sloped in chequered miles to the sea and the clustered roofs of Westover. But here, in this high valley, shut off from the Channel gales and open to the sun, the trees stood up in the bright air with a midland serenity: with an air, almost, of enchantment. The scene had the bright perfection and stillness of an apparition.

A fine inheritance; a fine rich inheritance. She hoped that Simon would do well by it. There were times when she had—no, not been afraid. Times perhaps when she had wondered. Simon had far too many sides to him; a quicksilver quality that did not go with a yeoman inheritance. Only Latchetts, of all the surrounding estates, still sheltered a local family and Bee hoped that it would go on sheltering Ashbys for centuries to come. Fair, small-boned, long-headed Ashbys like the ones round the table.

"Jane, must you splash fruit juice round like that?"

"I don't like rhubarb in inches, Aunt Bee, I like it in mush."

"Well, mush it more carefully."

When she had been Jane's age she had mushed up her rhubarb too, and at this same table. At this same table had eaten Ashbys who had died of fever in India, of wounds in the Crimea, of starvation in Queensland, of typhoid at the Cape, and of cirrhosis of the liver in the Straits Settlements. But always there had been an Ashby at Latchetts; and they had done well by the land. Here and there came a ne'er-do-well—like her cousin Walter—but Providence had seen to it that the worthless quality had been confined to younger sons, who could practise their waywardness on subjects remote from Latchetts.

No queens had come to Latchetts to dine; no cavaliers to hide. For three hundred years it had stood in its meadows very much as it stood now; a yeoman's dwelling. And for nearly two of those three hundred years Ashbys had lived in it.

"Simon, dear, see to the cona."

Perhaps its simplicity had saved it. It had pretended to nothing; had aspired to nothing. Its goodness had been dug back into the earth; its sap had returned to its roots. Across the valley the long white house of Clare stood in its park, gracious as a vicereine, but there were no Ledinghams there now. The Ledinghams had been prodigal of their talents and their riches; using Clare as a background, as a purse, as a decoration, as a refuge, but not as a home. For centuries they had peacocked over the world: as proconsuls, explorers, court jesters, rakes, and revolutionaries; and Clare had supported their extravagances. Now only their portraits remained. And the great house in the park was a boarding-school for the unmanageable children of parents with progressive ideas and large bank accounts.

But the Ashbys stayed at Latchetts.

Chapter 2

As Bee poured the coffee the twins disappeared on ploys of their own, this being their half-holiday; and Eleanor drank hers hastily and went back to the stables.

"Do you want the car this afternoon?" Simon asked. "I half promised old Gates that I would bring a calf out from Westover in one of our trailers. His own has collapsed."

"No, I don't need it," Bee said, wondering what had prompted Simon to so dull a chore. She hoped it was not the Gates daughter; who was very pretty, very silly, and very commonplace. Gates was the tenant of Wigsell, the smallest of the three farms; and Simon was not normally tolerant of his opportunism.

"If you really want to know," Simon said as he got up, "I want to see June Kaye's new picture. It's at the Empire."

The disarming frankness of this would have delighted anyone but Beatrice Ashby, who knew very well her nephew's habit of throwing up two balls to divert your attention from the third.

"Can I fetch you anything?"

"You might get one of the new bus timetables from the Westover and District offices if you have time. Eleanor says they have a new Clare service that goes round by Guessgate."

"Bee," said a voice in the hall. "Are you there. Bee?"

"Mrs. Peck," Simon said, going out to meet her.

"Come in, Nancy," Bee called. "Come and have coffee with me. The others have finished."

And the Rector's wife came into the room, put her empty basket on the sideboard, and sat down with a pleased sigh. "I could do with some," she said.

When people mentioned Mrs. Peck's name they still added: "Nancy Ledingham that was, you know"; although it was a decade since she had stunned the social world by marrying George Peck and burying herself in a country rectory. Nancy Ledingham had been more than the "débutante of her year," she had been a national possession. The penny Press had done for her what the penny post-card had done for Lily Langtry: her beauty was common property. If the public did not stand on chairs to see her pass they certainly stopped the traffic; her appearance as bridesmaid at a wedding was enough to give the authorities palpitations for a week beforehand. She had that serene unquestionable loveliness that defeats even a willing detractor. Indeed the only question seemed to be whether the ultimate coronet would have strawberry leaves or not. More than once the popular Press had supplied her with a crown, but this was generally considered mere wishful thinking; her public would settle for strawberry leaves.

And then, quite suddenly—between a *Tatler* and a *Tatler*, so to speak—she had married George Peck. The shattered Press, doing the best they could for a shattered public, had pulled out the *vox humana* stop and quavered about romance, but George had de-feated them. He was a tall, thin man with the face of a very intelli-gent and rather nice ape. Besides, as the society editor of the Clar-ion said: "A clergyman! I ask you! I could get more romance out of a cement-mixer!"

So the public let her go, into her chosen oblivion. Her aunt, who had been responsible for her coming-out, disinherited her. Her fa-ther died in a welter of chagrin and debts. And her old home, the great white house in the park, had become a school.

But after thirteen years of rectory life Nancy Peck was still serenely and unquestionably beautiful; and people still said: "Nancy Ledingham that was, you know."

"I've come for the eggs," she said, "but there's no hurry, is there? It's wonderful to sit and do nothing."

Bee's eyes slid sideways at her in a smile.

"You have such a nice face, Bee."

"Thank you. Ruth says it is a face like a very expensive cat."

"Nonsense. At least—not the furry kind. Oh, I know what she means! The long-necked, short-haired kind that show their small chins. Heraldic cats. Yes, Bee, darling, you have a face like a heraldic cat. Especially when you keep your head still and slide your eyes at people." She put her cup down and sighed again with plea-sure. "I can't think how the Nonconformists have failed to discover coffee."

"Discover it?"

"Yes. As a snare. It does far more for one than drink. And yet no one preaches about it, or signs pledges about it. Five mouthfuls and the world looks rosy."

"Was it very grey before?"

"A sort of mud colour. I was so happy this week because it was the first week this year that we hadn't needed sitting-room fires and I had no fires to do and no fireplaces to clean. But nothing—I repeat, nothing—will stop George from throwing his used matches into the fireplace. And as he takes fifteen matches to light one pipe—! The room swarms with waste-paper baskets and ash trays, but no, George must use the fireplace. He doesn't even *aim*, blast him. A fine careless flick of the wrist and the match lands anywhere from the fender to the farthest coal. And they have all got to be picked out again."

"And he says: why don't you leave them."

"He does. However, now that I've had some Latchetts coffee I have decided not to take a chopper to him after all."

"Poor Nan. These Christians."

"How are the coming-of-age preparations getting on?"

"The invitations are about to go to the printers; which is a nice definite stage to have arrived at. A dinner for intimates, here; and a dance for everyone in the barn. What is Alec's address, by the way?"

"I can't remember his latest one off-hand. I'll look it up for you. He has a different one almost every time he writes. I think he gets heaved out when he can't pay his rent. Not that I hear from him often, of course. He has never forgiven me for not marrying well, so that I could keep my only brother in the state to which he had been accustomed."

"Is he playing just now?"

"I don't know. He had a part in that silly comedy at the Savoy but it ran only a few weeks. He is so much a type that his parts are necessarily limited."

"Yes, I suppose so."

"No one could cast Alec as anything but Alec. You don't know how lucky you are, Bee, to have Ashbys to deal with. The incidence of rakes in the Ashby family is singularly low."

"There was Walter."

"A lone wolf crying in the wilderness. What became of Cousin Walter?"

"Oh, he died."

"In an odour of sanctity?"

"No. Carbolic. A workhouse ward, I think."

"Even Walter wasn't bad, you know. He just liked drink and hadn't the head for it. But when a Ledingham is a rake he is plain bad."

They sat together in a comfortable silence, considering their respective families. Bee was several years older than her friend: almost a generation older. But neither could remember a time when the other was not there; and the Ledingham children had gone in and out of Latchetts as if it were their home, as familiar with it as the Ashbys were with Clare.

"I have been thinking so often lately of Bill and Nora," Nancy said. "This would have been such a happy time for them."

"Yes," Bee said, reflectively; her eyes on the window. It was at that view she had been looking when it happened. On a day very like this and at this time of the year. Standing in the sitting-room window, thinking how lovely everything looked and if they would think that nothing they had seen in Europe was half as lovely. Wondering if Nora would look well again: she had been very pulled down after the twins' birth. Hoping she had been a good deputy for them, and yet a little pleased to be resuming her own life in London tomorrow.

The twins had been asleep, and the older children upstairs grooming themselves for the welcome and for the dinner they were to be allowed to stay up for. In half an hour or so the car would swing out from the avenue of lime trees and come to rest at the door and there they would be; in a flurry of laughter and embracing and present-giving and well-being.

The turning on of the wireless had been so absentminded a gesture that she did not know that she had done it. "The two o'clock plane from Paris to London," said the cool voice, "with nine passengers and a crew of three crashed this afternoon just after crossing the Kent coast. There were no survivors."

No. There had been no survivors.

"They were so wrapped up in the children," Nancy said. "They have been so much in my mind lately, now that Simon is going to be twenty-one."

"And Patrick has been in mine."

"Patrick?" Nancy sounded at a loss. "Oh, yes, of course. Poor Pat."

Bee looked at her curiously. "You had almost forgotten, hadn't you?"

"Well, it is a long time ago, Bee. And—well, I suppose one's mind tidies away the things it can't bear to remember. Bill and Nora—that was frightful, but it *was* something that happened to people. I mean, it was part of the ordinary risks of life. But Pat—that was different." She sat silent for a moment. "I have pushed it so far down in my mind that I can't even remember what he looked like any more. Was he as like Simon as Ruth is like Jane?"

"Oh, no. They weren't identical twins. Not much more alike than some brothers are. Though oddly enough they were much more in each other's pockets than Ruth and Jane are."

"Simon seems to have got over it. Do you think he remembers it often?"

"He must have remembered it very often lately."

"Yes. But it is a long way between thirteen and twenty-one. I expect even a twin grows shadowy at that distance."

This gave Bee pause. How shadowy was he to her: the kind solemn little boy who should have been coming into his inheritance next month? She tried to call up his face in front of her but there was only a blur. He had been small and immature for his age, but otherwise he was just an Ashby. Less an individual than a family resemblance. All she really remembered, now she thought about it, was that he was solemn and kind.

Kindness was not a common trait in small boys.

Simon had a careless generosity when it did not cost him inconvenience; but Patrick had had that inner kindness that not only gives but gives up.

"I still wonder," Bee said unhappily, "whether we should have allowed the body that was found on the Castleton beach to be buried over there. A pauper's burial, it was."

"But, Bee! It had been months in the water, hadn't it? They couldn't even tell what sex it was; could they? And Castleton is miles away. And they get all the corpses from the Atlantic founderings anyhow. I mean, the nearer ones. It is not sense to worry over—to identify it with—" Her dismayed voice died into silence.

"No, of course it isn't!" Bee said briskly. "I am just being morbid. Have some more coffee."

And as she poured the coffee she decided that when Nancy had gone she would unlock the private drawer of her desk and burn that pitiful note of Patrick's. It was morbid to keep it, even if she had not looked at it for years. She had never had the heart to tear it up because it had seemed part of Patrick. But of course that was absurd. It was no more part of Patrick than was the despair that had filled him when he wrote: "I'm sorry, but I can't bear it any longer. Don't be angry with me. Patrick." She would take it out and burn it. Burning it would not blot it from her mind, of course, but there was nothing she could do about that. The round schoolboy letters were printed there for always. Round, careful letters written with the stylograph that he had been so attached to. It was so like Patrick to apologise for taking his own life.

Nancy, watching her friend's face, proffered what she considered to be consolation. "They say, you know, that when you throw yourself from a high place you lose consciousness almost at once."

"I don't think he did it that way, Nan."

"No!" Nancy sounded staggered. "But that was where the note was found. I mean, the coat with the note in the pocket. On the cliff-top."

"Yes, but by the path. By the path down the Gap to the shore."

"Then what do you—?"

"I think he swam out."

"Till he couldn't come back, you mean?"

"Yes. When I was *in loco parentis* that time, when Bill and Nora were on holiday, we went several times to the Gap, the children and I; to swim and have a picnic. And once when we were there Patrick said that the best way to die—I think he called it the lovely way— would be to swim out until you were too tired to go any farther. He said it quite matter-of-factly, of course. In those days it was—a mere academic matter. When I pointed out that drowning would still be drowning, he said: 'But you would be so tired, you see; you wouldn't care any more. The water would just take you.' He loved the water."

She was silent for a little and then blurted out the thing that had been her private nightmare for years.

"I've always been afraid that when it was too late to come back he may have regretted."

"Oh. Bee, no!"

Bee's sidelong glance went to Nancy's beautiful, protesting face. "Morbid. I know. Forget I said it."

"I don't know now how I *could* have forgotten," Nancy said, wondering. "The worst of pushing horrible things down into one's subconscious is that when they pop up again they are as fresh as if they had been in a refrigerator. You haven't allowed time to get at them to—to mould them over a little."

"I think a great many people have almost forgotten that Simon had a twin," Bee said, excusing. "Or that he has not always been the heir. Certainly no one has mentioned Patrick to me since the coming-of-age celebrations have been in the air."

"Why was Patrick so inconsolable about his parents' death?"

"I didn't know he was. None of us did. All the children were wild with grief to begin with, of course. Sick with it. But none more than another. Patrick seemed bewildered rather than inconsolable. 'You mean: Latchetts belongs to me now?' I remember him saying, as if it were some strange idea, difficult to understand. Simon was impatient with him, I remember. Simon was always the brilliant one. I think that it was all too much for Patrick; too strange. The adrift feeling of being suddenly without his father and mother, and the weight of Latchetts on his shoulders. It was too much for him and he was so unhappy that he—took a way out."

"Poor Pat. Poor darling. It was wrong of me to forget him."

"Come; let us go get those eggs. You won't forget to let me have Alec's address, will you? A Ledingham must have an invitation."

"No, I'll look it up when I go back, and telephone it to you. Can your latest moron take a telephone message?"

"Just."

"Well, I'll stick to basic. You won't forget that he is Alec Loding on the stage, will you?" She picked up her basket from the sideboard. "I wonder if he would come. It is a long time since he has been to Clare. A country life is not Alec's idea of amusement. But an Ashby coming-of-age is surely something that would interest him."

Chapter 3

*B*ut Alec Loding's main interest in the Ashby coming-of-age was to blow the celebrations sky-high. Indeed, he was at this moment actively engaged in pulling strings to that end.

Or rather, trying to pull strings. The strings weren't pulling very well.

He was sitting in the back room at the Green Man, the remains of lunch spread before him, and beside him sat a young man. A boy, one would have said, but for something controlled and still that did not go with adolescence. Loding poured coffee for himself and sugared it liberally; casting a glance now and then at his companion, who was turning an almost empty beer glass round and round on the table. The movement was so deliberate that it hardly came under the heading of fidgeting.

"Well?" said Loding at last.

"No."

Loding took a mouthful of coffee.

"Squeamish?"

"I'm not an actor."

Something in the unaccented phrase seemed to sting Loding and he flushed a little.

"You're not asked to be emotional, if that is what you mean. There is no filial devotion to be simulated, you know. Only dutiful affection for an aunt you haven't seen for nearly ten years—which one would expect to be more dutiful than affectionate."

"No."

"You young idiot, I'm offering you a fortune."

"Half a fortune. And you're not offering me anything."

"If I'm not offering it to you, what am I doing?"

"Propositioning me," said the young man. He had not raised his eyes from his slowly-turning beer.

"Very well, I'm propositioning you, to use your barbarous idiom. What is wrong with the proposition?"

"It's crazy."

"What is crazy about it, given the initial advantage of your existence?"

"No one could bring it off."

"It is not so long since a famous general whose face was a household word—if you will forgive the metaphor—was impersonated quite successfully by an actor in broad daylight and in full view of the multitude."

"That is quite different."

"I agree. You aren't asked to impersonate anyone. Just to be yourself. A much easier task."

"No," said the young man.

Loding kept his temper with a visible effort. He had a pink, collapsed face that reminded one of the underside of fresh mushrooms. The flesh hung away from his good Ledingham bones with a discouraged slackness, and the incipient pouches under his eyes detracted from their undoubted intelligence. Managers who had once cast him for gay young rakes now offered him nothing but discredited roués.

"My God!" he said suddenly. "Your teeth!"

Even that did not startle the young man's face into any expression. He lifted his eyes for the first time, resting them incuriously on Loding. "What's the matter with my teeth?" he asked.

"It's how they identify people nowadays. A dentist keeps a record of work, you know. I wonder where those kids went. Something would have to be done about that. Are those front teeth your own?"

"The two middle ones are caps. They were kicked out."

"They went to someone here in town, I remember that much. There was a London trip to see the dentist twice a year; once before Christmas and once in the summer. They went to the dentist in the morning and to a show in the afternoon: pantomime in the winter and the Tournament at Olympia in the summer. These are the kind of things you would have to know, by the way."

"Yes?"

The gentle monosyllable maddened Loding.

"Look, Farrar, what are you frightened of? A strawberry mark? I bathed with that kid in the buff many a time and he hadn't as much as a mole on him. He was so ordinary that you could order him by the dozen from any prep. school in England. You are more like his brother at this moment than that kid ever was, twins though they were. I tell you, I thought for a moment that you *were* young Ashby. Isn't that good enough for you? You come and live with me for a fortnight and by the end of it there won't be anything you don't know about the village of Clare and its inhabitants. Nor anything about Latchetts. I know every last pantry in it. Nor anything about the Ashbys. Can you swim, by the way?"

The young man nodded. He had gone back to his glass of beer.

"Swim well?"

"Yes."

"Don't you ever qualify a statement?"

"Not unless it needs it."

"The kid could swim like an eel. There's the matter of ears, too. Yours look ordinary enough, and his must have been ordinary too or I should remember. Anyone who has worked in a life-class notices ears. But I must see what photographs of him exist. Front ones wouldn't matter, but a real close-up of an ear might be a giveaway. I think I must take a trip to Clare and do some prospecting."

"Don't bother on my account."

Loding was silent for a moment. Then he said, reasonably: "Tell me, do you believe my story at all?"

"Your story?"

"Do you believe that I am who I say I am, and that I come from a village called Clare, where there is someone who is practically your double? Do you believe that? Or do you think that this is just a way of getting you to come home with me?"

"No, I didn't think it was that. I believe your story."

"Well, thank heaven for that, at least," Loding said with a quirk of his eyebrow. "I know that my looks are not what they were, but I should be shattered to find that they suggested the predatory. Well, then. That settled, do you believe that you are as like young Ashby as I say?"

For a whole turn of the glass there was no answer. "I doubt it."

"Why?"

"On your own showing it is some time since you saw him."

"But you don't have to *be* young Ashby. Just look like him. And believe me you do! My God, how you do! It's something I wouldn't have believed unless I saw it with my own eyes; something I have imagined only happened in books. And it is worth a fortune to you. You have only to put out your hand and take it."

"Oh, no, I haven't."

"Metaphorically speaking. Do you realise that except for the first year or so your story would be truth? It would be your own story; able to stand up to any amount of checking." His voice twisted into a comedy note. "Or—would it?"

"Oh, yes, it would check."

"Well, then. You have only to stow away on the *Ira Jones* out of Westover instead of going for a day trip to Dieppe, *et voilà!*"

"How do you know there was a ship called the *Ira Jones* at Westover about then?"

" 'About then'! You do me scant justice, *amigo*. There was a ship of that repellent title at Westover the day the boy disappeared. I know because I spent most of the day painting her. On canvas, not on her plates, you understand. And the old scow went out before I had finished; bound for the Channel Islands. All my ships go out before I have finished painting them."

There was silence for a little.

"It's in your lap, Farrar."

"So is my table napkin."

"A fortune. A charming small estate. Security. A—"

"*Security*, did you say?"

"After the initial gamble, of course," Loding said smoothly.

The light eyes that looked at him for a moment held a faint amusement.

"Hadn't it occurred to you at all, Mr. Loding, that the gamble was yours?"

"Mine?"

"You're offering me the sweetest chance for a double-cross that I ever heard of. I take your coaching, pass the exam, and forget about you. And you wouldn't be able to do a thing about it. How did you figure to keep tabs on me?"

"I hadn't. No one with your Ashby looks could be a double-crosser. The Ashbys are monsters of rectitude."

The boy pushed away the glass.

"Which must be why I don't take kindly to the idea of being a phoney. Thank you for my lunch, Mr. Loding. If I had known what you had in mind when you asked me to lunch with you, I wouldn't have—"

"All right, all right. Don't apologise. And don't run away; we'll go together. You don't like my proposition; very good: so be it. But you, on the other hand, fascinate me. I can hardly take my eyes off you, or believe that anything so unique exists. And since you are sure that my improper proposal to you has nothing of the personal in it, there is nothing against our walking as far as the Underground together."

Loding paid for their lunch, and as they walked out of the Green Man he said: "I won't ask where you are living in case you think I want to hound you. But I shall give you my address in the hope that you will come to see me. Oh, no; not about the proposition. If it isn't your cup of tea then it isn't your cup of tea; and if you felt like that you certainly wouldn't make a success of it. No, not about the proposition. I have something in my rooms that I think would interest you."

He paused artistically while they negotiated a street crossing.

"When my old home, Clare, was sold—after my father's death—Nancy bundled together all the personal things in my room and sent them to me. A whole trunkful of rubbish, which I have never had the energy to get rid of, and a large proportion of it consists of snapshots and photographs of the companions of my youth. I think you would find it very interesting."

He glanced sideways at the uncommunicative profile of his companion.

"Tell me," he said as they stopped at the entrance to the Underground, "do you play cards?"

"Not with strangers," said the young man pleasantly.

"I just wondered. I had never met the perfect poker face until now, and I should be sorry if it was being wasted on some nonconformist abstainer. Ah, well. Here is my address. If by any chance I have fled from there the *Spotlight* will find me. I am truly sorry I couldn't sell you the idea of being an Ashby. You would have made an excellent master of Latchetts, I feel. Someone who was at home with horses, and used to an outdoor life."

The young man, who had made a gesture of farewell and was in the act of turning away, paused. "Horses?" he said.

"Yes," Loding said, vaguely surprised. "It's a stud, you know. Very well thought of, I understand."

"Oh." He paused a moment longer, and then turned away.

Loding watched him as he went down the street. "I missed something," he was thinking. "There was some bait he would have risen to, and I missed it. Why should he have nibbled at the word horse? He must be sick of them."

Ah, well; perhaps he would come to see what his double looked like.

Chapter 4

*T*he boy lay on his bed in the dark, fully dressed, and stared at the ceiling.

There were no street lamps outside to illuminate this back room under the slates; but the faint haze of light that hangs over London at night, emanation from a million arcs and gas-lights and paraffin lamps, shone ghost-like on the ceiling so that its cracks and stains showed like a world map.

The boy was looking at a map of the world too, but it was not on the ceiling. He was examining his odyssey; conducting a private inventory. That meeting to-day had shaken him. Somewhere, it seemed, there was another fellow so like him that for a moment they could be mistaken for each other. To one who had been very much alone all his life that was an amazing thought.

Indeed, it was the most surprising thing that had happened to him in all his twenty-one years. In a way it was as if all those years that had seemed so full and exciting at the time had been merely leading up to that moment when the actor chap had caught himself short in the street and said: "Hello, Simon."

"Oh! Sorry!" he had said at once. "Thought you were a friend of—" And then he had stopped and stared.

"Can I do something for you?" the boy had asked at last, since the man showed no sign of moving on.

"Yes. You could come and have lunch with me."

"Why?"

"It's lunch-time, and that's my favourite pub behind you."

"But why me?"

"Because you interest me. You are so like a friend of mine. My name is Loding, by the way. Alec Loding. I act a bad part in a bad farce at that very bad old theatre over there." He had nodded across the street. "But Equity, God bless them, has ordained a minimum fee for my labours, so the hire is considerably better than the part, I rejoice to say. Do you mind telling me your name?"

"Farrar."

"Farrell?"

"No. Farrar."

"Oh." The amused, considering look was still in his eye. "Is it long since you came back to England?"

"How did you know I had been out of it?"

"Your clothes, my boy. Clothes are my business. I have dressed too many parts not to recognise American tailoring when I see it. Even the admirably conservative tailoring that you so rightly wear."

"Then what makes you think I'm not American?"

At that the man had smiled quite broadly. "Ah, *that*," he said, "is the eternal mystery of the English. You watch a procession of monks in Italy and your eye singles out one and you say: 'Ha! An Englishman.' You come across five hoboes wrapped in gunny sacks sheltering from the rain in Wisconsin, and you notice the fifth and think: 'Dear goodness, that chap's English.' You see ten men stripped to the buff for the Foreign Legion doctor to pass judgement on, and you say—But come to lunch and we can explore the subject at leisure."

So he had gone to lunch, and the man had talked and been charming. But always behind the lively puffy eyes there had been that quizzical, amused, almost unbelieving look. That look was more eloquent than any of his subsequent arguments. Truly, he, Brat Farrar, *must* be like that other fellow to bring that look of half-incredulous amusement into someone's eyes.

He lay on the bed and thought about it. This sudden identification in an unbelonging life. He had a great desire to see this twin of his; this Ashby boy. Ashby. It was a nice name: a good English name. He would like to see the place too: this Latchetts, where his twin had grown up in belonging quiet while he had bucketed round the world, all the way from the orphanage to that moment in a London street, belonging nowhere.

The orphanage. It was no fault of the orphanage that he had not belonged. It was a very good orphanage; a great deal happier than many a home he had seen in passing since. The children had loved it. They had wept when they left and had come back for visits; they had sent contributions to the funds; they had invited the staff to their marriages, and brought their subsequent children for the matron's approval. There was never a day when some old girl or boy was not cluttering up the front door. Then why had he not felt like that?

Because he was a foundling? Was that why? Because no visitors ever came for him; no parcels or letters or invitations? But they had been very wise about that; very determined to prop his self-esteem. If anything he had been privileged beyond the other children by his foundling status. His Christmas present from Matron, he remembered, had been looked upon with envy by children whose only present came from an aunt or uncle; a mere relation, as it were. It was Matron who had taken him off the doorstep; and who saw to it that he heard how well-dressed and cared-for he had been. (He heard about this at judicious intervals for fifteen years but he had never been able to feel any satisfaction about it.) It was Matron who had determined his name with the aid of a pin and the telephone directory. The pin had come down on the word Farrell. Which had pleased Matron considerably; her pin had once, long ago, come down on the word Coffin, and she had had to cheat and try again.

There had never been any doubt about his first name, since he had arrived on the doorstep on St. Bartholomew's day. He had been Bart from the beginning. But the older children had changed that to Brat, and presently even the staff used the more familiar name (another device of Matron's to prevent his feeling "different"?) and the name had followed him to the grammar school.

The grammar school. Why had he not "belonged" there, then? Because his clothes were subtly different? Surely not. He had not been thin-skinned as a child; merely detached. Because he was a scholarship boy? Certainly not: half his form were scholarship boys. Then why had he decided that the school was not for him. Decided with such unboy-like finality that all Matron's arguments had died into ultimate silence, and she had countenanced his going to work.

There was no mystery about his not liking the work, of course. The office job had been fifty miles away, and since no ordinary lodgings could be paid for out of his salary he had had to stay in the local "boys' home." He had not known how good the orphanage was until he had sampled the boys' home. He could have supported either the job or the home, but not the two simultaneously. And of the two the office was by far the worse. It was, as a job, comfortable, leisurely, and graced with certain, if far-off, prospects; but to him it had been a prison. He was continually aware of time running past him; time that he was wasting. This was not what he wanted.

He had said good-bye to his office life almost accidentally; certainly without premeditation. DAY RETURN TO DIEPPE a bill had said, plastered against the glass of a newsagent's window; and the price, in large red figures, was exactly the amount of his savings to the nearest half-crown. Even so, he would have done nothing about it if it had not been for old Mr. Hendren's funeral. Mr. Hendren was the "retired" partner, and on the day of his funeral the office shut down "out of respect." And so, with a week's pay in his pocket and a whole week-day free, he had taken his savings and gone to see "abroad." He had had a grand time in Dieppe, where his first-year French was no deterrent to enjoyment, but it had not even crossed his mind to stay there until he was on his way home. He had reached the harbour before the shocking idea took hold of him.

Was it native honesty, he thought, staring at the Pimlico ceiling, or his good orphanage training that had made his unpaid laundry bill bulk so large in the subsequent mental struggle? A boy who had no money and no bed for the night should hardly have been concerned with the ethics of bilking a laundry of two-and-threepence.

The camion, rolling up from the harbour, had been his salvation. He had held up his thumb, and the brown, sweaty brigand at the wheel had grinned at this international gesture and slowed as he passed. He had run at the moving cliff-face, snatched and clung, and been hauled aboard. And all his old life was behind him.

He had planned to stay and work in France. Debated with himself during the long run to Havre, when gesture had given out and the driver's patois proved unintelligible, how best he might earn enough to eat. It was his neighbour in the Havre *bistro* who enlightened him. "My young friend," the man had said, fixing him with melancholy spaniel's eyes, "it is not sufficient to be a man in France in order to work. One has also to have papers."

"And where," he had asked, "does one not have papers? I mean, in what country? I can go anywhere." He was suddenly conscious of the world, and that he was free of it.

"God knows," the man had said. "Mankind grows every day more like sheep. Go to the harbour and take a ship."

"Which ship?"

"It is immaterial. Have you in English a game that—" He made descriptive gestures.

"A counting-out game? Oh, yes. Eenie, meenie, minie, moe."

"Good. Go to the harbour and do 'Eenie, meenie, minie, moe.' And when you go aboard 'moe' see that no one is looking. On ships they have a passion for papers that amounts to a madness."

"Moe" was the *Barfleur*, and he had not needed papers after all. He was the gift from heaven that the *Barfleur's* cook had been looking for for years.

Good old *Barfleur*, with her filthy pea-green galley smelling of over-used olive oil, and the grey seas combing up mountains high, and the continuous miracle of their harmless passing, and the cook's weekly drunk that left him acting unpaid cook, and learning to play a mouth organ, and the odd literature in the fo'c'sle. Good old *Barfleur*!

He had taken a lot away with him when he left her, but most important of all he took a new name. When he had written his name for the Captain, old Bourdet had taken the final double-L to be an R, and copied the name Farrar. And he had kept it so. Farrell came out of a telephone directory; and Farrar out of a tramp skipper's mistake. It was all one.

And then what?

Tampico and the smell of tallow. And the tally-man who had said: "You Englishman? You want shore job?"

He had gone to inspect the "job," expecting dishwashing.

Odd to think that he might still be living in that great quiet house with the tiled patio, and the bright scentless flowers, and the bare shadowed rooms with the beautiful furniture. Living in luxury, instead of lying on a broken-down bedstead in Pimlico. The old man had liked him, and wanted to adopt him; but he had not "belonged." He had enjoyed reading the English newspaper to him twice a day, the old man following with a slender yellow forefinger on his own copy; but it was not the life he was looking for. ("If he doesn't understand English, what's the good of reading English to him?" he had asked when the job was first explained to him; and they had made him understand that the old man knew "reading" English, having taught himself from a dictionary, but did not know how to pronounce it. He wanted to listen to it spoken by an Englishman.)

No, it had not been for him. It had been like living in a film set.

So he had gone as cook to a collection of botanists. And as he was packing to go the butler had said consolingly: "Better you go, after all. If you stay his mistress poison you."

It was the first he had heard of a mistress.

He had cooked his way steadily to the New Mexico border. That was the easy way into the States: where there was no river to stop you. He enjoyed this absurd, brilliant, angular country but, like the old aristocrat's home near Tampico, it was not what he was looking for.

After that it had been a slow crescendo of satisfaction.

Assistant cook for that outfit at Las Cruces. Their intolerance of any variation from the food they knew, and their delight in his accent. ("Say it again, Limey." And then their laughter and their delighted "Whaddya know!")

Cook to the Snake River round-up. And his discovery of horses. And the feeling it gave him of having come home.

Riding herd for the Santa Clara. And the discovery that "ornery" horses were less ornery when ridden by the limey kid.

A spell with the shoesmith at the Wilson ranch. He had had his first girl there, but it hadn't been half as exciting as seeing what he could do with the "hopeless lot" in the corral. "Nothing but shooting for them," the boss had said. And when he had suggested trying to do something about them, the boss had said unenthusiastically: "Go ahead; but don't expect me to pay hospital bills. You're hired as help to the farrier."

It was from that lot that Smoky came: his beautiful Smoky. The boss gave it him as a reward for what he had done with the hard cases. And when he went to the Lazy Y he took Smoky with him.

Breaking horses for the Lazy Y. That had been happiness. That had been happiness full up and running over. Nearly two years of it.

And then. That momentary slowness on his part; drowsy with heat or dazzled by the sun. And seeing the writhing brown back turning over on him. And hearing his thighbone crack.

The hospital at Edgemont. It had not been at all like the hospitals in films. There were no pretty nurses and no handsome internes. The ward had sage-green walls, the fittings were old and dingy, and the nurses over-worked. They alternately spoiled and ignored him.

The sudden stoppage of letters from the boys.

The sweat-making business of learning to walk again and the slow realisation that his leg had mended "short." That he was going to be permanently lame.

The letter from the boss that put an end to the Lazy Y.

Oil. They had struck oil. The first derrick was already going up not two hundred yards from the bunk house. The enclosed cheque would look after Brat till he was well again. Meanwhile, what should be done with Smoky?

What would a lame man do with a horse in an oil field?

He cried about Smoky; lying in the dark of the ward. It was the first time he had cried about anyone.

Well, he might be too slow to break horses any more, but he would be no servant to oil. There were other ways of living with horseflesh.

The dude ranch. That had not been like the films either.

Ungainly women in unseemly clothes punishing the saddles of broken-spirited horses until he wondered that they didn't break in two.

The woman who had wanted to marry him.

She had been not at all the kind of woman you'd imagine would want a "kept man." Not fat or silly or amorous. She was thin, and tired-looking, and rather nice; and she had owned the place up the hill from the dude ranch. She would get his leg right for him, she said. That was the bait she had offered.

The one good thing about the dude ranch was that you made money at it. He had never had so much money in his life as when he finished there. He planned to go East and spend it. And then something had happened to him. The smaller, greener country in the East, the smell of spring gardens, woke in him a nostalgia for England that dismayed him. He had no intention of going back to England for years yet.

For several restless weeks he fought the longing—it was a baby thing to want to go back—and then quite suddenly gave in. After all, he had never seen London. Going to see London was quite a legitimate reason for going to England.

And so to the back room in Pimlico and that meeting in the street.

Chapter 5

*H*e got up and took his cigarettes from the pocket of the coat that was hanging on the back of the door.

Why hadn't he been more shocked when Loding made his suggestion?

Because he had guessed that a proposition would be coming? Because the man's face had been warning enough that his interests would be shady? Because it quite simply had nothing to do with him, was not anything that he was likely to touch?

He had not been indignant with the man, had not said: "You swine, to think of cheating your friend out of his inheritance!" or words to that effect. But then he had never been interested in other people's concerns: their sins, their griefs, or their happiness. And anyhow, you couldn't be righteous with a man whose food you were eating.

He moved over to the window and stood looking out at the dim frieze of chimney-pots against the luminous haze. He was not broke yet but he had got the length of prospecting for a job, and the prospects were anything but encouraging. It seemed that there were far more people interested in stable jobs in England than stables to accommodate them. The horse world contracted as the horse lovers expanded. All those men who had lost their main interest in living when the cavalry was put down were still hale and active, and besieged stable entrances at the mere whiff of a vacancy.

Besides, he didn't want just to "do his two a day." If road engineering interested you you didn't pine to spend your days putting tar on the surface.

He had tried a few contacts, but none of the good places was interested in a lame stranger without references. Why should they be? They had their pick of England's best. And when he had mentioned that his experience of breaking had been in the States, that seemed to settle it. "Oh, cattle horses!" they said. They said it quite kindly and politely—he had forgotten until he came back how polite his countrymen were—but they had inferred in one way or another that Western kill-or-cure methods were not theirs. Since they never said so openly he could not explain that they were not his either. And anyhow, it wouldn't have been any good. They wanted to know something about you before they took you to work with them in this country. In America, where a man moved on every so often, it was different; but here a job was for life, and what you were mattered almost as much as what you could do.

The solution, of course, was to leave the country. But the real, the insurmountable trouble was that he didn't want to go. Now that he was back he realised that what he had thought of as free, purposeless wandering had merely been a long way round on the way back to England. He had come back, not via Dieppe, but via Las Cruces and points east; that was all. He had found what he wanted when he found horses; but he had no more sense of "belonging" in New Mexico than he had had at the grammar school. He had liked New Mexico better, that was all.

And better still, now that he looked at it, he liked England. He wanted to work with English horses in an English greenness on English turf.

In any case, it was much more difficult to get out of this country than to get into it, if you were broke. He had shared a table at the Coventry Street Lyons one day with a man who had been trying for eighteen months to work his passage somewhere or other. "Cards!" the little man had snarled. "That's all they ever say. Where is your card? If you don't happen to belong to the Amalgamated Union of Table-napkin Folders you can't as much as help a steward set a table. I'm just waiting to see them let a ship sink under them because no one aboard has the right card for manning a pump with."

He had looked at the Englishman's furious blue eyes and remembered the man in the Havre *bistro*. "One has also to have papers." Yes, the world was cluttered up with papers.

It was a pity that Loding's proposition was so very criminal.

Would he have listened to it with any more interest if Loding had mentioned the horses earlier?

No, of course not: that was absurd. The thing was criminal and he wouldn't touch it.

"It would be quite safe, you know," said a voice in him. "They wouldn't prosecute you even if they found out, because of the scandal. Loding said that."

"Shut up," he said. "The thing's criminal."

It might be amusing to go and see Loding act, one night. He had never met an actor before. It would be a new sensation to sit and watch the performance of someone you knew "off." How would Loding be as a partner?

"A very clever partner, believe me," said the voice.

"A plain bad lot," he said. "I don't want any part of him."

"You don't need any part of any of it," the voice said. "You have only to go to Latchetts and say: Take a look at me. Do I remind you of anyone? I was left on a doorstep on such-and-such a date, and as from to-day I want a job."

"Blackmail, 'm? And how much do you think I'd enjoy a job I'd blackmailed out of anyone? Don't be silly."

"They owe you something, don't they?"

"No, they don't. Not a bean."

"Oh, come off it! You're an Ashby and you know it."

"I don't know it. There have been doubles before. Hitler had several. *Lots* of famous people have doubles. The papers are for ever printing photographs of the humble doubles of great men. They all look like the great men with the character sponged out."

"Bunk. You're an Ashby. Where did you get your way with horses?"

"Lots of people have a way with horses."

"There were sixty-two kids at that orphanage, and did any of them go about spurning good jobs, and adoption by rich parents, so that they could find their way to horses?"

"I didn't know I was looking for horses."

"Of course you didn't know. Your Ashby blood knew."

"Oh, shut up."

To-morrow he would go down to Lewes and have a go at that jumping stable. He might be lame but he could still ride anything on four legs. They might be interested in someone who could ride at ten stone and didn't mind risking his neck.

"Risk your neck when you might be living in clover?"

"If it was clover I wanted I could have had it long ago."

"Ah, but not clover with horses in it."

"Shut up. You're wasting your time."

He began to undress, as if movement might put an end to the voice. Yes: he would go down to Lewes. It was a little too near his calf country, but no one would recognise him after those six years.

It wouldn't really matter, of course, if they did; but he didn't want to go backwards.

"You could always say: Sorry, my name is Ashby," mocked the voice.

"Will you be quiet!"

As he hung his jacket over the back of the chair he thought about that young Ashby who had bowed out. With everything in the world to live for he had gone and thrown himself off a cliff. It didn't make sense. Did parents matter all that much?

"No, he was a poor thing, and you'd make a much better job of Latchetts in his place."

He poured cold water into the basin and washed vigorously; an orphanage training being almost as lasting as a Regular Service one. And as he towelled himself on the thin turkish—so old that it was limp-wet before he was dry—he thought: "I wouldn't like it, anyhow. Butlers, and things." His idea of English middle-class life being derived from American films.

Anyhow, the thing was unthinkable.

And he'd better stop thinking about it.

Someone had said that if you thought about the unthinkable long enough it became quite reasonable.

But he would go some time and see those photographs of Loding's. There was no harm in that.

He must see what his "twin" looked like.

He didn't like Loding much, but just going to see him could do no harm, and he did want to see photographs of Latchetts.

Yes, he would go to see Loding.

The day after tomorrow perhaps; after he had been to Lewes.

Or even tomorrow.

Chapter 6

*M*r. Sandal, of Cosset, Thring and Noble, was nearing the end of his afternoon's work and his mind was beginning its daily debate as to whether it should be the 4.55 or the 5.15 that should bear him home. This was almost the only debate that ever exercised Mr. Sandal's mind. The clients of Cosset, Thring and Noble were of two kinds only: those who made up their own minds about a problem and told their solicitors in firm tones what they wanted done, and those who had no problems. The even pulse of the Georgian office in the shadow of the plane trees was never quickened by unexpected news or untoward happenings. Even the death of a client was not news: clients were expected to die; the appropriate will would be in the appropriate deed-box and things would go on as before.

Family solicitors; that is what Cosset, Thring and Noble were. Keepers of wills and protectors of secrets; but not wrestlers with problems. Which is why Mr. Sandal was by no means the best person to take what was coming to him.

"Is that all, Mercer?" he said to his clerk, who had been showing a visitor out.

"There's one client in the waiting-room, sir. Young Mr. Ashby."

"Ashby? Of Latchetts?"

"Yes, sir."

"Oh, good; good. Bring in a pot of tea, Mercer, will you?"

"Yes, sir." And to the client: "Will you come in, sir?"

The young man came in.

"Ah, Simon, my dear boy," Mr. Sandal said, shaking hands with him, "I'm delighted to see you. Are you up on business, or are you just—"

His voice died away uncertainly, and he stared, the gesture of his arm towards a chair arrested mid-way.

"God bless my soul," he said, "you are not Simon."

"No. I am not Simon."

"But—but you *are* an Ashby."

"If you think that, it makes things a whole lot easier for me."

"Yes? Do forgive me if I am a little confused. I didn't know that there were Ashby cousins."

"There aren't, as far as I know."

"No? Then—forgive me—which Ashby are you?"

"Patrick."

Mr. Sandal's neat mouth opened and shut like a goldfish's.

He stopped being a green thought in a green shade and became a very worried and staggered little lawyer.

For a long moment he looked into the light Ashby eyes so near his own without finding any words that seemed adequate to the occasion.

"I think we had better both sit down," he said at last. He indicated the visitors' chair, and subsided into his own with an air of being glad of an anchorage in a world suddenly at sea.

"Now, let us clarify the situation," he said. "The only Patrick Ashby died at the age of thirteen, some—let me see—eight years ago, it must be."

"What makes you think he died?"

"He committed suicide, and left a farewell note."

"Did the note mention suicide?"

"I am afraid I cannot recall the wording."

"Nor can I, exactly. But I can give you the sense of it. It said: 'I can't stand it any longer. Don't be angry with me.' "

"Yes. Yes, that was the tenor of the message."

"And where in that is the mention of suicide?"

"The suggestion surely is—One would naturally infer—The letter was found on the cliff-top with the boy's coat."

"The cliff path is the short-cut to the harbour."

"The harbour? You mean—"

"It was a running-away note; not a suicide one."

"But—but the coat?"

"You can't leave a note on the open down. The only way to leave it is in the pocket of something."

"Are you seriously suggesting that—that—that you are Patrick Ashby, and that you never committed suicide at all?"

The young man looked at him with those unrevealing eyes of his. "When I came in," he said, "you took me for my brother."

"Yes. They were twins. Not identical twins, but of course very—"

The full implication of what he was saying came home to him. "God bless my soul, so I did. So I did."

He sat for a moment or two staring in a helpless fashion. And while he stared Mercer came in with the tea.

"Do you take tea?" Mr. Sandal asked, the question being merely a reflex conditioned by the presence of the tea-tray.

"Thank you," said the young man. "No sugar."

"You do realise, don't you," Mr. Sandal said, half-appealingly, "that such a very startling and—and serious claim must be investigated? One cannot, you understand, merely accept your statement."

"I don't expect you to."

"Good. That is good. Very sensible of you. At some later date it may be possible—the fatted calf—but just now we have to be sensible about it. You do see that. Milk?"

"Thank you."

"For instance: you ran away, you say. Ran away to sea, I take it."

"Yes."

"On what ship?"

"The *Ira Jones*. She was lying in Westover harbour."

"You stowed away, of course."

"Yes."

"And where did the ship take you?" asked Mr. Sandal, making notes and beginning to feel that he wasn't doing so badly after all. This was quite the worst situation he had ever been in, and there was no question of catching the 5.15 now.

"The Channel Islands. St. Helier."

"Were you discovered on board?"

"No."

"You disembarked at St. Helier, undiscovered."

"Yes."

"And there?"

"I got the boat to St. Malo."

"You stowed away again?"

"No, I paid my fare."

"You remember what the boat was called?"

"No; it was the regular ferry service."

"I see. And then?"

"I went bus-riding. Buses always seemed to me more exciting than that old station wagon at Latchetts, but I never had a chance of riding in them."

"The station wagon. Ah, yes," said Mr. Sandal; and wrote: "Remembers car." "And then?"

"Let me see. I was garage-boy for a while at a hotel in a place called Villedieu."

"You remember the name of the hotel, perhaps?"

"The Dauphin, I think. From there I went across country and fetched up in Havre. In Havre I got a job as galley boy on a tramp steamer."

"The name? You remember it?"

"I'll never forget it! She was called the *Barfleur*. I joined her as Farrar. F-a-r-r-a-r. I stayed with her until I left her in Tampico. From there I worked my way north to the States. Would you like me to write down for you the places I worked at in the States?"

"That would be very kind of you. Here is—ah, you have a pen. If you would just write them here, in a list. Thank you. And you came back to England—?"

"On the second of last month. On the *Philadelphia*. As a passenger. I took a room in London and have lived there ever since. I'll write the address for you; you'll want to check that too."

"Yes. Thank you. Yes." Mr. Sandal had an odd feeling that it was this young man—who after all was on trial, so to speak—who was dominating the situation and not, as it certainly should be, himself. He pulled himself together.

"Have you attempted to communicate with your—I mean, with Miss Ashby?"

"No, is it difficult?" said the young man gently.

"What I mean is—"

"I've done nothing about my family, if that is what you mean. I thought this was the best way."

"Very wise. Very wise." There he was again, being forced into the position of chorus. "I shall get in touch with Miss Ashby at once, and inform her of your visit."

"Tell her that I'm alive, yes."

"Yes. Quite so." Was the young man making fun of him? Surely not.

"Meanwhile you will go on living at this address?"

"Yes, I shall be there." The young man got up, again taking the initiative from him.

"If your credentials prove to be good," Mr. Sandal said with an attempt at severity, "I shall be the first to welcome you back to England and to your home. In spite of the fact that your desertion of it has caused deep grief to all concerned. I find it inexplicable that you should not have communicated with your people before now."

"Perhaps I liked being dead."

"Being dead!"

"Anyhow you never did find me very explicable, did you?"

"Didn't I?"

"You thought it was because I was afraid that I cried, that day at Olympia, didn't you?"

"Olympia?"

"It wasn't you know. It was because the horses were so beautiful."

"Olympia! You mean . . . But that was . . . You remember, then?"

"I expect you'll let me know, Mr. Sandal, when you have checked my statements."

"What? Oh, yes; yes, certainly." Good heavens, even he himself had forgotten that children's party at the Tournament. Perhaps he had been altogether too cautious. If this young man—the owner of Latchetts—dear me! Perhaps he should not have been so—

"I hope you don't think—" he began.

But the young man was gone, letting himself out with cool decision and a brief nod to Mercer.

Mr. Sandal sat down in the inner office and mopped his brow.

And Brat, walking down the street, was shocked to find himself exhilarated. He had expected to be nervous and a little ashamed. And it had not been in the least like that. It had been one of the most exciting things he had ever done. A wonderful, tight-rope sort of thing. He had sat there and lied and not even been conscious that he was lying, it had been so thrilling. It was like riding a rogue; you had the same wary, strung-up feeling; the same satisfaction in avoiding an unexpected movement to destroy you. But nothing he had ever ridden had given him the mental excitement, the subsequent glow of achievement, that this had given him. He was drunk with it.

And greatly surprised.

So this, he thought, was what sent criminals back to their old ways when there was no material need. This breathless, step-picking excitement; this subsequent intoxication of achievement.

He went to have tea, according to Loding's instructions; but he could not eat. He felt as if he had already had food and drink. No previous experience of his had had this oddly satisfying effect. Normally, after the exciting things of life—riding, love-making, rescue, close calls—he was ravenously hungry. But now he just sat and looked at the food in front of him in a daze of content. The glow inside him left no room for food.

No one had followed him into the restaurant, and no one seemed to be taking any interest in him.

He paid his bill and went out. No one was loitering anywhere; the pavement was one long stream of hurrying people. He went to a telephone at Victoria.

"Well?" said Loding. "How did it go?"

"Wonderful."

"Have you been drinking?"

"No. Why?"

"That is the first time I have ever heard you use a superlative."

"I'm just pleased."

"My God, you must be. Does it show?"

"Show?"

"Is there any faint change in that poker face of yours?"

"How should I know? Don't you want to know about this afternoon?"

"I already know the most important thing."

"What is that?"

"You haven't been given in charge."

"Did you expect me to be?"

"There was always the chance. But I didn't really expect it. Not with our combined intelligences."

"Thanks."

"Did the old boy fall on your neck?"

"No. He nearly fell over. He's being very correct."

"Everything to be verified."

"Yes."

"How did he receive you?"

"He took me for Simon."

He heard Loding's amused laughter.

"Did you manage to use his Tournament party?"

"Yes."

"Oh, my God, don't go monosyllabic on me. You didn't have to rake it up, did you?"

"No. It fitted very neatly."

"Was he impressed?"

"It had him on the ropes."

"It didn't convince him, though?"

"I didn't wait to see. I was on my way out."

"You mean, that was your exit line? My boy, I take off my hat to you. You're a perishing marvel. After living in your pocket for the last fortnight I thought I was beginning to know you. But you're still surprising me to death."

"I surprise myself, if it's any consolation to you."

"I don't detect any bitterness in that line, do I?"

"No. Just surprise. Neat."

"Ah, well; we shall not be meeting for some time to come. It has been a privilege to know you, my boy. I shall never hear Kew Gardens mentioned without thinking tenderly of you. And I look forward, of course, to further privileges from knowing you in the future. Meanwhile, don't ring me up unless there is absolutely no alternative. You are as well briefed as I can make you. From now on you're on your own."

Loding was right: it had been a wonderful briefing. For a whole fortnight, from early morning till seven in the evening, rain or shine, they had sat in Kew Gardens and rehearsed the ways of Latchetts and Clare, the histories of Ashbys and Ledinghams, the lie of a land he had never seen. And that too had been exciting. He had always been what they called "good at exams"; and had always come to an examination paper with the same faint pleasure that an addict brings to a quiz party. And those fourteen days in Kew Gardens had been one glorified quiz party. Indeed, the last few days had had some of the tight-rope excitement that had characterised this afternoon. "Which arm did you bowl with?" "Go to the stables from the side door." "Did you sing?" "Could you play the piano?" "Who lived in the lodge at Clare?" "What colour was your mother's hair?" "How did your father make his money, apart from the estate?" "What was the name of his firm?" "What was your favourite food?" "The name of the tuck-shop owner in the village?" "Where is the Ashby pew in the church?" "Go from the great drawing-room to the butler's pantry in Clare." "What was the housekeeper's name?" "Could you ride a bicycle?" "What do you see from the south window in the attic?" Loding fired the questions at him through the long days, and it had been first amusing and then exciting to avoid being stumped.

Kew had been Loding's idea. "Your life since you came to London must be subject to the most searching scrutiny, if you will forgive the cliché. So you can't come and live with me as I suggested. You can't even be seen with me by anyone we know. Nor can I come to your Pimlico place. You must go on being unvisited there as you have been up till now." So the Kew scheme had been evolved. Kew Gardens, Loding said, had perfect cover and a wonderful field of fire. There was nowhere in London where you could see approaching figures at such a distance and still be unnoticed yourself. Nowhere in London offered the variety of meeting-places, the undisturbed quiet, that Kew did.

So each morning they had arrived separately, by different gates; had met at a new point and gone to a different region; and there for a fortnight Loding had primed him with photographs, maps, plans, drawings, and pencilled diagrams. He had begun with a one-inch Ordnance Survey map of Clare and its surroundings, progressed to a larger size, and thence to plans of the house; so that it was rather like coming down from above in a plane. First the lie of the country, then the details of fields and gardens, and then the close-up of the house so that the thing was whole in his mind from the beginning, and the details had merely to be pointed to on a picture already etched. It was methodical, careful teaching, and Brat appreciated it.

But the highlight, of course, was provided by the photographs. And it was not, oddly enough, the photograph of his "twin" that held his attention once he had seen them all. Simon, of course, was extraordinarily like him; and it gave him a strange, almost embarrassed, feeling to look at the pictured face so like his own. But it was not Simon who held his interest; it was the child who had not lived to grow up; the boy whose place he was going to take. He had an odd feeling of identity with Patrick.

Even he himself noticed this, and found it strange. He should have been filled with guilt when he considered Patrick. But his only emotion was one of partisanship; almost of alliance.

Crossing the courtyard at Victoria after telephoning, he wondered what had prompted him to say that about Patrick crying. Loding had told him merely that Patrick had cried for no known reason (he was seven then) and that old Sandal had been disgusted and had never taken the children out again. Loding had left the story with him to be used as and when he thought fit. What had prompted him to say that Patrick had cried because the horses were so beautiful? Was that, perhaps, why Patrick *had* cried?

Well, there was no going back now, whether he wanted to or not. That insistent voice that had talked to him in the dark of his room had fought for its head and got it. All he could do was sit in the saddle and hope for the best. But at least it would be a breath-taking ride; a unique, heart-stopping ride. Danger to life and limb he was used to; but far more exciting was this new mental danger, this pitting of wits.

This danger to his immortal soul, the orphanage would call it. But he had never believed in his immortal soul.

He couldn't go to Latchetts as a blackmailer, he wouldn't go as a suppliant, he would damn well go as an invader.

Chapter 7

*T*he telegraph wires swooped and the earth whirled round the carriage window; and Bee's mind swooped and whirled with them.

"I would have come down to see you, of course," Mr. Sandal had said on the telephone. "It is against all my principles to deal with such grave matters by telephone. But I was afraid that my presence might suggest to the children that there was something serious afoot. And it would be a pity to upset them if there is a chance that—that the trouble is temporary."

Poor dear old Sandal. He had been very kind; had asked her if she were sitting down, before he broke the news; and had said: "You're not feeling faint, are you, Miss Ashby?" when his shock had been administered.

She had not fainted. She had sat for a long time letting her knees get back their strength, and then she had gone to her room and looked for photographs of Patrick. Except for a studio group taken when Simon and Patrick were ten and Eleanor nine, she seemed to have nothing. She was not a snapshot-keeper.

Nora had been a passionate collector of her children's photographs, but she had spurned photograph albums, which she held to be "a great waste of time and space." (Nora had never wasted anything; it had been as if she was half conscious that her allotted time was short.) She had kept them all in a tattered and bursting manila envelope with O.H.M.S. on it, and the envelope went everywhere with her. It had gone to Europe on that holiday with her, and had made part of that blaze on the Kent coast.

Balked of photographs, Bee went up to the old nursery, as if there she would get nearer to the child Patrick, although she knew very well that nothing of Patrick's remained there. Simon had burned them all. It was the only sign he had given that his twin's death was more than he could well bear. Simon had gone away to

school after Patrick's death, and when he came back for the summer holidays he had behaved normally, if one took it for granted
that not mentioning Patrick was in the circumstances normal
enough. And then one day Bee had come on him tending a bonfire
where the children had made their "Red Indian" and campfires, beyond the shrubbery, and on the fire were Patrick's toys and other
small belongings. Even exercise books, she noticed, had been
brought down to feed the flames. Books and childish paintings and
the silly horse that had hung at the end of his bed; Simon was burning them all.

He had been furious when he saw her. He had moved between
her and the fire, standing at bay, as it were, and glared at her.

"I don't want them around," he had said, almost shouting.

"I understand, Simon," she had said, and had gone away.

So there was nothing of Patrick in the old nursery under the
eaves; and not very much of the other children, after all. When this
had been Bee's own nursery it had been ugly and individual and
furnished largely with rejections from the other parts of the house.
It had patterned linoleum, and a rag rug, and a cuckoo clock, and
crazy basket chairs, and a clothes-horse, and a deal table covered
with a red rep tablecloth trimmed with bobbles and marked with
ink-stains; and coloured prints of "Bubbles" and similar master-
pieces hung against a cabbage-rose wallpaper. But Nora had done
it over, so that it became an illustration from a homemaker maga-
zine, in powder-blue and white, with a wallpaper of nursery-rhyme
characters. Only the cuckoo clock had stayed.

The children had been happy there, but had left no mark on it.
Now that it was empty and tidy, it looked just like something in a
furniture shop window.

She had gone back to her own room, baffled and sick at heart,
and had packed a small bag for her use in the morning. Tomorrow
she must go up to town and face this new emergency in the history
of the Ashbys.

"Do you believe, yourself, that it is Patrick?" she had asked.

But Mr. Sandal could give her no assurance.

"He has not the air of a pretender," he allowed. "And if he is not
Patrick, then who is he? The Ashby family resemblance has always
been abnormally strong. And there is no other son of this generation."

"But Patrick would have written," she said.

That is the thought she always went back to. Patrick would never have left her in grief and doubt all those years. Patrick would have written. It couldn't be Patrick.

Then if it wasn't Patrick, who *was* it?

Round and round went her mind, swooping and whirling.

"You will be the best judge," Mr. Sandal had said. "Of those now living you are the one who knew the boy best."

"There is Simon," she had said.

"But Simon was a boy at the time and boys forget, don't they? You were grown up."

So the onus was being put upon her. But how was *she* to know? She who had loved Patrick but now could hardly remember what he looked like at thirteen. What test would there be?

Or would she know at once when she saw him that he was Patrick? Or that he—wasn't?

And if he wasn't and yet insisted that he was, what would happen? Would he bring a claim? Make a court action of it? Drag them all through the publicity of the daily Press?

And if he was Patrick, what of Simon? How would he take the resurrection of a brother he had not seen for eight years? The loss of a fortune. Would he be glad about it, fortune or no, or would he hate his brother?

The coming-of-age celebrations would have to be postponed, that was clear. They were much too close now for anything to be decided by that time. What excuse should they make?

But oh, if it *could*, by some miracle, be Patrick, she would be free of that haunting horror, that thought of the boy who regretted too late to come back.

Her mind was still swooping and swirling as she climbed the stairs to the offices of Cosset, Thring and Noble.

"Ah, Miss Ashby," Mr. Sandal said. "This is a shocking dilemma. A most unprecedented—Do sit down. You must be exhausted. A dreadful ordeal for you. Sit down, sit down. Mercer, some tea for Miss Ashby."

"Did he say why he didn't write, all those years?" she asked; this being the all-important thing in her mind.

"He said something about 'perhaps preferring to be dead.'"

"Oh."

"A psychological difficulty, no doubt," Mr. Sandal said, proffering comfort.

"Then you believe it *is* Patrick?"

"I mean, if it is Patrick, his 'preferring to be dead' would no doubt arise from the same psychological difficulty as did his running away."

"Yes. I see. I suppose so. Only—it is so unlike Patrick. Not to write, I mean."

"It was unlike Patrick to run away."

"Yes; there is that. He certainly wasn't a runner-away by nature. He was a sensitive child but very brave. Something must have gone very wrong." She sat silent for a moment. "And now he is back."

"We hope so; we hope so."

"Did he seem quite normal to you?"

"Excessively," said Mr. Sandal, with a hint of dryness in his tone.

"I looked for photographs of Patrick, but there is nothing later than this." She produced the studio group. "The children had studio portraits taken regularly every three years, from the time they were babies. This was the last of them. The new one would have been taken in the summer of the year that Bill and Nora were killed; the year Patrick—disappeared. Patrick is ten there."

She watched while Mr. Sandal studied the small immature face.

"No," he said at last. "It is impossible to say anything from so early a photograph. As I said before, the family likeness is very strong. At that age they are just young Ashbys, aren't they? Without any great individuality." He looked up from studying the photograph and went on: "I am hoping that when you yourself see the boy—the young man—you will have no doubt one way or another. After all, it is not entirely a matter of likeness, this recognition, is it? There is an aura of—of personality."

"But—but if I am not sure? What is to happen if I am not sure?"

"About that: I think I have found a way out. I dined last night with my young friend Kevin Macdermott."

"The K.C.?"

"Yes. I was greatly distressed, of course, and told him of my difficulty, and he comforted me greatly by assuring me that identification would be a quite simple matter. It was merely an affair of teeth."

"Teeth? But Patrick had quite ordinary teeth."

"Yes, yes. But he had no doubt been to a dentist, and dentists have records. Indeed, most dentists have a sort of visual memory, I understand, of mouths they have treated—a very grim thought— and would almost recognise one at sight. But the record will certainly show—" He caught the look on Bee's face and paused. "What is the matter?"

"The children went to Hammond."

"Hammond? Well? That is simple, isn't it? If you don't definitely identify the boy as Patrick, we have only to—" He broke off. "Hammond!" he said quietly. "Oh!"

"Yes," Bee said, agreeing with the tone of the monosyllable.

"Dear me, how unfortunate. How very unfortunate."

Into the subsequent silence Mr. Sandal said miserably: "I think I ought to tell you that Kevin Macdermott thinks the boy is lying."

"What could Mr. Macdermott possibly know about it," said Bee angrily. "He has not even seen him!" And as Mr. Sandal went on sitting in miserable silence, "Well?"

"It was only Kevin's opinion on the hypothesis."

"I know, but why did he think that?"

"He said it was a—a 'phoney thing to come straight to a lawyer.'"

"What nonsense! It was a very sensible thing to do."

"Yes. That was his point. It was too sensible. Too pat. Everything, Kevin said, was too pat for his liking. He said a boy coming home after years away would go home."

"Then he doesn't know Patrick. That is just what Patrick would have done: broken it gently by going to the family lawyer first. He was always the most thoughtful and unselfish of creatures. I don't think much of the clever Mr. Macdermott's analysis."

"I felt it only right to tell you everything," Mr. Sandal said, still miserably.

"Yes, of course," Bee said kindly, recovering her temper. "Did you tell Mr. Macdermott that Patrick—that the boy had remembered crying at Olympia? I mean, that he had volunteered the information."

"I did; yes."

"And he still thought the boy was lying?"

"That was part of the 'patness' he professed not to like."

Bee gave a small snort. "What a mind!" she said. "I suppose that is what a court practise does."

"It is a detached mind, that is all. One not emotionally engaged in the matter, as we are. It behooves us to keep our minds detached."

"Yes, of course," Bee said, sobered. "Well, now that poor old Hammond is to be of no help to us—they never found him, did you know? Everything was just blown to dust."

"Yes. Yes, so I heard; poor fellow."

"Now that we have no physical evidence, I suppose we have to rely on the boy's own story. I mean, on checking it. I suppose that can be done."

"Oh, quite easily. It is all quite straightforward, with dates and places. That is what Kevin found so—Yes. Yes. Of course it can be checked. And of course I am sure that it *will* check. He would not have offered us information which would be proved nonsense."

"So really there is nothing to wait for."

"No, I—No."

Bee braced herself.

"Then how soon can you arrange for me to meet him?"

"Well—I have been thinking about it, and I don't think, you know, that it should be arranged at all."

"What?"

"What I should like to do—with your permission and co-operation—would be to, as it were, walk in on him. Go and see him unannounced. So that you would see him as he is and not as he wants you to see him. If we made an appointment here at the office, he would—"

"Yes, I see. I understand. I agree to that. Can we go now?"

"I don't see why not. I really don't see why not," Mr. Sandal said in that regretful tone that lawyers use when they cannot see any reason why not. "There is, of course, the chance that he may be out. But we can at least go and see. Ah, here is your tea! Will you drink it while Mercer asks Simpson to ask Willett to get us a taxi?"

"You haven't got anything stronger, have you?" Bee asked.

"I'm afraid not; I'm afraid not. I have never succumbed to the transatlantic custom of the bottle in the office. But Willett will get you anything you may—"

"Oh, no, thank you; it's all right. I'll drink the tea. They say the effects are much more lasting, anyway."

Mr. Sandal looked as though he would like to pat her encouragingly on the shoulder, but could not make up his mind to it. He was really a very kind little man, she thought, but just—just not much of a *prop*.

"Did he explain why he chose the name Farrar?" she asked, when they were seated in the taxi.

"He didn't explain anything," Mr. Sandal said, falling back on his dry tone.

"Did you gather that he was badly off?"

"He did not mention money, but he seemed very well-dressed in a slightly un-English fashion."

"There was no suggestion of a loan?"

"Oh, no. Oh, dear me, no."

"Then he hasn't come back just because he is broke," Bee said, and felt somehow pleased. She sat back and relaxed a little. Perhaps everything was going to be all right.

"I have never quite understood why Pimlico descended so rapidly in the social scale," said Mr. Sandal, breaking the silence as they travelled down the avenues of pretentious porches. "It has fine wide streets, and little through-traffic, and no more smuts than its neighbours. Why should the well-to-do have deserted it and yet stayed in Belgravia? Very puzzling."

"There is a sort of suction about desertion," Bee said, trying to meet him on the small-talk level. "The local Lady Almighty occasions the draught by leaving, and the rest, in descending order of importance, follow in her wake. And the poorer people flood in from either side to fill the vacuum. Is this the place?"

Her dismay took possession of her again as she looked at the dismal front of the house; at the peeling paint and the stained stucco, the variety of drab curtains at the windows, the unswept doorway and the rubbed-out house-number on the horrible pillar.

The front door was open and they walked in.

A different card on each door in the hallway proclaimed the fact that the house was let out in single rooms.

"The address is 59K," Mr. Sandal said. "I take it that K is the number of the room."

"They begin on the ground floor and work upwards," Bee said. "This is B on my side." So they mounted.

"H," said Bee, peering at a first-floor door. "It's up the next flight."

The second floor was also the top one. They stood together on the dark landing listening to the silence. He is out, she thought, he is out, and I shall have to go through all this again.

"Have you a match?" she said.

"I and J," she read, on the two front-room doors.

Then it was the back one.

They stood in the dark for a moment, staring at it. Then Mr. Sandal moved purposively forward and knocked.

"Come in!" said a voice. It was a deep, boy's voice; quite unlike Simon's light sophisticated tones.

Bee, being half a head taller than Mr. Sandal, could see over his shoulder; and her first feeling was one of shock that he should be so much more like Simon than Patrick ever was. Her mind had been filled with images of Patrick: vague, blurred images that she strove to make clear so that she could compare them with the adult reality. Her whole being had been obsessed with Patrick for the last twenty-four hours.

And now here was someone just like Simon.

The boy got up from where he had been sitting on the edge of the bed, and with no haste or embarrassment pulled from off his left hand the sock he had been darning. She couldn't imagine Simon darning a sock.

"Good morning," he said.

"Good morning," said Mr. Sandal. "I hope you don't mind: I've brought you a visitor." He moved aside to let Bee come in. "Do you know who this is?"

Bee's heart hammered on her ribs as she met the boy's light calm gaze and watched him identify her.

"You do your hair differently," he said.

Yes, of course; hairdressing had changed completely in those eight years; of course he would see a difference.

"You recognise her, then?" Mr. Sandal said.

"Yes, of course. It's Aunt Bee."

She waited for him to come forward to greet her, but he made no move to. After a moment's pause he turned to find a seat for her.

"I'm afraid there is only one chair. It is all right if you don't lean back on it," he said, picking up one of those hard chairs with a black curved back and a tan seat with small holes in it. Bee was glad to sit down on it.

"Do you mind the bed?" he said to Mr. Sandal.

"I'll stand, thank you, I'll stand," Mr. Sandal said hastily.

The details of the face were not at all like Simon's, she thought; watching the boy stick the needle carefully in the sock. It was the general impression that was the same; once you really looked at him the startling resemblance vanished, and only the family likeness remained.

"Miss Ashby could not wait for a meeting at my office, so I brought her here," Mr. Sandal said. "You don't seem particularly—" He allowed the sentence to speak for itself.

The boy looked at her in a friendly unsmiling way and said: "I'm not very sure of my welcome."

It was a curiously immobile face. A face like a child's drawing, now she came to think of it. Everything in the right place and with the right proportions, but without animation. Even the mouth had the straight uncompromising line that is a child's version of a mouth.

He moved over to lay the socks on the dressing-table, and she saw that he was lame.

"Have you hurt your leg?" she asked.

"I broke it. Over in the States."

"But should you be walking about on it if it is still tender?"

"Oh, it doesn't hurt," he said. "It's just short."

"Short! You mean, permanently short?"

"It looks like it."

They were sensitive lips, she noticed, for all their thinness; they gave him away when he said that.

"But something can be done about that," she said. "It just means that it was mended badly. I expect you didn't have a very good surgeon."

"I don't remember a surgeon. Perhaps I passed out. They did all the correct things: hung weights on the end of it, and all that."

"But Pat—" she began, and failed to finish his name.

Into the hiatus he said: "You don't have to call me anything until you are sure."

"They do miracles in surgery nowadays," she said, covering her break. "How long ago is it since it happened?"

"I'd have to think. About a couple of years now, I think."

Except for the flat American *a*, his speech was without peculiarity.

"Well, we must see what can be done about it. A horse, was it?"

"Yes. I wasn't quick enough. How did you know it was a horse?"

"You told Mr. Sandal that you had worked with horses. Did you enjoy that?" Just like railway-carriage small-talk, she thought.

"It's the only life I do enjoy."

She forgot about small-talk. "Really?" she said pleased. "Were they good horses, those western ones?"

"Most of them were commoners, of course. Very good stuff for their work—which, after all, is being a good horse, I suppose. But every now and then you come across one with blood. Some of those are beauties. More—more individual than I ever remember English horses being."

"Perhaps in England we 'manner' the individuality out of them. I hadn't thought of it. Did you have a horse of your own at all?"

"Yes, I had one. Smoky."

She noticed the change in his voice when he said it. As audible as the flat note in the cracked bell of a chime.

"A grey?"

"Yes, a dark grey with black points. Not that hard, iron colour, you know. A soft, smoky colour. When he had a tantrum he was just a whirling cloud of smoke."

A whirling cloud of smoke. She could see it. He must love horses to be able to see them like that. He must particularly have loved his Smoky.

"What happened to Smoky?"

"I sold him."

No trespassers. Very well, she would not trespass. He had probably had to sell the horse when he broke his leg.

She began to hope very strenuously that this was Patrick.

The thought recalled her to the situation which she had begun to lose sight of. She looked doubtfully at Mr. Sandal.

Catching the appeal in her glance, Mr. Sandal said: "Miss Ashby is no doubt prepared to vouch for you, but you will understand that the matter needs more clarification. If it were a simple matter of a prodigal's homecoming, your aunt's acceptance of you would no doubt be sufficient to restore you to the bosom of your family. But in the present instance it is a matter of property. Of the ultimate destination of a fortune. And the law will require incontrovertible evidence of your identity before you could be allowed to succeed to anything that was Patrick Ashby's. I hope you understand our position."

"I understand perfectly. I shall, of course, stay here until you have made your enquiries and are satisfied."

"But you can't stay *here*," Bee said, looking with loathing at the room and the forest of chimney-pots beyond the window.

"I have stayed in a great many worse places."

"Perhaps. That is no reason for staying here. If you need money we can give you some, you know."

"I'll stay here, thanks."

"Are you just being independent?"

"No. It's quiet here. And handy. And bung full of privacy. When you have lived in bunk houses you put a high value on privacy."

"Very well, you stay here. Is there anything else we can—can stake you to?"

"I could do with another suit."

"Very well. Mr. Sandal will advance whatever you need for that." She suddenly remembered that if he went to the Ashby tailor there would be a sensation. So she added: "And he will give you the address of his tailor."

"Why not Walters?" said the boy.

For a moment she could not speak.

"Aren't they there any more?"

"Oh, yes; but there would be too many explanations if you went to Walters." She must keep a hold on herself. Anyone could find out who the Ashby tailor had been.

"Oh, yes. I see."

She fell back on small-talk and began to take her leave.

"We have not told the family about you," she said, as she prepared to go. "We thought it better not to, until things are—are what Mr. Sandal calls clarified."

A flash of amusement showed in his eyes at that. For a moment they were allied in a secret laughter.

"I understand."

She turned at the door to say good-bye. He was standing in the middle of the room watching her go, leaving Mr. Sandal to shepherd her out. He looked remote and lonely. And she thought: "If this *is* Patrick, Patrick come home again, and I am leaving him like this as if he were a casual acquaintance—" It was more than she could bear, the thought of the boy's loneliness.

She went back to him, took his face lightly in her gloved hand, and kissed his cheek. "Welcome back, my dear," she said.

Chapter 8

So Cosset, Thring and Noble began their investigations, and Bee went back to Latchetts to deal with the problem of postponing the coming-of-age celebrations.

Was she to tell the children now, before the thing was certain? And if not, what excuse could she possibly put forward for not celebrating at the proper time?

Mr. Sandal was against telling the children yet. The unknown Kevin's verdict had left a mark on him, it seemed; and he was entirely prepared to find a flaw in the so-complete dossier that had been handed to them. It would be inadvisable, he thought, to bring the children into this until the claim had been sifted through the finest mesh.

With that she agreed. If this thing passed—if that boy in the back room in Pimlico was not Patrick—they need never know anything about it. Simon would probably have to be told, so that he could be warned against future attempts at fraud, but by that time it would be of no more than academic interest; a quite impersonal affair. Her present difficulty was how to reconcile the children's ignorance with the postponing of the celebrations.

The person who rescued her from this dilemma was Great-uncle Charles, who cabled to announce his (long overdue) retirement, and his hope to be present at his great-nephew's coming-of-age party. He was on his way home from the Far East, and, since he refused to fly, his homecoming was likely to be a protracted one, but he hoped Simon would keep the champagne corked till he came.

Great-uncles do not normally cut much ice in the families in which they survive, but to the Ashbys Great-uncle Charles was much more than a great-uncle: he was a household word. Every birthday had been made iridescent and every Christmas a tingling expectation by the thought of Great-uncle Charles's present. There were reasonable bounds to the possible presents of parents; and Father Christmas's were merely the answer to indents.

But neither reason nor bounds had any connection with presents from Great-uncle Charles. Once he had sent a set of chop-sticks, which upset nursery discipline for a week. And once it had been the skin of a snake; the glory of owning the skin of a snake had made Simon dizzy for days. And Eleanor still ran to and from her bath in a pair of odd-smelling leather slippers that had come on her twelfth birthday. At least four times every year Great-uncle Charles became the most important factor in the Ashby family; and when you have been of first importance four times a year for twenty years your importance is pretty considerable. Simon might grumble and the others protest a little, but they would without doubt wait for Great-uncle Charles.

Besides, she had a shrewd idea that Simon would not be willing to offend the last-surviving Ashby of his generation. Charles was not rich—he had been far too liberal a giver all his life—but he was comfortably off; and Simon, for all his careless good nature and easy charm, was an exceedingly practical person.

So the postponement was taken by the family with resignation, and by Clare with equanimity. It was held to be a very proper thing that the Ashbys should wait until the old boy could be present. Bee spent her after-dinner leisure altering the date on the invitation cards, and thanking heaven for the mercifulness of chance.

Bee was at odds with herself these days. She wanted this boy to be Patrick; but it would be so much better for all concerned, she felt, if he proved not to be Patrick. Seven-eighths of her wanted Patrick back; warm, and alive, and dear; wanted it passionately. The other eighth shrank from the upheaval of the happy Ashby world that his return would bring with it. When she caught this renegade eighth at its work she reproved it and was suitably ashamed of herself; but she could not destroy it. And so she was distrait and short-tempered, and Ruth, commenting on it to Jane said:

"Do you think she can have a Secret Sorrow?"

"I expect the books won't balance," Jane said. "She's a very bad adder-up."

Mr. Sandal reported from time to time on the progress of the investigations, and the reports were uniform and monotonous. Everything seemed to confirm the boy's story.

"The most heartening thing, using the word in its sense of reassurance," Mr. Sandal said, "is that the young man seems to have no contacts since he came to England. He has lived at that address since the *Philadelphia*'s arrival, and he has had neither letters nor visitors. The woman who owns the house occupies one of the front rooms on the ground floor. She is one of those women who has nothing to do but sit back and watch her neighbours. The lives of her tenants seem to be an open book to the good lady. She is also accustomed to waiting for the postman and collecting the letters he drops. Nothing escapes her. Her description of myself was, I understand, hardly flattering but quite touching in its fidelity. The young man could therefore have hardly had visitors without her being aware of it. He was out all day, of course; as any young man in London would be. But there is no trace of that intimacy which would suggest connivance. He had no friends."

The young man came willingly to the office and answered questions freely. With Bee's consent, Kevin Macdermott had "sat in" at one of these office conferences, and even Kevin had been shaken. "What shakes me," Kevin had said, "is not the fellow's knowledge of the subject—all good con. men are glib—but the general cut of his jib. He's quite frankly not what I expected. After a little while in my job you develop a smell for a wrong 'un. This chap has me baffled. He doesn't smell like a crook to me, and yet the set-up stinks."

So the day came when Mr. Sandal announced to Bee that Cosset, Thring and Noble were now prepared to accept the claimant as Patrick Ashby, the eldest son of William Ashby of Latchetts, and to hand over to him everything that was due to him. There would be legal formalities, of course, since the fact of his death eight years ago had been presumed; but they would be automatic. As far as they, Cosset, Thring and Noble, were concerned, Patrick Ashby was free to go home whenever he pleased.

So the moment had come, and Bee was faced with breaking the news to the family.

Her instinct was to tell Simon first, privately; but she felt that anything that set him apart from the others in this matter of welcoming back his brother was to be avoided. It would be better to take for granted that for Simon, as for the others, the news would be a matter for unqualified happiness.

It was after lunch on a Sunday that she told them.

"I have something to tell you that will be rather a shock to you. But a nice kind of shock," she said. And went on from there. Patrick had not committed suicide as they had thought. He had merely run away. And now he had come back. He had been living for a little in London because, of course, he had to prove to the lawyers that he was Patrick. But he had had no difficulty in doing that. And now he was going to come home.

She had avoided looking at their faces as she talked; it was easier just to talk into space, impersonally. But in the startled silence that followed her story she looked across at Simon; and for a moment did not recognise him. The shrunk white face with the blazing eyes had no resemblance to the Simon she knew. She looked away hastily.

"Does it mean that this new brother will get all the money that is Simon's?" asked Jane, with her usual lack of finesse.

"Well, I think it was a horrible thing to do," Eleanor said bluntly.

"What was?"

"Running away and leaving us all thinking he was dead."

"He didn't know that, of course. I mean: that we would take his note to mean that he was going to kill himself."

"Even so. He left us all without a word for—for—how long is it? Seven years? Nearly eight years. And then comes back one day without warning, and expects us to welcome him."

"Is he nice?" asked Ruth.

"What do you mean by nice?" Bee asked, glad for once of Ruth's interest in the personal.

"Is he nice to look at? And does he talk nicely or has he a frightful accent?"

"He is exceedingly nice to look at, and he has no accent whatsoever."

"Where has he been all this time?" Eleanor asked.

"Mexico and the States, mostly."

"Mexico!" said Ruth. "How romantic! Does he wear a black sailor hat?"

"A what? No, of course he doesn't. He wears a hat like anyone else."

"How often have you seen him, Aunt Bee?" Eleanor asked.

"Just once. A few weeks ago."

"Why didn't you tell us about it then?"

"It seemed better to wait until the lawyers were finished with him and he was ready to come home. You couldn't all go rushing up to London to see him."

"No, I suppose not. But I expect Simon would have liked to go up and see him, wouldn't you, Simon, and we wouldn't have minded? After all, Patrick was his twin."

"I don't believe for one moment that it is Patrick," Simon said, in a tight, careful voice that was worse than shouting.

"But, Simon!" Eleanor said.

Bee sat in a dismayed silence. This was worse than she had anticipated.

"But, Simon! Aunt Bee has seen him. She must know."

"Aunt Bee seems to have adopted him."

Much worse than she had anticipated.

"The people who *have* adopted him, Simon, are Cosset, Thring and Noble. A not very emotional firm, I think you'll agree. If there had been the faintest doubt of his being Patrick, Cosset, Thring and Noble would have discovered it during those weeks. They have left no part of his life since he left England unaccounted for."

"Of *course* whoever it is has had a life that can be checked! What did they expect? But what possible reason can they have for believing that he is Patrick?"

"Well, for one thing, he is your double."

This was clearly unexpected. "My double?" he said vaguely.

"Yes. He is even more like you than when he went away."

The colour had come back to Simon's face and the stuff on the bones had begun to look like flesh again; but now he looked stupid, like a boxer who is taking too much punishment.

"Believe me, Simon dear," she said, "it *is* Patrick!"

"It isn't. I know it isn't. You are all being fooled!"

"But, Simon!" Eleanor said. "Why should you think that? I know it won't be easy for you to have Patrick back—it won't be easy for any of us—but there's no use making a fuss about it. The thing is there and we just have to accept it. You are only making things worse by trying to push it away."

"How did this—this creature who says he is Patrick, how did he get to Mexico? How did he leave England? And when? And where?"

"He left from Westover in a ship called the *Ira Jones*."

"Westover! Who says so?"

"He does. And according to the harbourmaster, a ship of that name did leave Westover on the night that Patrick went missing."

Since this seemed to leave Simon without speech, she went on: "And everything he did from then on has been checked. The hotel he worked at in Normandy is no longer there, but they have found the ship he sailed from Havre in—it's a tramp, but it belongs to a firm in Brest—and people have been shown photographs and identified him. And so on, all the way back to England. Till the day he walked into Mr. Sandal's office."

"Is that how he came back?" Eleanor asked. "Went to see old Mr. Sandal?"

"Yes."

"Well, I should say that proves that he is Patrick, if anyone is in any doubt about it. But I don't know why there should be doubt at all. After all, it would be very easy to catch him out if he wasn't Patrick, wouldn't it? All the family things he would know . . ."

"It *isn't* Patrick."

"It is a shock for you, Simon, my dear," Bee said, "and, as Eleanor says, it won't be easy for you. But I think it will be easier when you see him. Easier to accept him, I mean. He is so undeniably an Ashby, and so very like you."

"Patrick *wasn't* very like me."

Eleanor saved Bee from having to reply to that. "He was, Simon. Of course he was. He was your twin."

"If *I* ran away for years and years, would you believe I was me, Jane?" Ruth asked.

"You wouldn't stay away for years, and years, anyhow," Jane said.

"What makes you think I wouldn't?"

"You'd come home in no time at all."

"Why would I come home?"

"To see how everyone was taking your running away."

"When is he coming, Aunt Bee?" Eleanor asked.

"On Tuesday. At least that is what we had arranged. But if you would like to put it off a little—until you grow more used to the idea, I mean . . ." She glanced at Simon, who was looking sick and baffled. In her most apprehensive moments she had never pictured a reaction as serious as this.

"If you flatter yourself that I shall grow used to the idea, you are wrong," Simon said. "It makes no difference to me when the fellow comes. As far as I'm concerned he is not Patrick and he never will be."

And he walked out of the room. Walking, Bee noticed, not very steadily, as if he were drunk.

"I've never known Simon like that before," Eleanor said, puzzled.

"I should have broken it to him differently. I'm afraid it is my fault. I just—didn't want to make him different from anyone else."

"But he loved Patrick, didn't he? Why shouldn't he be glad about it? Even a *little* glad!"

"I think it is horrid that someone can come and take Simon's place, without warning, like that," Jane said. "Simply horrid. And I don't wonder that Simon is angry."

"Aunt Bee," said Ruth, "can I wear my blue on Tuesday when Patrick comes?"

Chapter 9

*B*ee waited till Evensong would be over, and then walked
across the fields to the Rectory. Ostensibly, she was going to
tell them the news; actually she was going to pour out her troubles
to George Peck. When George could withdraw his mind sufficiently from the classic world to focus it on the present one, he was
a comfortable person to talk to. Unemotional and unshockable. Bee
supposed that an intimate acquaintance with classic on-goings,
topped-off with a cure of souls in a country parish, had so conditioned him to shocks that he had long ago become immune from
further attack. Neither ancient iniquity nor modern English backsliding surprised him. So it was not to Nancy, her friend, that she
was taking her unquiet heart, but to the Rector. Nancy would wrap
her round with warm affection and sympathy, but it was not sympathy she needed; it was support. Besides, if she was to find understanding it would not be with Nancy, who had forgotten Patrick's
very existence, but with George Peck, who would most certainly remember the boy he had taught.

So she walked in the sunlight over the fields, through the
churchyard, and into the Rectory garden through the little iron gate
that had caused that terrific row in 1723. Very peaceful it all was
tonight, and very peaceful were the rival smiths, sleeping within
twelve feet of each other over there in the corner in good Clare
earth. Some day quite soon, she thought, pausing with her hand on
the delicate iron scroll, my trouble too will be just an old song; one
must try to keep things in proportion. But it was her head talking
to her heart, and her heart would not listen.

She found the Rector where she knew he would be. Always after Evensong it was his habit to go and stare at something in the
garden; usually at something at the farther end of the garden from
which he could not be too easily recalled to the trivialities of social
obligation. This evening he was staring at a purple lilac and pollut-

ing the fragrant air with a pipe that smelt like a damp bonfire. "There should be a by-law against pipes like George's," his wife had said, and the present sample was no exception. It depressed Bee still further.

He glanced up as she came down the path and went back to staring at the lilac. "Wonderful colour, isn't it," he said. "Odd to think that it is just an optical illusion. What colour is a lilac when you are not looking at it, I wonder?"

Bee remembered that the Rector had once broken it to the twins that a clock does not tick if no one is in the room. She had found Ruth being surreptitious in the hall, and Ruth, when asked what this noiseless progress was occasioned by, had said that she was "trying to sneak up on the drawing-room clock." She wanted to catch it not ticking.

Bee stood by the Rector in silence for a little, looking at the glory and trying to arrange her thoughts. But they would not arrange.

"George," she said at length, "you remember Patrick, don't you?"

"Pat Ashby? Of course." He turned to look at her.

"Well, he didn't die at all. He just ran away. That is what the note meant. And he is coming back. And Simon isn't pleased." A great round shameless tear slipped out of her eye and ran down her cheek. She brushed it off her chin and went on staring at the lilac.

George extended a bony forefinger and gently speared the front of her shoulder with it.

"Sit down," he said.

She sat down on the seat behind her, under the arch of the young green honeysuckle, and the Rector sat down beside her. "Now, tell me," he said; and she told him. All the bewildering story, in the proper order and with full detail; Mr. Sandal's telephone call, the journey to town, the top-floor-back in Pimlico, the investigations of Cosset, Thring and Noble, the rescue by Great-uncle Charles, the ultimate facing of the facts and announcing them to the family, the family reaction.

"Eleanor is a little cold about it, but reasonable as she always is. The thing is there and she is going to make the best of it. Jane, of course, is partisan, and sorry for Simon, but she will get over that when she meets her brother in the flesh. She is a friendly soul by nature."

"And Ruth?"

"Ruth is planning her wardrobe for Tuesday," Bee said, tartly.

The Rector smiled a little. "The happy ones of the earth, the Ruths."

"But Simon . . . How can one account for Simon?"

"I don't think that that is very difficult, you know. Simon would have had to be a saint to welcome back a brother who was going to supplant him. A brother, moreover, who has been dead to him since the age of thirteen."

"But, George, his twin! They were inseparable."

"I think that thirteen is further removed from twenty-one than almost any other equidistant points in life. It is a whole lifetime away. An association that ended at thirteen has little but sentimental value for the boy of twenty-one. Latchetts has been Simon's for—what is it?—eight years; he has known for eight years that he would come into his mother's money at twenty-one: to be deprived of all that without warning would upset a stronger character than Simon's."

"I expect I did it badly," Bee said. "The way I told them, I mean. I should have told Simon first, privately. But I did so want to keep them all on the same level. To pretend that they would all be equally glad. Taking Simon apart and telling him before the others would have—would have—"

"Anticipated the trouble."

"Yes. Something like that, I suppose. I suppose I had known quite well that his reaction would be—different from the others. And I just wanted to minimise the difference. I had never imagined for a moment, you see, that his reaction would be so violent. That he would go to the length of denying that Patrick was alive."

"That is only his method of pushing the unwelcome fact away from him."

"Unwelcome," Bee murmured.

"Yes, unwelcome. And very naturally unwelcome. You make things difficult for yourself if you don't accept that fundamental fact. *You* remember Patrick with your adult mind, and are rejoiced that he is still alive." He turned his head to look at her. "Or—are you?"

"Of *course* I am!" she said, a shade too emphatically. But he let it go.

"Simon doesn't remember him with an adult mind or adult emotions. To Simon he is a remembered emotion; not a present one. He has no present love to fight his present—hatred with."

"Oh, George."

"Yes; it is best to face it. It would take an almost divine love to combat the resentment that Simon must be feeling now; and there has never been anything in the least divine about Simon. Poor Simon. It is a wretched thing to have happened to him."

"And at the very worst moment. When we were all ready for celebration."

"At least this is the answer to something that has puzzled me for eight years."

"What is that?"

"The fact of Patrick's suicide. I could never reconcile it with the Patrick I knew. Patrick was a sensitive child, but he had a tremendous fund of good common sense; a balance. A far better equilibrium, for instance, than the less sensitive but more brilliant Simon. He had also, moreover, a great sense of obligation. If Latchetts was suddenly and unaccountably his he might be overwhelmed to the point of running away, but not unbalanced to the point of taking his life."

"Why did we all so unquestioningly accept the suicide theory?"

"The coat on the cliff-top. The note—which did read like a suicide one, undoubtedly. The complete lack of anyone who had seen him after old Abel met him between Tanbitches and the cliff. The persistence with which suicides use that particular part of the coast for their taking-off. It was the natural conclusion to come to. I don't remember that we ever questioned it. But it had always stayed in my mind as an unaccountable thing. Not the method, but the fact that Patrick should have taken his own life. It was unlike everything I knew about Patrick. And now we find that, after all, he did no such thing."

"I shut my eyes and the lilac is no colour; I open them and it is purple," Bee was saying to herself; which was her way of keeping her tears at bay. Just as she counted objects when in danger of crying at a play.

"Tell me, are you pleased with this adult Patrick who has come back?"

"Yes. Yes, I am pleased. He is in some ways very like the Patrick who went away. Very quiet. Self-contained. Very considerate. Do you remember how Patrick used to turn and say: 'Are you all right?' before he began whatever he was planning to do on his own? He still thinks of the other person. Didn't try to—rush me, or take his welcome for granted. And he still keeps his bad times to himself. Simon always came flying to one with his griefs and grievances, but

Patrick dealt with his own. He seems still to be able to deal with his own."

"Has he had a bad time, then, do you think?"

"I gather it hasn't been a bed of roses. I forgot to tell you that he is lame."

"Lame!"

"Yes. Just a little. Some accident with a horse. He is still mad about horses."

"That will make you happy," George said. He said it a little wryly, being no horseman.

"Yes," agreed Bee with a faint smile for the wryness. "It is good that Latchetts should go to a real lover."

"You rate Simon as a poor lover?"

"Not poor. Indifferent, perhaps. To Simon horses are a means of providing excitement. Of enhancing his prestige. A medium for trade; for profitable dickering. I doubt if it goes further than that. For horses as—people, if you know what I mean, he has little feeling. Their sicknesses bore him. Eleanor will stay up for nights on end with a horse that is ill, sharing the nursing fifty-fifty with Gregg. The only time Simon loses sleep is when a horse he wants to ride, or jump, or hunt, has a 'leg.' "

"Poor Simon," the Rector said reflectively. "Not the temperament to make a successful fight against jealousy. A very destructive emotion indeed, jealousy."

Before Bee could answer, Nancy appeared.

"Bee! How nice," she said. "Were you at Evensong, and did you see the latest contingent from our local school for scandalisers? Two adolescents who are 'studying the prevalent English superstitions': to wit, the Church of England. A boy, very hairy for fourteen, it seemed to me; and a girl with eleven combs keeping up her not very abundant wisps. What would you say a passion for combs was an indication of? A sense of insecurity?"

"Beatrice has come with a very wonderful piece of news," the Rector said.

"Don't tell me Simon has got himself engaged."

"No. It is not about Simon. It's about Patrick."

"Patrick?" Nancy said uncertainly.

"He is alive." And he told her how.

"Oh, Bee, my dear," Nancy said, putting her arms round her friend, "how glorious for you. Now you won't have to wonder any more."

That Nancy's first reaction was to remember that private night-mare of hers broke Bee down altogether.

"You need a drink," Nancy said, briskly. "Come along in and we'll finish what's left in the sherry bottle."

"A deplorable reason for drinking sherry," the Rector said.

"What is?"

"That one 'needs a drink.' "

"An even more deplorable reason is that if we don't drink it Mrs. Godkin will. She has had most of the rest of the bottle. Come along."

So Bee drank the Rectory sherry and listened while George en-lightened Nancy on the details of Patrick Ashby's return. Now that her weight of knowledge was shared with her own generation, the burden was suddenly lighter. Whatever difficulties lay ahead, there would be George and Nancy to support and comfort her.

"When is Patrick coming?" Nancy asked; and the Rector turned to Bee.

"On Tuesday," Bee told them. "What I can't decide is the best way of spreading the news in the district."

"That's easy," Nancy said. "Just tell Mrs. Gloom."

Mrs. Gloom kept the sweets-tobacco-and-newspaper shop in the village. Her real name was Bloom, but her relish for disaster caused her to be known, first by the Ledingham and Ashby chil-dren, and later by all and sundry, as Mrs. Gloom.

"Or you could send yourself a postcard. The post office is almost as good. That is what Jim Bowden did when he jilted the Heywood girl. Sent his mother a telegram announcing his wedding. The fuss was all over before he came back."

"I'm afraid we are going to be at the exact centre of the fuss un-til the nine days' wonder is over," Bee said. "One must just put up with it."

"Ah, well, my dear, it's a *nice* sort of fuss," Nancy said, comfort-ing.

"Yes. But the situation is so—so incalculable. It's like—like—"

"I know," Nancy said, agreeing. "Like walking on jelly."

"I was going to say picking one's way over a bog, but I think the jelly is a better description."

"Or one of those uneven floors at fun fairs," the Rector said un-expectedly, as Bee took her leave.

"How do you know about fun fairs, George?" his wife asked.

"They had one at the Westover Carnival a year or two ago, I seem to remember. A most interesting study in masochism."

"You see now why I have stuck to George," Nancy said, as she walked with Bee to the garden gate. "After thirteen years I am still finding out things about him. I wouldn't have believed that he even knew what a fun fair was. Can you picture George lost in contemplation of the Giant Racer?"

But it was not of Nancy's George that she was thinking as she walked away through the churchyard, but of the fun-fair floor that she was doomed to walk in the days ahead. She turned in at the south porch of the church and found the great oak door still unlocked. The light of the sunset flooded the grey vault with warmth, and the whole building held peace as a cup holds water. She sat down on a bench by the door and listened to the silence. A companionable silence which she shared with the figures on the tombs, the tattered banners, the names on the wall, the Legion's garish Union Jack, and the slow ticking of a clock. The tombs were all Ledingham ones: from the simple dignity of the Crusader to the marble family that wept with ostentatious opulence over the eighteenth-century politician. The Ashbys had no crusaders and no opulence. Their memorials were tablets on the wall. Bee sat there and read them for the thousandth time. "Of Latchetts" was the refrain. "Of Latchetts in this parish." No field-marshals, no chancellors, no poets, no reformers. Just the yeoman simplicity of Latchetts; the small-squire sufficiency of Latchetts.

And now Latchetts belonged to this unknown boy from half a world away.

"A great sense of obligation," the Rector had said, speaking of the Patrick he remembered. And that had been the Patrick that she, too, remembered. And that Patrick would have written to them.

Always she came back to that in her mind. The Patrick they knew would never have left them in grief and doubt for eight years.

"Some psychological difficulty," Mr. Sandal had said. And after all, he *had* run away. A sufficiently unlikely thing for Patrick to do. Perhaps he had been overcome by shame when he came to himself. And yet. And yet.

That kind child who so automatically asked: "Are you all right?" That child with the "great sense of obligation"?

Chapter 10

*A*nd while Bee sat and stared at the Ashby tablets in the church at Clare, Brat Farrar was standing in the back room in Pimlico in a brand-new suit and a state of panic.

How had he got himself into this? What could he have been thinking of? He, Brat Farrar. How did he ever think that he could go through with it? How had he ever in the first place consented to lend himself to such a plan?

It was the suit that had shocked him into realisation. The suit was wrong-doing made concrete and manifest. It was a wonderful suit. The kind of suit that he dreamed of possessing; so unremarkable, so unmistakable once you had remarked it: English tailoring at its unobtrusive best. But he stood looking at himself in the mirror in a kind of horror.

He couldn't do it, that was all. He just couldn't do it.

He would duck, before it was too late.

He would send back the goddamned suit to the tailor, and send a letter to that woman who had been so nice, and just duck out of sight.

"What!" said the voice. "And pass up the greatest adventure of your life? The greatest adventure that has happened to any man within living memory?"

"Adventure my foot. It's plain false pretences."

They wouldn't bother to look for him. They would be too relieved to have him out of their hair. He could duck without leaving a ripple.

"And leave a fortune behind?" said the voice.

"*Yes*, and leave a fortune behind. Who wants a fortune, anyhow?"

They would have his letter to insure them against any further nuisance from his side, and they would just let him go. He would write to that woman who, because she was kind, had kissed him before she was sure, and confess, and say he was sorry, and that would be that.

"And pass up the chance of owning a stud?"

"Who wants a stud? The world's lousy with horses."

"And you are going to own some, perhaps?"

"I may, some day. I may."

"Pigs may fly."

"Shut up."

He would write to Loding and tell him that he would be no party to his criminal schemes.

"And waste all that knowledge? All that training?"

"I should never have started it."

"But you did start it. You finished it. You are pinned to the gills with knowledge worth a fortune. You can't waste it, surely!"

Loding would have to whistle for that fifty per cent. How could he ever have thought of letting himself be an instrument in the hands of a crook like Loding!

"A very amusing and intelligent crook. On the highest level of crookery. Nothing to be ashamed of, believe me."

He would go to a travel agency to-morrow morning and get a berth out of the country. Anywhere out of the country.

"I thought you wanted to stay in England?"

He would put the sea between him and temptation.

"Did you say temptation? Don't tell me that you're still wavering!"

He hadn't enough left for a fare to America, but he had enough to take him quite a distance. The travel agency would offer him a choice of places. The world was wide and there was a lot of fun left in it. By Tuesday morning he would be out of England, and this time he would stay out.

"And never see Latchetts at all?"

He would find some—"What did you say?"

"I said: And never see Latchetts at all?"

He tried to think of an answer.

"Stumped you, haven't I!"

There must be an answer.

"Money, and horses, and fun, and adventure are common change. You can have them anywhere in the world. But if you pass up Latchetts now you pass it up for good. There won't be any going back."

"But what has Latchetts to do with me?"

"You ask that? You, with your Ashby face, and your Ashby bones, and your Ashby tastes, and your Ashby colouring, and your Ashby blood."

"I haven't any evidence at all that—"

"And your Ashby blood, I said. Why, you poor little brute of a foundling, Latchetts is your belonging-place, and you have the immortal gall to pretend that you don't care a rap about it!"

"I didn't say I didn't care. Of course I care."

"But you'll walk out of this country to-morrow, and leave Latchetts behind? For always? Because that is what it amounts to, my boy. That is the choice before you. Take the road of high adventure and on Tuesday morning you will see Latchetts, Duck, and you will never see it at all."

"But I'm not a crook! I can't do something that is criminal."

"Can't you? You've been giving a pretty good imitation of it these last few weeks. And enjoying it too. Remember how you enjoyed that tight-rope business on that first visit to old Sandal? How you enjoyed all the others? Even with a K.C. sitting across the table and doing a sort of mental X-ray on you. You loved it. All that is wrong with you just now is cold feet. Nerves. You want to see Latchetts as an Ashby. You want horses. You want adventure. You want a life in England. Go to Latchetts on Tuesday and they are all yours."

"But—"

"You came half across the world to that meeting with Loding. Was that just chance? Of course not. It was all meant. Your destiny is at Latchetts. Your destiny. What you were born for. Your destiny. At Latchetts. You're an Ashby. Half across a world to a place you never heard of. Destiny. You can't pass up destiny. . . ."

Brat got slowly out of the brand-new suit, and hung it up with orphanage neatness on its fine new hanger. Then he sat down on the edge of his bed and buried his face in his hands.

He was still sitting there when the darkness came.

Chapter 11

*I*t was a beautiful day, the day that Brat Farrar came to Latchetts, but a restless little wind kept turning the leaves over so that
in spite of the sunlight and the bright air the world was filled with
a vague unease and a promise of storm.

"Much too shiny!" thought Bee, looking at the landscape from
her bedroom window after breakfast. " 'Tears before night?' as Nannie used to say of too exuberant children. However. At least he will
arrive in sunshine."

She had been greatly exercised in her mind over that arrival. It
was to be as informal as possible; that was a thing that was agreed
to by all concerned. Someone would meet him at the station and
bring him home, and there would be luncheon with only the family present. The question was: Who was to meet him? The twins
had held that the whole family should go to the station, but that, of
course, was not to be thought of. The prodigal could hardly be
welcomed publicly on the platform at Guessgate for the entertainment of the railway staff and casual travellers between Westover
and Bures. She herself could not go without giving the returning
Patrick an air of being her protégé; which was something to be
avoided at all costs. She had not forgotten Simon's sneer about her
"adoption" of Patrick. Simon—the obvious choice for the role of
welcomer—was not available; since her announcement on Sunday
he had slept at home but had not otherwise taken part in Latchetts
activities, and Bee's attempt to talk to him in his room late on
Monday night had been futile.

So she had been relieved when Eleanor offered to drive the four
miles to the station at Guessgate and bring Patrick back.

The present load on her mind was that family meal after his arrival. If Simon did not turn up how was his absence to be explained? And if he did turn up what was that lunch going to be
like?

She turned to go down for one more rehearsal with the cook—their third cook in the last twelve months—when she was waylaid by Lana, their "help." Lana came from the village, and had gilt hair and varnished fingernails and the local version of the current makeup. She "obliged" only because her "boy-friend" worked in the stables. She would sweep and dust, she explained when she first came, because that was "all right," but she would not wait at table because that was "menial." Bee had longed to tell her that no one with her hands, or her breath, or her scent, or her manners, would ever be allowed to hand an Ashby a plate; but she had learned to be politic. She explained that there was, in any case, no question of waiting at table; the Ashbys always waited on themselves.

Lana had come to say that the "vacuum was vomiting instead of swallowing," and domestic worries closed once more over Bee's head and swamped domestic drama. She came to the surface in time to see Eleanor getting into her little two-seater.

"Aren't you taking the car?" she asked. "The car" was the family vehicle, Eleanor's disreputable little conveyance being known as "the bug."

"No. He'll have to take us as we are," Eleanor said.

Bee noticed that she had not bothered to change into a dress. She was wearing the breeches and gaiters in which she had begun the morning.

"Oh, take me, take me!" Ruth said, precipitating herself down the steps and on to the car, but taking good care, Bee noticed, to keep "her blue" away from the bug's dusty metal.

"No," Eleanor said firmly.

"I'm sure he would like me to be there. One of my generation, I mean. After all, he knows you. It won't be exciting for him to see you the way it would be for him to see—"

"No. And keep off if you don't want that dazzling outfit of yours to be mucked up."

"I do think it is selfish of Eleanor," Ruth said, dusting her palms as she watched the car grow small between the lime trees. "She just wants to keep the excitement to herself."

"Nonsense. It was arranged that you and Jane should wait here. Where is Jane, by the way?"

"In the stables, I think. She isn't interested in Patrick."

"I hope she comes in in good time for lunch."

"Oh, she will. She may not be interested in Patrick, but she is always ready for her meals. Is Simon going to be there, at lunch?"

"I hope so."

"What do you think he will say to Patrick?"

If the peace and happiness of Latchetts was going to break down into a welter of discord the twins must go away to school. They would be going to school in a year or two, anyhow; they had much better go now than live in an atmosphere of strain and hatred.

"Do you think there will be a scene?" Ruth asked, hopefully.

"Of course not, Ruth. I wish you wouldn't dramatise things."

But she wished too that she could count on there being no scene. And Eleanor, on her way to the station, was wishing the same thing. She was a little nervous of meeting this new brother, and annoyed with herself for being nervous. Her everyday clothes were her protest against her own excitement: a pretence that nothing of real moment was about to happen.

Guessgate, which served three villages but no town, was a small wayside station with a fairly heavy goods business but little passenger traffic, so that when Brat climbed down from his carriage there was no one on the platform but a fat countrywoman, a sweating porter, the ticket-collector, and Eleanor.

"Hullo," she said. "You are very like Simon." And she shook hands with him. He noticed that she wore no makeup. A little powdering of freckles went over the bridge of her nose.

"Eleanor," he said, identifying her.

"Yes. What about your luggage? I have just the small car but the dickey holds quite a lot."

"I have just this," he said, indicating his "grip."

"Is the rest coming later?"

"No, this is all I possess."

"Oh." She smiled just a little. "No moss."

"No," he said, "no moss," and began to like her very much.

"The car is out in the yard. Through this way."

"Been away, Mr. Ashby?" the ticket-collector said, accepting his piece of pasteboard.

"Yes, I've been away."

At the sound of his voice the ticket-collector looked up, puzzled.

"He took you for Simon," Eleanor said, as they got into the car; and smiled properly. Her two front teeth crossed just a little; which gave her face an endearing childishness. It was a cool, determined, small face when she was serious. "You couldn't have come home at a better time of the year," she said, as they scrunched over the gravel of the station yard and fled away into the landscape.

"Home," he thought. Her hair was the colour of corn so ripe that it was nearly white. Pale, silky stuff, very fine. It was brushed back into a knot, as if she could not be bothered to do anything else with it.

"The blossom is just beginning. And the first foals are here."

The knees in their worn whipcord were just like a boy's. But the bare arms protruding from the jacket she wore slung over her shoulders were delicately round.

"Honey has a filly foal that is going to make history. Wait till you see it. You won't know Honey, of course. She was after your time. Her real name is Greek Honey. By Hymettus out of a mare called Money For Jam. I hope you will be impressed with our horses."

"I expect to be," he said.

"Aunt Bee says that you're still interested in them. Horses, I mean."

"I haven't done much on the breeding side, of course. Just preparing horses for work."

They came to the village.

So this was Clare. This warm, living, smiling entity was what those little flat squares on the map had stood for. There was the White Hart; there was the Bell. And up there behind, on its knoll, was the church where the Ashby tablets hung.

"The village is looking nice, isn't it?" Eleanor said. "Not changed a bit since I can remember. Not changed since the Flood, if it comes to that. The names of the people in the houses come in the same order down the street as they did in the time of Richard the Second. But of course you know that! I keep thinking of you as a visitor."

Beyond the village, he knew, were the great gates of Clare Park. He waited, mildly curious, to see the entrance to what had been Alec Loding's home. It proved to be a sweeping curve of iron lace flanked by two enormous pillars bearing on each a lion passant. Astride the farther lion was a small boy clad in a leopard-skin rug with green baize edging, a seaside pail worn helmet-wise, and nothing else that was visible. A very long brass poker stood up lance-wise from its rest on his bare foot.

"It's all right," Eleanor said. "You did see it."

"That comforts me quite a bit."

"Did you know that Clare was a school nowadays?"

He had nearly said yes, when he remembered that this was

merely one of the things Loding had told him, not one of the things that he was supposed to know.

"What kind of school?"

"A school for dodgers."

"Dodgers?"

"Yes. Anyone who loathes hard work and has a parent with enough money to pay the fees makes a beeline for Clare. No one is forced to learn anything at Clare. Not even the multiplication table. The theory is that one day you'll feel the need of the multiplication table and be seized with a mad desire to acquire the nine-times. Of course, it doesn't work out like that at all."

"Doesn't it?"

"Of course not. No one who could get out of the nine-times would ever dream of acquiring it voluntarily."

"And if they don't do lessons what do they do all day?"

"Express their personalities. They draw things; or make things; or whitewash the coach-house; or dress up, like Antony Toselli. That was Tony on the lion. I teach some of them to ride. They like that. Riding, I mean. I think they are so bored with easy things that they find something a little difficult simply fascinating. But of course it has to be something out of the ordinary. The difficult thing, I mean. If it was a difficulty that everyone was supposed to overcome they wouldn't be interested. That would bring them down to the common level of you and me. They wouldn't be 'different' any longer."

"Nice people."

"Very profitable to Latchetts, anyhow. And here *is* Latchetts."

Brat's heart rose up into his throat. Eleanor turned slowly into the white gateway between the limes.

It was just as well that she was going slowly, for she had no sooner entered the green tunnel than something like a giant blue butterfly shot out from the boles of the trees and danced wildly in front of the car.

Eleanor braked and swore simultaneously.

"Hullo! Hullo!" shouted the butterfly, dancing to Brat's side of the car.

"You little idiot," Eleanor said. "You deserve to be killed. Don't you know that a driver doesn't see well coming into the avenue out of the sunlight?"

"Hullo! Hullo, Patrick! It's me! Ruth. How d'you do. I came to ride up with you. To the house, you know. Can I sit on your knee?

There isn't very much room in that awful old car of Eleanor's, and I don't want to crush my dress. I hope you like my dress. It is put on specially for your coming home. You're very good-looking, aren't you? Am I what you expected?"

She waited for an answer to that, so Brat said that he hadn't really thought about it.

"Oh," said Ruth, much dashed. "We thought about you," she said reprovingly. "No one has talked about anything else for days."

"Ah well," Brat said, "when *you* have run away for years and years people will talk about *you*."

"I shouldn't dream of doing anything so *outré*," Ruth said, unforgiving.

"Where did you get that word?" Eleanor asked.

"It's a very good word. Mrs. Peck uses it."

Brat felt that he ought to paint in a little local colour by saying: "How are the Pecks, by the way?" But he had no mind to spare for artifice. He was waiting for the moment when the limes would thin out and he would see Latchetts.

For the moment when he would be face to face with his "twin."

"Simon hasn't come back yet," he heard Ruth say; and saw her sideways glance at Eleanor. The glance, even more than the information, shook him.

So Simon wasn't waiting on the doorstep for him. Simon was "away" somewhere and the family was uneasy about it.

Alec Loding had disabused him of the idea that a feudal staff reception would await him at Latchetts; that there would be a line of servants, headed by the butler and descending in strict order to the latest tweeny, to welcome the Young Master to the ancestral home. That, Loding had said, had gone out with bustles, and Latchetts had never had a butler, anyhow. And he had known too that there would be no array of relations. The children's father had been an only son with one sister, Aunt Bee. The children's mother had been an only daughter with two brothers: both of them killed by the Germans before they were twenty. The only near Ashby relation was Great-uncle Charles, reported by Loding to be now nearing Singapore.

But it had not occurred to him that all the available Ashbys might not be there. That there might be dissenters. The ease of his meeting with Eleanor had fooled him. Metaphorically speaking, he picked up the reins that had been lying on his neck.

The car ran out of the thin spring green of the avenue into the wide sweep in front of the house, and there in the too-bright gusty sunlight stood Latchetts; very quiet, very friendly, very sure of itself. The gabled front of the original building had been altered by some eighteenth-century Ashby to conform with the times, so that only the tiled roof showed its age and origin. Built in the last days of Elizabeth, it was now blandly "Queen Anne." It stood there in its grasslands, undecorated and sufficient; needing no garden for its enhancement. The green of the small park flowered at its heart into the house itself, and any other flowering would have been redundant.

As Eleanor swept round towards the house, Brat saw Beatrice Ashby come out on the doorstep, and a sudden panic seized him; a mad desire to blurt out the truth to her and back out there and then; before he had put foot over the doorstep; before he was definitely "on" in the scene. It was going to be a damnably difficult and awkward scene and he had no idea how to play it.

It was Ruth who saved him from the worst moment of awkwardness. Before the car had come to a halt she was piping her triumph to the world, so that Brat's arrival somehow took second place to her own achievement.

"I met him after all, Aunt Bee! I met him after all. I came up from the gate with them. You don't mind, do you? I just strolled down as far as the gate and when I got there I saw them coming, and they stopped and gave me a lift and here we are and so I met him after all."

She linked her arm through Brat's and tumbled with him out of the car, dragging him behind her as if he were a find of her own. So that it was with a mutual shrug for this display of personality that Brat and Bee greeted each other. They were united for the moment in a rueful amusement, and by the time the amusement had passed so had the moment.

Before awkwardness could come flooding back, there was a second distraction. Jane came riding round the corner of the house on Fourposter on her way to the stables. The instant check of her hands on the reins when she saw the group at the door made it obvious that she had not planned on being one of that group. But it was too late now to back out, even if backing out had been possible. It was never possible to back away from anything that Fourposter might happen to be interested in; he had no mouth and an insatiable curiosity. So forward came the reluctant Jane on a highly interested pony. As Fourposter came to a halt she slid politely to the ground and stood there shy and defensive. When Bee introduced her she laid a small limp hand in Brat's and after a moment withdrew it.

"What is your pony's name?" Brat asked, aware of her antagonism.

"That's Fourposter," Ruth said, appropriating Jane's mount. "The Rector calls him the Equine Omnibus."

Brat put out his hand to the pony, who refused the advance by withdrawing a pace and looking contemptuously down his Roman nose. As a gesture it was pure burlesque; a Victorian gesture of repudiation from a Victorian drama.

"A comedian," remarked Brat; and Bee, delighted with his perception, laughed.

"He doesn't like people," Jane said, half-repressive, half-defending her friend.

But Brat kept his hand out, and presently Fourposter's curiosity overcame his stand-offishness and he dropped his head to the waiting hand. Brat made much of him, till Fourposter capitulated entirely and nuzzled him with elephantine playfulness.

"*Well!*" said Ruth, watching. "He never does that to *anyone!*"

Brat looked down into the small tight face by his elbow, at the small grubby hands clutching the reins so tightly.

"I expect he does to Jane when no one is around," he said.

"Jane, it is time you were cleaned up for lunch," Bee said, and turned to lead the way indoors.

And Brat followed her, over the threshold.

Chapter 12

I have put you in the old night nursery," Bee said. "I hope you don't mind. Simon has the room that he used to share with— that you used to share with him." Oh, dear, what a gaffe, she thought; shall I ever be able to think of him as Patrick? "And to give you one of the spare rooms was to treat you like a visitor."

Brat said that he would be glad to have the night nursery.

"Will you go up now, or will you have a drink first?"

"I'll go up now," Brat said, and turned to the stairway.

He knew that she had been waiting for this moment; waiting for the moment when he must show knowledge of the house. So he turned from her and led the way upstairs; up to the big first landing and down the narrow corridor to the north wing, and to the children's rooms facing west from it. He opened the third of the four doors and stood in the room that Nora Ashby had arranged for her children when they were small. One window looked west over the paddocks and the other north to the rise of the down. It was on the quiet side of the house, away from the stables and the approach from the road. He stood at the window looking at the soft blue English distances, thinking of the brilliant mountains beyond the whirling dust of the West, and very conscious of Bee Ashby behind him.

There was something else that he must take the initiative about.

"Where is Simon?" he said, and turned to face her.

"He is like Jane," she said. "Late for lunch. But he'll be in at any moment."

It was smoothly done, but he had seen her shy at his unheralded question, as if he had flicked a whip. Simon had not come to meet him; Simon had not been at Latchetts to greet him; Simon, it was to be deduced, was being difficult.

Before he could pursue the subject she took the initiative from him.

"You can have the nursery bathroom all to yourself, but *do* go slow on the hot water, will you? Fuel is a dreadful problem. Now wash and come down at once. The Pecks sent over some of the Rectory sherry."

"Aren't they coming to lunch?"

"No, they're coming to dinner to-night. Lunch is for family only."

She watched him turn to the fourth door, which he knew to be the bathroom of the nursery wing, and went away looking comforted. He knew why she was comforted: because he had known his way about the house. And he felt guilty and ill at ease. Fooling Mr. Sandal—with a K.C. sitting opposite you and gimletting holes in you with cynical Irish eyes—had been one thing; fooling Mr. Sandal had been fun. But fooling Bee Ashby was another thing altogether.

He washed absentmindedly, turning the soap in his hands with his eyes on the line of the down. There was the turf he had wanted to ride on; the turf he had sold his soul for. Presently he would get a horse and go up there and ride in the quiet, away from human relationships and this fantastic game of human poker, and up there it would once more seem right and worth while.

He went back to his room and found a brassy blonde in tight flowered rayon tweaking the wallflower in the bowl on the windowsill.

"Hullo," said the blonde. "Welcome home, and all that."

"Thanks," Brat said. Was this someone that he should know? Surely not!

"You're very like your brother, aren't you?"

"I suppose so." He took his brushes from his "grip" and put them on the dressing-table; it was a symbolical taking-possession.

"You won't know me, of course. I'm Lana Adams from the village. Adams the joiner was my father. I oblige because my boy-friend works in the stables."

So that is what she was: the help. He looked at her and was sorry for the boy-friend.

"You look a lot older than your brother, don't you? I suppose it's knocking about the world that does it. Having to look out for yourself, and all that. Not being spoilt like your brother. You'll excuse me saying it but spoilt he is. That's why he's made all this to-do about you coming back. Silly, I call it. You've only to look at you to know that you're an Ashby. Not much point in saying you're not, I should think. But you take my tip and stand up to him. He can't stand being stood up to. Been humoured all his life, I should say. Don't let it get you down."

As Brat went silently on with his unpacking, she paused; and before she could resume Eleanor's cool voice said from the doorway: "Have you everything you want?"

The blonde said hastily: "I was just welcoming Mr. Patrick back," and, having flung Brat a radiant smile, made a hip-swing exit from the room.

Brat wondered how much Eleanor had heard.

"It's a nice room this," Eleanor said, "except that it doesn't get the morning sun. That bed is from Clare Park. Aunt Bee sold the little ones and bought that one at the Clare sale. It's nice, isn't it? It was the one in Alec Ledingham's room. Except for that the room is just the same."

"Yes; the old wallpaper, I notice."

"Robinson Crusoe and company. Yes. I had a great weakness for Hereward the Wake. He had such an enchanting profile." She pointed to Hereward's place in the pattern of fictional heroes that Nora had chosen for her children's nightly entertainment.

"Is the nursery-rhyme paper still next door?"

"Yes, of course. Come and see."

He went with her, but while she rehearsed the pictured tales his mind was busy with the village girl's revelation about Simon and with the ironic fact that he was to sleep in Alec Loding's bed.

So Simon had refused to believe that he was Patrick.

"Not much point in saying you're not, I should think." That could only mean that Simon, in the face of all the evidence, refused to accept him.

Why?

He followed Eleanor downstairs, still wondering.

Eleanor led him into a big sunny sitting-room where Bee was pouring sherry, and Ruth was picking out a tune on a piano.

"Would you like to hear me play?" Ruth asked, inevitably.

"No," Eleanor said, "he wouldn't. We've been looking at the old wallpapers," she said to Bee. "I'd forgotten how in love with Hereward I used to be. It's just as well that I removed from him in time or he might have become a fixation or something."

"I never *liked* that baby stuff on the walls," Ruth said.

"*You* never *read*, so you couldn't know anything about them," Eleanor said.

"We gave up using the nursery wing when the twins ceased to have a Nanny," Bee said. "It was too far away from the rest of the house."

"It was a day's march to call the twins in the morning," Eleanor said, "and as Ruth always needed calling several times we had to move them into the normal family orbit."

"Delicate people need more sleep," Ruth said.

"Since when have you been delicate?" asked Eleanor.

"It's not that I'm delicate but that Jane's more robust, aren't you, Jane?" she said, appealing to Jane, who sidled into the room, the hair at her temples still damp from her hasty ablutions.

But Jane's eyes were on Bee.

"Simon is here," she said in a small voice; and crossed the room to stand near Bee as if for reassurance.

There was an instant of complete silence. In the moment of suspended animation only Ruth moved. Ruth sat up and sparkled with anticipation.

Then Bee's hand moved again and went on filling the glasses. "That is very nice," she said. "We needn't keep luncheon back after all."

It was so beautifully done that Brat, knowing what he knew now, felt like applauding.

"Where is Simon?" Eleanor asked casually.

"He was coming downstairs," Jane said; and her eyes went back to Bee.

The door opened and Simon Ashby came in.

He paused a moment, looking across at Brat, before closing the door behind him. "So you've come," he said.

There was no emphasis on the words; no apparent emotion in the tone.

He walked slowly across the room until he was standing face to face with Brat by the window. He had abnormally clear grey eyes with a darker rim to the iris, but they had no expression in them. Nor had his pale features any expression. He was so tightly strung, Brat thought, that if you plucked him with a finger he would twang.

And then quite suddenly the tightness went.

He stood for a moment searching Brat's face; and his own was suddenly slack with relief.

"They won't have told you?" he said, drawling a little, "but I was prepared to deny with my last breath that you were Patrick. Now

that I've seen you I take all that back. Of course you are Patrick."
He put out his hand. "Welcome home."

The stillness behind them broke in a flurry of movement and
competing voices. There was a babble of mutual congratulation, of
chinking glasses and laughter. Even Ruth, it seemed, stifled her disappointment at being done out of melodrama, and devoted her talents to wheedling a little more sherry into her glass than the "sip"
that was the twins' allowance for health-drinking.

But Brat, drinking the golden liquid and thanking heaven that
the moment was over, was puzzled. Why *relief?* he was thinking.

What had Ashby expected? What had he been afraid of?

He had denied the possibility of Brat's being Patrick. Had that
been just a defence against hope; an insurance against ultimate disappointment? Had he said to himself: I won't believe that Patrick
is alive, and so when it is proved that he isn't I won't have hoped for
nothing? And was that overwhelming relief a moment ago due
merely to the realisation that he was after all Patrick?

It didn't fit.

He watched Simon being the life of the party, and wondered
about him. A few moments ago Ashby had been steeled to face
something, and now it seemed he had been—let off. That was it.
That was what that sudden relief had been. The reaction of someone steeled to face the worst and suddenly reprieved.

Why should he feel reprieved?

He took the small puzzle into luncheon with him, and it lay at
the back of his mind while he dealt with the problems of Ashby
conversation and answered their crowding questions.

"You're in!" gloated the voice inside him. "You're in! You're sitting as of right at the Ashby table, and they're all tickled to death
about it."

Well, perhaps not all. Jane, loyal to Simon, was a small silent oa-
sis in the right talk. And it was not to be expected that Simon himself, for all his capitulation, was tickled to any great extent. But Bee,
entirely uncritical of that capitulation, was radiant; and Eleanor
melted moment by moment from conversational politeness to a
frank interest.

"But a Comanche bridle is a kind of twitch, isn't it?"

"No; just a gag. The rope goes through the mouth the way a bit
does. It's best for a led horse. He'll follow to lessen the pull."

Ruth, having quite forgiven his lack of speculation about her looks, paid assiduous court to him; and she was the only one who called him Patrick.

This became more noticeable as the meal went on, and her continual interjection of "Patrick!" as she claimed his attention contrasted with the others' half-conscious avoidance of the name. Brat wished that his sole "follower" had proved to be Jane and not Ruth. If he had ever had a small sister he would have liked her to be just like Jane. It annoyed him that he had difficulty in meeting Jane's eyes. It cost him the same effort to meet her regard with equanimity as it did to meet the eyes of the portrait behind her. The dining-room was positively papered with portraits, and the one behind Jane was of William Ashby the Seventh, wearing the uniform of the Westover Fencibles, in which he had proposed to resist the invasion of Napoleon the First. Brat had learned those portraits off by heart, sitting under the pagoda in Kew Gardens, and every time he lifted his eyes to those of William Ashby the Seventh he was plagued by the ridiculous notion that William knew all about the pagoda.

One thing helped him enormously, however, in this first difficult meeting with the Ashbys. The tale he had to tell, as Loding had pointed out during that meal at the Green Man, was, except for its beginnings, true; it was the tale of his own life. And since the whole family with one accord avoided any reference to the events which had catapulted him into that life, the conversational ground he moved on was firm. There was need for neither sidestepping nor manoeuvre.

Nor was there any need for him to "mind his manners"; and for that too Alec Loding had given loud thanks. It seemed that, short of a first-class and very strict Nannie, there was no more rigorous training in the civilised consumption of food than was to be had at a first-class orphanage. "My God," Loding had said, "if I ever have any change from a round of drinks I'll send it to that caravanserai of yours, as a mark of my gratitude that you were not brought up in some genteel suburb. Gentility is practically ineradicable, my boy. And whatever Pat Ashby might conceivably do, it is quite inconceivable that he should ever stick out his little finger when he drank."

So Brat had no social habits to unlearn. Indeed, his orthodoxy slightly disappointed Ruth, always on the lookout for the flamboyant.

"You don't eat with your fork," she said; and when he looked puzzled, added: "The way they do in American pictures; they cut things up with their knives and forks and then they change the fork over to their other hand and eat with it."

"I don't chew gum either," he pointed out.

"I wonder how that very elaborate method of dealing with their food arose," Bee said.

"Perhaps knives were scarce in the early days," Eleanor suggested.

"Knives were far too useful to be scarce in a pioneer society," Simon said. "It's much more likely that they lived so long on hash that when they got things in slices their instinct was to make hash of it as soon as possible."

Brat thought, listening to them, how very English it all was. Here he was, back from the dead, and they were calmly discussing American table manners. There was no blackslapping, congratulatory insistence on the situation as there would be in a transatlantic household. They avoided the do-you-remember theme as determinedly as Americans would have wallowed in it. Remembering his friends of the Lazy Y, he thought what a fine exhibition of Limey snootiness this would be from the point of view of Pete, and Hank, and Lefty.

But perhaps the happiness on Bee's face would have impressed even Lefty.

"Do you smoke?" Bee asked, when she had poured the coffee; and she pushed the cigarette box over to him. But Brat, who liked his own brand, took out his case and offered the contents to her.

"I've given them up," Bee said. "I have a bank balance instead."

So Brat offered the case to Eleanor.

Eleanor paused with her fingers touching the cigarettes and bent forward to read something engraved on the inside of the case.

"Brat Farrar," she said. "Who is that?"

"Me," said Brat.

"You? Oh, yes; Farrar, of course. But why Brat?"

"I don't know."

"Did they call you that? Brat, I mean?"

"Yes."

"Why Brat?"

"I don't know. Because I was small, I guess."

"Brat!" Ruth said delighted. "Do you mind if I call you Brat? Do you?"

"No. I haven't been called anything else for a large part of my life."

The door opened and Lana appeared to say that a young man had called to see Miss Ashby and she had put him in the library.

"Oh, what a nuisance," Bee said. "What does he want, do you know?"

"He says he's a reporter," Lana said, "but he doesn't look like a reporter to me. Quite tidy and clean and polite." Lana's experience of the Press, like Brat's knowledge of middle-class life, was derived solely from films.

"Oh, *no!*" Bee said. "Not the Press. Not already."

"The *Westover Times* he says he is."

"Did he say why he had come?"

"Come about Mr. Patrick, of course," Lana said, turning her thumb in Patrick's direction.

"Oh, God," Simon groaned, "and the fatted calf not half-way down our gullets. I suppose it had to come sooner or later!"

Bee drank the remains of her coffee. "Come on, Brat!" she said, putting out her hand and pulling him to his feet. "We might as well go and get it over. You too, Simon." She led Brat out of the room, laughing at him, and still hand in hand with him. The warm friendliness of her clasp sent a rush of emotion through him that he could not identify. It was like nothing he had so far experienced in life. And he was too busy with thoughts of the reporter to pause to analyse it.

The library was the dark room at the back of the house where Bee kept her roll-top desk, her accounts, and her reference books. A small young man in a neat blue suit was puzzling over a stud book. At their entrance he dropped the book and said in a rich Glasgow accent: "Miss Ashby? My name is Macallan. I'm working on the *Westover Times*. I'm awfully sorry about barging in like this, but I thought you'd have finished eating this long time."

"Well, we began late, and I'm afraid we lingered over things," Bee said.

"Uh, huh," said Mr. Macallan understandingly. "A very special occasion. I've no right to be spoiling it for you, but 'the first with the latest' is my motto, and just this minute you're the latest."

"I suppose you mean my nephew's homecoming."

"Just that."

"And how did you find out about it so soon, Mr. Macallan?"

"One of my contacts heard about it in one of the Clare pubs."

"A deplorable word," said Bee.

"Pub?" Mr. Macallan said, puzzled.

"No. Contact."

"Och, well one of my stooges, if you like that better," Mr. Macallan said agreeably. "Which of these young gentlemen is the returned prodigal, may I ask?"

Bee introduced Brat and Simon. Some of the cold tightness had come back to Simon's face; but Brat, who had been around when Nat Zucco had cut his throat in the kitchen of his ex-wife's eating-house and had witnessed the activities of the American Press on that occasion, was entranced by this glimpse of news-gathering in Britain. He answered the obvious questions put to him by Mr. Macallan and wondered if there would be any suggestion of a photograph. If so, he must get out of it somehow.

But it was Bee who saved him from that. No photograph, said Bee. No; positively *no* photograph. All the information he liked to ask for, but no photograph.

Mr. Macallan accepted this, but reluctantly. "The story of the missing twin won't be half so good without a photograph," he complained.

"You're not going to call it. 'The Missing Twin,' are you?" Bee said.

"No; he's going to call it 'Back From The Dead,' " Simon said, speaking for the first time. His cool drawl fell on the room like a shadow.

Mr. Macallan's pale blue eyes went to him, rested a moment on him consideringly, and then came back to Bee. "I *had* thought of 'Sensation at Clare,' " he said, "but I doubt the *Westover Times* would stand for it. A very conservative organ. But I expect the *Daily Clarion* will do better."

"The *Clarion!*" Bee said. "A London paper! But—but I hope there is no question of that. This is an entirely local—an entirely family matter."

"So was that affair in Hilldrop Crescent," Mr. Macallan said.

"What affair?"

"Crippen was the name. The world's Press is composed of family affairs, Miss Ashby."

"But this is of no possible interest to anyone but ourselves. When my nephew—disappeared, eight years ago, the *Westover Times* reported it quite—quite incidentally."

"Ay, I know. I looked it up. A small paragraph at the bottom of page three."

"I fail to see why my nephew's return should be of any more interest than his disappearance."

"It's the man-bites-dog affair over again. People go to their deaths every day, but the amount of people who come back from the dead is very small indeed, Miss Ashby. Coming back from the dead, in spite of the advances of modern science, is still a sensation. And that's why the *Daily Clarion* is going to be interested."

"But how should they hear about it?"

"Hear about it!" Mr. Macallan said, genuinely horrified. "Miss Ashby, this is my own *scoop*, don't you see."

"You mean you are going to send the story to the *Clarion*?"

"Assuredly."

"Mr. Macallan, you mustn't; you really must not."

"Listen, Miss Ashby," Mr. Macallan said patiently. "I agreed about the no-photographs prohibition, and I respect the agreement—I won't go sneaking around the countryside trying to snap the young gentleman unawares, or anything like that—but you can't ask me to give up a scoop like this. Not a scoop of 'London daily' dimensions." And as Bee, caught in the toils of her natural desire to be fair, hesitated, he added: "Even if I didn't send them the story, there's nothing to hinder a sub-editor lifting the story from the *Westover Times* and making it front-page news. You wouldn't be a scrap better off and I'd have lost my chance of doing a bit of good for myself."

"Oh, dear," Bee said, tacitly acknowledging that he was right, "I suppose that means swarms of newspaper men from London."

"Och, no. Only the *Clarion*. If it's the *Clarion*'s story none of the rest will bother. And whoever they send down you don't have to worry. They're all Balliol men, I understand."

With which flip at the English Press, Mr. Macallan looked round for his hat and made motions of departure.

"I'm very grateful to you, and to you, Mr. Ashby, for being so accommodating in the matter of information. I won't keep you any longer. May I offer you my congratulations on your happiness"—for a second the pale blue eyes rested in mild benevolence on Simon—"and my thanks for your kindness."

"You're a long way from home, aren't you, Mr. Macallan?" Bee said conversationally as she went to the front door with him.

"Home?"

"Scotland."

"Oh, I see. How did you know I was Scots? Oh, my name, of course. Ay, it's a far cry to Glasgow; but this is just the long way round to London, so to speak. If I'm going to work on an English paper it's as well to know something of the—the—"

"Aborigines?" suggested Bee.

"Local conditions, I *was* going to say," Mr. Macallan said solemnly.

"Haven't you a car?" Bee said, looking at the empty sweep in front of the door.

"I left it parked at the end of your drive there. I've never got used to sweeping up to strange houses as if I owned them."

With which startling exhibition of modesty the little man bowed, put on his hat, and walked away.

Chapter 13

*I*n the library, as the voices of Bee and Mr. Macallan faded down the hall and into the out-of-doors, there was silence. Brat, uncertain of the quality of that silence, turned to the shelves and began to consider the books.

"Well," said Simon, lounging in the window, "another hazard safely negotiated."

Brat waited, trying to analyse the sound of the words while they still hung in the air.

"Hazard?" he said at length.

"The snags and bunkers in the difficult business of coming back. It must have taken some nerve, all things considered. What moved you to it, Brat—homesickness?"

This was the first frank question he had been asked, and he suddenly liked Ashby the better for it.

"Not exactly. A realisation that my place was here, after all." He felt that that had a self-righteous sound, and added: "I mean, that my place in the world was here."

This was succeeded by another silence. Brat went on looking at books and hoped that he was not going to like young Ashby. That would be an unforeseen complication. It was bad enough not to be able to face the person he was supplanting, now that he was left alone in a room with him; but to find himself liking that person would make the situation intolerable.

It was Bee who broke the silence.

"I think we should have offered the poor little man a drink," she said, coming in. "However, it's too late now. He can get one from his 'contact' at the White Hart."

"The Bell, I suspect," Simon said.

"Why the Bell?"

"Our Lana frequents that in preference to the White Hart."

"Ah, well. The sooner everyone knows the sooner the fuss will be over." She smiled at Brat to take any sting from the words. "Let's go and look at the horses, shall we? Have you any riding clothes with you, Brat?"

"Not any that Latchetts would recognise as riding clothes," Brat said, noticing how thankfully she seized on the excuse not to call him Patrick.

"Come up with me," Simon said, "and I'll find you something."

"Good," said Bee, looking pleased with him. "I'll collect Eleanor."

"Did you like being given the old night nursery?" Simon asked, preceding Brat upstairs.

"Very much."

"Same old paper, I suppose you noticed."

"Yes."

"Do you remember the night we had an Ivanhoe-Hereward battle?"

"No; I don't remember that."

"No. Of course you wouldn't."

Again the words hung on the silence, teasing Brat's ear with an echo of their tone.

He followed young Ashby into the room he had shared with his brother, and noticed that there was no suggestion in the room that it had ever been shared by another person. It was, on the contrary, very much Simon's own room; being furnished with his possessions to an extent that made it as much a sitting-room as a bedroom. Shelves of books, rows of silver cups, framed sketches of horses on the walls, easy chairs, and a small desk with a telephone extension on it.

Brat moved over to the window while Simon rummaged among his clothes for appropriate garments. The window, as he knew, looked over the stables, but a green hedge of lilac and laburnum trees hid the buildings from view. Above them, in the middle distance, rose the tower of Clare church. On Sunday, he supposed, he would be taken to service there. Another hazard. Hazard had been an odd word for young Ashby to choose, surely?

Simon emerged from the cupboard with breeches and a tweed coat.

"I think these ought to do," he said, throwing them on the bed. "I'll find you a shirt." He opened a drawer of the chest which held his dressing mirror and toilet things. The chest stood by the window, and Brat, still uneasy in Ashby's vicinity, moved over to the fireplace and began to look at the silver cups on the mantelpiece. All of them were prizes for horsemanship, and they ranged from a hurdle race at the local point-to-point to Olympia. All of them except one were of a date too late to have concerned Patrick Ashby; the exception being a small and humble chalice that had been awarded to Simon Ashby on "Patience" for being the winner of the juvenile jumping class at the Bures Agricultural Show in the year before Patrick Ashby committed suicide.

Simon, looking round and seeing the small cup in Brat's hand, smiled and said: "I took that from you, if you remember."

"From me?" Brat said, unprepared.

"You would have won on Old Harry if I hadn't done you out of it by doing a perfect second round."

"Oh, yes," Brat said. And to lay a new scent: "You seem to have done well for yourself since."

"Not badly," Simon said, his attention going back to his shirt drawer. "But I'm going to do a lot better. Ballsbridge and all stops to Olympia." It was said absentmindedly, but with confidence; as if the money to buy good horseflesh would automatically be available. Brat wondered a little, but felt that this was no moment for discussing the financial future.

"Do you remember the object that used to hang at the end of your bed?" Simon asked casually, pushing the shirt drawer shut.

"The little horse?" Brat said. "Yes, of course. Travesty," he added, giving its name and mock breeding. "By Irish Peasant out of Bog Oak."

He turned from the exhibits on the mantelpiece, meaning to collect the clothes that Ashby had looked out for him; but as he turned he saw Ashby's face in the mirror, and the naked shock on that face stopped him in his tracks. Simon had been in the act of pushing the drawer shut, but the action was arrested half-way. It was, thought Brat, exactly the reaction of someone who has heard a telephone ring: the involuntary pause and then the resumed movement.

Simon turned to face him, slowly, the shirt hanging over his left forearm. "I think you'll find that all right," he said, taking the shirt in his right hand and holding it out to Brat but keeping his eyes on Brat's face. His expression was no longer shocked; he merely looked blank, as if his mind were elsewhere. As if, Brat thought, he were doing sums in his head.

Brat took the shirt, collected the rest of the clothes, expressed his thanks, and made for the door.

"Come down when you're ready," Simon said, still staring at him in that blank way. "We'll be waiting for you."

And Brat, making his way round the landing to his own room in the opposite wing, was shocked in his turn. Ashby hadn't expected him to know that. Ashby had been so certain, indeed, that he would not know about the toy horse that he had been rocked back on his heels when it was clear that he did know about it.

And that meant?

It could mean only one thing.

It meant that young Ashby had not believed for a moment that he was Patrick.

Brat shut the door of the peaceful old night nursery behind him and stood leaning against it, the clothes cascading slowly to the ground from his slackened arm.

Simon had not been fooled. That touching little scene over the sherry glasses had been only an act.

It was a staggering thought.

Why had Simon bothered to pretend?

Why had he not said at once, "You are not Patrick and nothing will make me believe that you are!"

That had been his original line, if Lana's report and the family atmosphere meant anything. Up to the last moment they had been unsure of his reaction to Brat's arrival; and he had gratified them all by a frank and charming capitulation.

Why the gratuitous capitulation?

Was it—was it a trap of some sort? Were the welcome and the charm merely the grass and green leaves laid over a pit he had prepared?

But he could not have known until the actual face-to-face meeting that he, Brat, was not Patrick. And he had apparently known instantly that the person he was facing was not his brother. Why then should he . . .

Brat stooped to pick up the clothes from the floor and straightened himself abruptly. He had remembered something. He had remembered that odd relaxing on Simon's part the moment he had had a good look at himself. That suggestion of relief. Of being "let off."

So that was it!

Simon had been afraid that it *was* Patrick.

When he found that he was faced with a mere impostor he must have had difficulty in refraining from embracing him.

But that still did not explain the capitulation.

Perhaps it was a mere postponement; a setting to partners. It might be that he planned a more dramatic *dénouement*; a more public discrediting.

If that were so, Brat thought, there were a few surprises in store for young Mr. Ashby. The more he thought about the surprises the better he began to feel about things. As he changed into riding clothes he recalled with something like pleasure that shocked face in the mirror. Simon had been unaware that he, Brat, had passed any "family" tests. He had not been present when Brat passed the searching test of knowing his way about the house; and he had not had any chance of being told about it. All that he knew was that Brat had satisfied the lawyers of his identity. Having been faced with, to him, an obvious impostor he must have looked forward with a delighted malice to baiting the pretender.

Yes; all ready to pull the wings off flies was young Mr. Ashby.

The first tentative pull had been about the Ivanhoe-Hereward battle. Something that only Patrick would know about. But something too that he might easily have forgotten.

The little wooden horse was something that only Patrick would know about and something that Patrick could in no circumstances have forgotten.

And Brat had known about it.

Not much wonder that Ashby had been shocked. Shocked and at sea. Not much wonder that he looked as if he were doing sums in his head.

Brat spared a kind thought for that master tutor, Alec Loding. Loding had missed his vocation; as a coach he was superb. Sometime, somewhere, something was going to turn up that Alec Loding had either forgotten to tell him about or had not himself known; and the moment was going to be a very sticky one; but so far he had known his lines. So far he was word perfect.

Even to the point of Travesty.

A little object of black bog oak, it had been. "Rudimentary and surrealist," Loding had said, "but recognisable as a horse." It had originally been yoked to a jaunting car, the whole turnout being one of those bog-oak souvenirs that tourists brought back from Ireland in the days before it was more advisable to bring home the bacon. The small car, being made of bits and pieces, soon went the way of all nursery objects; but the little horse, chunky and solid, had survived and had become Patrick's halidom and fetish. It was Alec

Loding who had been responsible for its naming; one winter evening over nursery tea. He and Nancy had looked in at Latchetts on their way home from some pony races, hoping for a drink; but finding no one at home except Nora, who was having tea upstairs with her children, they had joined the nursery party. And there, while they made toast, they had sought a name for Patrick's talisman. Patrick, who always referred to the object as "my little Irish horse," and was conscious of no need for a more particular description, rejected all suggestions.

"What would you call it, Alec?" his mother asked Loding, who had been too busy consuming buttered toast to care what a toy was called.

"Travesty," Alec had said, eyeing the thing. "By Irish Peasant out of Bog Oak."

The grown-ups had laughed, but Patrick, who was too young to know the meaning of the word, thought that Travesty was a fine, proud-sounding name. A name filled with the tramplings and prancings and curvettings of war horses, and worthy therefore of the little black object of his love.

"He kept it in a pocket," Loding had said in Queen Adelaide's sitting-room (it was raining that morning), "but when he grew too big for that it hung on a frayed Stewart tartan ribbon off a box of Edinburgh rock at the end of his bed."

Yes; not much wonder that Simon had been shaken to the core. No stranger to the Ashby family could have known about Travesty.

Brat, buttoning himself into Ashby garments and noticing how a well-cut article adapts itself even to an alien figure, wondered what Simon was making of the problem. He had no doubt learned by now that the "impostor" not only knew about the existence of Travesty but had walked about the house with the confidence of long acquaintance. A faint flare of excitement woke in Brat. The same excitement that had made those interviews with old Mr. Sandal so enjoyable. For the last couple of hours—ever since his arrival at Guessgate station—he had been received with kindness and welcome, and the result had been a faint queasiness, a sort of spiritual indigestion. What had been a dice game for dangerous stakes had become a mere taking candy from a baby. Now that Simon was his opponent, the thing was once more a contest.

Not dice, thought Brat, considering himself in the mirror. Chequers rather. A matter of cautious moves, of anticipating attack, of blocking an unforeseen thrust. Yes; chequers.

Brat went downstairs buoyed up with a new anticipation. He would not any more have to stand with his back to young Ashby because he was unable to face him. The pieces were laid out on the board and they faced each other across it.

Through the wide-open door of the hall he could see the Ashbys grouped in the sunlight on the steps and went forward to join them. Ruth, with her chronically roving eye, was the first to see him.

"Oh, doesn't he look nice," said Ruth, still paying court.

Brat was aware that he looked "nice" but wished that Ruth had not called attention to his borrowed finery. He wondered if anyone had ever smacked Ruth Ashby.

"You must get some riding clothes from Walters as soon as may be," Bee said. "These are almost a good enough fit to do as a pattern. Which would save you having to go to town for measurements only."

"Those breeches aren't Walters's," Simon said, eyeing the clothes lazily. "They're Gore and Bowen's. Walters never made a good pair of breeches in his life."

He was draped against the wall by the doorway, relaxed and apparently at peace with the world. His eyes travelled slowly up from Brat's boots to his shirt, and came to rest, with the same detached interest on his face.

"Well," he said amiably, pushing himself off the wall, "let's go and look at some horses."

Not chequers, thought Brat. No, not chequers. Poker.

"We'll show you the stables this afternoon," Bee said, "and leave the mares until after tea."

She ran an arm through Brat's and gathered Simon in with her other one, so that they went towards the stables arm-in-arm like old friends; Eleanor and the twins tailing along behind.

"Gregg is all agog to see you," she said. "Not that you'll notice any agogness, of course. His face doesn't permit anything like that. You'll just have to believe me that he is excited inside."

"What happened to old Malpas?" Brat asked, although he had heard all about old Malpas one afternoon outside the Orangery.

"He became very astigmatic," Bee said. "Figuratively speaking. We could never see eye to eye. He didn't really like taking orders from a woman. So he retired about eighteen months after I took over, and we've had Gregg ever since. He's a misanthropist, and a misogynist, and he has his perks, of course; but he doesn't let any of them interfere with the running of the stables. There was a noted drop in the fodder bills after old Malpas left. And the local people like Gregg better because he buys his hay direct from the farmers and not through a contractor. And I think on the whole he's a better horsemaster than Malpas was. Cleverer at getting a poor horse into condition. And a genius at doctoring a sick one."

Why doesn't he relax? she was thinking, feeling the boy's arm rigid under her fingers. The ordeal is over now, surely. Why doesn't he relax?

And Brat for his part was conscious of her fingers clasping his forearm as he had never been conscious before of a woman's hand. He was experiencing again that surge of an unrecognised emotion that had filled him when Bee had taken his hand to lead him to the interview with Mr. Macallan.

But his first sight of the stables distracted his attention from both emotional and ethical problems.

His reaction to the stable yard at Latchetts was very much the reaction of a merchant seaman to his first acquaintance with one of His Majesty's ships. A sort of contemptuous but kindly amusement. A wonder that the thing wasn't finished off with ribbons. Only the fact that several horses' heads protruded inquisitively from the loose boxes convinced him that the place was seriously used as a stable at all. It was like nothing so much as one of the toy models he had seen in expensive toy shops. He had always imagined that those gay little affairs with their bright paint and their flowers in tubs had been manufactured to a child's taste. But apparently they had been authentic copies of an actual article. He was looking at one of the articles at this moment, and being very much surprised.

Not even the dude ranch had prepared him for this. There was paint galore at the dude ranch, but there was also a tradition of toughness. The dude ranch would never have thought of mowing the bit of grass in the middle until it looked like a square of green baize, so neat-edged and trim that it looked as if you could roll it up and take it away. At the dude ranch there was still a suggestion of the mud, dung, sweat, and flies which are inseparable from a life alongside horseflesh.

The little building on the left of the yard entrance was the saddle room, and in the saddle-room door was the stud-groom, Gregg. Gregg had in the highest degree that disillusioned air common to those who make their living out of horses. He had also the horseman's quality of agelessness. He was probably fifty, but it would not be surprising to be told that he was thirty-five.

He took two paces forward and waited for them to come up to him. The two paces were his concession to good manners, and the waiting emphasised the fact that he was receiving them on his own ground. His clear blue eyes ran over Brat as Bee introduced them, but his expression remained polite and inscrutable. He gave Brat a conventional welcome and a crushing hand-clasp.

"I hear you've been riding horses in America," he said.

"Only western ones," Brat said. "Working horses."

"Oh, these work," Gregg said, inclining his head towards the boxes. Don't be in any doubt about it, the tone said. It was as if he had understood Brat's distrust of the spit and polish. His eyes went past Brat to Eleanor standing behind and he said: "Have you seen what's in the saddle room, Miss Eleanor?"

From the gloom of the saddle room there materialised as if in answer to his question the figure of a small boy. He materialised rather reluctantly as if uncertain of his welcome. In spite of a change of costume Brat recognised him as the rider of the stone lion at the gates of Clare. His present apparel, though less startling, was hardly more orthodox than his leopard-skin outfit. He was wearing a striped football jersey that clung to his tadpole body, a pair of jodhpurs so large that they hung in a fold above each skinny knee, a steeple-chasing jockey cap with the crash-lining showing at the back, and a pair of grubby red moccasins.

"Tony!" said Eleanor. "Tony, what are you doing here?"

"I've come for my ride," said Tony, his eyes darting to and fro among the group like lizards.

"But this isn't the day for your ride."

"Isn't it, Eleanor? I thought it was."

"You know quite well that you don't ride on a Tuesday."

"I thought this was Wednesday."

"You're a dreadful little liar, Tony," Eleanor said dispassionately. "You knew quite well this wasn't Wednesday. You just saw me in a car with a stranger and so you came along to find out who the stranger was."

"Eleanor," murmured Bee, deprecating.

"You don't know him," Eleanor said, as if the subject of discussion was not present. "His curiosity amounts to a mania. It's almost his only human attribute."

"If you take him to-day you won't have to take him to-morrow," Simon said, eyeing the Toselli child with distaste.

"He can't come and expect to ride just when he feels like it!" Eleanor said. "Besides, I said I wouldn't take him out again in these things. I told you to get a pair of boots, Tony."

The black eyes stopped being lizards and became two brimming pools of grief. "My father can't afford boots for me," said Tony with a catch in his alto, guaranteed to draw blood from a stone.

"Your father has £12,000 a year free of income tax," Eleanor said briskly.

"If you took him to-day, Nell," Bee said, "you'd be free to help me to-morrow when half the countryside comes dropping in to have a look at Brat." And, as Eleanor hesitated: "You might as well get it over now that he's here."

"And he'll still be wearing moccasins to-morrow," Simon drawled.

"Indian riders wear moccasins," Tony observed mildly, "and they are very good riders."

"I don't think your destitute father would be very pleased if you turned up with moccasins in the Row. You get a pair of boots. And if I take you this afternoon, Tony, you are not to think that you can make a habit of this."

"Oh, no, Eleanor."

"If you come on the wrong day again you'll just have to go away without a ride."

"Yes, Eleanor." The eyes were lizards again, darting and sliding.

"All right. Go and ask Arthur to saddle Spuds for you."

"Yes, Eleanor."

"No thanks, you'll observe," Eleanor said, watching him go.

"What is the crash helmet for?" Simon asked.

"His skull is as thin as cellophane, he says, and must be protected. I don't know how he got one that size. Out of a circus, I should imagine. What with his Indian longings I suppose I should be thankful that he doesn't turn up in a headband and a single feather."

"He will one day, when it occurs to him," Simon said.

"Oh, well, I suppose I'd better go and saddle Buster. I'm sorry, Brat," she said, smiling a little at him, "but it is really one of those blessings in disguise. The pony he rides will be a lot less fresh with him to-day than he would be to-morrow, after a day in the stable. And you don't really need three people to show you round. I'll go round the paddocks with you after tea."

Chapter 14

*B*rat's tendency to be patronising about spit and polish died painlessly and permanently somewhere between the fourth and fifth boxes. The pampered darlings that he had been prepared to find in these boxes did not exist. Thoroughbred, half-bred, cob, or pony, the shine on their coats came from condition and grooming and not from coddling in warm stables; Brat had lived long enough with horses to recognise that. The only ribbons that had ever been tied on these animals were rosettes of red or blue or yellow; and the rosettes were quite properly in the saddle room.

Bee did the honours, with Gregg as assistant; but since it is not possible for four horsemen to consider any given horse without entering into a discussion, the occasion soon lost the slight formality of its beginnings and degenerated into a friendly free-for-all. And presently Brat, always a little detached from his surroundings, noticed that Bee was leaving the discussion more and more to Simon. That it was Simon instead of Bee who said: "This is a throwout from a racing stable that Eleanor is schooling into a hack," or "Do you remember old Thora? This is a son of hers by Cold Steel." That Bee was quite deliberately edging herself out.

The twins had soon grown tired and evaporated; Ruth because horses bored her, and Jane because she knew all that was to be known about the horses and did not like the thought that they belonged to a person she did not know. And Gregg, congenitally taciturn, fell more and more into the background with Bee. So that in no time at all it was Simon's occasion; Simon's and Brat's.

Simon behaved as if he had not a care in the world. As if this were just another afternoon and Brat was just another visitor. A rather privileged and knowledgeable visitor; unquestionably welcome. Brat, coming to the surface every now and then from his beguilement with the horses, would listen to the light drawl discussing pedigree, conformation, character, or prospects; would watch the cool untroubled profile, and wonder. "A bit light in front," the cool voice would be saying, and the untroubled eyes would be running over the animal as if no more important matter clouded the sun. "Nice, though, don't you think?" or "This one should really be turned out: he's been hunted all the winter; but I'm going pothunting on him this summer. And anyhow Bee's awfully stingy with her pasture."

And Bee would put in her tuppenceworth and fade out again.

It was Bee who "ran" Latchetts, but the various interests involved were divided between the three Ashbys. Eleanor's chief concerns were the hacks and hunters, Simon's were hunters and show jumpers, and Bee's were the mares and the Shetland ponies. During Bill Ashby's lifetime, when Latchetts was purely a breeding establishment, the hacks and hunters in the stables had been there for family use and amusement. Occasionally, when there happened to be an extra-good horse in the stable, Bee, who was a better horsewoman than her brother, would come down from London for a week or two to school it and afterwards show it for him. It was good advertisement for Latchetts; not because Latchetts ever dealt in made horses but because the simple repetition of a name is of value in the commercial world, as the writers of advertisements have discovered. Nowadays the younger Ashbys, under Bee's supervision, had turned the stables into a profitable rival to the brood mares.

"Mr. Gates is asking if he can speak to you, sir," said the stableman to Gregg. And Gregg excused himself and went back to the saddle room.

Fourposter came to the door of his box, stared coldly at Brat for a moment, and then nudged him jocosely with his Roman nose.

"Has he always been Jane's?" Brat asked.

"No," Bee said, "he was bought for Simon's fourteenth birthday. But Simon grew so fast that in a year or so he had outgrown him, and Jane at four was already clamouring to ride a 'real' horse instead of a Shetland. So she fell heir to him. If he ever had any manners he has forgotten them, but he and Jane seem to understand each other."

Gregg came back to say that it was Miss Ashby that Gates wanted to see. It was about the fencing.

"All right, I'll come," Bee said. And as Gregg went away: "What he really wants to see is Brat, but he'll just wait till tomorrow like the rest of the countryside. It's so like Gates to try to steal a march.

Opportunism is his middle name. If you two go trying out any of the horses, do be back for tea. I want to go round the paddocks with Brat before it gets dark."

"Do you remember Gates?" Simon asked, opening the door of another box.

"No, I don't think so."

"He's the tenant of Wigsell."

"What became of Vidler, then?"

"He died. This man was married to his daughter and had a small farm the other side of Bures."

Well, Simon had dealt him the cards he needed that time. He looked at Simon to see how he had taken it, but Simon's whole interest seemed to be in the horse he was leading out of the box.

"These last three boxes are all new acquisitions, bought with an eye on the show ring. But this is the pick of the bunch. He's a four-year-old by High Wood out of a mare called Shout Aloud. His name is Timber."

Timber was a black without a brown hair in him. He had a rudimentary white star, and a ring of white on each coronet; and he was quite the handsomest thing in horseflesh that Brat had ever been at close quarters with. He came out of his box with an air of benevolent condescension, as if aware of his good looks and pleased that they should be the subject of tribute. There was something oddly demure about him, Brat thought, watching him. Perhaps it was just the way he was standing, with his forefeet close together. Whatever it was it didn't go with the self-confident, considering eye.

"Difficult to fault, isn't he?" Simon said.

Brat, lost in admiration of his physical conformation, was still puzzled by what he thought of as the butter-wouldn't-melt air.

"He has one of the best-looking heads I've ever seen on a horse," Simon said. "And just look at the bone." He led the horse round. "And a sweet mover too," he said.

Brat went on looking in silence, admiring and puzzled.

"Well?" Simon said, waiting for Brat's comment.

"Isn't he *conceited*!" said Brat.

Simon laughed.

"Yes, I suppose he is. But not without cause."

"No. He's a good-looker all right."

"He is more than that. He's a lovely ride. And he can jump anything you can see the sky over."

Brat moved forward to the horse and made friendly overtures.

Timber accepted the gesture without responding. He looked gratified but faintly bored.

"He should have been a tenor," Brat said.

"A tenor?" Simon said. "Oh, I see. The conceit." He considered
the horse afresh. "I suppose he is rather pleased with himself. I
hadn't thought about it before. Would you like to try him out, by
the way?"

"I certainly would."

"He ought to have some exercise to-day and he hasn't so far." He
hailed a stable-man. "Arthur, bring a saddle for Timber."

"Yes, sir. A double bridle, sir?"

"No; a snaffle." And, as the man went, to Brat: "He has a mouth
like a glove."

Brat wondered if he was merely reluctant to submit that tender
mouth to the ham hands of a Westerner with a curb rein at his disposal.

While Timber was being saddled they inspected the two remaining "acquisitions." They were a long-backed bay mare with a
good head and quarters ("Two good ends make up for a middle," as
Simon said) who was called Scapa; and Chevron, a bright chestnut
of great quality with a nervous eye.

"What are you riding?" Brat asked, as Simon led Chevron back
to his box.

Simon bolted the half-door and turned to face him.

"I thought you might like to have a look round by yourself," he
said. And as Brat, surprised by this piece of luck, was momentarily
wordless: "Don't let him get lit-up too much, will you, or he'll break
out again when he has been dried."

"No, I'll bring him back cool," Brat said and flung his leg across
his first English horse.

He took one of the two whips that Arthur was holding out for
his choosing, and turned the horse to the inner end of the yard.

"Where are you going?" Simon asked, as if surprised.

"Up to the down, I think," Brat said, as if Simon's question had
applied to his choice of a place to ride in.

If that gate at the north-west corner of the yard didn't still lead
to the short-cut to the downs, then Simon would have to tell him.
If it still did lead there, Simon would have one more item to worry
about.

"You haven't chosen a very good whip for shutting gates with,"

Simon said smoothly. "Or are you going to jump everything you come to?" You rodeo artist, the tone said.

"I'll shut the gates," Brat said equably.

He began to walk Timber to the corner of the yard.

"He has his tricks, so look out for him," Simon said, as an afterthought.

"I'll look out for him," Brat said, and rode away to the inner gate which Arthur was waiting to open for him.

Arthur grinned at him in a friendly fashion and said admiringly: "He's a fly one, that, sir."

As he turned to his right into the little lane he considered the implication of that very English adjective. It was a long time since he had heard anything called fly. "Fly" was "cute"—in the English sense, not in the American. Fly was something on the side. A fly cup. Something sly with a hint of cleverness in it.

A fly one, Timber was.

The fly one walked composedly up the track between the green banks netted with violets, his ears erect in anticipation of the turf ahead of them. As they came in sight of the gate at the far end he danced a little. "No," said Brat's hands, and he desisted at once. Someone had left the gate open, but since there was a notice saying PLEASE SHUT THE GATE neatly painted in the middle of it, Brat manoeuvred Timber into the appropriate position for closing it. Timber seemed as well acquainted with gates and their uses as a cow pony was with a rope, but never before had Brat had so delicate and so well-oiled a mechanism under him. Timber obeyed the slightest indication of hand or heel with a lack of questioning and a confidence that was new in Brat's experience. Surprised and delighted, Brat experimented with this new adaptability. And Timber, even with the turf in front of him, with the turf practically under his feet, moved sweetly and obediently under his hands.

"You wonder!" said Brat softly.

The ears flicked at him.

"You perishing marvel," he said, and closed his knees as he turned to face the down. Timber broke into a slow canter, headed for the clumps of gorse and juniper bushes that marked the skyline.

So this was what riding a good English horse was like, he thought. This communion, this being one half of a whole. This effortlessness. This magic.

The close, fine turf slipped by under them, and it was odd to see no little spurt of dust coming up as the shoes struck. England, England, England, said the shoes as they struck. A soft drum on the English turf.

I don't care, he thought, I don't care. I'm a criminal, and a heel, but I've got what I wanted, and it's worth it. By God, it's worth it. If I died to-morrow, it's worth it.

They came to the level top of the down and faced the double row of bushes that made a rough natural avenue, about fifty yards wide, along the crest. This was something that Alec Loding had forgotten to tell him about, and something that had not appeared on a map. Even the Ordnance Survey can hardly take note of juniper growths. He pulled up to consider it. But Timber was in no considering mood. Timber knew all about that level stretch of down between the rows of bushes.

"All right," said Brat, "let's see what you can do," and let him go.

Brat had ridden flyers before. Dozens of them. He had ridden sprinters and won money with them. He had been bolted with at the speed of jet propulsion. Mere speed no longer surprised him. What surprised him was the smoothness of the progress. It was like being carried through the air on a horse suspended to a merry-go-round.

The soft air parted round his face and tickled his ears and fled away behind them, smelling of grass with the sun on it and leather and gorse. Who cares, who cares, who cares! said the galloping feet. Who cares, who cares, who cares! said the blood in Brat's veins.

If he died to-morrow it was all the same to him.

As they came to the end of the stretch Timber began to pull up of his own accord, but it was against Brat's instincts to let a horse make the decisions, so he kept him going, turned him round the south end of the green corridor, and cantered him gently to a walk, and Timber responded without question.

"Brother," said Brat, running his fingers up the dark crest, "are there more like you in England, or do you rate special?"

Timber bent his head to the caress, still with the air of one receiving his due.

But as they walked back on the south side of the irregular green hedge Brat's attention and interest went to the countryside spread below them. Except that he was looking at it upside down, as it were—from the north, instead of from the south as one looks normally at a map—this was Clare as he had first become acquainted with it. All laid out below his eye in Ordnance Survey clarity and precision.

Down below him, a little to his left, were the crimson roofs of Latchetts, set in the neat squares of paddock. Farther to the left was the church, on its own small rise; and left of it again, the village of Clare, a huddle of roofs in pale green trees. Where the land sloped up from the village to make the south side of the small valley stood Clare Park, a long white house sheltered from the south-west Channel gales by the slope behind it.

Directly opposite him that slope rose into a smaller and tamer version of the down he was sitting on; a low green hill called Tanbitches. It was an open stretch of grazing, marked half-way up with the green scar of an old quarry, and crowned by the beeches that had given it its name. There were only seven beeches now instead of ten, but the clump made a decorative and satisfying climax to the southern side of the valley.

The other side of the Tanbitches hill, as he knew from the maps, ran away in a gentle slope for a mile and a half to the cliffs. To the cliffs where Patrick Ashby had put an end to his life. Behind the lower rise of the valley, on the reverse slope of Clare Park, were farms that merged imperceptibly in a mile or two into the suburbs of Westover. In the slight hollow that marked the Clare Park slope from Tanbitches hill was a path that led to the coast. The path that Patrick Ashby had taken on that day eight years ago.

It was suddenly more real to him than it had ever been so far: this tragedy which he was using to his advantage. More real even than it had been in the rooms that Patrick had lived in. In the house there had been other associations besides Patrick: associations more present and alive. There had been the distractions of human intercourse and of his own need to be constantly wary. Out here in the open and alone it had a reality that it had never had before. Up here, on that straggling path on the other side of the valley a boy had gone, so loaded with misery that this neat green English world had meant nothing to him. He had had horses like Timber, and friends and family, and a belonging-place, and it had all meant nothing to him.

For the first time in his detached existence Brat was personally aware of another's tragedy. When Loding had first told him the story, in that London pub, he had had nothing but contempt for the boy who had had so much and could not do without that little extra. A poor thing, he had thought. Then Loding had brought those photographs to Kew, and had shown him Patrick, and he had had that odd feeling of identification, of partisanship.

"That is Pat Ashby. He was about eleven there," Loding had said, his feet propped comfortably on the railings of the park, and had passed him the piece of paper. It was a snapshot taken with a Brownie 2A, and Brat had accepted it with a curiosity that was active but not urgent.

But Pat Ashby had not been the anonymous "poor thing" that he had so far held in his mind. He had been a real person. A likeable real person. A person who would have been, Brat felt, very much his cup of tea. From being vaguely anti-Patrick he had become Patrick's champion.

It was not, however, until this moment of quiet above Latchetts that he had been moved to sorrow for him.

Clink—clink! came the faint sound from the valley; and Brat's eyes travelled down from Tanbitches to the cottage at its foot. The blacksmith's, that was. A quarter of a mile west of the village. A tiny black square by the roadside it had been on the map; now it was a small building with a black chimney and an occupant who made musical sounds with a hammer.

The whole scene was very like the picture from which he had acquired his first-year French. *Voilà le forgeron.* It needed only a curé coming from the church. And a postman on a bicycle between the forge and the village.

Brat slid from Timber's back, from long habit loosened the girths as if he had saddled up hours ago, and sat down with his back to the gorse and juniper to feast his eyes on this primer of the English countryside.

Chapter 15

The great clouds sailed up and past, the sunlight flickered and ran, the uncertain soft wind edged in and out of the junipers and made soft scufflings in the grass. Timber made small sounds with his bit, and cropped turf in a tentative and superior fashion. Brat sank into a daze of pleasure and ceased altogether from conscious thought.

He was aroused by the swift fling-up of Timber's head, and almost at the same moment a female voice behind him said, as if it were a chant and rhymed:

> "Don't look,
> Don't move,
> Shut your eyes
> And guess who."

It was a slightly Cockney voice, and it dripped with archness.

Like anyone else in the circumstances Brat disobeyed the injunction automatically. He looked round into the face of a girl of sixteen or so. She was a large, plumpish girl, with bright auburn hair and prominent blue eyes. The eyes were remarkable in that they managed to be at once avid and sleepy. As they met Brat's they almost popped out altogether.

"Oh!" said the girl, in a half-shriek. "I thought you were Simon. You're not!"

"No," agreed Brat, beginning to get to his feet.

But before he could move she had dropped to the grass beside him.

"My, you gave me a shock. I bet I know who you are. You're the long-lost brother, aren't you? You must be; you're so like Simon. That's who you are, isn't it?"

Brat said that it was.

"You even wear the same kind of clothes."

Brat said that they were Simon's clothes. "You know Simon?"

"Of course I know Simon. I'm Sheila Parslow. I'm a boarder at Clare Park."

"Oh." The school for dodgers, Eleanor had called it. The place where no one had to learn the nine-times.

"I'm doing my best to have an *affaire* with Simon, but it's uphill work."

Brat did not know the correct rejoinder to this, but she did not need conversational encouragement.

"I have to do something to put some pep into life at Clare Park. You can't imagine the screaming boredom of it. You simply can't imagine. There is nothing, but I mean *nothing*, that you are forbidden to do. I once got so desperate I took off all my clothes and walked into Cedric's office—Cedric is our Leader, he doesn't like being called the Head, but that's what he is, of course—I walked in with nothing on, not a stitch, and all he said was: 'Have you ever thought of going on a diet, Sheila dear?' Just took a look at me and said: 'Have you ever thought of going on a diet?' and then went on with looking up *Who's Who*. He's always looking up *Who's Who*. You don't really stand much of a chance of fetching up at Clare Park unless your father is in *Who's Who*. Or your mother, of course. My father's not in it, but he has millions, my father, and that makes a very good substitute. Millions are a very good introduction, aren't they?"

Brat said that he supposed they were.

"I flapped Father's millions in front of Simon; Simon has a great respect for a good investment and I hoped it would weight my charms, so to speak; but he's a frightful snob, Simon, isn't he?"

"Is he?"

"Don't you *know*?"

"I've only met him to-day."

"Oh, of course. You've just come back. How exciting for you. I can understand Simon not being overjoyed, of course, but it must be exciting for you to put his nose out of joint."

Brat wondered if she too pulled the wings off flies.

"I may have more chance with Simon now that you've taken his fortune from him. I'll have to waylay him somewhere and see. I thought I was waylaying him now, when I saw Timber. He often comes up here because it's his favourite place for exercising the horses. He hates Tanbitches." She jerked her chin at the opposite side of the valley. "And this is a good place for getting him alone.

So I came up here on spec, and then I saw that black brute, and I thought I had him cold. But it was only you."

"I'm sorry," Brat said meekly.

She considered him.

"I suppose it's no good my trying to seduce you instead?" she said.

"I'm afraid not."

"Is it that I'm not your type, or is it not your line?"

"Not much in my line, I'm afraid."

"No, I suppose not," she said, agreeing with him. "You have a face like a monk. Funny you should look so like Simon and yet look so different. Simon's no monk; as that Gates girl over at Wigsell could tell you. I make images of that Gates girl and stick pins in them, but it doesn't do any good. She goes on blooming like a blasted peony and fascinating him like fly paper."

She was rather like a well-blown peony herself, he thought, looking at her wet red mouth and the buttons straining the cloth across her ample bust. A rather drooping and disappointed peony at the moment.

"Does Simon know that you are fond of him?" Brat asked.

"Fond of him? I'm not fond of him. I don't think I like him at all. I just want to have an *affaire* with him to brighten up the term a bit. Until I can leave this boring place."

"If you can do anything you like, why can't you leave now?" Brat asked reasonably.

"Well, I don't want to look too much of a fool, you know. I went to school at Ling Abbey, you see, and I made the place a hell so that my people would take me away and send me here. I thought I was going to have the time of my life here, with no lessons and no timetable and no rules or anything. I had no idea it would be so boring. I could weep with boredom."

"Isn't there anyone at Clare Park you would substitute for Simon? I mean, someone who would be more—accommodating?"

"No. I had a look at them first. Skinny and hairy and intellectual. Have you ever noticed how the intellect runs to hair? Some people get a kick out of disgust, but not me. I like them good-looking. And you have to admit Simon is very good-looking. There was an under-gardener at Ling Abbey that was almost as handsome, but he hadn't that lovely God-damn-you look that Simon has."

"Didn't the under-gardener keep you at the Abbey place?"

"Oh, no, they sacked him. It was easier than expelling me and having a scandal. But they had to expel me in any case, so they might as well have kept poor Albert. He was much better with his lobelias than he was with girls. But of course they couldn't be expected to know that. I suppose you wouldn't put in a good word for me with Simon? It would be such a pity to waste all the agony I've gone through trying to interest him."

"Agony?"

"You don't suppose I endure hours on those horrible quadrupeds just for *fun*, do you? With that cold stick of a sister of his looking down her nose at me. Oh, I forgot: she's your sister too, isn't she? But perhaps you've been away so long that you don't think of her the way a boy thinks of his sister."

"I certainly don't," Brat said; but she was not listening.

"I suppose you've ridden horses since you could crawl, so you have no idea what it is like to be bumped about on a great shapeless mountain of a thing that's far too high from the ground and has nothing to hold on to. It looks so easy when Simon does it. The horse looks so nice and *narrow* when you're standing on the ground. You think you could ride it the way you ride a bicycle. It's only when you get up you find that its back is simply acres across and you can make no impression on it at all. You just sit there and are bumped about, and your legs slip backwards and forwards instead of staying still like Simon's, and you get large blisters and can't sit down in the bath for weeks. You don't look quite so like a monk when you smile a bit."

Brat suggested that surely there were better ways of attracting favourable notice than being a tyro at something that the object of one's pursuit already did to perfection.

"Oh, I didn't think that I'd attract him that way. It just gave me an excuse for being round the stables. That sister of—your sister doesn't stand any hanging round if you haven't got business."

"Your sister," he thought, and liked the sound of it.

He had three sisters now, and at least two of them were the kind he would have indented for. Presently he must go down and make their further acquaintance.

"I'm afraid I must go," he said, getting up and putting the reins over Timber's head.

"I wish you didn't have to," she said, watching him tighten the girth. "You are quite the nicest person I have talked to since I came to Clare. It's a pity you aren't interested in women. You might cut

Simon out with the Gates girl, and then I'd have more chance. Do you know the Gates girl?"

"No," Brat said, getting up on Timber.

"Well, have a look at her. She's very pretty."

"I'll do that," Brat said.

"Now that you're home, I'll be running across you in the stables, I suppose."

"I expect so."

"You wouldn't like to give me one of my lessons instead of your sister, would you?"

"I'm afraid that's not my department."

"Oh, well." She sounded resigned. "You look very nice on that brute. I suppose *his* back is acres across too. They all are. It's a conspiracy."

"Good-bye," said Brat.

"Do you know, I don't know your name. Someone told me, of course, but I forget. What is it?"

"Patrick."

And as he said the word his mind went back to the path across the valley, and he forgot Miss Parslow almost instantly. He cantered back along the top of the down until he came level with Latchetts, and then began to walk Timber down. Below him, a green ride led through the paddocks to the west of the house and so to the sweep of gravel in front of it. It was by that way that Jane had come this morning, when she had become mixed up with his reception at the front door. The gate to the ride stood open, the gate lying flat against the stout paddock rails that bordered the ride. Brat rode down until the steepness of the down gave way to a gentle slope and then pressed Timber into a canter. The green tunnel of the ride with its soft floor was open before them, and he was not going to spoil it by stopping to shut another gate that someone else had left open.

It was due to no good riding on Brat's part that his left leg was still whole five seconds later. It was due entirely to the years of rough-riding that had made his physical reactions quicker than conscious thought. The swerve was so sudden and so wholehearted that the white rail was scraping along the saddle where his leg should have been before he realised that his leg was not there. That he had taken it away before he had time to think about it.

As Timber came away from the rails he settled back into the saddle and pulled the horse to a stop. Timber stopped obediently.

"Whew!" said Brat, expelling his pent breath. He looked down at Timber standing innocent and demure in the exact centre of the ride.

"You ornery thing, you," he said, amused.

Timber went on looking demure but the ears listened to him. A trifle apprehensively, Brat thought.

"I know men who'd beat the bejesus out of you for that," Brat said, and turned the horse's nose to the down again. Timber retraced his steps obediently, but was obviously not easy in his mind. When he was far enough away from the gate Brat took him into a canter once more and down to the opening. He had neither spurs nor curb but he was curious to see what Timber would do this time. Timber, as he had expected, swept good-manneredly into the ride, bisecting the distance from either rail with mathematical precision.

"What, me!" he seemed to be saying. "Do a thing like that on purpose? Me, with my perfect manners? Of course not. I just lost my balance for a moment, coming into the ride there. It can happen to the best of us."

"Well, well," thought Brat, pulling him to a walk. "Think you're smart, don't you," he said aloud, walking him down the ride. "Far smarter horses than you have tried to brush me off, take it from me. I've been brushed off horses that would make you look like five-cents worth of candy."

The black ears flickered, listening to him, analysing the sound of his voice, its tone; puzzled.

The mares came to the rails to watch them pass, pleased with this small event in their placid lives; and the foals ran round and round in a self-induced excitement. But Timber took no notice of them. He had lost any active interest in mares at a very early age, and just now his whole interest seemed to be in the fact that he had been outwitted, and that the outwitting one made sounds which he did not understand. His ears, which should have been pricked at the thought of his nearing stable, were restless and enquiring.

Brat rode round the front of the house, as Jane had that morning, but he saw no one. He went on to the stables and found Eleanor just riding in with a led horse, having given Tony his lesson and left him at Clare Park.

"Hullo!" she said, "have you been out on Timber?" She sounded a little surprised. "I hope Simon warned you about him."

"Yes, thank you, he warned me."

"One of my bad buys," she said ruefully, eyeing Timber as they rode side by side towards the yard.

"Yours?" he said.

"Yes. Didn't Simon tell you about that?"

"No."

"That was nice of him. I expect he didn't want you to find out too soon what a fool of a sister you have." She smiled a little at him, as if she were glad to be his sister. "I bought him at the Lerridge Hunt sale. It was Timber who killed old Felix. Old Felix Hunstanton, the Master, you know. Did Simon tell you?"

"No. No, he just told me about his tricks."

"Old Felix had some good horses, and when they were being sold I went over to see what I could pick up. None of the Lerridge Hunt regulars was bidding for Timber, but I thought it was because of sentiment, perhaps. I thought they probably didn't want to own the horse the Master was killed on. As if there was ever any sentiment about horse-dealing! I oughtn't to be let out alone. Even so, I ought to have wondered why I was getting him so cheap; with his looks and his breeding and his performance. It was only afterwards that we found that he had done the same thing to the huntsman a few days later, only the branches were small and broke, instead of braining him or sweeping him off."

"I see," said Brat, who was beginning to.

"Not that anyone needed convincing, apparently. No one who was there when Felix was killed believed it was an accident. It was a Lerridge Castle meet, and they had found in one of the Lerridge woods and gone away over the park. Good open galloping country with the trees isolated. And yet Timber took Felix under an oak, going an awful bat, and he was dead before he hit the ground. But of course we heard about all that later. All I knew when I was bidding for him was that Felix had hit his head on a branch during the hunt. Which is something that has been happening to people ever since William Rufus."

"Did anyone actually see it happen?"

"No, I don't think so. Everyone just knew that with the whole park to choose from Felix wouldn't have ridden under the oak. And when he tried the same thing on Samms, the huntsman, there was no doubt. So he is put into the sale with the rest of the lot and all the Lerridge regulars sit around in silence and watch Eleanor Ashby from over Clare way buying a pup."

"He's a very elegant pup, there's no denying," Brat said, rubbing Timber's neck.

"He's beautiful," Eleanor said. "And a faultless jumper. Did you jump him at all to-day? No? You must next time. He is safest jumping because his mind is distracted. He hasn't time to think up mischief. It's odd, isn't it; he doesn't *look* untrustworthy," she added, still eyeing her bad bargain with a puzzled eye.

"No."

She caught the tone and said: "You don't sound too sure."

"Well, I must allow he is the most conceited animal I've ever met."

This seemed to be as new an idea to Eleanor as it had been to Simon.

"Vain, is he? Yes, I suppose he is. I expect *I'd* be conceited if I were a horse and I had been clever enough to kill a man. Did he try any tricks to-day?"

"He swerved at the entrance to the ride, but that was all." He did not say: He took advantage of the first good stout piece of timber to mash my leg against. That was something between the horse and himself. He and Timber had a long acquaintanceship in front of them, and a lot to say to each other.

"He behaves like an angel most of the time," Eleanor said. "That is what is so lethal about him. We have all ridden him; Simon and Gregg and Arthur and me, and he has only twice played up. Once with Simon and once with Arthur. But, of course," she added with a grin, "we have always given trees a wide berth."

"He'd be a great success in the desert. Not a rail or a limb in a day's journey."

Eleanor looked sadly at the black horse as Brat drew up to let her precede him into the yard. "He'd think up something else, I expect."

And Brat, thinking it over, agreed with her. Timber was that rare thing in horses: a deliberate and intelligent rogue. Balked of his normal fun, he would think up something new. There was nothing small-time about Timber.

Nor was Simon exactly small-time. Simon had sent him out on a notorious rogue with a light remark about the horse "having its tricks." As neat a piece of vicarious manslaughter as anyone ever thought up.

Chapter 16

*B*eatrice Ashby looked down the dining-table at her nephew Patrick and thought how well he was doing it. The occasion must be an extraordinarily difficult one for him, but he was carrying it off beautifully. He was neither awkward nor exuberant. He brought to the situation the same quiet detachment that he had shown on their first meeting in that Pimlico room. It was a very adult quality, and a little surprising in a boy not yet twenty-one. He had great dignity this Patrick Ashby, she thought, watching him dealing with the Rector. Surely never before can anyone have been so silent by habit without appearing either stiff or stupid.

It was she who had brought Simon up, and she was pleased with the result. But this boy had brought himself up, and the result was even better, it seemed. Perhaps it was a case of "giving the first seven years" and the rest followed automatically. Or perhaps it was that the goodness in Patrick had been so innate that he had needed no other guidance. He had followed his own lights, and the result was this quiet, adult young man with the still face.

It was a mask of a face; a sad mask, on the whole. It was such a contrast to the similar set of features in Simon's mobile countenance that they reminded one of those reversible comedy-tragedy masks that are used to decorate the title-pages of plays.

Simon was being particularly gay tonight, and Bee's heart ached for him. He too was doing it well, and tonight she loved him almost without reservation. Simon was abdicating, and doing it with a grace and spontaneity that she would not have believed possible. She felt a little guilty that she had underrated him. She had not credited the selfish, acquisitive Simon with such a power of renunciation.

They were choosing a name for Honey's filly foal, and the conversation was growing ribald. Nancy was insisting that "honey" was an endearment, and should be translated as "poppet," and Eleanor said that no thoroughbred as good as Honey's present foal should be damned by a name like Poppet. If Eleanor had refused to dress especially for Patrick's arrival, she had now made up for it. It was a long time since Bee had seen her looking so well or so pretty. Eleanor belonged to a type which did not glow easily.

"Brat is in love with Honey," Eleanor said.

"I suppose Bee dragged you round the paddocks before you were well over the doorstep," said Nancy. "Were you impressed, Brat?"

She too had adopted the nickname. Only the Rector called him Patrick.

"I'm in love with the whole bunch," Brat said. "And I found an old friend."

"Oh? Who was that?"

"Regina."

"Oh, yes, of course. Poor old Regina. She must be about twenty!" Nancy said.

"Not so much of the 'poor,'" said Simon. "Regina has kept us shod and clothed for a whole generation. We ought to pay her a dividend."

"She takes her dividends out in pasture," Eleanor said. "She was always a greedy eater."

"When you drop foals like Regina year after year without a break, you're entitled to an appetite," Simon said.

Simon was drinking a great deal more than usual, but it seemed to be having little effect on him. Bee thought that the Rector looked at him now and then with pity in his eyes.

And Brat too, at the other end of the table, was watching Simon, but without pity. Pity was not an emotion that Brat indulged in very often: like everyone who despises self-pity he did not readily pity others; but it was not because of his native disinclination to pity that he withheld sympathy from Simon Ashby. It was not even because Simon was his declared enemy; he had admired enemies before now. It was because there was something about Simon Ashby that repelled him. There was something unaccountable about Simon. There he sat, being light-hearted and charming, and there sat his relations and friends silently applauding his nobility and his courage. They were applauding an "act," but they would all be staggered to know what an act Simon was really putting on for their benefit.

Watching him as he displayed his graces, Brat felt that Simon reminded him of someone that he had met quite lately. Someone who had just that air of breeding, and excellent good manners, and good looks, and that—unaccountability. Who could that have been?

He was maddened by that tip-of-the-tongue feeling. In one more second he would remember. Loding? No. Someone on the ship coming over? Not very likely. That lawyer chap: the K.C. chap, Macdermott? No. Then who could it—

"Don't you think so, Patrick?"

It was the Rector again. He must be careful with the old boy. He had been more afraid of meeting George Peck than of anyone but Simon. After a twin brother there is no one who is liable to remember so much about you or to remember that much so well as the man who taught you. There would be a score of small things that George Peck would know about Patrick Ashby that not even Patrick Ashby's mother would know. But the meeting had gone off very well. Nancy Peck had kissed him on both cheeks and said: "Oh, dear, you've got very grown-up and serious, haven't you!"

"Patrick always was," the Rector had said, and had shaken hands.

He had looked consideringly at Brat, but no more consideringly than was normal in a man examining an old pupil met after a decade of absence. And Brat, who had no love for the Cloth, found himself liking the Rector. He was still wary of him, but the wariness was due not to the Rector's calling but to his knowledge of Pat Ashby, and to the intelligence and penetration of the eyes in his simian face.

Considering that intelligence, Brat was glad that he was particularly well primed in the matter of Pat Ashby's schooling. The Rector was Alec Loding's brother-in-law, and Loding had had what he called a front-stall view of the Ashby twins' education.

As for Alec Loding's sister, she was the most beautiful woman that Brat had ever seen. He had never heard of the famous Nancy Ledingham, but her brother had been eloquent about her. "Could have had anyone in the world; any man would have been delighted to keep her just to look at; but she had to choose George Peck." He had been shown Nancy in every kind of garment, from a swimming suit to her court presentation gown, but none of the photographs had done justice to her serene beauty, her gaiety, her general niceness. He felt that George Peck must be all right if Nancy had married him.

"Was that the Toselli child you had out with you?" she was saying to Eleanor. "That object I met you with this afternoon?"

"That was Tony," Eleanor said.

"How he brought back the days of my youth!"

"Tony did? How?"

"You won't remember it, but there used to be things called cavalry regiments. And every regiment had a trick-riding team. And every trick-riding team had a 'comedy' member. And every comedy member of a trick-riding team looked just like Tony."

"So they did!" Bee said, delighted. "That was what he reminded me of this afternoon and I couldn't think of it at the time. That masterly irrelevance. The completely unrelated garments."

"You may wonder why I took him out at all," Eleanor remarked. "But after Sheila Parslow he's a positive holiday. He'll ride quite well some day, Tony."

"To the prospective horseman all things are forgiven, are they?" the Rector said, mocking mildly.

"Doesn't La Parslow get any better?" Simon asked.

"She will never get any better. She skates about in the saddle like a block of ice on a plate. I could weep for the horse all the time we are out. Luckily Cherrypicker has an indestructible frame and practically no feelings."

The move from the dining-room to the living-room produced an anti-climax. The talk ceased to flow and ran into aimless trickles. Brat was suddenly so tired that he could hardly stand up. He hoped that no one would spring anything on him now; his normally hard head was muzzy with unaccustomed wine, and his thoughts fumbled and stuck. The twins said good night and went upstairs. Bee poured the coffee which had been placed in readiness for them on a low table by the fire, and it was not as hot as it should have been. Bee made despairing grimaces at Nancy.

"Our Lana, is it?" Nancy asked, sympathetic.

"Yes. I suppose she had to meet our Arthur and couldn't wait another ten minutes."

Simon too fell silent, as if the effort he had been making seemed suddenly not worth while. Only Eleanor seemed to have brought from the dining-room the warmth and happiness that had made dinner a success. In the moments of silence between the slow spurts of talk the rain fell against the tall windows with a soft shush.

"You were right about the weather, Aunt Bee," Eleanor said. "She said this morning that it was that too-bright kind that would bring rain before night."

"Bee is perennially right," the Rector said, giving her a look that was half a smile, half a benediction.

"It sounds loathsome," Bee said.

Nancy waited until they had lingered properly over their coffee and then said: "It has been a very full day for Brat, Bee; and I expect you are all tired. We won't stay now, but you'll come over and see us when you can crawl out from under the crush, won't you, Brat?"

Simon fetched her wraps and they all went out to the doorstep to see their guests off. On the doorstep Nancy took off her evening shoes, tucked them under her arm, and stepped into a pair of wellingtons that she had left behind the door. Then she tucked her other arm under her husband's, huddled close to him under their single umbrella, and walked away with him into the night.

"Good old Nancy," Simon said. "You can't keep a Ledingham down." He sounded just a little drunk.

"Dear Nan," Bee said softly. She moved into the living-room and surveyed it in an absent fashion.

"I think Nan is right," she said. "It is time we all went to bed. It has been an exciting day for all of us."

"We don't want it to end so soon, do we?" Eleanor said.

"You have La Parslow at nine-thirty to-morrow," Simon reminded her. "I saw it in the book."

"What were *you* doing with the riding book?"

"I like to see that you're not cheating on your income tax."

"Oh, yes, let's go to bed," Eleanor said, with a wide happy yawn. "It's been a wonderful day."

She turned to Brat to say good night, became suddenly shy, gave him her hand and said: "Good night Brat. Sleep well," and went away upstairs.

Brat turned to Bee, but she said: "I shall come in to see you on my way up." So he turned back to face Simon.

"Good night, Simon." He met the clear cold eyes levelly.

"Good night to you—Patrick," Simon said, looking faintly amused. He had managed to make the name sound like a provocation.

"Are you coming up now?" Brat heard Bee ask him as he climbed the stairs.

"Not quite yet."

"Will you see that the lights are out, then? And make sure of the locks?"

"Yes, of course I'll do that. Good night, Bee darling."

As Brat turned on to the landing he saw Bee's arms go round Simon. And he was stabbed by a hot despairing jealousy that shocked him. What had it to do with him?

Bee followed him into the old night nursery in a few moments. She looked with a practised eye at the bed and said: "That moron promised to put in a hot-water bottle and she has forgotten to do it."

"Don't worry," Brat said. "I'd only have put it out again. I don't use the things."

"You must think us a crowd of soft-livers," she said.

"I think you're a nice crowd," he said.

"Tired?"

"Yes."

"Too tired for breakfast at eight-thirty?"

"That sounds luxuriously late to me."

"Did you enjoy it, that hard life—Brat?"

"Sure."

"I think you're nice too," she said, and kissed him lightly. "I wish you hadn't stayed away from us so long, but we are glad to have you back. Good night, my dear." And as she went out: "It's no use ringing a bell, of course, because no one will answer. But if you have a mad desire for fried shrimps, or iced water, or a copy of *The Pilgrim's Progress* or something, come along to my room. It is still the right-hand one in front."

"Good night," he said.

She stood for a moment outside his room, the doorknob still in her hand, and then moved away to Eleanor's door. She knocked and went in. For the last year or so Eleanor had been a great comfort to her. She had been so long alone in her need for judgement and resolution that it was refreshing to have the companionship of her own kind; to have Eleanor's unemotional good sense on tap when she wanted it.

"Hullo, Bee," Eleanor said, looking up through the hair she was brushing. She was beginning to drop the "aunt," as Simon did.

Bee sank into a chair and said: "Well, that's over."

"It turned out to be quite a success, didn't it," Eleanor said. "Simon behaved beautifully. Poor Simon."

"Yes. Poor Simon."

"Perhaps Brat—Patrick—will offer him some kind of partnership. Do you think? After all, Simon helped to make the stable. It wouldn't be fair to walk in and grab the lot after taking no interest for years and years."

"No. I don't know. I hope so."

"You sound tired."

"Aren't we all?"

"D'you know, Bee, I must confess I have the greatest difficulty in connecting the two."

"The two? Simon and Patrick?"

"No. Patrick and Brat."

There was a moment's silence, filled with the soft sound of the rain and the strokes of Eleanor's brush.

"You mean you—don't think he is Patrick?"

Eleanor stopped brushing and looked up, her eyes wide with surprise. "Of course he's Patrick," she said, astonished. "Who else would he be?" She put down the brush and began to tie up her hair in a blue ribbon. "It's just that I have no feeling of ever having met him before. Odd, isn't it? When we spent nearly twelve years of our lives together. I like him; don't you?"

"Yes," Bee said. "I like him." She too had no feeling of ever having met him before, and she too did not see "who else he could be."

"Did Patrick not smile very often?"

"No; he was a serious child."

"When Brat smiles I want to cry."

"Good heavens, Eleanor."

"You can 'good heaven' all you like, but I expect you know what I mean."

Bee thought that she did.

"Did he tell you why he didn't write to us all those years?"

"No. There wasn't much opportunity for confidences."

"I thought you might have asked him when you were going round the paddocks with him this evening."

"No. He was too interested in the horses."

"Why do *you* think he didn't take any interest in us after he left?"

"Perhaps he took what old Nannie used to call a 'scunner' to us. It's not so surprising, in a way, as the fact that he ran away in the first place. The urge to put Latchetts behind him must have been overwhelming."

"Yes. I suppose so. But he was such a kind person: Pat. And so fond of us all. He mightn't have wanted to come back, but you would have thought he'd want to let us know that he was safe."

Since this was her own private stumbling-block, Bee had no help to offer.

"It must have been difficult to come back," Eleanor said, running the comb through her brush. "He looked so tired tonight that he looked like a *dead* man. It's not a very lively face at the best of times, is it? If you chopped it off behind the ears and hung it on a wall, no one would know the difference."

Bee knew Eleanor well enough, and agreed with her sufficiently, to translate this successfully.

"You don't think he'll want to sheer off again once the excitement of coming home has worn off?"

"Oh, no, I'm quite sure he won't."

"You think he is here for keeps?"

"Of course I do."

But Brat, standing in the dark before the open window of his room and looking at the curve of the down in the wet starlight, was wondering about that very matter. The thing had succeeded beyond Loding's most extravagant promises, and now?

Where did he go from here? How long would it be before Simon had him cold? And if Simon failed, how long could he go on living a life where at any moment someone might spring a mine?

That is what he had set out to do, of course. But somehow he had not really looked beyond the first stages. In his heart he had been unable to believe that he would succeed. Now that success was his he felt rather like someone who has climbed a pinnacle and can't get down again. Elated but misgiving.

He turned from the window and switched the lamp on. His landlady in Pimlico used to say that she "was so tired that she felt as if she'd been through a mangle"; he knew now how good a description that had been. That was exactly how he felt. Wrung out and empty. So limp that it was an effort to lift a hand to undress. He pulled off his new suit—the suit that had made him feel so guilty in that other life way back in London—and made himself hang it up. He peeled off his underclothes and stumbled into his faded old pyjamas. He wondered for a moment whether they would mind if the rain came in and marked the carpet, but decided to risk it. So he left the window wide open and got into bed.

He lay for a long time listening to the quiet sound of rain and looking at the room. Now was the time for Pat Ashby's ghost to come and chill that room. He waited for the ghost but it did not come. The room was warm and welcoming. The figures on the wallpaper, the figures that those children had grown up with, looked friendly and alive. He turned his head to look at the groups by the bedside. To look for the one Eleanor had been in love with. The chap with the profile. He wondered if she was in love with anyone now.

His eyes went on to the wood of the bedstead, and he remembered that this was Alec Loding's bed, and was pleased once more by the irony of it all. It was fantastically right that he should come to Latchetts only to sleep in Alec Loding's bed. He must tell him one day. It was the kind of thing that Loding would appreciate.

He wondered whether it was Eleanor or Bee who had put the flowers in the bowl. Flowers to welcome him—home,

Latchetts, he said to himself, looking at the room. This is Latchetts. I'm here. This is Latchetts.

The sound of the word was a soporific; like the swing of a hammock. He put out his hand and switched off the light. In the dark the rain suddenly sounded louder.

This morning he had got up and dressed in that back room under the slates, with the crowding chimney-pots beyond the window. And here he was, going to sleep in Latchetts, with the sweet cold smell of the down blowing in on the damp air from the window.

As sleep drew him under he had an odd feeling of reassurance. A feeling that Pat Ashby didn't mind his being there; that he was on the contrary pleased about it all.

The unlikeliness of this roused him a little, and his thoughts, running on approval and disapproval, went to Bee. What was it that he felt when Bee took his hand to lead him to the interview this afternoon? What was different from any other of the thousand handclasps he had experienced in his time? Why the surge of warmth under his heart, and what kind of emotion was it anyway? He had suffered the same obscure gratification when Bee had thrust her arm through his on the way to the stables. What was so remarkable about a woman putting her hand on your arm? A woman, moreover, that you were not in love with, and were never likely to be in love with.

It *was* because she was a woman, of course, but the thing that made it remarkable was something else again. It had something to do with being taken for granted by her. No one else had taken his hand in just that way. Casual but—no, not possessive. Quite a few had been possessive with him, and he had not been gratified in the least. Casual but—what? Belonging. It had something to do with belonging. The hand had taken him for granted because he belonged. It was the unthinking friendliness of a woman to one of her family. Was it because he had never "belonged" before that made that commonplace gesture into a benediction?

He went on thinking of Bee as he fell asleep. Her sidelong glance when she was considering something; her courage; the way she had braced herself to meet him that day in the back room in Pimlico; the way she had kissed him before she was sure, just in case he was Patrick; the way she had dealt with the suspense of Simon's absence when he arrived today.

She was a lovely woman, Beatrice Ashby, and he loved her.

He had reached the toppling-over place of sleep when he was yanked of a sudden wide awake.

He had remembered something.

He knew now who it was that Simon Ashby reminded him of.

It was Timber.

Chapter 17

On Wednesday morning Bee took him to call on the tenants of the three farms: Frenchland, Upacres, and Wigsell. "Gates last; just to larn him," Bee said. Gates was last also in importance, since Wigsell was the smallest of the three farms. It had originally been the home farm of Latchetts and lay just beyond the Rectory, on the slope north of the village. It was almost too small a farm to be self-supporting, but Gates also ran the butcher's shop in the village (open twice a week) and was not dependent on what he made from Wigsell.

"Do you drive, Brat?" Bee asked, as they prepared to get into the car.

"Yes, but I'd rather you did. You know the"—"road" he had almost said—"the car better."

"Nice of you to call it a car. I expect you're used to left-hand drive."

"Yes."

"I'm sorry it had to be the bug. It isn't often the car goes wrong on us. Jameson has all its inside out on the garage floor, and is conducting a post-mortem in a silent fury."

"I like the bug. I came from the station in it yesterday."

"So you did. What a very long time ago that seems. Does it seem like that to you?"

"Yes." It seemed years away to him.

"Have you heard that we've been saved from the *Clarion*?" she asked, as they sped down the avenue to the accompaniment of the bug's sewing-machine song.

"No?"

"Are you not a consumer of the Press at breakfast?" asked Bee, who had breakfasted at eight o'clock.

"I never lived where we had papers to read at breakfast. We just switched on the radio."

"Oh, lord, yes. I forget that your generation doesn't have to read."

"How have we been saved?"

"We have been rescued by three people we never heard of, and are never likely to meet. The fourth wife of a Manchester dentist, the husband of a principal boy, and the owner of a black leather trunk." She pressed the horn and turned slowly to the right out of the avenue. "The owner of the trunk left it at Charing Cross with someone's arms and legs in it. Or, of course, it may be the owner's arms and legs. That is a question which will occupy the *Clarion* for some time to come, I expect. The husband of the principal boy is suing for alienation of affection, and none of the three people concerned has ever been bothered with an inhibition, which is very nice for the *Clarion*. Since the reports of divorce cases have been pruned the *Clarion* has been suffering from frustration, and a suit for alienation of affection is a gift from heaven. Especially when it is Tattie Thacker's affections." She looked with pleasure at the morning. "I do like a morning after rain."

"You've still one to come?"

"What?"

"The fourth wife of the Manchester dentist."

"Oh. Yes. She, poor wretch, has just been exhumed from a very expensive and elaborate tomb and found to be loaded with arsenic. Her husband is found to be missing."

"And you think that the *Clarion* will be too busy to bother about—us?"

"I'm sure of it. They haven't room as it is for all they want to do with Tattie. She had a whole page to herself this morning. If they ever bothered about the Ashbys they would print the report in a tiny paragraph at the bottom of a page, and five million people would read it and not be able to tell you two minutes later what was in it. I think we are quite safe. The *Westover Times* will have one of their usual discreet paragraphs this morning, and that will be the end of the matter."

Well, that was another snag out of the way. In the meantime he must keep his wits alive for the visits to Frenchland and Upacres. He was supposed to know these people.

Frenchland was farmed by a tall rosy old man and his tall sallow sister. "Everyone was terrified of Miss Hassell," Loding had said. "She had a face like a witch, and a tongue that took the skin off you. She didn't talk; just made one remark and you found that you were raw."

"Well, this is an honour," old Mr. Hassell said, coming to the garden gate and seeing whom Bee had with her. "Mr. Patrick, I'm glad to see you. I'm tarnation glad to see you." He took Brat's hand in his gnarled old fist and closed on it with his other one. There was no doubt that he was glad to see Patrick Ashby again.

It was difficult to know whether Miss Hassell was glad or not. She eyed Brat while she shook hands with him and said: "This is an unexpected pleasure." Her dry use of the conventional phrase and its wicked appropriateness amused Brat.

"Foreign parts don't seem to have changed you much," she said, as she set out glasses in the crowded little parlour.

"I've changed in one way," Brat said.

"You have?" She wasn't going to gratify him by asking in what way.

"I'm not frightened of you any more."

Old Mr. Hassell laughed.

"You beat me there, son. She still puts the fear of God in me. If I'm half an hour late getting home from market I creep up the lane with my tail down like I was a sheep-stealer."

Miss Hassell said nothing, but Brat thought there was a new interest in her glance; almost as if she were pleased with him. And she went away and fetched some short bread from the kitchen which she had obviously had no intention of producing before.

They drank a liquid called White Port Wine Type, and discussed Rhode Island Reds.

At Upacres there was only plump Mrs. Docket, and she was busy making butter in the dairy at the back.

"Come in, whoever you are!" she called, and they went down the cool tiled passage from the open front door, and turned into the chill of the dairy.

"I can't stop this," she said, looking round at them. "The butter is just—Oh, goodness, I didn't know! I just thought it was someone passing. The children are all at school and Carrie is out in the barn and—Goodness! To think of it!"

Bee automatically took her place at the churn while she shook hands with Brat.

"Well, well," said kind plump Mrs. Docket, "a fine, good-looking Ashby you are. You're more like Mr. Simon than ever you were."

Brat thought that Bee looked up with interest when she said that.

"It's a happy day for us all, Miss Ashby, isn't it? I could hardly believe it. I just said to Joe, I don't believe it, I said. It's the kind of thing that happens in books. And in pictures and plays. Not the kind of thing that would happen to quiet folk like us in a quiet place like Clare, I said. And yet here you are and it's really happened. My, Mr. Patrick, it's nice to see you again, and looking so well and bonny."

"Can I have a shot at that?" Brat asked, indicating the churn. "I've never handled one of those things."

"But of course you have!" Mrs. Docket said, looking taken aback. "You used to come in special on Saturday mornings to have a go at it."

Brat's heart missed a beat. "Did I?" he said. "I've forgotten that."

Always say quite frankly that you don't remember, Loding had advised. No one can deny that you don't remember, but they will certainly jump on you if you try to make-believe about anything.

"I thought you did this by electricity now," he heard Bee say as she made way for him at the churn.

"Oh, we do everything else by electricity, of course," Mrs. Docket said. "But I can't believe it makes good butter. No more home-made taste to it than you'd get at the International in Westover. Sometimes when I'm rushed I switch on the electricity, but I'm always sorry afterwards. Awful *mechanical*, it is. No artfulness about it."

They drank hot black tea and ate light floury scones and discussed the children's schooling.

"She's a darling, Mrs. Docket," Bee said as they drove away. "I think she is still of the opinion in her heart of hearts that electricity is an invention of the devil."

But Brat was thoughtful. He must stop himself from volunteering remarks. It was not important about the churn, but it quite easily might have been something vital. He must be less forthcoming.

"About Friday, Brat," Bee said, as they made their way back to Clare and to Wigsell.

"What is on Friday?" Brat said, out of his absorption.

Bee looked round and smiled at him. "Your birthday," she said.

Of course. He was now the possessor of a birthday.

"Had you forgotten that you are going to be twenty-one on Friday?" she asked.

"I had, almost." He caught her sidelong look at him. After a pause she said: "You came of age a long time ago, didn't you." She said it without smiling and it was not a question.

"About Friday," she went on. "I thought that since we have post-poned the celebrations for Uncle Charles's benefit, we wouldn't have a party on Friday. Mr. Sandal will be coming down with the papers he wants you to sign, so we shall have him to lunch, and make it just a quiet family party."

Papers to sign. Yes, he had known that there would be papers to sign sooner or later. He had even learned to make his capital letters the way Patrick did, thanks to an old exercise book that Loding had unearthed and filched from the Rectory. And, after all, signing a paper didn't make him any more of a heel than he was being at this moment. It just put him more surely in the Law's reverence, made the thing irrevocable.

"Is that how you would like it?"

"What? Oh, the birthday. Yes, of course. I don't want a party. I don't want a celebration, if it comes to that. Can't we just take this coming-of-age for granted?"

"I don't think the neighbourhood would be very pleased if we did. They are all looking forward to some kind of party. I think we shall have to give them one. Even the invitation cards are all ready. I altered the date to a fortnight after Charles's arrival. He is due in about twenty-three days. So you'll have to 'thole' it, as old Nannie used to say."

Yes, he would have to thole it. Anyhow, he could sit back now and relax for a little. He was not supposed to know the Gates family.

They were coming back to the village now; the white rails of the south paddocks on their left. It was a washed and shining morning, but it had an uneasy glitter. The sky was metallic, and the light had a silver edge to it.

As they passed the entrance to the Rectory Bee said: "Alec Lod-ing came down for the week-end not long ago."

"Oh? What is he doing now?"

"Still playing roué parts in dreadful little comedies and farces. You know: four characters, five doors, and one bed. I didn't see him, but Nancy said he had improved."

"In what way?"

"Oh, more interested in other people. Kindlier. He even made efforts to get on with George. Nancy thought age was beginning to tell. He was quite happy to sit for hours with a book in George's study when George was out. And when George was in they would yarn quite happily. Nancy was delighted. She had always been fond of Alec, but she used to dread his visits. The country bored him and George bored him even more, and he never bothered to hide it. So it was a pleasant change."

Half-way through the village they turned into the lane that led to Wigsell.

"You don't remember Emmy Vidler, do you?" she asked Brat. "She was brought up at Wigsell, and married Gates when he had a farm the other side of Bures. When her father died, Gates put a bailiff into his farm and took over Wigsell. And, of course, the butcher's shop. So they are very comfortably off. The boy couldn't stand his father, and got himself a job in the Midlands somewhere; engineering. But the girl lives at home, and is the apple of her father's eye. She went to an expensive boarding school, where I understand she was known as Margot. Her name is Peggy."

They swung into the farm entrance and came to rest on the small old cobbles of the yard. Two dogs rushed at them in wild self-importance, yelling their arrival to the world.

"I do wish Gates would train his dogs," said Bee, whose dogs were as well-trained as her horses.

The clamour brought Mrs. Gates to the front door. She was a faded and subdued little woman who must once have been very pretty.

"Glen! Joy! Be quiet!" she called, ineffectually, and came forward to greet them. But before she reached them Gates came round the corner of the house, and in a few strides had anticipated her. His pompous welcome drowned her more genuine pleasure, and she stood smiling gently at Brat while her husband trumpeted forth their satisfaction in seeing Patrick Ashby on their doorstep again.

Gates was a large, coarse individual, but Brat supposed that once he had had the youthful vigour and assurance that appealed to pretty, fragile little women like Emmy Vidler.

"They tell me that you've been making money in horses over there," he said to Brat.

"I've earned my living from them," Brat said.

"You come and see what I've got in *my* stable." He began to lead the way to the back of the house.

"But Harry, they must come in and sit down for a little," his wife protested.

"They'll sit down presently. They'd much rather look at a piece of good horseflesh than at your gewgaws. Come along, Mr. Patrick.

Come along, Miss Ashby. Alfred!" he bellowed as they went down the yard. "Turn out that new horse for Miss Ashby to see."

Mrs. Gates, tailing along behind, found herself side by side with Brat. "I'm so happy about this," she said quietly. "So happy about your coming back. I remember you when you were little; when I lived here in my father's day. Except for my own son I've never been so fond of a small boy as I was of you."

"Now then, Mr. Patrick, have a look at this here, have a look at this! Tell me if that doesn't fill the eye for you."

Gates swept his great limb of an arm at the stable door where Alfred was leading out a brown horse that looked oddly out of place in the small farmyard, even in a region where every small farmer kept a mount that would carry him across country in the winter. There was no denying it, the brown horse was something exceptional.

"There! What do you think of that, eh? What do you think of that?"

Bee, having looked, said: "But that, surely, is the horse that Dick Pope won the jumping on at the Bath Show last year."

"That's the horse," Gates said complacently. "And not only the jumping. The cup for the best riding horse in the show. Cost me a pretty penny, that did, but I can afford it and nothing's too good for my girl. Oh ah! It's for Peggy I bought it. That wouldn't carry me, that wouldn't." He gave an abrupt shout of laughter; at least Brat supposed it was laughter. "But my girl, now, she's a feather in the saddle. I don't have to tell you, Miss Ashby; you've seen her. There's no one in the county deserves a good horse better than my Peggy, and I don't grudge the money for it."

"You've certainly got a good horse, Mr. Gates," Bee said, with an enthusiasm in her voice that surprised Brat. He looked across at her and wondered why she was looking so pleased. After all, this brown horse was a potential rival to Timber, and all the other Latchetts' animals.

"Got a vet's certificate with it, I need hardly say. I don't buy pigs in pokes."

"Is Peggy going to show it this year?"

"Of course she is, of course she is. What did I buy it for but for her to show?"

Bee's face was positively blissful. "How nice!" she said, and she sounded rapturous.

"Do you like it, Miss Ashby?" Peggy Gates said, appearing at Brat's side.

Peggy was a very pretty creature. Pink and white and gold. Brat thought that if it were possible to cross Miss Parslow and Eleanor the result would probably be Peggy Gates. She accepted her introduction to Brat with composure, but managed to convey the impression that it was personally delightful to her to have Patrick home again. Her small hand lay in his with a soft pressure that was intimate rather than friendly. Brat shook it heartily and resisted a temptation to wipe his palm down his hip.

She accepted Bee's congratulations on her possession of the horse, allowed a decent interval for further contemplation of it, and then with an admirable display of social dexterity, lifted the whole family from the yard into the drawing-room of the house. It was called the drawing-room, and was furnished as such, but Bee, who remembered it as old Mrs. Vidler's parlour, thought the water-colours and wistaria wallpaper a poor exchange for the lustre jugs and framed engravings of Mrs. Vidler's day.

They drank very good madeira and talked about the Bures Agricultural Show.

And they drove home with Bee still looking as if someone had left her a fortune. She caught Brat's considering look at her and said: "Well?"

"You look like a cat that has been given cream," he said.

She gave him her sideways, amused glance. "Cream and fish and liver," she said; but did not tell him the translation.

"When all the fuss of Friday is over, Brat," she said, "you must go up to town and get yourself a wardrobe. Walkers will take weeks to make your evening things, and you'll need them for the celebration when Uncle Charles comes home."

"What shall I get?" he asked, at a loss for the first time.

"I should leave it to Walters, if I were you."

"Outfit for a young English gentleman," Brat said.

And she looked sideways again, surprised by the twist in his voice.

Chapter 18

*E*leanor came into the sitting-room as Bee was opening the midday post, and said: "She bumped!"

Bee looked up hazily, her mind still on the contents of her mail.

"She bumped, I tell you. For a whole fifty yards she bumped like a good 'un."

"The Parslow girl? Oh, congratulations, Nell, dear."

"I never thought I'd live to see this day. Is no one having sherry?"

"Brat and I have drunk sufficient strange liquids this morning to last us for the rest of the week."

"How did it go, Brat?" Eleanor asked, pouring herself some sherry.

"Not as badly as I'd been prepared for," Brat said, watching her thin capable hand manipulating the glasses. That hand wouldn't lie soft and confidential and insinuating in one's own.

"Did Docket tell you how he got his wound?"

"Docket was at market," Bee said. "But we had hot buttered scones from Mrs. Docket."

"Dear Mrs. Docket. What did Miss Hassell give you?"

"Shortbread. She wasn't going to give us that, but she succumbed to Brat's charms." So Bee had noticed that.

"I'm not surprised," Eleanor said, looking at Brat over her glass. "And Wigsell?"

"Do you remember that brown horse of Dick Pope's? The one he swept the board with at Bath last year?"

"Certainly."

"Gates has bought it for Peggy."

Eleanor stopped sipping sherry and thought about this in silence for a moment or two.

"For Peggy to show."

"Yes."

"Well, well!" said Eleanor slowly: and she looked amused and thoughtful. She looked at Bee, met Bee's glance, and looked away again. "Well, well!" she said again, and went on sipping sherry. After an interval broken only by the rip of paper as Bee opened envelopes, she said: "I don't know that that was such a very good move."

"No," said Bee, not looking up.

"I'm going to wash. What is for lunch?"

"Goulash."

"As made by our Mrs. Betts, that is just stew."

The twins came in from lessons at the Rectory, and Simon from the stables, and they went in to lunch.

Simon had come down so late to breakfast that Brat's only intercourse with him to-day had been to wish him good morning. He seemed amiable and relaxed, and enquired with what appeared to be genuine interest about the success of the morning. Bee provided an account, with periodic confirmation from Brat. When she came to Wigsell, Eleanor interrupted her to say:

"Did you know that Gates has bought Peggy a new horse?"

"No," Simon said, looking up with mild interest.

"He has bought her that brown horse of Dick Pope's."

"*Riding Light?*"

"Yes. Riding Light. She is going to show it this year."

For the first time since he had met him Brat saw Simon Ashby flush. He paused for a moment, and then went on with his lunch. The flush died, and the cool pale profile resumed its normal calm. Both Eleanor and Bee had avoided looking at him while he absorbed the news, but Ruth studied him with interest.

And Brat, eating Mrs. Betts's goulash, studied him with his mind. Simon Ashby was reputedly crazy about the Gates girl. But was he glad that the girl had been given a good horse? No. He was furious. And what was more, his womenfolk had known that he would be furious. They had known beforehand that he would find Peggy's entry as a rival unforgivable. They had, understandably, not wanted the Gates affair to last or to become serious; and they had recognised instantly, both of them, that Peggy's possession of Riding Light had saved them. What kind of creature was this Simon Ashby, who could not bear to be beaten by the girl he was in love with?

He remembered Bee's inordinate pleasure in the brown horse. He saw again Eleanor's slow amusement at the news. They had known at once that that was the end of the Peggy affair. Gates had bought that horse to be "upsides" with Latchetts; to give his daughter a mount as good as any owned by the man he hoped she would marry. And all he had done was to destroy any chance that Peggy ever had of being mistress of Latchetts.

Well, Simon was no longer master of Latchetts, so it would not matter to the Gates family that Simon resented Peggy's possession of the horse. But what kind of heel was Simon that he could not love a rival?

"What is Brat going to ride at the Bures Show," he heard Eleanor say, and brought his attention back to the lunch table.

"All of them," Simon said. And as Eleanor looked her question: "They are his horses."

This was the kind of thing that the English did not say. Simon must be very angry to desert the habit of a lifetime.

"I'm not going to 'show' any horses, if that is what you mean," Brat said. "That requires technique, and I haven't got it."

"But you used to be very good," Bee said.

"Did I? Oh, well, that is a long time ago. I certainly don't want to show any horses in the ring at Bures."

"The show isn't for nearly three weeks yet," Eleanor said. "Bee could coach you for a day or two, and you'd be as good as ever."

But Brat was not to be moved. It would have been fun to see what he could do against English horsemen; fun especially to jump the Latchetts horses and perhaps win with them; but he was not going to make any public appearance as Patrick Ashby of Latchetts if he could help it.

"Brat could ride in the races," Ruth said. "The races they end up with. He could beat everyone on Timber, couldn't he?"

"Timber is not going to be knocked about in any country bumpkins' race if I still have any say in the matter," Simon said, speaking into his plate. "He is going to Olympia, which is his proper place."

"I agree," Brat said. And the atmosphere ceased to be tense. Jane wanted to know why fractions were vulgar, and Ruth wanted a new bicycle tire, and the conversation became the normal family conversation of any mealtime in any home.

Before lunch was over the first of the visitors arrived; and the steady stream went on, from after-luncheon coffee, through tea, to six o'clock drinks. They had all come to inspect Brat, but he noticed that those who had known Patrick Ashby came with a genuine pleasure in welcoming him back. Each of them had some small memory of him to recount, and all of them had kept the memory green because they had liked Pat Ashby and grieved for him. And Brat caught himself being gratified in an absurd and proprietorial way, as if some protégé of his own was being praised. The light that had been shed on Simon this morning made him more than ever Patrick's champion. It was all wrong that Latchetts should have been Simon's all those years. It was Patrick's inheritance and it was all wrong that Patrick should not be here to inherit it. Patrick was all right. Patrick would not have gone sick with rage because his best girl had a better horse than he had. Patrick was all right.

So he accepted the small verbal gifts on Patrick's behalf and was pleased and gratified.

About the time when tea-cups were being mixed up with cock-tail glasses the local doctor appeared, and Brat ceased to be grati-fied, and became interested in Eleanor's reactions to the doctor. Eleanor seemed to like the doctor very much, and Brat, knowing nothing whatever about him, was straightway convinced that he was not good enough for her. The only guests left now were Colonel Smollett, the Chief Constable for the county; the two Misses Byrne, who occupied the Jacobean house at the far end of the village and, according to Bee, had their walls hung with "plates and warming-pans, and other kitchen utensils"; and Dr. Spence. Dr. Spence was young and red-haired and bony, and he had freck-les and a friendly manner. He was the successor of the old country doctor who had brought the whole Ashby family up, and he was, so Bee confided in an interval of tea-pouring, "much too brilliant to stay in a country practice." Brat wondered if he stayed for Eleanor's sake; he seemed to like Eleanor very much.

"You caused us a lot of trouble, young man," Colonel Smollett had said, greeting him; and Brat, after the polite evasions he had experienced so far, was glad of his frankness. Just as his notions of English middle-class had been derived from American films, so his idea of a colonel had been derived from the English Press, and was equally erroneous. Colonel Smollett was a small, thin man with a beaked nose and a self-effacing manner. What one noticed about him was his extraordinary neatness and his gay blue eyes.

The Colonel gave the Misses Byrne a lift in his car, but the doc-tor lingered, and it was only when Bee asked him to stay for dinner that he pulled himself together and went.

"Poor Dr. Spence," Bee said at dinner. "I'm sorry he wouldn't stay. I'm sure that landlady of his starves him."

"Nonsense," said Simon, who had recovered his good temper

and had been very bright all the afternoon; "that lean, red-haired type always look underfed. Besides, he wouldn't have eaten, anyhow. All he wants is to sit and look at Eleanor."

Which confirmed Brat's worst fears.

But all Eleanor said was: "Don't be absurd"; and she said it without heat and without interest.

They were all tired by dinner-time, and it was a quiet meal. The excitement of having Brat there had died into acceptance, and they no longer treated him as a newcomer. Even the unforthcoming Jane had stopped accusing him with her eyes. He was part of the landscape. It was wonderfully restful to be part of the landscape again. For the first time since he came to Latchetts he was hungry.

But as he got ready for bed he puzzled over the problem of Simon. Simon, who was quite sure that he was not Patrick, but had no intention of saying so. (Why? Because he would not be believed, and his protest would be put down to resentment at his brother's return? Because he had plans for a dramatic unveiling? Because he had some better way of dealing with an impostor who would not be unveiled?) Simon, who was so good a dissembler that he could fool his own family about his inmost feelings. Simon, who was so self-centered, so vain, that to come between him and the sun was to insult him. Simon, who had charm enough for ten men, and an appealing air of vulnerability. Simon, who was like Timber.

He stood again at the open window in the dark, looking at the curve of the down against the sky. Perhaps because he was less tired to-night he was no longer so afraid; but the incalculable factor in this life that he was due to lead was still Simon.

If Simon so resented Peggy Gates's owning a better horse than his, what, wondered Brat, could have been his reaction to Patrick's sudden succession to Latchetts?

He considered this a long time, staring into the dark.

And as he turned at last to put the light on, a voice in his mind said: I wonder where Simon was when Patrick went over the cliff.

But he noticed the heinousness of this at once, of course. What was he suggesting? Murder? In Latchetts? In Clare? By a boy of thirteen? He was letting his antipathy to Simon run away with his common sense.

The suicide of Patrick Ashby had been a police affair. An affair of inquest and evidence. The thing had been investigated, and the police had been satisfied that it was in truth suicide.

Satisfied? Or just without a case?

Where would that coroner's report be now? In the police records he supposed. And it was not easy for a civilian to persuade the police to satisfy an idle curiosity; they were busy people.

But the thing must have been reported in the local Press. It must have been a local sensation. Somewhere in the files there would be an account of that inquest, and he, Brat Farrar, would unearth it at the first opportunity.

Antipathy or no antipathy, common sense or no common sense, he wanted to know where Simon Ashby was when his twin went over the Westover cliffs.

Chapter 19

*M*r. Sandal was to come on Thursday night and stay over till after luncheon on Friday.

On Thursday morning Bee said that she was going into Westover to do some special shopping for Mr. Sandal's meals, and what would Brat like to do with his day?

Brat said that he would like to come with her and see Westover again, and Bee looked pleased.

"We can stop on the way through the village," she said, "and let Mrs. Gloom run her eye over you. It will be one less for you to meet after church on Sunday."

So they stopped at the newsagent's, and Brat was exhibited, and Mrs. Gloom sucked the last ounce of satisfaction out of the drama of his return, and they laughed together about her as they sped away to the sea.

"People who can't sing are horribly frustrated," Bee said, after a little.

Brat considered this *non sequitur.* "The highest mountain in Britain is Ben Nevis," he said, proffering one in his turn.

Bee laughed at that and said: "No, I just meant that I should like to sing at the top of my voice, but I can only croak. Can you sing?"

"No. I croak too. We could croak together."

"I doubt if it is legal to croak in a built-up area. One never knows nowadays. And anyhow, there is that." She waved her hand at a large sign which read:

MOTORISTS. PLEASE REFRAIN FROM USING
YOUR HORN. THIS IS A HOSPITAL.

Brat glanced up at the building, set on the slope above the town, and remarked that it was uncommonly pretty for a hospital.

"Yes; much less terrifying than the normal place. It is a great pity that *that* was allowed to happen." She jerked her chin at the row of cheap shops on the opposite side of the road; some of them not much better than shacks. Dingy cafés, a cobbler's, a bicycle "depot," a seller of wreaths and crosses, a rival seller of flowers, a greengrocer's, and anonymous businesses with windows painted half-way up and odd bills tacked in the windows.

They were running down the slope into the town, and this miscellaneous strip of roadside commerce was the last petering-out of the poorer suburbs. Beyond was Westover proper: clean and neat and shining in the reflected light from the sea.

As Bee turned into the car park she said: "You don't want to tail round looking at 'sea-food' for Mr. Sandal's consumption. Go away and amuse yourself, and we'll meet for lunch at the Angel about a quarter to one."

He was some distance away when she called him back. "I forgot to ask if you were short of money. I can lend you some if you—"

"Oh, no, thanks; I still have some of what Cosset, Thring and what-you-may-call-'em advanced me."

He went first to the harbour to see the place that he was supposed to have set out from eight years ago. It was filled with coastwise shipping and fishing boats, very gay in the dancing light. He leaned against the warm stones of the breakwater and contemplated it. It was here that Alec Loding had sat painting his "old scow" on the last day of Pat Ashby's life. It was over those cliffs away to the right that Pat Ashby had fallen to his death.

He pushed himself off the breakwater and went to look for the office of the *Westover Times*. It took him some time to find it because, although every citizen of Westover read the local paper, very few of them had occasion to seek it out in its home. Its home was a stone's throw from the harbour in a small old house in a small old street which still had its original cobbles. The entrance was so low that Brat instinctively ducked his head as he went in. Beyond, after the bright sunlight outside, there was blackness. But out of the blackness the unmistakable adolescent voice of an office boy said: "Yes?"

Brat said that he would like to see Mr. Macallan.

The voice said that Mr. Macallan was out.

"I suppose you couldn't tell me where I could find him?"

"The fourth table on the left upstairs at the Blue Bird."

"That's explicit."

"Can't help it; that's where he is. That's where he always is, this time of day."

The Blue Bird, it seemed, was a coffee-shop round the corner on the harbour front. And Mr. Macallan was indeed sitting at the fourth table on the left upstairs, which was the one by the far window. Mr. Macallan was sitting with a half-drunk cup of coffee in front of him, glowering down on the bright front. He greeted Brat amiably, however, as one old friend to another, and pulled out a chair for him.

"I'm afraid I haven't been much good to you," Brat said.

"The only way I'll ever get myself onto the front page of the *Clarion* is in a trunk," Mr. Macallan said.

"A trunk?"

"In sections. And I can't help feeling that would be a wee bit drastic." He spread out that morning's *Clarion* so that the shrieking black print screamed up from the table. The trunk murder was still front-page news after three days, it having been discovered that the legs in the case belonged to two different persons; a complication which put the present case *hors concours* in the trunk-murder class.

"What's horrible about murder," Mr. Macallan said reflectively, "is not that it happens, but that it happens to your Aunt Agnes, if you follow me. Hi! *Miss!* A cup of coffee for my friend here. Brother Johnny goes to the war and gets killed and it is all very sad, but no one is shocked—civilisation being what it is. But if someone bumps Aunt Agnes off on her way home one night that *is* a shock. That sort of thing doesn't happen to people you know."

"It must be worse when someone you know bumps off someone's Aunt Agnes."

"Ay," said Mr. Macallan, shooting an extra spoonful of sugar into his half-cold coffee and stirring it vigorously. "I've seen some of that. Families, you know. It's always the same; they just can't believe it. *Their* Johnny. That is the horror in murder. The domesticity of it." He took out his cigarette case and offered it. "And how do you like being Clare's white-headed boy? Are you glad to be back?"

"You can't imagine how glad."

"After that fine free life in Arizona or Texas or wherever it was? You mean you actually prefer this?" Mr. Macallan jerked his head at the Westover front filled with placid shoppers. And, as Brat nodded: "Mercy-be-here! I can't hardly credit it."

"Why? Don't you like the place?"

Mr. Macallan looked down at the southern English walking about in their southern English sunshine, and metaphorically spat. "They're so satisfied with themselves I can't take my eyes off them," he said.

"Satisfied with their lot, you mean? Why not?"

"Nothing in this world came out of satisfaction."

"Except the human race," said Brat.

Mr. Macallan grinned. "I'll allow you that." But he went on glowering down at the bright harbour scene. "I look at them and think: 'These people kept Scotland fighting for four hundred years,' and I can't find the answer."

"The answer, of course, is that they didn't."

"No? Let me tell you that my country—"

"They've been much too busy for the last thousand years keeping the shores of England. But for them your Scotland would be part of Spain to-day."

This was apparently a new idea to Mr. Macallan. He decided to let it ride.

"You weren't looking for me, were you? When you came to the Blue Bird?"

"Yes. I went to the office first and they told me you would be here. There's something I want and I thought that you might help me to it."

"Not publicity, I take it," Mr. Macallan said dryly.

"No, I want to read my obituary."

"Man, who doesn't! You're a privileged person, Mr. Ashby, a very privileged person."

"I suppose the *Westover Times* keeps back numbers."

"Och, yes, back to June the 18th, 1827. Or is it June the 28th? I forget. So you want to look at the files. Well, there's not much, but you'll find it very interesting of course. One's own death must be a fascinating subject to read about."

"You've read about it, then?"

"Och, yes. Before I went out to Latchetts on Tuesday, I naturally looked you up."

So it was that, when they stumbled down the dark stairs to the cellar of the *Westover Times* offices, Mr. Macallan was able to put his hand on the required copy without delay and without raising the dust of a hundred and fifty years about their ears.

"I'll leave you to it," Mr. Macallan said, spreading the volume open under the naked light above the old-fashioned sloping desk. "Have a good time. If there is anything else I can do for you, just let me know. And drop in when you feel like it."

He trotted up the stone stairs, and the scuffling sound of his shoes faded upwards into the world of men, and Brat was left alone with the past.

The *Westover Times* appeared twice a week: on Wednesdays and Saturdays. Patrick Ashby's death had occurred on a Saturday, so that a single Wednesday issue carried both the announcement of his death and the report of the inquest. As well as the usual announcement inserted by the family in the list of deaths, there was a short news item on the middle page. The *Westover Times* had been owned and run by a Westover family since its founding, and it still kept the stateliness, the good manners, and the reticence of an early Edwardian doctor's brougham plying between Harley Street and Knightsbridge. The paper announced the sad occurrence and offered its sympathy to the family in this great trial which had come to them so soon after the tragic death of Mr. and Mrs. Ashby in a flying accident. It offered no information beyond the fact that on Saturday afternoon or evening Patrick Ashby had met his death by falling over the cliffs to the west of the town. An account of the inquest would be found on page five.

On page five there was a whole column on the inquest. A column was not enough, of course, to do justice to the inquest in detail, but all the salient facts were there, and now and then a piece of evidence was reported verbatim.

Saturday afternoon was a holiday for the Ashby children and they were accustomed in the summer to take a "piece" with them and pursue their various interests in the countryside until it was time to come home to their evening meal. No alarm had been raised about Patrick's non-appearance in the evening until he had been missing for several hours. It was taken for granted that he had gone farther than he had intended in his latest hobby of bird-watching, and that he was merely late. When darkness closed down and he still had not come home, telephoned enquiries were sent all round the countryside in an effort to find someone who had seen him, so that if an accident had overtaken him rescue might be directed to the proper locality. When these enquiries proved barren, a search-party was organised to beat all the likely places for the missing boy. The search was conducted both on horse and on foot, and along the roads by car, without success.

In the first light of early morning the boy's jacket was found by a coastguard patrolling along the cliffs. Albert Potticary, the coastguard in question, gave evidence that the coat was lying about fifty yards from the cliff-edge, just where the path from Tanbitches began to descend through the gap to the harbour at Westover. It was lying a few yards off the path on the side nearest the cliff, and was weighted in its place by a stone. It was wet with dew when he picked it up, and the pockets were empty except for a note written in thin ink. The note was the one now shown him. He telephoned the news to the police and at once instituted a search for a body on the beach. No body was found. High tide the previous night had been at seven twenty-nine, and if the boy had fallen into the water, or if he had fallen before high-water so that his body was taken out by the tide, it would not be washed up again at Westover. No one drowned in the Westover district had ever been washed up nearer than Castleton, away to the west; and most of them farther west than that. He was therefore not hopeful of finding any body when he instituted the search. It was merely routine.

The last person to see Patrick Ashby turned out to be Abel Tusk, the shepherd. He had met the boy in the early afternoon, about half-way between Tanbitches and the cliff.

Q. What was he doing?

A. He was lying on his belly in the grass.

Q. Doing what?

A. Waiting for a lark.

Q. What kind of lark?

A. An English lark.

Q. Ah, you mean he was bird-watching. Did he appear his normal self?

Yes, Abel said, as far as he could judge Pat Ashby had looked much as usual. Never very "gabby" at any time. A quiet boy? Yes, a nice quiet boy. They discussed birds for a little and then parted. He, Abel Tusk, was on his way into Westover by the cliff path, it being also his own half-holiday. He did not get back until late at night and did not hear about the search for the boy until Sunday morning.

Asked if many people used that cliff path he said no. There were buses from the village that got you into Westover in a tenth of the time, but he didn't care for buses. It was rough walking, the cliff part of the path, and not suitable for the kind of shoes that people going to town would be wearing. So no one but someone like himself who was already on the sea side of Tanbitches hill would think of going to Westover that way.

Bee gave evidence that his parents' death had been a great shock to the boy, but that he had taken it well and had seemed to be recovering. She had no reason to think that he contemplated taking his own life. The children separated on Saturday afternoons because their interests were different, so that it was not unusual for Patrick to be alone.

Q. His twin did not accompany him?

A. No. Patrick was fascinated by birds, but Simon's tastes are mechanical.

Q. You have seen the note found in the boy's coat, and you recognise it as the handwriting of your nephew Patrick?

A. Oh, yes. Patrick had a very individual way of making his capital letters. And he was the only person I know who wrote with a stylograph.

She explained the nature of a stylograph. The one Patrick owned had been black vulcanite with a thin yellow spiral down the barrel. Yes, it was missing. He carried it always with him; it was one of his pet possessions.

Q. Can you think of any reason why this sudden desire to take his own life should overcome him, when he seemed to his friend, the shepherd, to be normally happy in the afternoon?

A. I can only suggest that he *was* normally happy during the afternoon, but that when it was time to turn homeward the thought of going back to a house empty of so much that had made life fine for him was suddenly too much, and that he was overcome by an impulse born of a moment's despair.

And that was the verdict of the court too. That the boy had succumbed to a passing impulse at a moment when the balance of his mind had been disturbed.

That was the end of the column and that was the end of Patrick Ashby. Brat turned over the pages of the next issue, filled with the small importances of summertime Westover: shows, bowling competitions, tennis tournaments, council meetings, trade outings; but there was no mention of Pat Ashby. Pat Ashby already belonged to the past.

Brat sat back in the dead quiet of the cellar and thought about it all. The boy lying in the summer grass waiting for his beloved larks to drop out of the sky. And the night coming. And no boy coming home across Tanbitches hill.

Mechanical interests. Bee had said, describing Simon's way of spending his half-holiday. That meant the internal combustion engine, he supposed. It was about the age of thirteen that one did begin to be interested in cars. Simon had probably been innocently

tinkering in the garage at Latchetts. Certainly there was no suggestion at the inquest, as reported in the Press, that his whereabouts
had been a matter for question.

When he joined Bee for lunch at the Angel he longed to ask her
bluntly where Simon had been that afternoon. But of course one
could not say: "Where was Simon the afternoon I ran away from
home?" It was an utterly pointless question. He must think up some
other way of bringing the subject into the conversation. He was distracted by the old head-waiter at the Angel, who had known all the
Ashby children and was shaken to the core, apparently, by Patrick's
unexpected return. His old hands trembled as they laid the various
dishes in front of him, and each dish was accompanied by a quavered "Mr. Patrick, sir," as if he was glad to use the name. But the
climax came with the sweet course. The sweet was fruit tart, and he
had already served both Bee and Brat, but he returned immediately
and with great empressement laid a large meringue on a silver dish
in front of Brat's place. Brat gazed at it in surprise and then looked
up to find the old man waiting for his comment with a proud smile
and tears in his eyes. His mind was so full of Simon that he was not
quick enough, and it was Bee who saved the situation.

"How wonderful of Daniel to remember that you always had
that!" she said, and Brat followed her lead and the old man went
away pleased and moved, mopping his eyes on a dazzling white
handkerchief that looked as large as a sheet.

"Thanks," Brat said to Bee. "I hadn't remembered that."

"Dear old Daniel. I think it is almost like seeing his own son
coming back. He had three, you know. They all died in one war, and
his grandsons all died in the following one. He was very fond of you
children, so I expect it is very wonderful for him to see anyone he
has loved come back from the dead. What have you been doing
with your morning?"

"Reading my obituary."

"How morbid of you. Or, no, of course, it isn't. It is what we all
want to do. Did you see little Mr. Macallan?"

"I did. He sent his best respects to you. Aunt Bee—"

"You are too old to begin calling me aunt."

"Bee, what were Simon's 'mechanical interests'?"

"Simon never had any mechanical interests as far as I know."

"You said at the inquest that he had."

"*I* did? I can't imagine what they could have been. What was it
apropos of?"

"To explain why we didn't do things together on a Saturday afternoon. What did Simon do when I went bird-watching?" He tried to make it sound like someone trying to remember an old way of life.

"Pottered about, I expect. Simon was always a potterer. His hobbies never lasted longer than a fortnight at the outside."

"So you don't remember what Simon was using for a hobby the day I ran away?"

"It's absurd of me, my dear, but I don't. I don't even remember where he was that day. When something dreadful happens, you know, you push it down in your mind and never bring it up again if you can help it. I do remember that he spent all night out on his pony looking frantically for you. Poor Simon. You did him a bad turn, Brat. I don't know if you realise it. Simon changed after you went. I don't know whether it was the shock of your going or the lack of your sober companionship, but he was a different person afterwards."

Since Brat had no answer to this he ate in silence, and presently she said: "And you did me a bad turn in never writing to me. Why didn't you, Brat?"

This was the weak spot in the whole structure, as Loding had continually pointed out.

"I don't *know*," he said. "Honestly, I don't *know*!"

The exasperation and desperation of his tone had an appropriateness that he had not foreseen.

"All right," she said. "I won't worry you, my dear. I didn't mean to. It is just something that has puzzled me. I was so very fond of you when you were small, and we were such very good friends. It was not like you to live a life of your own without once glancing back."

He raked up an offering from the depths of his own experience. "It's easier than you'd think to drop the past behind you when you are fourteen. If you are continually meeting fresh experience, I mean. The past has no greater reality than something you saw in a cinema. No personal reality, I mean."

"I must try running away one day," she said lightly. "There is a lot of the past I should like to drop behind me."

And Daniel came with the cheese, and they talked about other things.

Chapter 20

*B*rat had not been prepared to find birthday presents by his plate on Friday morning. He had not, in fact, reckoned with a birthday at all. "All celebration has been postponed until Mr. Charles Ashby comes back to this country," Mr. Sandal had said to him in London, and it was not until Bee had drawn his attention to it that he had remembered that, celebration apart, there would inevitably be a day on which he would become twenty-one. He had had so little experience of birthdays that he had taken it for granted that a postponement of celebration meant a simple verbal congratulation from each member of the family, and he was dismayed by the pile of parcels by his breakfast plate. He quailed at the thought of having to open them in public.

The sardonic light in Simon's eye braced him to the task. He had a suspicion that Simon's punctuality at breakfast this morning was due less to the presence of Mr. Sandal than to the prospect of enjoying his embarrassment over those presents.

"Happy birthday, Brat!" they said, as they came in. "Happy birthday, Brat!" One after another. So that the light benedictions fell round him like confetti.

He wished he didn't feel so bad about it. He wished that they were really his family, and that these were his presents by his plate, and that it was his birthday. It was a very nice thing, a family birthday.

"Are you an opener-before-breakfast or an opener-after, Brat?" Eleanor asked.

"After," he said promptly, and won a breathing-space.

After several cups of strong coffee he might feel braver.

Simon had, as well as presents, a pile of telegrams from the still large numbers of his acquaintances who had not heard of his twin's return, and he opened them as he ate and shared the contents. Having read each message aloud he added a postscript of comment.

"An exact shilling, the cheeseparing adding-machine! And I gave her a wonderful lunch last time I was in town. . . . What do you imagine Bobby is doing in Skye? He loathes mountains and is a martyr to midges . . . Gore and Bowen. I suppose that's to remind me to pay my bill. . . . I'm sure I don't know anyone called Bert Burt. Do you think he can be a bookie?"

When eventually Brat could no longer postpone the opening of his parcels, his task was made easier by the fact that his presents were for the most part replicas of those Simon was pulling out of his own pile. Mr. Sandal's Georgian sugar-sifter, Bee's silver flask, Eleanor's whip, and the twins' pocket-book, were all duplicated. Only the present from the Rectory was individual. It was a small wooden box that played a tune when the lid was opened. Brat had never seen or heard of such a thing before, and was so delighted with it that he forgot to be self-conscious and became absorbed in it.

"That came from Clare Park," Bee said.

And at that reminder of Loding he came back to reality and shut down the lid on the sweet frail melody.

This morning he was going to sign his soul away. It was no time for tinkling little tunes.

This signing-away was also the subject of surprise. He had imagined in his innocence that various papers would be put in front of him and he would sign them, and that would be that. A matter of twenty minutes at the most. But it proved to be a matter of hours. He and Mr. Sandal sat side by side at the big table in the library, and the whole economic history of Latchetts was laid open for his inspection. Cosset, Thring and Noble were accounting to their young client for the years of his minority.

Brat, a little bewildered but interested, toiled after Mr. Sandal in his progress through the years, and admired the way the old man handled this legal and mathematical exploration.

"Your dear mother's fortune is not what it was in the prosperous days when she inherited it, of course; but it will be sufficient to ensure that you may live at Latchetts in the future without anxiety. As you have observed, the margin of safety has often been very small during the years of your minority, but it was Miss Ashby's wish that there should be no borrowing on the strength of your inheritance from your mother. She was determined that that should come to you intact when you were twenty-one."

He went on laying statements in front of Brat, and for the first time Brat was aware of the struggle and the insecurity that lay behind the assured contentment that Latchetts presented to the eye.

"What happened that year?" he asked, putting his finger on a particularly black record.

Mr. Sandal flipped over some papers. "Ah, yes. I remember. That was a bad year. A very bad year. One of the mares died and two were barren, and a very fine foal broke a leg. A heart-breaking year. It is a precarious way of making a living. That year, for instance," his thin dry finger pointed out another unsatisfactory report, "everything went swimmingly at Latchetts but it happened to be a year when no one was buying and none of the yearlings made their reserve price at the sales. A matter of luck. Merely luck. You will observe that some of the years were exceedingly lucky ones, so that the losses were overtaken."

He left the stables and went on to the farms: the conditions of lease, the improvements, the standing of the tenants, the nature of the crops. Eventually he came to the matter of personal income.

"Your father made a very good income in his profession of consulting engineer, and there seemed, of course, nothing to prevent him making that large yearly sum for a lifetime to come. He therefore spent generously on Latchetts and on the horses that were his hobby. Bought expensive and finely bred mares, and so on, so that when he died his investments were not very extensive, and death duties had of course to be paid, so the investments had to go."

He slipped another sheet in front of Brat's eye, showing how the duty had been paid without mortgaging Latchetts.

"Miss Ashby has her own income and has never taken an allowance from the Latchetts estate. Except a housekeeping one, that is. The two elder children have had increasing allowances as they grew up. With the exception of some personal possessions—the children's ponies, for instance—the horses in the stable belong to the estate. When the children went to sales to buy for re-selling they were given money by Miss Ashby, and any profit on the improved horses went towards the expenses of Latchetts. I understand, however, that Simon has lately bought one or two with the result of profitable bets, and Eleanor with the result of her efforts as an instructress in the art of riding. Miss Ashby will no doubt tell you which these are. They do not appear in the relevant papers. The Shetland ponies were Miss Ashby's own venture, and are her own property. I hope that is all clear?"

Brat said that it was.

"Now about the future. It is the Bank's advice that the money left you by your mother should stay invested as it is now. Have you any objection to that?"

"I don't want any lump sum," Loding had said. "I should only blow it, in the first place. And in the second place, it would cause a shocking amount of heart-searching at the bank. We don't want any heart-searching once you're in the saddle. All I want is a cosy little weekly allowance for the rest of my life, so that I can thumb my nose at Equity, and managements, and producers who say that I'm always late for rehearsals. *And* landladies. Riches, my boy, don't consist in having things, but in not having to do something you don't want to do. And don't you forget it. Riches is being able to thumb your nose."

"What income would that bring me, as it is?" Brat asked Mr. Sandal, and Mr. Sandal told him.

That was all right. He could peel Loding's cut off that and still have enough to meet his obligations at Latchetts.

"These are the children's present allowances. The twins, of course, will be going away to school presently, and that will be a charge on the estate for a few years."

He was surprised by the smallness of the allowances. Why, he thought, I made more than that in three months at the dude ranch. It subtly altered his attitude to Simon that Simon in the matter of spending money should have been so much his inferior.

"They're not very big, are they?" he said to Mr. Sandal, and the old man looked taken aback.

"They are in accordance with the size of the estate," he said dryly.

"Well, I think they ought to be stepped up a bit now."

"Yes; that would be quite in order. But you cannot expect to carry two adults as passengers on the estate. It would not be just to the estate. They are both capable of earning their own living."

"What do you suggest, then?"

"I suggest that Eleanor be given a slightly increased allowance while she lives at Latchetts, or until she marries."

"Is she thinking of getting married?"

"My dear boy, all young ladies think of getting married, especially when they are as pleasant to look upon as your sister. I am not aware, however, that she has so far exhibited any specific interest in the matter."

"Oh. And Simon?"

"Simon's case is difficult. Until a few weeks ago he looked upon Latchetts as his. He is not likely to remain long at Latchetts now, but the slightly increased allowance you suggest could be paid to him while he gives you his services here."

"I don't think that is good enough," said Brat, who was surprised by Mr. Sandal's assumption that Simon would go. Simon showed no signs of going. "I think a bit of the estate is owing to him."

"Morally owing, you mean?"

"Yes, I suppose so."

"No doubt you are right, but it is a dangerous assumption which you cannot expect me to countenance. One cannot hand out bits of a financial estate and still keep the said estate in good heart. An allowance is one thing: it comes out of income. But the giving away of the fabric of the thing is to damage its whole structure."

"Well, I suggest that if Simon wants to go away and begin somewhere on his own that the money to start should be lent to him out of the estate at a nominal rate of interest. I suppose if I say without interest you'll jump down my throat."

The old man smiled on him, quite kindly. "I think there is nothing against that. I am looking forward to a period of great prosperity for Latchetts now that the lean years are over. I don't suppose a loan to Simon would greatly incommode the estate. There would be the saving of the allowance to balance it. Now, about the increase in the present allowances—"

They settled the amounts of that.

"Lastly," said Mr. Sandal, "the pensioners."

"Pensioners?"

"Yes. The various dependents of the family who have become too old to work."

For the fourth time that morning Brat was surprised. He looked at the long list and wondered if all established English families had this drain on their income. Mr. Sandal seemed to take it as a matter of course; as much a commonplace of honourable practice as paying one's income tax. Mr. Sandal had frowned on any extravagance where the family was concerned: able-bodied Ashbys must earn their own living. The obligation to support the aged and infirm retainers of the family he took for granted. There was Nannie, who was now ninety-two and lived in a place called New Deer in Scotland; there was an old groom of eighty-nine who lived in the village, and another at Guessgate; there was a cook who had cooked for them until she was sixty-eight and now lived with a daughter of sixty-nine in Horsham; and so on.

He thought of the brassy blonde in the flowered rayon who had bade him welcome to Latchetts. Who would pension her? The country, he supposed. For long and honourable service?

Brat agreed to the continuance of the pensions, and then Simon was called in to do his share of signing. It pleased Brat, who had found it a depressing morning, to notice the sudden widening of Simon's eye as it lighted on his own signature. It was nearly a decade since Simon had set eyes on those capital letters of Patrick's, and here they were blandly confronting him on the library table. That would "larn" him to be sardonic over Brat's efforts to carry off a birthday that was not his.

Then Bee came in, and Mr. Sandal explained the increased provisions in the matter of allowances and the plan for providing for Simon's future. When Simon heard of the plan he eyed Brat thoughtfully; and Brat could read quite plainly what the look said. "Bribery, is that it? Well, it won't work. I'm damned well staying here and you will damned well pay me that allowance." Whatever plans Simon had, they centred round Latchetts.

Bee seemed pleased, however. She put her arm through his to lead him to lunch, and squeezed it. "Dear Brat!" she said.

"I congratulated you both and gave you my good wishes at breakfast," Mr. Sandal said, picking up his glass of claret, "but I should like now to drink a toast." He lifted his glass to Brat. "To Patrick, who has not only succeeded to his inheritance but has accepted its obligations."

"To Patrick!" they said. "To Patrick!"

"To Patrick!" said Jane, last.

He looked at her and found that she was smiling at him.

Chapter 21

Simon took Mr. Sandal to the station in the afternoon, and when they had gone Bee said: "If you want to avoid the social life this afternoon I'll hold the fort for you. I have the books to do, anyhow. Perhaps you would like to take out one of the horses with Eleanor. She has gone back to the stables, I think."

There were few things in life that Brat would have liked so much as to go riding with Eleanor, but there was one thing that he wanted to do more. He wanted, on this day when Pat Ashby should have come into his inheritance, to walk over Tanbitches hill by the path that Pat had taken on the last day of his life.

"I want to go with Brat," Ruth said; and he noticed that Jane lingered to hear the result of this proposition, as if she too might have come. But Bee quashed the suggestion. Brat had had enough of his family for a little, she said.

"But he is going with Eleanor!" protested Ruth.

But Brat said no. He was going walking by himself.

He avoided the avenue, in case he might meet visitors bound for the house, and went down through the paddocks to the road. In one of the paddocks that bordered the avenue Eleanor was lunging a bay colt. He stood under the trees and watched her; her unruffled patience, her mastery of the puzzled and resentful youngster; the way she managed, even at the end of a long rein, to reassure him. He wondered if that doctor fellow knew anything about horses.

The turf on Tanbitches delighted him. He had not had turf like that underfoot since he was a child. He walked slowly upward, smelling the grassy smell and watching the great shadows flying before the wind. He bore away from the path towards the crown of beeches on the hilltop. If he went up there he would be able to see the whole slope of the countryside to the cliff edge; the countryside that Pat Ashby had shared with the larks.

As he came level with the green clump of bushes and young trees that marked the old quarry, he found an old man sitting in its shelter eating solid slabs of bread and jam, and gave him a greeting as he passed.

"Proud, a'nt yu!" said the old man tartly.

Brat swung on his heel and stared.

"Wonderful dentical and Frenchy furrin parts makes folks, surely."

He took another large bite and surveyed Brat from under the battered felt of his hat.

"Dunnamany nests you'd never seen but fur me."

"Abel!" said Brat.

"Well, that's summat," said the old man grudgingly.

"Abel!" said Brat, and sat down beside him. "Am I glad to see you!"

"Adone do!" Abel said to his dog, who came out from under the spread of his coat to sniff at the newcomer.

"Abel!" He could hardly believe that yesterday's occupant of a newspaper morgue was here in the flesh.

Abel began to exhibit signs of gratification at this undoubted enthusiasm for his society, and allowed that he had recognised him afar off. "Lame, are yu?"

"Just a bit."

"Bruck?"

"Yes."

"Weren't never one to make a pucker," Abel said, approving his laconic acceptance of bad luck.

Brat propped his back against the stout wooden fencing that kept the sheep from the quarry face, took out his cigarette case, and settled down for the afternoon.

In the hour that followed he learned a great deal about Pat Ashby, but nothing that helped to explain his suicide. Like everyone else, old Abel had been shocked and surprised by the boy's death, and now felt that his disbelief in a suicidal Patrick had been vindicated.

Patrick "weren't never one to make a pucker," no matter how "tedious bad" things were.

The old shepherd walked with him to the beeches, and Brat stayed there and watched man and dog grow small in the distance. Long after they were indistinguishable he stayed there, soothed by the loneliness and the great "hush" of the wind in the beech trees.

Then he followed them down into the green plain until he came to the path, and let it lead him back over the hill to Clare.

As he came down the north slope to the road, a familiar "clink-clink" came up to him on the wind. For a moment he was back on the Wilson ranch, with the forge glowing in the thin mountain air and—what was her name?—Cora waiting for him beyond the barn when he was tidied up after supper. Then he remembered where the forge was: in that cottage at the foot of the hill. It was early yet. He would go and see what an English smithy looked like.

It looked very like the Wilson one, when at last he stood in the doorway, except that the roof was a good deal lower. The smith was alone, his mate being no doubt an employee and subject to a rationing of labour, and he was fashioning horse-shoes. He looked up as Brat darkened the doorway, and gave him a greeting without pausing in his work. Brat watched him for a little in a companionable quiet, and then moved over to work the bellows for him. The man looked up and smiled. He finished what he was doing at the moment and then said: "I didn't know you against the light. I'm unaccountable glad to see you in my place again, Mr. Patrick."

"Thanks, Mr. Pilbeam."

"You're a deal handier with that thing than you used to be."

"I've earned my living at it since I saw you last."

"You have? Well, I'll be—!" He took a half-made shoe red-hot from the furnace and was about to resume work when he changed his mind and held it out with a grin to Brat. Brat accepted the challenge and made a good job of it, Mr. Pilbeam acting as mate with critical approval.

"Funny," he said, as Brat plunged the shoe into the water, "if any Ashby was to earn his living at this job it ought to have been your brother."

"Why?"

"You never showed much interest."

"And did Simon?"

"There was a time when I couldn't keep him out of this place. There wasn't anything he wasn't going to make, from a candlestick to gates for the avenue at Latchetts. Far as I remember, all he ever made was a sheep-crook, and that not over-well. But he was always round the place. It was a craze of his for the whole summer."

"Which summer was that?"

"Summer you left us, it was. I'd misremember about it, only he was here seeing us put an iron on a cartwheel the day you ran away. I had to shoo him home for his supper."

Brat considered the shoe he had made, while Mr. Pilbeam made ready to call it a day.

"I ought to hang that up," Mr. Pilbeam said, nodding at Brat's handiwork, "and label it: Made by Patrick Ashby of Latchetts. And I couldn't make a better one myself," he added handsomely.

"Give it to old Abel to nail on his door."

"Bless you, old Abel wouldn't have cold iron on his threshold. Keep his visitors away."

"Oh. Friendly with 'them,' is he?"

"Do all his washing up and keep his house clean, if you'd believe all you hear."

"I wouldn't put it past him," Brat said. And set out for Latchetts.

So Simon had an alibi. Simon had been nowhere near the cliffs that afternoon. He had never been out of the Clare valley.

And so that was that.

On his way home up the ride between the paddock he met Jane. Jane had every appearance of "hanging around," and he wondered if it was to intercept him that she lingered there. She was talking to Honey and her foal, and made no effort to efface herself as she had done hitherto at his approach.

"Hullo, Jane," he said, and joined in the intercourse with Honey to give her time. Her small pale face had flushed, and she was evidently struggling with a quite unusual emotion.

"It's about time we were going home to wash up," he suggested at last, as she seemed no nearer speech.

She dropped her hand from Honey's head and turned to face him, braced for effort.

"I wanted to say something to you. Do you mind?"

"Something you want me to do for you?"

"Oh, no. Nothing like that. It's just that I wasn't very nice to you when you came home from America, and I want to apologise."

"Oh, Jane," he said, wanting to take the small brave figure in his arms.

"It wasn't because I *wanted* to be horrid to you," she said, anxious that he should understand. "It was because—it was because—"

"I know why it was."

"Do you?"

"Yes, of course. It was a very natural thing to feel."

"Was it?"

"In fact, all things considered, it does you credit."

"Then you'll accept my apology?"

"I accept your apology," Brat said gravely, and they shook hands.

She did not immediately put her arm through his as Ruth would have done. She walked beside him in a grown-up fashion, talking politely about the chances of Honey's foal in the market, and what it should be called. The matter of the name was such an absorbing and exciting one that presently she forgot her self-consciousness, so that by the time they reached the house she was chattering unreservedly.

As they crossed the wide gravel sweep, Bee came to the door and stood there watching them come.

"You are going to be late for dinner, you two," she said.

Chapter 22

So Brat took possession of Latchetts and of everyone in it with the exception of Simon.

He went to church on Sunday and submitted to being stared at for an hour and a half with time off for prayers. The only people not in Clare Church that morning were the Nonconformists and three children who had measles. Indeed, there were, as Bee pointed out, several members of the congregation whose normal place of Sunday worship was the blue brick barn at the other end of the village, and who had decided to put up with ritual and prelacy this once in order to share in the sensation of his appearance. As for the orthodox flock, there were individuals there, Bee said, who had not entered a church since their last child was christened. There was even Lana Adams who, as far as anyone knew, had not been in any church since her own baptism in the blue brick barn some twenty years ago.

Brat sat between Bee and Eleanor, and Simon on the other side of Bee. The twins were beyond Eleanor; Ruth wallowing in the drama and singing hymns loudly with a rapt expression, and Jane looking at the congregation with stony disapproval. Brat read the Ashby tablets over and over again, and listened to the Rector's unemphatic voice providing the inhabitants of Clare with their weekly ration of the abstract. The Rector did not preach, in the accepted meaning of the term. He sounded as if he were arguing the matter out for himself; so that, if you shut your eyes, you could be in a chair at the other side of the Rectory fireplace listening to him talk. Brat thought of the fine variety of preachers who had come to take Sunday service at the orphanage: the shouters, the between-you-and-me-ers, the drama merchants who varied their tones and dropped their voices like amateur reciters, the hearties, the mincing aesthetes; and he thought that George Peck came very well out of the comparison. George Peck really did look as if he were not thinking about himself at all; as if he might conceivably have become a clergy-man even if there had been no such inducement as public appearances in a pulpit.

After service Brat went to Sunday lunch at the Rectory, but not until he had run the gamut of village good wishes. Bee had come out of church at his side ready to pilot him through the ordeal, but she was accosted by Mrs. Gloom, and he was left defenceless. He looked in panic at the first of these unknowns bearing down on him: a big apple-cheeked woman with pink roses in a crinoline hat. How was he going to pretend to remember her? Or all the others who were obviously lingering?

"You remember Sarah Godwin, who used to come on washing days," a voice said, and there was Eleanor at his elbow. She moved him on from one group to another as expertly as a social secretary, briefing him quickly in a muttered phrase as each new face loomed up. "Harry Watts. Used to mend our bicycles." "Miss Marchant. Village school." "Mrs. Stapley. Midwife." "Tommy Fitt. Used to be the gardener's boy." "Mrs. Stack. Rural industries."

She saw him safely to the little iron gate that led into the Rectory garden, opened it, pushed him through, and said: "Now you're safe. That's 'coolee.' "

"That's what?"

"Don't tell me you have forgotten that. In our hide-and-seek games a safe hide was always a 'coolee.' "

Some day, Brat Farrar, he thought as he walked down the path to the Rectory, you are going to be faced with something that you *couldn't possibly* have forgotten.

At luncheon he and his host sat in relaxed silence while Nancy entertained them, and afterwards he walked in the garden with the Rector and answered his questions about the life he had been leading these last eight years. One of George Peck's charms was that he listened to what was said to him.

On Monday he went to London and sat in a chair while rolls of cloth were exhibited several yards away from him, and were then brought forward to touching distance so that he might gauge the weight, texture, and wearing qualities of the cloth. He was fitted by Gore and Bowen, and measured by Walters, and assured by both that in record time he would have an outfit that no Englishman would blush to own. It was a revelation to him that shirts were made to measure. He had been pleased that he could present himself to the Ashby tailors in a suit as respect-worthy as that made for him by Mr. Sandal's tailor, and it was a shock to him to be sympathised with about the nice clean blue American shirt that he was wearing under it. However, when in Rome . . . So he was measured for shirts too.

He lunched with Mr. Sandal, who took him to meet the manager of his bank. He cashed a cheque at the bank, bought a registered envelope, and sent a fat wad of notes to Alec Loding. That had been the arrangement; "notes and no note," Loding had said. No telephones either. There must never be any communication between them again beyond the anonymous notes in the registered envelope.

This first payment to his partner in crime left a taste in his mouth that was not entirely due to the gum on the envelope that he had licked. He went and had a beer to wash it away, but it was still there. So he got on a 24 bus and went to have a look at his late lodgings in Pimlico, and immediately felt better.

He caught the 4.10 down, and Eleanor was waiting in the bug at Guessgate to meet him. His heart was no longer in his mouth, and Eleanor was no longer an abstraction and an enemy.

"It seemed a shame to let you wait for the bus when I was free to come to meet you," she said, and he got in beside her and she drove him home.

"Now you won't have to go away for a long time," she said.

"No. Except for a fitting and to the dentist."

"Yes; just up for the day. And perhaps Uncle Charles will expect someone to go up to meet him. But until then we can settle down and be quiet."

So he settled down.

He exercised the horses in the mornings, or schooled them over the jumps in the paddock. He rode out with Eleanor and the children from Clare Park; and so satisfied Antony Toselli's romantic soul that he arrived for his lesson one morning in a complete "child's riding outfit," to obtain which he had sent telegrams of a length and fluency that made history in the life of the Clare post office. He lunged the yearling for Eleanor, and watched while she taught a young thoroughbred from a racing stable to walk collected and carry his head like a gentleman. Nearly all his days were spent with Eleanor, and when they came in in the evenings it was to plan for to-morrow's task.

Bee watched this companionship with pleasure, but wished that Simon had more share in it. Simon found more and more excuses to be away from home from breakfast to dinner. He would school Timber or Scapa in the morning, and then find some excuse for going into Westover for lunch. Occasionally when he came home for dinner after being out all day Bee wondered whether he was quite sober. But except for the fact that he now took two drinks where once he would have taken one, he drank little at home, and so she decided that she must be mistaken. His alternate fits of moodiness and gaiety were nothing new: Simon had always been mercurial. She took it that his absence was his way of reducing the strain of a difficult situation, and hoped that presently he would make a third in the partnership that was blossoming so happily between Eleanor and Patrick.

"You'll have to do *something* at the Bures Show," Eleanor said one day as they came in tired from the stables. "Otherwise people will think it very odd."

"I could ride in a race, as Ruth suggested."

"But that is just fun. I mean, no one takes that seriously. You ought to show one of the horses. Your own riding things will be here in time, so there's no reason why you shouldn't."

"No."

"I'm getting to know that monosyllable of yours."

"It's no monopoly of mine."

"No. Just your speciality."

"What could I ride in the races?"

"Well, after Timber, Chevron is the fastest we have."

"But Chevron is Simon's."

"Oh, no. Chevron was bought by Bee with stable money. Have you ridden races at all?"

"Oh, yes. Often. Local ones, of course. For small stakes."

"Well, I think Bee plans to show Chevron as a hack, but that's no reason she shouldn't be entered for the races at the end of the day. She's very nervous and excitable, but she jumps clean and she's very fast."

They put the proposition to Bee at dinner, and Bee agreed to it. "What do you ride at, Brat?"

"Nine stone thirteen."

Bee looked at him reflectively as he ate his dinner. He was too fine-drawn. None of the Ashbys of the last two generations had run to weight, but there was a used-up look about the boy; especially at the end of the day. Presently, when the business of the celebration was all over, they must do something about his leg. Perhaps that ac-

counted for the strung look that marked his spareness. Both physically and psychologically it must be a drag on him. She must ask
Peter Spence about a good surgeon to consult.

Bee had been delighted to find that Brat had what Simon so
consciously lacked: an interest in the genus horse in the abstract.
Simon was knowledgeable about breeding in so far as it concerned
his own particular interests, but his theoretical study of the matter
was confined to *Racing Up to Date*. Brat, on the other hand, took to
stud books as some people take to detection. She had gone in one
evening to turn off a light that someone had evidently left on in the
library, and found Brat poring over a stud book. He was trying to
work back on Honey's pedigree, he said.

"You've got the wrong book," she said, and provided him with
the right one. She was busy with some W.R.I. matter and so she
left him to it and forgot him. But nearly two hours later she noticed
the light still there and went in to find Brat surrounded by tomes
of all kinds and so dead to the world that he did not hear her come
in.

"It's fascinating, Bee," he said. He was mooning over a photograph of Bend Or, and had propped various other volumes open at
photographs that gave him particular pleasure, so that the big table
looked like some secondhand bookstall with the plates exhibited to
entice the purchaser.

"You haven't got my favourite in your collection," she said, having examined his choice, and brought another tome from the
shelves. And then, finding that he was totally ignorant, she took
him back to the beginning and showed him the foundations—
Arab, Barb, and Turk—of the finished product. By midnight there
were more books on the floor than there were on the shelves but
they had both had a marvelous time.

After that if Brat was missing from the normal orbit, one could
always find him in the library, either working out something in a
stud book or going slowly through the photographs of remarkable
horses.

He sat openly at Gregg's feet, with the result that in a week
Gregg was according him a respect that he had never paid to Simon. Bee noticed that where he addressed Simon as "Mr. Simon,"
Brat was "Mr. Patrick, sir." There was never any trace of the defensive attitude of a stud-groom faced with a newcomer who was also
his master. Gregg recognised an enthusiast who did not think that
he already knew it all, and so Brat was "Mr. Patrick, sir." Bee would

smile as she passed the saddle room and heard the long monotone of Gregg's speech punctuated by Brat's monosyllables.

"Shoot him, I said, I'll do nothing of the kind, that horse'll walk out of here like a Christian inside a month, your blasted hounds can starve, I said, before they get their jaws on as good a piece of horse-flesh as ever looked through a bridle, so what do you think I did?"

"What?"

Bee was humbly grateful to fate not only for her nephew's return but for the form in which he had returned. Rehearsing in her mind all the shapes that Patrick might have reappeared in, she was filled with wonder that the actual one should be so cut-to-measure, so according to her own prescription. Brat was what she would have indented for if she could have chosen. He was too silent, of course; too reticent. One felt at peace in his company without having any feeling of knowing him. But his unchanging front was surely easier to deal with than Simon's fluidity.

She wrote a long letter to Uncle Charles, to meet him at Marseilles, describing this new nephew to him, and saying all that could not be said in the initial cables. It would not impress Charles, of course, that Brat was useful with horses, since Charles loathed horses; which he held to be animals of an invincible stupidity, uncontrolled imagination, and faulty deduction. Indeed, Charles claimed that a three-month-old child not actually suffering from encephalitis or other congenital incapacity was more capable of drawing a correct deduction than the most intelligent and most impeccably bred thoroughbred. Charles liked cats; and if ever against his better judgement he was lured within smell of a stable, he made friends with the stable cat and retired with it to some quiet corner until the process of horse exhibition was finished. He was rather like a cat himself; a large soft man with a soft round face that creased only sufficiently to hold an eyeglass; in either eye, according to which hand Charles had free at the moment. And although he was over six feet tall, he padded as lightly on his large feet as though he were partly filled with air.

Charles was devoted to his old home and to his family, but was fond of declaring himself a throw-back to a more virile age when a horse was simply a means of transport, capable of carrying a respectable weight, and it was not necessary for a man to develop bones that would disgrace a chicken so that brittle thoroughbreds should be induced to surmount unnecessary and unwarrantable obstacles.

A half-starved cat could out-jump any horse anyhow; and no one had to teach it to either.

But his brother's grandchildren were the apple of his eye, and he loved every brittle bone of them. And it was to this Charles that Bee commended his new nephew.

"In the short two weeks that he has been here, he has passed from being a complete stranger to being so much a part of Latchetts that one doesn't notice him. He has a peculiar trick of being part of the landscape, of course, but it is not just that he is self-effacing. It is that he has dropped into place. I notice that even country people, to whom he ought still to be strange and a matter for sideways-looking, treat him as if he had been here all along. He is very silent, and rarely volunteers a remark, but his mind is extraordinarily alive, and his comment when he makes one would be blistering sometimes if it were not uttered so gently. He speaks very correct American—which, dear Uncle Charles, is very correct English with a flat A—and drawls a little. It is quite a different drawl from Simon's. I mean, from the drawl Simon uses when he drawls. It is not a comment; just a method of production.

"His greatest conquest was Jane, who resented his coming bitterly, on Simon's behalf. She made a wide sweep round him for days, and then capitulated. Ruth made a tremendous fuss of him, but got little encouragement—I think he felt her disloyalty to Simon—and she is now a little 'off' him.

"George Peck seems pleased with him, but I think finds it hard to forgive his silence all those years. I do too, of course. I find it inexplicable. One can only try to understand the immensity of the upheaval that sent him away from us.

"Simon has been beyond praise. He has taken his relegation to second place with a fortitude and a grace that is touching. I think he is very unhappy, and finds it difficult to join up this new Patrick with the old one. The greatest wrong Pat did in keeping silence was the wrong to Simon. I can only suppose that he intended never to come back at all. I have tried to sound him about it, but he is not an easy person to talk to. He was a reserved child and he is even more reserved to-day. Perhaps he will talk to you when you come.

"We are busy preparing for the Bures Show—which, you will be glad to hear, occurs at least three days before you are even due to arrive in England—and have hopes of a little successful publicity for Latchetts. We have three new horses that are well above average, and we are hoping that at least two of them are of Olympia standard. We shall see what their ring manners are like when we take them to Bures. Patrick has refused to take any part in this year's showing, leaving all the kudos to Simon and Eleanor—to whom, of course, it belongs. I think that, more than anything, describes this Patrick who has come home to us."

Chapter 23

Because it was Simon who would show Timber and jump him, Brat left his schooling entirely to him, and shared his attentions between the other horses. But there were days, especially now that Simon absented himself more and more, when someone else had to exercise Timber, and Brat looked forward to those days more than he acknowledged even to himself. He liked most of the Latchetts horses, despised a few, and had an affection for the lively Chevron, the kind, sensible Scapa, and Eleanor's aged hack, Buster: a disillusioned but lovable old gentleman. But Timber was something else again. Timber was challenge, and excitement, and satisfaction; Timber was question and glory.

He planned to cure Timber of brushing people off his back, but he would do nothing yet a while. It was important, if he was going to be jumped at Bures, that nothing should be done to damage his self-confidence. Some day, if Brat had anything to do with it, Timber was going to feel very small indeed, but meanwhile let Simon have at his command every jot of that lordly assurance. So Brat exercised him mildly, and as he rode round the countryside kept his eyes open for a likely curing-place for Timber when the time came. The beeches on Tanbitches had no branches low enough for his purpose, and there was no room on that hill-top to get up the necessary speed. He wanted some open country with isolated or bunched trees with their lowest branches the right height from the ground to tempt Timber of his undoing. He remembered that Timber's most spectacular exploit had been in Lerridge Park and over there was Clare Park, with its surrounding stretch of turf and trees.

"Do the Clare Park people mind if we ride through the park?" he asked Eleanor one day when there were still seven days before the Bures Show.

Eleanor said no, provided they kept away from the playing fields.

"They don't play anything because organised games are dreadful unless they are organised by Russians in Russia, but they keep the playing fields because they look well in the prospectus."

So Brat took Timber to the other side of the valley, and cantered him gently on the centuries-old turf of Clare Park, keeping well away from the trees. Then he walked him round the various clumps, gauging the height of the lowest limbs from the ground. The manoeuvre was received by Timber with a puzzled but passionate interest. One could almost see him trying to work it out. What was this for? What did the man come and look at large trees for? With a horse's abnormal memory, he was well aware that large trees were associated with private delights of his own, but, being a horse, he was also incapable of drawing any reasonable deduction from his rider's interest in the same kind of trees.

He walked up to each clump with a mannerly grace, until they approached the large oak which had been for five hundred years the pride of Clare Park. As they came within its flung shadow Timber propped himself suddenly on his forelegs and snorted with fright. Brat was puzzled. What did he remember about the oak that would cause a reaction as strong as that? He looked at the ears that were sticking up as stiff as horns. Perhaps it wasn't a memory. Perhaps there was something in the grass.

"Do you always sneak up on girls under trees?" said a voice from the shadows, and from the grass there emerged the seal-like form of Miss Parslow. She propped herself on an elbow and surveyed the pair. Brat was a little surprised that she was alone. "Don't you ever ride anything but that black brute?"

Brat said that he did, quite often.

"I suppose it would be too much to expect that you were looking for me when you came over to the park to ride?"

Brat said that he was looking for a place to teach Timber manners.

"What's the matter with his manners?"

"He has a habit of diving suddenly under a tree so that he scrapes his rider off."

Miss Parslow propped herself a little further up and looked with new interest at the horse. "You don't say! I never thought the brutes had that much sense. How are you going to stop him?"

"I'm going to make riding under trees a painful experience for him."

"You mean you'll beat him when he tries to do it?"

"Oh, no. That wouldn't do much good."

"After he has actually done it, then?"

"No. He mightn't associate the beating with a tree at all." He rubbed his whip up Timber's dark crest, and Timber bowed. "You'd be surprised at the odd things they associate."

"Nothing would surprise me to any extent about horses. How are you going to do it then?"

"Let him go full bat near a nice tempting tree, and when he swerves under it give him a cut on the belly that he'll remember all his life."

"Oh, no, that's too bad. The poor brute."

"It will be just too bad if I don't time my slip sideways on the saddle properly," Brat said dryly.

"And will that cure him?"

"I hope so. Next time he sees a likely tree he'll remember that it hurt like the blazes last time he tried it."

"But he'll hate you."

Brat smiled. "I'd be very surprised if he associated me with the business at all. I'd be surprised if he even associated it with the whip. Horses don't think like humans."

"What will he think hurt him, then?"

"The trees, more than likely."

"I always *thought* they were awfully silly animals."

It occurred to Brat that she had not made one of those riding parties on which he had accompanied Eleanor. Nor had he seen her about the stables lately. He asked how her riding was getting on.

"I've given it up."

"Altogether?"

"Uh-huh."

"But you were getting on well, weren't you? Eleanor said you had learned to bump."

"It was a very slithery bump, and it hurt me far more than it hurt the horse." She pulled a long grass and began to chew it, eyeing him with a sly amusement. "I don't have to hang around the stables any more. If I want to see Simon I know where to find him nowadays."

"Where?" said Brat before he could stop himself.

"The upstairs bar at the Angel."

"In Westover? But are you allowed to go to Westover when you like?"

"I'm attending a Westover dentist," she giggled. "Or rather, I was. The school made the first appointment for me, of course, but after that I just told them when I had to go next. I've reckoned that I have about thirty teeth, which should last me till the end of the term quite nicely." She opened her red mouth wide and laughed. They were excellent teeth. "That's what I'm doing at the moment. Putting off time till the Westover bus is due. I could have gone with the earlier one but there is a very good-looking conductor on this one. He's got the length of asking me to the pictures one night next week. If Simon was going on the way he has been all those months, not knowing I'm alive, I'd maybe have done something about the conductor boy—he has lashes about an inch long—but now that Simon has stopped looking down his nose I think I'll give the conductor boy a miss." She chewed the stalk provocatively. "Got quite matey, Simon has."

"Oh."

"Have you been seducing the Gates girl from him, like I suggested?"

"I have not."

"That's funny. He's distinctly off her. And he's not awfully enamoured of you, if it comes to that. So I thought you'd been cutting him out with that Peggy woman. But I suppose it's just that you cut him out of Latchetts."

"You're going to miss your bus, aren't you?"

"You can be just as squashing as Simon, in your own way."

"I was only pointing out that the bus is almost at the smithy. It will be at the Park gates in—"

"What!" she shrieked, exploding to her feet in one enormous convulsion, so that Timber whirled in alarm from the wild eruption. "Oh, great heavens! Oh, for the love of . . . ! Oh! Oh!"

She fled down the park to the avenue gates, screaming her distress as she went. Brat watched the green bus skim along the road past the white gates of Latchetts and slow down as it came to the gates of Clare Park. She was going to catch it after all, and her day would not be wasted. She would find Simon. At the Angel. In the upstairs bar.

That Simon should spend his time in Westover in the Angel bar was distressing but not, in the circumstances, surprising. What was surprising was the emergence of a Simon who was "matey" with Sheila Parslow. In Simon's eyes the Parslow girl had always been something beneath contempt; a lower form of life. He dismissed her with a gibe when her name was mentioned and in her presence was, as she had said herself, unaware that she was alive. What had happened to Simon that he was not only resigned to her companionship, but was "matey"? The girl was not lying about it. If her glowing self-satisfaction was not sufficient evidence, there was the obvious fact that Simon could avoid her by changing his drinking place. There was no lack of pubs in Westover; most of them more exclusively masculine haunts than the very social and female-ridden Angel.

Brat tried to imagine Simon with Sheila Parslow and failed.

What had come over Simon—the fastidious, critical Simon—that he found it possible to endure her? To spend hours in her company?

Was it a sort of "larning" his family for the disappointment he had been caused? A sort of you-don't-like-me-therefore-I'll-take-up-with-Sheila-Parslow? A sorry-when-I'm-dead reaction? There was a very childish side to Simon.

There was also, Brat thought from all he had heard, a very practical side, and Sheila Parslow had money, and Simon needed it. But somehow Brat could not believe that Simon, even in his most deplorable moments, would ever consider pawning his life to a nymphomaniacal moron.

As he walked Timber home he considered yet once more the general oddity of Simon, but as usual came to no conclusions.

He handed Timber over to Arthur to be rubbed down, and went down with Eleanor to inspect Regina's new foal.

"She's an old marvel, isn't she," Eleanor said, watching the new arrival stagger about on its out-of-proportion legs. "It's another good one. Not much wonder that she looks complacent. People have been coming to admire her foals for practically a lifetime, the old duchess. I think foals to her are just a means of achieving this annual homage. She doesn't care a rap about the foal."

"It's not any better than Honey's," Brat said, looking at the foal without enthusiasm.

"You and your Honey."

"And you wait and see what Honey will produce next year with this new mating. A foal that will make history."

"Your enthusiasm for Honey borders on the indecent."

"You heard Bee say that."

"How did you know?"

"I heard her too."

They laughed a little, and she said: "It's so nice to have you here, Brat." He noticed that she did not say: It is so nice to have you back, Patrick; but he realised that she herself was unaware of any oddity in the form she used.

"Is that doctor chap going over to Bures for the show?"

"I shouldn't think so. He's much too busy. What made you think of him?"

Brat did not know.

They pottered round the paddocks for so long that they came in for tea very late, and had it by themselves. Jane was pounding her way through a Chopin valse with conscientious accuracy, and stopped with undisguised relief when they came in.

"Could I say twenty-five minutes was half an hour, Eleanor?" she asked. "It's twenty-five-and-a-half minutes really."

"You can say anything you like as long as we don't have to listen to that valse while we eat."

So Jane slid off the piano-stool, removed the glasses that gave her such an owl-like look, pushed them into her breeches pocket, and disappeared thankfully into the out-of-doors.

"Ruth puts in all the tiddley bits and the expression and doesn't mind how many wrong notes she strikes, but with Jane it is accuracy or nothing. I don't know which Chopin would have hated more," Eleanor said, folding bread and butter into a thickness that would match her appetite.

Brat watched her pour the tea with a delight in her clean unhurried movements. Some day the foundation of the life he was living here would give way; Simon would achieve the plan he was devising to undo him, or some incautious word of his own would bring the whole structure crashing down; and then there would be no more Eleanor.

It was not the least of his fears for the future.

They ate in a friendly silence, dropping unrelated remarks into the quiet as they happened to occur to them.

Presently Eleanor said: "Did you ask Bee about colours for the race next week?"

Brat said that he had forgotten.

"Let's go and look them out now. They are in that locker in the saddle room."

So they went back to the stables. The saddle room was empty; Gregg had gone home to his supper; but Eleanor knew where the key was.

"They are practically in ribbons, they are so old," she said as she spread the colours on the table. "They were actually made for Father, and then they were taken in a bit for Simon to wear at points-to-points when he was narrower than he is now. And then let out again when he grew. So they are just hanging together. Perhaps now we'll be able to afford—" She pulled herself up.

"Yes. We'll have a new set."

"I think violet and primrose are nice colours, don't you; but they do fade an unattractive shade. Simon goes blue with cold in the winter, and he says the colours were designed to tone with his face."

They rummaged in the chest, turning up souvenirs of old races. They moved round the saddle room studying the long row of ribbon rosettes, each with its tab under it telling where and how it had been won.

At last Eleanor shut the chest, saying: "It is time we got ready for dinner." She locked the chest and hung up the key. "We'll take the colours with us. I expect they'll fit you all right, since Simon was the last to wear them. But they'll have to be pressed."

She took the colours in her arms, and together they walked out of the saddle-room door and came face to face with Simon.

"Oh, you're back, Simon," Eleanor was beginning, when she caught sight of his face.

"*Who had Timber out?*" he said, furious.

"I had," Brat said.

"Timber is my business and you have no right to have him out when my back is turned."

"Someone had to exercise him to-day," Brat said mildly.

"*No one* exercises Timber but me. *No one.* If I'm going to be responsible for jumping him, then I say when he is to be exercised, and *I* do the exercising."

"But, Simon," Eleanor said, "that is absurd. There are—"

"Shut up!" he said, through his teeth.

"I will *not* shut up! The horses are Brat's, and if anyone says who does what and when, then it is—"

"Shut up, I tell you. I won't have a ham-headed lout from the backwoods ruining a good piece of horseflesh like Timber."

"Simon! *Really!*"

"Coming from nowhere and interfering in the stables as if he had lived here all his life!"

"You must be drunk, Simon, to talk like that about your own brother."

"My brother! *That!* Why, you poor little fool, he isn't even an Ashby. God knows what he is. Somebody's groom, I have no doubt.

And that is what he should be doing. Sweeping out stables. Not lording it round the countryside on my best horses. After this, you damned little upstart, you leave the horses I intend to ride in their stables unless I say they are to be taken out, and if I say they are to be taken out it is not you who will ride them. We have plenty of other stablemen."

His chin was sticking out about two feet from Brat's face, and Brat could have brought one from the ground that would have lifted him half over the saddle room. He longed to do it, but not with Eleanor there. And not now, perhaps. Better not do anything that he could not foresee the consequences of.

"Well? Did you hear me?" shouted Simon, maddened by his silence.

"I heard you," Brat said.

"Well, see that you remember what I said. Timber is my business, and you don't put a leg across him again until I say so."

And he flung away from them towards the house.

Eleanor looked stricken.

"Oh, Brat, I'm sorry. I'm so sorry. He had that mad notion about your not being Patrick before he ever saw you, and now that he has been drinking I suppose it came from the back of his mind and he said it because he was angry. He always did say a lot of things he didn't mean when he was in a temper, you know."

It was Brat's experience that, on the contrary, it was only when a person was in a temper that they said exactly what they did mean. But he refrained from telling Eleanor that.

"He *has* been drinking, you know," she went on. "I know he doesn't look as if he has, but I can tell from his eyes. And he would never have behaved like that when he was sober, even in a temper. I do apologise for him."

Brat said that everyone made a fool of themselves some time or other when they had "drink taken," and she was not to bother about it.

They followed Simon to the house soberly, the happiness of their long afternoon together vanished as if it had not been.

As he changed into what he still thought of as "his good suit" Brat thought that if the cracks that were showing in Simon widened sufficiently he might one day show his hand, and he would find out what Simon's plans for him were. He wondered if Simon would be sober enough to behave normally at dinner.

But there was no Simon at dinner, and when Eleanor asked

where he was, Bee said that he had gone over to the pub at Guess-gate to meet a friend who was staying there. Someone had tele-phoned just before dinner, it appeared.

Bee looked equable, and Brat decided that Simon had seemed normal to her and that she had believed his story of the friend stay-ing the night at the Guessgate inn.

And in the morning Simon came down to breakfast his usual sunny self.

"I'm afraid I was tight last night," he said. "And very objection-able, I'm afraid. I apologise unreservedly."

He regarded Brat and Eleanor, the only other people at the table, with friendly confidence. "I ought never to drink gin," he said. "It obscures the judgement and destroys the soul."

"You were quite horrible," Eleanor said coldly.

But the atmosphere cleared, and the day was just another day. Bee came in from out-of-doors for her second cup of coffee; Jane arrived clutching to her stomach the bowl of porridge which she had fetched from the kitchen for herself, according to Latchetts routine; Ruth came flying in very late with a "diamond" clasp in her hair and was sent back to take the thing off.

"Where did she get that loathsome object," Bee said when Ruth had disappeared with wild cries that Bee was going to make her late for lessons.

"She bought it at Woolworth's last time we were in Westover," Jane said. "They're not real diamonds, you know, but it seemed a bargain for one-and-sixpence."

"Why didn't you buy one then, Jane?" Bee asked, looking at the aged kirby-grip that kept Jane's hair off her face.

"Oh, I don't think I'm the diamond type," Jane said.

So the Ashby household settled back to its normal placidity, and to its preparations for that day at Bures that was to alter all their lives.

Chapter 24

*B*ures was a little market town, set north of Westover and almost in the middle of the county. It was like almost every
other little market town in the south of England, except perhaps
that it stood in slightly richer and more unspoiled country than
most. For which reason the Bures Agricultural Show, although a
small country affair, had a standing and reputation considerably
greater than its size alone would warrant. Every year animals would
appear at the Bures show on their way to more mature triumphs
elsewhere, and it was common for someone, watching an exhibit at
one of the great shows, to say: "I remember that when it was a
novice at Bures three years ago."

It was a pleasant, civilised little town, with a minister, some
fine old inns, a High Street both broad and gay, and no self-
consciousness whatsoever. The farmers who brought their wares to
its markets would have annoyed Mr. Macallan exceedingly by their
content with their lot, and their evident unawareness that there
were other worlds to conquer. An air of well-being came off the
Bures pavements like reflected sunlight. Bad years there might be,
for both tradespeople and farmers, but that was a risk that was incidental in a life that was satisfying and good.

The annual show, in the early summer, was a social reunion as
well as a business affair, and the day ended with a "ball" in the assembly room of the Chequers, at which farmers' wives who hadn't
seen each other since New Year swopped gossip, and young blades
who had not met since the Combined Hunts Ball swopped horses.
The combined hunts, between them, embraced the town; the Lerridge to the south and the Kenley Vale to the north; and did much
to ensure that the horses exhibited at Bures should be worth more
than a passing glance. And since almost every farmer well enough
off to own both a horse and a tractor belonged to one or other of
the hunts, there was never any lack of competition.

In the early days of the show, when transport was still by horse and slow, it was the custom to stay overnight at Bures; and the Chequers, the Rose and Crown, the Wellington, and the Kenley Arms packed them in three to a bed. But with the coming of the motor all that changed. It was more fun to go home nine-to-a-car in the summer dawn than to sleep three-to-a-bed in the Wellington. It was not always a successful method of getting home, of course, and more than one young farmer had spent his summer months in hospital after the Bures Show, but to the younger generation it was inconceivable that they should sleep in an inn when their home was less than forty miles away. So only the older exhibitors, who clung to tradition, or those who lived at an inconvenient distance from Bures, or could not, owing to difficult communications, get their animals away on the evening of the show, still stayed overnight at Bures. And of these most stayed at the Chequers.

The Ashbys had had the same bedrooms at the Chequers for the night of the Bures Show since the days of William Ashby the Seventh: he who had joined the Westover Fencibles to resist the expected invasion of Napoleon the First. They were not the best bedrooms, because in those days the best bedrooms went to the Ledinghams of Clare, who also, of course, had a yearly reservation for the night of the show. What the Ledinghams left went to the Shirleys of Penbury and the Hallands of Hallands House. The Hallands, on whose lands on the outskirts of the town the show was held, had used the bedrooms only for their overflow of guests, but a Hallands guest rated a great deal higher, of course, than any Ashby in the flesh.

Penbury was now the possession of the nation in the shape of the National Trust; a shillingsworth of uplift for coachloads who didn't know Gibbons from Adams and wanted their tea. Hallands House was also the possession of the nation, in the shape of a Government department. No one quite knew what this alien community did. Mrs. Thrale, who ran the Singing Kettle tea-rooms out on the Westover road, once boldly asked a young Government employee who was drinking her coffee what her task was at the moment, and was told that it was "arranging the translation of *Tom Jones* into Turkish": but this was held to be merely a misunderstanding on Mrs. Thrale's part, and no one had the heart to question the aliens further. They kept themselves to themselves very determinedly, and it was no longer possible for the people of Bures to walk through Hallands Park.

It would have been possible long ago for the Ashbys on their annual visit to have some of the finer bedrooms at the Chequers, but no such idea ever crossed an Ashby mind. The difference between Number Three and Number Seventeen was not that one was a fine room with a pleasant out-look and good furniture and the other a back room looking on to the roof of the assembly room, but that one wasn't "their" room and the other was. So they still had the three little rooms in the older wing, which, since the bathroom had been added at the end of the passage, made it practically an Ashby apartment.

Gregg took the horses over to Bures on Tuesday evening. Arthur followed on Wednesday morning with the ponies and Eleanor's hack, Buster, who hated any box but his own, and was liable to kick a strange stable to pieces. Simon and the twins went in the car with Bee; and Brat shared the bug with Eleanor and Tony Toselli, who had insisted on being allowed to compete in the Best Child Rider class. ("My father will commit suicide if I am not allowed to try.")

Brat wished that this tadpole creature was not sitting between himself and Eleanor. The feeling that his time with Eleanor was short was constantly with him, making each indifferent moment a matter of consequence. But Eleanor seemed happy enough to feel charitable even to Tony Toselli.

"It's going to be perfect weather," she said, looking at the high arch of the sky with no clouds in it. "I can remember only one real soaker at Bures and that's years ago. They've always been awfully lucky. Did I put my string gloves in the locker?"

"Yes."

"What are you going to do all the morning? Look at Mrs. Godwin's jam exhibit?"

"I'm going to walk the course."

"Canny Brat," she said, approving. "How right you are."

"The other fellows probably know every inch of it."

"Oh, yes. For most of them it is an annual. In fact, if you started the horses off they'd probably go round by themselves, they are so used to it. Did Bee remember to give you your stand ticket?"

"Yes."

"And have you got it with you?"

"I have."

"I sound a fusser this morning, don't I? You are a nice reassuring person to be with. Do you never get excited, Brat?"

"Oh, yes."

"Inside-churning excited?"

"Inside turning over and over."

"That's interesting. It just doesn't show, I suppose."

"I suppose not."

"It's an extraordinarily useful sort of face to have. Mine goes a dull unhealthy pink as you can see."

He thought the warm childish flush on her normally cool features touching and endearing.

"I hear that Peggy Gates has a new outfit for the occasion. Have you ever seen her on a horse? I can't remember."

"No."

"She looks nice," Eleanor said approvingly. "She rides very well. I think she will do justice to that horse of Dick Pope's."

It was typical of Eleanor that her judgement was independent of her emotions.

The High Street of Bures glittered in the low morning sunlight. Large Motoring Association signs encouraged the traveller, and fluttering advertisements cajoled him. "Carr's Meal for Calves," said a banner. "Saffo, the Safe Disinfectant!" screamed a chimney-to-chimney pendant. "Pett's Dip," said a placard quietly, taking it for granted that the Dip was sufficiently famous to explain itself.

In the dim hall of the Chequers Bee was waiting for them. Simon had gone round to the stables, she said.

"The rooms are Number Seventeen, Eighteen, and Nineteen, Brat. You are sharing Seventeen with Simon, Nell and I have Eighteen, and the twins are in the connecting one, Nineteen."

Sharing a room with Simon was something he had not reckoned with, but there was nothing he could do about it. He picked up Eleanor's bag and his own and went upstairs with them, since the hall was a flurry of arriving guests. Eleanor came with him and showed him where the rooms were.

"The first time I came here and was allowed to stay the night I thought life had nothing left to offer," she said. "Put it down there, Brat, thank you, and I'll unpack it at once or my frock will be ruined."

In Number Seventeen Simon's things were already strewn all over the room, including the second bed. It was odd how these inanimate belongings of Simon's had, even in his absence, a kind of arrogance.

Brat cleared his own bed and unpacked, hanging his new evening things carefully in the still empty wardrobe.

To-night for the first time in his life he would wear evening clothes.

"In case you get lost, Brat," Bee said to him when he came down, "lunch is at twelve-thirty in the luncheon tent. The last table to your left as you come in. What do you plan to do this morning? Poke the pigs?"

"No, he is going to walk the course," Eleanor said.

"All right. Don't stray off it into any Government holy-of-holies and get yourself arrested, will you?"

Tony was handed over to Mrs. Stack, who, being interested solely in rural industries, represented a Fixed Point in the flux of an agricultural show.

"If he tells you that his father is dying and he is urgently wanted at home, don't believe him," Eleanor said.

"Is his father ill, then?"

"No, but Tony may grow bored before half-past twelve. I'll come and fetch him for lunch."

Brat walked into the High Street of Bures with a feeling of escape. For the first time for nearly a month he was his own master, free to be himself. He had forgotten what it was like to walk about without care. For nearly three hours he could go where he liked, ask what he wanted, and answer without a curb on his tongue.

"Hallands Park," said the direction sign on a bus, so he got on the bus and went there. He had never been to a country show before, and he went round the exhibits with an interest that was at once fresh and critical, comparing all he saw with similar things seen elsewhere. Homespuns in Arizona, farm implements in Normandy, rams in Zacatecas, Herefords after American air, pottery in New Mexico. Occasionally someone looked at him curiously, and more than one hand was half lifted in salutation only to fall again. He was too like an Ashby ever to be completely free in Bures. But, speaking generally, people were too absorbed in the exhibits and in their own cares at that hour of the morning to take much interest in the passersby.

Having exhausted the exhibition, he walked out into the park, where the red flags marked out the temporary racecourse. It was a straight, fast-galloping course over hurdles for the first half-mile through the park, then it went out into the country in a wide curve of a mile or more, came back to the park about half a mile from the stands, and from then on was another series of hurdles up to the finish in front of the stands. Except for the sharp turns and a few very blind fences in the country, it was not a difficult course. The hurdles in the park stretches were regulation racing ones, and the turf was wonderful. Brat's heart lifted.

It was very peaceful out there in the country, and he came back to the show with a sense of reluctance. But he was surprised to find how glad he was to see the familiar faces round the table in the luncheon tent when he got there; how glad he was to sink into the place kept for him, and be part of this family again.

People came up to their table to welcome him back to Bures Show, to England. People who had known Bill and Nora Ashby, and Bill's father before him. None of them expected him to remember them, and he had merely to be polite.

Chapter 25

I think I'm going to be sick," Ruth said, when she and Brat were
left alone in the stands.

"I don't wonder," said Brat.

"Why?" she was surprised into saying, this being not at all the reaction she expected.

"Three ices on top of dressed crab."

"It is not anything I *ate*," she said, repressive. "It's that I have a
delicate nervous system. Excitement makes me feel ill. I get sick
with it."

"I should go and get it over," Brat advised.

"Be sick, you mean!"

"Yes. It's a wonderful feeling."

"If I sit very still I may feel better," Ruth said, giving up.

Ruth was feeling her lack of importance to-day. She avoided
horses too consistently for the rest of the year to claim any right to
exhibit any on this one day at Bures, so she sat in the stands in her
neat grey flannel and looked on. It was to her credit that she did not
grudge her twin her well-earned place in the sun, and was passionately anxious that Jane should come first in her class.

"There's Roger Clint with Eleanor."

Brat looked for the couple and found them.

"Who is Roger Clint?"

"He has a big farm near here."

Roger Clint was a black-browed young man, and he was being
old-friendly with Eleanor.

"He's in love with Eleanor," said Ruth, having failed with one try
for drama.

"A very good person to be in love with," Brat said, but his heart
contracted.

"It would be a very good thing if she married him. He has lots
of money and a lovely big house and simply scads of horses."

Against his will Brat asked if Eleanor were thinking of it.

Ruth considered the pros and cons of this as they fitted into her dramatic framework.

"She is making him serve his seven years for her. You know: like Jacob. He is simply frantic about it, poor Roger, but she is La Belle Dame Sans Merci."

La Belle Dame Sans Merci bade Mr. Clint a temporary farewell and came up to join them in the stands as the Novices under Ten filed into the ring.

"Do you know that Tony scraped into this by the skin of his teeth," she said, sitting down by Brat. "He is going to be ten the day after to-morrow."

There were eleven novices, the youngest being a fat child of four in a black velvet jockey cap, who bounced about on a solid pony of which she had no control whatever.

"Well, at least Tony never looked as awful as that, even in his bad days," Eleanor said.

"Tony looks wonderful," Ruth said, and Tony did indeed look wonderful. As Eleanor had said on an earlier occasion, Tony had the root of the matter in him.

The novices walked, and trotted, and cantered, under the lenient eye of the judges, and presently the seeding began. Even from the stands the fanatic determination in Tony's snail-black eyes was plain to see. He was going to be in the money or die in the attempt. From being six possibles they were narrowed down to four, but these four kept the judges puzzled. Again and again they were sent out to canter and brought back for inspection, and sent out to canter again. There were only three prizes and one must go.

It was at this stage that Tony played what he evidently considered his ace. As he cantered along in front of the stands he got to his knees in the saddle and with a slight scramble stood up in it, straight and proud.

"Oh, God," said Eleanor reverently and with feeling.

A ripple of laughter went through the stands. But Tony had another shot in his locker. He slipped to his knees, grabbed the front edge of the saddle, and stood on his head, his thin spider-legs waving rather uncertainly in the air.

At that a gale of laughter and applause broke out, and Tony, much gratified, resumed his seat and urged his astonished pony, who had slowed to a trot, into a canter again.

That of course settled the matter very nicely for the judges, and

Tony had the mortification of seeing the three rosettes handed to his rivals. But his mortification was nothing to the mortification he had already inflicted on his preceptress.

"I hope I don't see that child until I cool off," she said, "or I am liable to take an axe to him."

But Tony, having handed his pony over to Arthur, came blithely to the stands to find her.

"Tony, you little *idiot*," she said, "what made you do a thing like that?"

"I wanted to show how I could ride, Eleanor."

"And where did you learn to do those circus tricks?"

"I practised on the pony that mows the lawn. At school, you know. He has a much broader back than Muffet, and that's why I wasn't so steady to-day. I don't think these people appreciate good riding," he added, nodding his head at the offending judges.

Eleanor was speechless.

Brat presented him with a coin and told him to go and buy himself an ice.

"If I didn't want to see Jane ride," Eleanor said, "I would go and bury my shame in the ladies' room. I'm *curdled* with humiliation."

Jane, on Rajah, in her best riding things, was a pleasant sight. Brat had never seen her in anything but the shabby jodhpurs and shapeless jersey that she wore at home, and was surprised by this trim little figure.

"Jane has the best seat of all the Ashbys," Eleanor said affectionately, watching the serious and efficient Jane making Rajah change his leg to order. "That is her only rival: that tall girl on the grey."

The tall girl was fifteen and the grey very handsome, but the judges preferred Jane and Rajah. Jane might have lost for all the emotion she showed, but Ruth was rapturous.

"Good old Jane," Simon said, appearing beside them. "A veteran at nine."

"Oh, Simon, did you *see!*" Eleanor said, in agony again as she remembered.

"Cheer up, Nell," he said, dropping a commiserating hand on her shoulder. "It might have been worse."

"How *could* it be worse?"

"He didn't yodel," Simon said.

At that she began to laugh, and went on laughing. "Oh, I suppose it is very funny," she said, wiping her eyes, "and I expect I shall laugh over it for years, but at the moment I just wish I could be in Australia for the rest of the afternoon."

"Come on, Nell," he said. "It's time to collect the horses," and they went away together as Jane came to sit in the stands.

"This is the exciting class coming now. It isn't very much to win a Fifteen and Under," was her answer to Brat's congratulations. "Some day I'll be down there with *them*. With Aunt Bee, and Eleanor, and Simon, and Peggy, and Roger Clint, and all of them."

Yes, there was Roger Clint. Eleanor was riding the long-backed bay mare Scapa, and Roger Clint was standing next to her on a chestnut with four of the longest and whitest stockings Brat had ever seen. While the judges walked down the row he and Eleanor talked quietly together.

"Who do you think will be first?" Jane asked.

Brat took his eyes from Eleanor and Clint and forced himself to consider the entry. The judge had sent Bee out to canter Chevron, the chestnut he was going to race this afternoon, and she was coming down in front of the stands now. He had never seen Bee in formal riding clothes, and was surprised again, as he had been with Jane. It was a new, serious, rather intimidating Bee.

"Who do you think, Brat?" Jane said again.

"Timber, of course."

"Not Peggy's horse? The one Dick Pope had?"

"Riding Light? No. He may win the jumping, but not this."

And he was right. This was the judges' first sight of Timber and they were too much impressed to be seduced even by the looks and reputation of Riding Light.

And it was a popular verdict. As Simon cantered Timber down in front of the stands after accepting the rosette the applause broke into cheering.

"Isn't that the brute that killed old Felix?" a voice behind said. "They ought to shoot it instead of giving it prizes."

Second was Peggy on Riding Light, looking flushed and pleased; her father's extravagance had been justified. Third, rather unexpectedly, was Bee on Chevron.

"The Ashbys cleaning up as usual," the voice said, and was instantly shushed and the proximity of the Ashbys presumably indicated.

It was when the Open Jumping Class began that the real excitement of the day was reached, and Bee came to sit in the stands and share it with them.

"Number One, please," said the loud-speaker, and Eleanor came into the ring on Scapa. Scapa was a careful and unemotional jumper, but could never be persuaded into standing away from her fences. By dint of patient schooling with a guard rail, Eleanor hoped that she had now persuaded her into better ways. And for half a round it worked, until Scapa noticed that there was no plaguey obstruction to beware of at the foot of these jumps, and began to go close in again, with the inevitable result. Nothing Eleanor could do would make her take off in time. She jumped "fit to hit the moon," but came down in the wrong place, and the little battens of white-painted wood came down with her.

"Poor Nell," said Bee. "After all her schooling."

Number Two and Number Three did not appear to have been schooled at all.

"Number Four, please," said the loud-speaker, and Riding Light appeared. Peggy's "new outfit" consisted of a dark snuff-coloured coat a little too tight in the waist, and a pair of buff breeches a little too pale in the buff, but she looked well on the brown horse and handled him beautifully. Or rather, she sat still and let Riding Light do his stuff. He was a finished jumper who took the obstacles in his stride, propelling himself into the air in a long effortless curve and tucking his hind feet after him like a cat. He went out having done a perfect round.

"Number Five, please," said the loud-speaker.

Number Five was Roger Clint's mount with the long white stockings. "Do you know what he calls it?" Bee said. "Operation Stockings."

"It's very ugly," Brat said. "Looks as if he had walked through a trough of whitewash."

"He can jump, though."

He could certainly jump, but he had phobia about water.

"Poor Roger," laughed Bee, watching Stockings refuse the water. "He has been jumping him backwards and forwards across the duck pond at home in the hope of curing him, and now he does this!" Stockings continued to refuse, and Clint had to take him out, in a burst of sympathetic applause.

Numbers Six and Seven had one fault each.

Number Eight was Simon on Timber.

The black horse came into the ring exactly as he had come out of his box on the day Brat first saw him, pleased with himself and ready for homage. His excited, flickering ears pricked into attention as he caught sight of the jumps. Simon took him into a canter and moved down to the first one. Even from where he was sitting, Brat could feel the smoothness of that action. The smoothness that had astonished him that first day at Latchetts when he had ridden on the top of the down. Smoothly the black horse rose into the air and came down on the far side of the jump, and a murmur of admiration came from the crowd at the almost feline beauty of it. Brat, with the most wholehearted respect, watched Simon's body swing with the black horse's rise and fall as though he were part of it. It was right that Simon should ride it. He would never attain that perfection if he lived to be a hundred. A great silence settled on the crowd as one by one the jumps fled away behind Timber. It would be monstrous if this beauty were to fail or be faulted. It was so quiet when he faced the water jump that the voice of a paper-seller far away at the main gate was the only sound to be heard. And when he landed smoothly and neatly on the far bank, a great sigh went up from them. They had seen a perfect thing. They had not been cheated of it after all.

So moved were they that Simon was almost out of the ring before the applause broke out.

The last three entries had been scratched, and Simon was the final performer, so the second round began as soon as he had left.

Eleanor came back on Scapa, and by dint of voice and spur managed to make the unwilling mare take off at the proper place, and so did something to retrieve her self-respect. The crowd, appreciating what had been wrong in the first place and what she had now succeeded in doing, gave her credit for it.

Number Two did a wild but lucky round, and Number Three a wild and unlucky one; and then Peggy again, still flushed from the pleasure of her perfect round.

Again she had the sense to sit still while Riding Light heaved her into the air with the thrust of his tremendous quarters, sailed over the jump, and made for the next one with his ears erect and confident. It seemed that there was nothing to hinder the brown horse doing this all day. There was an air of routine about the business that somehow detracted from his performance; he made it look too easy. There seemed little doubt that he would do another perfect round. His judgement of distance was faultless. He never had to stop and put in a short one to bring him to the proper taking-off point; he arrived at the taking-off point by some computing of his own, taking the jumps in his stride as if they were hurdles. He was coming up to the wall now, and they waited to see if he would treat that too like a hurdle.

"Thump! Thump! Thump!" said the drum of the Bures Silver Band, as the preliminary to *Colonel Bogey* and their entry into the front gate of the show for their afternoon performance. Riding Light's ears flickered in question, in doubt. His mind was distracted from that rapidly nearing wall. His ears shot forward again in alarm as he saw it almost upon him. He shortened his stride, trying to fit it into the remaining space, but he had misjudged it. He rose at it with determination and landed on the other side, flinging his quarters upwards in a successful effort to avoid hitting the fence that was now too close under him. But the shoe of his near fore had touched the wall as he rose to it, and a billet slid out of place, wavered a moment on the edge, and then dropped to the ground.

"A-a-ah!" said the crowd in quick sympathy, and Peggy looked back to see what had happened. She saw the little gap in the top of the wall, but it did not rattle her. She collected Riding Light, patted him encouragingly on the neck, and headed him for the next.

"Good girl, Peggy!" murmured Bee.

The distant band was now playing *Colonel Bogey*, and Riding Light took no further notice of it; he knew all about bands. Bands had been the accompaniment to some of his best performances. He settled down again to his routine, and finished by taking the water jump with a margin that made the crowd gasp.

"Simon will never beat that," Bee said. "That perfect round of Timber's was a miracle in the first place."

The four long stockings of Roger Clint's mount flashed round the ring in a brisk and willing fashion until they came to the water. Faced with the long distance to the last jump, Stockings stopped and pondered. Clint argued amiably with him, but Stockings would have none of it. "I know what is behind that hedge quite well, and I *don't like it!*" he seemed to be saying. And then, with that perennial unreasonableness of horses, he decided to have a go at it. Of his own accord he turned towards the jump and began to canter. Roger sat down and drove him at it, and Stockings went flying down to it with purpose in every line of him. In the last half-second he changed his mind just as suddenly as he had made it up, stuck both toes in hard, and skidded to a stop up against the fence.

The crowd laughed, and so did Roger Clint. He hauled himself back into the saddle from his position round his mount's neck. He took Stockings round to the other side of the fence and showed him the water. He took him up to it and let him inspect it at close quarters. He walked him round it and let him look at the other edge. And then he took him back to the far end of the ring and turned him to the jump. With an air of "Oh, well, let's get this thing over with," Stockings jumped off his haunches, tore down the ring, and fled over the water with a yard or two to spare.

The crowd laughed delightedly, and the white teeth showed in Clint's brown face. He lifted his hat to the applause without looking at them, as a cricketer lifts his cap, and rode out of the ring, well satisfied to have ignored the judge's disqualifying eye long enough to have induced Stockings to cross the hated obstacle.

Number Six had two faults. Number Seven two-and-a-half. "Number Eight, please," said the loud-speaker, and Jane shivered and put her hand in Bee's. For once Ruth did not have to manufacture drama to suit her; her mouth was open with suspense and she was entirely oblivious of Ruth Ashby.

Timber had neither the experience nor the machine-like power of Riding Light. He had to be ridden. It rested as much on Simon's judgement as on Timber's powers whether they could beat the almost faultless performance of Peggy Gates's horse. Brat thought that Simon looked very white about the mouth. There was more in this for Simon than winning a cup at a small country show. He had to take that prize from the girl who had tried to be up-sides with him by introducing a made winner to beat his own untried horses.

Timber came in looking puzzled. It was as if he said: "I've *done* this." His ears pricked at the sight of the jumps and then flickered in question. There was no eagerness to go at them as there had been when it was a new experience. But he went good-manneredly down to the first and cleared it in his effortless fluid fashion. Brat thought that he could hear the Ashby hearts thumping alongside him. He could certainly hear his own; it was making a noise like the Bures Silver Band's drum. Simon was half-way round. Ruth had shut her mouth and her eyes and looked as if she were praying. She opened her eyes in time to see Timber clear the gate; a smooth river of black pouring over the white barrier. "Oh, thank you, God," said Ruth. There was only the wall and the water left.

As Timber turned at the far end of the ring to come back to the wall a gust of wind lifted Simon's hat from his head and sent it bowling along the ground behind him. Brat was of the opinion that Simon was not even aware of it. Not even Tony Toselli had shown a concentration like Simon's. For Simon there quite patently existed nothing in this world but himself, the black horse, and the jumps. No one, *no one*, was going to come between Simon Ashby and the sun and get away with it.

Everything that Simon knew of riding, everything he had learned since he first sat on a pony at the age of two, was devoted to getting Timber safely over the wall. Timber did not like hard bare obstacles.

He had started his canter to the wall when a shrieking white terrier shot out from the stand in pursuit of the distant hat, streaking across in front of the advancing Timber like a hard-kicked ball, and yelling its excitement as only a terrier can.

Timber swerved from this terror and broke into a sweat.

Ruth shut her eyes again and resorted to further prayer. Simon soothed Timber patiently, cantering him round and making much of him while someone retrieved the dog and brought it back to its owner. (Who said: "Poor darling Scottie, he might have been killed!") Patiently, while the unforgiving seconds ticked on, Simon worked to reassure Timber. He must know that time was running out, that the dog incident was now officially over and each additional second's delay piling up against him.

Brat had marvelled often at Simon's powers of self-control, but he had never seen a more remarkable sample of it. The temptation to take Timber to the jump as he was must be enormous. But Simon was taking no chances with Timber. He was pawning time to gain a little better odds for Timber.

And then, having apparently calculated his time to the nearest possible margin, he brought Timber, still sweating but collected, to the wall again. Just before he came to the fence Timber hesitated a little.

And Simon sat still.

If it had been possible for Brat to like Simon Ashby he would have liked him at that moment.

The horse, undistracted from the task in front of him, gathered himself together and catapulted himself over the hated obstacle. And then, relieved to have it behind him, he raced on delightedly to the water and rocketed across it like a blackbird.

Simon had done it.

Jane took her hand out of Bee's, and wiped her palms on a screwed-up ball of handkerchief.

Bee slipped her arm through Brat's and squeezed it.

The great burst of cheering made speech inaudible.

In the quiet that succeeded it Ruth said, as one remembering an awkward engagement: "Oh, dear! I've pawned my month's allowance."

"To whom?" asked her aunt.

"God," said Ruth.

Chapter 26

*B*rat surveyed himself in the small cracked mirror of the Gent's Temporary Dressing-room and decided that primrose and violet did not become him any better than they became Simon. It would take Roger Clint's dark face to do justice to those springtime glories. Roger Clint would probably look dashing in them. He was in no mood to look favourably on Roger Clint. Whenever he had caught sight of Eleanor this afternoon it seemed that she was in the company of Mr. Clint, and what is more, seemed to be enjoying the company.

Brat tugged the yellow visor a little farther over his eyes. A sick misery burned in him; a spiritual heartburn.

"What's it got to do with you?" said a voice in him. "You're her brother: remember?"

"Shut up!"

"Can't have your cake and eat it, you know."

"*Shut up!*"

He walked out of the almost deserted dressing-room and went to find Chevron. The serious business of the day was over and there was an air of relaxation. In the shade of the trees competitors who had taken part in the sober events were now walking ponies and coffee-housing while they waited for the bending race. Alone for the moment, on a solid dun pony, was Peggy Gates, her eyes roving over the crowd in search of someone. She looked tired and discouraged. As Brat came level with her he paused and said:

"That was very bad luck."

"Oh, hullo, Mr. Ashby! What was?"

"The big drum."

"Oh, that!" she said, and smiled at him. "Oh, that was just one of those things."

She sounded quite philosophical about it, and yet Brat could have sworn that when he came up she had tears in her eyes.

"Good luck to the race," she said.

Brat thanked her and was moving away when she said: "Mr. Ashby, have I done anything to offend Simon, do you know?"

Brat said no, not that he knew.

"Oh. It's just that he seems to be avoiding me lately, and I'm not aware of having done anything—anything that he wouldn't—"

There were undoubted tears in her eyes now.

"Oh, you *know*," she said, tried a smile, didn't manage it very well, and moved away with a wave of her hand.

So it had not been a desire to be mistress of Latchetts that had moved pretty Peggy; it was devotion to Simon. Poor Peggy. Simon would never forgive her for Riding Light.

Eleanor was waiting under the trees on Buster, but stirrup to stirrup with her was Roger Clint, who had also found a pony for the bending race. Roger was pouring out a long story and Eleanor was nodding sympathetically; Brat gave them a wide berth and betook himself to the stables. In the stables he found Bee and Gregg. Gregg saw him weighed out and saddled Chevron, who was nervous and unhappy.

"It's the sound of the crowd that worries her," Gregg said. "Something she hears and can't understand. If I were you, Mr. Patrick, sir, I'd take her out and walk her. Take her out and show her the crowds and she'll be so interested she'll forget her nerves."

So Brat took the dithering chestnut out into the park, and she became gradually quieter, as Gregg had known she would. Presently Simon found him and suggested that it was time to be going down to the start.

"Did you remember to sign the book?" he asked.

"Book?" said Brat. "Sign for what?"

"To show that you consent to your horse running."

"I never heard of anyone signing a book. The horse was entered, wasn't it?"

"Yes, but in previous years they had trouble with gate-crashers. Some bright sparks who took out horses that didn't belong to them, when their owners didn't intend to run them. Had a free jaunt on them, and in at least one case broke the already tired horse down."

"All right. Where is the book?"

"In the weighing-room place. I'll look after Chevron till you come back. No need to take her into that mêlée."

In the little office, sitting behind the desk, was Colonel Smollett.

"Well, young Ashby, your family has been doing very well today, eh? Three firsts, no less. Are you going to add a fourth? Book? What book? Oh, the paper. Yes, yes. Here it is."

Brat, signing the single sheet of paper that was presented to him, said that he had never heard of this procedure.

"Probably not. Never heard of it myself. But it does insure the show against loss to a certain extent. That fellow whose horse was ridden unbeknownst to him last year, he sued the Show for damages. Very nearly got them too. So your brother suggested this method of insurance."

"My brother? Simon suggested it?"

"Yes. Got a head on him, Simon. Now no one can say that his horse was pulled out without his permission."

"I see."

He went back and retrieved Chevron from Arthur's custody.

"Mr. Simon said he couldn't wait, Mr. Patrick, but he said to wish you luck. He's gone back to the stands with the rest of the family to watch the finish."

"All right, Arthur; thanks."

"Would you like me to come to the start with you, sir?"

"Oh, no, thanks."

"In that case, I'll go and see about getting myself a place to see from. Good luck, sir. We're betting on you."

And he hurried off through the crowd.

Brat put the reins over Chevron's head and was just about to mount when he thought that he would take one more look at the girth. He had already tightened it, but perhaps he had made it too tight.

But someone had loosened the girth.

Brat stood holding up the flap with his hand and stared. Someone had loosened it since he left the mare with Simon. He put his hand under the girth and tested its degree of slackness. He reckoned that it would have got him out of the park into the country and would have lasted perhaps another two fences. After that, the saddle would have slipped round on the highly excitable Chevron and she would have gone crazy.

Arthur? No, not Arthur. Simon almost certainly.

He tightened the girth and made for the start. As he arrived he was overtaken by Roger Clint in white and scarlet on Operation Stockings.

"You're Patrick Ashby, aren't you?" he said. "My name is Roger

Clint." He leaned over and shook hands. "Very nice to have you at Bures again."

"Who won the bending race?" Brat asked.

"I did. By a short head from Nell."

"Nell" indeed!

"She won it last year on Buster, so it is just as well that the thing should go round. And I wanted a silver cup, anyway."

Brat had no time to ask why he had this longing for a silver cup. They were lining up, and he was Number Five, and Roger Clint was away on the outside. There were fourteen runners and a considerable amount of jostling. There was no gate, of course, the start being by flag.

Brat was in no hurry at the start. He let the others lead him so that he could gauge the opposition. At least five, he decided, were horses that had been ridden so much to-day that they were of no consequence and were merely cluttering up the course and spoiling things for their betters. Three more he had seen jumped in a junior competition, and had no belief that they would ever get round the course. That left five possibles, and of those three were dangerous: a bay charger ridden by his officer owner; a great raking brown youngster ridden by a young farmer; and Roger Clint's mount.

They took the hurdles at a tearing pace, and two of the over worked lot, fighting for position, struck into each other and rolled into a third. One of the "junior" jumpers came a frightful purler over the first fence going into the country, and brought down the other two over-tired animals. Which cleared the field very happily.

Chevron liked seeing her horses in front of her, and was patently enjoying herself. She loved jumping and was taking her fences with an off-handed confidence. One could almost hear her humming. She watched the other two "junior" jumpers fail to get over a blind fence and flicked her heels in their faces.

The field was thinning out very nicely.

Brat began to move up.

He passed the fifth of the possibles without effort. The fourth was making a noise like a pipe band but seemed good for a little yet. In front of him at the farthest point of the course were the soldier on the bay charger, the farmer on the big young brown horse, and Roger Clint on the chestnut with the white stockings. Apart from his own Chevron, Clint's was probably the best quality horse in the race, but the soldier was riding like a veteran, and the farmer like someone who has no respect for his neck.

It was a right-handed course, and the farmer's young horse jumped consistently to the right, so that no one could with any safety come up on the inside of him as long as he hugged the turns tightly. And since no one wanted to go wider than they need at the turns they dallied a little behind the big brown until they could come into the straight and pass him without disadvantage. It was going to be a race when they came back to that last half-mile of park.

Gradually the pipe band that had been so long at his left ear faded backwards into the distance, and when they came back to the park there were only four of them in it: the soldier, the farmer, Clint, and himself. He didn't mind about the other two, but he wanted very much to beat Roger Clint.

Clint had a look round as they left the country behind, and flashed a friendly smile to him. After that there was no time for courtesies. The pace was turned on with the suddenness of a tap, and the four of them pounded down the green avenue between the fluttering red flags as if classic honours were waiting for them at the other end. The big young brown horse began to sprawl; and the charger, though steady as a rock and apparently tireless, seemed to have no turn of speed to finish with. Brat decided to keep Chevron's nose level with the chestnut's quarters and see what transpired. To-gether they forged ahead of the bay and the brown. The farmer was using his whip and his horse sprawled more at every lift of it. The soldier was sitting still on the bay and evidently hoping that stam-ina would tell in the end.

Brat had a good look at Stockings and decided that he was tir-ing rapidly and that Clint, from the careful way he was riding him, knew it. There were two hurdles to go. He had no idea how much speed or stamina Chevron might have left, so he decided that the safest method was to try to trick Clint out of it. He shook Chevron up and took her up level with Stockings as if he were making his effort. Clint increased his speed to match, and together they crossed the last two obstacles, Brat still by his own choice a little in the rear, and therefore out of Clint's vision. Then Brat eased the pressure momentarily, and Clint, taking it for granted that a falling back so near the post argued failing stamina, was glad that he would not have to ask his mount for the last ounce and relaxed a little. Brat gathered Chevron together with all his strength and came like a rocket from behind him. Clint looked, startled, and set Stockings alight again, but it was too late. They were far too near the post for that, as Brat reckoned. He had stolen the race.

"Of all the 'old soldier' tricks to fall for!" laughed Clint, as they walked their horses together to the weighing-room. "I ought to have my head examined."

And Brat felt that whether Eleanor was going to marry him or not he really did like Roger Clint quite a lot.

Chapter 27

*B*rat had expected that Simon's success would have shored up his disintegrating spiritual structure and that the cracks would have disappeared. But it seemed that the very opposite had happened. The strain of the afternoon followed by the triumph of having beaten a performer like Riding Light had eaten away a little more of the foundation and shaken his equilibrium still further.

"I've never seen Simon so cock-a-hoop," Eleanor said, watching Simon over Brat's shoulder as they danced together that night. She said it as one making an apology. "He is usually so off-hand about his triumphs."

Brat said that it was probably the champagne, and turned her away from her view of Simon.

He had looked forward all day to dancing with Eleanor but it was with Bee that he had danced first. Just as he had given up his first chance of a ride with Eleanor to walk on Tanbitches with the ghost of Pat Ashby, so when faced with the moment of his first chance with Eleanor he had found something else that he wanted more. He had crossed the room to Bee and said: "Will you dance with me?" They had danced together in a happy quiet, her only remark being: "Who taught you to cheat someone out of a race like that?"

"I didn't have to be taught. It's original sin."

She laughed a little and patted him with the hand that was lying on his shoulder. She was a lovely woman, Bee Ashby, and he loved her. The only other person he had ever loved was a horse called Smoky.

"I haven't seen much of you this afternoon since that awful exhibition of Tony's," Eleanor said.

Brat said that he had wanted to talk to her before the race but that she was in deep conversation with Roger Clint.

"Oh, yes. I remember. His uncle wants him to give up the farm and go and live in Ulster. His uncle is Tim Connell, you know, who has the Kilbarty stud. Tim wants to retire, and would lease the place to Roger, but Roger doesn't want to leave England."

Understandably, Brat thought. England and Eleanor together was heaven enough. "I don't see him here tonight?"

"No, he didn't stay for the dance. He just came to get a silver cup to take home to his wife."

"His *wife!*"

"Yes, she had their first baby last week, and she sent him to the show to get a christening mug for it. What is the matter?" she asked.

"Remind me sometime to break Ruth's neck," he said, beginning to dance again.

She looked amused and said: "Has Ruth been romancing?"

"She said he wanted to marry you."

"Oh, well, he did have an idea like that but it's a long time ago. And of course he wasn't married last year, so Ruth probably didn't know about it. Are you going to be all patriarchal and supervise my marriage plans?"

"Have you any?"

"None at all."

As the night wore on and he danced more and more with Eleanor, she said: "You really must dance with someone else, Brat."

"I have."

"Only with Peggy Gates."

"So you've been keeping track of me. Am I keeping you from dancing with someone you want to dance with?"

"No. I love dancing with you."

"All right, then."

This was perhaps the first and the last night he would ever dance with Eleanor. A little before midnight they went up together to the buffet, filled their plates, and took them to one of the little tables in the balcony. The buffet was part of the actual hotel building, and the balcony, a piece of Regency ironwork, looked down on the little garden at the side of the hotel. Chinese lanterns hung in the garden and above the tables in the balcony.

"I'm too happy to eat," Eleanor said, and drank her champagne in a dreamy silence. "You look very nice in your evening things, Brat."

"Thank you."

"Do you like my frock?"

"It's the most beautiful frock I ever saw."

"I did hope you would like it."

"Have you had supper already to-night?"

"No. Only some drinks and a sandwich."

"Better eat, then."

She ate in an uninterested fashion that was new in Eleanor.

"It has been an Ashby occasion, hasn't it, the Seventy-fourth Annual Show of the Bures Agricultural. . . . Stay still for a moment, you have a gnat crawling down your collar."

She leant over and struck the back of his neck lightly. "Oh, it's going down!" In a rough sisterly fashion she bent his head aside with one hand while she retrieved the insect with the other.

"Got it?" he said.

But she was silent, and he looked up at her.

"You're *not* my brother!" she said. "I couldn't feel the way I—" She stopped, horrified.

In the silence the beat of the distant drums came up from the assembly room.

"Oh. Brat, I'm sorry! I didn't mean that! I think I must have drunk too much." She began to sob. "Oh, Brat, I'm sorry!" She gathered up her bag from the table and stumbled from the dim balcony into the buffet room. "I'll go and lie down and get sober."

Brat let her go and sought counsel in the bar. There was some sort of stunt in the assembly room at midnight, and the bar was deserted except for Simon, all by himself with a bottle of champagne at a table in the far corner.

"Ah! My big brother," said Simon. "Are you not interested in the lottery drawing? Have a drink."

"Thanks. I'll buy my own."

He bought a drink at the bar and carried it down the long room to Simon's table.

"I suppose lottery odds are too long for you," Simon said. "You want the table rigged before you bet."

Brat ignored that. "I haven't had a chance of congratulating you on your win with Timber."

"I don't need praise from you."

Simon was certainly drunk.

"That was very rude of me, wasn't it?" he said like a pleased child. "But I enjoy being rude. I'm behaving very badly to-night, aren't I? I seem to be slipping. Have a drink."

"I've got one."

"You don't like me, do you?" He looked pleased by Brat's dislike.

"Not very much."

"Why not?"

"I suppose because you are the only one who doesn't believe that I am Patrick."

"You mean, don't you, that I'm the only one who *knows* you're not?"

There was a long silence while Brat searched the shining eyes with their odd dark rim.

"You killed him," he said, suddenly sure of it.

"Of course I did." He leaned forward and looked delightedly at Brat. "But you'll never be able to say so, will you? Because of course Patrick isn't dead at all. He's alive, and I'm talking to him."

"How did you do it?"

"You'd like to know, wouldn't you? Well, I'll tell you. It's very simple." He leaned still closer and said in a mock-confidential undertone: "You see, I'm a witch. I can be in two places at once."

He sat back and enjoyed Brat's discomfiture.

"You must think that I'm a lot drunker than I am, my friend," he said. "I've told you about Patrick, because you are my posthumous accomplice. A wonderful epithet, that, and I managed it very well. But if you think that I am to make you free of the details, you are mistaken."

"Then, why did you do it?"

"He was a very stupid little boy," he said in his airy "Simon" tone, "and not worthy of Latchetts." Then he added, without façade: "I hated him, if you want to know."

He poured himself another glass of the Ayala, and drank it. He laughed under his breath, and said: "It's a wonderful spiritual twinship, isn't it? I can't tell about you and you can't tell about me!"

"You have the advantage of me, though."

"I have? How?"

"You have no scruples."

"Yes; I suppose it is an advantage."

"I have to put up with you, but you have no intention of putting up with me, have you? You did your best to kill me this afternoon."

"Not my best."

"You'll improve on it, I take it?"

"I'll improve."

"I expect you will. A person who can be in two places at once can do better than a loosened girth."

"Oh, much better. But one has to accept the means to hand."

"I see."

"I suppose you wouldn't like, in return for my confidences, to tell *me* something?"

"Tell you what?"

"Who you are?"

Brat sat looking at him for a long time.

"Don't you recognise me?" he said.

"No. Who are you?"

"Retribution," said Brat, and finished his drink.

He walked out of the bar and hung for a little over the banisters until his insides settled down and his breath came more easily. He tried to think of some place where he could be alone to think this thing out. There was nowhere in the hotel; even in his bedroom Simon might join him at any moment; he would have to go out.

He went to get his coat from Number Seventeen, and on the way back again he met Bee.

"Has everyone gone crazy?" Bee said angrily. "Eleanor is upstairs crying, Simon is getting drunk in the bar, and now you look as if you had seen a ghost. What is the matter with everyone? Have you had a quarrel?"

"A quarrel, no. Eleanor and Simon have had a wearing day, I expect."

"And what makes *you* so white about the gills?"

"Ballroom air. I'm from the wide open spaces: remember?"

"I've always understood that the wide open spaces were just seething with dance halls."

"Do you mind if I take the car, Bee?"

"Take it where?"

"I want to see the sun rise over Kenley Vale."

"Alone?"

"Definitely alone."

"Put on your coat," she said. "It's cold out."

At the top of the rise looking over Kenley Vale he stopped the car and shut off the engine. It was still dark and would be dark for some time yet. He got out and stood on the grass verge, leaning against the bonnet, and listened to the silence. The earth and grass smelt strong in the cool damp after the sun of yesterday. The air was motionless. Far away across the Vale a train whistled.

He had a cigarette, and his stomach felt better. But the turmoil had merely moved up. The turmoil was now in his head.

He had been right about Simon. He had been right in seeing the resemblance to Timber: the well-bred creature with the beautiful manners who was also a rogue. Simon had told the truth, back there in the bar. He had been glad to tell him the truth. They said all killers wanted to boast about their killings; Simon must have longed often to tell someone how clever he had been. But he could never tell until now; when he had a "safe" listener.

He, Brat Farrar, was the "safe" listener.

He, Brat Farrar, owned Latchetts, and Simon took it for granted that he would keep what he had taken. That he would keep it as Simon's accessory.

But that, of course, was not possible. The unholy alliance with Loding was one thing; but the alliance that Simon took so mockingly for granted was not possible. It was monstrous. Unthinkable.

And that being that, what was he going to do about it?

Go to the police and say: Look, I'm not Patrick Ashby at all. Patrick Ashby was killed by his brother eight years ago. I know, because he told me so when he was a little drunk.

And then they would point out that in the course of their investigation into the death of Patrick Ashby it was proved that Simon Ashby had spent the relevant hours in the smith's company in Clare.

He could tell them the truth about himself, but nothing would be changed except his own life. Patrick Ashby would remain a suicide.

How had Simon done it?

"One has to accept the means at hand," he had said, about his slackening of the girth.

What "means at hand" had there been that day eight years ago?

The slackening of the girth had been a combination of planning and improvisation. The "signing the book" suggestion had been a long shot. If it worked successfully to get him out of the way, then Simon was free to complete the rest of his plan. If it did not work, then no harm was done. The set-up was innocent to the observer's eye.

That was the way Simon's mind had worked about the girth, and that was the way it had worked eight years ago, undoubtedly. The set-up that was innocent and unquestionable. The using of the means at hand.

How, eight years ago, had Simon used an innocent set of circumstances to provide him with the chance he wanted?

Brat's mind was still toiling round and round the problem when the first sight of the stirring air told him that the dawn was coming. Presently the wind came again, lifting the leaves this time and ruffling the grass, and the east was grey. He watched the light come. The first bird notes dropped into the quiet.

He had been there for hours and he was no nearer a solution of the problem that faced him.

A policeman came along at leisure, pushing a bicycle, and paused to ask if he were in trouble. Brat said that he was getting some fresh air after a dance.

The policeman looked at his starched linen and accepted his explanation without remark. He looked at the interior of the car and said: "First time I ever saw a young gentleman getting fresh air alone after a dance. You haven't made away with her, by any chance, have you, sir?"

Brat wondered what he would say if he said: "No, but I'm accessory after the fact to another murder."

"She turned me down," he said.

"Ah. I see. Nursing your grief. Take it from me, sir, a week from now you'll be so thankful you'll feel like dancing in the street."

And he pushed his bicycle away along the ridge.

Brat began to shiver.

He got into the car and headed after the policeman. Where could he get something hot, he asked?

There was an all-night café at the main crossroads two miles ahead, the policeman said.

At the café, warm and bright and mundane after the grey spaces of the dawn, he drank scalding coffee. A buxom woman was frying sausages for two lorry-drivers, and a third was trying his luck at a penny-in-the-slot game in the corner. They glanced incuriously at his dance clothes, but beyond exchanging greetings with him they left him alone.

He came back to Bures at breakfast time, and put the car in the garage. The Chequers vestibule had a littered look; it was still only half-past seven, and show people notoriously made a night of it. He went up to Number Seventeen and found Simon fast asleep with all his clothes in one single heap on the floor just as he peeled them off. He changed into his day clothes, quietly at first and then less carefully as he realised that only long shaking would awaken Simon in his present condition. He looked down at Simon and marvelled. He slept quietly, like a child. Had he grown so used to the thing after eight years that it no longer troubled him, or was it that it never had been a monstrous thing in his estimation?

It was a charming face, except perhaps for the pettish mouth. A delightful face; delicately made and proportioned. There was no more suggestion of wrong-doing about it than there was in the beauty that was Timber.

He went downstairs and washed, wishing that he had thought in time of having a bath. He had been too obsessed by the desire to change clothes without having to talk to Simon.

When he came into the dining-room he found Bee and the twins having breakfast, and joined them.

"Nell and Simon are still asleep," Bee said. "You'd better come back with me and the twins in the car, and let Eleanor take Simon when they waken."

"What about Tony?"

"Oh, he went back yesterday with Mrs. Stack."

It was a relief to know that he could go back to Latchetts with Bee in peace.

The twins began to talk about Tony's exploit, which was patently going to be part of Latchetts history, and he did not have to make conversation. Bee asked if the dawn had come up to expectation, and remarked that he was looking the better of it.

Through the green early-morning countryside they drove home to Clare, and Brat caught himself looking at it with the emotions of someone who has only a short time to live. He looked at things with a that-will-still-be-there attitude.

He would never come to Bures. He might never even drive with Bee again.

Whatever else Simon's confession meant, it meant the end of his life at Latchetts.

Chapter 28

*I*t was Thursday morning and on Sunday Charles Ashby would come sailing up Southampton Water, and nothing would stop the subsequent celebrations. He followed Bee into the hall at Latchetts feeling desperate.

"Do you mind if I desert you and go into Westover?" he asked Bee.

"No, I think you are due a little rest from the family. Simon is for ever running away."

So he took the bus into Westover and waited until it was time for Mr. Macallan to be having his mid-morning coffee. He went to the *Westover Times* office and asked to see the files. The office boy, who showed no sign of ever having seen him before, took him to the cellar and showed him where they were, Brat read the report of the inquest all over again, but could find no help there.

Perhaps in the full report there would be something?

He went out and looked up Colonel Smollett in the telephone book. Where, he asked the Colonel, would the report of the inquest on himself be now? With the police? Well, would he make it easy for him to see it?

The Colonel would, but he considered it a most morbid and undesirable ambition, and implored young Ashby to think again.

So armed with the Colonel's telephoned introduction, he went to see a highly amused police force, who sat him down in a leather chair and offered him cigarettes, and set before him the coroner's report of eight years ago with the empressement of a conjurer who has produced the rabbit from the hat.

He read it all through several times. It was merely the *Westover Times's* report in greater detail.

He thanked the police, offered them cigarettes in his turn, and went away as empty of suggestion as he had come. He went down to the harbour and hung over the wall, staring westward at the cliffs.

He had a fixed point, anyhow. A fixed point that could not be altered. Simon Ashby was in Clare that day. That was held to by a man who had no reason for lying, and no suspicion that the fact was of any importance. Simon had never been long enough away from Mr. Pilbeam's vicinity to make his absence felt.

Pat Ashby must have been killed between the time that old Abel met him in the early afternoon and the moment when Mr. Pilbeam had to chase Simon home for six o'clock supper.

Well, there was that old saying about Mahomet and the mountain.

He thought the Mahomet theory over, but was stumped by the coat on the cliff-top. It was Simon who had written that note, but Simon was never out of Clare.

It was two o'clock when he came to himself, and he went to have lunch at a small pub in the harbour. They had nothing much left, but it did not matter because he sat staring at his plate until they put the bill in front of him.

He went back to Latchetts and without going to the house went to the stables aad took out one of the horses that had not been at Bures. There was no one about but Arthur, who reported that all the horses were safely back and all well except that Buster had an overreach.

"Taking him out like that, sir?" Arthur asked, nodding at Brat's tweed suit. And Brat said that he was.

He turned up to the down as he had that first morning when he took out Timber, and did again what he had done on Timber's back. But all the glory was gone. The whole world looked sick. Life itself tasted bad.

He dismounted and sat down where he had sat that morning a month ago, looking out over the small green valley. It had seemed paradise to him then. Even that silly girl who had come and talked to him had not sufficed to spoil it for him. He remembered how her eyes had popped when she found he was not Simon. She had come there sure of seeing Simon because it was his favourite place for exercising the horses. Because he . . .

The horse by his side threw up his head as Brat's sudden movement jerked the bit in his mouth.

Because he . . . ?

He listened to the girl's voice in his mind. Then he got slowly to his feet and stood a long time staring across the valley.

He knew now how Simon had done it. And he also knew the answer to something that had puzzled him. He knew why Simon had been afraid that, by some miracle, it was the real Patrick who had come back.

He got on the horse and went back to the stables. The great clouds were racing up from the south-west and it was beginning to rain. In the saddle room he took a sheet of writing paper from the desk and wrote on it: "Out for dinner. Leave the front door on the latch for me, and don't worry if I am late." He put it in an envelope, addressed it to Bee, and asked Arthur to hand it in at the house when he was passing. He took his burberry from the back of the saddle-room door, and went out into the rain, away from Latchetts. He had the knowledge now. What was he going to do with it?

He walked without conscious purpose, unaware of anything but the dreadful question to be answered. He came to the smithy where Mr. Pilbeam was still working, and greeted him, and exchanged opinions on the work in hand and on the weather to come, without having for a moment ceased to battle with the thing in his mind.

He walked up the path to Tanbitches and up the hill over the wet grass to the crown of beeches, and walked there to and fro among the great boles of the trees, distracted and stricken.

How could he bring this thing on Bee?

On Eleanor? On Latchetts?

Had he not already done Latchetts sufficient harm?

Would it matter so much if Simon were left in possession as he had been for eight years?

Who had been harmed by that? Only one person: Patrick.

If Simon was to be brought to justice for Patrick's death, it would mean horror beyond horror for Bee and the rest.

He didn't have to do it at all. He could go away; stage a suicide. After all, Simon had staged Patrick's suicide, and it had passed a police investigation. If a boy of thirteen could do that he could do it. He could just drop out, and things would be as they were a month ago.

And—Pat Ashby?

But Pat, if he could choose, would not want justice on Simon at the cost of his family's ruin. Not Pat, who had been kind and always thought first of others.

And Simon?

Was he to make good Simon's monstrous supposition that he would do nothing? Was Simon to spend a long life as the owner of Latchetts? Were Simon's children to inherit Latchetts?

But they would still be Ashbys. If Simon were brought to justice there would be no more Ashbys at Latchetts.

And how would it advantage Latchetts to have its inheritance made safe by the condoning of murder?

Was it not, perhaps, to uncover that murder that he had come by such strange ways to Latchetts?

He had come half across a world to that meeting with Loding in the street, and he had said to himself that so strange a chance must be destiny. But he had not imagined it to be an important destiny. Now, it would seem, it was an all-important one.

What was he to do? Who could advise him? Decide for him? It was not fair that this should be put on his shoulders. He had not the wisdom, the experience, to deal with a thing of this magnitude.

"I am retribution," he had said to Simon, and meant it. But that was before he had the weapon of retribution in his hand.

What was he to do?

Go to the police to-night? To-morrow?

Do nothing, and let the celebrations begin when Charles Ashby came home?

What was he to do?

It was late that night that George Peck, sitting in his study and conscious every now and then even from his distant vantage point in Thebes of the lashing rain on the window of the Rectory in Clare, heard a tapping at that window, and came back from Thebes and went to the front door. It was by no means the first time that people had tapped on that window late at night.

In the light from the hall he saw one of the Ashbys, he could not tell which because the soaked hat almost obscured the face.

"Rector, may I come in and talk to you?"

"Of course, Patrick. Come in."

Brat stood on the step, the rain sluicing from his coat.

"I'm afraid I'm very wet," he said vaguely.

The Rector looked down and saw that the grey tweed of his trousers was black, and his shoes an oozing pulp. His eyes went sharply to the boy's face. Brat had taken off his limp hat and the rain-water from his soaked hair was running down his face.

"Take off your coat and leave it here," the Rector said. "I'll give you another one when you are ready to go." He went to the hall cloakroom and came back with a towel. "Rub your head with that."

Brat did as he was told, with the obedient air and fumbling

movements of a child. The Rector went through to the empty kitchen and brought a kettle of water.

"Come in," he said. "Just drop the towel where your wet coat is." He led the way into his study and put the kettle on an electric ring. "That will be hot in no time. I often make tea for myself when I sit up late. What was it you wanted to talk to me about?"

"A pit in Dothan."

"What?"

"I'm sorry. My mind has stopped working. Have you a drink of any kind?"

The Rector had meant to put the whisky in the tea, as a toddy, but he poured a stiff one now and Brat drank it.

"Thank you. I am sorry to come and worry you like this, but I had to talk to you. I hope you don't mind."

"I am here to be talked to. Some more whisky?"

"No, thanks."

"Then let me give you some dry shoes."

"Oh, no, thank you. I'm used to being wet, you know. Rector, I want your advice about something very important, but can I talk to you as if—as if it were confessional I mean, without your feeling that you must do something about it."

"Whatever you say I shall treat as confession, certainly."

"Well, first I have to tell you something. I am not Patrick Ashby."

"No," agreed the Rector. And Brat stared.

"You mean—you mean, you *knew* I wasn't Patrick?"

"I rather thought that you weren't."

"Why?"

"There is more to any person than a physical presence; there is an aura, a personality, a being. And I was almost sure the first time I met you that I had never met you before. There was nothing in you that I recognised, although you have many things in common with Patrick as well as your appearance."

"And you did nothing about it!"

"What do you suggest that I should have done? Your lawyer, your family, and your friends had all accepted and welcomed you. I had no evidence to show that you were not Patrick. Nothing but my own belief that you weren't. What good would it have done to express my disbelief? It did not seem to me that it would be long before the situation resolved itself without my interference."

"You mean: that I should be found out."

"No. I mean that you did not seem to me someone who would be happy in the life you had chosen. Judging by your visit to-night, I was right."

"But I didn't come here to-night just to confess to not being Patrick."

"No?"

"No, that is only—I had to tell you that because it was the only way you could understand what has—I wish my mind was clearer. I've been walking about trying to get things straight."

"Perhaps if you told me first how you came to Latchetts at all, it would at least clear *my* mind."

"I—I met someone in America who had lived in Clare. They—she thought I looked like an Ashby, and suggested that I should pretend to be Patrick."

"And you were to pay her a share of the proceeds of the deception."

"Yes."

"I can only say that she earned her percentage whatever it was. As a tutor she must be remarkable. I have never seen a better piece of coaching. Are you American, then?"

"No," said Brat, and the Rector smiled faintly at the emphasis. "I was brought up in an orphanage. I was left on its doorstep."

And he sketched for the Rector the story of his life.

"I have heard of your orphanage," the Rector said when he had finished. "It explains one thing that puzzled me: your good up-bringing." He poured tea, and added whisky. "Would you like something more substantial than biscuits, by the way? No? Then have the oatmeal ones; they are very filling."

"I had to tell you all this because of something I found out. Patrick didn't commit suicide. He was murdered."

The Rector set down the cup he was holding. For the first time he looked startled.

"Murdered? By whom?"

"His brother."

"*Simon?*"

"Yes."

"But Patrick! That—What is your name by the way?"

"You forget I haven't got one. I've always been called Brat. It was a corruption of Bartholomew."

"But my dear fellow, that is absurd. What evidence have you of anything so incredible?"

"I have Simon's word for it."

"*Simon* told you?"

"He boasted about it. He said that I could never do anything about it because it would mean giving myself away. He knew as soon as he saw me that I wasn't Patrick, you see."

"When did this extraordinary conversation take place?"

"Last night, at the Bures ball. It wasn't as sudden as it sounds. I began to wonder about Simon long before that, and I challenged him about it because of something he said about *knowing* I wasn't Patrick, and he laughed and boasted about it."

"I think that the setting of this scene does a lot to explain it."

"You mean you think we were drunk?"

"Not exactly. Elated, shall we say. And you challenged Simon on the subject, and Simon with his perverted sense of mischief provided you with what you expected from him."

"Do you really believe I have as little intelligence as that?" Brat asked quietly.

"It surprises me, I must admit. I have always considered you to be highly intelligent."

"Then believe me, I am not here because of a piece of fooling on Simon's part. Patrick didn't commit suicide. Simon killed him. Deliberately. And what is more, I know how he did it."

And he told him.

"But Brat, you have no evidence even now. That is theory, what you have just told me. An ingenious and likely theory, I admit. It has the merit of simplicity. But you have no evidence whatsoever."

"We can get the evidence, if the police once know the truth. But that isn't what I want to know. What I want advice about is—well, whether to let sleeping dogs lie."

And he explained his dilemma.

But the Rector, rather surprisingly in view of his silence about his doubts of Brat's identity, had no doubts on the subject at all. If murder had been done, then the law must be invoked. Anything else was anarchy.

His point was that Brat had no case against Simon. His mind had run on murder, he had taunted Simon with it, Simon had one of his well-known impish moments and confessed, and Brat after long thought had found a theory to fit the alleged confession.

"And you think that I've been walking about in the rain since four o'clock because of a little joke of Simon's? You think that I came here to-night and confessed to not being Patrick because of a little joke of Simon's?" The Rector was silent. "Tell me, Rector, were you surprised when Pat committed suicide?"

"Exceedingly."

"Do you know anyone who wasn't surprised?"

"No. But suicide *is* a surprising thing."

"I give up," Brat said.

In the contemplative silence that followed, the Rector said: "I see what you meant by the pit in Dothan. That was an excellent upbringing at the orphanage."

"It was a very thoroughly Biblical one, if that is what you mean. Simon knows that story too, by the way."

"I expect so, but how do you happen to know?"

"When he heard that Patrick had come back he couldn't help, in spite of his denials, a fear that it might be true. There had been that other case, you see. That time the victim had survived by a miracle. He was afraid that by some miracle Patrick had survived. I know, because he came into that room, the first day I was there, strung up to face something dreadful. And his relief when he saw me was almost funny."

He drank down the rest of his tea and looked quizzically at the Rector. In spite of himself he was beginning to feel better.

"Another of Simon's little jokes was to send me out that first day on Timber, without telling me he was a rogue. But I suppose that was just his 'perverted sense of mischief.' And still another of his little jokes was to loosen my girth yesterday before I started a race on Chevron. But I suppose that was just one of his 'well-known impish moments.' "

The Rector's deep eyes considered Brat.

"I am not defending Simon—he has never been an admirable character—but tricks played on an interloper, a pretender—even dangerous tricks, are one thing, and the murder of a well-loved brother is quite another. Why, by the way, did Simon not denounce you at once if he did not believe you were his brother?"

"For the same reason that you didn't."

"I see. He would merely be held to be—difficult."

"And of course, having got rid of one Patrick with impunity, he looked forward with confidence to getting rid of another."

"Brat, I wish I could convince you that this is a figment of your imagination."

"You must have a great respect for my imaginative powers."

"If you look back, critically and honestly, you must see how the thing grew in your mind from quite small beginnings. An edifice of your own making."

And that, when Brat took his leave towards two o'clock in the morning, was still the Rector's opinion.

He offered Brat a bed, but Brat compromised on the loan of a waterproof and a torch, and found his way back to Latchetts by the soaking field-path with the rain still pouring hopelessly down.

"Come and see me again before you decide anything," the Rector had said; but he had at least been helpful in one direction. He had answered Brat's main question. If it was a choice between love and justice, the choice had to be justice.

He found the front door of Latchetts unlocked, a note from Bee on the hall table, saying: "Soup on the ring in the pantry," and a silver cup on an ebony stand bearing a card in Eleanor's writing which said: "You forgot this, you blasé rodeo hound!"

He put out the lights and crept up through the silent house to his bed in the old night nursery. Someone had put a hot-water bottle in his bed. He was asleep almost before his head touched the pillow.

Chapter 29

On Friday morning Simon came bright and cheerful to breakfast and greeted Brat with pleasure. He commented on the process of the "trunk" murder investigations, the character of Tattie Thacker (whose value had been estimated by the court at one halfpenny) and the iniquity of poisoning as a means of ridding oneself of a human encumbrance. Except for an occasional gleam in the eye he showed no awareness of their changed relationship. He was taking their "spiritual twinship" for granted.

Eleanor too seemed to be back on the old footing, although she seemed shy, like someone who had made a social gaffe. She suggested that in the afternoon they should take the four silver cups into Westover and give instructions for their engraving.

"It will be nice to have 'Patrick Ashby' on a cup again," she said.

"Yes, won't it!" Simon said.

Simon evidently looked forward to years of baiting his spiritual twin. But when Brat said, in answer to Bee, that he had talked late with the Rector, Simon's head came up as if he had heard a warning. And after that Brat caught Simon's glance at him every now and then.

When Eleanor and Brat were setting off for Westover in the afternoon, he appeared and insisted on making a third in the bug's scanty space. One of the cups was his own unaided work, he said, and he had a right to say what was to go on it, and whether it should be in Roman, Arabic, Hebrew, Greek, or Cyrillic script, or mere shorthand.

So powerful was Simon's indifferent charm that even Brat found himself on the verge of wondering whether the Rector had been right and he had built his story out of whole cloth. But he remembered the horse that Farmer Gates had bought his daughter, Peggy, and concluded that that was a more reliable guide to Simon than anything Simon himself might provide.

When they had decided on the lettering for the names on the cups, Simon and Eleanor went to tea, but Brat said that he had some shopping to do. Brat had decided what he had to do in the present impasse. He could not go to the police with his story in its present form with any more hope of being believed than he had been by the Rector. If the Rector, who knew Simon's weaknesses, refused to believe without concrete evidence, how much more would the police refuse to believe, when Simon to them was not a wayward boy but Mr. Ashby of Latchetts?

Brat therefore proposed to provide them with the evidence.

He went down to the harbour and sought a chandler's, and there, after some consultation and a deal of choosing, bought two hundred feet of rope. The rope was so thin that it was not much thicker than stout string, but its breaking-point under tension was very much that of steel. He asked them to pack it in a cardboard box and deliver it to the Angel garage, where the bug was. He received it at the garage and packed it away in the luggage compartment.

When the others arrived to go home he was waiting innocently in the car with an evening paper.

They had packed themselves into the bug and were preparing to go when Simon said: "Whoa! We've forgotten to leave that old tire with them," and he got out and opened the rear compartment to get the tire.

"What is in the box, Nell?"

"I didn't put any box there," Eleanor said, not moving. "It can't be for us."

"It's mine," Brat said.

"What is it?"

"Secret."

"James Fryer and Son, Ship Chandlers," said Simon's voice.

Oh, God! There was a label on the box that he had not noticed.

Simon shut the luggage compartment with a bang and came back to his seat. "What have you been buying, Brat? One of those ships in a bottle? No, it is a little too large for that. One of those ships not in a bottle. One of those full-sailed galleons that sit on suburban sideboards to delight the heart of our Island Race and comfort it for being sick on the trip to Margate."

"Don't be a fool, Simon. What is it, Brat? Is it really a secret?"

If Simon wanted to find out what was in the box he most certainly would, by one method or another. And to make a mystery of it was to call attention to it. Far better to be apparently frank about it.

"If you must know. I'm afraid I'll lose the knack of spinning a rope, so I've bought some to practise on."

Eleanor was delighted. Brat must show them some spinning that very evening.

"No. Not till I've tried it out in camera first."

"You'll teach me how, won't you?"

Yes, he would teach her how to throw a rope. She was going to hate him one day soon, if that rope did what it was bought for.

When they arrived back at Latchetts he took the rope out and left it openly in the hall. Bee asked about it, and accepted the explanation of its presence, and no one took any more notice of it. He wished that his last short time at Latchetts did not have to be spent in lying. It was odd that, having spent his whole time at Latchetts lying like a Levantine, he should mind so much about this smaller deception.

There was still time to do nothing about it. To leave the rope there, and not ask it to answer any question. It was the wrong kind of rope for throwing, but he could change it for the right kind.

But when night came, and he was alone in his room, he knew that he had no choice. This was what he had come half across a world to do, and he was going to do it.

The household went early to bed, still tired from their excitements at Bures, and he gave them till half-past twelve, and then prospected. There seemed to be no light anywhere. There was certainly no sound. He went downstairs and took the rope from its corner. He unlatched the dining-room window, stepped over the sill into the night, and drew it gently down again behind him. He waited for any reaction, but there was none.

He made his way softly over the gravel to the grass, sat down in the shelter of the first paddock trees, out of the range of the windows, and without need of any light, deftly knotted footholds at intervals down the length of rope. It was a pleasant reassuring thing to feel the familiar touch of rope after so long. It was a well-bred rope and answered sweetly to his demands. He felt grateful to James Fryer and Son.

He wound the rope and put the coil of it over his shoulder. In half an hour the moon would be up. It was a young moon, and not much of a lamp, but he had two good torches in his pocket and he did not very much desire a full moon's frankness to-night.

Every five minutes he stopped and waited to see if he had been followed. But nothing at all moved in the night. Not even a cat.

The grey light of the coming moon greeted him as he came towards the foot of Tanbitches, and he found the path to Westover without having to flick a torch. He followed it up a little and then, when he could see the beech-crown of the hill against the sky, he struck off it until he reached the thicket on the upper side of the old quarry. There he sat down and waited. But again there was no sound in all the sleeping countryside except the sudden cry of a sheep on the hill. He tied the rope round the bole of the largest of the young beeches that had seeded themselves there, and let it uncoil itself until it fell over the edge of the quarry into the green thickness below. This was the steep side of the quarry. The lower side had had a narrow entrance, but it had long ago fallen together and become overgrown with an impenetrable denseness of briars. Old Abel had told him all about it the day they had sat there and talked of Patrick. Abel knew all about the quarry because he had once rescued a sheep from it. It was much easier to go down the sheer face, Abel said, than in at the lower side. In fact, to go in at the lower side, or any other side, was plumb impossible. No, there was no water in it; at least there wasn't any twenty years ago, which was when last he went down after a sheep; the water all drained away under the hill to the sea.

Brat tested the rope several times, and felt for it fraying. But the bole of the tree was smooth, and where it went over the lips of the quarry he had padded it. He slid over the edge and felt for his first toe-hold. Now that he was level with the ground he was more aware of the brightness of the sky. He could see the dark shape of the low thicket against it, and the larger darkness of the tree above him.

He had found his first foothold in the rope now, but his hands were still on the rope where it lay taut on the turf.

"I should hate," said Simon's voice in its most "Simon" drawl, "to let you go without an appropriate farewell. I mean, I could just cut the rope and let you think, if you had time to think at all, that it had broken. But that wouldn't be any fun, would it?"

Brat could see his bulk against the sky. From the shape of it, he was half-kneeling on the edge, by the rope. Brat could touch him by putting out a hand.

Fool that he had been to underrate Simon. Simon had taken no chances. He hadn't even taken the chance of following him. He had come first and waited.

"Cutting the rope won't do much good," he said. "I'll yell my head off until someone comes."

"I know better than that. A personal acquaintance of mine, this quarry is. Almost a relation, one might say." He expelled his breath in a whispered laugh. "A sheer drop to the ground, half a hillside away."

Brat wondered if he had time to slide down the rope in one swift rush before Simon cut it. The footholds had been for coming up again. He could just ignore them and slide. Would he be near enough the bottom before Simon realised what he had done?

Or would it be better—? Yes. His hand tightened on the rope and he pressed on his toe-hold and lifted himself until he had almost got one knee on the turf again. But Simon must have his hand on the rope somewhere. He had felt the movement.

"Oh, no, you don't!" he said, and brought his heel down on Brat's hand. Brat grabbed the foot with his other hand and hung on, his fingers in the opening of the shoe. Simon brought his knife down on Brat's wrist and Brat yelled, but continued to hang on. He dragged his right hand from under Simon's shoe and caught him round the back of the ankle. He was covering with his body the rope in front of Simon and as long as he held on Simon could not turn to cut the rope behind him. It is very upsetting to have one's foot grasped from below when one is standing on the very edge of a precipice.

"Let go!" said Simon, stabbing frantically.

"If you don't stop that," panted Brat, "I'll drag you over with me."

"Let go! Let go!" Simon said, hitting wildly in blind panic and not listening.

Brat removed the hand that was holding on to the edge of the shoe and caught the knife-hand as it came down. He now had his right hand round Simon's left ankle, and his left hand was clutching Simon's right wrist.

Simon screamed and pulled away, but Brat hung his weight on the wrist. He had the confidence of a toe-hold, but Simon had nothing to brace himself against. Simon tore at the hand that was hanging on to his knife-wrist, and Brat, with a great heave, took his right hand from Simon's foot and caught Simon's left hand with it. He had now got Simon by both wrists, and Simon was bent over like a bow above him.

"Drop that knife!" he said.

As he said it he felt the turf at the quarry edge settle a little and slide forward. It made no difference to him, except to press him out a little from the face of the cliff. But to Simon, already bent over by the weight of Brat's arms and body, it was fatal.

Horrified, Brat saw the dark mass come forward on top of him. It struck him from his toe-hold, and he fell down with it into darkness.

A great light exploded in his head, and he ceased to know anything.

Chapter 30

*B*ee sat in the dingy café with a cup of slopped coffee in front of her and read the sign on the other side of the road for the hundredth time in the last forty-eight hours. The sign said: MOTORISTS. PLEASE REFRAIN FROM USING YOUR HORN. THIS IS A HOSPITAL. It was only seven o'clock in the morning, but the café opened at six, and there was always at least one other customer having a meal as she sat there. She did not notice them. She just sat with a cup of coffee in front of her and stared at the hospital wall opposite. She was an old inhabitant of the café by now. "Better go out and have a meal," they would say kindly, and she would cross the road and sit for a little with a cup of coffee in front of her and then go back again.

Her life had narrowed down to this pendulum existence between the hospital and café. She found it difficult to remember a past, and quite impossible to visualise a future. There was only the "now," a dreary half-world of grey misery. Last night they had given her a cot in one of the sisters' rooms, and the night before that she had spent in the hospital waiting-room. There were two phrases that they used to her, and they were as sickeningly familiar as the sign on their wall: "No, no change," they would say, or, "Better go out and get a meal."

The slatternly girl came and pushed a fresh cup of coffee in front of her and took away the one she had. "That one's cold," said the slatternly girl, "and you haven't even touched it." The fresh cup was slopped over too. She was grateful to the slatternly girl but felt outraged by her sympathy. She was enjoying the vicarious drama of her presence in the café, and its implications.

MOTORISTS. PLEASE REFRAIN FROM USING—She must stop reading that thing. Must look at something else. The blue-checked pattern of the plastic tablecloth, perhaps. One, two, three, four, five, six—Oh, no. Not counting things.

The door opened and Dr. Spence came in, his red hair tumbled and his chin unshaved. He said "Coffee!" to the girl, and slid into the seat beside her.

"Well?" she said.

"Still alive."

"Conscious?"

"No. But there are better indications. I mean, of a chance of his regaining consciousness, not necessarily of—his living."

"I see."

"We know about the skull fracture, but there are no means of telling what other injuries there may be."

"No."

"You oughtn't to be living on cups of coffee. That's all you've been having, isn't it?"

"She hasn't been having that," said the slatternly girl, putting down his full cup. "She just sits and looks at them."

A wave of weary anger rose in her at the slatternly girl's appropriation of her concerns.

"Better let me take you downtown and give you a meal."

"No. No, thank you."

"The Angel is only a mile away, and you can rest properly there and—"

"No. No, I can't go as far away as that. I'll drink this cup. It's nice and hot."

Spence gulped down his coffee and paid for it. He hesitated a moment as if reluctant to leave her. "I have to go back to Clare now. You know I shouldn't leave him if he wasn't in good hands, don't you? They'll do more for him than I ever could."

"You've done wonders for all of us," she said. "I shall never forget it."

Now that she had begun drinking the coffee she went on drinking it, and did not look up when the doors opened again. It would not be another message from the hospital already, and nothing had any importance for her that was not a message from the hospital. She was surprised when George Peck sat down beside her.

"Spence told me I should find you here."

"George!" she said. "What are you doing in Westover at this hour of the morning?"

"I have come to bring you comfort that Simon is dead."

"Comfort?"

"Yes."

He took something from an envelope and laid it in front of her on the table. It was weatherworn but recognisable. It was a slender black stylograph with a decoration consisting of a thin yellow spiral.

She looked at it a long time without touching it, then looked up at the Rector.

"Then they have found—it?"

"Yes. It was there. Do you want to talk about it here? Wouldn't you prefer to go back to the hospital?"

"What difference does it make? They are both just places where one waits."

"Coffee?" said the slatternly girl, appearing at George's shoulder.

"No; no, thank you."

"Righteeo!"

"What—what *is* there? I mean, what—what is left? What did they find?"

"Just bones, my dear. A skeleton. Under three feet of leaf mould. And some shreds of cloth."

"And his pen?"

"That was separate," he said carefully.

"You mean, it—had been—that it had been thrown down after?"

"Not necessarily, but—probably."

"I see."

"I don't know whether you will find it comforting or not—I think it is—but the police surgeon is of the opinion that he was not alive—or perhaps it would be more accurate to say not conscious—when he—"

"When he was thrown over," Bee said for him.

"Yes. The nature of the skull injury, I understand, leads him to that conclusion."

"Yes. Yes, I am glad, of course. He probably knew nothing about it. Just ended quite happy on a summer afternoon."

"There were some small objects in the cloth. Things that he probably had in his trousers pockets. But the police have kept these. Colonel Smollett gave me this," he picked up the stylograph and put it back in its envelope, "and asked me to show it to you so that you might identify it. What news from the hospital? Spence was driving away when I saw him."

"None. He is not conscious."

"I blame myself greatly for that, you know," the Rector said. "If

I had listened with understanding he would not have been driven to this *sub rosa* proceeding, to that crazy night-time search."

"George, we must do something to find out who he is."

"But I understand that the orphanage—"

"Oh, I know. They made the usual enquiries. But I don't suppose they were very persistent ones. We could do much better, surely."

"Starting from the pre-supposition that he has Ashby blood in him?"

"Yes. I can't believe that a resemblance like that could exist without it. The coincidence would be too great."

"Very well, my dear. Do you want it put in hand—now?"

"Yes. Especially now. Time may be precious."

"I'll speak to Colonel Smollett about it. He'll know how to go about it. I talked to him about the inquest, and he thinks it may be possible to manage without your appearing. Nancy told me to ask you if you would like her to come into Westover to be with you, or if it would only worry you to have someone around."

"Dear Nan. Say it is easier alone, will you? But thank her. Tell her to stand by Eleanor, rather. It must be dreadful for Nell, having to toil with unimportant things in the stables."

"I think it must be a soothing thing to have to devote oneself to the routine demands of the animal world."

"Did you break the news to her, as you promised? The news that Brat was not Patrick?"

"Yes. I dreaded it, Bee, I confess frankly. You had given me one of the hardest tasks of my life. She was still fresh from the shock of knowing that Simon had been killed. I dreaded it. But the event was surprising."

"What did she do?"

"She kissed me."

The door opened, and a probationer, flushed and young and pretty, and looking in her lilac print and spreading white linen like a visitor from another world, stood in the dim opening. She saw Bee and came over to her.

"Are you Miss Ashby, please?"

"Yes?" said Bee, half rising.

"Miss *Beatrice* Ashby? Oh, that's nice. Your nephew is conscious now, but he doesn't recognise anyone or where he is; he just keeps talking about someone called Bee, and we thought it might be you. So Sister sent me across to see if I could find you. I'm sorry to interrupt you, and you haven't finished your coffee, have you, but you see—"

"Yes, yes," said Bee, already at the door.

"He may be quieter, you see, if you are there," the probationer said, following her out. "They often are, when someone they know is there, even if they don't actually recognise them. It's funny. It's as if they could see them through their skin. I've noticed it often. They'll say, Eileen?—or whoever it is. And Eileen says, Yes. And then they're quiet for a bit. But if anyone else says yes, nine times out of ten they're not fooled at all, and get restless and fractious. It's very strange."

What really was strange was to hear that steady stream of words from the lips of the normally silent Brat. For a day and a night and a day again she sat by his bed and listened to that restless torrent of talk. "Bee?" he would say, just as the little probationer had recounted to her. And she would say: "Yes, I'm here," and he would go back reassured to whatever world he was wandering in.

His most constant belief was that this was the time he had broken his leg, and this the same hospital; and he was torn with anxiety about it. "I'll be able to ride again, won't I? There's nothing really wrong with my leg, is there? They won't take it off, will they?"

"No," she would say, "everything is all right."

And once, when he was quieter: "Are you very angry with me, Bee?"

"No, I'm not angry with you. Go to sleep."

The world went on outside the hospital; ships arrived in Southampton Water, inquests were held, bodies were consigned to the earth, but for Bee the world had narrowed to the room where Brat was and her cot in the Sister's room.

On Wednesday morning Charles Ashby arrived at the hospital, padding lightly down the polished corridors on his large noiseless feet. Bee went down to receive him and took him up to Brat's room. He had hugged her as he used to when she was a little girl, and she felt warm and comforted.

"Dear Uncle Charles. I'm so glad you were fifteen years younger than Father, or you wouldn't be here to be a comfort to us all."

"The great point in being fifteen years younger than your brother is that you don't have to wear his cast-offs," Charles said.

"He's asleep just now," she said, pausing outside Brat's room, "so you'll be very quiet, won't you?"

Charles took one look at the young face with the slack jaw, the blue shadows under the closed eyes, and the grey haze of stubble, and said: "Walter."

"His name is Brat."

"I know. I wasn't addressing him. I was merely pointing out the resemblance to Walter. That is exactly what Walter used to look like, at his age, when he had a hangover."

Bee came nearer and looked. "*Walter's* son?"

"Undoubtedly."

"I don't see any resemblance, somehow. He doesn't look like anyone but himself, now."

"You never saw Walter sleeping it off." He looked at the boy a little longer. "A better face than Walter's, though. A good face." He followed her into the corridor. "I hear you all liked him."

"We loved him," she said.

"Well, it's all very sad, very sad. Who was his accomplice, do you know?"

"Someone in America."

"Yes, so George Peck told me. But who would that be? Who went to America from Clare?"

"The Willett family went to Canada. And they had daughters. It was a woman, you know. Perhaps they finished up in the States."

"If it was a woman I'll eat my hat."

"I feel that way too."

"Do you? Good girl. You're an admirably intelligent woman, Bee. Nice-looking too. What are we going to do about the boy? For the future, I mean."

"We don't know yet if he has a future," she said.

Chapter 31

Only the Rector, Bee, Charles, Eleanor, and the firm of Coset, Thring and Noble knew, so far, that Brat was not Patrick Ashby.

And the police.

The police, that is, at what is known as "the highest level."

The police had been told everything, and they were now engaged in their own admirable fashion in smoothing out the mess to the best of their ability without breaking any of the laws which they were engaged to uphold. Simon Ashby was dead. It was to no one's advantage to uncover the story of his crime. By a process of not saying too much, the ritual of the Law might be complied with, leaving unwanted truths still buried; a harrow dragging over earth that held below its surface unexploded bombs.

The coroner sat on the poor bones found in the quarry, and adjourned the inquest *sine die*. No one in the neighbourhood had ever been reported missing. Tanbitches, on the other hand, was a favourite camping ground for gipsies, who were not given to reporting accidents to the police. Nothing remained of the clothing but a few scraps of unrecognisable cloth. The objects found in the vicinity of the bones were unidentifiable; they consisted of a corroded piece of metal that might once have been a whistle, another corroded piece still recognisable as a knife, and several coins of small denominations.

"George!" said Bee. "What became of the pen?"

"The stylograph? I lost it."

"*George!*"

"Someone had to lose it, my dear. Colonel Smollett couldn't; he's a soldier, with a soldier's sense of duty. The police couldn't; they have their self-respect and their duty to the public to consider. But my conscience is between me and my God. I think they were touchingly grateful to me in their tacit way."

The adjourned inquest on Simon Ashby came later, since it had been postponed until Brat was capable of being interviewed in hospital. The policeman who had interviewed him reported that Mr. Ashby could remember nothing about the accident, or why he should have gone there with his brother at that hour to climb down into the quarry. He had an idea that it was the result of a bet. Something about whether there was water in the old quarry or not, he thought; but could not take his oath on it since his recollection was vague. He had serious head injuries and was still very ill. He did know, however, that he had found out from Abel Tusk that there was no water there; and Simon probably had said that that was highly unlikely, and so the contest may have arisen.

Abel Tusk corroborated the fact that Patrick Ashby had asked him about water in the quarry, and that it was an unusual thing to find the floor of an old quarry dry. It was Abel Tusk who had given the first alarm of the accident. He had been out on the hill with his sheep and had heard what he took to be cries for help from the direction of the quarry, and had gone there as fast as he could and found the undamaged rope, and had gone down to the blacksmith's and used his telephone to call the police.

Bee, replying to the coroner, agreed that she would most certainly have taken steps to put an end to any such plan had she heard about it. And the coroner expressed his opinion that it was for that reason that the thing had been done *sub rosa*.

The verdict was death by misadventure, and the coroner expressed his sympathy with the family on the loss of this high-spirited young man.

So the problem of Simon was settled. Simon, who, before he was fourteen, had killed his brother, calmly written a note on that brother's behalf, tossed the pen into the abyss after his brother's body, and gone home calmly to six o'clock supper when he was chased out of the smithy. Who had joined the night search for his brother on his pony, and some time during that long night had taken his brother's coat to the cliff-top and left it there with the note in the pocket. Who was now to be mourned by the countryside as a high-spirited young man of memorable charm.

The problem of Brat remained.

Not the problem of who he was, but the problem of his future. The doctors had decided that, having against all probability lived so long, he was likely to go on living. He would need long care, however, and a peaceful life if he was to recover properly.

"Uncle Charles came to see you one day when you were ill." Bee said to him when he was well enough to keep his attention on a subject. "He was astonished by your resemblance to Walter Ashby. My cousin."

"Yes?" said Brat. He was not interested. What did it matter now?

"We began enquires about you."

"The police did that," he said wearily. "Years ago."

"Yes, but they had very little to come and go on. Only that a young girl had arrived by train with a baby, and gone away by train without one. The train had come from the crowded Birmingham district with all its ramifications. We started at the other end. Walter's end. We went back to where Walter was, somewhere about twenty-two years ago, and began from there. Walter was a rolling stone, so it wasn't easy, but we did find out that among his other jobs, he was in charge of a stable in Gloucestershire for a couple of months while the owner was away having an operation. The household was a housekeeper and a young girl who cooked. She was a very good cook, but her real ambition was to be a hospital nurse. The housekeeper liked her and so did the owner, and when they found she was going to have a baby they let her stay on, and she had her baby in the local maternity home. The housekeeper always believed that it was Walter's child, but the girl would not say. She did not want to get married; she wanted to be a nurse. She said that she was taking the baby home for the christening—she came from Evesham way—and she didn't come back. But the housekeeper had a letter from her long afterwards, thanking her for her goodness and telling her that the girl had realised her ambition and was a nurse. "No one knows about my baby," she said, "but I have seen that he is well looked after."

She glanced at Brat. He was lying with his eyes on the ceiling, but he appeared to be listening.

"Her name was Mary Woodward. She was an even better nurse than she was a cook. She was killed during the war, taking patients out of a ward to safety in a shelter."

There was a long silence.

"I seem to have inherited my cooking talents too," he said; and she could not tell whether the words were bitter or not.

"I was very fond of Walter. He was a dear; very kind. He had only one fault; he had no head for drink, and he liked drink very much. I don't believe for a moment that Walter knew about the girl.

He was the kind who would have rushed to marry her. I think she didn't want him to know."

She had another look at Brat. Perhaps she had told him all this too soon, before he was strong enough to be interested. But she had hoped that it would give him an interest in life.

"I'm afraid that is as near as we can get, Brat. But none of us have any doubt about it. Charles took one look at you and said, 'Walter.' And I think myself you look a little like your mother. That is Mary Woodward. It was taken in her second year at St. Luke's."

She gave him the photograph, and left it with him.

A week or two later she said to Eleanor: "Nell, I'm going to leave you. I've taken a lease on Tim Connell's stud at Kilbarty."

"Oh, Bee!"

"Not immediately, but when Brat is able to travel."

"You're taking Brat there? Oh, yes, of course you must go! Oh, that is a wonderful idea, Bee. It solves such a lot of problems, doesn't it? But can you afford it? Shall I lend you money for it?"

"No, Uncle Charles is doing that. Lovely to think of Charles supporting horses, isn't it? You'll need all you have to pay death duty, my dear. Mr. Sandal has broken it to the Bank that the place belonged to Simon all the time."

"What shall we do about letting people know about Brat? I mean, about his not being Patrick."

"I don't think we'll have to do anything about it. The facts will inevitably *ooze*. They always do. I think we just do nothing to prevent the leak. The fact that we are making him part of the family instead of starting prosecutions and things will take a lot of the fun out of it for the scandal-mongers. We'll survive, Nell. And so will he."

"Of course we will. And the first time someone mentions it boldly to me, I shall say: My cousin? Yes, he did pretend to be my brother. He *is* very like Patrick, isn't he? As if we were discussing creamcakes." She paused a moment and then added: "But I should like the news to get round before I'm too old to marry him."

"Are you thinking of it?" Bee said, taken aback.

"I'm set on it."

Bee hesitated; then decided to let the future take care of itself.

"Don't worry. It will get round," she said.

"Now that Uncle Charles is here, and is going to settle down at Latchetts," she said later to Brat, "I can go back to having a life of my own somewhere else."

His eyes came away from the ceiling, and watched her.

"There's a place in Ulster I have my eye on. Tim Connell's place at Kilbarty."

She saw his fingers begin to play with the sheet, unhappily.

"Are you going away to Ulster, then?" he asked.

"Only if you will come with me, and run the stable for me."

The easy tears of the newly convalescent rose in his eyes and ran down his cheek.

"Oh, Bee!" he said.

"I take it that means that my offer is accepted," she said.

THE
DAUGHTER
OF TIME

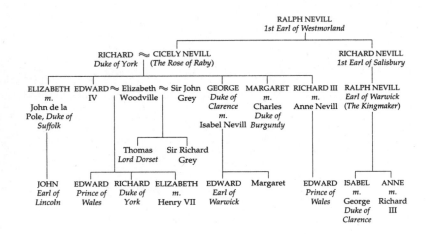

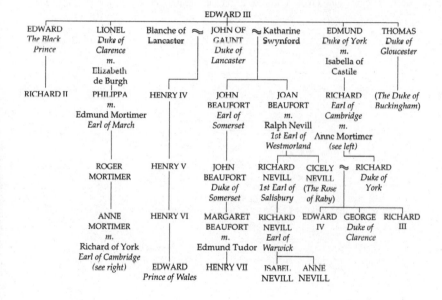

EDWARD III

EDWARD *The Black Prince* — LIONEL *Duke of Clarence m. Elizabeth de Burgh* — Blanche of Lancaster ≈ JOHN OF GAUNT *Duke of Lancaster* ≈ Katharine Swynford — EDMUND *Duke of York m. Isabella of Castile* — THOMAS *Duke of Gloucester*

RICHARD II

PHILIPPA *m. Edmund Mortimer Earl of March*

HENRY IV

JOHN BEAUFORT *Earl of Somerset*

JOAN BEAUFORT *m. Ralph Nevill 1st Earl of Westmorland*

RICHARD *Earl of Cambridge m. Anne Mortimer (see left)*

(The Duke of Buckingham)

ROGER MORTIMER

HENRY V

JOHN BEAUFORT *Duke of Somerset*

RICHARD NEVILL *1st Earl of Salisbury*

CICELY NEVILL ≈ RICHARD *(The Rose of Raby) Duke of York*

ANNE MORTIMER *m. Richard of York Earl of Cambridge (see right)*

HENRY VI

MARGARET BEAUFORT *m. Edmund Tudor*

RICHARD NEVILL *Earl of Warwick*

EDWARD IV — GEORGE *Duke of Clarence* — RICHARD III

EDWARD *Prince of Wales*

HENRY VII

ISABEL NEVILL   ANNE NEVILL

Truth is the daughter of time.

—*Old Proverb*

Chapter 1

Grant lay on his high white cot and stared at the ceiling. Stared at it with loathing. He knew by heart every last minute crack on its nice clean surface. He had made maps of the ceiling and gone exploring on them; rivers, islands, and continents. He had made guessing games of it and discovered hidden objects; faces, birds, and fishes. He had made mathematical calculations of it and rediscovered his childhood; theorems, angles, and triangles. There was practically nothing else he could do but look at it. He hated the sight of it.

He had suggested to The Midget that she might turn his bed around a little so that he could have a new patch of ceiling to explore. But it seemed that that would spoil the symmetry of the room, and in hospitals symmetry ranked just a short head behind cleanliness and a whole length in front of Godliness. Anything out of the parallel was hospital profanity. Why didn't he read? she asked. Why didn't he go on reading some of those expensive brand-new novels that his friends kept on bringing him?

"There are far too many people born into the world, and far too many words written. Millions and millions of them pouring from the presses every minute. It's a horrible thought."

"You sound constipated," said The Midget.

The Midget was Nurse Ingham, and she was in sober fact a very nice five-feet-two, with everything in just proportion. Grant called her The Midget to compensate himself for being bossed around by a piece of Dresden china which he could pick up in one hand. When he was on his feet, this is to say. It was not only that she told him what he might or might not do, but she dealt with his six-feet-odd with an off-hand ease that Grant found humiliating. Weights meant nothing, apparently, to The Midget. She tossed mattresses around with the absent-minded grace of a plate spinner. When she was off duty he was attended to by The Amazon, a goddess with arms like the limb of a beech tree. The Amazon was Nurse Darroll, who came from Gloucestershire and was homesick each daffodil season. (The Midget came from Lytham St. Anne's, and there was no daffodil nonsense about her.) She had large soft hands and large soft cow's eyes and she always looked very sorry for you, but the slightest physical exertion set her breathing like a suction-pump. On the whole Grant found it even more humiliating to be treated as a dead weight than to be treated as if he were no weight at all.

Grant was bed-borne, and a charge on The Midget and The Amazon, because he had fallen through a trap-door. This, of course, was the absolute in humiliation; compared with which the heavings of The Amazon and the light slingings of The Midget were a mere corollary. To fall through a trap-door was the ultimate in absurdity; pantomimic, bathetic, grotesque. At the moment of his disappearance from the normal level of perambulation he had been in hot pursuit of Benny Skoll, and the fact that Benny had careened round the next corner slap into the arms of Sergeant Williams provided the one small crumb of comfort in an intolerable situation.

Benny was now "away" for three years, which was very satisfactory for the lieges, but Benny would get time off for good behaviour. In hospitals there was no time off for good behaviour.

Grant stopped staring at the ceiling, and slid his eyes sideways at the pile of books on his bedside table; the gay expensive pile that The Midget had been urging on his attention. The top one, with the pretty picture of Valetta in unlikely pink, was Lavinia Fitch's annual account of a blameless heroine's tribulations. In view of the representation of the Grand Harbour on the cover, the present Valerie or Angela or Cecile or Denise must be a naval wife. He had opened the book only to read the kind message that Lavinia had written inside.

The Sweat and the Furrow was Silas Weekley being earthly and spade-conscious all over seven hundred pages. The situation, to judge from the first paragraph, had not materially changed since Silas's last book: mother lying-in with her eleventh upstairs, father laid-out after his ninth downstairs, eldest son lying to the Government in the cow-shed, eldest daughter lying with her lover in the hayloft, everyone else lying low in the barn. The rain dripped from the thatch, and the manure steamed in the midden. Silas never omitted the manure. It was not Silas's fault that its steam provided the only uprising element in the picture. If Silas could have discovered a brand of steam that steamed downwards, Silas would have introduced it.

Under the harsh shadows and highlights of Silas's jacket was an elegant affair of Edwardian curlicues and Baroque nonsense, entitled *Bells on Her Toes*. Which was Rupert Rouge being arch about vice. Rupert Rouge always seduced you into laughter for the first three pages. About Page Three you noticed that Rupert had learned from that very arch (but of course not vicious) creature George Bernard Shaw that the easiest way to sound witty was to use that cheap and convenient method, the paradox. After that you could see the jokes coming three sentences away.

The thing with a red gun-flash across a night-green cover was Oscar Oakley's latest. Toughs talking out of the corners of their mouths in synthetic American that had neither the wit nor the pungency of the real thing. Blondes, chromium bars, breakneck chases. Very remarkably bunk.

The Case of the Missing Tin-Opener, by John James Mark, had three errors of procedure in the first two pages, and had at least provided Grant with a pleasant five minutes while he composed an imaginary letter to its author.

He could not remember what the thin blue book at the bottom of the pile was. Something earnest and statistical, he thought. Tsetse flies, or calories, or sex behaviour, or something.

Even in that, you knew what to expect on the next page. Did no one, any more, no one in all this wide world, change their record now and then? Was everyone nowadays thirled to a formula? Authors today wrote so much to a pattern that their public expected it. The public talked about "a new Silas Weekley" or "a new Lavinia Fitch" exactly as they talked about "a new brick" or "a new hairbrush." They never said "a new book by" whoever it might be. Their interest was not in the book but in its newness. They knew quite well what the book would be like.

It might be a good thing, Grant thought as he turned his nauseated gaze away from the motley pile, if all the presses of the world were stopped for a generation. There ought to be a literary moratorium. Some Superman ought to invent a ray that would stop them all simultaneously. Then people wouldn't send you a lot of fool nonsense when you were flat on your back, and bossy bits of Meissen wouldn't expect you to read them.

He heard the door open, but did not stir himself to look. He had turned his face to the wall, literally and metaphorically.

He heard someone come across to his bed, and closed his eyes against possible conversation. He wanted neither Gloucestershire sympathy nor Lancashire briskness just now. In the succeeding pause a faint enticement, a nostalgic breath of all the fields of Grasse, teased his nostrils and swam about his brain. He savoured it and considered. The Midget smelt of lavender dusting powder, and The Amazon of soap and iodoform. What was floating expensively about his nostrils was *L'Enclos Numéro Cinq*. Only one person of his acquaintance used L'Enclos Number Five. Marta Hallard.

He opened an eye and squinted up at her. She had evidently bent over to see if he was asleep, and was now standing in an irresolute way—if anything Marta did could be said to be irresolute—with her attention on the heap of all too obviously virgin publications on the table. In one arm she was carrying two new books, and in the other a great sheaf of white lilac. He wondered whether she had chosen white lilac because it was her idea of the proper floral offering for winter (it adorned her dressing-room at the theatre from December to March) or whether she had taken it because it would not detract from her black-and-white chic. She was wearing a new hat and her usual pearls; the pearls which he had once been the means of recovering for her. She looked very handsome, very Parisian, and blessedly unhospital-like.

"Did I waken you, Alan?"

"No. I wasn't asleep."

"I seem to be bringing the proverbial coals," she said, dropping the two books alongside their despised brethren. "I hope you will find these more interesting than you seem to have found that lot. Didn't you even try a little teensy taste of our Lavinia?"

"I can't read anything."

"Are you in pain?"

"Agony. But it's neither my leg nor my back."

"What then?"

"It's what my cousin Laura calls 'the prickles of boredom.' "

"Poor Alan. And how right your Laura is." She picked a bunch of narcissi out of a glass that was much too large for them, dropped them with one of her best gestures into the washbasin, and proceeded to substitute the lilac. "One would expect boredom to be a great yawning emotion, but it isn't, of course. It's a small niggling thing."

"Small nothing. It's like being beaten with nettles."

"Why don't you take up something?"

"Improve the shining hour?"

"Improve your mind. To say nothing of your soul and your temper. You might study one of the philosophies. Yoga, or something like that. But I suppose an analytical mind is not the best kind to bring to the consideration of the abstract."

"I did think of going back to algebra. I have an idea that I never did algebra justice, at school. But I've done so much geometry on that damned ceiling that I'm a little off mathematics."

"Well, I suppose it is no use suggesting jig-saws to someone in your position. How about cross-words. I could get you a book of them, if you like."

"God forbid."

"You could invent them, of course. I have heard that that is more fun than solving them."

"Perhaps. But a dictionary weighs several pounds. Besides, I always did hate looking up something in a reference book."

"Do you play chess? I don't remember. How about chess problems? White to play and mate in three moves, or something like that."

"My only interest in chess is pictorial."

"Pictorial?"

"Very decorative things, knights and pawns and what-not. Very elegant."

"Charming. I *could* bring you along a set to play with. All right, no chess. You could do some academic investigating. That's a sort of mathematics. Finding a solution to an unsolved problem."

"Crime, you mean? I know all the case-histories by heart. And there is nothing more that can be done about any of them. Certainly not by someone who is flat on his back."

"I didn't mean something out of the files at the Yard. I meant something more—what's the word?—something classic. Something that has puzzled the world for ages."

"As what, for instance?"

"Say, the casket letters."

"Oh, *not* Mary Queen of Scots!"

"Why not?" asked Marta, who like all actresses saw Mary Stuart through a haze of white veils.

"I could be interested in a bad woman but never in a silly one."

"*Silly?*" said Marta in her best lower-register Electra voice.

"*Very* silly."

"Oh, Alan, how can you!"

"If she had worn another kind of headdress no one would ever have bothered about her. It's that cap that seduces people."

"You think she would have loved less greatly in a sun-bonnet?"

"She never loved greatly at all, in any kind of bonnet."

Marta looked as scandalised as a lifetime in the theatre and an hour of careful make-up allowed her to.

"Why do you think that?"

"Mary Stuart was six feet tall. Nearly all out-size women are sexually cold. Ask any doctor."

And as he said it he wondered why, in all the years since Marta had first adopted him as a spare escort when she needed one, it had not occurred to him to wonder whether her notorious level-headedness about men had something to do with her inches. But Marta had not drawn any parallels; her mind was still on her favourite queen.

"At least she was a martyr. You'll have to allow her that."

"Martyr to what?"

"Her religion."

"The only thing she was a martyr to was rheumatism. She married Darnley without the Pope's dispensation, and Bothwell by Protestant rites."

"In a moment you'll be telling me she wasn't a prisoner!"

"The trouble with you is that you think of her in a little room at the top of a castle, with bars on the windows and a faithful old attendant to share her prayers with her. In actual fact she had a personal household of sixty persons. She complained bitterly when it was reduced to a beggarly thirty, and nearly died of chagrin when it was reduced to two male secretaries, several women, an embroiderer, and a cook or two. And Elizabeth had to pay for all that out of her own purse. For twenty years she paid, and for twenty years Mary Stuart hawked the crown of Scotland round Europe to anyone who would start a revolution and put her back on the throne that she had lost; or, alternatively, on the one Elizabeth was sitting on."

He looked at Marta and found that she was smiling.

"Are they a little better now?" she asked.

"Are what better?"

"The prickles."

He laughed.

"Yes. For a whole minute I had forgotten about them. That is at least one good thing to put down to Mary Stuart's account!"

"How do you know so much about Mary?"

"I did an essay about her in my last year at school."

"And didn't like her, I take it."

"Didn't like what I found out about her."

"You don't think her tragic, then."

"Oh, yes, very. But not tragic in any of the ways that popular belief makes her tragic. Her tragedy was that she was born a queen with the outlook of a suburban house-wife. Scoring off Mrs. Tudor in the next street is harmless and amusing; it may lead you into unwarrantable indulgence in hire-purchase, but it affects only yourself. When you use the same technique on kingdoms the result is disastrous. If you are willing to put a country of ten million people in pawn in order to score off a royal rival, then you end by being a friendless failure." He lay thinking about it for a little. "She would have been a wild success as a mistress at a girls' school."

"Beast!"

"I meant it nicely. The staff would have liked her, and all the little girls would have adored her. That is what I meant about her being tragic."

"Ah, well. No casket letters, it seems. What else is there? The Man in the Iron Mask?"

"I can't remember who that was, but I couldn't be interested in anyone who was being coy behind some tin-plate. I couldn't be interested in anyone at all unless I could see his face."

"Ah, yes. I forgot your passion for faces. The Borgias had wonderful faces. I should think they would provide a little mystery or two for you to dabble in if you looked them up. Or there was Perkin Warbeck, of course. Imposture is always fascinating. Was he or wasn't he? A lovely game. The balance can never come down wholly on one side or the other. You push it over and up it comes again, like one of those weighted toys."

The door opened and Mrs. Tinker's homely face appeared in the aperture surmounted by her still more homely and historic hat. Mrs. Tinker had worn the same hat since first she began to "do" for Grant, and he could not imagine her in any other. That she did possess another one he knew, because it went with something that she referred to as "me blue." Her "blue" was an occasional affair, in both senses, and never appeared at 19 Tenby Court. It was worn with a ritualistic awareness, and having been worn it was used in the event as a yardstick by which to judge the proceedings. ("Did you enjoy it, Tink? What was it like?" "Not worth putting on me blue for.") She had worn it to Princess Elizabeth's wedding, and to various other royal functions, and had indeed figured in it for two flashing seconds in a newsreel shot of the Duchess of Kent cutting a ribbon, but to Grant it was a mere report; a criterion of the social worth of an occasion. A thing was or was not worth putting on "me blue" for.

"I 'eard you 'ad a visitor," said Mrs. Tinker, "and I was all set to go away again when I thought the voice sounded familiar like, and I says to meself: 'It's only Miss Hallard,' I says, so I come in."

She was carrying various paper bags and a small tight bunch of anemones. She greeted Marta as woman to woman, having been in her time a dresser and having therefore no exaggerated reverence for the goddesses of the theatre world, and looked askance at the beautiful arrangement of lilac sprays that had blossomed under Marta's ministrations. Marta did not see the glance but she saw the little bunch of anemones and took over the situation as if it were something already rehearsed.

"I squander my vagabond's hire on white lilac for you, and then Mrs. Tinker puts my nose out of joint by bringing you the Lilies of the Field."

"Lilies?" said Mrs. Tinker, doubtfully.

"Those are the Solomon in all his glory things. The ones that toiled not, neither did they spin."

Mrs. Tinker went to church only for weddings and christenings, but she belonged to a generation that had been sent to Sunday school. She looked with a new interest at the little handful of glory incased by her woollen glove.

"Well, now. I never knew that. Makes more sense that way, don't it? I always pictured them arums. Fields and fields of arums. Awful expensive, you know, but a bit depressing. So they was coloured? Well, why can't they say so? What do they have to call them lilies for!"

And they went on to talk about translation, and how misleading Holy Writ could be ("I always wondered what bread on the waters was," Mrs. Tinker said) and the awkward moment was over.

While they were still busy with the Bible, The Midget came in with extra flower vases. Grant noticed that the vases were designed to hold white lilac and not anemones. They were tribute to Marta; a passport to further communing. But Marta never bothered about women unless she had an immediate use for them; her tack with Mrs. Tinker had been mere *savoir faire;* a conditioned reflex. So The Midget was reduced to being functional instead of social. She collected the discarded narcissi from the washbasin and meekly put them back into a vase. The Midget being meek was the most beautiful sight that had gladdened Grant's eyes for a long time.

"Well," Marta said, having finished her arrangement of the lilac and placed the result where he could see it, "I shall leave Mrs. Tinker to feed you all the titbits out of those paper bags. It couldn't be, could it, Mrs. Tinker darling, that one of those bags contains any of your wonderful bachelor's buttons?"

Mrs. Tinker glowed.

"You'd like one or two maybe? Fresh outa me oven?"

"Well, of course I shall have to do penance for it afterwards—those little rich cakes are death on the waist—but just give me a couple to put in my bag for my tea at the theatre."

She chose two with a flattering deliberation ("I like them a little brown at the edges"), dropped them into her handbag, and said: "Well, au revoir, Alan. I shall look in, in a day or two, and start you on a sock. There is nothing so soothing, I understand, as knitting. Isn't that so, Nurse?"

"Oh, yes, indeed. A lot of my gentlemen patients take to knitting. They find it whiles away the time very nicely."

Marta blew him a kiss from the door and was gone, followed by the respectful Midget.

"I'd be surprised if that hussy is any better than she ought to be," Mrs. Tinker said, beginning to open the paper bags. She was not referring to Marta.

Chapter 2

*B*ut when Marta came back two days later it was not with knitting needles and wool. She breezed in, very dashing in a Cossack hat worn at a casual rake that must have taken her several minutes at her mirror, just after lunch.

"I haven't come to stay, my dear, I'm on my way to the theatre. It's matinée day, God help me. Tea trays and morons. And we've got to the frightful stage when the lines have ceased to have any meaning at all for us. I don't think this play is ever coming off. It's going to be like those New York ones that run by the decade instead of by the year. It's too frightening. One's mind just won't stay on the thing. Geoffrey dried up in the middle of the second act last night. His eyes nearly popped out of his head. I thought for a moment he was having a stroke. He said afterwards that he had no recollection of anything that happened between his entrance and the point where he came to and found himself half-way through the act."

"A black-out, you mean?"

"No. Oh, no. Just being an automaton. Saying the lines and doing the business and thinking of something else all the time."

"If all reports are true that's no unusual matter where actors are concerned."

"Oh, in moderation, no. Johnny Garson can tell you how much paper there is in the house while he is sobbing his heart out on someone's lap. But that's different from being 'away' for half an act. Do you realise that Geoffrey had turned his son out of the house, quarrelled with his mistress, and accused his wife of having an affaire with his best friend all without being aware of it?"

"What *was* he aware of?"

"He says he had decided to lease his Park Lane flat to Dolly Dacre and buy that Charles the Second house at Richmond that the Latimers are giving up because he has got that Governor's appointment. He had thought about the lack of bathrooms and decided that the little upstairs room, with the eighteenth-century Chinese paper, would make a very good one. They could remove the beautiful paper and use it to decorate that dull little room downstairs at the back. It's full of Victorian paneling, the dull little room. He had also reviewed the drainage, wondered if he had enough money to take the old tiling off and replace it, and speculated as to what kind of cooking range they had in the kitchen. He had just decided to get rid of the shrubbery at the gate when he found himself face to face with me, on a stage, in the presence of nine hundred and eighty-seven people, in the middle of a speech. Do you wonder that his eyes popped? I see that you have managed to read at least one of the books I brought you—if the rumpled jacket is any criterion."

"Yes. The mountain one. It was a godsend. I lay for hours looking at the pictures. Nothing puts things in perspective as quickly as a mountain."

"The stars are better, I find."

"Oh, *no*. The stars merely reduce one to the status of an amoeba. The stars take the last vestige of human pride, the last spark of confidence, from one. But a snow mountain is a nice human-size yardstick. I lay and looked at Everest and thanked God that I wasn't climbing those slopes. A hospital bed was a haven of warmth and rest and security by comparison, and The Midget and The Amazon two of the highest achievements of civilisation."

"Ah, well, here are some more pictures for you."

Marta up-ended the quarto envelope she was carrying, and spilled a collection of paper sheets over his chest.

"What is this?"

"Faces," said Marta, delightedly. "Dozens of faces for you. Men, women, and children. All sorts, conditions, and sizes."

He picked a sheet off his chest and looked at it. It was an engraving of a fifteenth-century portrait. A woman.

"Who is this?"

"Lucrezia Borgia. Isn't she a duck?"

"Perhaps, but are you suggesting that there was any mystery about her?"

"Oh, yes. No one has ever decided whether she was her brother's tool or his accomplice."

He discarded Lucrezia, and picked up a second sheet. This proved to be the portrait of a small boy in late-eighteenth-century clothes, and under it in faint capitals were printed the words: Louis XVII.

"Now there's a *beautiful* mystery for you," Marta said. "The Dauphin. Did he escape or did he die in captivity?"

"Where did you get all these?"

"I routed James out of his cubby-hole at the Victoria and Albert, and made him take me to a print shop. I knew he would know about that sort of thing, and I'm sure he has nothing to interest him at the V. and A."

It was so like Marta to take it for granted that a Civil Servant, because he happened also to be a playwright and an authority on portraits, should be willing to leave his work and delve about in print shops for her pleasure.

He turned up the photograph of an Elizabethan portrait. A man in velvet and pearls. He turned the back to see who this might be and found that it was the Earl of Leicester.

"So that is Elizabeth's Robin," he said. "I don't think I ever saw a portrait of him before."

Marta looked down on the virile fleshy face and said: "It occurs to me for the first time that one of the major tragedies of history is that the best painters didn't paint you till you were past your best. Robin must have been quite a man. They say Henry the Eighth was dazzling as a young man, but what is he now? Something on a playing card. Nowadays we *know* what Tennyson was like before he grew that frightful beard. I must fly. I'm late as it is. I've been lunching at the Blague, and so many people came up to talk that I couldn't get away as early as I meant to."

"I hope your host was impressed," Grant said, with a glance at the hat.

"Oh, yes. She knows about hats. She took one look and said, 'Jacques Tous, I take it.'"

"She!" said Grant, surprised.

"Yes. Madeleine March. And it was I who was giving her luncheon. Don't look so astonished: it isn't tactful. I'm hoping, if you must know, that she'll write me that play about Lady Blessington. But there was such a to-ing and fro-ing that I had no chance to make any impression on her. However, I gave her a wonderful meal. Which reminds me that Tony Bittmaker was entertaining a party of seven. Magnums galore. How do you imagine he keeps going?"

"Lack of evidence," Grant said, and she laughed and went away.

In the silence he went back to considering Elizabeth's Robin. What mystery was there about Robin?

Oh, yes. Amy Robsart, of course.

Well, he wasn't interested in Amy Robsart. He didn't care how she had fallen down stairs, or why.

But he spent a very happy afternoon with the rest of the faces. Long before he had entered the Force he had taken a delight in faces, and in his years at the Yard that interest had proved both a private entertainment and a professional advantage. He had once in his early days dropped in with his Superintendent at an identification parade. It was not his case, and they were both there on other business, but they lingered in the background and watched while a man and a woman, separately, walked down the line of twelve nondescript men, looking for the one they hoped to recognise.

"Which is Chummy, do you know?" the Super had whispered to him.

"I don't know," Grant had said, "but I can guess."

"You can? Which do you make it?"

"The third from the left."

"What is the charge?"

"I don't know. Don't know anything about it."

His chief had cast him an amused glance. But when both the man and the woman had failed to identify anyone and had gone away, and the line broke into a chattering group, hitching collars and settling ties preparatory to going back to the street and the world of every day from which they had been summoned to assist the Law, the one who did not move was the third man from the left. The third man from the left waited submissively for his escort and was led to his cell again.

"Strewth!" the Superintendent had said. "One chance out of twelve, and you made it. That was good going. He picked your man out of the bunch," he said in explanation to the local Inspector.

"Did you know him?" the Inspector said, a little surprised. "He's never been in trouble before, as far as we know."

"No, I never saw him before. I don't even know what the charge is."

"Then what made you pick him?"

Grant had hesitated, analysing for the first time his process of selection. It had not been a matter of reasoning. He had not said: "That man's face has this characteristic or that characteristic, therefore he is the accused person." His choice had been almost instinctive; the reason was in his subconscious. At last, having delved into his subconscious, he blurted: "He was the only one of the twelve with no lines on his face."

They had laughed at that. But Grant, once he had pulled the thing into the light, saw how his instinct had worked and recognised the reasoning behind it. "It sounds silly, but it isn't," he said. "The only adult entirely without face lines is the idiot."

"Freeman's no idiot, take it from me," the Inspector broke in. "A very wide-awake boy he is, believe me."

"I didn't mean that. I mean that the idiot is irresponsible. The idiot is the standard of irresponsibility. All those twelve men in that parade were thirty-ish, but only one had an irresponsible face. So I picked him at once."

After that it had become a mild joke at the Yard that Grant could "pick them at sight." And the Assistant Commissioner had once said teasingly: "Don't tell me that you believe that there is such a thing as a criminal face, Inspector."

But Grant had said no, he wasn't as simple as that. "If there was only one kind of crime, sir, it might be possible; but crimes being as wide as human nature, if a policeman started to put faces into categories he would be sunk. You can tell what the normal run of over-sexed women look like by a walk down Bond Street any day between five and six, and yet the most notorious nymphomaniac in London looks like a cold saint."

"Not so saintly of late; she's drinking too much these days," the A.C. had said, identifying the lady without difficulty; and the conversation had gone on to other things.

But Grant's interest in faces had remained and enlarged until it became a conscious study. A matter of case records and comparisons. It was, as he had said, not possible to put faces into any kind of category, but it was possible to characterise individual faces. In a reprint of a famous trial, for instance, where photographs of the principal actors in the case were displayed for the public's interest, there was never any doubt as to which was the accused and which the judge. Occasionally, one of the counsel might on looks have changed places with the prisoner in the dock—counsel were after all a mere cross-section of humanity, as liable to passion and greed as the rest of the world, but a judge had a special quality; an integrity and a detachment. So, even without a wig, one did not confuse him with the man in the dock, who had had neither integrity nor detachment.

Marta's James, having been dragged from his "cubby-hole," had evidently enjoyed himself, and a fine selection of offenders, or their victims, kept Grant entertained until The Midget brought his tea. As he tidied the sheets together to put them away in his locker his hand came in contact with one that had slipped off his chest and had lain all afternoon unnoticed on the counterpane. He picked it up and looked at it.

It was the portrait of a man. A man dressed in the velvet cap and slashed doublet of the late fifteenth century. A man about thirty-five or thirty-six years old, lean and clean-shaven. He wore a rich jewelled collar, and was in the act of putting a ring on the little finger of his right hand. But he was not looking at the ring. He was looking off into space.

Of all the portraits Grant had seen this afternoon this was the most individual. It was as if the artist had striven to put on canvas something that his talent was not sufficient to translate into paint. The expression in the eyes—that most arresting and individual expression—had defeated him. So had the mouth: he had not known how to make lips so thin and so wide look mobile, so the mouth was wooden and a failure. What he had best succeeded in was the bone structure of the face: the strong cheekbones, the hollows below them, the chin too large for strength.

Grant paused in the act of turning the thing over, to consider the face a moment longer. A judge? A soldier? A prince? Someone used to great responsibility, and responsible in his authority. Someone too conscientious. A worrier; perhaps a perfectionist. A man at ease in a large design, but anxious over details. A candidate for gastric ulcer. Someone, too, who had suffered ill-health as a child. He had that incommunicable, that indescribable look that childhood suffering leaves behind it, less positive than the look on a cripple's face, but as inescapable. This the artist had both understood and translated into terms of paint. The slight fullness of the lower eyelid, like a child that has slept too heavily; the texture of the skin; the old-man look in a young face.

He turned the portrait over to look for a caption.

On the back was printed: *Richard the Third. From the portrait in the National Portrait Gallery. Artist Unknown.*

Richard the Third.

So that was who it was. Richard the Third. Crouchback. The monster of nursery stories. The destroyer of innocence. A synonym for villainy.

He turned the paper over and looked again. Was that what the artist had tried to convey when he had painted those eyes? Had what he had seen in those eyes been the look of a man haunted?

He lay a long time looking at that face; at those extraordinary eyes. They were long eyes, set close under the brows; the brows slightly drawn in that worried, over-conscientious frown. At first glance they appeared to be peering; but as one looked one found that they were in fact withdrawn, almost absent-minded.

When The Midget came back for his tray he was still staring at the portrait. Nothing like this had come his way for years. It made La Gioconda look like a poster.

The Midget examined his virgin teacup, put a practised hand against the teapot's tepid cheek, and pouted. She had better things to do, she conveyed, than bring him trays for him to ignore.

He pushed the portrait at her.

What did she think of it? If that man were her patient what would be her verdict?

"Liver," she said crisply, and bore away the tray in heel-tapping protest, all starch and blond curls.

But the surgeon strolling in against her draught, kindly and casual, had other views. He looked at the portrait, as invited, and said after a moment's scrutiny:

"Poliomyelitis."

"Infantile paralysis?" Grant said; and remembered all of a sudden that Richard III had a withered arm.

"Who is it?" the surgeon asked.

"Richard the Third."

"Really? That's interesting."

"Did you know that he had a withered arm?"

"Had he? I didn't remember that. I thought he was a hunchback."

"So he was."

"What I do remember is that he was born with a full set of teeth and ate live frogs. Well, my diagnosis seems to be abnormally accurate."

"Uncanny. What made you choose polio?"

"I don't quite know, now that you ask me to be definitive. Just the look of the face, I suppose. It's the look one sees on the face of a crippled child. If he was born hunchbacked that probably accounts for it and not polio. I notice the artist has left out the hump."

"Yes. Court painters have to have a modicum of tact. It wasn't until Cromwell that sitters asked for 'warts and all.' "

"If you ask me," the surgeon said, absent-mindedly considering the splint on Grant's leg, "Cromwell started that inverted snobbery from which we are all suffering today. 'I'm a plain man, I am; no nonsense about *me*.' And no manners, grace, or generosity, either." He pinched Grant's toe with detached interest. "It's a raging disease. A horrible perversion. In some parts of the States, I understand, it's as much as a man's political life is worth to go to some constituencies with his tie and his coat on. That's being stuffed-shirt. The beau ideal is to be one of the boys. That's looking very healthy," he added, referring to Grant's big toe, and came back of his own accord to the portrait lying on the counterpane.

"Interesting," he said, "that about the polio. Perhaps it really was polio, and that accounts for the shrunken arm." He went on considering it, making no movement to go. "Interesting, anyhow. Portrait of a murderer. Does he run to type, would you say?"

"There isn't a murder type. People murder for too many different reasons. But I can't remember any murderer, either in my own experience, or in case-histories, who resembled him."

"Of course he was *hors-concours* in his class, wasn't he? He couldn't have known the meaning of scruple."

"No."

"I once saw Olivier play him. The most dazzling exhibition of sheer evil, it was. Always on the verge of toppling over into the grotesque, and never doing it."

"When I showed you the portrait," Grant said, "before you knew who it was, did you think of villainy?"

"No," said the surgeon, "no, I thought of illness."

"It's odd, isn't it? I didn't think of villainy either. And now that I know who it is, now that I've read the name on the back, I can't think of it as anything but villainous."

"I suppose villainy, like beauty, is in the eye of the beholder. Well, I'll look in again towards the end of the week. No pain to speak of now?"

And he went away, kindly and casual as he had come.

It was only after he had given the portrait further puzzled consideration (it piqued him to have mistaken one of the most notorious murderers of all time for a judge; to have transferred a subject from the dock to the bench was a shocking piece of ineptitude) that it occurred to Grant that the portrait had been provided as the illustration to a piece of detection.

What mystery was there about Richard III?

And then he remembered. Richard had murdered his two boy nephews, but no one knew how. They had merely disappeared. They had disappeared, if he remembered rightly, while Richard was away from London. Richard had sent someone to do the deed. But the mystery of the children's actual fate had never been solved. Two skeletons had turned up—under some stairs?—in Charles II's day, and had been buried. It was taken for granted that the skeletons were the remains of the young princes, but nothing had ever been proved.

It was shocking how little history remained with one after a good education. All he knew about Richard III was that he was the younger brother of Edward IV. That Edward was a blond six-footer with remarkable good looks and a still more remarkable way with women; and that Richard was a hunchback who usurped the throne on his brother's death in place of the boy heir, and arranged the death of that heir and his small brother to save himself any further trouble. He also knew that Richard had died at the battle of Bosworth yelling for a horse, and that he was the last of his line. The last Plantagenet.

Every schoolboy turned over the final page of Richard III with relief, because now at last the Wars of the Roses were over and they could get on to the Tudors, who were dull but easy to follow.

When The Midget came to tidy him up for the night, Grant said: "You don't happen to have a history book, by any chance, do you?"

"A history book? No. What would I be doing with a history book." It was not a question, so Grant did not try to provide an answer. His silence seemed to fret her.

"If you really want a history book," she said presently, "you could ask Nurse Darroll when she brings your supper. She has all her school books on a shelf in her room and it's quite possible she has a history among them."

How like The Amazon to keep her school books! he thought. She was still homesick for school as she was homesick for Gloucestershire every time the daffodils bloomed. When she lumbered into the room, bearing his cheese pudding and stewed rhubarb, he looked at her with a tolerance that bordered on the benevolent. She ceased to be a large female who breathed like a suction-pump and became a potential dispenser of delight.

Oh, yes, she had a history book, she said. Indeed, she rather thought that she had two. She had kept all her school books, because she had loved school.

It was on the tip of Grant's tongue to ask her if she had kept her dolls, but he stopped himself in time.

"And of course I loved history," she said. "It was my favourite subject. Richard the Lionheart was my hero."

"An intolerable bounder," Grant said.

"Oh, no!" she said, looking wounded.

"A hyperthyroid type," Grant said pitilessly. "Rocketing to and fro about the earth like a badly made firework. Are you going off duty now?"

"Whenever I've finished my trays."

"Could you find that book for me tonight?"

"You're supposed to be going to sleep, not staying awake over history books."

"I might as well read history as look at the ceiling—which is the alternative. Will you get it for me?"

"I don't think I could go all the way up to the Nurses' Block and back again tonight for someone who is rude about the Lionheart."

"All right," he said. "I'm not the stuff that martyrs are made of. As far as I'm concerned Coeur-de-Lion is the pattern of chivalry, the *chevalier sans peur et sans reproche*, a faultless commander and a triple D.S.O. Now will you get the book?"

"It seems to me you've sore need to read a little history," she said, smoothing a mitred sheet-corner with a large admiring hand, "so I'll bring you the book when I come past. I'm going out to the pictures anyhow."

It was nearly an hour before she reappeared, immense in a camel-hair coat. The room lights had been put out and she materialised into the light of his reading-lamp like some kindly genie.

"I was hoping you'd be asleep," she said. "I don't really think you should start on these tonight."

"If there is anything that is likely to put me to sleep," he said, "it would be an English history book. So you can hold hands with a clear conscience."

"I'm going with Nurse Burrows."

"You can still hold hands."

"I've no patience with you," she said patiently and faded backwards into the gloom.

She had brought two books.

One was the kind of history book known as a Historical Reader. It bore the same relation to history as Stories from the Bible bears to Holy Writ. Canute rebuked his courtiers on the shore, Alfred burned the cakes, Raleigh spread his cloak for Elizabeth, Nelson took leave of Hardy in his cabin on the *Victory*, all in nice clear large print and one-sentence paragraphs. To each episode went one full-page illustration.

There was something curiously touching in the fact that The Amazon should treasure this childish literature. He turned to the fly-leaf to see if her name was there. On the fly-leaf was written:

> Ella Darroll,
> Form III
> Newbridge High School
> Newbridge,
> Gloucestershire.
> England
> Europe,
> The World
> The Universe.

This was surrounded by a fine section of coloured transfers.

Did all children do that, he wondered. Write their names like that, and spend their time in class making transfers? He certainly had. And the sight of those squares of bright primitive colour brought back his childhood as nothing had for many years. He had forgotten the excitement of transfers. That wonderfully satisfying moment when you began the peeling-off and saw that it was coming perfectly. The adult world held few such gratifications. A clean smacking drive at golf, perhaps, was the nearest. Or the moment when your line tightened and you knew that the fish had struck.

The little book pleased him so much that he went through it at his leisure. Solemnly reading each childish story. This, after all, was the history that every adult remembered. This was what remained in their minds when tonnage and poundage, and ship money, and Laud's Liturgy, and the Rye House Plot, and the Triennial Acts, and all the long muddle of schism and shindy, treaty and treason, had faded from their consciousness.

The Richard III story, when he came to it, was called *The Princes in the Tower*, and it seemed that young Ella had found the Princes a poor substitute for Coeur-de-Lion, since she had filled every small O throughout the tale with neat pencil shading. The two golden-haired boys who played together in the sunbeam from the barred window in the accompanying picture had each been provided with a pair of anachronistic spectacles, and on the blank back of the picture-page someone had been playing Noughts and Crosses. As far as young Ella was concerned the Princes were a dead loss.

And yet it was a sufficiently arresting little story. Macabre enough to delight any child's heart. The innocent children; the wicked uncle. The classic ingredients in a tale of classic simplicity.

It had also a moral. It was the perfect cautionary tale.

But the King won no profit from his wicked deed. The people of England were shocked by his coldblooded cruelty and decided that they would no longer have him for King. They sent for a distant cousin of Richard's, Henry Tudor, who was living in France, to come and be crowned King in his stead. Richard died bravely in the battle which resulted, but he had made his name hated throughout the country and many deserted him to fight for his rival.

Well, it was neat but not gaudy. Reporting at its simplest.

He turned to the second book.

The second book was the School History proper. The two thousand years of England's story were neatly parcelled into compartments for ready reference. The compartments, as usual, were reigns. It was no wonder that one pinned a personality to a reign, forgetful that that personality had known and lived under other kings. One put them in pigeon-holes automatically. Pepys: Charles II. Shakespeare: Elizabeth. Marlborough: Queen Anne. It never crossed one's mind that someone who had seen Queen Elizabeth could also have seen George I. One had been conditioned to the reign idea from childhood.

However it did simplify things when you were just a policeman with a game leg and a concussed spine hunting up some information on dead and gone royalties to keep yourself from going crazy.

He was surprised to find the reign of Richard III so short. To have made oneself one of the best-known rulers in all those two thousand years of England's history, and to have had only two years to do it in, surely augured a towering personality. If Richard had not made friends he had certainly influenced people.

The history book, too, thought that he had personality.

Richard was a man of great ability, but quite unscrupulous as to his means. He boldly claimed the crown on the absurd grounds that his brother's marriage with Elizabeth Woodville had been illegal and the children of it illegitimate. He was accepted by the people, who dreaded a minority, and began his reign by making a progress through the south, where he was well received. During this progress, however, the two young Princes who were living in the Tower, disappeared, and were believed to have been murdered. A serious rebellion followed, which Richard put down with great ferocity. In order to recover some of his lost popularity he held a Parliament, which passed useful statutes against Benevolences, Maintenance, and Livery.

But a second rebellion followed. This took the form of an invasion, with French troops, by the head of the Lancaster branch, Henry Tudor. He encountered Richard at Bosworth, near Leicester, where the treachery of the Stanleys gave the day to Henry. Richard was killed in battle, fighting courageously, leaving behind him a name hardly less infamous than that of John.

What on earth were Benevolences, Maintenance, and Livery?

And how did the English like having the succession decided for them by French troops?

But, of course, in the days of the Roses, France was still a sort of semi-detached part of England; a country much less foreign to an Englishman than Ireland was. A fifteenth-century Englishman went to France as a matter of course; but to Ireland only under protest.

He lay and thought about that England. The England over which the Wars of the Roses had been fought. A green, green England; with not a chimney-stack from Cumberland to Cornwall. An England still unhedged, with great forests alive with game, and wide marshes thick with wild-fowl. An England with the same small group of dwellings repeated every few miles in endless permutation: castle, church, and cottages; monastery, church, and cottages; manor, church, and cottages. The strips of cultivation round the cluster of dwellings, and beyond that the greenness. The unbroken greenness. The deep-rutted lanes that ran from group to group, mired to bog in the winter and white with dust in the summer; decorated with wild roses or red with hawthorn as the seasons came and went.

For thirty years, over this green uncrowded land, the Wars of the Roses had been fought. But it had been more of a blood feud than a war. A Montague and Capulet affair; of no great concern to the average Englishman. No one pushed in at your door to demand whether you were York or Lancaster and to hale you off to a concentration camp if your answer proved to be the wrong one for the occasion. It was a small concentrated war; almost a private party. They fought a battle in your lower meadow, and turned your kitchen into a dressing-station, and then moved off somewhere or other to fight a battle somewhere else, and a few weeks later you would hear what had happened at that battle, and you would have a family row about the result because your wife was probably Lancaster and you were perhaps York, and it was all rather like following rival football teams. No one persecuted you for being a Lancastrian or a Yorkist, any more than you would be persecuted for being an Arsenal fan or a Chelsea follower.

He was still thinking of the green England when he fell asleep.

And he was not a whit wiser about the two young Princes and their fate.

Chapter 3

"Can't you find something more cheerful to look at than that thing?" The Midget asked next morning, referring to the Richard portrait which Grant had propped up against the pile of books on his bed-side table.

"You don't find it an interesting face?"

"Interesting! It gives me the willies. A proper Dismal Desmond."

"According to the history books he was a man of great ability."

"So was Bluebeard."

"And considerable popularity, it would seem."

"So was Bluebeard."

"A very fine soldier, too," Grant said wickedly, and waited. "No Bluebeard offers?"

"What do you want to look at that face for? Who was he anyway?"

"Richard the Third."

"Oh, well, I ask you!"

"You mean that's what you expected him to look like."

"Exactly."

"Why?"

"A murdering brute, wasn't he?"

"You seem to know your history."

"Everyone knows that. Did away with his two little nephews, poor brats. Had them smothered."

"Smothered?" said Grant, interested. "I didn't know that."

"Smothered with pillows." She banged his own pillows with a fragile vigorous fist, and replaced them with speed and precision.

"Why smothering? Why not poison?" Grant inquired.

"Don't ask me. I didn't arrange it."

"Who said they were smothered?"

"My history book at school said it."

"Yes, but whom was the history book quoting?"

"Quoting? It wasn't quoting anything. It was just giving facts."

"Who smothered them, did it say?"

"A man called Tyrrel. Didn't you do any history, at school?"

"I attended history lessons. It is not the same thing. Who was Tyrrel?"

"I haven't the remotest. A friend of Richard's."

"How did anyone know it was Tyrrel?"

"He confessed."

"Confessed?"

"After he had been found guilty, of course. Before he was hanged."

"You mean that this Tyrrel was actually hanged for the murder of the two Princes?"

"Yes, of course. Shall I take that dreary face away and put up something gayer? There were quite a lot of nice faces in that bundle Miss Hallard brought you yesterday."

"I'm not interested in nice faces. I'm interested only in dreary ones; in 'murdering brutes' who are 'men of great ability.' "

"Well, there's no accounting for tastes," said The Midget inevitably. "And *I* don't have to look at it, thank goodness. But in my humble estimation it's enough to prevent bones knitting, so help me it is."

"Well, if my fracture doesn't mend you can put it down to Richard III's account. Another little item on that account won't be noticed, it seems to me."

He must ask Marta when next she looked in if she too knew about this Tyrrel. Her general knowledge was not very great, but she had been educated very expensively at a highly approved school and perhaps some of it had stuck.

But the first visitor to penetrate from the outside world proved to be Sergeant Williams, large and pink and scrubbed-looking; and for a little Grant forgot about battles long ago and considered wide boys alive today. Williams sat planted on the small hard visitors' chair, his knees apart and his pale blue eyes blinking like a contented cat's in the light from the window, and Grant regarded him with affection. It was pleasant to talk shop again; to use that elliptical, allusive speech that one uses only with another of one's trade. It was pleasant to hear the professional gossip, to talk professional politics; to learn who was on the mat and who was on the skids.

"The Super sent his regards," Williams said as he got up to go, "and said if there was anything he could do for you to let him know." His eyes, no longer dazzled by the light, went to the photograph propped against the books. He leant his head sideways at it. "Who's the bloke?"

Grant was just about to tell him when it occurred to him that here was a fellow policeman. A man as used, professionally, to faces as he was himself. Someone to whom faces were of daily importance.

"Portrait of a man by an unknown fifteenth-century painter," he said. "What do you make of it?"

"I don't know the first thing about painting."

"I didn't mean that. I meant what do you make of the subject?"

"Oh. Oh, I see." Williams bent forward and drew his bland brows into a travesty of concentration. "How do you mean: make of it?"

"Well, where would you place him? In the dock or on the bench?"

Williams considered for a moment, and then said with confidence: "Oh, on the bench."

"You would?"

"Certainly. Why? Wouldn't you?"

"Yes. But the odd thing is that we're both wrong. He belongs in the dock."

"You surprise me," Williams said, peering again. "Do you know who he was, then?"

"Yes. Richard the Third."

Williams whistled.

"So that's who it is, is it! Well, well. The Princes in the Tower, and all that. The original Wicked Uncle. I suppose, once you know, you can see it, but offhand it wouldn't occur to you. I mean, that he was a crook. He's the spit of old Halsbury, come to think of it, and if Halsbury had a fault at all it was that he was too soft with the bastards in the dock. He used to lean over backwards to give them the benefit in his summing-up."

"Do you know how the Princes were murdered?"

"I don't know a thing about Richard III except that his mother was two years conceiving him."

"What! Where did you get that tale?"

"In my school history, I suppose."

"You must have gone to a very remarkable school. Conception was not mentioned in any history book of mine. That is what made Shakespeare and the Bible so refreshing as lessons; the facts of life were always turning up. Did you ever hear of a man called Tyrrel?"

"Yes; he was a con man on the P. & O. boats. Drowned in the *Egypt*."

"No; I mean in history."

"I tell you, I never knew any history except 1066 and 1603."

"What happened in 1603?" Grant asked, his mind still on Tyrrel.

"We had the Scots tied to our tails for good."

"Better than having them at our throats every five minutes. Tyrrel is said to be the man who put the boys out of the way."

"The nephews? No, it doesn't ring a bell. Well, I must be getting along. Anything I can do for you?"

"Did you say you were going to Charing Cross Road?"

"To the Phoenix, yes."

"You could do something for me."

"What is that?"

"Go into one of the bookshops and buy me a History of England. An adult one. And a Life of Richard III, if you can find one."

"Sure, I'll do that."

As he was going out he encountered The Amazon, and looked startled to find anything as large as himself in nurse's uniform. He murmured a good-morning in an abashed way, cast a questioning glance at Grant, and faded into the corridor.

The Amazon said that she was supposed to be giving Number Four her blanket bath but that she had to look in to see if he was convinced.

"Convinced?"

About the nobility of Richard Coeur-de-Lion.

"I haven't got round to Richard the First yet. But keep Number Four waiting a few moments longer and tell me what you know about Richard III."

"Ah, those poor lambs!" she said, her great cow's eyes soft with pity.

"Who?"

"Those two precious little boys. It used to be my nightmare when I was a kiddie. That someone would come and put a pillow over my face when I was asleep."

"Is that how it was done: the murder?"

"Oh, yes. Didn't you know? Sir James Tyrrel rode back to London when the court was at Warwick, and told Dighton and Forrest to kill them, and then they buried them at the foot of some stairs under a great mound of stones."

"But it doesn't say that in the book you lent me."

"Oh, that book is just history-for-exams, if you know what I mean. You don't get really interesting history in swot books like that."

"And where did you get the juicy gossip about Tyrrel, may one ask?"

"It isn't gossip," she said, hurt. "You'll find it in Sir Thomas More's history of his time. And you can't find a more respected or trustworthy person in the whole of history than Sir Thomas More, now can you?"

"No. It would be bad manners to contradict Sir Thomas."

"Well, that's what Sir Thomas says, and, after all, he was alive then and knew all those people to talk to."

"Dighton and Forrest?"

"No, of course not. But Richard, and the poor Queen, and those."

"The Queen? Richard's Queen?"

"Yes."

"Why 'poor'?"

"He led her an awful life. They say he poisoned her. He wanted to marry his niece."

"Why?"

"Because she was the heir to the throne."

"I see. He got rid of the two boys, and then wanted to marry their eldest sister."

"Yes. He couldn't marry either of the boys, you see."

"No, I suppose even Richard the Third never thought of that one."

"So he wanted to marry Elizabeth so as to feel safer on the throne. Actually, of course, she married his successor. She was Queen Elizabeth's grandmother. It always used to please me that Elizabeth was a little bit Plantagenet. I never was very fond of the Tudor side. Now I must go, or Matron will be here on her round before I have Number Four tidied up."

"That would be the end of the world."

"It would be the end of *me*," she said, and went away.

Grant took the book she had left him off the pile again, and tried to make head or tail of the Wars of the Roses. He failed. Armies marched and counter-marched. York and Lancaster succeeded each other as victors in a bewildering repetition. It was as meaningless as watching a crowd of dodgem cars bumping and whirling at a fair.

But it seemed to him that the whole trouble was implicit, the germ of it sown, nearly a hundred years earlier, when the direct line was broken by the deposition of Richard II. He knew all about that because he had in his youth seen *Richard of Bordeaux* at the New Theatre; four times he had seen it. For three generations the usurping Lancasters had ruled England: Richard of Bordeaux's Henry unhappily but with fair efficiency, Shakespeare's Prince Hal with Agincourt for glory and the stake for zeal, and his son in half-witted muddle and failure. It was no wonder if men hankered after the legitimate line again, as they watched poor Henry VI's inept friends frittering away the victories in France while Henry nursed his new foundation of Eton and besought the ladies at court to cover up their bosoms.

All three Lancasters had had an unlovely fanaticism which contrasted sharply with the liberalism of the Court which had died with Richard II. Richard's live-and-let-live methods had given place, almost overnight, to the burning of heretics. For three generations heretics had burned. It was no wonder if a less public fire of discontent had begun to smoulder in the heart of the man on the street.

Especially since there, before their eyes, was the Duke of York. Able, sensible, influential, gifted, a great prince in his own right, and by blood the heir of Richard II. They might not desire that York should take the place of poor silly Henry, but they did wish that he would take over the running of the country and clean up the mess.

York tried it, and died in battle for his pains, and his family spent much time in exile or sanctuary as a result.

But when the tumult and the shouting was all over, there on the throne of England was the son who had fought alongside him in that struggle, and the country settled back happily under that tall, flaxen, wenching, exceedingly beautiful but most remarkably shrewd young man, Edward IV.

And that was as near as Grant would ever come to understanding the Wars of the Roses.

He looked up from his book to find Matron standing in the middle of the room.

"I did knock," she said, "but you were lost in your book."

She stood there, slender and remote; as elegant in her way as Marta was; her white-cuffed hands clasped loosely in front of her narrow waist; her white veil spreading itself in imperishable dignity;

her only ornament the small silver badge of her diploma. Grant wondered if there was anywhere in this world a more unshakable poise than that achieved by the matron of a great hospital.

"I've taken to history," he said. "Rather late in the day."

"An admirable choice," she said. "It puts things in perspective." Her eyes lighted on the portrait and she said: "Are you York or Lancaster?"

"So you recognise the portrait."

"Oh, yes. When I was a probationer I used to spend a lot of time in the National. I had very little money and very sore feet, and it was warm in the Gallery and quiet and it had plenty of seats." She smiled a very little, looking back from her present consequence to that young, tired, earnest creature she had been. "I liked the Portrait Gallery best because it gave one the same sense of proportion that reading history does. All those Importances who had made such a to-do over so much in their day. All just names. Just canvas and paint. I saw a lot of that portrait in those days." Her attention went back to the picture. "A most unhappy creature," she said.

"My surgeon thinks it is poliomyelitis."

"Polio?" She considered it. "Perhaps. I hadn't thought of it before. But to me it has always seemed to be intense unhappiness. It is the most desperately unhappy face that I have ever encountered—and I have encountered a great many."

"You think it was painted later than the murder, then?"

"Oh, yes. Obviously. He is not a type that would do anything lightly. A man of that calibre. He must have been well aware of how—heinous the crime was."

"You think he belonged to the type who can't live with themselves any more."

"What a good description! Yes. The kind who want something badly, and then discover that the price they have paid for it is too high."

"So you don't think he was an out-and-out villain?"

"No; oh, no. Villains don't suffer, and that face is full of the most dreadful pain."

They considered the portrait in silence for a moment or two.

"It must have seemed like retribution, you know. Losing his only boy so soon after. And his wife's death. Being stripped of his own personal world in so short a time. It must have seemed like Divine justice."

"Would he care about his wife?"

"She was his cousin, and they had known each other from child-hood. So whether he loved her or not, she must have been a companion for him. When you sit on a throne I suspect that companionship is a rare blessing. Now I must go and see how my hospital is getting on. I have not even asked the question that I came to ask. Which was how you felt this morning. But it is a very healthy sign that you have interest to spare for a man dead these four hundred years."

She had not moved from the position in which he had first caught sight of her. Now she smiled her faint, withdrawn smile, and with her hands still clasped lightly in front of her belt-buckle moved toward the door. She had a transcendental repose. Like a nun. Like a queen.

Chapter 4

*I*t was after luncheon before Sergeant Williams reappeared, breathless, bearing two fat volumes.

"You should have left them with the porter," Grant said. "I didn't mean you to come sweating up here with them."

"I had to come up and explain. I had only time to go to one shop, but it's the biggest in the street. That's the best history of England they have in stock. It's the best there is anywhere, they say." He laid down a severe-looking sage-green tome, with an air of taking no responsibility for it. "They had no separate history of Richard III. I mean, no life of him. But they gave me this." This was a gay affair with a coat of arms on the wrapper. It was called *The Rose of Raby*.

"What is this?"

"She was his mother, it seems. The Rose in question, I mean. I can't wait: I'm due at the Yard in five minutes from now and the Super will flay me alive if I'm late. Sorry I couldn't do better. I'll look in again, first time I'm passing, and if these are no good I'll see what else I can get."

Grant was grateful and said so.

To the sound of Williams's brisk departing footsteps he began his inspection of the "best history of England there is." It turned out to be what is known as a "constitutional" history; a sober compilation lightened with improving illustrations. An illumination from the Luttrell Psalter decorated the husbandry of the fourteenth century, and a contemporary map of London bisected the Great Fire. Kings and queens were mentioned only incidentally. Tanner's Constitutional History was concerned only with social progress and political evolution; with the Black Death, and the invention of printing, and the use of gunpowder, and the formation of the Trade Guilds, and so forth. But here and there Mr. Tanner was forced, by a horrid germaneness, to mention a king or his relations. And one such germaneness occurred in connection with the invention of printing.

A man called Caxton came out of the Weald of Kent as draper's apprentice to a future Lord Mayor of London, and then went to Bruges with the twenty marks his master left him in his will. And when, in the dreary autumn rain of the Low Countries, two young refugees from England fetched up on those low shores, in very low water, it was the successful merchant from the Weald of Kent who gave them succour. The refugees were Edward IV and his brother Richard; and when in the turn of the wheel Edward came back to rule England, Caxton came too, and the first books printed in England were printed for Edward IV and written by Edward's brother-in-law.

He turned the pages and marvelled how dull information is deprived of personality. The sorrows of humanity are no one's sorrows, as newspaper readers long ago found out. A *frisson* of horror may go down one's spine at wholesale destruction but one's heart stays unmoved. A thousand people drowned in floods in China are news: a solitary child drowned in a pond is tragedy. So Mr. Tanner's account of the progress of the English race was admirable but unexciting. But here and there where he could not avoid the personal his narrative flowered into a more immediate interest. In extracts from the Pastons' letters, for instance. The Pastons had a habit of sandwiching scraps of history between orders for salad oil and inquiries as to how Clement was doing at Cambridge. And between two of those domesticities appeared the small item that the two little York boys, George and Richard, were living in the Pastons' London lodgings, and that their brother Edward came every day to see them.

Surely, thought Grant, dropping the book for a moment on the counterpane and staring up at the now invisible ceiling, surely never before can anyone have come to the throne of England with so personal an experience of the ordinary man's life as Edward IV and his brother Richard. And perhaps only Charles II after them. And Charles, even in poverty and flight, had always been a King's son, a man apart. The two little boys who were living in the Pastons' lodgings were merely the babies of the York family. Of no particular importance at the best of times and at the moment when the Pastons' letter was written without a home and possibly without a future.

Grant reached for The Amazon's history book to find out what Edward was about in London at that date, and learned that he was collecting an army. "London was always Yorkist in temper, and men flocked with enthusiasm to the banner of the youthful Edward," said the history book.

And yet young Edward, aged eighteen, idol of a capital city and on the way to the first of his victories, found time to come every day to see his small brothers.

Was it now, Grant wondered, that the remarkable devotion of Richard to his elder brother was born? An unwavering life-long devotion that the history books not only did not deny but actually used in order to point the moral. "Up to the moment of his brother's death Richard had been in all vicissitudes his loyal and faithful help-meet, but the opportunity of a crown proved too much for him." Or in the simpler words of the Historical Reader: "He had been a good brother to Edward but when he saw that he might become King greed hardened his heart."

Grant took a sideways look at the portrait and decided that the Historical Reader was off the beam. Whatever had hardened Richard's heart to the point of murder had not been greed. Or did the Historical Reader mean greed for power? Probably. Probably.

But surely Richard must have had all the power that mortal man could wish. He was the King's brother, and rich. Was that short step further so important that he could murder his brother's children to achieve it?

It was an odd set-up altogether.

He was still mulling it over in his mind when Mrs. Tinker came in with fresh pyjamas for him and her daily précis of the newspaper headlines. Mrs. Tinker never read past the third headline of a report unless it happened to be a murder, in which case she read every word and bought an evening paper for herself on the way home to cook Tinker's supper.

Today the gentle burble of her comment on a Yorkshire arsenic-and-exhumation case flowed over him unbroken until she caught sight of the morning paper lying in its virgin condition alongside the books on the table. This brought her to a sudden halt.

"You not feelin' so good today?" she asked in a concerned way.

"I'm fine, Tink, fine. Why?"

"You 'aven't as much as opened your paper. That's 'ow my sister's gel started her decline. Not takin' no notice of what was in the paper."

"Don't worry. I'm on the up-grade. Even my temper has improved. I forgot about the paper because I've been reading history stories. Ever heard of the Princes in the Tower?"

"*Everyone's* 'eard of the Princes in the Tower."

"And do you know how they met their end?"

"Course I do. He put a pillow on their faces when they was asleep."

"Who did?"

"Their wicked uncle. Richard the Third. You didn't ought to think of things like that when you're poorly. You ought to be reading something nice and cheerful."

"Are you in a hurry to get home, Tink, or could you go round by St. Martin's Lane for me?"

"No, I've plenty of time. Is it Miss Hallard? She won't be at the theatre till six-about."

"No, I know. But you might leave a note for her and she'll get it when she comes in."

He reached for his scribbling pad and pencil and wrote:

"For the love of Mike find me a copy of Thomas More's *History of Richard III*."

He tore off the page, folded it, and scribbled Marta's name on it.

"You can give it to old Saxton at the stage-door. He'll see that she gets it."

"If I can get near the stage-door what with the stools for the queue," Mrs. Tinker said; in comment rather than in truth. "That thing's going to run for ever."

She put the folded paper carefully away in the cheap pseudo-leather handbag with the shabby edges that was as much a part of her as her hat. Grant had, Christmas by Christmas, provided her with a new bag; each of them a work of art in the best tradition of English leatherworking, an article so admirable in design and so perfect in execution that Marta Hallard might have carried it to luncheon at the Blague. But that was the last he had ever seen of any of them. Since Mrs. Tinker regarded a pawnshop as one degree more disgraceful than prison, he absolved her from any suspicion of cashing in on her presents. He deduced that the handbags were safely laid away in a drawer somewhere, still wrapped up in the original tissue paper. Perhaps she took them out to show people sometimes, sometimes perhaps just to gloat over; or perhaps the knowledge that they were there enriched her, as the knowledge of "something put by for my funeral" might enrich another. Next Christmas he was going to open this shabby sack of hers, this perennial satchel *à toute faire*, and put something in the money compartment. She would fritter it away, of course, in small unimportances; so that in the end she would not know what she had done with it; but perhaps a series of small satisfactions scattered like sequins over the texture of everyday life was of greater worth than the academic satisfaction of owning a collection of fine objects at the back of a drawer.

When she had gone creaking away, in a shoes-and-corset concerto, he went back to Mr. Tanner and tried to improve his mind by acquiring some of Mr. Tanner's interest in the human race. But he found it an effort. Neither by nature nor by profession was he interested in mankind in the large. His bias, native and acquired, was towards the personal. He waded through Mr. Tanner's statistics and longed for a king in an oak tree, or a broom tied to a masthead, or a Highlander hanging on to a trooper's stirrup in a charge. But at least he had the satisfaction of learning that the Englishman of the fifteenth century "drank water only as a penance." The English labourer of Richard III's day was, it seemed, the admiration of the continent. Mr. Tanner quoted a contemporary, writing in France.

The King of France will allow no one to use salt, but what is bought of himself at his own arbitrary price. The troops pay for nothing, and treat the people barbarously if they are not satisfied. All growers of vines must give a fourth to the King. All the towns must pay the King great yearly sums for his men-at-arms. The peasants live in great hardship and misery. They wear no woollen. Their clothing consists of little short jerkins of sackcloth, no trowse but from the knees up, and legs exposed and naked. The women all go barefoot. The people eat no meat, except the fat of bacon in their soup. Nor are the gentry much better off. If an accusation is brought against them they are examined in private, and perhaps never more heard of.

In England it is very different. No one can abide in another man's house without his leave. The King cannot put on taxes, nor alter the laws, nor make new ones. The English never drink water except for penance. They eat all sorts of flesh and fish. They are clothed throughout in good woollens, and are provided with all sorts of house-hold goods. An Englishman cannot be sued except before the ordinary judge.

And it seemed to Grant that if you were very hard up and wanted to go to see what your Lizzie's firstborn looked like it must have been reassuring to know that there was shelter and a hand-out at every religious house, instead of wondering how you were going to raise the train fare. That green England he had fallen asleep with last night had a lot to be said for it.

He thumbed through the pages on the fifteenth century, looking for personal items; for individual reports that might, in their single vividness, illumine the scene for him as a "spot" lights the desired part of a stage. But the story was distressingly devoted to the general. According to Mr. Tanner, Richard III's only Parliament was the most liberal and progressive within record; and he regretted, did the worthy Mr. Tanner, that his private crimes should have militated against his patent desire for the common weal. And that seemed to be all that Mr. Tanner had to say about Richard III. Except for the Pastons, chatting indestructibly through the centuries, there was a dearth of human beings in this record of humanity.

He let the book slide off his chest, and searched with his hand until he found *The Rose of Raby.*

Chapter 5

The Rose of Raby proved to be fiction, but it was at least easier to hold than Tanner's Constitutional History of England. It was, moreover, the almost-respectable form of historical fiction which is merely history-with-conversation, so to speak. An imaginative biography rather than an imagined story. Evelyn Payne-Ellis, whoever she might be, had provided portraits and a family tree, and had made no attempt, it seemed, to what he and his cousin Laura used to call in their childhood "write forsoothly." There were no "by our Ladys," no "nathelesses" or "varlets." It was an honest affair according to its lights.

And its lights were more illuminating than Mr. Tanner.

Much more illuminating.

It was Grant's belief that if you could not find out about a man, the next best way to arrive at an estimate of him was to find out about his mother.

So until Marta could provide him with the sainted and infallible Thomas More's personal account of Richard, he would do very happily with Cicely Nevill, Duchess of York.

He glanced at the family tree, and thought that if the two York brothers, Edward and Richard, were, as kings, unique in their experience of ordinary life they were no less unique in their Englishness. He looked at their breeding and marvelled. Nevill, Fitzalan, Percy, Holland, Mortimer, Clifford, and Audley, as well as Plantagenet. Queen Elizabeth (who made it her boast) was all English; if one counted the Welsh streak as English. But among all the half-bred monarchs who had graced the throne between the Conquest and Farmer George—half-French, half-Spanish, half-Danish, half-Dutch, half-Portuguese—Edward IV and Richard III were remarkable in their home-bred quality.

They were also, he noted, as royally bred on their mother's side as on their father's. Cicely Nevill's grandfather was John of Gaunt, the first of the Lancasters; third son of Edward III. Her husband's two grandfathers were two other sons of Edward III. So three of Edward III's five sons had contributed to the making of the two York brothers.

"To be a Nevill," said Miss Payne-Ellis, "was to be of some importance since they were great landowners. To be a Nevill was almost certainly to be handsome, since they were a good-looking family. To be a Nevill was to have personality, since they excelled in displays of both character and temperament. To unite all three Nevill gifts, in their finest quality, in one person was the good fortune of Cicely Nevill, who was the sole Rose of the north long before that north was forced to choose between White Roses and Red."

It was Miss Payne-Ellis's contention that the marriage with Richard Plantagenet, Duke of York, was a love match. Grant received this theory with a scepticism bordering on scorn until he noticed the results of that marriage. To have a yearly addition to the family was not, in the fifteenth century, evidence of anything but fertility. And the long family produced by Cicely Nevill to her charming husband augured nothing nearer love than co-habitation. But in a time when the wife's rôle was to stay meekly at home and see to her still-room, Cicely Nevill's constant travelings about in her husband's company were surely remarkable enough to suggest an abnormal pleasure in that company. The extent and constancy of that travel was witnessed to by the birthplaces of her children. Anne, her first, was born in Fotheringhay, the family home in Northamptonshire. Henry, who died as a baby, at Hatfield. Edward at Rouen, where the Duke was on active service. Edmund and Elizabeth also at Rouen. Margaret at Fotheringhay. John, who died young, at Neath in Wales. George in Dublin (and could it be, wondered Grant, that that accounted for the almost Irish perverseness of the ineffable George?). Richard at Fotheringhay.

Cicely Nevill had not sat at home in Northamptonshire waiting for her lord and master to visit her when it seemed good to him. She had accompanied him about the world of their inhabiting. There was a strong presumption in favour of Miss Payne-Ellis's theory. At the very canniest reckoning it was patently a very successful marriage.

Which perhaps accounted for the family devotion of those daily visits of Edward to his small brothers in the Pastons' lodgings. The York family, even before tribulations, was a united one.

This was borne out unexpectedly when, spurting the pages from under his thumb, he came on a letter. It was a letter from the two elder boys, Edward and Edmund, to their father. The boys were at Ludlow Castle, undergoing their education, and on a Saturday in Easter week, taking advantage of a courier who was going back, they burst out in loud complaint of their tutor and his "odiousness" and begged their father to listen to the tale of the courier, William Smyth, who was fully charged with the details of their oppression. This S.O.S. was introduced and ended in respectful padding, the formality of which was a little marred by their pointing out that it was nice of him to send the clothes but that he had forgotten their breviary.

The conscientious Miss Payne-Ellis had given the reference for this letter (one of the Cotton manuscripts, it appeared) and he thumbed more slowly, in search of more. Factual evidence was a policeman's meat.

He could not find any, but he came on a family tableau which held him for a moment.

The Duchess moved out into the thin sharp sunlight of a London December morning, and stood on the steps to watch them go: her husband, her brother, and her son. Dirk and his nephews brought the horses into the courtyard, scattering the pigeons and the fussing sparrows from the cobbles. She watched her husband mount, equable and deliberate as always, and thought that for all the emotion he showed he might be riding down to Fotheringhay to look at some new rams instead of setting out on a campaign. Salisbury, her brother, was being Nevill and temperamental; a little conscious of the occasion and living up to it. She looked at them both and smiled in her mind at them. But it was Edmund who caught at her heart. Edmund at seventeen, very slender, very untried, very vulnerable. Flushed with pride and excitement at this setting-out to his first campaigning. She wanted to say to her husband: "Take care of Edmund," but she could not do that. Her husband would not understand; and Edmund, if he were to suspect, would be furious. If Edward, only a year older, was commanding an army of his own on the borders of Wales at this very minute, then he, Edmund, was more than old enough to see a war at first-hand.

She glanced behind her at the three younger children who had come out in her wake; Margaret and George, the two solid fair ones, and behind them, a pace in the rear as always, her changeling baby, Richard; his dark brows and brown hair making him look like a visitor. Good-natured untidy Margaret watched with all the moist-eyed emotion of fourteen; George in a passionate envy and wild rebellion that he was only eleven and of no consequence in this martial moment. Thin little Richard showed no excitement at all, but his mother thought that he vibrated like a softly tapped drum.

The three horses moved out of the courtyard in a clatter of slipping hooves and jingling accoutrements, to join the servants waiting for them in the roadway, and the children called and danced and waved them out of the gate.

And Cicely, who in her time had seen so many men, and so many of her family, go off to war, went back to the house with an unaccustomed weight at her bosom. Which of them, said the voice in her unwilling mind, which of them was it who was not coming back?

Her imagination did not compass anything so horrible as the fact that none of them was coming back again. That she would never see any one of them again.

That before the year was ended her husband's severed head, crowned for insult with a paper crown, would be nailed above the Micklegate Bar in York, and the heads of her brother and her son on the two other gates.

Well, that might be fiction, but it was an illuminating glimpse of Richard. The dark one in a blond family. The one who "looked like a visitor." The "changeling."

He abandoned Cicely Nevill for the moment, and went hunting through the book for her son Richard. But Miss Payne-Ellis seemed not to be greatly interested in Richard. He was merely the tail-end of the family. The magnificent young creature who flourished at the other end was more to her taste. Edward was much to the fore. With his Nevill cousin Warwick, Salisbury's son, he won the battle of Towton, and, with the memory of Lancastrian ferocity still fresh and his father's head still nailed to the Micklegate Bar, gave evidence of that tolerance that was to be characteristic of him. There was quarter at Towton for all who asked. He was crowned King of England in Westminster Abbey (and two small boys, home from exile in Utrecht, were created respectively Duke of Clarence and Duke of Gloucester). And he buried his father and his brother

Edmund with great magnificence in the church at Fotheringhay (though it was Richard, aged thirteen, who convoyed that sad procession from Yorkshire, through the bright glory of five July days, to Northamptonshire; nearly six years after he had stood on the steps of Baynard's Castle in London to watch them ride away).

It was not until Edward had been King for some time that Miss Payne-Ellis allowed Richard to come back into the story. He was then being educated with his Nevill cousins at Middleham, in Yorkshire.

As Richard rode into the shadow of the keep, out of the broad sunlight and flying winds of Wensleydale, it seemed to him that there was an atmosphere of strangeness about the place. The guards were talking in loud excitement in the gatehouse and seemed abashed at his presence. From their sudden silence he rode on into a silent court that should have been bustling with activity at this hour of the day. It would soon be supper time, and both habit and hunger brought all the inhabitants of Middleham home from their various occupations, as they were bringing him back from his hawking, for the evening meal. This hush, this desertion, was unusual. He walked his horse to the stables, but there was no one there to give it to. As he unsaddled he noticed a hard-ridden bay in the next stall; a horse that did not belong to Middleham; a horse so tired that he had not eaten up and his head hung in a despondent beaten way between his knees.

Richard wiped his horse down and rugged him, brought him some hay and fresh water, and left him; wondering about that beaten horse and the uncanny silence. As he paused in the doorway he could hear voices in the distance of the great hall; and debated whether he should go there and investigate before going upstairs to his own quarters. As he hesitated a voice from the stairs above him said: "Z-z-zt."

He looked up to see his cousin Anne's head peering over the banisters, her two long fair plaits hanging down like bell-ropes.

"Richard!" she said, half whispering. "Have you heard?"

"Is something wrong?" he asked. "What is it?"

As he moved up to her she grabbed his hand and dragged him upwards towards their schoolroom in the roof.

"But what is it?" he asked, leaning back in protest against her urgency. "What has happened? Is it something so awful that you can't tell me here?"

She swept him into the schoolroom and shut the door.

"It's Edward!"

"Edward? Is he ill?"

"No! *Scandal!*"

"Oh," said Richard, relieved. Scandal and Edward were never far apart. "What is it? Has he a new mistress?"

"Much worse than that! Oh, much, *much* worse. He's married."

"Married?" said Richard, so unbelieving that he sounded calm. "He can't be."

"But he is. The news came from London an hour ago."

"He can't be married," Richard insisted. "For a King marriage is a long affair. A matter of contracts, and agreements. A matter for Parliament, even, I think. What made you think he had got married?"

"I don't *think*," Anne said, out of patience at this sober reception of her broadside. "The whole family is raging together in the Great Hall over the affair."

"Anne! have you been listening at the door?"

"Oh, don't be so righteous. I didn't have to listen very hard, anyhow. You could hear them on the other side of the river. He has married Lady Grey!"

"Who is Lady Grey? Lady Grey of Groby?"

"Yes."

"But he can't. She has two children and she's quite old."

"She is five years older than Edward, and she is wonderfully beautiful—so I overhear."

"When did this happen?"

"They've been married five months. They got married in secret down in Northamptonshire."

"But I thought he was going to marry the King of France's sister."

"So," said Anne, in a tone full of meaning, "did my father."

"Yes; yes, it makes things very awkward for him, doesn't it; after all the negotiating."

"According to the messenger from London he is throwing fits. It isn't only the making him look a fool. It seems she has cohorts of relations and he hates every one of them."

"Edward must be possessed." In Richard's hero-worshipping eyes everything Edward did had always been right. This folly, this undeniable, this inexcusable folly, could come only from possession.

"It will break my mother's heart," he said. He thought of his mother's courage when his father and Edmund had been killed, and the Lancastrian army was almost at the gates of London. She had not wept nor wrapped herself in protective veils of self-pity. She had arranged that he and George should go to Utrecht, as if she were arranging for them to go away to school. They might never see each other again, but she had busied herself about warm clothes for their winter voyage across the Channel with a calm and dry-eyed practicality.

How would she bear this; this further blow? This destructive folly. This shattering foolishness.

"Yes," said Anne, softening. "Poor Aunt Cicely. It is monstrous of Edward to hurt everyone so. Monstrous."

But Edward was still the infallible. If Edward had done wrong it was because he was ill, or possessed, or bewitched. Edward still had Richard's allegiance; his heart-whole and worshipping allegiance.

Nor in after years was that allegiance—an adult allegiance of recognition and acceptance—ever less than heart-whole.

And then the story went on to Cicely Nevill's tribulation, and her efforts to bring some kind of order into the relations between her son Edward, half-pleased, half-ashamed, and her nephew War-wick, wholly furious. There was also a long description of that in-destructibly virtuous beauty with the famous "gilt" hair, who had succeeded where more complaisant beauties had failed; and of her enthroning at Reading Abbey (led to the throne by a silently protesting Warwick, who could not but note the large array of Woodvilles, come to see their sister Elizabeth acknowledged Queen of England).

The next time Richard turned up in the tale he was setting out from Lynn without a penny in his pocket, in a Dutch vessel that happened to be in the harbour when it was needed. Along with him was his brother Edward, Edward's friend Lord Hastings, and a few followers. None of them had anything except what they stood up in, and after some argument the ship's captain agreed to accept Ed-ward's fur-lined cape as fare.

Warwick had finally decided that the Woodville clan was more than he could stomach. He had helped to put his cousin Edward on the throne of England; he could just as easily unseat him. For the achievement of this he had the help of the whole Nevill brood; and, incredibly, the active assistance of the ineffable George. Who had decided that falling heir to half the lands of Montague, Nevill, and

Beauchamp, by marrying Warwick's other daughter Isabel, was a better bet than being loyal to his brother Edward. In eleven days Warwick was master of a surprised England, and Edward and Richard were squelching through the October mud between Alkmaar and The Hague.

From then on, Richard was always in the background of the story. Through that dreary winter in Bruges. Staying with Margaret in Burgundy—for that kind moist-eyed Margaret who had stood on the steps of Baynard's Castle with himself and George to watch their father ride away was now the very new Duchess of Burgundy. Margaret, kind Margaret, was saddened and dismayed—as many people in future were to be saddened and dismayed—by George's inexplicable conduct, and set herself to missionary work what time she got together funds for her two more admirable brothers.

Not even Miss Payne-Ellis's interest in the magnificent Edward allowed her to conceal that the real work of outfitting the ships hired with Margaret's money was done by Richard; a Richard not yet eighteen. And when Edward with an absurd handful of followers found himself once more camped in an English meadow, facing George with an army, it was Richard who went over to George's camp and talked the Margaret-weakened George into alliance again and so left the road to London open to them.

Not, Grant thought, that this last was any great achievement. George could obviously be talked into anything. He was the born missionee.

Chapter 6

*H*e had not nearly exhausted *The Rose of Raby* and the illicit joys of fiction when, next morning about eleven, a parcel arrived from Marta containing the more respectable entertainment of history as recorded by the sainted Sir Thomas.

With the book was a note in Marta's large sprawling writing on Marta's stiff expensive notepaper.

> Have to send this instead of bringing it. Frantically busy. Think I have got M.M. to the sticking point re Blessington. No T. More in any of the bookshops, so tried Public Library. Can't think why one never thinks of Public Libraries. Probably because books expected to be soupy. Think this looks quite clean and unsoupy. You get fourteen days. Sounds like a sentence rather than a loan. Hope this interest in Crouchback means that the prickles are less nettlish. Till soon.
>
> Marta

The book did indeed look clean and unsoupy, if a little elderly. But after the light going of *The Rose* its print looked unexciting and its solid paragraphs forbidding. Nevertheless he attacked it with interest. This was, after all, where Richard III was concerned, "the horse's mouth."

He came to the surface an hour later, vaguely puzzled and ill at ease. It was not that the matter surprised him; the facts were very much what he had expected them to be. It was that this was not how he had expected Sir Thomas to write.

He took ill rest at nights, lay long waking and musing; sore wearied with care and watch, he slumbered rather than slept. So was his restless heart continually tossed and tumbled with the tedious impression and stormy remembrance of his most abominable deeds.

That was all right. But when he added that "this he had from such as were secret with his chamberers" one was suddenly repelled. An aroma of back-stair gossip and servants' spying came off the page. So that one's sympathy tilted before one was aware of it from the smug commentator to the tortured creature sleeping on his bed. The murderer seemed of greater stature than the man who was writing of him.

Which was all wrong.

Grant was conscious too of the same unease that filled him when he listened to a witness telling a perfect story that he knew to be flawed somewhere.

And that was very puzzling indeed. What could possibly be wrong with the personal account of a man revered for his integrity as Thomas More had been revered for four centuries?

The Richard who appeared in More's account was, Grant thought, one that Matron would have recognised. A man highly-strung and capable of both great evil and great suffering. "He was never quiet in his mind, never thought himself secure. His eyes whirled about, his body was privily fenced, his hand ever on his dagger, his countenance and manner like one always ready to strike again."

And of course there was the dramatic, not to say hysterical, scene that Grant remembered from his school-days; that every schoolboy probably remembered. The council scene in the Tower before he laid claim to the crown. Richard's sudden challenge to Hastings as to what was the proper fate for a man who plotted the death of the Protector of the Kingdom. The insane claim that Edward's wife and Edward's mistress (Jane Shore) were responsible for his withered arm by their sorcery. The smiting of the table in his rage, which was the signal for his armed satellites to burst in and arrest Lord Hastings, Lord Stanley, and John Morton, Bishop of Ely. The rushing of Hastings down into the courtyard and his beheading on a handy log of wood after bare time to confess himself to the first priest who could be found.

That was certainly the picture of a man who would act first—in fury, in fear, in revenge—and repent afterwards.

But it seemed that he was capable of more calculated iniquity. He caused a sermon to be preached by a certain Dr. Shaw, brother of the Lord Mayor, at Paul's Cross, on June 22, on the text: "Bastard slips shall take no root." Wherein Dr. Shaw maintained that both Edward and George were sons of the Duchess of York by some unknown man, and that Richard was the only legitimate son of the Duke and Duchess of York.

This was so unlikely, so inherently absurd, that Grant went back and read it over again. But it still said the same thing. That Richard had traduced his mother, in public and for his own material advantage, with an unbelievable infamy.

Well, Sir Thomas More said it. And if anyone should know it would be Thomas More. And if anyone should know how to pick and choose between the credibilities in the reporting of a story it ought to be Thomas More, Lord Chancellor of England.

Richard's mother, said Sir Thomas, complained bitterly of the slander with which her son had smirched her. Understandably, on the whole, Grant thought.

As for Dr. Shaw, he was overcome with remorse. So much so that "within a few days he withered and consumed away."

Had a stroke, probably, Grant considered. And little wonder. To have stood up and told that tale to a London crowd must have taken some nerve.

Sir Thomas's account of the Princes in the Tower was the same as The Amazon's, but Sir Thomas's version was more detailed. Richard had suggested to Robert Brackenbury, Constable of the Tower, that it might be a good thing if the Princes disappeared, but Brackenbury would have no part in such an act. Richard therefore waited until he was at Warwick, during his progress through England after his coronation, and then sent Tyrrel to London with orders that he was to receive the keys of the Tower for one night. During that night two ruffians, Dighton and Forrest, one a groom and one a warder, smothered the two boys.

At this point The Midget came in with his lunch and removed the book from his grasp; and while he forked the shepherd's pie from plate to mouth he considered again the face of the man in the dock. The faithful and patient small brother who had turned into a monster.

When The Midget came back for his tray he said: "Did you know that Richard III was a very popular person in his day? Before he came to the throne, I mean."

The Midget cast a baleful glance at the picture.

"Always was a snake in the grass, if you ask me. Smooth, that's what he was: smooth. Biding his time."

Biding his time for what? he wondered, as she tapped away down the corridor. He could not have known that his brother Edward would die unexpectedly at the early age of forty. He could not have foreseen (even after a childhood shared with him in uncommon intimacy) that George's ongoings would end in attainder and the debarring of his two children from the succession. There seemed little point in "biding one's time" if there was nothing to bide for. The indestructible virtuous beauty with the gilt hair had, except for her incurable nepotism, proved an admirable Queen and had provided Edward with a large brood of healthy children, including two boys. The whole of that brood, together with George and his son and daughter, stood between Richard and the throne. It was surely unlikely that a man busy with the administration of the North of England, or campaigning (with dazzling success) against the Scots, would have much spare interest in being "smooth."

What then had changed him so fundamentally in so short a time?

Grant reached for *The Rose of Raby* to see what Miss Payne-Ellis had had to say about the unhappy metamorphosis of Cicely Nevill's youngest son. But that wily author had burked the issue. She had wanted the book to be a happy one, and to have carried it to its logical conclusion would have made it unredeemed tragedy. She had therefore wound it up with a fine resounding major chord by making her last chapter the coming-out of young Elizabeth, Edward's eldest child. This avoided both the tragedy of Elizabeth's young brothers and the defeat and death of Richard in battle.

So the book ended with a Palace party, and a flushed and happy young Elizabeth, very magnificent in a new white dress and her first pearls, dancing the soles out of her slippers like the princesses in the fairy-tale. Richard and Anne, and their delicate little son, had come up from Middleham for the occasion. But neither George nor Isabel was there. Isabel had died in childbirth years ago, obscurely and as far as George was concerned unmourned. George too had died obscurely, but with that perverseness that was so peculiarly George's, had by that very obscurity won for himself imperishable fame.

George's life had been a progression from one spectacular piece of spiritual extravagance to the next. Each time, his family must have said: "Well, that at last is the summit of frightfulness; even George cannot think of anything more fantastic than that." And each time George had surprised them. There was no limit to George's antic capacity.

The seed was perhaps sown when, during his first backsliding in the company of his father-in-law, Warwick had created him heir to the poor crazy puppet-King, Henry VI, whom Warwick had dumped back on the throne to spite his cousin Edward. Both Warwick's hopes of seeing his daughter a Queen and George's royal pretensions had gone down the drain on that night when Richard had gone over to the Lancastrian camp and talked to George. But the taste of importance had perhaps proved too much for a natural sweet-tooth. In the years to come the family were always heading George off from unexpected vagaries, or rescuing him from his latest caper.

When Isabel died he had been certain that she had been poisoned by her waiting woman, and that his baby son had been poisoned by another. Edward, thinking the affair important enough to be tried before a London court, sent down a writ; only to find that George had tried them both at a petty sessions of his own magistrates and hanged them. The furious Edward, by way of rapping him over the knuckles, had two members of George's household tried for treason; but instead of taking the hint George declared that this was just judicial murder, and went about saying so in loud tones and a fine blaze of *lèse-majesté*.

Then he decided that he wanted to marry the richest heiress in Europe; who was Margaret's stepdaughter, young Mary of Burgundy. Kind Margaret thought that it would be nice to have her brother in Burgundy, but Edward had arranged to back Maximilian of Austria's suit, and George was a continual embarrassment.

When the Burgundy intrigue came to nothing, the family hoped for a little peace. After all, George owned half the Nevill lands and had no need to marry again either for fortune or children. But George had a new scheme for marrying Margaret, the sister of James III of Scotland.

At last his *folie de grandeur* graduated from secret negotiation undertaken on his own behalf with foreign courts to open display of the Lancastrian act of Parliament which had declared him heir to the throne after Henry VI. This, inevitably, landed him before another Parliament, and a much less amenable one.

The trial was chiefly remarkable for a flaming and wordy row between the two brothers, Edward and George, but when the expected attainder was passed, there was a pause. Depriving George of his standing was one thing: desirable and indeed necessary. But executing him was something else again.

As the days went by without sentence being carried out, the Commons sent a reminder. And next day it was announced that George, Duke of Clarence, had died in the Tower.

"Drowned in a butt of malmsey," said London. And what was merely a Cockney's comment on a drunkard's end passed into history and made the undeserving George immortal.

So George was not at that party at Westminster, and the emphasis in Miss Payne-Ellis's final chapter was not on Cicely Nevill as the mother of sons, but on Cicely Nevill the grandmother of a fine brood. George might have died discredited, on a dried-leaf heap of worn-out friendships, but his son, young Warwick, was a fine upstanding boy, and little Margaret at ten was already showing signs of the traditional Nevill beauty. Edmund, dead in battle at seventeen, might seem a wanton waste of young life, but there to balance it was the delicate baby whom she had never thought to rear; and he had a son to follow him. Richard in his twenties still looked as though one could break him in two, but he was as tough as a heather root, and perhaps his fragile-looking son would grow up to be as resilient. As for Edward, her tall blond Edward, his beauty might be blurring into grossness and his amiability into sloth, but his two small sons and his five girls had all the character and good looks of their combined ancestry.

As a grandmother she could look on that crowd of children with a personal pride, and as a Princess of England she could look on them with assurance. The crown was safe in the York line for generations to come.

If anyone, looking in a crystal ball at that party, had told Cicely Nevill that in four years not only the York line but the whole Plantagenet dynasty would have gone forever, she would have held it to be either madness or treason.

But what Miss Payne-Ellis had not sought to gloss over was the prevalence of the Woodville clan in a Nevill-Plantagenet gathering.

She looked round the room and wished that her daughter-in-law Elizabeth had been blessed either with a less generous heart or with fewer relations. The Woodville match had turned out far more happily than anyone had dared to hope; Elizabeth had been an admirable wife; but the by-products had not been so fortunate. It was perhaps inevitable that the governorship of the two boys should have gone to her eldest brother; and Rivers, if a little nouveau riche in his liking for display and a little too obviously ambitious, was a cultured creature and an admirable person to have the boys in charge during their schoolroom days at Ludlow. But as for the rest: four brothers, seven sisters, and two sons by her first husband, were really too many by half to have brought into the marriage market in her wake.

Cicely looked across the laughing mêlée of the children's blind man's buff to the grown-ups standing round the supper table. Anne Woodville married to the Earl of Essex's heir. Eleanor Woodville married to the Earl of Kent's heir. Margaret Woodville married to the Earl of Arundel's heir. Catherine Woodville married to the Duke of Buckingham. Jacquette Woodville to Lord Strange. Mary Woodville to Lord Herbert's heir. And John Woodville, disgracefully, to the Dowager of Norfolk who was old enough to be his grandmother. It was good that new blood should strengthen the old families—new blood had always seeped in—but it was not good that it should come suddenly and in a flood from one particular source. It was like a fever in the political blood of the country; a foreign introduction, difficult to be assimilated. Unwise and regrettable.

However. There were long years ahead in which that influx could be assimilated. This new sudden power in the body politic would cease to be so concentrated, would spread out, would settle down, would cease to be dangerous and upsetting. Edward for all his amiability had a shrewd common sense; he would keep the country on an even keel as he had kept it for nearly twenty years. No one had run England with a more despotic power or a lighter hand than her acute, lazy, woman-loving Edward.

It would be all right eventually.

She was about to rise and join them in their discussion of sweetmeats—they must not think that she was being critical or aloof—when her granddaughter Elizabeth came breathless and laughing out of the scrimmage and swept into the seat beside her.

"I am much too old for this sort of thing," she said between her gasps, "and it is ruinous to one's clothes. Do you like my dress, grandmother? I had to coax it out of Father. He said my old tawny satin would do. The one I had when Aunt Margaret came from Burgundy to visit us. That is the worst of having a father who notices what women wear. He knows too much about one's wardrobe. Did you hear that the Dauphin has jilted me? Father is in a pet, but I am so happy. I lighted ten candles to St. Catherine. It took all I had left of my allowance. I don't want to leave England. I want never to leave England ever. Can you arrange that for me, grandmother?"

Cicely smiled and said that she would try.

"Old Ankaret, who tells fortunes, says that I am to be a Queen. But since there is no prince to marry me I do not see how that may be." She paused, and added in a smaller voice: "She said Queen of England. But I expect she was just a little tipsy. She is very fond of hippocras."

It was unfair, not to say inartistic, of Miss Payne-Ellis to hint at Elizabeth's future as the wife of Henry VII if as author she was not prepared to face the unpleasantness that lay between. To presuppose in her readers a knowledge of Elizabeth's marriage to the first Tudor king, was also to presuppose their awareness of her brothers' murder. So that a dark reminding shadow fell across the festive scene with which she had chosen to end her story.

But on the whole, Grant thought, she had made a good enough job of the story, judging by what he had read of it. He might even go back sometime and read the bits he had skipped.

Chapter 7

Grant had switched off his bedside light that night, and was half asleep, when a voice in his mind said, "But Thomas More was Henry the Eighth."

This brought him wide awake. He flicked the light on again.

What the voice had meant, of course, was not that Thomas More and Henry the Eighth were one and the same person, but that, in that business of putting personalities into pigeon-holes according to reigns, Thomas More belonged to the reign of Henry the Eighth.

Grant lay looking at the pool of light that his lamp threw on the ceiling, and reckoned. If Thomas More was Henry VIII's Chancellor, then he must have lived through the whole of Henry VII's long reign as well as Richard III's. There was something wrong somewhere.

He reached for More's *History of Richard III*. It had as preface a short life of More which he had not bothered to read. Now he turned to it to find out how More could have been both Richard III's historian and Henry VIII's Chancellor. How old was More when Richard succeeded?

He was five.

When that dramatic council scene had taken place at the Tower, Thomas More had been five years old. He had been only eight when Richard died at Bosworth.

Everything in that history had been hearsay.

And if there was one word that a policeman loathed more than another it was hearsay. Especially when applied to evidence.

He was so disgusted that he flung the precious book on to the floor before he remembered that it was the property of a Public Library and his only by grace and for fourteen days.

More had never known Richard III at all. He had indeed grown up under a Tudor administration. That book was the Bible of the whole historical world on the subject of Richard III—it was from that account that Holinshed had taken his material, and from that that Shakespeare had written his—and except that More believed what he wrote to be true it was of no more value than what the soldier said. It was what his cousin Laura called "snow on their boots." A "gospel-true" event seen by someone other than the teller. That More had a critical mind and an admirable integrity did not make the story acceptable evidence. A great many otherwise admirable minds had accepted that story of the Russian troops passing through Britain. Grant had dealt too long with the human intelligence to accept as truth someone's report of someone's report of what that someone remembered to have seen or been told.

He was disgusted.

At the first opportunity he must get an actual contemporary account of the events of Richard's short reign. The Public Library could have Sir Thomas More back tomorrow and be damned to their fourteen days. The fact that Sir Thomas was a martyr and a Great Mind did not cut any ice at all with him, Alan Grant. He, Alan Grant, had known Great Minds so uncritical that they would believe a story that would make a con man blush for shame. He had known a great scientist who was convinced that a piece of butter muslin was his great-aunt Sophia because an illiterate medium from the back streets of Plymouth told him so. He had known a great authority on the Human Mind and Its Evolution who had been taken for all he had by an incurable knave because he "judged for himself and not on police stories." As far as he, Alan Grant, was concerned there was nothing so uncritical or so damn-silly as your Great Mind. As far as he, Alan Grant, was concerned Thomas More was washed out, cancelled, deleted; and he, Alan Grant, was beginning from scratch again tomorrow morning.

He was still illogically fuming when he fell asleep and he woke fuming.

"Do you know that your Sir Thomas More knew nothing about Richard III at all?" he said, accusing, to The Amazon the moment her large person appeared in the doorway.

She looked startled, not at his news but at his ferocity. Her eyes looked as if they might brim with tears at another rough word.

"But of *course* he knew!" she protested. "He *lived* then."

"He was eight when Richard died," Grant said, relentless. "And all he knew was what he had been told. Like me. Like you. Like Will Rogers of blessed memory. There is nothing hallowed at all about Sir Thomas More's history of Richard III. It's a damned piece of hearsay and a swindle."

"Aren't you feeling so well this morning?" she asked anxiously. "Do you think you've got a temperature?"

"I don't know about a temperature, but my blood pressure's away up."

"Oh, dear, dear," she said, taking this literally. "And you were doing so very well. Nurse Ingham will be so distressed. She has been boasting about your good recovery."

That The Midget should have found him a subject for boasting was a new idea to Grant, but it was not one that gave him any gratification. He resolved to have a temperature in earnest if he could manage it, just to score off The Midget.

But the morning visit of Marta distracted him from this experiment in the power of mind over matter.

Marta, it seemed, was pluming herself on his mental health very much as The Midget was pluming herself on his physical improvement. She was delighted that her pokings-about with James in the print shop had been so effective.

"Have you decided on Perkin Warbeck, then?" she asked.

"No. Not Warbeck. Tell me: what made you bring me a portrait of Richard III? There's no mystery about Richard, is there?"

"No. I suppose we took it as illustration to the Warbeck story. No, wait a moment. I remember, James turned it up and said: 'If he's mad about faces, there's one for him!' He said: 'That's the most notorious murderer in history, and yet his face is in my estimation the face of a saint.' "

"A saint!" Grant said; and then remembered something. " 'Over-conscientious,' " he said.

"What?"

"Nothing. I was just remembering my first impressions of it. Is that how it seemed to you: the face of a saint?"

She looked across to the picture, propped up against the pile of books. "I can't see it against the light," she said, and picked it up for a closer scrutiny.

He was suddenly reminded that to Marta, as to Sergeant Williams, faces were a professional matter. The slant of an eyebrow, the set of a mouth, was just as much an evidence of character to Marta as to Williams. Indeed she actually made herself faces to match the characters she played.

"Nurse Ingham thinks he's dreary. Nurse Darroll thinks he's a horror. My surgeon thinks he's a polio victim. Sergeant Williams thinks he's a born judge. Matron thinks he's a soul in torment."

Marta said nothing for a little. Then she said: "It's odd, you know. When you first look at it you think it a mean, suspicious face. Even cantankerous. But when you look at it a little longer you find that it isn't like that at all. It is quite calm. It is really quite a gentle face. Perhaps that is what James meant by being saintlike."

"No. No, I don't think so. What he meant was the subservience to conscience."

"Whatever it is, it is a *face*, isn't it! Not just a collection of organs for seeing, breathing, and eating with. A wonderful face. With very little alteration, you know, it might be a portrait of Lorenzo the Magnificent."

"You don't suppose that it *is* Lorenzo and that we're considering the wrong man altogether?"

"Of course not. Why should you think that?"

"Because nothing in the face fits the facts of history. And pictures have got shuffled before now."

"Oh, yes, of course they have. But that is Richard all right. The original—or what is supposed to be the original—is at Windsor Castle, James told me. It is included in Henry VIII's inventory, so it has been there for four hundred years or so. And there are duplicates at Hatfield and Albury."

"It's Richard," Grant said resignedly. "I just don't know anything about faces. Do you know anyone at the B. M.?"

"At the British Museum?" Marta asked, her attention still on the portrait. "No. I don't think so. Not that I can think of at the moment. I went there once to look at some Egyptian jewellery, when I was playing Cleopatra with Geoffrey—did you ever see Geoffrey's Antony? It was superlatively genteel—but the place frightens me rather. Such a garnering of the ages. It made me feel the way the stars make you feel: small and no-account. What do you want of the B. M.?"

"I wanted some information about history written in Richard III's day. Contemporary accounts."

"Isn't the sainted Sir Thomas any good, then?"

"The sainted Sir Thomas is nothing but an old gossip," Grant said with venom. He had taken a wild dislike to the much-admired More.

"Oh, dear. And the nice man at the Library seemed so reverent about him. The Gospel of Richard III according to St. Thomas More, and all that."

"Gospel nothing," Grant said rudely. "He was writing down in a Tudor England what someone had told him about events that happened in a Plantagenet England when he himself was five."

"Five years old?"

"Yes."

"Oh, dear. Not exactly the horse's mouth."

"Not even straight from the course. Come to think of it, it's as reliable as a bookie's tips would be. He's on the wrong side of the rails altogether. If he was a Tudor servant he was on the laying side where Richard III was concerned."

"Yes. Yes, I suppose so. What do you want to find out about Richard, when there is no mystery to investigate?"

"I want to know what made him tick. That is a more profound mystery than anything I have come up against of late. What changed him almost overnight? Up to the moment of his brother's death he seems to have been entirely admirable. And devoted to his brother."

"I suppose the supreme honour must always be a temptation."

"He was Regent until the boy came of age. Protector of England. With his previous history, you would think that would have been enough for him. You would have thought, indeed, that it would have been very much his cup of tea: guardian to both Edward's son and the kingdom."

"Perhaps the brat was unbearable, and Richard longed to 'larn' him. Isn't it odd how we never think of victims as anything but white innocents. Like Joseph in the Bible. I'm sure he was a quite intolerable young man, actually, and long overdue for that pushing into the pit. Perhaps young Edward was just sitting up and begging to be quietly put down."

"There were two of them," Grant reminded her.

"Yes, of course. Of course there isn't an explanation. It was the ultimate barbarism. Poor little woolly lambs! Oh!"

"What was the 'Oh' for?"

"I've just thought of something. Woolly lambs made me think of it."

"Well?"

"No, I won't tell you in case it doesn't come off. I must fly."

"Have you charmed Madeleine March into agreeing to write the play?"

"Well, she hasn't actually signed a contract yet, but I think she is sold on the idea. Au revoir, my dear, I shall look in soon again."

She went away, sped on her way by a blushing Amazon, and Grant did not remember anything about woolly lambs until the woolly lamb actually turned up in his room next evening. The woolly lamb was wearing horn-rimmed spectacles, which in some odd way emphasized the resemblance instead of detracting from it. Grant had been dozing, more at peace with the world than he had been for some time; history was, as Matron had pointed out, an excellent way of acquiring a sense of perspective. The tap at his door was so tentative that he had decided that he had imagined it. Taps on hospital doors are not apt to be tentative. But something made him say: "Come in!" and there in the opening was something that was so unmistakably Marta's woolly lamb that Grant laughed aloud before he could stop himself.

The young man looked abashed, smiled nervously, propped the spectacles on his nose with a long thin forefinger, cleared his throat, and said:

"Mr. Grant? My name is Carradine. Brent Carradine. I hope I haven't disturbed you when you were resting."

"No, no. Come in, Mr. Carradine. I am delighted to see you."

"Marta—Miss Hallard, that is—sent me. She said I could be of some help to you."

"Did she say how? Do sit down. You'll find a chair over there behind the door. Bring it over."

He was a tall boy, hatless, with soft fair curls crowning a high forehead and a much too big tweed coat hanging unfastened round him in negligent folds, American-wise. Indeed, it was obvious that he was in fact American. He brought over the chair, planted himself on it with the coat spread round him like some royal robe and looked at Grant with kind brown eyes whose luminous charm not even the horn-rims could dim.

"Marta—Miss Hallard, that is—said that you wanted something looked up."

"And are you a looker-upper?"

"I'm doing research, here in London. Historical research, I mean. And she said something about your wanting something in that line. She knows I work at the B. M. most mornings. I'd be very pleased, Mr. Grant, to do anything I can to help you."

"That's very kind of you; very kind indeed. What is it that you are working on? Your research, I mean."

"The Peasants' Revolt."

"Oh, Richard II."

"Yes."

"Are you interested in social conditions?"

The young man grinned suddenly in a very unstudent-like way and said: "No, I'm interested in staying in England."

"And you can't stay in England without doing research?"

"Not very easily. I've got to have an alibi. My pop thinks I should go into the family business. It's furniture. Wholesale furniture. You order it by mail. Out of a book. Don't misunderstand me, Mr. Grant: it's very good furniture. Lasts for ever. It's just that I can't take much interest in furnishing-units."

"And, short of Polar exploration, the British Museum was the best hideaway you could think of."

"Well, it's warm. And I really do like history. I majored in it. And—well, Mr. Grant, if you really want to know, I just had to follow Atlanta Shergold to England. She's the dumb blonde in Marta's—I mean, in Miss Hallard's play. I mean she *plays* the dumb blonde. She's not at all dumb, Atlanta."

"No, indeed. A very gifted young woman indeed."

"You've seen her?"

"I shouldn't think there is anyone in London who hasn't seen her."

"No, I suppose not. It does go on and on, doesn't it? We didn't think—Atlanta and me—that it would run for more than a few weeks, so we just waved each other goodbye and said: See you at the beginning of the month! It was when we found that it was going on indefinitely that I just had to find an excuse to come to England."

"Wasn't Atlanta sufficient excuse?"

"Not for my pop! The family are very snooty about Atlanta, but Pop is the worst of the bunch. When he can bring himself to mention her he refers to her as 'that young actress acquaintance of yours.' You see, Pop is Carradine the Third, and Atlanta's father is very much Shergold the First. A little grocery store on Main Street, as a matter of fact. And the salt of the earth, in case you're interested. And of course Atlanta hadn't really done very much, back in the States. I mean, on the stage. This is her first big success. That is why she didn't want to break her contract and come back home. As a matter of fact it'll be quite a fight to get her back home at all. She says we never appreciated her."

"So you took to research."

"I had to think of something that I could do only in London, you see. And I had done some research at college. So the B. M. seemed to be what you call my cup of tea. I could enjoy myself and yet show my father that I was really working, both at the same time."

"Yes. It's as nice an alibi as ever I met with. Why the Peasants' Revolt, by the way?"

"Well, it's an interesting time. And I thought it would please Pop."

"Is *he* interested in social reform, then?"

"No, but he hates kings."

"Carradine the Third?"

"Yes, it's a laugh, isn't it? I wouldn't put it past him to have a crown in one of his safe deposit boxes. I bet he takes out the parcel every now and then and sneaks over to Grand Central and tries it on in the men's washroom. I'm afraid I'm tiring you, Mr. Grant; gabbing on about my own affairs like this. I didn't come for that. I came to—"

"Whatever you came for, you're manna straight from heaven. So relax, if you're not in a hurry."

"I'm never in a hurry," the young man said, unfolding his legs and laying them out in front of him. As he did it his feet, at the far extremity of his long limbs, touched the bedside table and shook the portrait of Richard III from its precarious position, so that it dropped to the floor.

"Oh, pardon me! That was careless of me. I haven't really got used to the length of my legs yet. You'd think a fellow would be used to his growth by twenty-two, wouldn't you?" He picked up the photograph, dusted it carefully with the cuff of his sleeve, and looked at it with interest. "Richardus III. Ang. Rex.," he read aloud.

"You're the first person to have noticed that background writing," Grant said.

"Well, I suppose it isn't visible unless you look into it. You're the first person I ever met who had a king for a pinup."

"No beauty, is he?"

"I don't know," said the boy slowly. "It's not a bad face, as faces go. I had a prof. at college who looked rather like him. He lived on bismuth and glasses of milk so he had a slightly jaundiced outlook on life, but he was the kindest creature imaginable. Is it about Richard that you wanted information?"

"Yes. Nothing very abstruse or difficult. Just to know what the contemporary authority is."

"Well, that should be easy enough. It isn't very far from my own time. I mean my research period. Indeed, the modern authority for Richard II—Sir Cuthbert Oliphant—stretches over both. Have you read Oliphant?" Grant said that he had read nothing but school books and Sir Thomas More.

"More? Henry VIII's Chancellor?"

"Yes."

"I take it that that was a bit of special pleading!"

"It read to me more like a party pamphlet," Grant said, realising for the first time that that was the taste that had been left in his mouth. It had not read like a statesman's account; it had read like a party throw-away.

No, it read like a columnist. Like a columnist who got his information below-stairs.

"Do you know anything about Richard III?"

"Nothing except that he croaked his nephews, and offered his kingdom for a horse. And that he had two stooges known as the Cat and the Rat."

"What!"

"You know: 'The Cat, the Rat, and Love Our Dog, Rule all England under a Hog.'"

"Yes, of course. I'd forgotten that. What does it mean, do you know?"

"No, I've no idea. I don't know that period very well. How did you get interested in Richard III?"

"Marta suggested that I should do some academic investigating, since I can't do any practical investigating for some time to come. And because I find faces interesting she brought me portraits of all the principals. Principals in the various mysteries she suggested, I mean. Richard got in more or less by accident, but he proved the biggest mystery of the lot."

"He did? In what way?"

"He is the author of the most revolting crime in history, and he has the face of a great judge; a great administrator. Moreover he was by all accounts an abnormally civilised and well-living creature. He actually *was* a good administrator, by the way. He governed the North of England and did it excellently. He was a good staff officer and a good soldier. And nothing is known against his private life. His brother, perhaps you know, was—bar Charles II—our most wench-ridden royal product."

"Edward IV. Yes, I know. A six-foot hunk of male beauty. Perhaps Richard suffered from resentment at the contrast. And that accounts for his willingness to blot out his brother's seed."

This was something that Grant had not thought of.

"You're suggesting that Richard had a suppressed hate for his brother?"

"Why suppressed?"

"Because even his worst detractors admit that he was devoted to Edward. They were together in everything from the time that Richard was twelve or thirteen. The other brother was no good to anyone. George."

"Who was George?"

"The Duke of Clarence."

"Oh. Him! Butt-of-malmsey Clarence."

"That's the one. So there were just the two of them—Edward and Richard, I mean. And there was a ten-year gap in their ages. Just the right difference for hero worship."

"If I were a hunchback," young Carradine said musingly, "I sure would hate a brother who took my credit and my women and my place in the sun."

"It's possible," Grant said after an interval. "It's the best explanation I've come on so far."

"It mightn't have been an overt thing at all, you know. It mightn't have been even a conscious thing. It may just have all boiled up in him when he saw the chance of a crown. He may have said—I mean his blood may have said: 'Here's my chance! All those years of fetching and carrying and standing one pace in the rear, and no thanks for them. Here's where I take my pay. Here's where I settle accounts.' "

Grant noticed that by sheer chance Carradine had used the same imagined description of Richard as Miss Payne-Ellis. Standing one pace in the rear. That is how the novelist had seen him, standing with the fair, solid Margaret and George, on the steps of Baynard's Castle watching their father go away to war. One pace in the rear, "as always."

"That's very interesting, though, what you say about Richard being apparently a good sort up to the time of the crime," Carradine said, propping one leg of his horn-rims with a long forefinger in his characteristic gesture. "Makes him more of a person. That Shakespeare version of him, you know, that's just a caricature. Not a man at all. I'll be very pleased to do any investigating you want, Mr. Grant. It'll make a nice change from the Peasants."

"The Cat and the Rat instead of John Ball and Wat Tyler."

"That's it."

"Well, it's very nice of you. I'd be glad of anything you can rake up. But at the moment all I pine for is a contemporary account of events. They must have been country-rocking events. I want to read a contemporary's account of them. Not what someone heard-tell about events that happened when he was five, and under another regime altogether."

"I'll find out who the contemporary historian is. Fabyan, perhaps. Or is he Henry VII? Anyway, I'll find out. And meanwhile perhaps you'd like a look at Oliphant. He's the modern authority on the period, or so I understand."

Grant said that he would be delighted to take a look at Sir Cuthbert.

"I'll drop him in when I'm passing tomorrow—I suppose it'll be all right if I leave him in the office for you?—and as soon as I find out about the contemporary writers I'll be in with the news. That suit you?"

Grant said that that was perfect.

Young Carradine went suddenly shy, reminding Grant of the woolly lamb which he had quite forgotten in the interest of this new approach to Richard. He said goodnight in a quiet smothered way, and ambled out of the room followed by the sweeping skirts of his topcoat.

Grant thought that, the Carradine fortune apart, Atlanta Shergold looked like being on a good thing.

Chapter 8

"*W*ell," said Marta, when she came again, "what did you think of my woolly lamb?"

"It was *very* kind of you to find him for me."

"I didn't have to find him. He's continually underfoot. He practically lives at the theatre. He must have seen *To Sea in a Bowl* five hundred times; when he isn't in Atlanta's dressing-room he's in front. I wish they'd get married, and then we might see less of him. They're not even living together, you know. It's all pure idyll." She dropped her "actress" voice for a moment and said: "They're rather sweet together. In some ways they are more like twins than lovers. They have that utter trust in each other; that dependence on the other half to make a proper whole. And they never have rows—or even quarrels, that I can see. An idyll, as I said. Was it Brent who brought you this?"

She poked the solid bulk of Oliphant with a doubtful finger.

"Yes, he left it with the porter for me."

"It looks very indigestible."

"A bit unappetising, let us say. It is quite easily digested once you have swallowed it. History for the student. Set out in detailed fact."

"Ugh!"

"At least I've discovered where the revered and sainted Sir Thomas More got his account of Richard."

"Yes? Where?"

"From one John Morton."

"Never heard of him."

"Neither did I, but that's our ignorance."

"Who was he?"

"He was Henry VII's Archbishop of Canterbury. And Richard's bitterest enemy."

If Marta had been capable of whistling, she would have whistled in comment.

"So *that* was the horse's mouth!" she said.

"That was the horse's mouth. And it is on that account of Richard that all the later ones were built. It is on that story that Holinshed fashioned his history, and on that story that Shakespeare fashioned his character."

"So it is the version of someone who hated Richard. I didn't know that. Why did the sainted Sir Thomas report Morton rather than someone else?"

"Whoever he reported, it would be a Tudor version. But he reported Morton, it seems, because he had been in Morton's household as a boy. And of course Morton had been very much 'in on the act,' so it was natural to write down the version of an eyewitness whose account he could have at first hand."

Marta poked her finger at Oliphant again. "Does your dull fat historian acknowledge that it is a biassed version?"

"Oliphant? Only by implication. He is, to be honest, in a sad muddle himself about Richard. On the same page he says that he was an admirable administrator and general, with an excellent reputation, staid and good-living, very popular by contrast with the Woodville upstarts (the Queen's relations) and that he was 'perfectly unscrupulous and ready to wade through any depth of bloodshed to the crown which lay within his grasp.' On one page he says grudgingly: 'There are reasons for supposing that he was not destitute of a conscience' and then on a later page reports More's picture of a man so tormented by his own deed that he could not sleep. And so on."

"Does your dull fat Oliphant prefer his roses red, then?"

"Oh, I don't think so. I don't think he is consciously Lancastrian. Though now that I think of it he *is* very tolerant of Henry VII's usurpation. I can't remember his saying anywhere, brutally, that Henry hadn't a vestige of a shadow of a claim to the throne."

"Who put him there, then? Henry, I mean."

"The Lancastrian remnant and the upstart Woodvilles, backed, I suppose, by a country revolted by the boys' murder. Apparently anyone with a spice of Lancastrian blood in their veins would do. Henry himself was canny enough to put 'conquest' first in his claim to the throne, and his Lancaster blood second, *'De jure belli et de jure Lancastriae.'* His mother was the heir of an illegitimate son of the third son of Edward III."

"All I know about Henry VII is that he was fantastically rich and fantastically mean. Do you know the lovely Kipling story about his knighting the craftsman not for having done beautiful work but for having saved him the cost of some scroll-work?"

"With a rusty sword from behind the arras. You must be one of the few women who know their Kipling."

"Oh, I'm a very remarkable woman in many ways. So you are no nearer finding out about Richard's personality than you were?"

"No. I'm as completely bewildered as Sir Cuthbert Oliphant, bless his heart. The only difference between us is that I know I'm bewildered and he doesn't seem to be aware of it."

"Have you seen much of my woolly lamb?"

"I've seen nothing of him since his first visit, and that's three days ago. I'm beginning to wonder whether he has repented of his promise."

"Oh, no. I'm sure not. Faithfulness is his banner and creed."

"Like Richard."

"Richard?"

"His motto was *'Loyaulté me lie.'* Loyalty binds me."

There was a tentative tap at the door, and in answer to Grant's invitation, Brent Carradine appeared, hung around with topcoat as usual.

"Oh! I seem to be butting in. I didn't know you were here, Miss Hallard. I met the Statue of Liberty in the corridor there, and she seemed to think you were alone, Mr. Grant."

Grant identified the Statue of Liberty without difficulty. Marta said that she was in the act of going, and that in any case Brent was a much more welcome visitor than she was nowadays. She would leave them in peace to pursue their search for the soul of a murderer.

When he had bowed her politely to the door Brent came back and sat himself down in the visitor's chair with exactly the same air that an Englishman wears when he sits down to his port after the women have left the table. Grant wondered if even the female-ridden American felt a subconscious relief at settling down to a stag party. In answer to Brent's inquiry as to how he was getting on with Oliphant, he said he found Sir Cuthbert admirably lucid.

"I've discovered who the Cat and the Rat were, incidentally. They were entirely respectable knights of the realm: William Catesby and Richard Ratcliffe. Catesby was Speaker of the House of Commons, and Ratcliffe was one of the Commissioners of Peace with Scotland. It's odd how the very sound of words makes a political jingle vicious. The Hog of course was Richard's badge. The White Boar. Do you frequent our English pubs?"

"Sure. They're one of the things I think you do better than us."

"You forgive us our plumbing for the sake of the beer at the Boar."

"I wouldn't go as far as to say I forgive it. I discount it, shall we say?"

"Magnanimous of you. Well, there's something else you've got to discount. That theory of yours that Richard hated his brother because of the contrast between his beauty and Richard's hunchbacked state. According to Sir Cuthbert, the hunchback is a myth. So is the withered arm. It appears that he had no visible deformity. At least none that mattered. His left shoulder was lower than his right, that was all. Did you find out who the contemporary historian is?"

"There isn't one."

"None at *all?*"

"Not in the sense that you mean it. There *were* writers who were contemporaries of Richard, but they wrote after his death. For the Tudors. Which puts them out of court. There is a monkish chronicle in Latin somewhere that is contemporary, but I haven't been able to get hold of it yet. One thing I have discovered though: that account of Richard III is called Sir Thomas More's not because he wrote it but because the manuscript was found among his papers. It was an unfinished copy of an account that appears elsewhere in finished form."

"Well!" Grant considered this with interest. "You mean it was More's own manuscript copy?"

"Yes. In his own writing. Made when he was about thirty-five. In those days, before printing was general, manuscript copies of books were the usual thing."

"Yes. So, if the information came from John Morton, as it did, it is just as likely that the thing was written by Morton."

"Yes."

"Which would certainly account for the—the lack of sensibility. A climber like Morton wouldn't be at all abashed by back-stairs gossip. Do you know about Morton?"

"No."

"He was a lawyer turned churchman, and the greatest pluralist on record. He chose the Lancastrian side and stayed with it until it was clear that Edward IV was home and dried. Then he made his peace with the York side and Edward made him Bishop of Ely. And vicar of God knows how many parishes besides. But after Richard's accession he backed first the Woodvilles and then Henry Tudor and ended up with a cardinal's hat as Henry VII's Archbishop of—"

"Wait a minute!" said the boy, amused. "Of *course* I know Morton. He was Morton of 'Morton's Fork.' 'You can't be spending much so how about something for the King; you're spending such a lot you must be very rich so how about something for the King.'"

"Yes. That's Morton. Henry's best thumb-screw. And I've just thought of a reason why he might have a personal hatred for Richard long before the murder of the boys."

"Yes?"

"Edward took a large bribe from Louis XI to make a dishonourable peace in France. Richard was very angry about that—it really was a disgraceful affair—and washed his hands of the business. Which included refusing a large cash offer. But Morton was very much in favour both of the deal and the cash. Indeed he took a pension from Louis. A very nice pension it was. Two thousand crowns a year. I don't suppose Richard's outspoken comments went down very well, even with good gold for a chaser."

"No. I guess not."

"And of course there would be no preferment for Morton under the strait-laced Richard as there had been under the easy-going Edward. So he would have taken the Woodville side, even if there had been no murder."

"About that murder—" the boy said; and paused.

"Yes?"

"About that murder—the murder of those two boys—isn't it odd that no one talks of it?"

"How do you mean; no one talks of it?"

"These last three days I've been going through contemporary papers; letters and what not. And no one mentions them at all."

"Perhaps they were afraid to. It was a time when it paid to be discreet."

"Yes; but I'll tell you something even odder. You know that Henry brought a Bill of Attainder against Richard, after Bosworth. Before Parliament, I mean. Well, he accuses Richard of cruelty and tyranny but doesn't even mention the murder."

"What!" said Grant, startled.

"Yes, you may well look startled."

"Are you sure!"

"Quite sure."

"But Henry got possession of the Tower immediately on his arrival in London after Bosworth. If the boys were missing it is incredible that he should not publish the fact immediately. It was the trump card in his hand." He lay in surprised silence for a little. The sparrows on the windowsill quarrelled loudly. "I can't make sense of it," he said. "What possible explanation can there be for his omission to make capital out of the fact that the boys were missing?"

Brent shifted his long legs to a more comfortable position. "There is only one explanation," he said. "And that is that the boys weren't missing."

There was a still longer silence this time, while they stared at each other.

"Oh, no, it's nonsense," Grant said. "There must be some obvious explanation that we are failing to see."

"As what, for instance?"

"I don't know. I haven't had time to think."

"I've had nearly three days to think, and I still haven't thought up a reason that will fit. *Nothing* will fit the facts except the conclusion that the boys were alive when Henry took over the Tower. It was a completely unscrupulous Act of Attainder; it accused Richard's followers—the loyal followers of an anointed King fighting against an invader—of treason. Every accusation that Henry could possibly make with any hope of getting away with it was put into the Bill. And the very worst he could accuse Richard of was the usual cruelty and tyranny. The boys aren't even mentioned."

"It's fantastic."

"It's unbelievable. But it is fact."

"What it means is that there was *no contemporary accusation at all.*"

"That's about it."

"But—but wait a minute. Tyrrel was *hanged* for the murder. He actually confessed to it before he died. Wait a minute." He reached for Oliphant and sped through the pages looking for the place. "There's a full account of it here somewhere. There was no mystery about it. Even the Statue of Liberty knew about it."

"*Who?*"

"The nurse you met in the corridor. It was Tyrrel who committed the murder and he was found guilty and confessed before his death."

"Was that when Henry took over in London, then?"

"Wait a moment. Here it is." He skimmed down the paragraph. "No, it was in 1502." He realised all of a sudden what he had just said, and repeated in a new, bewildered tone: "In—1502."

"But—but—but that was—"

"Yes. Nearly twenty years afterwards."

Brent fumbled for his cigarette case, took it out, and then put it hastily away again.

"Smoke if you like," Grant said. "It's a good stiff drink I need. I don't think my brain can be working very well. I feel the way I used to feel as a child when I was blindfolded and whirled round before beginning a blindman's-buff game."

"Yes," said Carradine. He took out a cigarette and lighted it. "Completely in the dark, and more than a little dizzy."

He sat staring at the sparrows.

"Forty million school books can't be wrong," Grant said after a little.

"Can't they?"

"Well, can they!"

"I used to think so, but I'm not so sure nowadays."

"Aren't you being a little sudden in your scepticism?"

"Oh, it wasn't this that shook me."

"What then?"

"A little affair called the Boston Massacre. Ever heard of it?"

"Of course."

"Well, I discovered quite by accident, when I was looking up something at college, that the Boston Massacre consisted of a mob throwing stones at a sentry. The total casualties were four. I was brought up on the Boston Massacre, Mr. Grant. My twenty-eight-inch chest used to swell at the very memory of it. My good red spinach-laden blood used to seethe at the thought of helpless civilians mowed down by the fire of British troops. You can't imagine what a shock it was to find that all it added up to in actual fact was a brawl that wouldn't get more than local reporting in a clash between police and strikers in any American lock-out."

As Grant made no reply to this, he squinted his eyes against the light to see how Grant was taking it. But Grant was staring at the ceiling as if he were watching patterns forming there.

"That's partly why I like to research so much," Carradine volunteered, and settled back to staring at the sparrows.

Presently Grant put his hand out, wordlessly, and Carradine gave him a cigarette and lighted it for him.

They smoked in silence.

It was Grant who interrupted the sparrows' performance.

"Tonypandy," he said.

"How's that?"

But Grant was still far away.

"After all, I've seen the thing at work in my own day, haven't I?" He said, not to Carradine but to the ceiling, "It's Tonypandy."

"And what in heck is Tonypandy?" Brent asked. "It sounds like a patent medicine. Does your child get out of sorts? Does the little face get flushed, the temper short, and the limbs easily tired? Give the little one Tonypandy, and see the radiant results." And then, as Grant made no answer: "All right, then; keep your Tonypandy. I wouldn't have it as a gift."

"Tonypandy," Grant said, still in that sleep-walking voice, "is a place in the South of Wales."

"I knew it was some kind of physic."

"If you go to South Wales you will hear that, in 1910, the Government used troops to shoot down Welsh miners who were striking for their rights. You'll probably hear that Winston Churchill, who was Home Secretary at the time, was responsible. South Wales, you will be told, will never forget Tonypandy!"

Carradine had dropped his flippant air.

"And it wasn't a bit like that?"

"The actual facts are these. The rougher section of the Rhondda valley crowd had got quite out of hand. Shops were being looted and property destroyed. The Chief Constable of Glamorgan sent a request to the Home Office for troops to protect the lieges. If a Chief Constable thinks a situation serious enough to ask for the help of the military a Home Secretary has very little choice in the matter. But Churchill was so horrified at the possibility of the troops coming face to face with a crowd of rioters and having to fire on them, that he stopped the movement of the troops and sent instead a body of plain, solid Metropolitan Police, armed with nothing but their rolled-up mackintoshes. The troops were kept in reserve, and all contact with the rioters was made by unarmed London police. The only bloodshed in the whole affair was a bloody nose or two. The Home Secretary was severely criticised in the House of Commons incidentally for his 'unprecedented intervention.' That was Tonypandy. That is the shooting down by troops that Wales will never forget."

"Yes," Carradine said, considering. "Yes. It's almost a parallel to the Boston affair. Someone blowing up a simple affair to huge proportions for a political end."

"The point is not that it is a parallel. The point is that *every single man* who was there knows that the story is nonsense, and yet it has never been contradicted. It will never be overtaken now. It is a completely untrue story grown to legend while the men who knew it to be untrue looked on and said nothing."

"Yes. That's very interesting; very. History as it is made."

"Yes. History."

"Give me research. After all, the truth of anything at all doesn't lie in someone's account of it. It lies in all the small facts of the time. An advertisement in a paper. The sale of a house. The price of a ring."

Grant went on looking at the ceiling, and the sparrows' clamour came back into the room.

"What amuses you?" Grant said, turning his head at last and catching the expression on his visitor's face.

"This is the first time I've seen you look like a policeman."

"I'm feeling like a policeman. I'm *thinking* like a policeman. I'm asking myself the question that every policeman asks in every case of murder: Who benefits? And for the first time it occurs to me that the glib theory that Richard got rid of the boys to make himself safer on the throne is so much nonsense. Supposing he had got rid of the boys. There were still the boys' five sisters between him and the throne. To say nothing of George's two: the boy and girl. George's son and daughter were barred by their father's attainder; but I take it that an attainder can be reversed, or annulled, or something. If Richard's claim was shaky, all those lives stood between him and safety."

"And did they all survive him?"

"I don't know. But I shall make it my business to find out. The boys' eldest sister certainly did because she became Queen of England as Henry's wife."

"Look, Mr. Grant, let's you and I start at the very beginning of this thing. Without history books, or modern versions, or anyone's opinion about anything. Truth isn't in accounts but in account books."

"A neat phrase," Grant said, complimentary. "Does it mean anything?"

"It means everything. The real history is written in forms not meant as history. In Wardrobe accounts, in Privy Purse expenses, in personal letters, in estate books. If someone, say, insists that Lady Whosit never had a child, and you find in the account book the entry: 'For the son born to my lady on Michaelmas eve: five yards of blue ribbon, fourpence halfpenny' it's a reasonably fair deduction that my lady had a son on Michaelmas eve."

"Yes. I see. All right, where do we begin?"

"You're the investigator. I'm only the looker-upper."

"Research Worker."

"Thanks. What do you want to know?"

"Well, for a start, it would be useful, not to say enlightening, to know how the principals in the case reacted to Edward's death, Edward IV. I mean, Edward died unexpectedly, and his death must have caught everyone on the hop. I'd like to know how the people concerned reacted."

"That's straightforward and easy. I take it you mean what they did and not what they thought."

·"Yes, of course."

"Only historians tell you what they thought. Research workers stick to what they did."

"What they did is all I want to know. I've always been a believer in the old saw that actions speak louder than words."

"Incidentally, what does the sainted Sir Thomas say that Richard did when he heard that his brother was dead?" Brent wanted to know.

"The sainted Sir Thomas (alias John Morton) says that Richard got busy being charming to the Queen and persuading her not to send a large bodyguard to escort the boy prince from Ludlow, meanwhile cooking up a plot to kidnap the boy on his way to London."

"According to the sainted More, then, Richard meant from the very first to supplant the boy."

"Oh, yes."

"Well, we shall find out, at least, who was where and doing what, whether we can deduce their intentions or not."

"That's what I want. Exactly."

"Policeman," jibed the boy. " 'Where were you at five P.M. on the night of the fifteenth inst.?' "

"It works," Grant assured him. "It works."

"Well, I'll go away and work too. I'll be in again as soon as I have got the information you want. I'm very grateful to you, Mr. Grant. This is a lot better than the Peasants."

He floated away into the gathering dusk of the winter afternoon, his train-like coat giving an academic sweep and dignity to his thin young figure.

Grant switched on his lamp, and examined the pattern it made on the ceiling as if he had never seen it before.

It was a unique and engaging problem that the boy had dropped so casually into his lap. As unexpected as it was baffling.

What possible reason could there be for that lack of contemporary accusation?

Henry had not even needed proof that Richard was himself responsible. The boys were in Richard's care. If they were not to be found when the Tower was taken over, then that was far finer, thicker mud to throw at his dead rival than the routine accusations of cruelty and tyranny.

Grant ate his supper without for one moment being conscious either of its taste or its nature.

It was only when The Amazon, taking away his tray, said kindly: "Come now, that's a very good sign. Both rissoles all eaten up to the last crumb!" that he became aware that he had partaken of a meal.

For another hour he watched the lamp-pattern on the ceiling, going over the thing in his mind; going round and round it looking for some small crack that might indicate a way into the heart of the matter.

In the end he withdrew his attention altogether from the problem. Which was his habit when a conundrum proved too round and smooth and solid for immediate solution. If he slept on the proposition it might, tomorrow, show a facet that he had missed.

He looked for something that might stop his mind from harking back to that Act of Attainder, and saw the pile of letters waiting to be acknowledged. Kind, well-wishing letters from all sorts of people, including a few old lags. The really likable old lags were an outmoded type, growing fewer and fewer daily. Their place had been taken by brash young thugs with not a spark of humanity in their egocentric souls, as illiterate as puppies and as pitiless as a circular saw. The old professional burglar was apt to be as individual as the member of any other profession, and as little vicious. Quiet little domestic men, interested in family holidays and the children's tonsils; or odd bachelors devoted to cage-birds, or second-hand bookshops, or complicated and infallible betting systems. Old-fashioned types.

No modern thug would write to say that he was sorry that a

"busy" was laid aside. No such idea would ever cross a modern thug's mind.

Writing a letter when lying on one's back is a laborious business, and Grant shied away from it. But the top envelope on the pile bore the writing of his cousin Laura, and Laura would become anxious if she had no answer at all from him. Laura and he had shared summer holidays as children, and had been a little in love with each other all through one Highland summer, and that made a bond between them that had never been broken. He had better send Laura a note to say that he was alive.

He read her letter again, smiling a little; and the waters of the Turlie sounded in his ears and slid under his eyes, and he could smell the sweet cold smell of a Highland moor in winter and he forgot for a little that he was a hospital patient and that life was sordid and boring and claustrophobic.

Pat sends what would be his love if he were a little older or just a little younger. Being nine, he says: "Tell Alan I was asking for him," and has a fly of his own invention waiting to be presented to you when you come on sick-leave. He is a little in disgrace at the moment in school, having learned for the first time that the Scots sold Charles the First to the English and having decided that he can no longer belong to such a nation. He is therefore, I understand, conducting a one-man protest strike against all things Scottish, and will learn no history, sing no song, nor memorise any geography pertaining to so deplorable a country. He announced going to bed last night that he has decided to apply for Norwegian citizenship.

Grant took his letter pad from the table and wrote in pencil:

Dearest Laura,
    Would you be unbearably surprised to learn that the Princes in the Tower survived Richard III?

As ever
Alan.

P.S. I am nearly well again.

Chapter 9

"Do you know that the Bill attainting Richard III before Parliament didn't mention the murder of the Princes in the Tower?" Grant asked the surgeon next morning.

"Really?" said the surgeon. "That's odd, isn't it?"

"Extremely odd. Can you think of an explanation?"

"Probably trying to minimise the scandal. For the sake of the family."

"He wasn't succeeded by one of his family. He was the last of his line. His successor was the first Tudor. Henry VII."

"Yes, of course. I'd forgotten. I was never any good at history. I used to use the history period to do my home algebra. They don't manage to make history very interesting in schools. Perhaps more portraits might help." He glanced up at the Richard portrait and went back to his professional inspection. "That is looking very nice and healthy, I'm glad to say. No pain to speak of now?"

And he went away, kindly and casual. He was interested in faces because they were part of his trade, but history was just something that he used for other purposes; something that he set aside in favour of algebra under the desk. He had living bodies in his care, and the future in his hands; he had no thought to spare for problems academic.

Matron, too, had more immediate worries. She listened politely while he put his difficulty to her, but he had the impression that she might say: "I should see the almoner about it if I were you." It was not her affair. She looked down from her regal eminence at the great hive below her buzzing with activity, all of it urgent and important; she could hardly be expected to focus her gaze on something more than four hundred years away.

He wanted to say: "But you of all people should be interested in what can happen to royalty; in the frailness of your reputation's worth. Tomorrow a whisper may destroy you." But he was already guiltily conscious that to hinder a Matron with irrelevances was to lengthen her already lengthy morning round without reason or excuse.

The Midget did not know what an Attainder was, and made it clear that she did not care.

"It's becoming an obsession with you, that thing," she said, leaning her head at the portrait. "It's not healthy. Why don't you read some of those nice books?"

Even Marta, to whose visit he had looked forward so that he could put this odd, new proposition to her and see her reaction, even Marta was too full of wrath with Madeleine March to pay attention to him.

"After practically promising me that she would write it! After all our get-togethers and my plans for when this endless thing finally comes to an end. I had even talked to Jacques about clothes! And now she decides that she must write one of her awful little detective stories. She says she must write it while it is fresh—whatever it is."

He listened to Marta's grieving with sympathy—good plays were the scarcest commodity in the world and good playwrights worth their weight in platinum—but it was like watching something through a window. The fifteenth century was more actual to him this morning than any ongoings in Shaftesbury Avenue.

"I don't suppose it will take her long to write her detective book," he said comfortingly.

"Oh, no. She does them in six weeks or so. But now that she's off the chain how do I know that I'll ever get her on again? Tony Savilla wants her to write a Marlborough play for him, and you know what Tony is when he sets his heart on something. He'd talk the pigeons off the Admiralty Arch."

She came back to the Attainder problem, briefly, before she took her leave.

"There's sure to be some explanation, my dear," she said from the door.

Of *course* there's an explanation, he wanted to shout after her, but what is it? The thing is against all likelihood and sense. Historians say that the murder caused a great revulsion of feeling against Richard, that he was hated for the crime by the common people of England, and that was why they welcomed a stranger in his place. And yet when the tale of his wrongdoing is placed before Parliament there is no mention of the crime.

Richard was dead when that complaint was drawn up, and his followers in flight or exile; his enemies were free to bring against him any charge they could think of. And they *had not thought of that spectacular murder.*

Why?

The country was reputedly ringing with the scandal of the boys' disappearance. The very recent scandal. And when his enemies collected his alleged offences against morality and the State they had not included Richard's most spectacular piece of infamy.

Why?

Henry needed every small featherweight of advantage in the precarious newness of his accession. He was unknown to the country at large and he had no right by blood to be where he was. But he hadn't used the overwhelming advantage that Richard's published crime would have given him.

Why?

He was succeeding a man of great reputation, known personally to the people from the Marches of Wales to the Scots border, a man universally liked and admired until the disappearance of his nephews. And yet he omitted to use the one real advantage he had against Richard, the unforgivable, the abhorred thing.

Why?

Only The Amazon seemed concerned about the oddity that was engaging his mind; and she not out of any feeling for Richard but because her conscientious soul was distressed at any possibility of mistake. The Amazon would go all the way down the corridor and back again to tear off a page in a loose-leaf calendar that someone had forgotten to remove. But her instinct to be worried was less strong than her instinct to comfort.

"You don't need to worry about it," she said, soothing. "There'll be some quite simple explanation that you haven't thought of. It'll come to you sometime when you're thinking of something else altogether. That's usually how I remember where something I've mislaid is. I'll be putting the kettle on in the pantry, or counting the sterile dressings as Sister doles them out, and suddenly I'll think: 'Goodness, I left it in my Burberry pocket.' Whatever the thing was, I mean. So you don't have to worry about it."

Sergeant Williams was in the wilds of Essex helping the local constabulary to decide who had hit an old shop-keeper over the head with a brass scale-weight and left her dead among the shoelaces and liquorice all-sorts, so there was no help from the Yard.

There was no help from anyone until young Carradine turned up again three days later. Grant thought that his normal insouciance had a deeper tinge than usual; there was almost an air of self-congratulation about him. Being a well-brought-up child he inquired politely about Grant's physical progress, and having been reassured on that point he pulled some notes out of the capacious pocket of his coat and beamed through his horn-rims at his colleague.

"I wouldn't have the sainted More as a present," he observed pleasantly.

"You're not being offered him. There are no takers."

"He's way off the beam. Way off."

"I suspected as much. Let us have the facts. Can you begin on the day Edward died?"

"Sure. Edward died on April the 9th, 1483. In London. I mean, in Westminster; which wasn't the same thing then. The Queen and the daughters were living there, *and* the younger boy. I think. The young Prince was doing lessons at Ludlow Castle in charge of the Queen's brother, Lord Rivers. The Queen's relations are very much to the fore, did you know? The place is just lousy with Woodvilles."

"Yes, I know. Go on. Where was Richard?"

"On the Scottish border."

"What!"

"Yes, I said: on the Scottish border. Caught away off base. But does he yell for a horse and go posting off to London? He does not."

"What did he do?"

"He arranged for a requiem mass at York, to which all the nobility of the North were summoned, and in his presence they took an oath of loyalty to the young Prince."

"Interesting," Grant said dryly. "What did Rivers do? The Queen's brother?"

"On the 24th of April he set out with the Prince for London. With two thousand men and a large supply of arms."

"What did he want the arms for?"

"Don't ask me. I'm only a research worker. Dorset, the elder of the Queen's two sons by her first marriage, took over both the arsenal and the treasure in the Tower and began to fit up ships to command the Channel. And Council orders were issued *in the name of Rivers and Dorset*—'*avunculus Regis*' *and* '*frater Regis uteri-nus*' respectively—with no mention of Richard. Which was decid-edly off-colour when you remember—if you ever knew—that in his will Edward had appointed Richard guardian of the boy and Pro-tector of the Kingdom in case of any minority. Richard alone, mind you, without a colleague."

"Yes, that is in character, at least. He must always have had com-plete faith in Richard. Both as a person and as an administrator. Did Richard come south with a young army too?"

"No. He came with six hundred gentlemen of the North, all in deep mourning. He arrived at Northampton on April the 29th. He had apparently expected to join up with the Ludlow crowd there; but that is report and you have only a historian's word for it. But the Ludlow procession—Rivers and the young Prince—had gone on to Stoney Stratford without waiting for him. The person who actually met him at Northampton was the Duke of Buckingham with three hundred men. Do you know Buckingham?"

"We have a nodding acquaintance. He was a friend of Edward's."

"Yes. He arrived post haste from London."

"With the news of what was going on."

"It's a fair deduction. He wouldn't bring three hundred men just to express his condolences. Anyhow a Council was held there and then—he had all the human material for a proper Council in his own train and Buckingham's, and Rivers and his three aides were arrested and sent to the North, while Richard went on with the young Prince to London. They arrived in London on the 4th of May."

"Well, that is very nice and clear. And what is clearest of all is that, considering time and distances, the sainted More's account of his writing sweet letters to the Queen to induce her to send only a small escort for the boy, is nonsense."

"Bunk."

"Indeed, Richard did just what one would expect him to do. He must of course have known the provisions of Edward's will. What his actions suggest is just what one would expect them to suggest, his own sorrow and his care for the boy. A requiem mass and an oath of allegiance."

"Yes."

"Where does the break in this orthodox pattern come? I mean: in Richard's behaviour."

"Oh, not for a long time. When he arrived in London he found that the Queen, the younger boy, the daughters, and her first-marriage son, Dorset, had all bolted into sanctuary at Westminster. But apart from that things seem to have been normal."

"Did he take the boy to the Tower?"

Carradine riffled through his notes. "I don't remember. Perhaps I didn't get that. I was only—Oh, yes, here it is. No, he took the boy to the Bishop's Palace in St. Paul's Churchyard, and he himself went to stay with his mother at Baynard's Castle. Do you know where that was? I don't."

"Yes. It was the Yorks' town house. It stood on the bank of the river just a little way west of St. Paul's."

"Oh. Well, he stayed there until June the 5th, when his wife arrived from the North and they went to stay in a house called Crosby Place."

"It is still called Crosby Place. It has been moved to Chelsea, and the window Richard put into it may not still be there—I haven't seen it lately—but the building is there."

"It is?" Carradine said, delighted. "I'll go and see it right away. It's a very domestic tale when you think of it, isn't it? Staying with his mother until his wife gets to town and then moving in with her. Was Crosby Place theirs, then?"

"Richard had leased it, I think. It belonged to one of the Aldermen of London. So there is no suggestion of opposition to his Protectorship, or of change of plans, when he arrived in London."

"Oh, no. He was acknowledged Protector before he ever arrived in London."

"How do you know that?"

"In the Patent Rolls he is called Protector on two occasions—let me see—April 21st (that's less than a fortnight after Edward's death) and May the 2nd (that's two days before he arrived in London at all)."

"All right; I'm sold. And no fuss? No hint of trouble?"

"Not that I can find. On the 5th of June he gave detailed orders for the boy's coronation on the 22nd. He even had letters of summons sent out to the forty squires who would be made knights of the Bath. It seems it was the custom for the King to knight them on the occasion of his coronation."

"The 5th," Grant said musingly. "And he fixed the coronation for the 22nd. He wasn't leaving himself much time for a switch-over."

"No. There's even a record of the order for the boy's coronation clothes."

"And then what?"

"Well," Carradine said, apologetic, "that's as far as I've got. Something happened at a Council—on the 8th of June, I think—but the contemporary account is in the *Mémoires* of Philippe de Comines and I haven't been able to get hold of a copy so far. But someone promised to let me see a copy of Mandrot's 1901 printing of it tomorrow. It seems that the Bishop of Bath broke some news to the Council on June the 8th. Do you know the Bishop of Bath? His name was Stillington."

"Never heard of him."

"He was a fellow of All Souls, whatever that is, and a Canon of York, whatever *that* may be."

"Both learned and respectable, it appears."

"Well, we'll see."

"Have you turned up any contemporary historians—other than Comines?"

"Not any, so far, who wrote before Richard's death. Comines has a French bias but not a Tudor one, so he's more trustworthy than an Englishman writing about Richard under the Tudors would be. But I've got a lovely sample for you of how history is made. I found it when I was looking up the contemporary writers. You know that one of the things they tell about Richard III is that he killed Henry VI's only son in cold blood after the battle of Tewkesbury? Well, believe it or not, that story is made up out of whole cloth. You can trace it from the very time it was first told. It's the perfect answer to people who say there's no smoke without fire. Believe me, this smoke was made by rubbing two pieces of dry stick together."

"But Richard was just a boy at the time of Tewkesbury."

"He was eighteen, I think. And a very bonny fighter by all contemporary accounts. They were the same age, Henry's son and Richard. Well, *all* the contemporary accounts, of whatever complexion, are unanimous in saying that he was killed during the battle. Then the fun begins."

Carradine fluttered through his notes impatiently.

"Goldarn it, what did I do with it? Ah. Here we are. Now. Fabyan, writing for Henry VII, says that the boy was captured and brought before Edward IV, was struck in the face by Edward with his gauntlet and immediately slain by the King's servants. Nice? But Polydore Virgil goes one better. He says that the murder was done in person by George, Duke of Clarence, Richard, Duke of Gloucester, and William, Lord Hastings. Hall adds Dorset to the murderers. But that didn't satisfy Holinshed: Holinshed reports that it was Richard, Duke of Gloucester, who struck the first blow. How do you like that? Best quality Tonypandy, isn't it?"

"Pure Tonypandy. A dramatic story with not a word of truth in it. If you can bear to listen to a few sentences of the sainted More, I'll give you another sample of how history is made."

"The sainted More makes me sick at the stomach but I'll listen." Grant looked for the paragraph he wanted, and read:

Some wise men also ween that his drift [that is, Richard's drift] covertly conveyed, lacked not in helping forth his brother Clarence to his death; which he resisted openly, howbeit somewhat, as men deemed, more faintly than he that were heartily minded to his weal. And they who deem thus think that he, long time in King Edward's life, forethought to be King in case that the King his brother (whose life he looked that evil diet should shorten) should happen to decease (as indeed he did) while his children were young. And they deem that for this intent he was glad of his brother Clarence's death, whose life must needs have hindered him so intending whether the same Clarence had kept true to his nephew the young King or enterprised to be King himself. But of all this point there is no certainty, and whoso divineth upon conjectures may as well shoot too far as too short.

"The mean, burbling, insinuating old bastard," said Carradine sweetly.

"Were you clever enough to pick out the one positive statement in all that speculation?"

"Oh, yes."

"You spotted it? That was smart of you. I had to read it three times before I got the one unqualified fact."

"That Richard protested openly against his brother George being put to death."

"Yes."

"Of course, with all that 'men say' stuff," Carradine observed, "the impression that is left is just the opposite. I told you. I wouldn't have the sainted More as a present."

"I think we ought to remember that it is John Morton's account and not the sainted More's."

"The sainted More sounds better. Besides, he liked the thing well enough to be copying it out."

Grant, the one-time soldier, lay thinking of the expert handling of that very sticky situation at Northampton.

"It was neat of him to mop up Rivers's two thousand without any open clash."

"I expect they preferred the King's brother to the Queen's brother, if they were faced with it."

"Yes. And of course a fighting man has a better chance with troops than a man who writes books."

"Did Rivers write books?"

"He wrote the first book printed in England. Very cultured, he was."

"Huh. It doesn't seem to have taught him not to try conclusions with a man who was a brigadier at eighteen and general before he was twenty-five. That's one thing that has surprised me, you know."

"Richard's qualities as a soldier?"

"No, his youth. I'd always thought of him as a middle-aged grouch. He was only thirty-two when he was killed at Bosworth."

"Tell me: when Richard took over the boy's guardianship, at Stoney Stratford, did he make a clean sweep of the Ludlow crowd? I mean, was the boy separated from all the people he had been growing up with?"

"Oh, no. His tutor, Dr. Alcock, came on to London with him, for one."

"So there was no panic clearing-out of everyone who might be on the Woodville side: everyone who might influence the boy against him."

"Seems not. Just the four arrests."

"Yes. A very neat, discriminating operation altogether. I felicitate Richard Plantagenet."

"I'm positively beginning to like the guy. Well. I'm going along now to look at Crosby Place. I'm tickled pink at the thought of actually looking at a place he lived in. And tomorrow I'll have that copy of Comines, and let you know what he says about events in England in 1483, and what Robert Stillington, Bishop of Bath, told the Council in June of that year."

Chapter 10

*W*hat Stillington told the Council on that summer day in 1483 was, Grant learned, that he had married Edward IV to Lady Eleanor Butler, a daughter of the first Earl of Shrewsbury, before Edward married Elizabeth Woodville.

"Why had he kept it to himself so long?" he asked when he had digested the news.

"Edward had commanded him to keep it secret. Naturally."

"Edward seems to have made a habit of secret marriages," Grant said dryly.

"Well, it must have been difficult for him, you know, when he came up against unassailable virtue. There was nothing for it but marriage. And he was so used to getting his own way with women—what with his looks and his crown—that he couldn't have taken very resignedly to frustration."

"Yes. That was the pattern of the Woodville marriage. The indestructibly virtuous beauty with the gilt hair, and the secret wedding. So Edward had used the same formula on a previous occasion, if Stillington's story was true. Was it true?"

"Well, in Edward's time, it seems, he was in turn both Privy Seal and Lord Chancellor, and he had been an ambassador to Brittany. So Edward either owed him something or liked him. And he, on his part, had no reason to cook up anything against Edward. Supposing he was the cooking sort."

"No, I suppose not."

"Anyway, the thing was put to Parliament so we don't have to take just Stillington's word for it."

"To Parliament!"

"Sure. Everything was open and above board. There was a very long meeting of the Lords at Westminster on the 9th. Stillington brought in his evidence and his witnesses, and a report was prepared to put before Parliament when it assembled on the 25th. On the 10th Richard sent a letter to the city of York asking for troops to protect and support him."

"Ha! Trouble at last."

"Yes. On the 11th he sent a similar letter to his cousin Lord Nevill. So the danger was real."

"It must have been real. A man who dealt so economically with that unexpected and very nasty situation at Northampton wouldn't be one to lose his head at a threat."

"On the 20th he went with a small body of retainers to the Tower—did you know that the Tower was the royal residence in London, and not a prison at all?"

"Yes, I knew that. It got its prison meaning only because nowadays being sent to the Tower has one meaning only. And of course because, being the royal castle in London, and the only strong keep, offenders were sent there for safe keeping in the days before we had His Majesty's Prisons. What did Richard go to the Tower for?"

"He went to interrupt a meeting of the conspirators, and arrested Lord Hastings, Lord Stanley, and one John Morton, Bishop of Ely."

"I thought we would arrive at John Morton sooner or later!"

"A proclamation was issued, giving details of the plot to murder Richard, but apparently no copy now exists. Only one of the conspirators was beheaded, and that one, oddly enough, seems to have been an old friend of both Edward and Richard. Lord Hastings."

"Yes, according to the sainted More he was rushed down to the courtyard and beheaded on the nearest log."

"Rushed nothing," said Carradine disgustedly. "He was beheaded a week later. There's a contemporary letter about it that gives the date. Moreover, Richard couldn't have done it out of sheer vindictiveness, because he granted Hastings's forfeited estates to his widow, and restored the children's right of succession to them— which they had automatically lost."

"No, the death of Hastings must have been inevitable," said Grant, who was thumbing through More's *Richard III.* "Even the sainted More says: 'Undoubtedly the Protector loved him well, and was loth to have lost him.' What happened to Stanley and to John Morton?"

"Stanley was pardoned—what are you groaning about?"

"Poor Richard. That was his death warrant."

"Death warrant? How could pardoning Stanley be his death warrant?"

"Because it was Stanley's sudden decision to go over to the other side that lost Richard the battle of Bosworth."

"You don't say."

"Odd to think that if Richard had seen to it that Stanley went to the block like his much-loved Hastings, he would have won the battle of Bosworth, there would never have been any Tudors, and the hunchbacked monster that appears in Tudor tradition would never have been invented. On his previous showing he would probably have had the best and most enlightened reign in history. What was done to Morton?"

"Nothing."

"Another mistake."

"Or at least nothing to signify. He was put into gentlemanly detention under the care of Buckingham. The people who did go to the block were the heads of the conspiracy that Richard had arrested at Northampton: Rivers and Co. And Jane Shore was sentenced to do penance."

"Jane Shore? What on earth has she got to do with the case? I thought she was Edward's mistress?"

"So she was. But Hastings inherited her from Edward, it seems. Or rather—let me see—Dorset did. And she was go-between the Hastings side of the conspiracy and the Woodville side. One of Richard's letters existing today is about her. About Jane Shore."

"What about her?"

"His Solicitor-General wanted to marry her; when he was King, I mean."

"And he agreed?"

"He agreed. It's a lovely letter. More in sorrow than in anger—with a kind of twinkle in it."

" 'Lord, what fools these mortals be!' "

"That's it exactly."

"No vindictiveness there, either, it seems."

"No. Quite the opposite. You know, I know it isn't my business to think or draw deductions—I'm just the Research Worker—but it does strike me that Richard's ambition was to put an end to the York-Lancaster fight once and for all."

"What makes you think that?"

"Well, I've been looking at his coronation lists. It was the best-attended coronation on record, incidentally. You can't help being struck by the fact that practically nobody stayed away. Lancaster *or* York."

"Including the weather-cock Stanley, I suppose."

"I suppose so. I don't know them well enough to remember them individually."

"Perhaps you're right about his wanting a final end to the York-Lancaster feud. Perhaps his lenience with Stanley was due to that very thing."

"Was Stanley a Lancastrian, then?"

"No, but he was married to an abnormally rabid one. His wife was Margaret Beaufort, and the Beauforts were the reverse side, so to speak—the illegitimate side—of the Lancaster family. Not that her by-blow side worried her. *Or* her son."

"Who was her son?"

"Henry VII."

Carradine whistled, long and low.

"You actually mean to say that Lady Stanley was Henry's mother."

"She was. By her first husband Edmund Tudor."

"But—but Lady Stanley had a place of honour at Richard's coronation. She carried the Queen's train. I noticed that because I thought it quaint. Carrying the train, I mean. In our country we don't carry trains. It's an honour, I take it."

"It's a thundering great honour. Poor Richard. Poor Richard. It didn't work."

"What didn't?"

"Magnanimity." He lay thinking about it while Carradine shuffled through his notes. "So Parliament accepted the evidence of Stillington."

"They did more. They incorporated it into an Act, giving Richard the title to the crown. It was called Titulus Regius."

"For a holy man of God, Stillington wasn't cutting a very glorious figure. But I suppose that to have talked sooner would have been to compass his own ruin."

"You're a bit hard on him, aren't you? There wasn't any need to talk sooner. No harm was being done anyone."

"What about Lady Eleanor Butler?"

"She died in a convent. She's buried in the Church of the White Carmelites at Norwich, in case you're interested. As long as Edward was alive no wrong was being done anyone. But when it came to the question of succession, then he *had* to talk, whatever kind of figure he cut."

"Yes. Of course you're right. So the children were proclaimed illegitimate, in open Parliament. And Richard was crowned. With all the nobility of England in attendance. Was the Queen still in sanctuary?"

"Yes. But she had let the younger boy join his brother."

"When was that?"

Carradine searched through his notes. "On June the 16th. I've put: 'At the request of the Archbishop of Canterbury. Both boys living at the Tower.' "

"That was after the news had broken. The news that they were illegitimate."

"Yes." He tidied his notes into some kind of neatness and put them away in the enormous pocket. "That seems to be all, to date. But here's the pay-off." He gathered his train from either side of him on to his knees with a gesture that both Marta and King Richard might have envied. "You know that Act, that Titulus Regius."

"Yes; what about it?"

"Well, when Henry VII came to the throne he ordered that the Act should be repealed, without being read. He ordered that the Act itself should be destroyed, and forbade any copies to be kept. Anyone who kept a copy was to be fined and imprisoned during his pleasure."

Grant stared in great astonishment.

"*Henry VII!*" he said. "Why? What possible difference could it make to him?"

"I haven't a glimmer of an idea. But I mean to find out before I'm much older. Meanwhile, here is something to keep you amused till the Statue of Liberty brings your British tea."

He dropped a paper on to Grant's chest.

"What is this?" Grant said, looking at the torn-out page of a note-book.

"It's that letter of Richard's about Jane Shore. I'll be seeing you."

Left alone by himself in the quiet, Grant turned over the page and read.

The contrast between the sprawling childish handwriting and the formal phrases of Richard's imagining was piquant in the extreme. But what neither the untidy modern script nor the dignified phrases could destroy was the flavour of the letter. The bouquet of good humour that came up from the page as a bouquet comes up from a good-humoured wine. Translated into modern terms it said:

I hear to my great astonishment that Tom Lynom wants to marry Will Shore's wife. Apparently he is infatuated with her, and is quite determined about it. Do, my dear Bishop, send for him and see if you can talk some sense into his silly head. If you can't, and if there is no bar to their marriage from the Church's point of view, then I agree to it, but tell him to postpone the marriage till I am back in London. Meanwhile this will suffice to secure her release, on surety for her good behaviour, and I suggest that you hand her over for the time being to the care of her father, or anyone else who seems good to you.

It was certainly, as young Carradine had said, "more in sorrow than in anger." Indeed, considering that it was written about a woman who had done him a deadly wrong, its kindness and good temper were remarkable. And this was a case where no personal advantage could come to him from magnanimity. The broadmindedness that had sought for a York-Lancaster peace might not have been disinterested; it would have been enormously to his advantage to have a united country to rule. But this letter to the Bishop of Lincoln was a small private matter, and the release of Jane Shore of no importance to anyone but the infatuated Tom Lynom. Richard had nothing to gain by his generosity. His instinct to see a friend happy was apparently greater than his instinct for revenge.

Indeed, this instinct for revenge seemed to be lacking to a degree that would be surprising in any red-blooded male, and quite astonishing in the case of that reputed monster Richard III.

Chapter 11

*T*he letter lasted Grant very nicely until The Amazon brought his tea. He listened to the twentieth-century sparrows on his windowsill and marvelled that he should be reading phrases that formed in a man's mind more than four hundred years ago. What a fantastic idea it would have seemed to Richard that anyone would be reading that short, intimate letter about Shore's wife, and wondering about him, four hundred years afterwards.

"There's a letter for you, now isn't that nice?" The Amazon said, coming in with his two pieces of bread-and-butter and a rock bun.

Grant took his eyes from the uncompromising healthiness of the rock bun and saw that the letter was from Laura.

He opened it with pleasure.

Dear Alan [said Laura]

Nothing (repeat: nothing) would surprise me about history. Scotland has large monuments to two women martyrs drowned for their faith, in spite of the fact that they weren't drowned at all and neither was a martyr anyway. They were convicted of treason—fifth column work for the projected invasion from Holland, I think. Anyhow on a purely civil charge. They were reprieved *on their own petition* by the Privy Council, and the reprieve is in the Privy Council Register to this day.

This, of course, hasn't daunted the Scottish collectors of martyrs, and the tale of their sad end, complete with heart-rending dialogue, is to be found in every Scottish bookcase. Entirely different dialogue in each collection. And the gravestone of one of the women, in Wigtown churchyard, reads:

Murdered for owning Christ supreme
Head of his Church, and no more crime
But her not owning Prelacy

And not abjuring Presbytry
Within the sea tied to a stake
She suffered for Christ Jesus sake.

They are even a subject for fine Presbyterian sermons, I understand—though on that point I speak from hearsay. And tourists come and shake their heads over the monuments with their moving inscriptions, and a very profitable time is had by all.

All this in spite of the fact that the original collector of the material, canvassing the Wigtown district only forty years after the supposed martyrdom and at the height of the Presbyterian triumph, complains that "many deny that this happened"; and couldn't find any eyewitnesses at all.

It is very good news that you are convalescent, and a great relief to us all. If you manage it well your sick leave can coincide with the spring run. The water is very low at the moment, but by the time you are better it should be deep enough to please both the fish and you.

Love from us all,
Laura

P.S. It's an odd thing but when you tell someone the true facts of a mythical tale they are indignant not with the teller but with you. They don't *want* to have their ideas upset. It rouses some vague uneasiness in them, I think, and they resent it. So they reject it and refuse to think about it. If they were merely indifferent it would be natural and understandable. But it is much stronger than that, much more positive. They are annoyed.

Very odd, isn't it?

More Tonypandy, he thought.

He began to wonder just how much of the school book which up to now had represented British history for him was Tonypandy.

He went back, now that he knew a few facts, to read the sainted More again. To see how the relevant passages sounded now.

If, when he had read them merely by the light of his own critical mind, they had seemed to him curiously tattling, and in places absurd, they now read plain abominable. He was what Laura's small

Pat was in the habit of calling "scunnered." And he was also puzzled.

This was Morton's account. Morton the eyewitness, the participant. Morton must have known with minute accuracy what took place between the beginning and end of June that year. And yet there was no mention of Lady Eleanor Butler; no mention of Titulus Regius. According to Morton, Richard's case has been that Edward was previously married to his mistress Elizabeth Lucy. But Elizabeth Lucy, Morton pointed out, had denied that she was ever married to the King.

Why did Morton set up a ninepin just to knock it down again?

Why the substitution of Elizabeth Lucy for Eleanor Butler?

Because he could deny with truth that Lucy was ever married to the King, but could not do the same in the case of Eleanor Butler?

Surely the presumption was that it was very important to someone or other that Richard's claim that the children were illegitimate should be shown to be untenable.

And since Morton—in the handwriting of the sainted More—was writing for Henry VII, then that someone was presumably Henry VII. The Henry VII who had destroyed Titulus Regius and forbidden anyone to keep a copy.

Something Carradine had said came back into Grant's mind.

Henry had caused the Act to be repealed *without being read*.

It was so important to Henry that the contents of the Act should not be brought to mind that he had specially provided for its unquoted destruction.

Why should it be of such importance to Henry VII?

How could it matter to *Henry* what Richard's rights were? It was not as if he could say: Richard's claim was a trumped-up one, therefore mine is good. Whatever wretched small claim Henry Tudor might have was a Lancastrian one, and the heirs of York did not enter into the matter.

Then why should it have been of such paramount importance to Henry that the contents of Titulus Regius should be forgotten?

Why hide away Eleanor Butler, and bring in her place a mistress whom no one ever suggested was married to the King?

This problem lasted Grant very happily till just before supper, when the porter came in with a note for him.

"The front hall says that young American friend of yours left this for you," the porter said, handing him a folded sheet of paper.

"Thank you," said Grant. "What do you know about Richard the Third?"

"Is there a prize?"

"What for?"

"The quiz."

"No, just the satisfaction of intellectual curiosity. What *do* you know about Richard III?"

"He was the first multiple murderer."

"Multiple? I thought it was two nephews?"

"No, oh, no. I don't know much history but I do know that. Murdered his brother, and his cousin, and the poor old King in the Tower, and then finished off with his little nephews. A wholesale performer."

Grant considered this.

"If I told you that he never murdered anyone at all, what would you say?"

"I'd say that you're perfectly entitled to your opinion. Some people believe the earth is flat. Some people believe the world is going to end in A.D. 2000. Some people believe that it began less than five thousand years ago. You'll hear far funnier things than that at Marble Arch of a Sunday."

"So you wouldn't even entertain the idea for a moment?"

"I find it entertaining all right, but not what you might call very plausible, shall we say? But don't let me stand in your way. Try it out on a better bombing range. You take it to Marble Arch one Sunday, and I'll bet you'll find followers aplenty. Maybe start a movement."

He made a gay sketchy half-salute with his hand and went away humming to himself, secure and impervious.

So help me, Grant thought, I'm not far off it. If I get any deeper into this thing I *will* be standing on a soapbox at Marble Arch.

He unfolded the message from Carradine, and read: "You said that you wanted to know whether the other heirs to the throne survived Richard. As well as the boys, I mean. I forgot to say: would you make out a list of them for me, so that I can look them up. I think it's going to be important."

Well, if the world in general went on its humming way, brisk and uncaring, at least he had young America on his side.

He put aside the sainted More, with its Sunday-paper accounts of hysterical scenes and wild accusations, and reached for the sober student's account of history so that he might catalogue the possible rivals to Richard III in the English succession.

And as he put down More-Morton, he was reminded of something.

That hysterical scene during the Council in the Tower which was reported by More, that frantic outburst on Richard's part against the sorcery that had withered his arm, had been against Jane Shore.

The contrast between the reported scene, pointless and repellent even to a disinterested reader, and the kind, tolerant, almost casual air of the letter that Richard had actually written about her, was staggering.

So help me, he thought again, if I had to choose between the man who wrote that account and the man who wrote that letter I'd take the man who wrote the letter, whatever either of them had done besides.

The thought of Morton made him postpone his listing of the York heirs until he had found out what eventually became of John Morton. It seemed that, having used his leisure as Buckingham's guest to organise a joint Woodville-Lancastrian effort (in which Henry Tudor would bring ships and troops from France and Dorset and the rest of the Woodville tribe would meet him with what English malcontents they could induce to follow them), he escaped to his old hunting ground in the Ely district, and from there to the continent. And did not come back until he came in the wake of a Henry who had won both Bosworth and a crown; being himself on the way to Canterbury and a cardinal's hat and immortality as Morton of "Morton's Fork." Almost the only thing that any schoolboy remembered about his master Henry VII.

For the rest of the evening Grant pottered happily through the history book, collecting heirs.

There was no lack of them. Edward's five, George's boy and girl. And if these were discounted, the first through illegitimacy and the second through attainder, there was another possible: his elder sister Elizabeth's boy. Elizabeth was Duchess of Suffolk, and her son was John de la Pole, Earl of Lincoln.

There was, too, in the family, a boy whose existence Grant had not suspected. It appeared that the delicate child at Middleham was not Richard's only son. He had a love-child; a boy called John. John of Gloucester. A boy of no importance in rank but acknowledged and living in the household. It was an age when a bend sinister was accepted without grief. Indeed the Conqueror had made it fashionable. And conquerors from then on had advertised its lack of disadvantage. By way of compensation, perhaps.

Edward	Elizabeth	George	Richard
Edward, Prince of Wales	John de la Pole, Earl of Lincoln	Edward, Earl of Warwick	John of Gloucester
Richard, Duke of York		Margaret, Countess of Salisbury	
Elizabeth			
Cicely			
Anne			
Katherine			
Bridget			

He copied it out again for young Carradine's use, wondering how it could ever have occurred to anyone, Richard most of all, that the elimination of Edward's two boys would have kept him safe from rebellion. The place was what young Carradine would call just lousy with heirs. Swarming with focuses (or was it foci?) for disaffection.

It was brought home to him for the first time not only what a useless thing the murder of the boys would have been, but what a *silly thing*.

And if there was anything that Richard of Gloucester was not, beyond a shadow of doubt, it was silly.

He looked up Oliphant to see what Oliphant had to say on this obvious crack in the story.

"It is strange," said Oliphant, "that Richard does not seem to have published any version of their deaths."

It was more than strange: it was incomprehensible.

If Richard had wanted to murder his brother's sons then he most certainly would have done it expertly. They would have died of a fever, and their bodies would have been exposed to the public gaze as royal bodies habitually were, so that all men would know that they were in fact departed from this life.

No one can say that a man is incapable of murder—after long years on the Embankment Grant knew that only too well—but one can be sure to within one degree of the absolute when a man is incapable of silliness.

Oliphant had no doubts about the murder, nevertheless. Richard, according to Oliphant, was Richard the Monster. Perhaps when an historian was covering a field as large as the Middle Ages and the Renaissance he had no time to stop and analyse detail. Oliphant accepted the sainted More, even while he paused in flight to wonder at an oddity here and there. Not seeing that the oddities ate away at the very foundations of his theory.

Having Oliphant in his hand, he went on with Oliphant. On through the triumphal progress through England after the coronation. Oxford, Gloucester, Worcester, Warwick. No dissentient voice was recorded on that tour. Only a chorus of blessing and thanksgiving. A rejoicing that good government was to be the order of the day for a lifetime to come. That, after all, Edward's sudden death had not condemned them to years of faction and a new civil struggle over the person of his son.

And yet it was during this triumph, this unanimous acclamation, this universal hosanna, that (according to Oliphant, riding in the pocket of the sainted More) Richard sent Tyrrel back to London to make away with the boys who were doing lessons in the Tower. Between July 7th and 15th: At Warwick. In the very summer of his safety, in the heart of the York country on the borders of Wales, he planned the destruction of two discredited children.

It was a highly unlikely story.

He began to wonder whether historians were possessed of minds any more commonsensical than those Great Minds he had encountered, who had been so credulous.

He must find out without delay why, if Tyrrel did that job in 1485, he wasn't brought to book until twenty years afterwards. Where had he been in the meantime?

But Richard's summer was like an April day. Full of a promise that came to nothing. In the autumn he had to face that Woodville-Lancastrian invasion which Morton had cooked up before leaving these shores himself. The Lancastrian part of the affair did Morton proud: they came with a fleet of French ships and a French army. But the Woodville side could provide nothing better than sporadic little gatherings in widely separated centres: Guildford, Salisbury, Maidstone, Newbury, Exeter, and Brecon. The English wanted no part of Henry Tudor, whom they knew only too well. Even the English weather would have none of them. And Dorset's hope of seeing his half-sister Elizabeth queen of England as Henry Tudor's wife was washed away in Severn floods. Henry tried to land in the West, but found Devon and Cornwall up in indignant arms at the idea. He therefore sailed away to France again, to wait for a luckier day. And Dorset went to join in the growing crowd of Woodville exiles hanging around the French court.

So Morton's plan was washed away in autumn rain and English indifference, and Richard could be at peace for a little; but with the spring came a grief that nothing could wash away. The death of his son.

"The King is said to have shown signs of desperate grief; he was not such an unnatural monster as to be destitute of the feeling of a father," said the historian.

Nor of a husband, it seemed. The same marks of suffering were reported of him less than a year later, when Anne died.

And after that there was nothing but the waiting for the renewal of the invasion that had failed; the keeping of England in a state of defence, and the anxiety that that drain on the Exchequer brought him.

He had done what good he could. He had given his name to a model Parliament. He had made peace at last with Scotland and arranged a marriage between his niece and James III's son. He had tried very hard for a peace with France, but had failed. At the French court was Henry Tudor, and Henry Tudor was France's white-headed boy. It would be only a matter of time before Henry landed in England, this time with better backing.

Grant suddenly remembered Lady Stanley, the ardent Lancastrian mother of Henry. What part had Lady Stanley had in that autumn invasion that had put paid to Richard's summer?

He hunted through the solid print until he found it.

Lady Stanley had been found guilty of treasonable correspondence with her son.

But again Richard had proved too lenient for his own good, it seemed. Her estates were forfeit, but they were handed over to her husband. And so was Lady Stanley. For safe keeping. The bitter joke being that Stanley had almost certainly been as knowledgeable about the invasion as his wife.

Truly, the monster was not running according to form.

As Grant was falling asleep a voice said in his mind: "If the boys were murdered in July, and the Woodville-Lancastrian invasion took place in October, why didn't they use the murder of the children as a rallying call?"

The invasion had, of course, been planned before there was any question of murder; it was a full-dress affair of fifteen ships and five thousand mercenaries and must have taken a long time to prepare.

But by the time of the rising the rumours of Richard's infamy must have been widespread if there were any rumours at all. Why had they not gone shouting his crime through England, so that the horror of it brought men flocking to their cause?

Chapter 12

"Cool off, cool off," he said to himself when he woke next morning, "you're beginning to be partisan. That's no way to conduct an investigation."

So, by way of moral discipline, he became prosecutor.

Supposing that the Butler story was a frame-up. A story concocted with Stillington's help. Supposing that both Lords and Commons were willing to be hoodwinked in the hope of stable Government to come.

Did that bring one any nearer the murder of the two boys?

It didn't, did it?

If the story was false, the person to be got rid of was Stillington. Lady Eleanor had died in her convent long ago, so was not there to blow Titulus Regius to pieces any time she had a mind. But Stillington could. And Stillington evidently showed no difficulty in going on living. He survived the man he had put on the throne.

The sudden jar in the proceedings, the abrupt break in the pattern of the coronation preparation, was either wonderful stage-managing or just what one would expect if the thunderclap of Stillington's confession descended on unprepared ears. Richard was—what? Eleven? Twelve?—when the Butler contract was signed and witnessed; it was unlikely that he knew anything of it.

If the Butler story was an invention to oblige Richard, then Richard must have rewarded Stillington. But there was no sign of Stillington's being obliged with a cardinal's hat, or preferment, or office.

But the surest evidence that the Butler story was true lay in Henry VII's urgent need to destroy it. If it were false, then all he had to do to discredit Richard was to bring it into the open and make Stillington eat his words. Instead he hushed it up.

At this point Grant realised with disgust that he was back on the Defence side again. He decided to give it up. He would take to

Lavinia Fitch, or Rupert Rouge, or some other of the fashionable authors lying in such expensive neglect on his table, and forget Richard Plantagenet until such time as young Carradine appeared to renew the inquisition.

He put the family-tree sketch of Cicely Nevill's grandchildren into an envelope and addressed it to Carradine, and gave it to The Midget to post. Then he turned down the portrait that was leaning against the books, so that he should not be seduced by that face which Sergeant Williams had placed, without hesitation, on the bench, and reached for Silas Weekley's *The Sweat and the Furrow.* Thereafter he went from Silas's seamy wrestlings to Lavinia's tea-cups, and from Lavinia's teacups to Rupert's cavortings in the *coulisses,* with a growing dissatisfaction, until Brent Carradine once more turned up in his life.

Carradine regarded him anxiously and said: "You don't look so bright as last time I saw you, Mr. Grant. You not doing so well?"

"Not where Richard is concerned, I'm not," Grant said. "But I've got a new piece of Tonypandy for you."

And he handed him Laura's letter about the drowned women who were never drowned.

Carradine read it with a delight that grew on him like slow sunlight coming out, until eventually he glowed.

"My, but that's wonderful. That's very superior, first growth, dyed-in-the-wool Tonypandy, isn't it? Lovely, lovely. You didn't know about this before? And you a Scotsman?"

"I'm only a Scot once removed," Grant pointed out. "No; I knew that none of these Covenanters died 'for the Faith,' of course; but I didn't know that one of them—or rather, two of them—hadn't died at all."

"They didn't die for their Faith?" Carradine repeated, bewildered. "D'you mean that the *whole thing's* Tonypandy?"

Grant laughed. "I suppose it is," he said, surprised. "I never thought about it before. I've known so long that the 'martyrs' were no more martyrs than that thug who is going to his death for killing that old shop-keeper in Essex, that I've ceased to think about it. No one in Scotland went to his death for anything but civil crime."

"But I thought they were very holy people—the Covenanters, I mean."

"You've been looking at nineteenth-century pictures of conventicles. The reverent little gathering in the heather listening to the preacher; young rapt faces, and white hair blowing in the winds of

God. The Covenanters were the exact equivalent of the I.R.A. in Ireland. A small irreconcilable minority, and as bloodthirsty a crowd as ever disgraced a Christian nation. If you went to church on Sunday instead of to a conventicle, you were liable to wake on Monday to find your barn burned or your horses ham-strung. If you were more open in your disapproval you were shot. The men who shot Archbishop Sharp in his daughter's presence, in broad daylight on a road in Fife, were the heroes of the movement. 'Men of courage and zeal for the cause of God,' according to their admiring followers. They lived safe and swaggering among their Covenanting fans in the West for years. It was a 'preacher of the gospel' who shot Bishop Honeyman in an Edinburgh street. And they shot the old parish priest of Carsphairn on his own doorstep."

"It does sound like Ireland, doesn't it?" Carradine said.

"They were actually worse than the I.R.A. because there was a fifth column element on it. They were financed from Holland, and their arms came from Holland. There was nothing forlorn about their movement, you know. They expected to take over the Government any day, and rule Scotland. All their preaching was pure sedition. The most violent incitement to crime you could imagine. No modern Government could afford to be so patient with such a menace as the Government of the time were. The Covenanters were continually being offered amnesties."

"Well, well. And I thought they were fighting for freedom to worship God their own way."

"No one ever stopped them from worshipping God any way they pleased. What they were out to do was to impose their method of church government not only on Scotland but on England, believe it or not. You should read the Covenant some day. Freedom of worship was not to be allowed to anyone according to the Covenanting creed—except the Covenanters, of course."

"And all those gravestones and monuments that tourists go to see—"

"All Tonypandy. If you ever read on a gravestone that John Whosit 'suffered death for his adherence to the Word of God and Scotland's Covenanted work of Reformation,' with a touching little verse underneath about 'dust sacrificed to tyranny,' you can be sure that the said John Whosit was found guilty before a properly constituted court, of a civil crime punishable by death and that his death had nothing whatever to do with the Word of God." He laughed a little under his breath. "It's the final irony, you know, that a group whose name was anathema to the rest of Scotland in their own time should have been elevated into the position of saints and martyrs."

"I wouldn't wonder if it wasn't onomatopoeic," Carradine said thoughtfully.

"What?"

"Like the Cat and the Rat, you know."

"What are you talking about?"

" 'Member you said, about that Cat and Rat lampoon, that rhyme, that the sound of it made it an offence?"

"Yes; made it venomous."

"Well, the word dragoon does the same thing. I take it that the dragoons were just the policemen of the time."

"Yes. Mounted infantry."

"Well, to me—and I suspect to every other person reading about it—dragoons sound dreadful. They've come to mean something that they never were."

"Yes, I see. Force majeure in being. Actually the Government had only a tiny handful of men to police an enormous area, so the odds were all on the Covenanters' side. In more ways than one. A dragoon (read policeman) couldn't arrest anyone without a warrant (he couldn't stable his horse without the owner's permission, if it comes to that), but there was nothing to hinder a Covenanter lying snug in the heather and picking off dragoons at his leisure. Which they did, of course. And now there's a whole literature about the poor ill-used saint in the heather with his pistol; and the dragoon who died in the course of his duty is a Monster."

"Like Richard."

"Like Richard. How have you been getting on with our own particular Tonypandy?"

"Well, I still haven't managed to find out why Henry was so anxious to hush up that Act as well as repeal it. The thing *was* hushed up and for years it was forgotten, until the original draft turned up, just by chance, in the Tower records. It was printed in 1611. Speed printed the full text of it in his *History of Great Britain*."

"Oh. So there's no question at all about Titulus Regius. Richard succeeded as the Act says, and the sainted More's account is nonsense. There never was an Elizabeth Lucy in the matter."

"Lucy? Who's Elizabeth Lucy?"

"Oh, I forgot. You weren't on in that act. According to the

sainted More, Richard claimed that Edward was married to one of his mistresses, one Elizabeth Lucy."

The disgusted look that the mention of the sainted More always caused on young Carradine's mild face made him look almost nauseated.

"That's nonsense."

"So the sainted More smugly pointed out."

"Why did they want to hide Eleanor Butler?" Carradine said, seeing the point.

"Because she really had married Edward, and the children really were illegitimate. And if the children really were illegitimate, by the way, then no one could rise in their favour and they were no danger to Richard. Have you noticed that the Woodville-Lancastrian invasion was in Henry's favour, and not in the boys'—although Dorset was their half-brother? And that was before any rumours of their nonexistence could have reached him. As far as the leaders of the Dorset-Morton rebellion were concerned the boys were of no account. They were backing Henry. That way, Dorset would have a brother-in-law on the throne of England, and the Queen would be his half-sister. Which would be a nice reversal of form for a penniless fugitive."

"Yes. Yes, that's a point, all right; that about Dorset not fighting to restore his half-brother. If there had been a chance at all that England would have accepted the boy, he surely would have backed the boy. I'll tell you another interesting thing I found. The Queen and her daughters came out of sanctuary quite soon. It's your talking about her son Dorset that reminded me. She not only came out of sanctuary but settled down as if nothing had happened. Her daughters went to festivities at the Palace. And do you know what the pay-off is?"

"No."

"That was *after the Princes had been 'murdered.'* Yes, and I'll tell you something else. With her two boys done to death by their wicked uncle, she writes to her other son, in France—Dorset—and asks him to come home and make his peace with Richard, who will treat him well."

There was silence.

There were no sparrows to talk today. Only the soft sound of the rain against the window.

"No comment," Carradine said at last.

"You know," Grant said, "from the police point of view there is no case against Richard at all. And I mean that literally. It isn't that the case isn't good enough. Good enough to bring into court, I mean. There, quite literally, isn't any case against him at all."

"I'll say there isn't. Especially when I tell you that every single one of those people whose names you sent me were alive and prosperous, and *free*, when Richard was killed at Bosworth. They were not only free, they were very well cared for. Edward's children not only danced at the Palace, they had pensions. He appointed one of the crowd his heir when his own boy died."

"Which one?"

"George's boy."

"So he meant to reverse the attainder on his brother's children."

"Yes. He had protested about his being condemned, if you remember."

"According to even the sainted More, he did. So all the heirs to the throne of England were going about their business, free and unfettered, during the reign of Richard III, the Monster."

"They were more. They were part of the general scheme of things. I mean, part of the family and the general economy of the realm. I've been reading a collection of York records by a man Davies, records of the town of York, I mean; not the family. Both young Warwick—George's son—and his cousin, young Lincoln, were members of the Council. The town addressed a letter to them. In 1485, that was. What's more, Richard knighted young Warwick at the same time as he knighted his own son, at a splendid 'do' at York." He paused a long moment, and then blurted out: "Mr. Grant, do you want to write a book about this?"

"A book!" Grant said, astonished. "God forbid. Why?"

"Because I should like to write one. It would make a much better book than the Peasants."

"Write away."

"You see, I'd like to have something to show my father. Pop thinks I'm no good because I can't take an interest in furniture, and marketing, and graphs of sales. If he could actually handle a book that I had written he might believe that I wasn't so hopeless a bet after all. In fact, I wouldn't put it past him to begin to boast about me for a change."

Grant looked at him with benevolence.

"I forgot to ask you what you thought of Crosby Place," he said.

"Oh, fine, fine. If Carradine the Third ever sees it he'll want to take it back with him and rebuild it in the Adirondacks some-where."

"If you write that book about Richard, he most certainly will. He'll feel like a part-owner. What are you going to call it?"

"The book?"

"Yes."

"I'm going to borrow a phrase from Henry Ford, and call it *History Is the Bunk*."

"Excellent."

"However, I'll have a lot more reading to do and a lot more re-search, before I can start writing."

"Most assuredly you have. You haven't arrived yet at the real question."

"What is that?"

"Who *did* murder the boys?"

"Yes, of course."

"If the boys were alive when Henry took over the Tower what happened to them?"

"Yes. I'll get on to that. I still want to know why it was so impor-tant to Henry to hush up the contents of Titulus Regius."

He got up to go, and then noticed the portrait that was lying on its face on the table. He reached over and restored the photograph to its original place, propping it with a concerned care against the pile of books.

"You stay there," he said to the painted Richard. "I'm going to put you back where you belong."

As he went out the door, Grant said:

"I've just thought of a piece of history which is *not* Tonypandy."

"Yes?" said Carradine, lingering.

"The massacre of Glencoe."

"That really did happen?"

"That really did happen. And—Brent!"

Brent put his head back inside the door.

"Yes?"

"The man who gave the order for it was an ardent Covenanter."

Chapter 13

*C*arradine had not been gone more than twenty minutes when Marta appeared, laden with flowers, books, candy, and goodwill. She found Grant deep in the fifteenth century as reported by Sir Cuthbert Oliphant. He greeted her with an absent-mindedness to which she was not accustomed.

"If your two sons had been murdered by your brother-in-law, would you take a handsome pension from him?"

"I take it that the question is rhetorical," Marta said, putting down her sheaf of flowers and looking round to see which of the already occupied vases would best suit their type.

"Honestly, I think historians are all mad. Listen to this:

> The conduct of the Queen-Dowager is hard to explain; whether she feared to be taken from sanctuary by force, or whether she was merely tired of her forlorn existence at Westminster, and had resolved to be reconciled to the murder of her sons out of mere callous apathy, seems uncertain."

"Merciful Heaven!" said Marta, pausing with a delft jar in one hand and a glass cylinder in the other, and looking at him in wild surmise.

"Do you think historians really *listen* to what they are saying?"

"Who was the said Queen-Dowager?"

"Elizabeth Woodville. Edward IV's wife."

"Oh, yes. I played her once. It was a 'bit.' In a play about Warwick the Kingmaker."

"Of course I'm only a policeman," Grant said. "Perhaps I never moved in the right circles. It may be that I've met only nice people. Where would one have to go to meet a woman who became matey with the murderer of her two boys?"

"Greece, I should think," Marta said. "*Ancient* Greece."

"I can't remember a sample even there."

"Or a lunatic asylum, perhaps. Was there any sign of idiocy about Elizabeth Woodville?"

"Not that anyone ever noticed. And she was Queen for twenty years or so."

"Of course the thing is farce, I hope you see," Marta said, going on with her flower arranging. "Not tragedy at all. 'Yes, I know he did kill Edward and little Richard, but he really is a rather charming creature and it is so bad for my rheumatism living in rooms with a north light.' "

Grant laughed, and his good temper came back.

"Yes, of course. It's the height of absurdity. It belongs to Ruthless Rhymes, not to sober history. That is why historians surprise me. They seem to have no talent for the *likeliness* of any situation. They see history like a peepshow; with two-dimensional figures against a distant background."

"Perhaps when you are grubbing about with tattered records you haven't time to learn about people. I don't mean about the people in the records, but just about People. Flesh and blood. And how they react to circumstances."

"How would you play her?" Grant asked, remembering that the understanding of motive was Marta's trade.

"Play who?"

"The woman who came out of sanctuary and made friends with her children's murderer for seven hundred marks per annum and the right to go to parties at the Palace."

"I couldn't. There is no such woman outside Euripides or a delinquents' home. One could only play her as a rag. She'd make a very good burlesque, now I think of it. A take-off of poetic tragedy. The blank verse kind. I must try it sometime. For a charity matinée, or something. I hope you don't hate mimosa. It's odd, considering how long I've known you, how little I know your likes and dislikes. Who invented the woman who became buddies with her sons' murderer?"

"No one invented her. Elizabeth Woodville did come out of sanctuary, and did accept a pension from Richard. The pension was not only granted, it was paid. Her daughters went to parties at the Palace and she wrote to her other son—her first-marriage son—to come home from France and make his peace with Richard. Oliphant's only suggestion as to the reason for this is that she was either frightened of being dragged out of sanctuary (did you ever know of anyone who was dragged out of sanctuary? The man who did that would be excommunicated—and Richard was a very good son of Holy Church) or that she was bored with sanctuary life."

"And what is your theory about so odd a proceeding?"

"The obvious explanation is that the boys were alive and well. No one at that time ever suggested otherwise."

Marta considered the sprays of mimosa. "Yes, of course. You said that there was no accusation in that Bill of Attainder. After Richard's death, I mean." Her eyes went from the mimosa to the portrait on the table and then to Grant. "You think, then, you really soberly think, as a policeman, that Richard didn't have anything to do with the boys' deaths."

"I'm quite sure that they were alive and well when Henry took over the Tower on his arrival in London. There is *nothing* that would explain his omission to make a scandal of it if the boys were missing. Can you think of anything?"

"No. No, of course not. It is quite inexplicable. I have always taken it for granted that there was a terrific scandal about it. That it would be one of the main accusations against Richard. You and my woolly lamb seem to be having a lovely time with history. When I suggested a little investigation to pass the time and stop the prickles I had no idea that I was contributing to the rewriting of history. Which reminds me. Atlanta Shergold is gunning for you."

"For me? I've never even met her."

"Nevertheless she is looking for you with a gun. She says that Brent's attitude to the B. M. has become the attitude of an addict to his drug. She can't drag him away from it. If she takes him away from it physically, he spends the time harking back to it in his mind; so that she mightn't exist as far as he is concerned. He has even stopped sitting through *To Sea in a Bowl*. Do you see much of him?"

"He was here a few minutes before you came. But I don't expect to hear from him again for some days to come."

But in that he was wrong.

Just before supper-time the porter appeared with a telegram.

Grant put his thumb under the dainty Post Office lick on the flap and extracted two sheets of telegram. The telegram was from Brent.

Hell and damnation an awful thing has happened (stop) you know that chronicle in Latin I talked about (stop) the chronicle written by the monk at Croyland Abbey (stop) well

I've just seen it and the rumour is there the rumour about the boys being dead (stop) the thing is written before Richard's death so we are sunk aren't we and I specially am sunk and that fine book of mine will never be written (stop) is anyone allowed to commit suicide in your river or is it reserved for the British

Brent

Into the silence the voice of the porter said: "It's reply-paid, sir. Do you want to send an answer?"

"What? Oh. No. Not right away. I'll send it down presently."

"Very good, sir," said the porter, looking respectfully at the two sheets of telegram—in the porter's family a telegram was confined to one sheet only—and went away, not humming this time.

Grant considered the news conveyed with such transatlantic extravagance in the matter of telegraphic communication. He read the thing again.

"Croyland," he said, considering. Why did that ring a bell? No one had mentioned Croyland so far in this case. Carradine had talked merely of a monkish chronicle somewhere.

He had been too often, in his professional life, faced with a fact that apparently destroyed his whole case to be dismayed now. He reacted as he would have reacted in a professional investigation. He took out the upsetting small fact and looked at it. Calmly. Dispassionately. With none of poor Carradine's wild dismay.

"Croyland," he said again. Croyland was somewhere in Cambridgeshire. Or was it Norfolk? Somewhere on the borders there, in the flat country.

The Midget came in with his supper, and propped the flat bowl-like plate where he could eat from it with a modicum of comfort, but he was not aware of her.

"Can you reach your pudding easily from there?" she asked. And as he did not answer: "Mr. Grant, can you reach your pudding if I leave it on the edge there?"

"*Ely!*" he shouted at her.

"What?"

"Ely," he said, softly to the ceiling.

"Mr. Grant, aren't you feeling well?"

He became conscious of The Midget's well-powdered and concerned little face as it intruded between him and the familiar cracks.

"I'm fine, fine. Better than I've ever been in my life. Wait just a moment, there's a good girl, and send a telegram down for me. Give me my writing-pad. I can't reach it with that mess of rice pudding in the way."

She gave him the pad and pencil, and on the reply-paid form he wrote:

Can you find me a similar rumour in France at about the same date?

Grant

After that he ate his supper with a good appetite, and settled down to a good night's sleep. He was floating in that delicious half-way stage on the way to unconsciousness when he became aware that someone was leaning over to inspect him. He opened his eyes to see who it might be, and looked straight into the anxious yearning brown irises of The Amazon, looking larger and more cowlike than ever in the soft lamplight. She was holding in her hand a yellow envelope.

"I didn't quite know what to do," she said. "I didn't want to disturb you and yet I didn't know whether it mightn't be important. A telegram, you know. You never can tell. And if you didn't have it tonight it would mean a whole twelve hours' delay. Nurse Ingham has gone off duty, so there was no one to ask till Nurse Briggs comes on at ten. I hope I haven't wakened you up. But you weren't really asleep, were you?"

Grant assured her that she had done the right thing and she let out a sigh that nearly blew the portrait of Richard over. She stood by while he read the telegram, with an air of being ready to support him in any evil news that it might contain. To The Amazon all telegrams conveyed evil tidings.

The telegram was from Carradine.

It said: "You mean you want repeat want that there should be another repeat another accusation question-mark—Brent."

Grant took the reply-paid form and wrote: "Yes. Preferably in France."

Then he said to The Amazon: "You can turn out the light, I think. I'm going to sleep until seven tomorrow morning."

He fell asleep wondering how long it would be before he saw Carradine again, and what the odds were against that much desired instance of a second rumour.

But it was not so long after all until Carradine turned up again, and he turned up looking anything but suicidal. Indeed he seemed in some queer way to have broadened out. His coat seemed less of an appendage and more of a garment. He beamed at Grant.

"Mr. Grant, you're a wonder. Do they have more like you at Scotland Yard? Or do you rate special?"

Grant looked at him almost unbelieving. "Don't tell me you've turned up a French instance!"

"Didn't you want me to?"

"Yes. But I hardly dared hope for it. The odds against seemed tremendous. What form did the rumour take in France? A chronicle? A letter?"

"No. Something much more surprising. Something much more dismaying, actually. It seems that the Chancellor of France, in a speech to the States-General at Tours, spoke of the rumour. Indeed he was quite eloquent about it. In a way, his eloquence was the one scrap of comfort I could find in the situation."

"Why?"

"Well, it sounded more to my mind like a Senator being hasty about someone who had brought in a measure his own people back home wouldn't like. More like politics than State, if you know what I mean."

"You should be at the Yard, Brent. What did the Chancellor say?"

"Well, it's in French and my French isn't very good so perhaps you'd better read it for yourself."

He handed over a sheet of childish writing and Grant read:

Regardez, je vous prie, les événements qui après la mort du roi Edouard sont arrivés dans ce pays. Contemplez ses enfants, déjà grands et braves, massacrés impunément, et la couronne transportée à l'assassin par la faveur des peuples.

" 'Ce pays,' " said Grant. "Then he was in full flood against England. He even suggests that it was with the will of the English people that the boys were 'massacred.' We are being held up as a barbarous race."

"Yes. That's what I meant. It's a Congressman scoring a point. Actually, the French Regency sent an embassy to Richard that same year—about six months later—so they had probably found that the rumour wasn't true. Richard signed a safe-conduct for their visit.

He wouldn't have done that if they had been still slanging him as a murdering untouchable."

"No. Can you give me the dates of the two libels?"

"Sure. I have them here. The monk at Croyland wrote about events in the late summer of 1483. He says that there was a rumour that the boys had been put to death but no one knew how. The nasty slap in the meeting of the States-General was in January 1484."

"Perfect," said Grant.

"*Why* did you want there to have been another instance of rumour?"

"As a cross-check. Do you know where Croyland is?"

"Yes. In the Fen country."

"In the Fen country. Near Ely. And it was in the Fen country that Morton was hiding out after his escape from Buckingham's charge."

"Morton! Yes, of course."

"If Morton was the carrier, then there had to be another outbreak on the Continent, when he moved on there. Morton escaped from England in the autumn of 1483, and the rumour appears promptly in January 1484. Croyland is a very isolated place, incidentally; it would be an ideal place for a fugitive bishop to hide out till he could arrange transport abroad."

"Morton!" said Carradine again, rolling the name over on his tongue. "Wherever there's hanky-panky in this business you stub your toe against Morton."

"So you've noticed that too."

"He was the heart of that conspiracy to murder Richard before he could be crowned, he was in the back of the rebellion against Richard once he *was* crowned, and his trail to the Continent is sticky as a snail's with—with subversion."

"We-ll, the snail part is mere deduction. It wouldn't stand up in court. But there's no peradventure about his activities once he was across the channel. He settled down to a whole-time job of subversion. He and a buddy of his called Christopher Urswick worked like beavers in Henry's interest; 'sending preuie letters and cloked messengers' to England to stir up hostility to Richard."

"Yes? I don't know as much as you about what stands up in court and what won't but it seems to me that that snail's trail is a very allowable deduction—if you'll allow me. I don't suppose Morton waited till he was overseas before beginning his undermining."

"No. No, of course he didn't. It was life and death to Morton that Richard should go. Unless Richard went, John Morton's career was over. He was finished. It wasn't even that there would be no preferment for him now. There would be nothing. He would be stripped of his numerous livings and be reduced to his plain priest's frock. He, John Morton. Who had been within touching distance of an archbishopric. But if he could help Henry Tudor to a throne then he might still become not only Archbishop of Canterbury but a Cardinal besides. Oh, yes; it was desperately, overwhelmingly important to Morton that Richard should not have the governing of England."

"Well," said Brent, "he was the right man for a job of subversion. I don't suppose he knew what a scruple was. A little rumour like infanticide must have been child's play to him."

"There's always the odd chance that he believed it, of course," Grant said, his habit of weighing evidence overcoming even his dislike of Morton.

"Believed that the boys were murdered?"

"Yes. It may have been someone else's invention. After all, the country must have been swarming with Lancastrian tales, part mere ill-will, part propaganda. He may have been merely passing on the latest sample."

"Huh! I wouldn't put it past him to be paving the way for their future murder," Brent said tartly.

Grant laughed. "I wouldn't, at that," he said. "What else did you get from your monk at Croyland?"

"A little comfort, too. I found after I had written that panic wire to you that he wasn't at all to be taken as gospel. He just put down what gossip came his way from the outer world. He says, for instance, that Richard had a second coronation, at York; and that of course just isn't true. If he can be wrong about a big, known fact like a coronation, then he's not to be trusted as a reporter. But he did know about Titulus Regius, by the way. He recorded the whole tenor of it, including Lady Eleanor."

"That's interesting. Even a monk at Croyland had heard who Edward was supposed to have been married to."

"Yes. The sainted More must have dreamed up Elizabeth Lucy a good deal later."

"To say nothing of the unspeakable story that Richard based his claim on his mother's shame."

"What?"

"He says that Richard caused a sermon to be preached claiming that Edward and George were his mother's sons by some other father, and that he, Richard, was the only legitimate son and therefore the only true heir."

"The sainted More might have thought up a more convincing one," young Carradine said dryly.

"Yes. Especially when Richard was living in his mother's house at the time of the libel!"

"So he was. I'd forgotten that. I don't have a proper police brain. That's very neat, what you say about Morton being the carrier of the rumour. But suppose the rumour turns up somewhere else, even yet?"

"It's possible, of course. But I'm willing to lay you fifties to any amount that it won't. I don't for one moment believe that there was any general rumour that the boys were missing."

"Why not?"

"For a reason that I hold to be unanswerable. If there had been any general uneasiness, any obviously subversive rumours or action, Richard would have taken immediate steps to checkmate them. When the rumour went round, later, that he was proposing to marry his niece Elizabeth—the boys' eldest sister—he was on to it like a hawk. He not only sent letters to the various towns denying the rumour in no uncertain terms, he was so furious (and evidently thought it of such importance that he should not be traduced) that he summoned the 'heid yins' of London to the biggest hall he could find (so that he could get them all in at one time) and told them face to face what he thought about the affair."

"Yes. Of course you're right. Richard would have made a public denial of the rumour if the rumour was general. After all, it was a much more horrifying one than the one that he was going to marry his niece."

"Yes; actually you could get a dispensation to marry your niece in those days. Perhaps you still can, for all I know. That's not my department at the Yard. What is certain is that if Richard went to such lengths to contradict the marriage rumour then he most certainly would have gone to much greater lengths to put a stop to the murder one, if it had existed. The conclusion is inevitable; there *was* no general rumour of disappearance or foul play where the boys were concerned."

"Just a thin little trickle between the Fens and France."

"Just a thin little trickle between the Fens and France. Nothing in the picture suggests any worry about the boys. I mean: in a police investigation you look for any abnormalities in behaviour among the suspects in a crime. Why did X, who always goes to the movies on a Thursday night, decide on that night of all nights not to go? Why did Y take a return half as usual and very unusually not use it? That sort of thing. But in the short time between Richard's succession and his death everyone behaves quite normally. The boys' mother comes out of sanctuary and makes her peace with Richard. The girls resume their court life. The boys are presumably still doing their lessons that their father's death had interrupted. Their young cousins have a place on the Council and are of sufficient importance for the town of York to be addressing letters to them. It's all quite a normal, peaceful scene, with everyone going about their ordinary business, and no suggestion anywhere that a spectacular and unnecessary murder has just taken place in the family."

"It looks as if I might write that book after all, Mr. Grant."

"Most certainly you will write it. You have not only Richard to rescue from calumny; you have to clear Elizabeth Woodville of the imputation of condoning her sons' murder for seven hundred marks a year and perks."

"I can't write the book and leave it in the air like that, of course. I'll have to have at least a theory as to what became of the boys."

"You will."

Carradine's mild gaze came away from the small woolly clouds over the Thames and considered Grant with a question in it.

"Why that tone?" he asked. "Why are you looking like a cat with cream?"

"Well, I've been proceeding along police lines. During those empty days while I was waiting for you to turn up again."

"Police lines?"

"Yes. Who benefits, and all that. We've discovered that it wouldn't be a pin's-worth of advantage to Richard that the boys should die. So we go on looking round to see whom, in that case, it *would* benefit. And this is where Titulus Regius comes in."

"What has Titulus Regius got to do with the murder?"

"Henry VII married the boys' eldest sister. Elizabeth."

"Yes."

"By way of reconciling the Yorkists to his occupation of the throne."

"Yes."

"By repealing Titulus Regius, he made her legitimate."

"Sure."

"But by making the children legitimate he automatically made the two boys heir to the throne before her. In fact, by repealing Titulus Regius he made the elder of the two King of England."

Carradine made a little clicking sound with his tongue. His eyes behind their horn-rims were glowing with pleasure.

"So," said Grant, "I propose that we proceed with investigation along those lines."

"Sure. What do you want?"

"I want to know a lot more about that confession of Tyrrel's. But first, and most of all, I'd like to know how the people concerned acted. What happened to them; not what anyone reported of anyone. Just as we did in the case of Richard's succession after Edward's unexpected death."

"Fine. What do you want to know?"

"I want to know what became of all the York heirs that Richard left so alive and well and prosperous. Every single one of them. Can you do that for me?"

"Sure. That's elementary."

"And I could bear to know more about Tyrrel. About the man himself, I mean. Who he was, and what he had done."

"I'll do that." Carradine got up with such an on-with-the-charge air that for one moment Grant thought that he was actually going to button his coat. "Mr. Grant, I'm so grateful to you for all this—this—"

"This fun and games?"

"When you're on your feet again, I'll—I'll—I'll take you round the Tower of London."

"Make it Greenwich-and-back by boat. Our island race have a passion for the nautical."

"How long do they reckon it will be before you're out of bed, do you know?"

"I'll probably be up before you come back with the news about the heirs and Tyrrel."

Chapter 14

Grant was not, as it happened, out of bed when Carradine came again, but he was sitting up.

"You can't imagine," he said to Brent, "how fascinating the opposite wall looks, after the ceiling. And how small and queer the world looks right way up."

He was touched by Carradine's obvious pleasure in this progress and it was some time before they got down to business. It was Grant who had to say: "Well, how did the York heirs make out under Henry VII?"

"Oh, yes," said the boy, pulling out his usual wad of notes and drawing up a chair by hooking his right toe in the crossbar. He sat down on the chair. "Where shall I begin?"

"Well, about Elizabeth we know. He married her, and she was Queen of England until she died and he made a bid for the mad Juana of Spain."

"Yes. She was married to Henry in the spring of 1486—in January, rather; five months after Bosworth—and she died in the spring of 1503."

"Seventeen years. Poor Elizabeth. With Henry it must have seemed like seventy. He was what is euphemistically referred to as 'unuxorious.' Let us go on down the family. Edward's children, I mean. Fate of the two boys unknown. What happened to Cicely?"

"She was married to his old uncle Lord Welles, and sent away to live in Lincolnshire. Anne and Katherine, who were children, were married when they were old enough to be good Lancastrians. Bridget, the youngest, became a nun at Dartford."

"Orthodox enough, so far. Who comes next? George's boy."

"Yes. Young Warwick. Shut up for life in the Tower, and executed for allegedly planning to escape."

"So. And George's daughter? Margaret."

"She became the Countess of Salisbury. Her execution by Henry

VIII on a trumped-up charge is apparently the classic sample of judicial murder."

"Elizabeth's son? The alternative heir?"

"John de la Pole. He went to live with his aunt in Burgundy until—"

"To live with Margaret, Richard's sister."

"Yes. He died in the Simnel rising. But he had a younger brother that you didn't put in that list. He was executed by Henry VIII. He had surrendered to Henry VII under a safe-conduct, so Henry, I suppose, thought that it might break his luck to ignore that. In any case he had about used up his quota. Henry VIII took no chances. He didn't stop at de la Pole. There were four more that you missed out of that list. Exeter, Surrey, Buckingham, and Montague. He got rid of the lot."

"And Richard's son? John? The bastard one."

"Henry VII granted him a pension of £20 a year, but he was the first of the lot to go."

"On what charge?"

"On having been suspected of receiving an invitation to go to Ireland."

"You're joking."

"I'm not. Ireland was the focus of loyalist rebellion. The York family were very popular in Ireland, and to get an invitation from that direction was as good as a death warrant in Henry's eyes. Though I can't think why even Henry would have bothered about young John. 'An active, well-disposed boy,' he was, by the way, according to the 'Foedera.' "

"His claim was better than Henry's," Grant said, very tart. "He was the illegitimate only son of a King. Henry was the great-grandson of an illegitimate son of a younger son of a King."

There was silence for some time.

Then Carradine, out of the silence, said: "Yes."

"Yes to what?"

"To what you are thinking."

"It does look like it, doesn't it? They're the only two who are missing from the list."

There was another silence.

"They were all judicial murders," Grant said presently. "Murders under the form of law. But you can't bring a capital charge against a pair of children."

"No," agreed Carradine, and went on watching the sparrows.

"No, it would have to be done some other way. After all, they were the important ones."

"The vital ones."

"How do we start?"

"As we did with Richard's succession. Find out where everyone was in the first months of Henry's reign and what they were doing. Say the first year of his reign. There will be a break in the pattern somewhere, just as there was a break in the preparations for the boy's coronation."

"Right."

"Did you find out anything about Tyrrel? Who he was?"

"Yes. He wasn't at all what I had imagined. I'd imagined him as a sort of hanger-on; hadn't you?"

"Yes, I think I did. Wasn't he?"

"No. He was a person of importance. He was Sir James Tyrrel of Gipping. He had been on various—committees, I suppose you'd call them, for Edward IV. And he was created a Knight Banneret, whatever that is, at the siege of Berwick. And he did well for himself under Richard, though I can't find that he was at the battle of Bosworth. A lot of people came too late for the battle—did you know?—so I don't suppose that means anything particular. Anyhow, he wasn't that lackey-on-the-make person that I'd always pictured."

"That's interesting. How did he make out under Henry VII?"

"Well, that's the *really* interesting thing. For such a very good and successful servant of the York family, he seems to have fairly blossomed under Henry. Henry appointed him Constable of Guisnes. Then he was sent as ambassador to Rome. He was one of the Commissioners for negotiating the Treaty of Etaples. And Henry gave him a grant for life of the revenues of some lands in Wales, but made him exchange them for revenues of the county of Guisnes of equal value—I can't think why."

"I can," said Grant.

"You can?"

"Has it struck you that all his honours and his commissions are outside England? Even the reward of land revenues."

"Yes, so they are. What does that convey to you?"

"Nothing at the moment. Perhaps he just found Guisnes better for his bronchial catarrh. It is possible to read too much into historical transactions. Like Shakespeare's plays, they are capable of almost endless interpretations. How long did this honeymoon with Henry VII last?"

"Oh, quite a long time. Everything was just grand until 1502."

"What happened in 1502?"

"Henry heard that he had been ready to help one of the York crowd in the Tower to escape to Germany. He sent the whole garrison of Calais to besiege the castle at Guisnes. That wasn't quick enough for him, so he sent his Lord Privy Seal—know what that is?"

Grant nodded.

"Sent his Lord Privy Seal—what names you English have dreamed up for your Elks officials—to offer him safe conduct if he would come aboard a ship at Calais and confer with the Chancellor of the Exchequer."

"Don't tell me."

"I don't need to, do I? He finished up in a dungeon in the Tower. And was beheaded 'in great haste and without trial' on May 6, 1502."

"And what about his confession?"

"There wasn't one."

"What!"

"Don't look at me like that. I'm not responsible."

"But I thought he confessed to the murder of the boys."

"Yes, according to various accounts. But they are accounts of a confession, not—not a transcript, if you see what I mean."

"You mean, Henry didn't publish a confession?"

"No. His paid historian, Polydore Virgil, gave an account of how the murder was done. After Tyrrel was dead."

"But if Tyrrel confessed that he murdered the boys at Richard's instigation, why wasn't he charged with the crime and publicly tried for it?"

"I can't imagine."

"Let me get this straight. Nothing was heard of Tyrrel's confession until Tyrrel was dead."

"No."

"Tyrrel confesses that way back in 1483, nearly twenty years ago, he pelted up to London from Warwick, got the keys of the Tower from the Constable—I forget his name—"

"Brackenbury. Sir Robert Brackenbury."

"Yes. Got the keys of the Tower from Sir Robert Brackenbury for one night, murdered the boys, handed back the keys, and reported back to Richard. He confesses this, and so puts an end to what must have been a much canvassed mystery, and yet nothing public is done with him."

"Not a thing."

"I'd hate to go into court with a story like that."

"I wouldn't even consider it, myself. It's as phony a tale as ever I heard."

"Didn't they even bring Brackenbury in to affirm or deny the story of the keys being handed over?"

"Brackenbury was killed at Bosworth."

"So he was conveniently dead too, was he?" He lay and thought about it. "You know, if Brackenbury died at Bosworth, then we have one more small piece of evidence on our side."

"How? What?"

"If that had really happened; I mean: if the keys were handed over for a night on Richard's order, then a lot of junior officials at the Tower must have been aware of it. It is quite inconceivable that one or other of them wouldn't be ready to tell the tale of Henry when he took over the Tower. Especially if the boys were missing. Brackenbury was dead. Richard was dead. The next in command at the Tower would be expected to produce the boys. When they weren't producible, he *must* have said: 'The Constable handed over the keys, one night, and since then the boys have not been seen.' There would have been the most ruthless hue and cry after the man who had been given the keys. He would have been Exhibit A in the case against Richard, and to produce him would have been a feather in Henry's cap."

"Not only that, but Tyrrel was too well known to the people at the Tower to have passed unrecognised. In the small London of that day he must have been quite a well-known figure."

"Yes. If that story were true Tyrrel would have been tried and executed for the boys' murder, openly, in 1485. He had no one to protect him." He reached for his cigarettes. "So what we're left with is that Henry executed Tyrrel in 1502, and then announced by way of his tame historians that Tyrrel had confessed that twenty years before he had murdered the Princes."

"Yes."

"And he didn't offer, anywhere, at any time, any reason for trying Tyrrel for this atrocious thing he had confessed."

"No. Not as far as I can make out. He was sideways as a crab, you know. He never went straight at anything, even murder. It had to be covered up to look like something else. He waited years to find some sort of legal excuse that would camouflage a murder. He had a mind like a corkscrew. Do you know what his first official action as Henry VII was?"

"No."

"To execute some of the men fighting for Richard at Bosworth *on a charge of treason.* And do you know how he managed to make it legally treason? By dating his reign from the day before Bosworth. A mind that was capable of a piece of sharp practice of that calibre was capable of anything." He took the cigarette that Grant was offering him. "But he didn't get away with it," he added, with sober joy. "Oh, no, he didn't get away with it. The English, bless them, drew the line at that. They told him where he got off."

"How?"

"They presented him, in that nice polite English way, with an Act of Parliament that said that no one serving the Sovereign Lord of the land for the time being should be convicted of treason or suffer either forfeiture or imprisonment, and they made him consent to it. That's terribly English, that ruthless politeness. No yelling in the street or throwing stones because they didn't like his little bit of cheating. Just a nice polite reasonable Act for him to swallow and like it. I bet he did a slow burn about that one. Well, I must be on my way. It's sure nice to see you sitting up and taking notice. We'll be having that trip to Greenwich in no time at all, I see. What's at Greenwich?"

"Some very fine architecture and a fine stretch of muddy river."

"That all?"

"And some good pubs."

"We're going to Greenwich."

When he had gone Grant slid down in bed and smoked one cigarette after another while he considered the tale of those heirs of York who had prospered under Richard III, and gone to their graves under Henry VII.

Some of them may have "asked for it." Carradine's report had, after all, been a précis; innocent of qualification, insusceptible to halftones. But it was surely a thundering great coincidence that all the lives who stood between the Tudors and the throne had been cut short so conveniently.

He looked, with no great enthusiasm, at the book that young Carradine had brought him. It was called *The Life and Reign of Richard III,* by someone named James Gairdner. Carradine had assured him that he would find Dr. Gairdner well worth his while. Dr. Gairdner was, according to Brent, "a scream."

The book did not appear to Grant to be markedly hilarious, but anything about Richard was better than something about anyone else, so he began to glance through it, and presently he became aware just what Brent had meant by saying that the good Doctor was a "scream." Dr. Gairdner obstinately believed Richard to be a murderer, but since he was a writer honest, learned, and according to his lights impartial, it was not in him to suppress facts. The spectacle of Dr. Gairdner trying to make his facts fit his theory was the most entertaining thing in gymnastics that Grant had witnessed for some time.

Dr. Gairdner acknowledged with no apparent sense of incongruity Richard's great wisdom, his generosity, and his courage, his ability, his charm, his popularity, and the trust that he inspired even in his beaten enemies; and in the same breath reported his vile slander of his mother and his slaughter of two helpless children. Tradition says, said the worthy Doctor; and solemnly reported the horrible tradition and subscribed to it. There was nothing mean or paltry in his character, according to the Doctor—but he was a murderer of innocent children. Even his enemies had confidence in his justice—but he murdered his own nephews. His integrity was remarkable—but he killed for gain.

As a contortionist Dr. Gairdner was the original boneless wonder. More than ever Grant wondered with what part of their brains historians reasoned. It was certainly by no process of reasoning known to ordinary mortals that they arrived at their conclusions. Nowhere in life had he met any human being remotely resembling either Dr. Gairdner's Richard or Oliphant's Elizabeth Woodville.

Perhaps there was something in Laura's theory that human nature found it difficult to give up preconceived beliefs. That there was some vague inward opposition to, and resentment of, a reversal of accepted fact. Certainly Dr. Gairdner dragged like a frightened child on the hand that was pulling him towards the inevitable.

That charming men of great integrity had committed murder in their day Grant knew only too well. But not that kind of murder and not for that kind of reason. The kind of man whom Dr. Gairdner had drawn in his *Life and History of Richard III* would commit murder only when his personal life had been *bouleversé* by some earthquake. He would murder his wife for unfaithfulness suddenly discovered, perhaps. Or kill the partner whose secret speculation had ruined their firm and the future of his children. Whatever murder he committed would be the result of acute emotion, it would never be planned; and it would never be a base murder.

One could not say: Because Richard possessed this quality and that, therefore he was incapable of murder. But one could say: Because Richard possessed these qualities, therefore he is incapable of this murder.

It would have been a silly murder, that murder of the boy Princes; and Richard was a remarkably able man. It was base beyond description; and he was a man of great integrity. It was callous; and he was noted for his warm-heartedness.

One could go through the catalogue of his acknowledged virtues, and find that each of them, individually, made his part in the murder unlikely in the extreme. Taken together they amounted to a wall of impossibility that towered into fantasy.

Chapter 15

*T*here was one person you forgot to ask for," Carradine said, breezing in, very gay, some days later. "In your list of kind inquiries."

"Hullo. Who was that?"

"Stillington."

"Of course! The worthy Bishop of Bath. If Henry hated Titulus Regius, as a witness of Richard's integrity and his own wife's illegitimacy, he must still more have disliked the presence of its instigator. What happened to old Stillington? Judicial murder?"

"Apparently the old boy wouldn't play."

"Wouldn't play what?"

"Henry's pet game. Out goes he. Either he was a wily old bird, or he was too innocent to see the snare at all. It's my belief—if a mere Research Worker is entitled to a belief—that he was so innocent that no agent provocateur could provoke him to anything. Not anything that could be made a capital charge, anyhow."

"Are you telling me that he defeated Henry?"

"No. Oh, no. No one ever defeated Henry. Henry put him on a charge and conveniently forgot to release him. And never home came he. Who was that? Mary on the sands of Dee?"

"You're very bright this morning, not to say exhilarated."

"Don't say it in that suspicious tone. They're not open yet. This effervescence that you observe in me is intellectual carbonisation. Spiritual rejoicing. An entirely cerebral scintillation."

"Well? Sit down and cough up. What is so good? I take it that something is?"

"Good is hardly the proper word. It's beautiful, perfectly-holy beautiful."

"I think you *have* been drinking."

"I couldn't drink this morning if I tried. I'm bung full, full up to the gullet's edge, with satisfaction."

"I take it you found that break in the pattern we were looking for."

"Yes, I found it, but it was later than we had thought. Later in time, I mean. Further on. In the first months everyone did what you would expect them to do. Henry took over—not a word about the boys—and cleaned up, got married to the boys' sister. Got his own attainder reversed by a Parliament of his own attainted followers— no mention of the boys—and got an act of attainder through against Richard and his loyal subjects whose service was so neatly made treason by that one day's antedating. That brought a fine heap of forfeited estates into the kitty in one go. The Croyland monk was terribly scandalised, by the way, at Henry's sharp practice in the matter of treason. 'O God,' he says, 'what security are our kings to have henceforth in the day of battle if their loyal followers may in defeat be deprived of life, fortune, and inheritance?' "

"He reckoned without his countrymen."

"Yes. He might have known that the English would get round to that matter sooner or later. Perhaps he was an alien. Anyhow, everything went on just as you would expect things to go with Henry in charge. He succeeded in August of 1485, and married Elizabeth in the following January. Elizabeth had her first child at Winchester, and her mother was there with her and was present at the baptism. That was in September 1486. Then she came back to London—the Queen-Dowager, I mean—in the autumn. And in February—hold on to everything—in February she was shut up in a convent for the rest of her life."

"*Elizabeth Woodville?*" Grant said, in the greatest astonishment. This was the very last thing he had expected.

"Yes. Elizabeth Woodville. The boys' mother."

"How do you know that she didn't go voluntarily?" Grant asked, when he had thought of it for a little. "It was not an uncommon thing for great ladies who were tired of court life to retire into an Order. It was not a severe existence, you know. Indeed, I have an idea it was fairly comfortable for rich women."

"Henry stripped her of everything she owned, and ordered her into the nunnery at Bermondsey. And that, by the way, *did* create a sensation. There was 'much wondering,' it appears."

"I'm not surprised. What an extraordinary thing. Did he give a reason?"

"Yes."

"What did he say he was ruining her for?"

"For being nice to Richard."

"Are you serious?"

"Sure."

"Is that the official wording?"

"No. That's the version of Henry's pet historian."

"Virgil?"

"Yes. The actual order of council that shut her up, said it was 'for various considerations.' "

"Are you quoting?" asked Grant, incredulous.

"I'm quoting. That's what it said: 'For various considerations.' "

After a moment Grant said: "He had no talent for excuses, had he? In his place I would have thought up six better ones."

"Either he couldn't be bothered or he thought other people very credulous. Mark you, her niceness to Richard didn't worry him until eighteen months after he succeeded Richard. Up till then everything had apparently been smooth as silk. He had even given her presents, manors and what not, when he succeeded Richard."

"What was his real reason? Have you any suggestion?"

"Well, I've another little item that may give you ideas. It certainly gave me one hell of a big idea."

"Go on."

"In June of that year —"

"Which year?"

"The first year of Elizabeth's marriage. 1486. The year when she was married in January and had Prince Arthur at Winchester in September, with her mother dancing attendance."

"All right. Yes."

"In June of that year, Sir James Tyrrel received a general pardon. On the 16th June."

"But that means very little, you know. It was quite a usual thing. At the end of a period of service. Or on setting out on a new one. It merely meant that you were quit of anything that anyone might think of raking up against you afterwards."

"Yes, I know. I know that. The first pardon isn't the surprising one."

"The *first* pardon? Was there a second one?"

"Yes. That's the pay-off. There was a second general pardon to Sir James exactly a month later. To be exact on the 16th of July, 1486."

"Yes," Grant said, thinking it over. "That really is extraordinary."

"It's highly unusual, anyway. I asked an old boy who works next to me at the B. M.—he does historical research and he's been a wonderful help to me I don't mind telling you—and he said he had never come across another instance. I showed him the two entries—in the *Memorials of Henry VII*—and he mooned over them like a lover."

Grant said, considering: "On the 16th June, Tyrrel is given a general pardon. On the 16th July he is given a second general pardon. In November or thereabouts the boys' mother comes back to town. And in February she is immured for life."

"Suggestive?"

"Very."

"You think he did it? Tyrrel."

"It could be. It's very suggestive, isn't it, that when we find the break in the normal pattern that we've been looking for, Tyrrel is there, on the spot, with a most unconscionable break in his own pattern. When did the rumour that the boys were missing first become general? I mean, something to be talked openly about."

"Quite early in Henry's reign, it would seem."

"Yes; it fits. It would certainly explain the thing that has puzzled us from the beginning in this affair."

"What do you mean?"

"It would explain why there was no fuss when the boys disappeared. It's always been a puzzling thing, even to people who thought that Richard did it. Indeed, when you come to think of it it would be impossible for Richard to get away with it. There was a large, and very active, and very powerful opposition party in Richard's day, and he left them all free and scattered up and down the country to carry on as they liked. He had all the Woodville-Lancaster crowd to deal with if the boys had gone missing. But where interference or undue curiosity was concerned Henry was sitting pretty. Henry had got *his* opposition party safely in jail. The only possible danger was his mother-in-law, and at the very moment when she becomes capable of being a prying nuisance she too is put under hatches and battened down."

"Yes. Wouldn't you think that there was *something* she could have done? When she found that she was being prevented from getting news of the boys."

"She may never have known that they were missing. He may just have said: 'It is my wish that you should not see them. I think you are a bad influence on them: you who came out of sanctuary and let your daughters go to that man's parties!' "

"Yes, that's so, of course. He didn't have to wait until she actually became suspicious. The whole thing might have been one move. 'You're a bad woman, and a bad mother; I am sending you into a convent to save your soul and your children from the contamination of your presence.' "

"Yes. And where the rest of England were concerned, he was as safe as any murderer ever could be. After his happy thought about the 'treason' accusation, no one was going to stick his neck out by inquiring particularly about the boys' health. Everyone must have been walking on eggs as it was. No one knowing what Henry might think of next to make into a retrospective offence that would send their lives into limbo and their estates into Henry's kitty. No, it was no time to be overcurious about anything that didn't directly concern oneself. Not that it would be easy, in any case, to satisfy one's curiosity."

"With the boys living at the Tower, you mean."

"With the boys living in a Tower officialled by Henry's men. There was none of Richard's get-together live-and-let-live attitude about Henry. No York-Lancaster alliance for Henry. The people at the Tower would be Henry's men."

"Yes. Of course they would. Did you know that Henry was the first English King to have a bodyguard? I wonder what he told his wife about her brothers."

"Yes. That would be interesting to know. He may even have told her the truth."

"*Henry!* Never! It would cost Henry a spiritual struggle, Mr. Grant, to acknowledge that two and two were four. I tell you, he was a crab; he never went straight at anything."

"If he were a sadist he could tell her with impunity, you know. There was practically nothing she could do about it. Even if she wanted to. She mightn't have wanted to all that much. She had just produced an heir to the throne of England and was getting ready to produce another. She might not have the spare interest for a crusade; especially a crusade that would knock the ground from under her own feet."

"He wasn't a sadist, Henry," young Carradine said sadly. Sad at having to grant Henry even a negative virtue. "In a way he was just the opposite. He didn't enjoy murder at all. He had to pretty it up before he could bear the thought of it. Dress it up in legal ribbons. If you think that Henry got a kick out of boasting to Elizabeth in bed about what he had done with her brothers, I think you're wrong."

"Yes, probably," Grant said. And lay thinking about Henry. "I've just thought of the right adjective for Henry," he said presently. "Shabby. He was a shabby creature."

"Yes. Even his hair was thin and scanty."

"I didn't mean it physically."

"I know you didn't."

"Everything that he did was shabby. Come to think of it, 'Morton's Fork' is the shabbiest piece of revenue-raising in history. But it wasn't only his greed for money. Everything about him is shabby, isn't it?"

"Yes. Dr. Gairdner wouldn't have any trouble in making *his* actions fit his character. How did you get on with the Doctor?"

"A fascinating study. But for the grace of God I think the worthy Doctor might have made a living as a criminal."

"Because he cheated?"

"Because he didn't cheat. He was as honest as the day. He just couldn't reason from B to C."

"All right, I'll buy."

"Everyone can reason from A to B—even a child. And most adults can reason from B to C. But a lot can't. Most criminals can't. You may not believe it—I know it's an awful come-down from the popular conception of the criminal as a dashing and cute character—but the criminal mind is an essentially silly one. You can't imagine how silly sometimes. You'd have to experience it to believe their lack of reasoning powers. They arrive at B, but they're quite incapable of making the jump to C. They'll lay two completely incompatible things side by side and contemplate them with the most unquestioning content. You can't make them see that they can't have both, any more than you can make a man of no taste see that bits of plywood nailed on to a gable to simulate Tudor beams are impossible. Have you started your own book?"

"Well—I've made a sort of tentative beginning. I know the way I *want* to write it. I mean the form. I hope you won't mind."

"Why should I mind?"

"I want to write it the way it happened. You know; about my coming to see you, and our starting the Richard thing quite casually and not knowing what we were getting into, and how we stuck to things that actually happened and not what someone reported afterwards about it, and how we looked for the break in the normal pattern that would indicate where the mischief was, like bubbles coming up from a diver way below, and that sort of thing."

"I think it's a grand idea."

"You do?"

"I do indeed."

"Well, that's fine, then. I'll get on with it. I'm going to do some research on Henry, just as garnish. I'd like to be able to put their actual records side by side, you see. So that people can compare them for themselves. Did you know that Henry invented the Star Chamber?"

"Was it Henry? I'd forgotten that. Morton's Fork and the Star Chamber. The classic sample of sharp practice, and the classic sample of tyranny. You're not going to have any difficulty in differentiating the rival portraits, are you? Morton's Fork and the Star Chamber make a nice contrast to the granting of the right to bail, and the prevention of the intimidation of juries."

"Was that Richard's Parliament? Golly, what a lot of reading I have to do. Atlanta's not speaking to me. She hates your marrow. She says I'm about as much use to a girl as last year's *Vogue*. But honestly, Mr. Grant, this is the first time in my life that anything exciting has happened to me. Important, I mean. Not exciting meaning exciting. Atlanta's exciting. She's all the excitement I ever want. But neither of us is important, the way I mean important—if you can understand what I mean."

"Yes, I understand. You've found something worth doing."

"That's it. I've found something worth doing. And it's me that's doing it; that's what's wonderful about it. Me. Mrs. Carradine's little boy. I come over here with Atlanta, with no idea about anything but using that research gag as an alibi. I walked into the B. M. to get me some dope to keep Pop quiet, and I walk out with a mission. Doesn't that shake you!" He eyed Grant in a considering way. "You're quite sure, Mr. Grant, that you don't want to write this book yourself? After all, it's quite a thing to do."

"I shall *never* write a book," Grant said firmly. "Not even *My Twenty Years at the Yard*."

"What! Not even your autobiography?"

"Not even my autobiography. It is my considered opinion that far too many books are written as it is."

"But this is one that must be written," Carradine said, looking slightly hurt.

"Of course it is. This one must be written. Tell me: there's something I forgot to ask you. How soon after that double did Tyrrel get that appointment in France? How soon after his supposed service to Henry in July 1486 did he become Constable of the Castle of Guisnes?"

Carradine stopped looking hurt and looked as malicious as it was possible for his kind woolly-lamb face to look.

"I was wondering when you were going to ask that," he said. "I was going to throw it at you on my way out if you forgot to ask. The answer is: almost right away."

"So. Another appropriate little pebble in the mosaic. I wonder whether the constableship just happened to be vacant, or whether it was a French appointment because Henry wanted him out of England."

"I bet it was the other way about, and it was Tyrrel who wanted to get out of England. If I were being ruled by Henry VII, I'd sure prefer to be ruled by remote control. Especially if I had done a secret job for Henry that might make it convenient for Henry if I didn't live to too venerable an age."

"Yes, perhaps you're right. He didn't only go abroad, he stayed abroad—as we have already observed. Interesting."

"He wasn't the only one who stayed abroad. John Dighton did too. I couldn't find out who all the people who were supposed to be involved in the murder actually were. All the Tudor accounts are different, I suppose you know. Indeed most of them are so different that they contradict each other flat. Henry's pet historian, Polydore Virgil, says the deed was done when Richard was at York. According to the sainted More it was during an earlier trip altogether, when Richard was at Warwick. And the personnel changes with each account. So that it's difficult to sort them out. I don't know who Will Slater was—Black Will to you, and another piece of onomatopoesis—or Miles Forrest. But there *was* a John Dighton. Grafton says he lived for long at Calais 'no less disdained than pointed at' and died there in great misery. How they relished a good moral, didn't they? The Victorians had nothing on them."

"If Dighton was destitute it doesn't look as if he had done any job for Henry. What was he by trade?"

"Well, if it's the same John Dighton, he was a priest, and he was anything but destitute. He was living very comfortably on the proceeds of a sinecure. Henry gave a John Dighton the living of Fulbeck, near Grantham—that's in Lincolnshire—on the 2nd of May, 1487."

"Well, well," Grant said, drawling. "1487. And he, too, lives abroad and in comfort."

"Uh-huh. Lovely, isn't it?"

"It's beautiful. And does anyone explain how the much-pointed-at Dighton wasn't haled home by the scruff of his neck to hang for regicide?"

"Oh, no. Nothing like that. Tudor historians didn't any of them think from B to C."

Grant laughed. "I see you're being educated."

"Sure. I'm not only learning history, I'm sitting at the feet of Scotland Yard on the subject of the human mind. Well, that will be about all for now. If you feel strong enough I'll read you the first two chapters of the book next time I come." He paused and said: "Would you mind, Mr. Grant, if I dedicated it to you?"

"I think you had better dedicate it to Carradine the Third," Grant said lightly.

But Carradine apparently did not feel it to be a light matter.

"I don't use soft soap as a dedication," he said, with a hint of stiffness.

"Oh, not soft soap," Grant said in haste. "A matter of policy merely."

"I'd never have started on this thing if it hadn't been for you, Mr. Grant," Carradine said, standing in the middle of the floor all formal and emotional and American and surrounded by the sweeping folds of his topcoat, "and I should like to make due acknowledgement of my indebtedness."

"I should be delighted, of course," murmured Grant, and the royal figure in the middle of the floor relaxed to boyhood again and the awkward moment was over. Carradine went away joyous and light-footed as he had come, looking thirty pounds heavier and twelve inches more round the chest than he had done three weeks ago.

And Grant took out the new knowledge that had been given him, hung it on the opposite wall, and stared at it.

Chapter 16

*S*he had been shut away from the world, that indestructibly virtuous beauty with the gilt hair.

Why gilt, he wondered for the first time. Silver-gilt probably; she had been radiantly fair. A pity that the word blonde had degenerated to the point where it had almost a secondary meaning.

She had been walled up to end her days where she could be no trouble to anyone. An eddy of trouble had moved with her all through her life. Her marriage to Edward had rocked England. She had been the passive means of Warwick's ruin. Her kindnesses to her family had built a whole new party in England and had prevented Richard's peaceful succession. Bosworth was implicit in that scanty little ceremony in the wilds of Northamptonshire when she became Edward's wife. But no one seemed to have borne her malice. Even the sinned-against Richard had forgiven her her relations' enormities. No one—until Henry came.

She had disappeared into obscurity. Elizabeth Woodville. The Queen-Dowager who was mother of the Queen of England. The mother of the Princes in the Tower, who had lived free and prosperous under Richard III.

That was an ugly break in the pattern, wasn't it?

He took his mind away from personal histories and began to think police-fashion. It was time he tidied up his case. Put it shipshape for presenting. It would help the boy with his book, and better still it would clear his own mind. It would be down in black and white where he could see it.

He reached for his writing-pad and pen, and made a neat entry:

CASE: Disappearance of two boys (Edward, Prince of Wales; Richard, Duke of York) from the Tower of London, 1485 or thereabouts.

He wondered whether it would be better to do the two suspects in parallel columns or successively. Perhaps it was better to finish with Richard first. So he made another neat headline, and began on his summing-up:

RICHARD III

Previous Record:
Good. Has excellent record in public service, and good reputation in private life. Salient characteristic as indicated by his actions: good sense.

In the matter of the presumed crime:
(a) He did not stand to benefit; there were nine other heirs to the house of York, including three males.
(b) There is no contemporary accusation.
(c) The boys' mother continued on friendly terms with him until his death, and her daughters attended Palace festivities.
(d) He showed no fear of the other heirs of York, providing generously for their upkeep and granting all of them their royal state.
(e) His own right to the crown was unassailable, approved by Act of Parliament and public acclamation; the boys were out of the succession and of no danger to him.
(f) If he had been nervous about disaffection then the person to have got rid of was not the two boys, but the person who really was next in succession to him: young Warwick. Whom he publicly created his heir when his own son died.

HENRY VII

Previous Record:
An adventurer, living at foreign courts. Son of an ambitious mother. Nothing known against his private life. No public office or employment. Salient characteristic as indicated by his actions: subtlety.

In the matter of the presumed crime:
(a) It was of great importance to him that the boys should not continue to live. By repealing the Act acknowledging the

children's illegitimacy, he made the elder boy King of England, and the youngest boy the next heir.

(b) In the Act which he brought before Parliament for the attainting of Richard he accused Richard of the conventional tyranny and cruelty but made no mention of the two young Princes. The conclusion is inevitable that at that time the two boys were alive and their whereabouts known.

(c) The boys' mother was deprived of her living and consigned to a nunnery eighteen months after his succession.

(d) He took immediate steps to secure the persons of all the other heirs to the crown, and kept them in close arrest until he could with the minimum of scandal get rid of them.

(e) He had no right whatever to the throne. Since the death of Richard, young Warwick was *de jure* King of England.

It occurred to Grant for the first time, as he wrote it out, that it had been within Richard's power to legitimise his bastard son John, and foist him on the nation. There was no lack of precedent for such a course. After all, the whole Beaufort clan (including Henry's mother) were the descendants not only of an illegitimate union but of a double adultery. There was nothing to hinder Richard from legitimising that "active and well-disposed" boy who lived in recognised state in his household. It was surely the measure of Richard that no such course had apparently crossed his mind. He had appointed as his heir his brother's boy. Even in the destitution of his own grief, good sense was his ruling characteristic. Good sense and family feeling. No base-born son, however active and well-disposed, was going to sit in the Plantagenets' seat while his brother's son was there to occupy it.

It was remarkable how that atmosphere of family feeling permeated the whole story. All the way from Cicely's journeyings about in her husband's company to her son's free acknowledgement of his brother George's boy as his heir.

And it occurred to him too for the first time in full force just how that family atmosphere strengthened the case for Richard's innocence. The boys whom he was supposed to have put down as he would put down twin foals were Edward's sons, children he must have known personally and well. To Henry, on the other hand, they were mere symbols. Obstacles on a path. He may never even have set eyes on them. All questions of character apart, the choice between the two men as suspects might almost be decided on that alone.

It was wonderfully clearing to the head to see it neat and tidy as *(a)*, *(b)*, and *(c)*. He had not noticed before how doubly suspect was Henry's behaviour over Titulus Regius. If, as Henry had insisted, Richard's claim was absurd, then surely the obvious thing to do was to have the thing reread in public and demonstrate its falsity. But he did no such thing. He went to endless pains to obliterate even the memory of it. The conclusion was inevitable that Richard's title to the crown as shown in Titulus Regius was unassailable.

Chapter 17

On the afternoon when Carradine reappeared in the room at the hospital Grant had walked to the window and back again, and was so cock-a-hoop about it that The Midget was moved to remind him that it was a thing that a child of eighteen months could do. But nothing could subdue Grant today.

"Thought you'd have me here for months, didn't you?" he crowed.

"We are very glad to see you better so quickly," she said primly; and added: "We are, of course, very glad, too, to have your bed."

And she clicked away down the corridor, all blond curls and starch.

Grant lay on his bed and looked at his little prison room with something approaching benevolence. Neither a man who has stood at the Pole nor a man who has stood on Everest has anything on a man who has stood at a window after weeks of being merely twelve stones of destitution. Or so Grant felt.

Tomorrow he was going home. Going home to be cosseted by Mrs. Tinker. He would have to spend half of each day in bed and he would be able to walk only with the aid of sticks, but he would be his own man again. At the bidding of no one. In tutelage to no half-pint piece of efficiency, yearned over by no lump of outsized benevolence.

It was a glorious prospect.

He had already unloaded his hallelujahs all over Sergeant Williams, who had looked in on the completion of his chore in Essex, and he was now yearning for Marta to drop in so that he could peacock in front of her in his new-found manhood.

"How did you get on with the history books?" Williams had asked.

"Couldn't be better. I've proved them all wrong."

Williams had grinned. "I expect there's a law against that," he said. "MI 5 won't like it. Treason or lèse-majesté or something like that it might turn out to be. You never know nowadays. I'd be careful if I was you."

"I'll never again believe anything I read in a history book, as long as I live, so help me."

"You'll have to make exceptions," Williams pointed out with Williams's dogged reasonableness. "Queen Victoria was true, and I suppose Julius Caesar did invade Britain. And there's 1066."

"I'm beginning to have the gravest doubts about 1066. I see you've tied up the Essex job. What is Chummy like?"

"A thorough little bastard. Been treated soft all his life since he started stealing change from his Ma at the age of nine. A good belting at the age of twelve might have saved his life. Now he'll hang before the almond blossoms' out. It's going to be an early spring. I've been working every evening in the garden this last few days, now that the days are drawing out. You'll be glad to sniff fresh air again."

And he had gone away, rosy and sane and balanced, as befitted a man who was belted for his good in his youth.

So Grant was longing for some other visitor from the outside world that he was so soon to be a part of again, and he was delighted when the familiar tentative tap came on his door.

"Come in, Brent!" he called, joyfully.

And Brent came in.

But it was not the Brent who had last gone out.

Gone was the jubilation. Gone was his newly acquired breadth.

He was no longer Carradine the pioneer, the blazer of trails.

He was just a thin boy in a very long, very large overcoat. He looked young, and shocked, and bereaved.

Grant watched him in dismay as he crossed the room with his listless uncoordinated walk. There was no bundle of paper sticking out of his mail-sack of a pocket today.

Oh, well, thought Grant philosophically; it had been fun while it lasted. There was bound to be a snag somewhere. One couldn't do serious research in that light-hearted amateur way and hope to prove anything by it. One wouldn't expect an amateur to walk into the Yard and solve a case that had defeated the pros; so why should he have thought himself smarter than the historians. He had wanted to prove to himself that he was right in his face-reading of the portrait; he had wanted to blot out the shame of having put a criminal on the bench instead of in the dock. But he would have to accept his mistake, and like it. Perhaps he had asked for it. Perhaps, in his heart of hearts, he had been growing a little pleased with himself about his eye for faces.

"Hullo, Mr. Grant."

"Hullo, Brent."

Actually it was worse for the boy. He was at the age when he expected miracles to happen. He was still at the age when he was surprised that a balloon should burst.

"You look saddish," he said cheerfully to the boy. "Something come unstuck?"

"Everything."

Carradine sat down on the chair and stared at the window.

"Don't these damned sparrows get you down?" he asked, fretfully.

"What is it? Have you discovered that there was a general rumour about the boys before Richard's death, after all?"

"Oh, much worse than that."

"Oh. Something in print? A letter?"

"No, it isn't that sort of thing at all. It's something much worse. Something quite—quite fundamental. I don't know how to tell you." He glowered at the quarrelling sparrows. "These damned birds. I'll never write that book now, Mr. Grant."

"Why not, Brent?"

"Because it isn't new to anyone. Everyone has known all about those things all along."

"Known? About what?"

"About Richard not having killed the boys at all, and all that."

"They've *known*? Since when!"

"Oh, hundreds and hundreds of years."

"Pull yourself together, chum. It's only four hundred years altogether since the thing happened."

"I know. But it doesn't make any difference. People have known about Richard's not doing it for hundreds and hundreds—"

"Will you stop that keening and talk sense. When did this—this rehabilitation first begin?"

"Begin? Oh, at the first available moment."

"When was that?"

"As soon as the Tudors were gone and it was safe to talk."

"In Stuart times, you mean?"

"Yes, I suppose—yes. A man Buck wrote a vindication in the seventeenth century. And Horace Walpole in the eighteenth. And someone called Markham in the nineteenth."

"And who in the twentieth?"

"No one that I know of."

"Then what's wrong with your doing it?"

"But it won't be the same, don't you see? It won't be a great discovery!" He said it in capitals. A Great Discovery.

Grant smiled at him. "Oh, come! You can't expect to pick Great Discoveries off bushes. If you can't be a pioneer what's wrong with leading a crusade?"

"A crusade?"

"Certainly."

"Against what?"

"Tonypandy."

The boy's face lost its blankness. It looked suddenly amused, like someone who has just seen a joke.

"It's the damnedest silliest name, isn't it!" he remarked.

"If people have been pointing out for three hundred and fifty years that Richard didn't murder his nephews and a school book can still say, in words of one syllable and without qualification, that he did, then it seems to me that Tonypandy has a long lead on you. It's time you got busy."

"But what can *I* do when people like Walpole and those have failed?"

"There's that old saying about constant water and its effect on stone."

"Mr. Grant, right now I feel an awfully feeble little trickle."

"You look it, I must say. I've never seen such self-pity. That's no mood to start bucking the British public in. You'll be giving enough weight away as it is."

"Because I've not written a book before, you mean?"

"No, that doesn't matter at all. Most people's first books are their best anyway; it's the one they wanted most to write. No, I meant that all the people who've never read a history book since they left school will feel themselves qualified to pontificate about what you've written. They'll accuse you of whitewashing Richard: 'whitewashing' has a derogatory sound that 'rehabilitation' hasn't, so they'll call it whitewashing. A few will look up the *Britannica*, and feel themselves competent to go a little further in the matter. These will slay you instead of flaying you. And the serious historians won't even bother to notice you."

"By God, I'll make them notice me!" Carradine said.

"Come! That sounds a little more like the spirit that won the Empire."

"We haven't got an Empire," Carradine reminded him.

"Oh, yes, you have," Grant said equably. "The only difference between ours and yours is that you acquire yours, economically, in the one latitude, while we got ours in bits all over the world. Had you written any of the book before the awful knowledge of its unoriginality hit you?"

"Yes, I'd done two chapters."

"What have you done with them? You haven't thrown them away, have you?"

"No. I nearly did. I nearly threw them in the fire."

"What stopped you?"

"It was an electric fire." Carradine stretched out his long legs in a relaxing movement and began to laugh. "Brother, I feel better already. I can't wait to land the British public one in the kisser with a few home truths. Carradine the First is just raging in my blood."

"A very virulent fever, it sounds."

"He was the most ruthless old blackguard that ever felled timber. He started as a logger and ended up with a Renaissance castle, two yachts, and a private car. Railroad car, you know. It had green silk curtains with bobbles on them and inlay woodwork that had to be seen to be believed. It has been popularly supposed, not least by Carradine the Third, that the Carradine blood was growing thin. But right now I'm all Carradine the First. I know just how the old boy felt when he wanted to buy a particular forest and someone said that he couldn't have it. Brother, I'm going to town."

"That's nice," Grant said, mildly. "I was looking forward to that dedication." He took his writing-pad from the table and held it out. "I've been doing a policeman's summing-up. Perhaps it may help you when you come to your peroration."

Carradine took it and looked at it with respect.

"Tear it off and take it with you. I've finished with it."

"I suppose in a week or two you'll be too busy with real investigations to care about a—an academic one," Carradine said, a little wistfully.

"I'll never enjoy one more than I've enjoyed this," Grant said, with truth. He glanced sideways at the portrait which was still propped against the books. "I was more dashed than you would believe when you came in all despondent, and I thought it had come to pieces." He looked back at the portrait and said: "Marta thinks he is a little like Lorenzo the Magnificent. Her friend James thinks it is the face of a saint. My surgeon thinks it is the face of a cripple. Sergeant Williams thinks he looks like a great judge. But I think, perhaps, Matron comes nearest the heart of the matter."

"What does she say?"

"She says it is a face full of the most dreadful suffering."

"Yes. Yes, I suppose it is. And would you wonder, after all?"

"No. No, there was little he was spared. Those last two years of his life must have happened with the suddenness and weight of an avalanche. Everything had been going along so nicely. England on an even keel at last. The civil war fading out of mind, a good firm government to keep things peaceful and a good brisk trade to keep things prosperous. It must have seemed a good outlook, looking out from Middleham across Wensleydale. And in two short years—his wife, his son, and his peace."

"I know one thing he was spared."

"What?"

"The knowledge that his name was to be a hissing and a byword down the centuries."

"Yes. That would have been the final heart-break. Do you know what I personally find *the* convincing thing in the case for Richard's innocence of any design for usurpation?"

"No. What?"

"The fact that he had to send for those troops from the North when Stillington broke his news. If he had any fore-knowledge of what Stillington was going to say, or even any plans to concoct a story with Stillington's help, he would have brought those troops with him. If not to London then to the Home Counties where they would be handy. That he had to send urgently first to York and then to his Nevill cousins for men is proof that Stillington's confession took him entirely unawares."

"Yes. He came up with his train of gentlemen, expecting to take over the Regency. He met the news of the Woodville trouble when he came to Northampton, but that didn't rattle him. He mopped up the Woodville two thousand and went on to London as if nothing had happened. There was still nothing but an orthodox Coronation in front of him as far as he knew. It wasn't until Stillington confessed to the council that he sends for troops of his own. And he has to send all the way to the North of England at a critical moment. Yes, you're right, of course. He was taken aback." He propped the leg of his spectacles with a forefinger in the old tentative gesture, and proffered a companion piece. "Know what I find the convincing thing in the case for Henry's guilt?"

"What?"

"The mystery."

"Mystery?"

"The mysteriousness. The hush-hush. The hole-and-corner stuff."

"Because it is in character, you mean?"

"No, no; nothing as subtle as that. Don't you see: Richard had no need of any mystery; but Henry's whole case depended on the boys' end being mysterious. No one has ever been able to think up a reason for such a hole-and-corner method as Richard was supposed to have used. It was a quite mad way to do it. He couldn't hope to get away with it. Sooner or later he was going to have to account for the boys not being there. As far as he knew he had a long reign in front of him. No one has ever been able to think why he should have chosen so difficult and dangerous a way when he had so many simpler methods at hand. He had only to have the boys suffocated, and let them lie in state while the whole of London walked by and wept over two young things dead before their time of fever. That is the way he *would* have done it, too. Goodness, *the whole point* of Richard's killing the boys was to prevent any rising in their favour, and to get any benefit from the murder the fact of their deaths would *have* to be made public, and as soon as possible. It would defeat the whole plan if people didn't *know* that they were dead. But Henry, now. Henry *had* to find a way to push them out of sight. Henry *had* to be mysterious. Henry *had* to hide the facts of when and how they died. *Henry's whole case depended* on no one's knowing what exactly happened to the boys."

"It did indeed, Brent; it did indeed," Grant said, smiling at counsel's eager young face. "You ought to be at the Yard, Mr. Carradine!"

Brent laughed.

"I'll stick to Tonypandy," he said. "I bet there's a lot more of it that we don't know about. I bet history books are just riddled with it."

"You'd better take Sir Cuthbert Oliphant with you, by the way." Grant took the fat respectable-looking volume from his locker. "Historians should be compelled to fake a course in psychology before they are allowed to write."

"Huh. That wouldn't do anything for them. A man who is interested in what makes people tick doesn't write history. He writes novels, or becomes an alienist, or a magistrate—"

"Or a confidence man."

"Or a confidence man. Or a fortune-teller. A man who understands about people hasn't any yen to write history. History is toy soldiers."

"Oh, come. Aren't you being a little severe? It's a very learned and erudite—"

"Oh, I didn't mean it that way. I mean: it's moving little figures about on a flat surface. It's half-way to mathematics, when you come to think about it."

"Then if it's mathematics they've no right to drag in back-stairs gossip," Grant said, suddenly vicious. The memory of the sainted More continued to upset him. He thumbed through the fat respectable Sir Cuthbert in a farewell review. As he came to the final pages the progress of the paper from under his thumb slackened, and presently stopped.

"Odd," he said, "how willing they are to grant a man the quality of courage in battle. They have only tradition to go on, and yet not one of them questions it. Not one of them, in fact, fails to stress it."

"It was an enemy's tribute," Carradine reminded him. "The tradition began with a ballad written by the other side."

"Yes. By a man of the Stanleys 'Then a knight to King Richard gan say.' It's here somewhere." He turned over a leaf or two, until he found what he was looking for. "It was 'good Sir William Harrington,' it seems. The knight in question.

There may no man their strokes abide, the Stanleys dints
they be so strong [the treacherous bastards!]
Ye may come back at another tide, methinks ye tarry here
too long.
Your horse at your hand is ready, another day you may worship win
And come to reign with royalty, and wear your crown and
be our king.
'Nay, give me my battle-axe in my hand, set the crown of
England on my head so high.
For by Him that made both sea and land, King of England
this day I will die.
One foot I will never flee whilst the breath is my breast
within.'
As he said so did it be—if he lost his life he died a King."

" 'Set the crown of England on my head,' " said Carradine, musing. "That was the crown that was found in a hawthorn bush afterwards."

"Yes. Set aside for plunder probably."

"I used to picture it one of those high plush things that King George got crowned in, but it seems it was just a gold circlet."

"Yes. It could be worn outside the battle helmet."

"Gosh," said Carradine with sudden feeling, "I sure would have hated to wear that crown if I had been Henry! I sure would have hated it!" He was silent for a little, and then he said: "Do you know what the town of York wrote—wrote in their records, you know—about the battle of Bosworth?"

"No."

"They wrote: 'This day was our good King Richard piteously slain and murdered; to the great heaviness of this city.' "

The chatter of the sparrows was loud in the quiet.

"Hardly the obituary of a hated usurper," Grant said at last, very dry.

"No," said Carradine. "No. 'To the great heaviness of this city,' " he repeated slowly, rolling the phrase over in his mind. "They cared so much about it that even with a new régime in the offing and the future not to be guessed at they put down in black and white in the town record their opinion that it was murder and their sorrow at it."

"Perhaps they had just heard about the indignities perpetrated on the King's dead body and were feeling a little sick."

"Yes. Yes. You don't like to think of a man you've known and admired flung stripped and dangling across a pony like a dead animal."

"One wouldn't like to think of even an enemy so. But sensibility is not a quality that one would look for among the Henry-Morton crowd."

"Huh. Morton!" said Brent, spitting out the word as if it were a bad taste. "No one was 'heavy' when Morton died, believe me. Know what the Chronicler wrote of him? The London one, I mean. He wrote: 'In our time was no man like to be compared with him in all things; albeit that he lived not without the great disdain and hatred of the Commons of this land.' "

Grant turned to look at the portrait which had kept him company through so many days and nights.

"You know," he said, "for all his success and his Cardinal's hat I think Morton was the loser in that fight with Richard III. In spite of his defeat and his long traducing, Richard came off the better of these two. He was loved in his day."

"That's no bad epitaph," the boy said soberly.

"No. Not at all a bad epitaph," Grant said, shutting Oliphant for the last time. "Not many men would ask for a better." He handed over the book to its owner. "Few men have earned so much," he said.

When Carradine had gone Grant began to sort out the things on his table, preparatory to his homegoing on the morrow. The unread fashionable novels could go to the hospital library to gladden other hearts than his. But he would keep the book with the mountain pictures. And he must remember to give The Amazon back her two history books. He took them out so that he could give them to her when she brought in his supper. And he read again, for the first time since he began his search for the truth about Richard, the school book tale of his villainy. There it was, in unequivocal black and white, the infamous story. Without a perhaps or a peradventure. Without a qualification or a question.

As he was about to shut the senior of the two educators his eye fell on the beginning of Henry VII's reign, and he read: "It was the settled and considered policy of the Tudors to rid themselves of all rivals to the throne, more especially those heirs of York who remained alive on the succession of Henry VII. In this they were successful, although it was left to Henry VIII to get rid of the last of them."

He stared at this bald announcement. This placid acceptance of wholesale murder. This simple acknowledgement of a process of family elimination.

Richard III had been credited with the elimination of two nephews, and his name was a synonym for evil. But Henry VII, whose "settled and considered policy" was to eliminate a whole family was regarded as a shrewd and far-seeing monarch. Not very lovable perhaps, but constructive and painstaking, and very successful withal.

Grant gave up. History was something that he would never understand.

The values of historians differed so radically from any values with which he was acquainted that he could never hope to meet them on any common ground. He would go back to the Yard, where murderers were murderers and what went for Cox went equally for Box.

He put the two books tidily together and when The Amazon came in with his mince and stewed prunes he handed them over with a neat little speech of gratitude. He really was very grateful to The Amazon. If she had not kept her school books he might never have started on the road that led to his knowledge of Richard Plantagenet.

She looked confused by his kindness, and he wondered if he had been such a bear in his illness that she expected nothing but carping from him. It was a humiliating thought.

"We'll miss you, you know," she said, and her big eyes looked as if they might brim with tears. "We've grown used to having you here. We've even got used to *that*." And she moved an elbow in the direction of the portrait.

A thought stirred in him.

"Will you do something for me?" he asked.

"Of course. Anything I can do."

"Will you take that photograph to the window and look at it in a good light as long as it takes to count a pulse?"

"Yes, of course, if you want me to. But why?"

"Never mind why. You just do it to please me. I'll time you."

She took up the portrait and moved into the light of the window. He watched the second-hand of his watch.

He gave her forty-five seconds and then said: "Well?" And as there was no immediate answer he said again: "Well?"

"Funny," she said. "When you look at it for a little it's really quite a nice face, isn't it?"

About the Author

ELIZABETH MACKINTOSH used two pen names during her writing career: Josephine Tey, who was also her Suffolk great-great-grandmother, and Gordon Daviot. She was born in 1897 in Inverness, Scotland, where she attended the Royal Academy. Miss MacKintosh later trained for three years at the Anstey Physical Training College in Birmingham, then began her teaching career as a physical training instructor. She gave up teaching to keep house for her father, who lived near Loch Ness, and pursue her writing. Her first book was *The Man in the Queue* (1929), published under the Gordon Daviot pseudonym, and it introduced the character of Inspector Grant, familiar now from the Tey novels. The author wrote chiefly under the signature of Gordon Daviot from 1929 to 1946, during which time her works included the play *Richard of Bordeaux* (1933), which ran for a year with John Gielgud in the lead part. The first of the Josephine Tey mysteries, *A Shilling for Candles*, was published in 1936 and was eventually followed by *Miss Pym Disposes* in 1947. Also included among the Tey mysteries are *The Franchise Affair* (1949), *Brat Farrar* (1949), *To Love and Be Wise* (1950), *The Daughter of Time* (1951), and *The Singing Sands* (1952). Elizabeth MacKintosh died in London on February 13, 1952.